C000129032

PAUL C HILL

RISE
OF THE
CHIMERA
THE CHIMERA SAGA

authorHOUSE®

AuthorHouse™ UK
1663 Liberty Drive
Bloomington, IN 47403 USA
www.authorhouse.co.uk
Phone: 0800.197.4150

© *2019 Paul C Hill. All rights reserved.*

No part of this book may be reproduced, stored in a retrieval system, or transmitted by any means without the written permission of the author.

Published by AuthorHouse 01/10/2019

ISBN: 978-1-7283-8209-8 (sc)
ISBN: 978-1-7283-8208-1 (e)

Print information available on the last page.

Any people depicted in stock imagery provided by Getty Images are models, and such images are being used for illustrative purposes only. Certain stock imagery © Getty Images.

This book is printed on acid-free paper.

Because of the dynamic nature of the Internet, any web addresses or links contained in this book may have changed since publication and may no longer be valid. The views expressed in this work are solely those of the author and do not necessarily reflect the views of the publisher, and the publisher hereby disclaims any responsibility for them.

chi•me•ra or chi•mae•ra (kɪˈmɪər ə, kaɪ-) - Noun (Ki mere a or Sh mare a)

1. (*often cap.*) a monster of classical myth, commonly represented with a lion's head, a goat's body and a serpent's tail.
2. any horrible or grotesque imaginary creature.
3. a fancy or dream.
4. an organism composed of two or more genetically distinct tissues.

CHAPTER 1

NIGHT TIME IN BIRMINGHAM

The spring night was muggy in the rundown area of Birmingham, the overcast sky inviting clouds to idle by and obscure both the moon and stars, making it a great night for hunting. The city air was crammed full of odours, both appetising and disturbing; all useful in concealing a predator's scent from their prey, but also creating an excellent atmosphere for a Friday night out for people to enjoy the busy nightlife and absorb the ambience.

The terrified woman's scream cut through the night's adolescent babble echoing around the empty spaces, reaching out for help as she ran to escape down the cluttered and poorly lit alley she'd been using as a cut through to home. Her breath was ragged, stuttering; both harsh in her ears. She desperately looked ahead, avoiding dangerous obstacles hidden by the shadows and scanning for an escape route from her pursuers.

In her early twenties, her mid-length skirt, low cut silk top, and the newly purchased boots had been intended to fit the latest trend. Instead, it had attracted the wrong kind of attention. The boot's heels were not particularly high, but not flat enough to allow her to run at full speed, especially as the alley ahead was strewn with broken glass, empty boxes, and crushed cans. Her assailants had ambushed her from the shadows on opposing sides of the cobblestone lane, specifically aiming for her bag, which she barely managed to keep safe. Now she ran desperately back towards the main road in the improbable hope of reaching safety.

Her attackers, dressed in their gang's plain black hoodies and white trainers, hung back far enough to give their prey hope, knowing they could overtake her anytime; certainly before she could escape. If she'd given them her bag, it would have been enough, but having put up resistance they now wanted more; payment for their effort, some 'fun' with her. They whooped, taunting her; making her flinch and squeal with occasional bursts of speed, designed to terrify her. She was in for an exciting time, once they took her back to the den that was certain.

None of them spotted another figure, high up on one of the shadow-covered alley walls, crouching low, head cocked listening, eyes following the scene intently, seeing it in seemingly normal daylight, strange flickering symbols surrounding the viewed image.

The undeniably female figure, perfectly filled a one-piece dark grey catsuit, made of a matt material, accentuating her lithe figure and allowing full freedom of movement. Two slim coiled whips, a utility belt full of unknown items completed the outfit; its overall effect being one of sleek efficiency. Pale, eerily glowing, gold-flecked green eyes peering over a half face mask were the only sign anything lay in the shadows to the casual observer.

The figure's hands clenched in anger at the unfolding scene; this had supposed to be a meeting, not a rescue. Still, she could do with venting some anger on the two targets. She watched for a few more seconds, gauging their speed and strength, suddenly launching herself along the wall, sprinting and leaping in elegant silent precision towards the pursuit.

The panicking woman threw a blind, backhanded bag-swipe at the nearest man, who dodged out of its way laughing gruffly. With fear building inside her, she carried on running, guessing what was coming and realising safety was beyond her reach. She flung a last hoarse screech for help into the night, as one of the attackers made a grab for her, the same instant a whip-crack slashed through the air.

The attacker's laughter died in their throats, as the snatching hand instead of grasping the woman wrestled with a strange pulsing metallic whip-line, painfully digging into its wrist drawing drips of blood; the line extending into the shadows of a small doorway just behind the trio.

The whole chaotic procession came to a shocked halt, the woman half turning at the unexpected cessation of sound; more fearful that a new threat might be emerging than anything else.

"The lady would like you to leave her alone," came a slightly muffled, but commanding, voice from the darkness, followed by a tall, lithe figure slinking from the inky shadows. The catsuit made a dim outline in the night and more than human eyes emitting a rich, golden glow, with an intense predatory quality.

"In fact, she insists!" added the figure, tugging the whip with minimal effort. Despite that, the yank was brutally strong the ensnared assailant staggering towards the wielder. He wrestled with the line around his wrist, trying to detach it, being interrupted by another jerk from the strange presence before them. Another whip-line cracked out, wrapping itself around the hood of the second thug; tiny barbs digging into his throat, gripping tightly and painfully, forcing his hands to involuntarily grasp the cruel wire as he tried to scream, the restricting line choking it off resulting in a muted gurgling.

"You're dead, bitch!" snarled the leader, a large ape of a man, with a black mass of beard, beady eyes, and sweaty skin, "my gang will slice you up and feed you your own guts, deep-fried." He grasped the thin wire and hauled back hard, expecting to break free and grab his tormentor, instead finding the line simply tightened, the length biting deeper into his flesh, causing him to bleed more and halting his aggressive movement. He looked disbelievingly at the blood seeping in thick, crimson, globs from his wrist. Shaking his head to clear the pain, he looked hopefully at the other attacker. They nodded together, simultaneously heaving back against the figure, hoping to overbalance and grab her. To their surprise, however, she resisted steadily, remaining totally unmoved, her whips drawing painfully tighter; making their blood flow freely.

"One more pull like that, and I expect you'll be either crippled or dead," came a cold, emotionless, almost icy observation. "My whips will slice clean through your flesh, and both of you will rapidly bleed to death. That is not what I really want but if that's the way you want it," she shrugged. She stepped deliberately towards them, loosening the tension a fraction, "now stay still," she commanded.

The tall rescuer half turned to look at the woman, who had frozen in shock during the exchange. "Call the police and, if you're feeling generous, an ambulance. There's a phone booth that way that's still working," she flicked her head back to the main road.

The grateful woman nodded, "thank you," she whispered; bolting, clutching her handbag, but not looking back. That woman's ice-cold voice frightened her every bit as much, if not more than, the attackers had.

While the figure was distracted, the bearded attacker surreptitiously reached into his pocket with his free hand drawing a lock knife and reaching towards the whip line in an attempt to cut through it and free himself.

"Unwise, my little man," snapped that flat voice over her shoulder, sensing the change in tension in the line. "The line cannot be cut, and if you try, you'll probably lose that hand, bones and all."

The man froze but did not put the knife away pausing as if planning something else. As the masked face turned, its' green and gold-flecked eyes locked on to his, seeming to gaze deep into his pitch-black soul; the knife trembled, then dropped, and a large wet patch spread near the crotch of his jeans. Continuing to gaze into his eyes, the figure asked "now, what shall we do with you?" The question was rhetorical, and the man found that he could not say anything, not even beg for his life. "Well, I suppose it would be better if you both slept, rather than died. The police don't like finding dead bodies; they're much too messy."

She hooked her first whip onto her belt, then raising and dropped her freed hand, propelling a glass sphere against the tarmac in front of the two pacified attackers, white gas erupting around them. Their vision swam, both men dropping in short unceremonious arcs to the pathway and quickly losing consciousness, their crumpled forms seeming to satisfy the grey figure, as she darted next to the leader.

"Thugs like you want people to be afraid of you, enjoy the power that the fear gives you. Now let's see who is afraid." The voice was calm, but the undertone in it was one of resolve and determination. As she concluded her pronouncement, the light of consciousness left his eyes. She would be remembered, vividly, she was sure.

Once she was confident they were both entirely unconscious she released the whip lines pulling them carefully through their sliced skin and bandaging their wounds crudely, but effectively; she was not a trained medic after all. Crouching down, she rifled through their pockets for information; names, addresses, and any evidence of criminal activity they might have perpetrated spotting several small

3

packets of unidentified drugs. She scrutinised them, then tucked a sample into one of her belt pouches for analysis later, leaving the rest for the crown prosecution. The police would need the knife as evidence too, so she bagged that for them, being careful not to smudge the fingerprints on it. She left their money and legal belongings; she was no thief after all.

Checking their arms and necks, the revealed gang tattoo was also of interest. Hidden under their hoodies and the full length of their forearms, a black feathered bird-like creature, topped by an ugly human face on its feathered; a motif identifying them as the "Highfield Harpies."

"Hmmm, that name's familiar," she murmured. The gang had been on the news recently as an up-and-coming threat in urban cities linked to murders, drugs, gang warfare, and, of particular interest to the figure, occult connections. There were the usual minimal clues to their gang's hide-out, although the group was more associated with Oxfordshire, Buckinghamshire and Greater London than West Midlands.

One object, however, was of great interest; a nightclub ticket for the Oxford branch of a club chain called "The Black Rooms." She gazed at the stub, with its' pentagram symbol, for a few seconds, as if considering the possibilities, then put it into another belt pouch for future investigation.

"Perhaps you went there? Or were taken. But why there?" it explained the thugs but not the reason for them being here, nor the reason she'd been directed here initially, she thought as she waited. It would be bad form if the men had an allergic reaction to the knockout gas she'd used and a death was the last thing she wanted; she was no murderer, any more than she was a thief. She was sure, however, that the resulting pounding headache would be ample reminder of their encounter with her; along with the scars from the whips. It might even deter them from re-offending, however unlikely that seemed.

She stayed until she heard the emergency services' sirens before standing up to leave, "they're all yours GhostKnight," she said looking up slightly, a faint outline against the stars shimmered slightly, "see you back at base."

"Confirmed Chi'mera, thanks for the assist," came a deeply resonant masculine voice, filled with warmth and gratitude. It was the thugs that should be grateful, if he'd had to deal with them, they would probably be dead by now; she knew the bad blood between him and gangs was too ingrained for him to be so, reserved. Satisfied with her handy work and that the woman was safe, she vanished, with a feint whining-pop.

At the end of the alley, a police van and an ambulance arrived, guided in by the partially traumatised victim. As the first police officer approached the two unconscious men, he spotted their injuries and the bandages on their wrists.

"Oh great," he reached for his radio, "Five-One-Four to Control. Code 6, need a van, code 9, for Ambulance. Oh, and tell the CO, it's another for SCG." He picked up the contents of the thugs' pockets in gloved hands and put it all into an evidence bag, "I hate the weird ones."

In a distant building, the figure appeared in a toilet cubical and promptly changed. Off slipped the grey outfit, gloves, mask, and whips, all folding tightly into a slim rucksack; quickly stashed in the raised ceiling, through a tightly fitting tile. On went the lab coat, security badge, labelled, Dr. C Clerk, and safety spectacles; utilitarian and straightforward, hiding the lithe figure under the loose fitting, plain white coat.

The statuesque blonde, some 6' 1" tall, with those startling green and gold-flecked eyes, obscured by the tinted Perspex protective lenses, swept the toilet room as she came out of the cubicle, ensuring there was no one there to observe her sudden appearance. Her movements were deliberate, controlled, simple, graceful, and fluid; the lithe gait of a tiger entering its' lair. All clear, she stepped out of the toilets, rounding a corner to join the main laboratory area again, her demeanour changing as soon as she approached the security guard at the door; her body stooping slightly, leaning over her standard, white, metallic clipboard, her gait changing, becoming more hesitant, almost clumsy, covering half its normal stride.

"Ah well, back to the lab," she muttered, feeling strangely unenthusiastic about going back to the environment that once she'd loved with a passion.

She would have little time to do more work today on the new batch of Nanites before the meeting with the project manager. She shuffled past the security guard, having his flask of coffee, flashing her badge and clocking into her lab.

The labs at the international conglomerate Advanced Bio Chem., A.B.C. for short, were not as cosy as those at her old labs, Advanced Genetic Engineering, but they were much more modern; the equipment much more powerful. Still, that was a trivial consideration really; she had a job to do here, and she needed to get on with it. Military Intelligence Ten, or M.I.X., needed the information that only she could obtain and quickly.

As the security doors closed behind her, she put a finger to her ear.

"Chi'mera to Base. I have some clues in the other case. I will report back in eight hours." The communications earpiece was virtually invisible to regular sight but powerful enough to cut through even this company's electronic shielding to reach the M.I.X. Network.

"Confirmed Chi'mera. Bringing it home in eight. Understood." It was Helena, her ever vigilant boss, friend, and fellow M.I.X. agent.

It was sad really. She understood just how much she'd lost in the last two months. Still, there had been gains too. She looked back for a moment. Had it really been just eight weeks since that day in April? And yet so much more time had passed, so much more, and she remembered just how traumatic the revelation of her true nature had been to her. And it all started in that first lab ...

JUST A NORMAL DAY—TWO MONTHS AGO

Dr. Charlene Klerk was having a normal day in the high-tech laboratory where she lived and worked. That is, it was the same as every other day she'd had since leaving university at the age of sixteen with her doctorate in biochemistry and joining A.G.E. Her life was filled with her love of work, study, and discipline;

all she had really since she'd no family having lost her parents in an accident. She had no recollection of the incident, although she'd been told by her mentor, Dr. Trafford, that it had been a tragic set of events; but her family would have wanted her to continue with her studies and be happy.

So, she honoured their memory by throwing herself into her work with a zeal and fire that continued to burn. Only occasionally did she see something that triggered faded memories of her early years with her parents – mostly happy ones with her father, but, rarely, darker ones with her mother.

She had no false modesty about herself or rancour about her lot in life. Charlene knew she was a biochemist of rare talent and dedication, happily living a life that, she was privately informed by her mentor, most people would view as luxury. Others commented that she was living in virtual slavery, locked in a laboratory twenty-four hours a day, seven days a week, baring the odd emergency meeting with the boss. But it did not really enter her mind that others might consider her life strange in any way, except for the lack of relatives. She was happy, blissfully happy, and wouldn't change a thing.

She'd been offered a career with A.G.E. as soon as she left university. She suspected it was not solely because of her genius in biology and chemistry but also because her mentor and adoptive father, Dr. Miles Trafford, an eminent neurobiologist and founder of the high-tech research company, had vouched for her.

She'd soon made a name for herself in the company by discovering a family of chemicals that could rapidly and effectively treat several early-stage cancers, and for her dedication to her work. That dedication had been a source of gossip early in her career until Dr. Trafford suggested that perhaps Charlene should view taking a coffee break as an opportunity to gather information, help others, and expand her technical contacts list rather than as a waste of time.

After she started to leave her lab spot on ten in the morning and again at three in the afternoon, people found that this daunting, cool, and intensely precise genius could be friendly, if a little incomprehensible at times. The list of people who'd had problems solved, tips passed on, and occasionally miraculous solutions handed to them began to grow. Word within the building spread that she – Char as they called her – could be not only of tremendous help but was also intelligent, engaging, and actually funny if a little naïve. Those who tried to take advantage of that were rather unceremoniously asked to clear their desk, not that Dr. Klerk ever saw them. The professional community knew of her successes, even if public and commercial credit was the company's.

She did not care about that in the slightest, except in that the patent for the drugs earned the company money that could be used to purchase better equipment for her. Let them have the rights as long as she could focus on her task in hand.

She, in effect, lived at the company labs in Oxford, reporting to her project manager/mentor weekly. Her flat was linked to the lab via a personal airlock. It contained an unused galley kitchen, a separate exercise area, a modern bathroom, and a wonderfully comfy bedroom.

The kitchen was a modern masterpiece fitted with top-spec appliances, spices, workspace, and cutlery that all went totally unused due to Charlene's habit of ordering food in, to save work time. The company installed it before she'd arrived as an incentive, only to find she did not know how to cook anything except chemicals and microwave meals.

The bathroom, however, was a must, needed for those long evening soaks that she took after her frequently frustrating day's work was over. It consisted of a frosted shower cubicle, extra-large bath, sink, and a drier cubicle; the latter something she'd come up with to save towelling-down time. Of the whole place, this had some personal selections of items. Her choice of soaps, shampoos, candles, and oils helped her rather delicate skin withstand her more corrosive experiments.

The bedroom consisted of a massive bed with a comfortable mattress. An unadorned bedside table was lit by a radiant, wall-mounted reading lamp for her evening routine and the beauty sleep her late father informed her would be essential later in life. He'd passed away before explaining why this would be so critical. Still, she considered herself an obedient daughter, so she incorporated those nine hours into her daily routine.

She frequently still missed her dad, despite her lack of any solid memories of him. Every once in a while, she remembered steady hands, deep green eyes, and a calm voice guiding her through whichever experiment he was teaching her at the time. She sighed every time she realised, she still missed him so much. Unlike her mother, the bitch. Her memories of her mother were dark, pain-filled episodes of suffering, blood, and relentless discipline. Although she knew they had happened, she tried very hard to forget.

The well-stocked lab sported many of the latest high-tech, computerised versions of standard equipment to aid in her quest for an instrument or mechanism to deal with otherwise inoperable cancers: computers, chemical vats, electron microscopes, heaters, fuges—the works. It was her little glass palace, right down to the toughened glass, double security doors, pressure seals, and not-so-stylish clean suits. She even had a dedicated server and internet connection to buy the goods she needed, teleconference with her contacts, and order her takeaways. She rarely had to go anywhere except to report serious problems or important discoveries.

On those exceedingly rare occasions, she needed to go somewhere to talk to someone face-to-face, there was her chauffeur-bodyguard to help her get around. She privately thought he had overly developed musculature and thought of him as 'Muscles,' but officially called him 'Driver,' though he looked more like a soldier than a chauffeur. It was a standing joke with herself that his IQ was probably not much higher than her bust size. And she was so amused by the way he took his job seriously, wanting to open every door and to check every room before she entered. She guessed he thought she could not take care of herself, although he was probably well paid for his services. One day she would show him! He was, in effect, the human face of the company, and she found herself liking him, albeit in a big-brother kind of way.

She remembered how she'd started at the company; Dr. Trafford's introducing her to everyone, meeting the security people, seeing the new equipment, and skimming through the masses of introductory company literature.

Charlene had struggled slightly in those initial days to come to grips with her new circumstances until they'd finally let her get down to doing the real work, where she was comfortable. Her initial bugbear had been the programming of the Nanites; she'd memorised their design on the first day. They'd given her the language manual, and she'd read it quickly enough. But as she tried the logical way to program tasks, she realised that the commands seemed illogical, at least to her, and her programs failed. Charlene mentally noted how she would set up each function with organic Nanites, detailing the basics in her encrypted lab tablet as she worked. She kept the complicated details in her head; not because she was afraid that it would be stolen by A.G.E., as they already owned the rights, but more because she was still working out the intricate molecular structures.

The work started slowly, with the 'bots initially flawed design, a minor propulsion issue which her work and tips from other sources corrected. Once that was fixed, the pace of work accelerated towards the initial goal: navigation of the Nanobot to the primary cancer-cell cluster. Adding the nutrient bait payload to the Nanites had been the next step and critical breakthrough, allowing them to draw migrating cancer cells to more easily accessible areas for treatment. The bonus Charlene received from her mentor for that suggestion had been some expensive Chinese silk evening dresses from some designer she'd never heard of. Then Dr. Trafford realised she would never wear them, not being interested in the city's nightlife or in socialising. After that, she suggested that she select her own rewards, which tended to be extra tech or new top-of-the-range tablets or servers to aid her work.

Though, according to Dr. Trafford, some would say she lay in the lap of luxury, she did not see it that way. And if you don't comprehend something, does it exist? Charlene did not see the money around her or the walls that surrounded and imprisoned her. All she saw was her work and her dedication to it—and to the ultimate goal of eradicating cancer.

Her current subjects of study were the company's commercial nanotech offerings. She was examining and analysing their statistics and limitations to see if any could aid her in her work. All she'd found so far was that mechanical nanotechnology was a different kettle of fish from the biological systems she was knowledgeable in. Still, she was smart and bridging the knowledge gap fast, although it tested her patience and discipline to their limits.

After much consideration, her selected avenue of investigation was a nanobot that lay hollow carbon tubes containing a coating of synthetic T-cells into a targeted cancerous area. With the bait, this would hopefully cause channelling of the cancerous growth to a more operable location, while stopping the cancer from spreading from the target area. It was in its preliminary stages, but it looked promising. The main problem was programming the nanotech correctly. Charlene had worked hard on that for the past week with only moderate progress. It was tough going even for her. Many would have given up, but her disciplined approach to work was winning through. The main problem was that the manual for the programming language was poorly organised and omitted several essential points.

"Now is it the 'engage' subroutine or the 'activate' function, that is being ignored?", She muttered, sighing gently, looking at the nanobot just sat there, in the electron microscope viewer. She thought she had programmed it to power up and perform its' task. But, for the third time in as many days, the thing had stopped just after starting, as though the program had triggered the wrong routine; blasted computerised technology.

She checked the notes on her tablet, which had been a godsend for someone as organised as Charlene, although she'd had one more rugged than commercially available. She'd recently developed a tendency to slam them down when frustrated.

She flicked an intruding blonde hair out of her eyes, a habit that her mother had tried to break her of, but had never fully succeeded; "Tie it. No flicking!" she had ordered constantly, trying to teach her daughter proper control. Charlene had eventually started to tie the long, unruly, mop when she had visited her mother, but still flicked it elsewhere. Her dad had worried more about the glorious hair falling into his, or her, experiments when she'd been with him. She'd worn a cap then; control was one thing, prudence another.

Charlene's distraction caused her to shake her head, thus dislodging the hair again, much to her building annoyance. Grrr, she was losing focus, something happening more and more of late, as the darn nanobots refused her control, and found herself on the verge of launching the latest tablet at the microscope. Sheesh, she was getting just like her mother: Perish the thought!

The afternoon was moving along, so she abandoned the errant nanobots and logged on to the internet to research the command processor manual, again. She'd been on it so often she had it as a favourite, which it most certainly was not. If she'd thought that her university chemistry exam at twelve had been hard, this gibberish was ten times worse.

She spent an hour rummaging through expert examples of complex nanobot programming and contacted one of the primary designers of the processor, Yen So from the industrial giant Che'namami Industries in Japan, talking with him for another hour trying to get the intricacies of the Nanobots' task programmed correctly. The two scientists had had previous enjoyable discussions on nano-robotics and she admired his precision of thought, especially as they shared a general interest in robotics and related subjects. From their discussions today, it seemed that the Nanobots' programming language had limitations that had not been apparent. By five in the evening, she had a good idea as to what was needed and the modifications that were necessary for her programming; however, as she saw the time, she started to tidy up. Five pm was warm-down time.

She had a strict regime and used her discipline to follow it. On weekdays, she had a simple nine to five work-regime, in the lab, followed by relaxation and study in her quarters. The weekends had less actual work but increased study time. For the bulk of her life, she had followed those rules; the routine serving her well. For both schedules, five was the end of the workday, after which she moved on to enjoying some hard-earned relaxation.

She addressed the lab mic, "Dr. Klerk authorisation, one seven five six nine alpha, clearance level four, de-activate Lab System."

"Thank you, Doctor. See you in the morning," came the voice, and all the systems started shutting off one by one, the lights dimming as she reached her private exit to the lab.

Charlene entered the airlock, stripped off her clean suit, and placed it into the transport module that would remove it from the lab to be replaced by a new one at the other side of the sealed unit, along with her freshly pressed evening suit. She stepped lightly into her living area, away from the cameras; they were not needed here as the whole area was security sealed, with no way out except the entrance.

The floor was spotlessly clean, lit in a pleasantly bright pale blue wave of colour. The tiled floor was pleasantly warm, rather than cool, hinting at special heating systems or other levels below. A faint caress of gentle instrumental music filled the air as she moved to the bathroom.

From five to half five she bathed, scrubbing off the chemicals from her hair and skin. The laboratory was ostensibly a clean room however she'd found that even the most controlled reactions in the sealed vacuum cupboards released gases and odours into the wider laboratory, escapes too faint to trigger the alarms or the neutralising agents for the more powerful chemicals. She'd gotten used to the fact that the leaks occurred; A.G.E. was not the biggest company capable of affording the best equipment, and only the best allowed everything to remain clean. She was semi-convinced that several of the problems she was having were caused by those tiny gaseous emanations.

After half five, Charlene dried off in a blast of air and changed into the red and gold kimono used for her next three relaxation sessions; meditation, gymnastics, and judo. She did not really know why this pattern had fixed in her mind as a fitness routine, other than the fact that she'd done several of them with her mother, when the 'Dark Queen' had taken her away on her visiting days, something she had never revealed to her father. The memories were full of the pain from her mother's training techniques and the discretely hidden wounds they had inflicted on her, so it was weird that they felt such an integral part of her, as though some inner sight sensed the need to continue the routine, despite its associated disturbing memories.

She strode into the Bedroom and settled down for her meditation, the warmth of the bath still glowing in her limbs and body. The oils she used in the burners were designed to refresh the senses; a tip gleaned from the internet, along with the gymnastics routine and the judo kata. Her initial use of them had necessitated a change in the fire detectors used in the installation. She'd almost enjoyed the fuss that had caused, probably a trait from the 'Dark Queen.' As she usually did, she started with her mental relaxation; reciting the periodic table, various chemical families and programming commands. Slowly, her heart rate dropped, her mind calmed; readying her for the next stage.

Padding, barefoot, into the mini gymnasium which had been installed for her, she grabbed two ribbons from the wall rack and began stretching ready to start her acrobatic routine. They reminded her again of the whips with which she'd been trained. It was a sad thing that, during the daytime, she thought of her father; in the evening it was mostly her mother; even if they were both gone. She had no real illusions about her physical skills, having no true athletic ability, other than her build, lifestyle and routine. She started by leaping high, shooting the ribbons out as far as they could go, then darting, apparently manically, around the room with the ribbons trailing, then on to the tumble sequence. She'd spent hours perfecting the ribbon's patterns, crisscrossing the tumbling line and not getting tangled. As she landed the third tumble, she launched herself into the air, and the silk crossed beneath her body followed by the final somersault and forward roll landing. She was breathing quite regularly, with just a few extra heartbeats to show for the minutes of rapid acrobatics. After a minute's recovery, she reluctantly put aside the ribbons. One day she'd have the courage to use whips, but for now she was content with just ribbons; after all, occasionally she had accidents; with whips that really smarted.

Finally, came the judo; a relatively complex self-defence kata she'd located on one of her web searches. Her main reason for doing this was to keep up certain parts of her musculature that the gymnastics could not, especially when she was indoors all the time. All in all, it was not a bad lifestyle; her work kept her mind active, while the exercise kept her body healthy. She saw the news occasionally, knowing many people could not do even this.

After her katas, She had a shower and started her evening routine with a leisurely tea. Most days, she ordered in a Chinese take away from a local shop she'd discovered, today's special being a beautiful chicken chow mien; a local recipe which was healthy, unlike the European equivalent or the shops' microwave versions. She had the takeaway's green tea too, even though the whole building was raving about the latest fad tea, Cha-mer. She found its' smell literally stung her palette and made her eyes water.

Two hours of study followed in her bedroom including more checking into the latest Nano-technology, miniature equipment, chemical engineering design theory and similar subjects. Very occasionally at this point, she needed to call one of her contacts, to consult on problems she did not have the expertise for, and they would discuss technical matters. Additionally, two of them were keen chess players, one of them always having a game on the go with her. After her latest move, Charlene looked up at the clock and saw it was rapidly approaching nine in the evening. She sighed, the game would have to wait until tomorrow.

The hour between nine and ten was wind down time, and she slid into her night silks, powered down her tablet and dimmed her bedroom lights. Her bed was a wondrously large king-sized four-poster, with a thick memory foam mattress, plump pillows, and a double-helix patterned duvet, with night lights above and a lace curtain surround, to block any residual light from the lab. Books were stacked neatly on the other side of the bed while the rest of the room was plain and functional; wardrobes and stools in front of a small, unused, dressing table. The one thing that contrasted the whole thing was the stuffed toy on her side of the bed, a large fluffy brown bear, worn, but clean, given to her on her fourth birthday; two years before her parents split up. Her father had always said that she would be a strong as a bear one day. She'd never seen it in herself, but then he'd always been a bit of a romantic. She lay down, meditating, to help her to drift off to sleep.

Tonight, the same as every other night, the sleep came easily, and she started to dream. Tonight, she was standing in the air in front of Big Ben; the clock just ticking, over and over again, the feeling was that time just kept drifting ever onwards. The crowds went past below following their usual routines; no one even noticing her floating there.

Then the scene changed, and instead of London, she was in Cornwall, near her father's ancestral home. The old clock tower, in the garden, ticked loudly and the clouds speeding overhead; time starting to accelerate, gathering pace.

She looked down and, instead of grass, she stood on dry, undulating sand. Looking up, she stood near one of the great Egyptian Pyramids, in the ruins of a small mud house with only a small stool to sit on; a large wooden hourglass in her hands, its sands running down, Faster and faster until the sands were lost in a blur.

The scene shifted again, and she was standing in a large empty building, in India, in front of the Taj Mahal and, seeing the world turn, again and again, slowing again now. Next, she was in the mountains of Tibet where, finally, the frenetic pace of the dream slowed. A frail old man came wandering into the large hall, walking slowly, but without aid, to where she now sat still. He did not look familiar, but he seemed to know her as his hand cupped her face and he looked deep into her eyes. The words came into her head, rather than him speaking, "Be patient, child. Your time is coming."

Charlene awoke at seven on the dot, not really needing a watch, or alarm clock, with her regime so ingrained. Gliding to the shower, something dark caught her eye on the floor; a few dark specks on the otherwise spotless floor. Was that dirt? Or sand? She peered closer, then laughed at the absurdity of the question. Of course, it was dirt; gritty to be sure, but just dirt, she'd probably brought it in from the lab and not noticed.

Peeling off her night clothes, she poured herself into the shower although she actually felt refreshed. Still, the sensation of the water running down her back was always welcome, and today, it flowed just right, getting her thinking of the problem-set for the day. The command flow for the deployment subroutine needed routing properly; it needed initiating at the command node, for processing at the unloading subroutine.

Fifteen minutes of pure luxury later, she stepped out of the shower and into the drier; a quick blast of warm air forcing her hair straight. Then she was back into the bedroom, donning her clothes, grabbing her tablet, and moving towards the lab in one smooth flowing motion; ready for the day ahead. She entered the airlock seal and went back to the cameras, and her battle with the Nanobots.

"Dr. Charlene Klerk, authorisation, one seven five six nine alpha clearance level four. Activate lab systems," she prompted to the comms unit, on the wall.

"Good morning, Dr. Klerk," came the reply from the speakers in the ceiling. The lights flickered on and lab. systems began powering up, with the usual "Systems Booting" message. "There you are, Doctor. Just call, as usual, if you need anything. We had a new batch of tea arrive yesterday if you want to try it," came a perkier than usual comment. He must have received a pay rise or something.

"No thanks, just the usual please." And so, the day began as normal once again.

She planted herself at the main terminal, with her trusty tablet next to her, logged in, and started typing, with intense precision, equations that filled the screen to be transmitted to the test software. The emulation software seemed to indicate that the modification would work correctly, with the tech simulation confirming that. However, in her experience, Mother Nature was the final judge and jury, in matters of whether the technology would work in an organic system. All finished, she transferred the program to her arm unit.

"If this were an organic system, I'd be running human trials on the dam' cure by now," she tutted to herself, "but NOooo! They say 'mechanical nanotech is the future,'" she grumbled softly, then tapped the programming unit they had given her to control the little blighters again. "Now, pretty please, off you go and fix the nanotubes to the tissue sample so we can go to the next stage.".

She adjusted the focus of the scope and, as instructed, the little bot trundled off to do as it had been told; in the opposite direction.

"UUUUwwww." Charlene's heel stumped the ground hard in frustration. "Darn blasted polarity," she muttered tapping harder on her pad, to its' protesting bleeps, entering several of the less familiar commands again and adding the appropriate mathematical signing.

"This is the last time I tell you, THAT WAY," she ground out from between her teeth. The bot obediently followed the command this time and reached the edge of the tissue sample, then kept going. Charlene was about to rip the controller off her arm in frustration when the bot stopped, delivering its payload smack in the heart of the skin cell's cancer.

She froze. It had worked. It had actually worked. Her programming actually worked. The 'bot had homed in on the core of the cancer and started building the channel, she had a result. She broke into a sudden smile of both relief and disbelief, a strange moaning, laugh escaped her mouth and her feet paddled a little on the spot.

"Well, I'll be," a little squeal of joy, followed the laugh, then she rapidly copied the correct code to the central computer, along with a copy of the instructions needed, as her discipline reasserted itself.

Of course, this was just another stage. Now she needed to use the enhanced tubes to see if the nutrient lining that she had devised accelerated the cancers travel down the tubes, to allow a more efficient cure delivery in life improving timescale. It would be a step on the road to getting cancers off the deadly diseases list. If she could do that, she could perhaps aim for the Nobel prize for Chemistry or even Medicine.

After another few hours, the results came in. There was notable progress of the cancer through the tubes, and the growth suppressant was working at the entry end. If that progress continued as per the model, it would mean that the cancer could be relocated.

Once, she'd noted it all down on her tablet and slipped it in her going out coat, she set off to report this progress to Dr. Trafford at a conference somewhere in Kent. She did not fancy the journey, but she had strict instructions to report to him, directly, should she make any significant progress. A little strange, but then most of the people in her life seemed to have strangeness built-in, much like herself. She sometimes wondered if the people seemed weird because she was, or she was strange because she'd always been surrounded by peculiar people herself.

She changed quickly from the clean suit, into her business one; apparently from a top store, fully tailored and the height of current fashion, not that she cared. No matter what she wore, she still seemed to 'reek of Geek,' as she'd caught Driver saying to another of the security guards one time. Of course, hunched over her tablet and wearing a lab coat most of the time hardly allowed her to exude an air of business authority.

Grabbing a transport case, she loaded the necessities into it, including a samples case that Dr. Trafford had apparently forgotten to take with him, logged the contents, time and transport arrangements, and awaited the security door opening to allow Driver to take her to her destination. She must make sure to get a takeaway for the journey as Driver would want to take her straight there and she had not eaten in, well, she forgot how long.

The driver appeared at the door, as usual, precisely ten minutes later. He was always prompt, but then he needed to be; the first driver had been a few minutes late during her fourth day and been immediately dismissed, at least she'd never seen him again. The current one was snug in his chauffeur suit, indicating an extremely muscular build, but without a bodybuilder's exaggerated walk. His face was a bit plain, but with an experienced brawler's rugged looks and gleaming white teeth that broadcast a professional smile. There was a slight turn of his eyes that showed he was not entirely comfortable with the cap though, perhaps because it was slightly too small for him.

"G'Day, Ma'am. The car is ready." His speech was a little formal, but, being honest with herself, she kind of liked that simple rote phrase he used. His manner was friendly enough, although she was ambivalent about his looks.

"Thanks, Driver," Charlene replied, trying to recall if she actually knew his name and was a little surprised when she realised, she did not.

They headed out of the labs building, passing through the other security doors and gates, collecting her bags, properly tagged and registered to leave the building.

The waiting car was a long sleek black affair, but not knowing much about cars, she only knew the make because of the logo. The corporate people used them for travel these days she'd heard, instead of the more luxurious cars her father had raved about.

The driver opened the door for her, and she slid in with the case secured to her wrist by handcuffs; standard practice for something so potentially valuable. She may not be relishing the thought of the journey, but it was always a little exciting to see the outside world, and that, plus the feeling of her progress, made her forget to order the food. The driver stacked the other cases in the boot, took his seat and set off smoothly at a fast, but comfortable, pace.

Traffic towards the conference centre was heavy, nothing unusual there, but Charlene had a nagging feeling that this was not going to be a usual day; just something in the air perhaps, or maybe the quick progress, but the atmosphere thick with something she could not identify; impinging at her awareness like a buzzing mosquito. The sky was bright, a light breeze with just a few clouds. Perhaps she was just not used to the air out here, after all, her lab was fully sealed, and the air conditioning was negatively pressured, due to the nature of her work; did not want anything escaping decontamination, especially the more exciting chemicals that were in use in the lab. Perhaps it was just the normal atmospheric pollution that people chatted about on the medical forums.

The driver, John, was honestly feeling more than a little bored of this assignment. He worked for the private security company, DriveSec, who were sub-contracted by A.G.E. to protect its' critical assets. They had offered him an attractive, bodyguard, role. This was definitely not that; babysitting a scientist, albeit a pretty one provided little of interest.

The briefing proved interesting enough, regarding the situational assessment. Apparently, a key staff member had disappeared, and they needed someone to protect their crucial asset from any similar occurrence. Dr. Rampton had not left, fallen sick, or died; he'd just vanished without a trace. He'd departed work one day and not come back the next. Checks by the company had found his car missing from home, the milk stacking up outside, and concerned neighbours about to call the police. They'd taken care of that, but the police had said to keep it under wraps while they investigated. It seemed that there was an ongoing investigation, including similar occurrences at other companies.

He'd been briefed not to let her out of his sight, although because she was female, there was some leeway. It had been made abundantly clear that she was his priority, and that any failure would mean the end of not only his contract but his career; that's what made it interesting. But, so far, she'd been out of her lab once, to the central office to provide a monthly report. She had almost entirely ignored him, her small talk being virtually none existent. When he'd tried to hold a conversation with her, the answers were so convoluted that she might as well have been talking Swahili if she'd actually been talking to him, it'd been hard to tell. The pay was good, but not enough to endure such repetitive boredom.

Still, something piqued his interest. When they had travelled to the office, there had been glimpses, just glimpses mind you, of someone, that might have been following them. They'd been fleeting and infrequent, but just frequent enough to impinge on his awareness and create a feeling of disquiet. It might have been someone on a similar journey, or just the same make and colour of car, or any number of other coincidental associated recollections. But given his brief, he was not inclined to believe in coincidence. If they were being followed, they were very good, and it could be a prelude to an abduction like Rampton, or any number of other things.

He remembered all of the training he'd taken to get to his current security rating; awareness, anti-terror, firearms, tazer, first aid and, of course, defensive and advanced driving courses. All that, just to sit in the driver's seat to a junior scientist, no matter how vital the company thought she was, was wasteful. Still, he was a professional, like his father before him, so he kept his opinions to himself; at least until he handed in his notice at the end of this trip, unless that phantom tail suddenly decided to make his life more interesting. He'd never really subscribed to the saying 'be careful what you wish for.'

The traffic started getting heavier, with many more trucks filling the second lane, until, finally, the traffic began to slow to a crawl, just as they hit the southeast section of the M25.

Charlene sighed; this is why she did most of her conferences by Vidcom. The real world was full of all sorts obstacles that were beyond her control, and she hated that. Control, mainly self-control, was the one part of her mother's personality that she actually appreciated and used; although she admitted to herself that she needed more of it.

As the traffic slowed, even more, John started to get a little concerned. He'd checked the SatNav. before they departed and there'd been no accidents reported along this stretch of the motorway network, but ahead were flashing blue lights, and that meant trouble. An apparently unreported incident made him a bit nervous, and when he became nervous, he became both more suspicious, and alert. He started to track significant movements in the surrounding area, scrutinising the car's cams and mirrors more frequently. His hawk-eyed passenger soon spotted the change in his behaviour.

"A problem, Driver?" God, he hated the way she called him that.

He knew she thought he was like the previous driver, who'd been just that; a driver and a poorly organised one at that. John was a trained personal protection professional, and his driving skills would put some racers to shame. He'd show her one day, but he had more important things to worry about now; he'd been given his orders and, as far as his employers were concerned, she was John's number one priority.

"No, Ma'am. It's just that we are running a bit later than I'd like and you know how the M25 can clog the local routes around here when it's like this." He hated himself for saying that; she would NOT know that, but she would pretend to, just to seem clued up. Besides, it really sounded like a lame excuse even to him; her attitude was getting him wound up and making him sloppy. He would have to register for that darn Situational Awareness course again if this carried on. He sighed once more, making it even more apparent to himself that he needed that refresher. As they arrived at the incident, he noticed a few things in rapid succession that set off his alarm bells for real.

The incident lay across the middle lane, definitely not cleared properly, with the queue having built up there for several minutes, something the police and motorway agency tried to avoid at all costs. While it was coned off, there was no one guiding traffic through; the 'police' sitting in a marked BMW, supposedly talking details from people in the back, but actual paying more attention to the passing cars.

However, the current motorway response cars were the sports Subaru, with the upgraded engines. More importantly, the crashed car's roof was still intact, with no fire engines in attendance to evacuate the damaged vehicle and none could be heard approaching. All this and it was unreported? This stank. If only one of these points were present, he would have been slightly suspicious; with all three, it screamed - "SETUP"!

Subconsciously, he undid his firearms' holster catch and cleared access to his alert button, while trying to appear nonchalant.

"This traffic IS getting very heavy, Ma'am. I think I'd best take an alternate route, perhaps the one I saw one back there a short-ways," he said, putting on his best poker face, while shifting out of lane, in a tight, off-side turn manoeuvre, that took them out of the queue fastest, much to the annoyance of nearby drivers. He quickly executed the rattling turn a little fast for the corner and bumped the edge of the curb, even though he had to cross the hard shoulder and hashed lines to do it. A quick glance in the mirrors indicated that the police had spotted his departure and were on the radio to someone, although they were not trying to follow. This only confirmed that the situation was not what it had, at first, appeared to be and that it could still escalate, really fast.

Charlene was more a little startled by the sudden jostling, even more so by the bump; things suddenly seemed more dangerous than a simple reporting trip, or an accident. She had to admit, she kind of liked the adrenaline rush; it was so, exciting. She shook herself; the attitude was so unprofessional, and that thought made her stop cold. That thought was so like the 'Dark Queen,' it was almost as if she could hear her mother saying the oft-repeated phrases.

"Charlene, just remember, be professionally detached at all times. For a business person or scientist, it is probably the greatest advantage we have, over other people. They think themselves professional even when they actually are not. You must guard against enjoying a situation. Analyse, Adapt and Achieve, then you are in control." She'd said it so many times that Charlene had it on a plaque in her lab, one of the few personal items there. "Analyse, Adapt and Achieve." It was uncanny, the way the words she heard in her head, were accompanied by that same nasally superior tone the 'Dark Queen' had always used.

After a few minutes, it became apparent, even to the ultra-suspicious John, that there was no pursuit coming. Whatever the imposters had planned had either failed or was happening elsewhere. He relaxed, slightly, as they appeared to be safe for the moment, or at least not in immediate danger. Half turning to his passenger he said, "We'll be at the conference in about thirty-five minutes, Ma'am," trying to put her back at ease.

The driver was starting his usual scan of the locale as they approached their destination, Charlene noticed. His eyes were rapidly viewing the surrounding streets as they drew up to the main conference building, almost subconsciously, as if he did not even know he was doing it. It did not occur to her that she was doing a very similar thing, subconsciously watching the driver's every action. It was strange that she knew many of his mannerisms without understanding how. If he'd noticed that she was watching him so intently, he might even have started to get jittery in a different way.

As they pulled up to the hotel acting as the conference hall, several labourers outside moved sluggishly out of the way of the car. The driver, scowled at them until they were ushered inside by a suited corporate type.

The venue was a spacious multi-story affair, with a low side extension, where the conference was apparently being held. A crowd of well-dressed business people milled around outside, bleating to one another and plush vehicles frequently pulled up at the large reception area to disgorge more. Some large trucks, of the kind they had seen on the motorway, were unloading around the back, presumably delivering equipment, presentation stands and catering staff for the delegates, and corporate show. The front of the hotel showed its royal pedigree, compared to the lower conference area, as, through the main doors, a wide-based, grand, staircase leading to the upper floors where the bedrooms could be seen.

John drew up in a parking bay, a short way from the entrance of the hotel. The park was filled with company cars belonging to the various subsidiaries and partners of Biotecknica, A.G.E.'s parent company. He stepped out keeping his eyes sharp for anything suspicious, stowed his keys and striding around the car to open the door for his passenger.

"Here we are, Ma'am," he confirmed, as he opened the door; closing it smartly, once she'd lithely slid out; he had not previously noticed how graceful she was.

"Never been to one of these places before," she said to him in a forced conversational tone, "wonder where the Gym is?"

John thought that she was obviously unsettled as she rarely left A.G.E. The rapid departure from the motorway had probably not helped

"You'll be close?" Now what had made her say that?

"Of course, Ma'am. That's my job." Although his tone was one of professional indifference, John noted the quaver in her voice, feeling a little sympathy for her.

"I'm not one for science talk, so I'll just mingle. But I won't be more than a short dash away." He flashed her a practiced reassuring smile, and they walked together into the foyer of the hotel.

The reception desk was to the right as they entered, the staff seemingly fully engaged with various business customers, as ushers guided businessmen either left, up the main staircase to their rooms or straight ahead to the presentations. The Reception area itself was filled with the usual pre-conference chaos of milling scientists, executives and the odd entertainer or two, who were probably part of the corporate entertainment provided by the centre. They tried to move through the large, high ceilinged, room full of mahogany woods and polished brasses which usually warmed the room making it almost homely in the evening sunlight.

This evening, with the sun setting outside, the wood looked more like a deep blood red; though looking up, the crystal chandeliers, offset that redness, turning it almost into a dreamy pink; a fascinatingly romantic effect appreciated by John, but lost on his charge.

The two picked up their conference badges from the company reception desk, John noting that he was registered as a "Bodyguard" rather than the Chauffeur. He wished people would tell him if they were going to advertise his full skill set so that he could get the going rate and stock up on body armour.

However, Charlene noted something strange as well; Dr. Trafford had not arrived yet, even though according to the company he'd already checked in. She looked around to see if she could spot him but failed in the milling crowd. She did spot, or rather hear, one particular individual male making a bit of a scene.

"Don't you know who I am?" demanded the irate and very vocal man, of the Duty Manager. "I am here to reveal an important scientific breakthrough, and I need something much better than that, closet assigned to me."

Almost immediately, a massive security guard appeared at the man's shoulder.

"Is there a problem here, Sir?" he asked, casually put a hand on the loud guests' arm. Although the man did not move immediately, it was obvious, from the strained look on his face, that the guard was exerting a gradually increasing pressure on the arm, attempting to guide him away from the reception area. "Come along, sir, let's take this matter to the managers' office, where we can get it dealt with, quietly."

The man shot the guard a look of pure hatred, "get off me you ape," and he tried to struggle, to no effect.

John muttered a ripple of the shoulders showed he was watching the situation too.

"Bloody amateurs. They should have removed that idiot the moment he started to open his mouth." He shook his head in disapproval, then turned to his charge coming back to the reason they were here, "Room or Presentation first?".

She looked around and grabbed a program for the event from a stand. "I think that we should check out the amenities first, then decide," he noted with surprise his inclusion in the decision process. He'd been speaking rhetorically.

She moved deliberately towards the main hall, scanning the program on the way, bypassing a busy Cha-mér tea promotion stall on the way, trailing her bodyguard a few steps behind. Perhaps Dr. Trafford had gone straight into the main hall to present something, or just to hob-knob, after all, he was the kind of person that learned things about people by talking to other people about the weather; it was why he was sent to these kinds of does.

John had never really noticed how gracefully Dr. Klerk moved before; of course, he'd rarely seen her without her lab-coat, let alone in a tailor-made business suit before. Lithe was the best description, but there was something else in the way she walked; she moved with precision, balance, and care he'd not seen in others. He slowed more and at that point did a slight mental adjustment of his opinion of her. It was not something in her main profile, but she must have had some martial arts training. Not recently, as he knew she did not go to any club or mentor; unless she practiced in the lab sometime, but she definitely moved in that clipped, controlled and fluid way. This one was not a typical scientist, woman or charge, in fact, he suddenly had a deep gut feeling that she was not a typical anything. He should have asked for more on his contract. He followed her with his eyes noting how she scanned the room, avoiding conversations on the one hand and deflecting others with a curt glance. She suddenly had all the hallmarks of a class A problem, just waiting to happen. How had he not seen this before? What else had he missed? That Situational Awareness course now seemed a much more important item on his agenda.

Charlene glanced at the schedule. There were several different stages to this evening's events; all starting with a welcome from Biotecknica by the CEO, followed by a large number of presentations, of scientific interest, three which she actually wanted to see, all interspersed by acts from an Illusionist, Harry Hidden, and ending with a magic talent show that the illusionist would compare.

Well, the rounds would allow her time to talk to the other attending scientists; although, she noticed that there were quite a few seats that were empty. Each place had a name tag on it, and she was surprised by some of the absentees. She knew them, even if only over Skype, or by their work, and they reputedly never missed any such gatherings; if for no other reason than to gloat about their most recent achievements to their fellow scientists. One of those missing people was Dr. Trafford.

Maybe there'd been an emergency that required his knowledge and skill, or perhaps he'd been called back now that she was present. She was starting to get concerned about Dr. Trafford; he had not been seen him, and she had critical information she needed to give to him alone, and it was getting late.

She drifted across to a group of people who were sampling the buffet. One young man was in earnest discussion with older delegates, although they did not have the scientist's technical talk, nor the CEO's business suits. She ignored them and moved on hearing someone to her left muttering about one of the presentations being of interest, something about a new power source, one she'd looked into too. Charlene moved a little closer and listened more intently.

"Hmmm I wonder if the power frequency could be adjusted to match the resonance coupling of the mark three," speculated the stranger. The person he was talking to appeared much less interested and was attempting to politely move off towards the succulent looking buffet bar. The speaker seemed in his mid to late twenties but dressed more like someone twice his age, with a Tweed jacket, mismatched trousers, and two different scuffed light brown shoes. He was however rather handsome, certainly more so than anyone else here, except Driver of course; the comparison was instinctive and, almost, casually dismissed.

Charlene muttered almost to herself; "Or perhaps you could adjust the power coupling interface to match the power source frequency and thus only need to do it once. Given the output claimed for the power source, it would easily give you many times more amps to power your device than any current power source, short of a static power plant."

The strangers' turned slightly to face her, allowing the other person to escape, unnoticed by the remaining pair. The speaker locked eyes with her for a second, quickly appraising the well-dressed woman before him and recognising a kindred spirit, smiled slightly.

"Yes, but I'd need some sort of governing unit, to guard against excessive feed, and surges," challenging the newcomer, more than talking to her.

"Unless you had a second stage to the coupling, that bypasses the main unit to an inverter. Then, any excess power from the feed would counter the main feed, balancing the power, so that, the greater the overload, the more contra-power would be channelled to block it, thus protecting the main unit."

His smile grew Wider. "Yes. Hello?" he raised his hand in a tentative greeting.

"Dr. Charlene Klerk, Biochemistry and Nanotechnology," the stranger's eyes shot up, in apparent recognition of her name.

"Hello?" she smiled back at him, mimicking the tone and question, taking his hand and giving it a gentle squeeze.

"Professor Simon Caruthers. Human/Robotic interaction and Cybernetics". His name too was familiar to her.

"I did not realise you were so young," they said simultaneously, laughing in tandem.

The professor looked down to his notepad, "The articles you published, on 'aspects of nano-filament transport,' did not actually mention you were a woman either, and an attractive one at that." He was a little surprised to see her actually blush; something few women did these days.

"Well I would like to mention that YOUR article on 'lightweight robotic arms for mobility impaired servicemen' did not say that you are perhaps the youngest professor I have ever seen," she smiled even more, "of course, I rarely get out, so you're also probably the ONLY young professor I have seen, in person".

"Beauty, Brains, and Candour, in one so youthful. You are an interesting and complicated young lady Dr. Klerk; but one that most men would mark as someone to get to know," he complimented her. She looked indifferent to the compliment, as he handed her his card. "Perhaps we can compare notes on this new power source at some point. My card." She glanced at it, as she tucked it away in her suit.

"You have a business card? Humph. I've never had a business card," she was a trifle disgruntled at that, but she hid it well.

"Of course, the company tends to deal with all the business aspects of my work. I'm usually too busy on the sales side of things anyway."

There was a flurry of activity behind them, as the crowd started to settle into their seats in front of the stage. Reluctantly, she turned towards the wooden chairs at the back of the arrangement.

"See you around professor Caruthers," and she wafted away, aiming for the seat with her name on it.

He did not bother with his seat, he was more into robotic engineering, material sciences, and microelectronics than the particle physics and nanotech this conference advertised. He was only really here because his university did not have the staff spare to attend the nano-tech presentations they needed the feedback and literature from; especially as some that might have been asked to come had called in ill with some dubiously exotic symptoms. He was suspicious that they were crying off, because, like him, they expected it would be more than moderately dull, despite the later presentations having promise. The new power source being hinted at was of particular interest, especially after his conversation with Dr. Klerk, but he could hear about that from the side as easily as from in the audience, perhaps even better. He was not comfortable with crowds of people and did not want to mix too much with them. He suspected Dr. Klerk was the same, as she skirted the larger groups when weaving her way to the seats. He noticed her seat was right at the back, no doubt positioned so she could bolt as soon as it was over.

He had read her latest works and, while she was remarkably young for someone with her reputation and achievements, she had a mature technical insight. He tried to remember the rest of her history, but it was fuzzy, and he was not the kind to pry into people's past.

John drifted around the presentation area and stood near the entrance doing a visual inspection of the courtyard. Before him, congregated a mass of 'geek,' his term for those with high IQ's and low common sense, in their stiff business attire and overconfident superiority. While the left side was open to an inner courtyard, along the other side's length, was a cream draped buffet table, which looked rather appealing right now.

Opposite him stood the raised presentation stage, partially concealed by a couple of thick, deep red, drape curtains, suspended from a rich mahogany support frame, flanked by a medium-sized sound setup. Little was actually set up on the stage, although there were a few illusionist boxes and props stacked along the sides, probably for the show later. He assumed that everything had been cleared by the local security team, but he still he ran his eyes over them, just to be thorough. He did not want any surprises because he'd been unable to do his job, or they had failed to do theirs.

The yard had several rows of rather elegant padded wooden chairs, set out for the audience who were now settling in for the opening presentation, from the CEO of BioTechnica, Niles Wallice.

Leaning against the wall near the entrance, John took stock of the situation; nothing unusual at the moment, but after this morning he was on edge, and he was not usually this jittery, but, oh he didn't know, perhaps he was just getting paranoid after his company brief.

A stranger wandered past, stopping near to him, seemingly trying to avoid the scientists still clustered around the edges of the room as much as John had. He sported a smart leather jacket and matching dark trousers, with a fancy, ruffled, white shirt. He was dark skinned, which was smooth but showed a kind of tightness that made him look wiry. His eyes spoke of intelligence, without the geeky look of those around him; the sort of wary look of someone who'd been on the streets, that John knew so well. It was a look that could not be faked; it was on his face every morning and frequently appeared on the faces of people he worked with, on both sides of the law.

"Scientists!" muttered the stranger, as much to himself, or the room, as to anyone in particular. "They always seem to believe their eyes," there was a hint of derision in the tone.

John nodded slightly, looking up at the stage and awaiting the CEO to explain why they were all here, probably at great length. "Yup! Boring as hell too," he muttered, more to himself than to the other.

The bystander turned slightly, and seemed to notice John for the first time, giving him an appraising look; then produced a deck of cards from nowhere. John thought he was going to offer a game of poker or something, but once the pack was opened the other said, "pick a card!"

John looked at the cards and frowned. Then it dawned on him, the stranger was one of the entertainers, waiting their turn. He must be a magician. John backed away slightly, pretending to ward off both cards and trickster, evoking a wry, amused smile from the stranger.

"Oh no! I know better than to play card games with a magician," he said quietly. The man looked both hurt and amused, but he stowed the cards away in a flash of movement.

"Ah well another time perhaps," although his tone was one of resignation, that this 'victim' was not one he would catch out. He held out his hand, pulling back the sleeve of his costume in a sign that he had nothing up his sleeves, a blatant deception not lost on John.

"Harry Hidden, Illusionist," and he emphasised the word, "and Escapologist!"

John shook the hand, trying not to crush the others', much smaller, hand, "John."

Trying not to wince at the casual strength of the bodyguards' grip, the entertainer complained, "Wow, hell of a grip you have there, not surprising but still," he said, pantomiming having a crushed hand and producing a bandage from nowhere.

John smiled, "Pretty good, and surprisingly useful, trick that. If I need one, I'll come to find you". Harry smiled and just winked at him as they both settled next to the wall to await the start of the presentations.

The presentations started with bright spotlights, fanfare and the scientists' conversations died as they watched Niles Wallice's entrance. It was the standard corporation format, and John barely noticed, as the CEO started by welcoming everyone and listing the company's achievements for the year, from a small tablet in his hand. He followed that by introducing the special guest, an eminent scientist announcing his latest discovery; a new form of matter, z443, that promised to be many times more powerful than any known trans-uranic element. The scientist had apparently produced and was testing it in the CERN laboratories, in France. As he started with the technical details, the CEO bowed out, leaving the rather pompous scientist to wax lyrical about his theories on Chromatic creation, using this substance. Many of the audience sat hypnotised by the scientific details, but others, including John, started to get a bit fidgety towards the middle of the overly long talk.

While most of those attending watched the presentation, John noticed two that definitely were not. He did not know why they stood out, but, just at the edge of the yard, by the buffet table, two figures talked quietly with their backs to the stage in relatively plain sight. One was unknown to John, but the other was vaguely familiar; the middle-aged man, who had made the scene earlier at the reception. The skin on the back of his neck started to crawl, a sure sign trouble was brewing. John began to surreptitiously towards the pair manoeuvring his way between them and his charge. The unknown man talked for a few minutes with the other, then handed the other a business card. Near the end, John overheard one thing that concerned him.

"Perhaps you could visit sometime and demonstrate it to my investors?" That seemed to imply that he was leaving his current employers, AdvancedBioChem; that smacked of industrial espionage to John. He was about to go to security and point out the pair when he noticed Charlene trying to catch his attention.

Something unusual was going on here, besides the conspirators, as she rarely bothered with him. Of course, she'd never been at an event like this before. Perhaps she needed him to find her room, or to get him to take her bags there.

Something, or rather someone, had caught Charlene's eye. A particularly unkempt man came staggering into the presentation area from the open side, with an air of both determination and desperation. Charlene had never seen him before, but he stood out in his plain, worn and stain covered long coat. He'd the air of trouble waiting to happen.

She surreptitiously kept an eye on him, as she tried to attract Driver's attention, which seemed to be on the buffet bar at the moment. The man took a swig of some sort of brew, from a silver flask, then staggered closer to the CEO and as he staggered further across the area, he started to sweat and twitch slightly. Upon reaching the CEO's group, he began to argue with him, past the bodyguards, who immediately trying to intervene. Their voices carried over the now somewhat distracted presentation.

"Easy there, Leonard. We can discuss this outside, quietly. Let's not disturb the event," said the CEO authoritatively, while the guiding hands of his minders, tried to get the man towards the exit, although they seemed to be having a bit a trouble with that, the whole procession moving slowly to the exit. While that group continued to try and get the man out the area, the first presentation concluded to polite applause, drowning out the kafuffle at the side and allowing the first round of the magic show to start.

Harry Hidden had quite a few tricks up his sleeves it seemed; some that Charlene had seen, others that eluded even her sharp eyes, but she was a little distracted, and the ten-minute slot had finished when she finally caught the eye of Driver.

John got to her quickly, and she explained what she'd seen. John was not happy. Several things were going on that suggested that there was more going on in this place than just a science conference, and his alarm bells were starting to ring.

The argument between the man and the CEO was more subdued now, as the minders continued to guide the rank man away from the stage. As they did, John became aware of more people, that looked out of place, entering the room from the open side, acting suspiciously; as though they were scanning the area for someone.

Charlene saw them too but stayed focused on the main altercation.

"See if you can follow them and find out what's going on," she said, just behind his own resolve to do so. He was torn between following a potential threat to its source, and leaving her behind, potentially unprotected. Still, there were more people here than just Charlene, and he was curious as to what these people were doing and what trouble could a bunch of scientists be to a group of armed security.

John moved carefully, trying not to alert the people to the fact that they were being deliberately followed. Instead, he used the natural trickle of people between the yard and the reception after the magic act, to head to the foyer, and outside where they were heading. He'd never been so glad of his police training before, as he casually and inconspicuously followed the others out.

Chapter 2

CONFERENCE CHAOS

Harry Hidden had finished the first part of his act with a theatrical flourish and was just relaxing before the other entertainers began the magic competition. He'd found that, for scientists and businessmen, the audience was quite appreciative of his first corporate performance, despite the distractions. He was standing on the left side of the stage while one of the other performers, The White Witch, was performing. She seemed to have a flare for illusions and was currently levitating a wand across the stage. A standard stage trick, although, he had to admit, he could not see how she was doing it, primarily through the hoops and Perspex tunnels layout.

From his vantage point, he could see the bodyguard he'd talked to, John, entering the hotel, and his passenger peering over the crowd, towards the commotion with dishevelled tramp burbling away over the open side of the building, behind the chairs. He looked towards the group, trying to make out what was going on. Finally, the company security guards lost their patience and started to man-handle the intruder out of the conference, with what appeared to be increasing difficulty; as though he was putting up more resistance the closer to the exit he got. He was trying to figure out how the man was doing that, when the group exploded, bodies flying left and right, as the other figure erupted into violence.

At the same time, John had arrived at the reception, to see several people, that were all pale and more than a little sweaty like the other tramp, being restrained by a host of security guards. As the group reached the exit, right in front of him, the tramps all started to convulse, having some kind of fit. He thought it was just the light at first, but as they continued to writhe, he could not deny what was happening; they were changing, growing in stature, their faces and bodies twisting and changing in different ways, distorting into gruesome mockeries of canine snouts, furred faces and twisted animal limbs. Some seemed to change completely, others seemed to only get halfway then get stuck part-beast, part-human; all of them looked powerful and deadly. They had transformed into what can only be described as Were-creatures, and they were effectively blocking the entrance to the hotel, where all the delegates were now trapped.

In the yard, a security guard was flung high into the air, arms flailing until he landed, crashing loudly down into the middle of the chairs, amid screams of confusion from the audience, who suddenly became aware of the threat in their midst. The CEO's other guards, clung desperately onto the much larger creature, suddenly towering above the crowd; like a shadow of doom. Also, the lights had started to flicker, turning the yard into a nightmare scene from a horror movie, filled with stroboscope glimpses of monsters, screams of terror and snarls of madness.

As another minder was shaken off, the huge creature in the scattering crowd, rose to its full eight feet height and howled; whether in anger, pain, or just because it could, no one knew. The sound silenced the screams and shouts, for a few seconds; then the screams erupted again even louder than before, and a wave of people roiled towards the nearest exits.

Charlene made a split-second decision to run for the door rather than out into the yard, heading towards Driver and at least potential safety. However, halfway there, three new creatures started to make a bloody entrance to the room, fighting against a tide of panicked people. The monstrosities picked up two of the security guards stood by the door and efficiently ripped out their throats, before dismissively dropping them to the floor, without even a second glance.

So, food was not their motivation, Charlene thought while noticing that her escape route was now effectively blocked. She turned left, stopping before reaching the doorway, crouching next to the wall, looking at the scene and evaluating. Where was Driver? If ever she needed him, it was now, as the largest of the monsters started to slash at the people around it, wading towards the CEO, who was trying to slip away while it was distracted by the bodyguards, and more importantly her.

However, after a few seconds, a strange calm enveloped her thoughts; not shock, but more a filter, as though a different person viewed the unfolding events. The horror of the slaughter in the room seemed to diminish, as another presence, or instinct, began to guide her actions.

The scene paled even more, even though she could still see it, her limbs were now being guided by something entirely different, something with experience or skills to deal with even this situation. Charlene's body dropped to the floor into a perfectly balanced crouch, controlled by that other force, rather than her own thoughts, and it started unloading items from her backpack, cataloguing her resources. From the backpack came Charlene's thumb-print sealed steel demonstration case, which contained several chemicals, that might be useful against these things. In her own mind, she wanted desperately to study these creatures; the abilities to change so quickly, to alter appearance, to gain strength and to grow were phenomenal. The effect on the lights might be connected, but somehow, that did not fit with the creatures observed physiology.

Her hand selected a flask of concentrated acid and with the aid of a practised mind, launched it at the nearest of the monstrosities by the doorway, aiming for its head.

The projectile arced accurately but was diverted mid-flight, by a side light dislodged by the creature, causing the thick glass to be diverted from being an accurate strike, to hit an unfortunate scientist.

The man staggered from the impact on his shoulder, his clothes smouldering for a few seconds, before he started screaming, as the acid began boiling on his skin. He struggled clumsily to throw off his jacket to stop the acid from melting his skin. It was regrettable that he did that just as a creature arrived right next to him, turning to grab him.

With an audible crunch, the slavering creature snapped his neck and, realising that it was under attack, dropped a heavily bleeding minder from its other hand, to start striding towards the crouching human female. It bared its teeth ready to sink them into some tender, raw, flesh.

Still guided this other force, Charlene's chemical barrage continued. She selected another acid bottle, launched it and this time struck home, the creature's skin starting to burn and fizzle. However, the attack was not nearly as effective as she'd expected. Instead of stopping and screaming in agony the creature barely noticed the effect on its skin. Indeed the creature's skin resisted being severely damaged, the acid barely making a mark.

The creature screamed, not in pain, but in rage and continued its advance, trying to swipe at its' antagonist, the claw passing overhead as reflexes caused Charlene to rapidly duck. In the near distance, gunshots started to report from the yards' entrance, and a creature nearby was lifted over a chair by a bullet impact. From the main doorway, came more volleys, from powerful sounding handguns and the creature advancing on Charlene dropped. An armed security guard, appeared; standing behind the falling monster, with a strange smirk on his face,

"Silver bullets do it every time."

Werewolves and silver bullets; Charlene's mind leapt on that statement and performed a quick catalogue of her demonstration kit, remembering a mirror experiment; Silver Nitrate might work, where the acid had not. Her hand grabbed the appropriately marked bottle, leapt forward and doused the struggling creature with the contents. The effect was just like acid, perhaps even more so, melting the skin from the muscles, then the sinew from the bone. The snarling stopped replaced by howls of pain and looks of confusion, both being short-lived, as it started to revert to a human form; falling apart until only a mass of bloody flesh landed on the floor marking its' passage. Turning slightly, Charlene noticed that the larger creature too had started to revert, slowly shrinking back to his normal size and form. Hmm, the smaller creature's state seemed to be linked to the larger creature's state? Fascinating.

Driver bowled into the area behind the other bodyguard and finally reached her side. The strange view of the room faded, as the other presence seemed to release her, her thoughts clearing, becoming her own again. The driver was speaking to her, but the words did not register. She shook her head to vanquish the last of the mental haze and get an idea of what was going on.

"I said, are you ok? Are you injured?" Driver was shaking her shoulders gently, desperately looking her over for tell-tale claw marks. She blinked, then nodded, just about registering the fact that she'd just killed someone, even if it was in self-defence.

"You two, come with us, and cover our backs," ordered the CEO., starting towards the door

She blinked again, and brushed the driver's hand off her, "I'm fine. Let's get out of here," she said, rapidly clicking closed her case, slamming it into her rucksack, and standing as they both bolted after the CEO and his bodyguard, peripherally noticing as they did so that the tramp was swigging again from his silver flask.

The four raced towards the exit at a frantic pace, Charlene racing between two more creatures entering the room behind the two bodyguards, the others somehow evading them as well.

The group of four sprinted down the corridor, littered with dismembered scientists, guards and catering staff; the two armed ones clearing the path, with controlled volleys of silver bullets at the newly invigorated creatures. A few of the fallen were moaning, in the final throes of life with blood dripping from great gashes in their throats and torsos; obviously too far gone to help.

Charlene's hands twitched to aid them, but the guards were moving fast, and she needed their protection. All of this showed Charlene a glimpse of the world she thought she'd been removed from forever; deeply buried memories stirring within her mind. A cold feeling settled in the pit of her stomach, and the thought came "They will be coming for you," whoever they were. She needed to prepare herself, but first, she had to survive this insanity.

The group headed towards the staircase, charging up the steps.

"Where are we heading?" yelled Charlene, as the two guards shot a creature trying to come at them, from behind the reception counter. "The Entrance is just over there," she pointed at the door; just as another group of creatures came through it, snarling, searching for something. "Oh, Gotcha!" and continued after the rest of them, at top speed. Never mind escape, at the moment; the top priority was survival. She could plan what to do after that, assuming there was an after.

From a door, near the staircase, Harry Hidden and Dr. Caruthers pelted out, coming after the group, glancing fretfully behind. Harry had acquired a burn mark on his shoulder, clean through his clothes, showing burnt skin and blood.

"What happened to you two?" Charlene asked in a shocked and puzzled voice, looking meaningfully at the burn. It seemed strange to her as there was little blood, and the radius of the wound was near perfectly circular.

Harry looked at her in exasperation and gasped, "never mind that now, just run," glancing behind himself again.

The augmented group reached the upstairs landing and slowed to a swift jog. Harry glanced at the scientist and saw she was still awaiting an explanation. He looked to the ceiling in exaggerated consternation and gave in. In a tone that brooked no interruption, he began to explain, as they moved down the corridor and went up another broad set of stairs.

It appeared other things were happening, besides the Were-creature attacks, that the others were unaware of.

As the initial slaughter had started, the deformed creatures erupting into violence; a strange, fey, sensation had manifested on the stage. It was similar to the tingling you get when you hear a peculiar sound and almost know what it is, but don't really want to.

Then, as the first attacker had fallen at the door, a massive detonation, of deep purple energy, had tempestuously blown open the stage curtains, washing over the people there, bathing them in a warm, rippling, wave of ephemeral ether. It felt like a lover's first touch, or the warmth of a steaming bath after a trip in the sand dunes, or the hot breath of a hungry beast surrounding your neck. Harry yelled for everyone to evacuate; although the order was drowned out by the cacophony of the surrounding chaos.

He recalled what happened next very well. As the wave quickly passed him, the other magician on the stage gave an ear-numbing scream, as the device she was holding instantaneously changed; its length telescoping violently to six foot, and thickening, from a small stage wand, into a mighty, iron-shod, wooden staff. It started to glow and hum, pouring bolts of light towards a group of creatures, who were laying about them, with claws and fangs, at all within reach.

The woman convulsively grasped the ornate, rune-covered, staff, unable to release it. It was as if the thing had a mind of its own, as it jumped, and jigged, in her hands. A glowing fire-like aura surrounded her, and she seemed as startled at this, as she was with the staves weird, pulsing dance, and energy discharges.

Jack was not usually the brave kind, having grown up as a coloured South African child, in a gang-controlled block of flats, but, he was used to having to do whatever it took to survive; usually involving lots of running. However, the stranger's distress pulled at his heart, and he moved to try and prise the energised staff from her hands, or to help her at least control it better.

He moved carefully forward, planted his feet and tried to pull the staff down and away from the female magician, which proved to be a mistake. Having been discharging in various direction, the mystical device now decided that the newcomer was a much more attractive and immediate target. The bolts of power, having been going in all directions, suddenly all seemed to align on Harry, lighting him up, in a pulsing pink aura for a second, before slamming him down across the stage, miraculously unhurt. Jack did a double-take. A bolt of electricity like that should have killed him; it must have been something entirely different. At first his head was ringing from the effects of bouncing off the stage; fortunately, his landing was cushioned by a box of costumes prepared for one of the amateur acts, the landing relatively soft. Recovering, Jack began to notice that, for all the lights were flickering and dimming all over the place, he could now see an eerie, purple, pulsing light, with lines and waves fluxing around the staff and a few people in the room; including himself.

He'd just adjusted his eyes to focus on the rippling new sights when a large half-formed Were-creature landed on the stage. Now, Jack was a sensible guy usually, and typically, he would have tried to evade the creature; however, fate intervened. As the creature looked around for something to eat, or vent its rage on, it saw nothing, as Jack slipped on a silk cloth, and vanished out of sight of the monstrosity, just as it gazed in his direction. He also clunked his head on the stage fully and was momentarily out for the count, so he did not see the pretty young magician, stood not two feet from him, blast the werewolf with a huge pulse of white flame.; the oily stench it produced was one of burnt dog.

As he came to, the female magician held out her hand helping him up. "We need to get out of here!" She said, grasping the staff in one hand and offering him her other.

However, even as she did so, another figure entered the room, its eyes glowing deepest dark red, just bright enough to mark its location, exactly. The darkness hid the figure's features, mostly, but one thing was clear, it was raising its arm and pointing at the stage with strangely malformed gauntlets; a thin purple bolt of energy shot from the creatures hand, aimed dirrectly at the pair there. Before the pairs' hands linked the bolt of energy struck Jack's shoulder, knocking him back away from the rescuer's hand and prone again.

Agony erupted along his side and shoulder, and fire ignited his costume. He desperately beat them out then examined himself briefly to determine just how bad the bolt had hurt him. He grimaced with pain caused by the injury, but he was used to pain, from his days on the streets, and he quickly extinguished the flames. He used his fall's momentum, to roll off the stage into the shadows below, where he was better concealed.

The attacker stepped stridently across the room and up the stairs onto the stage, holding something resembling a picture in its' left hand, easily smashing away a were-creature that got too close with the other, only to find both its targets gone. It saw the dead were-creature turn human on stage, comparing it against the human female's picture it held. No, it was not the one it sought; the eyes were common brown, not the Gold-flecked Green of the target. If it had been here, it was either dead or gone.

Harry was a little surprised, as he'd not seen, or heard, which way Helena had left. However, he did spot, with eyes used to observing things frequently missed by others, that Simon was similarly hiding in the shadows, just the opposite side of the door that the attacker had come out of. He tried to surreptitiously attract the young professor's attention while remaining hidden from the attacker.

As the figure turned to leave the room again, Jack managed to catch Simon's attention and indicated that they should go through a side door to escape the yard, one that lead to reception, but not currently being blocked by still active creatures. A subtle nod and the two of them rabbited, as soon as the coast cleared; Simon dipping at one point, to pick up a strange rock, that the attacker had dropped. The two ran as fast as they could to the door, and, although it was locked, Jack's lock skills soon had them through, and sprinting down the corridors towards the entrance and freedom. In the distance, they could see another group, that included Charlene and John, just making it up the stairs.

"Let's follow them, they might know a safe way out of here," suggested Harry.

"Yes, let's," agreed Simon quickly.

"And that's what happened. Honest," although he saw that Charlene's look was only slightly sceptical. She looked at Simon, and he nodded confirmation, and she shook her head slightly, but was her story any less surreal? She doubted it.

After reaching the top of the stairs, and weaving their way through several twisting corridors, the group finally reached a room, for which the company executive produced an electronic pass key. He swiped the door key quickly, and he and his bodyguard piled in.

"Impossible!" came an exclamation from within the room, "where's she gone?"

The rest of the group started to enter the room, however, at that moment, another sound made itself audible from behind them at the end of the corridor; a heavy jagged breathing and dreadful scrapping of huge claws against brick. The corridoor-filling Werewolf came stalking around the corner with blood and drool dripping from his jaws, and glaring directly at the group, in the flickering lights.

"Oh, my, GOD," said Simon fearfully.

"I don't think so," said Jack, in a similarly terrified tone. They exchanged a brief glance then simultaneously bolted into the room, diving under the bed side by side; in an attempt to hide, from the nightmarish apparition.

John anticipating that the creature was going to attack, drew his gun, smoothly reloaded it with the silver bullets, and rapidly unleashed a volley. Each bullet hit but barely seemed the slow the brute, although the sound, attracted the attention of the other bodyguard, who also drew his gun and began peppering the hairy beast with rounds, as it started to accelerate down the corridor; like a blood-soaked juggernaut.

Charlene had no such firepower, and she was reasonably certain that the executive did not either as, seeing the beast charging down the corridor, he grabbed a large wooden case from beside the bed, gave a final strange look around the room and sprinted out, turning down a side corridor, presumably towards a fire escape.

Charlene felt herself follow him initially, but after a few strides, a feeling of unease enveloped her, dragging on her like a thick molasse, slowing her to a walk, instead of running blindly after him. She tried to apply logic to the situation, but the feeling remained, forcing her to stop.

She unlimbered her backpack, looking for something that might be used as a weapon, doing a double take as she did so; two of the flasks were gone. How had they gone missing? She shook her head. There were too many things going on here, even for her. As she looked again at the pack, her eyes fixing on the last bottle of acid. It was concentrated Hydrochloric acid, not the fastest working, nor the most painful, but it would have to do, and as she thought it, a shadow appeared at the exit the man was running towards s.

Another bodyguard came around the corner, the executive calling for him to help the others. Charlene started to hope that they were saved, then realised that the guard was moving strangely, jerking stiffly, as though his joints were stiff or fixed in some way; certainly not naturally. She belatedly yelled a warning, as the features of the other bodyguard resolved themselves in the low light.

The hulking mass of flesh, already sliced and rent, slammed its putrid flesh into the executive, knocking the dazed man back; towards to Charlene.

That made her subsequent action easy to select, as the person next to her was severely wounded, and he needed immediate aid if he were to survive. Fortunately, she'd just the thing. Reaching into her kit, she withdrew an experimental medical Nanite dispenser and slammed it against the stunned man's legs, the automatic sensor activating and dosing the man's bloodstream with the Nanites; almost immediately, the wounds on his neck and shoulder started to knit together, and his breathing eased.

She did not stay still, to see the rest of the miraculous healing that her Nanites were working. Instead, she grabbed his' hand and started to pull him towards another room, hoping that he could get the door open before the rotting creature reached them.

Unfortunately, as the door opened to allow the pair through, the creature managed to land a second, more substantial blow, on the already injured man. The maul-like hand crushed the executive's skull, and he collapsed next to her. Charlene had no time to register the shock she knew she should feel at his death next to her. To avoid being roommates with this creature, she reversed her forward motion and, grabbing the case that the man had been carrying on the way out, using her Gymnastic skills to bounce off the chest of the monster, knocking it back and propelling herself at maximum velocity towards John and relative safety.

Meanwhile, John and the other Bodyguard were trying to drop the Alpha were-creature. At first, it had seemed that the creature would not make it down the hall, as the two guards focused volleys of bullets down the corridor, scoring hit after hit and continually reloading. However, it was soon apparent that, despite the number of hits, the creature was too powerful, and moving too quickly, to be stopped before he reached the pair. It was John who received the education in pain, that the creature seemed so determined to deliver. A huge claw raking cleanly across his chest and face and sending him reeling through the open bedroom door, splattering the pale carpet with his blood.

As he thudded to the floor, a head popped briefly out of the wall wardrobe; apparently, others were hiding in the room, besides Simon and Harry. The face looked at the groaning person on the floor, quickly around the room, then just as quickly vanished back into the shadows. Harry briefly spotted an obviously exceedingly pregnant woman ensconced in the wardrobe. As the wardrobe doors closed, in a fantastic show of agility, another body dived through the doorway, right passed the occupied creature.

Charlene entered the room at breakneck speed and was shocked to see the state of her bodyguard. She started to move forward to aid him, but at that moment another body staggered through the doorway, still battling the beast.

The creature looked severely wounded, and, having reached the doorway, seemed to slow, either weakening or becoming afraid, and staggering back, and around the corner.

The remaining bodyguard, although badly wounded, hesitated, then decided that the creature was now on its last legs. In an insane or exceedingly courageous move, he followed the beast, shooting even faster.

Charlene reached John, wrenching open her case and administering first aid. She thought that the 'Dark Queen' would probably have felt more at home here. Still, she finished her bandaging just as things outside the room went quiet, chillingly quiet.

That's when the gas grenades started to come through the open window, two at a time, shouting of battle orders drifting in as well, but the gas seemed to make everything hazy, and all in the room saw little more than shadows moving through the windows and doorways before they fell to the floor unconscious.

"Hello there," came a female voice from Charlene's blurred vision. She tried to formula an enquiry, which came out as a groan of complaint.

"Just Stun gas Dr. Klerk, so you'll be fine in a second or two," came a reply to a question she'd only formulated in her head.

As others staggered to get up, or out from under the bed, they turned their heads towards the voice near the doorway. There stood a rather imposing young woman, with a head of white hair a shiny sheathed dagger; more the size of a short sword, with a large red jewel on the pommel. The gem glowed slightly with a strange inner light. The woman raised herself to his full height; of about five-foot-six inches tall.

She regarded all of them with old, hard and judgemental eyes.

"I know what you're thinking," she glowered at them. "This is all very strange. Yes, I suppose to you normal humans it is, but that's ok, I'm here to sort it all out now, and you can be sure I'll do that as efficiently as I can. My name is Whisper, or that is what you can call me. Or Ma'am"

She moved slightly into the room, just as the other bodyguard staggered into the room. She signalled down the corridor, where others dressed like her, ran fleetly; checking rooms and carrying out any bodies found, including that of the huge, barely moving bloody creature.

"And before you make any comments, let me just say that your fate is in my hands." She looked down at his hands, "Aye, these things," she wiggled and wafted them at the people to indicate that they should all move into the room and sit.

"Well now, don't we have ourselves a little pickle. You see, as a rule, your kind is not allowed to know about our kind, and I and my fellows out there and me, enforce that rule." She indicated the window, and Simon glancing outside, saw a host of indistinct figures surrounding the hotel, others removing downed attackers and people en-mass.

"That's the rule. However, an acquaintance of mine has presented a compelling case that you are more valuable as you are." She tapped her lips with the tip of one finger. "Yes, a dilemma indeed. Do we let you off and make you forget it all, or leave you be and trust you to keep your mouths shut?" She looked around the group. Finally, Charlene stood up and moved to sit on the bed, keeping a wary eye on the strange woman.

"Oh, and while we're at it lets do something about those nasty wounds," she held up a bracelet and waved the injured people to receive one.

She snapped one on John's arm, and another appeared, from a bag of them behind her. She moved towards the bed and snapped it on Charlene's' wrist. She frowned and as she did, the woman pointed to the cloth Charlene had used to treat her bodyguard, and she noticed a smudge of blood on one finger. Her eyes snapped to hers, and she nodded, slowly. Whatever she was worried about, it was something in the blood; she'd been infected with something in just that simple act of mercy. One of life's main rules; mercy can get you killed. Something her mother HAD tried to teach her, but that her father did not believe in; score one for 'Dark Queen' this time. That thought made Charlene shudder a little.

"These are family heirlooms, guaranteed to allow wounds to heal naturally, rather than causing you to bleed to death, or to infect you with such creature's condition. We cannot be having that happen now, can we?" She smirked a little, "that would pollute the Eldarin bloodline, with Human DNA, and that would never do."

Simon piped up finally, "So what exactly is going on here? These strange creatures, silver bullets, strange glowing-eyed creatures, and all hell breaks loose. I don't understand, Ma'am!" the tone being part entreaty, part sarcasm, and all confusion.

Two people emerged from the wardrobe, a burly and the well-dressed lady Jack had glimpsed earlier, her belly impossibly large.

"Perhaps I can explain a portion of that," said the bodyguard, as the woman moved and sat on the bed; Simon's and Jack's hiding place.

Charlene saw her, and eyes went momentarily wide, "Demon," she whispered.

Only Whisper heard her; she shook his head slightly, but Charlene fixed her eyes on the bump of the woman, and only reluctantly pulled them away from it.

The woman looked hard at the human female, there was something disturbingly familiar about her face. Unusually, she could not quite place the resemblance, despite her exceptional memory. She'd have to try and recall where she'd seen her likeness before.

"The whole thing with the creatures began about two months ago," started the bodyguard, in a hushed tone. "Frank, one of our researchers, was doing research on a blood sample from a body found in an old mass grave. Nothing unusual about that, we do things like that all the time, except, this time the sample contained a rare gene with an active cellular stabilising factor." The guard looked at the woman, who nodded some kind of permission.

"The main problem was that the researcher was an Eldarin; a werewolf in this case, and he'd fallen in love with a human," he nodded at the woman. "He attempted to use the stabilising factor in a serum for himself so that he could be with her safely. It all seemed to be going so right for them, that they got carried away," the woman bowed her head, "and the unforeseen happened, she became pregnant. So, he used more time trying to find what he was looking for," the man sighed.

"At that point, however, his boss found out about the research and immediately took control of it, redirecting it into a darker direction: Weaponisation." The bodyguard shook his head, "it could not have gone worse for us; the research went surprisingly well, and the solutions, in that case, were the product. The researcher tried to sabotage the work, but it still progressed at a great speed, and the boss discovered the man's attempts to delay the project. He then discovered that his boss had kidnapped his girlfriend and was holding her hostage, to ensure his good behaviour and cooperation. He was ordered to begin testing his work on people."

The man grinned viciously. "The boss underestimated the strength of the Eldarin and the solution. The researcher started testing alright, administering the solution to the test subjects, but doctoring the feeds, allowing him to use his own Eldarin powers to control them; hence all the creatures here today. So here they came, not understanding why; not quite fully under his control, but with the same purpose, to find and kill the boss, release his woman and their child, and finally escape." He looked around at the results and shrugged, "and so here we are."

"We will take care of them now," said the woman opening a window and signalling outside. The bodyguard and woman were escorted out of the building by two black dressed guards sporting an intimidating array of weapons.

Whisper turned to her left a little, cocking her head slightly as if listening to something. She frowned and nodded a few times, then muttered a few indistinct words apparently to thin air. Finally, her face cleared and she nodded.

"Well now; we've have come to a decision," the woman looked at the assembled humans. "You get to keep your memories, on the solemn promise that nothing is said to anyone about this incident," accepting their frantic nods as agreement, handing each a card.

"This is my friend's name and address. He will be expecting you after you have treated your various wounds and been interviewed by the police. Don't disappoint him."

Then she stepped back near the door. "We will be watching you from now on." She smiled a little smile, giving one final glance at Charlene frowning, then faded from view.

The room was silent for one more moment, then the sound of crying, alarms, and sirens crashed in on the group once again. It was John that broke their stunned silence.

"Well, I don't know about you but, I need to get to a hospital; these wounds need a serious number of stitches, and I, for one, would like to have some sleep, to try and make sense of the past few minutes." He staggered to his feet, Charlene jumping up and supporting him, as he moved out the door.

She still clutched the wooden case, that the Executive had come upstairs for. "Well, at least we have some evidence if this is what she said it was."

The others followed, and they all joined the walking wounded downstairs and outside; where armed police were just leaving the building, having secured the area. Medics rushed in, followed by unarmed detectives, forensic teams and plain clothed officers.

"Follow us please all of you. We'll need statements from everybody, especially the bodyguards, and those from the main room," directed a particularly authoritative Detective Sergeant.

The main group of people all followed numbly, those who'd been in the main room and somehow survived by either hiding or just by blind luck. Those from upstairs were just as bewildered but tried to keep their wits about them as the next few hours would require a certain amount of creative truthfulness if they were to avoid being locked up, one way or another.

For Charlene and her group, the rest of the night was split between the essential visit to the hospital and the required interviews at the police station. The rush to the hospital was a blur, Charlene hovering over John as the ambulance rushed him to the Emergency Department, blood seeping through the hastily packed bandage. While the others were seen by junior doctors, Charlene made sure that John received the best private treatment that the corporate card could afford and managed to sneak off for a few minutes too, doing a quick analysis of the removed bandages trying to determine any foreign substances therein. She was sure the medical staff would do their best. However the tests she was doing were much more detailed, and specifically for things, she was looking for. She had her suspicions about the wounds that the were-creatures had inflicted on John. Sure enough, there was a venom, in the claw marks of the creature, with some unusual properties that needed further study. She was a little surprised that she too had contracted something just from the blood sample, she'd casually taken.

After the treatment at the hospital was completed, the police who'd accompanied them took them to the incident centre set up at the local station. It was in chaos for, although the constabulary was not a small one, the building was not designed for the number of people packed into it. Outside, a large incident-control truck was parked, along with a dozen vans and cars, providing makeshift interview areas and bringing more officers to the investigation.

There were a group of detectives that wanted answers to many questions; about the violence, and the chaos which had consumed so many lives. There were twenty dead, twelve injured and some guests that were unaccounted for. The missing ones were more disturbing to the authorities, but no answers were forthcoming from any of the other stunned attendees as they were simply bewildered. Charlene was much more concerned that Dr. Trafford had was one counted as missing; meaning he'd got to the conference, then just vanished.

Chief Inspector Blackmoore was looking through the on-scene reports from the incident. The conference had been attacked by an unknown number of assailants, apparently bent on killing everyone in sight. The last four seemed to have been luckier than many, only one getting injured at all despite having allegedly tried to fight off the largest of the attackers. He hated amateurs and had some serious questions for each of them.

There were lots of things that did not make sense about the whole incident. There were signs that the attack was well coordinated, with a large number of attackers getting past the on-door security, yet the results seemed chaotic. At the scene, the objective remained unclear. If the attackers were there to kill someone why so many where a single attacker would have managed just as well. If they were after high-tech equipment, it might have been understandable, as many of the companies had brought demonstration models of their latest tech; except, none of them was missing. If it was terror then they had succeeded, but the coverage appearing on the web was mostly of four of the delegates, the last four remaining to be questioned.

He carried the dossiers on the last four and frowned. None were marked as having criminal records, although some had a lot in their folders. Having read three, it was not for the reasons that would fit with this incident and some even contra-indicated; peculiar. Still he, or rather his detectives, had an investigation to do, and he should be about it. He called in his detectives, passing them each a folder and giving them their instructions.

"Gently does it with these last four. Several have high powered lawyers on standby, and their companies are itching to get them back. We need to know what happened though, so go softly, softly."

The four groups of officers left. Moments after they had gone, the room was empty.

The first D.I., Portland, a severe and stocky looking officer, checked at his folder, as he entered the brightly lit interview room, while Jack Somerfelt, a.k.a. Harry Hidden; illusionist and escapologist, sat patiently awaiting the veteran officer. The BioTecknica Corporation had hired him to entertain the conference, despite him just starting out in the business, judging by the fact that there no other previous venues he'd performed at.

The notes showed no previous convictions, though there were numerous notes on times where he'd been around other incidents in Birmingham; as a witness, a passerby or just in the general vicinity. It was noted that he'd previously provided, almost casually, some surprisingly useful witness statement, some would say suspiciously good, given that he was just a passer-by, during several incidents. The coincidences mounted up rapidly when you viewed the number of entries in the file.

He'd been brought up as the youngest in a large family, and, while they were all unemployed, they had managed, almost miraculously given the neighbourhood, to stay out of the prevailing gang culture, and just about survive on benefits. His father and grandfather had both died serving their country in the army. Nobody remarkable really, and few others in the community either knew him or saw him much, in fact, he rarely left his house except to visit a lockup garage nearby, presumably, where he practised his illusions and tricks. The D.I. doubted he'd get a warrant to search that location unless he had other evidence that implicated him.

Jack was well dressed, someone might say overdressed, in top hat and tails that complimented his rich dark brown skin and his poise, creating an overall air of a gentleman of African descent. That made the D.I. nervous. Nowadays people played the race card too easily to confound and annoy the police. However, the D.I. was not as wary of him for what he was, but because there was something about the way he looked at you, not so much the person, but his eyes; they always seemed to be starring right at your soul.

To allow himself to relax a little, the D.I. flicked through the rather thin folder of information on the incident; it read like the synopsis of a horror novel.

Jack himself looked a little nervous, although, from the description of the victims, from forensics, the D.I. thought it was totally understandable; it was the worst he'd ever read, and the state of the conference area was described as being like an abattoir. Another strange thing was that there was no sign upstairs, and none of the attackers had been found, despite the bodyguards swearing they'd dropped quite a few.

"Don't I get a lawyer?" asked Jack, looking quickly around the interview room, still in a slightly shocked state. He'd seen some pretty bad things on the streets when dealing with, or rather avoiding, the gangs; but this beat them all hands down. He did some deep breathing exercises, designed to calm himself.

"Ah, no. You are not under caution here, sir. We are just gathering information on the events, leading up to and during the alleged attack. This is just a witness interview." The D.I. said casually, trying to calm the obviously agitated man. "It's only if you have direct, or indirect, criminal involvement, that you need legal defence or caution."

"Fair enough," Jack said, mostly to himself, and tried to relax. He produced a handkerchief from thin air, with a flourish, to wipe his nose with. The D.I. did a double take, then just ignored it, starting the recorder.

"Interview starts 11:30 am Tuesday 19 April 2014. D.I. Portland and Officer Bartlet in attendance. Your name is Jack Somerfield, is that that correct?"

"Somerfelt," Jack said, with some annoyance, despite his current state. "My surname is South African, by derivation, and I'm proud of that," his voice was deep, and, although not deliberately menacing, certainly invoked an air of respect. This was not someone to take lightly.

"You are from Birmingham, and have no previous convictions, is THAT correct?" The detective seemed to have his back up a bit after being corrected. Jack nodded, "for the record, the interviewee nodded."

Jack looked at the tape, "am I under caution, Detective?" he asked, still not entirely sure of this situation.

"Detective Inspector, mister Somerfelt," the D.I. corrected. "and no, you are just making a statement, at the moment. But the details are all recorded; for evidential reasons."

Jack conceded his mistake, with a slight shrug of apology.

"Very well, mister Somerfelt. In your own words can you tell me what actually happened tonight, after the power problems?" the inspector looked eager.

"What actually happened?" Jack suddenly seemed unsure of himself, "er, no. I cannot."

"Explain!" The D.I. commanded, losing patience with him.

Jack clasped his hands together and looked directly at the D.I. "The problem is, there was a lot actually happening and, I only saw a fraction, probably because I was trying to get out of there, as fast as I could. I can tell you what I saw, heard and think happened."

Jack thought he could hear the detective grinding his teeth, and was close to grinning, but thought better of it. His mother would not approve of him winding up officials, after all the effort he'd put in historically avoiding trouble with them.

"Ok," said the Detective, through thin lips, "'please,' tell me what you saw, and heard happen." The intensity in his voice was designed to try and make the witness focus. Jack looked right back at the detective and started to describe what he could.

"After my arrival, I was given the timetable and assigned a location to set up. I set up the equipment, tested it, the usual pre-show routine." He tried to sound professional about it.

"But you've never had a show before," the detective pointed out.

"True, but I'm trying to get into the habit," he said calmly, "if you'll let me continue?"

The detective waved him on.

"I tried avoiding the scientists, and I only talked casually to a few others,"

"Including John Brickman?" the detective, interjected.

"John? Brickman is his surname?" Jack asked.

"You did not know him?" the D.I. countered.

"No. He was avoiding the scientists too," the D.I. noted that down on his warrant pad, "and, he seemed as bored as I was with the tech talk. As I'd been paid to entertain, I tried to show him a trick. He declined." The memory brought a faint smile to his lips.

"Anyway, after that, I'd just finished my routine, and the audience was applauding, when a fight broke out between security, and, I believe, an intruder; behind the audience, to the right of the stage." His eyes screwed up a little as he recalled the scene.

"The lights went out, or rather flickered randomly, for about fifteen minutes; there was a panic and lots of screaming. There were lots of fighting, and some shooting, that I heard. I shouted to everyone to evacuate the building, trying to get people to safety; and that's about it before I banged my head. After that it's pretty distorted," the truth; his strange vision distorted everything, "and one of the attendees guided me out of the presentation area. After that, I hid until I heard the sirens." He saw the detective look at the bandage on his arm.

"Well, I made contact with a power outlet, on the stage, receiving this; but in magic that's just part of the show. As long as either the audience doesn't notice, or you make them think it's part of the show, it's ok."

"It seemed there was quite a show tonight, Jack." The detective sensed that the man was hiding something. "Did you see anything that might indicate who attacked the conference?"

The detective gave him a long hard look; Jack just shrugged. The D.I. could not prove anything; if he could, the questions he would ask would be of more interest to Jack, than his answers were to the DI. Jack did not dignify the question with a response, but the D.I. pressed.

"You ever had any gang involvement, Jack? Birmingham is full of gangs and the like, and they have previously been involved in such things; mass riots, kidnapping, and killings. Or perhaps an initiation gone wrong?"

"Detective, if I were involved in gangs, which I am not, I would not talk about it. City gangs are terribly unforgiving with informants. More to the point is that you would know, if I did talk about such things, I would be singled out for special treatment."

The detective tried to lean on him, shifting forward in his seat, staring intently at his eyes; trying to read the body language.

"No. I have never been involved in the gangs; too dangerous, the same with Cults," at which the detective gave a strange twitch in his left eye. Jack marked it but carried on, wondering at the reaction, "and they would more likely leave calling cards, I would think." The entertainer had indeed heard of such things but never been part of the culture that promoted such violence.

He produced a small handkerchief, with an embroidered dove and olive branch on it, and place it on the table in front of him. "I am a peaceful man, who has a deep love of entertainment and illusions. I don't have time for anything else. My art is like a Scientist's studies, Detective, and your job; it consumes all my time, which is mostly used practising and innovating to hopefully pay the bills in the future."

The detective still looked sceptical, so Jack produced a sheaf of papers to prove the point, much to the genuine surprise of the detective. Jack again looked deep into his eyes.

"I honestly cannot tell you what happened last night, and I genuinely hope I never truly know." Jack stood up, "may I go now?". D.I. Portland just nodded and wondered how the other interviews were going.

"Interview terminated. 11:40 am."

D.I. Carter-Lea sat, casually, on the interview seat. The man opposite seemed shaken, almost withdrawn. The D.I. thought that she'd have to be careful to get anything out of this one.

She'd reviewed his profile before entering; his family was in the upper echelons of the old families of Scotland and Northern England, and they had political connections across the party lines, and with many of the other families too. He was well respected in his scientific community, and his work involved prosthetics and advanced robotics for military veterans. Other than that, and a few clippings from magazines, about his work, there was little to suggest that he'd have anything except eyewitness details to contribute.

"Interview starts, 11:34 am, Tuesday, 19th April 2014. P.C. Staning and D.I. Carter-Lea in attendance. Your name is Simon Caruthers, is that that correct?"

"Professor Simon Caruthers, yes. Professor of Robotics and Human Interaction, at Cambridge University, Detective Inspector." His manner was clipped and precise. Oh boy.

"Well, mister Caruthers," the D.I. started.

"That's Professor Caruthers, Detective Inspector Carter-Lea. I don't miss out your title; you don't miss out mine." The, otherwise congenial, professor was not in the mood for being mistreated by someone who thought themselves, in any way, his superior.

"I think you're being a bit defensive, professor, are you trying,"

"Detective Inspector! I am not a bit defensive, I'm offended is what I am. You want information? I will give it. I will even be cooperative if you stop trying to treat me like I am some sort of ignoramus." His face became stern, "it's called professional courtesy, and you WILL extend it to me. Or, you will find that I am worse than any criminal, in my ability to speak to you and tell absolutely you nothing. Are we clear?"

The detective started to speak, then thought better of it. She kind of flexed her body, showing her discomfort, and took a deep breath, to calm herself. This one was not someone to trifle with.

"I'm sorry professor, it's years of dealing with stubborn criminals that sours me and makes me forget my manners," the D.I. showed genuine contrition.

"No problem detective," the simple courtesy, seemed to immediately mollify the man and, modify his attitude. "In truth, however, I did not see much. For most of the incident, I was hiding, running, head down or in darkness. For the rest of it, I was under a bed, concealing myself from whatever it was growling and bellowing so loudly."

"As a professor did you recognise what was making the sounds?" the D.I. asked.

"I'm not like Dr. Klerk, who has extensive knowledge of biology and the animal kingdom, no doubt. I cannot identify the difference between a dog, and a wolf hybrid," the man stopped, he'd nearly said, "or werewolf." He'd promised not to say anything, and he kept his promises. The detective saw the sincere face of the young man, "I truly hope I never hear that kind of growling and slavering again; or the screams of dying people."

"If I think of anything, I will tell you, wait, there was something." The detective leaned forward at that. "There was a man, making a fuss in the centre of the room, and the guards seem to move to take him away. That's when it all kicked off, and he was kind of manic, I did not see the full thing, fortunately. I do know that he was brutally strong; he managed to throw someone nearly twice his weight nearly fifteen feet, or so. After that, I did not see anything, clearly. That's all detective. Honestly, it is," and he stood and walked out of the room without asking permission; the detective did not stop him.

"Interview ended, 11:40 am." That was short and sweat to be sure. She hoped the others got more from their interviewees, although she doubted that somehow.

As he left, Simon fingered the small stone in his pocket, the one he'd picked up from the floor as he'd run from the strange figure who'd shot Jack. He would have to check it out, but he'd seen it glow, in some fashion; that meant it was, or contained, a power source of some kind and he needed to know what kind. He'd never seen anything like it before.

D.I. Dilock held the service record of the one really trustworthy and reliable witness of the whole incident. John 'Brick' Brickman, ex-police officer, firearms and close protection trained; now private bodyguard, and, it seemed, hero. Judging by the other bodyguard's statements and CCTV footage he'd held off the attackers, saved several bystanders and his own ward. Although other moments indicated he might also have hit some bystanders as well, the reported injuries did not match up. Something else was going on, and he was going to get the truth out.

He looked at John's career to date; an exceptional officer, marksman and self-defence trainer, before a disciplinary incident put pay to his career. He could not really blame him for striking the superior officer, who had subsequently been imprisoned on corruption charges. However, the discipline needed to be seen to be maintained, and he'd had actually done quite well off it. Bodyguards with his gun skills and background were in high demand by the big corporations and were paid well for their services. Mostly, it was babysitting, however, when it was not, they earned their pay; today was one of those days.

The problem was that the disciplinary action was against an officer who'd been a favourite of their current Chief Inspector, Blackmoore, and he was a stickler for discipline and details. Brickman had no surviving family, no siblings and was by all accounts a bit of a loner, but his record was all Dilock needed to see; he was an exceptional officer.

"Interview starts 11:40 am Tuesday 19 April 2014. D.I. Dilock and Officer Wakely in attendance."

"'Brick' is that correct?" the officer tried to be casual with a fellow officer, even an Ex.

"That is what they all call me," said John, presenting his ID card for inspection.

"John Brickman, Close Protection," the detective read along for the tape, trying not to sound impressed; the man seemed terribly young for assignment to Close Protection. But then he did have a look; that something in the eyes that spoke volumes, to those who'd been in the police as long as Dilock had. The look that made even a seasoned officer think; this man would do what was necessary.

"So, Brick, can you tell me what happened at," the D.I. started.

Brick interrupted with a raised hand, "before we start, I'd just like you to know a few things. I am talented with weapons and have an amiable personality. I'm no guardian angel really, and I don't bootlick," the officer bridled a little at that. "I call a spade a spade, and that's it. With that said, what would you like to know?" He straightened in his chair, feeling a bit naked without his sidearm; currently being analysed by the police forensics experts.

"You should know. I want the truth of what happened," D.I. Dilock seemed decidedly agitated after John's little speech.

"OK. Having arrived and received our conference badges, we went to the main presentation area and split up, talking with the people we'd eventually end up saving. My client, Dr. Klerk, noticed something out of the ordinary, and, at her insistence, I went to investigate. I noticed some people looking out of place and tried to get more information, but before I could act on the intel. they initiated hostile action. Apparently, the meeting was infiltrated by several people who were possibly under the influence of a drug or something else, that caused them to go berserk."

"That ties up with what the medics said, the wounds were pretty severe," interrupted Dilock, unaware perhaps that he was speaking out loud, John nodded.

"It was pretty scary, so I tried to get back to my charge; she's not the strongest or the most worldly person around, and the infiltrators were everywhere. The threat of guns did not seem to scare them, and several bodyguards started to deal with them." John shook his head. "Whatever they were on, they were getting hit, just not going down; of course, when you are running you have no time to really see if they go down, but it did not seem so at the time."

"How many did you kill?" Dilock asked. It was provocative, but he needed to get some information.

"Me. None. I shot at the attackers, but they did not drop. I don't know why; perhaps they were wearing body armour, or my aim was off," although his voice indicated he'd not really thought that. "They were certainly wearing masks, of some kind too, like Halloween or Animal masks." Dilock's eyes narrowed; that 'might' explain the other statements, better than anything he'd come up with.

"Anyway, I rescued my client, and we headed out, with another conference member, and we diverted upstairs, at his insistence, and to avoid more intruders at the entrance. The fighting blocked the other obvious escape routes anyway. The problem was that the leader of the group followed us up, and, another bodyguard and I tried to stop him."

"We finally drove him off with concerted volley fire, but unfortunately he managed to catch me with this," he indicated the bandage on his ribs, "and the conference member, with a fatal blow. After that, the rest of us fled the building, and that's the whole story."

"Any idea who they were, why they were there and what the whole thing was about?" Dilock was hopeful that a professional would have spotted something the tech people had not. The scene was remarkably clean of clues, for one which had so much blood and so many dead bodies. John thought carefully. Could he direct this in a safe direction?

"I did not get close to any of the other infiltrators, but they looked more hired thugs than anything, at a distance. They were unshaven, and they had long coats, the kind that criminals usually use to hide weapons. From several wounds like my own, it seems that they used some kind of Chinese weapons, like the Zhua. That would kind of lead us to believe that it might have been a Triad strike; they like to use ancient weapons and masks."

"One of the speakers said something about prospective clients coming to see him. It could be that someone turned up to do more than see him." John nodded again, as the more he thought about it, the more it sounded logical. "My guess would be; he had funding from them, and when he'd finally achieved the required results, they wanted to get the merchandise from him, to recoup the investment."

Dilock thought about this. It made sense and explained so much that otherwise would be inexplicable, the use of the strange weapons causing the wounds, the fact that the attackers were not afraid of guns, the fanatical mayhem designed to terrify opposition and the authorities.

"Interesting theory 'Brick.' Is that all?" Dilock looked intently.

John decided to try and re-enforce his theory with a bit more speculation. "It looked like it was an inside job. They seemed to have arranged to have the electrics sabotaged, to hide the attack, and they also must have arranged an escape route, that avoided the main routes, else you'd have probably seen them on the way in; after all, there were a fair few of them."

Dilock went over the statement again and tried to get more details from him, but the truth be told he only reiterated the same information unti, l after about an hour, they started to get tired of the process. "Can I go now? I'm exhausted, and the docs said I need to rest for the stitches to heal up properly."

Dilock waved him away; "Interview ended, 12:55 am."

He had some interesting calls to make. C.I.D. might have to be brought in on this one, maybe even Interpol, although if it were the Triads, they would put this in the SOC or intelligence agencies purview, rather than local law enforcement.

That just left the girl to talk to, and it was going to require a much more, gentle, approach. He'd read her file, and if he did this wrong, the media would have a field day.

She'd been through enough ordeals with her parents having been murdered in similar circumstances. He hoped that meant she might have some pertinent incites that the others did not.

She had been eight; living on Brae in the Shetland Isles, with her father, when her mother had visited, apparently trying to patch the marriage up. Although she'd been at a family friend's house when the incident had occurred, the fact she had lost both patents to murderers, had been a traumatic shock her. So much so that the doctors said she'd a certain amount of retrograde amnesia; the extent of which was not evident at the time, as she'd been catatonic. Afterwards, she just remembered being at the other house all night and that she'd lost her parents to an accident.

The usual strange stories were published in the tabloid papers, he knew, the sensationalist type; although, this time, corroborated by the investigating officers and the evidence. The coroner's report was graphic, and indeed the most terrible and disturbing thing to read; the parents were dismembered, few pieces identifiable and several parts had claw marks on them, similar to the ones on the bodies here. But the DNA had been confirmed as theirs' by their government employers, although the actual results were classified above his level, not surprising given where her father worked and the mother working in the foreign service.

Still, there were rumours, that a cult had been present on the island and had taken them. Eventually, the investigation was dropped, and the girl, supported by an uncle on her fathers' side, was brought under the state wing until she was old enough to be sponsored by A.G.E. and there the story faded. This was going to be difficult.

"Interview starts 12:20 am Tuesday 19 April 2014. D.I. Dilock and Officer Staning in attendance. Thank you for coming miss Clerk," he started. The look she gave him was one of severe impatience.

"That's Dr. Klerk, D.I. Dilock" said the young girl, with more maturity and weight than her appearance suggested. "It took a great deal of time and effort to get my title, please don't treat me like a child. Especially today. I'm not in the mood for the usual bias over age and maturity," the detective, was a little startled by the iron in her voice. Had she read him in some manner? Her comments paralleled his own thoughts.

"Hmmm. I see that you are indeed capable of answering intelligent questions," he saw that she relaxed, at the explicit compliment, "So I will ask you simply, in your own words, what happened?"

Charlene started to speak when suddenly her head began to buzz; the distant sound of angry wasps, and superimposed over the room, and the police around, was a different scene, one she recognised only vaguely. Charlene shook her head, and the scene vanished.

"Dr. Klerk are you ok?" the D.I. sounded genuinely concerned. "Would you like some water?" he started to reach for a jug on the table.

"I'm OK," although her colour showed otherwise, "It's just that, although the hospital cleared me, I don't feel quite myself," she was looking a little out of sorts, almost as if she thought she was OK, but knew better.

"Perhaps we should talk tomorrow," the D.I. found himself saying.

"No D.I. I would much rather tell you what happened," she said with more strength than she felt.

"OK. Dr. What happened?" He remembered that she'd been through this kind of trauma before, so his voice was much softer than usual.

As she started to speak, her thoughts began to scatter again, another presence attempting to take control of her actions, as one had at the conference. However, it was not the kindly influence of her father. The colder, more demanding tones of the 'Dark Queen' filled her head; so loudly that Charlene was almost overwhelmed by her presence. The buzzing became much louder, yet, after a couple of seconds she finally shook it off.

She'd remembered the mental training that her mother had drilled into her, during her younger years, to ensure her daughter was fit, talented and resilient; before things had gotten serious, and her mother had started to hurt her. She would never forgive the 'Dark Queen' for selecting the whip as a training method, the whips and many hours of hard practice that now, ironically, she enforced on herself. She also remembered well the punishments for the slight mistakes, and occasionally absences that her father's timing had caused. Charlene had known that her mother was a disciplinarian, as her father had called her, but Charlene believed she'd actually enjoyed it when she trained her daughter and disciplining her when she things went wrong; and that hurt more than any whip. She flicked her hair irritably, dismissing her reveille and the other presence in one action.

"D.I. Dilock, the conference was going great when a yob, on some sort of drug I think, crashed the conference. I told Driver, and he went off to deal with him. Then others appeared and just seemed to lay about themselves with glee. It was horrible."

"What about your use of the chemicals, seen on the CCTV." D.I. Dilock asked carefully. The medical reports, from her parent's murders, stated that she had retrograde amnesia, but it did not say if she was still on medication.

"I honestly don't remember that. I had my sample case, but I thought I dropped it and that several yobs had started throwing them around. I don't actually remember getting out the flasks and throwing them. I managed to get the case away from the yobs, with the help of another bodyguard at the conference, then we just ran".

"Why did you bother with the case?" the detective was understandable curious, "with your life in danger? Why not just run?" The look she returned was strangely unconfused.

"The case contained my life's work, D.I. If I'd have left it behind, I might as well have died." She was serious. There was something else in the woman's eyes and body though; for some reason, she was lying; the body signals did not match up. That thought vanished as C.I. Blackmoore had entered the room, with a lawyer in tow, a strange look quickly concealed on his face.

"For the tape Chief Inspector Blackmoore and the lawyer for A.G.E. have entered the room." The C.I. gave the D.I. a black look and turned the tape off.

"Mr. Glandon here," the other man bowed, "has asked that he sit in on the interview. The company wants to ensure that no industrial secrets are revealed during your questioning."

D.I. Dilock hated his superior's fawning manner with the corporations, but he indicated that the lawyer should sit.

"Actually, I don't really have much more to say," Charlene stated.

"What about the box that you had when you left the conference?" Dilock queried quickly. Charlene was about to say something, but the lawyer jumped in.

"My Client cannot comment on the contents of the company owned transport case, and I can assure you that its contents are legitimate and safe chemical samples, not involved in the incident, in any way."

"I have cleared the case to be released from the evidence storeroom," stated the C.I. with a meaningful look at the D.I. When he started to object, the sentence was quashed with an even more withering look.

"I see no reason to detain my client any further then," the lawyer added cheerfully. The D.I. started to talk again but was interrupted by the C.I.

"Of course. I'm sure Dr. Klerk would like to re-join her driver and get a hotel room in the local area to recover." He gave Dilock another glare, and the D.I.'s shoulders slumped in surrender.

He turned the tape back on. "Interview terminated 12:35 am," and slammed his chair under the table, leaving the room in a rush, before he did something he regretted.

D.I. Dilock was confused at what had just happened. Blackmoore had let her go without allowing him to obtain the answers to burning questions he had. Something stranger than the attack was going on, but he just could not see what, especially with Blackmoore involved. He'd have to get closer to this group and get the truth from them unofficially. He knew that his boss would block him, but he'd some leave coming up, and he could use it to better effect following them, than staying here; under the hawk eyes of C.I. Blackmoore and his cronies.

C I Blackmoore cursed himself for not reading the fourth folder when he had the chance. If he had, he could have handled this quietly instead of passing her to be questioned by the one person in the team that he knew could not be controlled. Too late now, but at least the Coven had found her at last. A strange dark thrill went through him; after nearly a decade of searching, they had found the master's sacrifice again. Charlene Klerk was within their grasp, and only her wounded bodyguard stood in their way.

Eventually, after several interminable delays, the investigating police detectives and officers had all the details, evidence and photographs that the group and the other witnesses could, or were willing, to give them. By 1am, they were all heartily relieved when they were told they were to be released.

John now looked stronger, and he planned to book into a hotel in the area, before returning to their laboratory, with Charlene; although, with the executive being killed in the incident, Charlene had indicated that there might be an internal investigation into the incident too; what a drag.

The group was gathered together in a waiting room before they were allowed to depart the incident control. In walked D.I. Dilock, asking the duty officer to leave, quietly. Detective Inspector Dilock looked at the group and spoke in a calm and menacing tone.

"I have been told, by my superiors, to let you all go. That is not my choice. If I had my way, I'd have you all in the nick, until you gave up even your mother's secrets. Understand this. I, know! I know that you are hiding things. I know that you know much more, and, that you are not telling us the whole story. Just so you know. I will be watching you. CLOSELY."

He glared at everyone, particularly Jack.

"I will be your shadow; and if you do anything wrong, say anything untoward or you try to leave the country, you'll be in prison so fast you'll bounce off the walls of the cell as I throw you in there. Don't think you've got away with anything. I will be your second skin from now on until I have found out what is REALLY going on," he then stomped out of the room.

The group looked at each other, and all kind of shrugged. It seemed as if they would have another new companion, or at least, a tail, from now on.

Charlene thought that they might as well create a Twitter page and start the whole thing off properly. The thought made, the normally staid, Charlene giggle a little; and the answering smiles showed the others thought the detective was ridiculously melodramatic too.

And they still had their mysterious new best friend to go meet; but that would have to wait for a day as they all agreed to meet, not on the next day, but on the day after that; to give themselves time to recover from both the trauma and the journey.

Harry and Simon, nodded to Charlene and John as they walked off towards a nearby budget hotel. Charlene, however, still had her company card, so she booked adjoining rooms in the closest five Star she could find. For one thing, Driver needed a bit of comfort to heal well.

As the others disappeared from view, she caught a glimpse of a smart-suited person leaving in the same direction; ah, there was their tail. She was confident she would see the same thing, if they looked behind them when they left, not that she cared.

John wearily drove them to the rooms, but as the car reached the hotel, John finally gave in to fatigue, and as he walked around the car to open his passenger's door, he slumped to the bonnet for a second. But, as Charlene started to reach for the door handle herself, he stood up proudly and gave her a withering look; causing her hand to drop back to her side.

He opened the door, as usual, and as she passed, he muttered, "thanks".

He was a strange one, she thought, but more helpful than the rest of the people at the lab, that treated her like she was not there at all. Of course, that was his job; still, it was apparently more than that with him.

They collected their keys from the reception, and went straight to their rooms, the bellhop lifting their light luggage load without comment. All the way up, Driver acted normally; not as though he'd just done ten rounds with a monster twice his size. As they entered the rooms, the bellhop waited for a tip, just outside driver's, and Charlene, without money, waved her card at him, a sign that she'd leave him something suitable on the bill. He nodded, and left discretely, at which point, Driver sagged visibly, and Charlene caught him, struggling to support his heavy muscular body and guide him through the room until he could get close to the bed; at which point he just flopped heavily onto it. Charlene, remembering the car door incident, averted her gaze and closed the door behind her, as she ambled into her adjacent room.

The medics had indicated that he would be alright so she just hoped that bracelet would do its job. She knew a little about were-folk legends and did not want another of those creatures giving her a visit later in the night.

Yesterday she'd been so innocent. All she'd had to worry about was getting a few Nanobots to work.

She changed into her Judo uniform and started her evening routine. An hour of Judo kata, an hours' worth of gymnastics and, finally, her hot bath; to soothe out the day's aches and pains. Today, however, none of the exercises calmed her, and, strangely, even with the bracelet that the Sheriff had given her, she had a tingling inside her, like pins and needles, but all over. She'd performed a few rudimentary tests at the hospital, to check her blood and cellular systems for problems and pathogens; they had all proven negative, but she knew that the equipment in the hospital was unlikely to spot the kind of thing responsible for that tonight. She needed her lab equipment and her usual Bio-Analysis software, as she was sure that only that would be powerful enough to identify any problems.

Finally, utterly exhausted, for the first time in years, she put her head down and descended into sleep; at least that was her intention.

As Charlene finally started to drift into sleep, a faint buzzing started in her ears, almost like a mosquito, or crane fly, zipping around the room. As it continued, she, gradually, slipped into a dream-like state.

The child Charlene stood in a corridor dimly lit by sickly green fluorescent lights. She was walking down an empty corridor towards the hospital's operating theatre, and the buzzing was loud, persistent and coming from ahead; somewhere beyond the doors.

She moved slowly; knowing that she had to go through those doors, but dreading what she was going to find there. Still, her father had said that she should never be afraid to move forward, so she walked forward resolutely.

She started to raise her hand to open the door and leaned forward to shove it open when the buzzing stopped. She hesitated, her heart pounding and the breath in her ears deepened, like that of a wounded beast in its death throes. She had the sense of something behind her. She did not look, but knew it was advancing; tracking or hunting her. Time seemed to slow as she knew that the next decision was crucial. At first, she hesitated, but then she moved forward resolving to face her fear, hearing distantly in her head a familiar voice, "that's my girl. Never be afraid".

The doors opened, and the scene she saw made her young eyes bulge and her heart stutter; it could not be. It was totally impossible. She felt herself pull air into her lungs and …

… she bolted upright screaming. She screamed, but she did not know why the air in her lungs ran out. She took a deep, gasping, breath, to release another scream when John burst through the door.

"What?" He had his Taser drawn, scanning the room, as he searched for the attacker, or whatever was causing her distress.

She looked at him, in a dazed fashion, tried to talk, then merely dropped back on to her bed, in a dead faint. He saw nothing in the night light lit room, not even a shadow. John looked at Charlene and sighed, all of this was too much for her frail spirit. He was more robust than that, but even he now felt the strain of recent events.

He tucked her back into bed and went back to his room to sleep. Tomorrow would be a better day; he hoped.

Chapter 3

A CHANGE OF DIRECTION

Charlene woke and immediately came to her senses. Something had happened after she'd gone to sleep last night; she'd had a terrible nightmare, but she could not remember the details.

Her head was feeling a little fuzzy; not the alcohol-induced fuzzy of people who'd had a heavy night or lack of sleep. No. This was a heavy mental confusion stopping her thinking straight at all. It was weird and entirely foreign to her. She had the distinct feeling that she'd caught something unnatural at the conference. She needed to get to her lab, and test herself; meticulously. A broad-spectrum antibiotic would also be a good idea, a stiff dose of ultraviolet radiation a better one.

She looked at herself in the mirror, and her skin looked strange; she could not put her finger on the difference, but there was one. Her skin felt softer, but not the delicate softness of cotton wool or a fur rug, but the raw sensitivity of a bruise or a wound.

Dressing quickly, she started her morning meditation, preparing her for her days' work. A couple of off days, no matter how bad, would not stop her from getting her research done and published today. Perhaps they could get it to the Nobel evaluation panel by the end of the week, in time for this years' prizes; perhaps.

She knocked on the door to the adjacent room and was startled when it immediately flew open. John was already up and ready for breakfast and obviously very alert.

"How are you feeling, Ma'am?" he enquired, as infuriatingly polite as ever. The look he gave her was a quick scan, for any sign of injury or trauma from the previous evening's ordeal.

"Fine," she lied unconvincingly. He coughed disbelievingly, "Ok, actually a bit rough," she added more honesty; a telling sign to any that knew her that she was seriously out of kilter. Oh yes, that would be just him.

"I feel like you look; like I was stomped on by a large angry bull elephant." She smiled a wane little smile, but the frown John gave her was indicative that he was really worried.

"Anything we can do?" Yup, he was worried and the fact that he showed it indicated the just how concerned he was.

"We need to get to the lab, and see what the hell is going on with us," she said straight out. He merely nodded, and they hurriedly checked out and got to the car. They could get breakfast at the lab, then sort out what to do next.

The traffic was light, on the way back to the company laboratories and they did not really talk as they travelled. What was there that they could say? Both were feeling the after effects of a severe dose of unreality, and neither really wanted to ask the other's opinion, in case the other confirmed it had all been real.

Charlene glanced out the window, as John turned a corner onto the main road; a brightly coloured area with many people moving about in the sunny centre of town … and looked straight into the eyes of the 'Dark Queen'. Time stopped dead. That was impossible!

The dark green eyes, almost black, stabbed out from a stern, but beautiful, face directly at her with a piercing concentration; as though through that look she trying to tell Charlene something. The moment stretched out as Charlene's mind raced. Who was the apparition? Could it really be her long-lost mother, or her ghost, or had Charlene finally fallen over the edge into insanity. The rest of the people around the figure were somehow almost transparent; pushed to the back of her mind. In her head, she heard her mother's voice, "remember. Remember. REMEMBER!" The thought pounding into her head, for what seemed like a minute, but what must have been mere fractions of a second. Remember what? What was she saying really? Fleeting memories passed before her eyes, although she did not really see them, the after images were disturbing and twisted; enough to send a shiver through her body, mind, and soul, but not enough to force her to do whatever it was the spectre was attempting to command her to do.

Then another car passed between the elegant figure and her, and, at that moment, she was gone. Charlene blinked, her eyes rapidly scanning the pavement, up and down, but the car quickly travelled beyond the spot. Even turning slightly, there was no sign of the woman; vanished into the crowd, or maybe never having been there in the first place.

The driver called over his shoulder, "see something, Ma'am?" His tone was concerned, and there was a focused point to the question, which Charlene found even more disturbing.

"No. Nothing really. It just I thought I saw someone I used to know; must have been mistaken," even to her, the explanation seemed uncertain. The driver frowned, then just shrugged.

In a sheltered section of the street, a shadowy figure talked to someone on her phone.

"Yes?" The tone was casual to any observing person, but the strain in her voice would have betrayed, to any experienced observer, that she was being interrogated.

"You were successful?" The male voice on the phone was intense but distorted by some kind of modulator.

"Of course. The mental conditioning that I implanted in her mind when young is fully intact. Even the shock of the confrontation could not shake so strong an enchantment. Besides, she is my blood and that bond binds her to me more than mere power, even that which you wield."

As she said it, she knew that she'd made a mistake. The silence down the phone line lasted for a few seconds, and she gritted her teeth in anticipation of the response. As expected, her head exploded in agony, forcing her to clamp her temples and grind her teeth as it continued.

"Remember your place witch! The master needs your power and knowledge, but just because he needs it now, it does not mean I have to put up with your insolence," the pain continued to build, and build.

"P... Please, please!" hating him as he sent her own stolen power pulsing through her head. While she knew its source, without her daughter, and line of sight, she could not resist the Coven's combined power.

"BEG!" Demanded the voice coldly, "BEG for forgiveness," the voice was both emotionless and remorseless, deep within her head.

"I BEG YOU! Forgive me my impudence!" The pain grew greater, "I BEG YOU!!!"

The pain dulled, finally, although she was receiving a few strange looks from nearby people, curled up against the wall.

"Since you have begged I relent," the voice was so quickly back to normal that even her spirit quailed momentarily; at the sure use of power and the magnitude needed to get past her usually impenetrable protective wards. Of course, he was using her own power against her; so, her wards were not really there for him.

"Move on to the next stage of the plan, and, don't get above your station and definitely, don't fail." The call ended.

Sylvia stood slowly, rubbing her temples. The ache would last a long while, and she now felt incredibly weak; but was also in need of a scapegoat, to vent her rage.

An old lady was close and moved towards her with a concerned look.

"You alright dear? Look like you received some bad news. Can I help?" The lady looked like a street tramp but seemed sincere about the offer.

Sylvia looked at the lady and said, in a slow and measured voice, "well as you offer, there is something," she looked around; the street had suddenly become relatively empty.

She started to cast a spell, "I just need your soul".

The old woman screamed, silently, for a long time. Her soul had little vitality left, but it satisfied the need in Sylvia, to punish someone; for her need to do what she did.

As the A.G.E. pair returned to Oxford, John noticed a car keeping pace with them, about three cars back, but in a sign of how out of sorts he really was, he did not switch to evasive driving; he just ploughed through the traffic, as fast as the speed limits and the traffic allowed. Let the police trail them if they wanted, they would only get the answers they wanted if John, and Charlene, could get the answers for them. Fortunately, either the tail lost them, or they did not want to make an issue of the speed they'd been travelling at.

As they neared the lab, their tail decided they knew where the couple was headed, and they parked up a few doors down from the public entrance to the A.G.E. labs.

The labs looked the same as usual, and John opened the external door for Charlene with a resigned look. Her answering look was wane, and he was genuinely concerned for her. He had not seen her ill before, and it seemed like she was actually coming down with something serious.

They reached the reception desk and nodded to the receptionist. She returned it with one of surprise, and perhaps a little uncertainty, as she put her tea down.

John moved ahead and swiped his card receiving a burp of failure instead of the usual affirmative beep. He paused, thinking perhaps the strange electronic field of the previous night had affected his security card then turned to the reader and tried it again; slower this time and looking at the readout panel. The burp came again, and this time he saw the readout and his eyes raised in surprise. He looked at the receptionist, now accompanied by two uniformed security guards, regarding her monitor.

"I'm, sorry sir. It appears that your clearance has been suspended. You've been placed on the inactive register until you have been cleared to work again, by medical." John glanced at Charlene, the question in his eyes. The receptionist nodded, "the Dr. too, sir. It was a recommendation from the government Biotechnology and Biological Sciences Research Council, sir. You are on paid leave until the pair of you has been given the all clear by them."

"And," John paused slightly, for emphasis, "who will give us the all clear; since Dr. Clerk is one of their advisors? Her laboratory is upstairs, and she cannot get to it to give the all clear," his voice betraying his exasperation. It was obviously a ridiculous situation, but it was one he could not see any way out of. He glanced at Charlene, looking for an out, but all she could manage was, "let's see what our new acquaintance has to say about this," in a hushed tone for him only. She nodded to the receptionist and turned to seek answers elsewhere.

John had forgotten about the cards the enigmatic woman from last night had passed to him. Charlene's hand was in her suit pocket and already fiddling with it, a sign of her own agitation.

As the pair turned to walk out the building, with their former colleges observing the pair; an aura of anger and indignation surrounding them, one poor soul yelping as Charlene slammed open the door on the way out, practically right into him. She recognised a junior technician, from an adjacent lab, and gave him a pat on the head, as she passed.

He shrank back, and suddenly Charlene had a sense of power she'd never felt before. She stopped and turned towards the man, who looked ready to bolt.

"Hello, George," she purred, the man's eyes going wide and starting to look for a way into the building past her.

"Dr. Klerk we," he stammered, panicking.

"Do me a favour," she leaned forward as he backed off. "Take care of the lab until I get back. I really don't want to have to rearrange things when I do," she raised her hand to his chin, but, before it made contact, the man's courage failed him, and he ducked under her outstretched arm and ploughed into the building, whimpering like a terrified puppy. Charlene shook her head. What had just happened? John was looking strangely at her.

"What?" she said, a little perplexed at his look.

"That was cruel," was all he said. He walked off towardsthe car, muttering to himself, but still keeping his eyes open. Charlene arrived at the car door and waited for the Driver to open the door, which, to her obvious surprise, he did. "Still getting paid. Still delivering the service," he said leaving her in no doubt of his disapproval of her treatment of the technician.

She slinked into the car as always, but today seemed different, almost like leaving home again; the first time had been traumatic enough. As the car started off to the destination on the card, her mind started to wander back to that first occasion.

She'd been six. Her parents were always on the move, for one reason or another and always too busy to explain why; mainly because they were working, or teaching her something, or arguing about where to move next.

Her father was, in her extremely biased opinion, a kind, scholarly man; serious, but fair. He was tall and very handsome. He always found time to play with her, whatever he was working on, to answer her sometimes silly questions.

He would smile at her, give her a real answer, then a silly answer to the same thing, to open her mind. Sometimes, the real answers had seemed right, but others, she asked why he was being silly with the real answer he gave. When they were alone, it was a game for Charlene to figure out which response was the silly one. Later, several of the ones she thought were silly made her father frown. "What makes you think that is silly Charlene?" he'd asked; not just, "don't be silly".

One time she'd answered heatedly, "it just is daddy. Your answer just does not make sense," and she'd tried to move on to the next question. He'd paused, looking strangely at her, then scribbled a couple of strange symbols on the pieces of paper he'd been writing on.

"Sweetheart, I want you to look at this, and tell me if it's right." There was an intensity in his eyes she'd only seen once in his eyes before; when the men that he worked with had come, with an urgent problem they'd had. She was a little worried by the look but being an obedient child, she looked down at the scribble; something daddy had said one time was an equation. It was several lines long, and there were lots of letters, numbers, and symbols in it.

She read it all, then thought carefully; the first few lines all seemed ok. Then she checked the next few, and another set of strange slightly wavering letters and numbers appeared on the page above them. She frowned and reached for a pen looking to her father for permission; he nodded, in a kind of bewildered haze. She turned back, filled with a kind of joy, and proceeded to cross out the wrong characters, replacing them with the others. More and more of them jumped out at her and, after three minutes, the bottom half of the equation was replaced with a neater, more concise, alternative.

She'd turned to face him. "There; that's right now, daddy." There'd been a note of satisfaction in her voice that told him she had done her best. After he'd read the changes, a look of astonished wonder lit his face. With a little moan, he traced the new symbology and grasped what she'd done; a huge smile of genuine pride lit his face.

"You did it," he muttered, "my little girl is a genius!" He regarded her for a second, then whooped a joyous yell, standing and hoisting her over his head, in his great long arms, and spinning her around. She squealed with laughter "Daddy, what have I done?" She had rarely seen him so, animated.

"My dear girl. You have just solved a problem that has eluded me for years. It may help daddy immensely and probably many other people too." He finally put her down and cuddled her for a moment. Then he became serious, and she knew there was a but coming.

He looked deep into her eyes as if searching for something.

"You must make me a promise, Sweetheart," he said in his, 'please listen' tone. She nodded. "Don't do this trick with mummy around. She must not know about this till you are much older, ok?" She nodded again.

"Why Daddy? Does she not need things fixing?" She'd asked

He looked at her harder. "No Sweetheart, it's just that mummy and me do not agree on some things, and we are going somewhere new soon. She does not need to know. Understand." She nodded. "Promise?"

"I promise Daddy," she smiled, and it was all done. She had made her promise, and from then onwards she'd kept it.

A few weeks later, he had taken her on a trip to their new home on the island Brae, in Scotland, and left her mother behind. Oh, her mother had visited her without daddy knowing, and occasionally she had even gone to the 'Dark Queen's' company flat, where she'd trained in many things. Even there, she'd not revealed her talent to her mother.

This was one of the few real memories she still had of her father after she lost her parent's. The rest was a blur, other than the facts that she loved her father, and hated the 'Dark Queen'. It was, perhaps, that thought that triggered the subsequent strange daydream.

She was in a room; it was dark, and she was in the centre, although she could not see the sides of it. There were two open doors; both had her mother in the doorway.

One was dressed all in white; the other in black.

"This way, now, you lady. You must come with me to do your training," the woman in black commanded.

"Now dear, you know you don't want to go that way, don't you?" said the other.

Charlene looked at both of them and felt compelled to go to the woman in black, and even started to move her foot to step that way.

"Trust your instincts, my dear," repeated the other one; and her foot stopped.

She wanted to go to the lady in white, but all her training was to do as she was told. Then she thought about it, as logically as she could. Do as you are told, came the thought again. The lady in white had said trust her instincts; her instincts were to go to the lady in white. The lady in black was also Sylvia. Sylvia had commanded her to come. So, she would go to Sylvia.

With teeth gritted, she stepped forward towards the lady in white, and kept on walking, despite the howl of anger and frustration coming from the other.

Then darkness descended on her thoughts.

Charlene had drifted off, for more than a few minutes, and the Driver was getting a bit worried when she suddenly piped up.

"Driver, what is your real name?" The question threw him totally. So much so that he'd to swerve a little to get back in lane. "You've guarded me for weeks, and I don't even know your name," she leaned forward, apparently awaiting the answer.

"Guards are trained to stay a discrete distance from their clients, Ma'am," he said in his best professional voice, "it avoids several knottier complications that can arise from, familiarity." He was staring straight ahead and avoiding her gaze, in the mirror, too. "It's not wise for us to get on a first name basis, especially with what we now know is going on."

His shoulder gave a strange twitch, "however, it might help, say if we ran into something like those wolf things again, if you call me by name. I'm John."

"Ok, John. Thank you, for the other night, and everything," she said quietly.

John barked a little laugh, "As I remember it, it was you who was treating me and holding the other creature at bay, no one else. So, thank you," Charlene emphasised a little as most of her help had been by accident, or coincidence, rather than intent; still, it was a nice thought on his part.

A short time later, John's glancing in his mirror spotted something amiss.

"Uh, oh," John started, distracting Charlene from her social awkwardness.

"What is it?" She asked, in a suddenly interested, but in a voice filled with trepidation.

"We lost our tail!" John said as he flicked between all his car's mirrors and cameras.

"That's good, isn't it?" she asked, puzzled by his apparent deep concern.

"That was a government tail. You don't lose that kind of people, except for an exceptional reason." He was now accelerating, moving along a straight stretch of motorway, suspiciously light of traffic. The only two vehicles behind also started to accelerate, doing so faster than their heavier car.

"And in this case, it seems, it's because someone else took them out, probably so they could get at us."

Their car was primarily built for comfort, not speed, while the two vehicles rapidly approaching, were sporty black Mercedes, whose windows now wound down to waist level sprouting multiple silencers, allowing the occupants to target them; shots following immediately, ricocheting off the road near their target's rear tyres.

John veered left, bouncing off the front wing of the lead car; while the second pursuing car dropped back a wheel's length, its displayed barrels trying again for the tyres, from directly behind.

John switched tack, and swerved right, straight in front of the other car, slamming the brakes on, using the extra weight of his heavier car to try and cripple the other. The second car slammed into the back but carried on going despite the substantial damage to the engine. John floored the accelerator, and spun the car into the opposite direction, aided by the other car's shove from behind.

"Hold on; we are going off-road," John warned his passenger, over his shoulder.

"What do you mean off-road?" Charlene asked, not understanding.

"Oh, for heaven sake," he muttered, "HOLD ON TIGHT!" he yelled as the car fell off the road onto a steep verge. The other vehicles swerved to follow, having failed to see the underpass coming up, that John was about to 'acquaint' them with. Car one went off the other side safely, the right-hand verge being only a few feet down. However the drop on the left-hand side was significant, and the second car having initially maintained its level, was jostled into a roll, about halfway down the forty-foot incline, and flipped at full speed as it hit the field below, tumbling end over end for three full lengths. Needless to say, the driver's airbag was deployed, at precisely the wrong time, and the driver was killed instantly. The passenger was catapulted out of the open window and learned how to fly, for all of five seconds. He flew thirty feet into the air but failed to learn how to land safely in that time. The medics would find a broken spine, and several vital organs ruptured, as he landed with a sickening crunch on a flattened safety railing, back first.

The other car tried to follow after the Mercedes, closing in behind and to the left, when it a concrete manhole cover, surrounding a water main, slamming the car into the air, on one side; smashing the concrete, bursting the tyre, twisting the chassis, dislocating the drive shaft and in effect crippling the car.

The bone-jarring landing onto the road below was worse for the driver and passengers, as both airbags fired off and wrenched them into the already twisted section of the car. Both were instantly rendered unconscious.

In the meantime, John carried on his evasive driving, at speed, down the now totally clear road, still looking around and checking to see if they were still in danger.

"You lost them!" Charlene's voice had a note of relief in her voice.

"I'm just making sure they were alone," he said, in a tone that meant that he thought that unlikely.

"Why would they send more, just for us?" Charlene was truly puzzled.

"Because, my dear Dr. Klerk, if what our friend from last night said was true, you are carrying in that wooden case, a weapon of a terrible kind, that is exceedingly valuable to the wrong kind of people; and you can assume that they are the wrong kind of people. That makes us target number one at the moment."

John carried on looking around; they'd caught him out once; they were not going to do it again. He made a mental note that the Situational Awareness course was no longer necessary; he'd just passed the exam.

After a few minutes, they passed the scene of a multi-car pileup, surrounded by a dozen police cars, ambulances, and a rescue tender just arriving.

"I think those cars are what's left of our tail and it seems that, like our attackers back there, they were not bothered about bystanders or witnesses; that's not professional, and nor is the single hit squad." John's mind was working at maximum speed now.

"But there were two cars." Charlene pointed out.

"That's just one squad. They probably thought it would be enough with just the driver to deal with. Obviously, they did not check out who was driving, else they'd have used a helicopter; so not an inside job," he thought intensely; running through possible suspects.

"Looks like, whoever was really behind your nasty concoction there, either, has some poor competition, or, they are not the only ones out for us." John gave a grim smile, "It always helps to have more people after you, especially if they are after different things. It means they tend to get in each other's way." He lowered his voice, "and it also means I get more target practice too". He tried to sound relaxed about the thought and, funnily enough, he really did. He was a professional and knowing that the opposition was not, gave him an edge and the feeling that he was going to enjoy their next encounter, an awful lot more than they were.

In a distant location, a robed man sat, in a dark, and incense filled, room, pondering the events of the past few hours. He'd finally located his quarry, after so many years of fruitless search and sent her mother out to trigger her homing command; the mental command had been sent, received and that meant the target should have been waiting outside the hotel for his people to take her away. However, something had gone terribly wrong. Somehow the command had been resisted, blocked or cancelled. Then, he'd sent a quartet of cars to capture her en-route; only to find that the target had a specialist bodyguard, and had not been alone. A formidable tailing unit had managed to kill at least three of the four teams sent. The final squad had neutralised them, but were repelled, or neutralised, by her guard. Those that survived would spend many days in agony, begging for release before him, until he granted them the sweet oblivion of death. His quarry had not been taken, and the bodyguard had spirited her away, to who knew where. He closed his eyes; this would not sit well with the Master.

As if on cue, a dark and disturbing presence started to gather in the room, like a choking fog.

"Geroth!" A deeply resonant voice echoed within his head, and his spirit quailed, as it always did when his master spoke to him.

"Master!" His left hand was placed to his temple, revealing the pentagram ring about his third finger, its' contact with his head, reducing the effort needed to send his thoughts to his master.

"I await your gift to me, Geroth, of the First Coven," the evil voice made him feel both powerful and weak, at the same time. Every word, filling him with mystic power while ageing his body; the master's power had its price, an obvious consequence of dealing with his kind.

"We have found and made contact master; but others dare to interfere with your plan," explained the man, his black tunic and rob gathered about him, as the air in the sanctuary room became cold, with impending manifestation; his master was impatient for his gift.

"An Age have I waited for this one, Geroth," boomed the voice, more physical than mental now, a dark cloud gathering in the centre of the room, not quite in the form of a vast, distorted face, but the shape was disturbing enough to make the man try to back away.

"I need that soul, Geroth, to gain the ultimate power I seek." The cloud did not achieve solidity, but loitered, almost silently staring at the underling, the surface bubbling away, exuding a noxious stench and palpable menace. Then it seemed to diminish slowly, like an impression of a person's face on a balloon's surface. His master did not yet have the strength to establish a full manifestation at present; something for which the man was profoundly grateful.

"Do not fail me Geroth; or your death will be eons in the planning, and your suffering without end, throughout all of eternity." The voice faded more, then was gone. He was alone again; as alone as he could get anyway.

The High Priest slumped in his chair for a second then, as he always did, he looked in the mirror, opposite him. The reflection thus presented shocked him as, instead of the forty-five-year-old he'd been a moment ago, he saw a decrepit old man in his eighties.

"You have been warned!" whispered the voice of his master, as the illusion faded.

He saw his actual face again, as he was, but there were still more wrinkles there than there should be. At the age of thirty-five, he now looked ten years older than his actual age; ironic, as he'd joined the Cult to gain eternal youth. Instead, he now aged with every new contact and, indeed he knew he would continue to age until the Master received his gift; nothing like a little incentive, to motivate your workforce, he thought. It was his own work ethic when he was about his usual business, now being used against him by his master, who it seemed, shared his twisted and cruel sense of humour.

But thinking about work now gave him an idea. If the police were present at the incident, then there would be official reports filed with information on the quarry, and her guard. His agents would be able to locate any other interfering factions and neutralise them. Then, they could re-acquire the target and deliver her for the Autumn Solstice.

"Impatient wasn't he," intruded a female voice, as the 'Dark Queen' entered the room; his second-in-command, his Priestess, and Arch-rival in the Coven.

"Spare me your prattle, woman," he started to rise, but his head swam, and he felt dizzy, so he sat back down, raising his hand to his head again, needing the ring's power to steady himself and stop the room from spinning.

"His presence does that to mortals," crowed the woman, as she floated gracefully into the room, wearing a rich purple bodice decorated with masses of interwoven gold thread. His purple cloak was similar but had blood-red veins, interleaved with the gold thread adoring it. "I imagine that even his whisper would make you swoon, without the ring you wield," she said pointing to the golden pentagram adored ring around his finger.

"I do wield it, however," he snarled, as he stood up, and pointed it at her. She bowed, perhaps an inch, in submission.

"Of that, I am well aware, mighty High Priest". Then, raising her head she suddenly, locked eyes with him.

"Your theft of my ring gained you the power to command me," her voice rang in his head, "but not to destroy me. We are in a deadly embrace, until the master releases both of us, one way or another," and her voice departed his head.

Strangely, her presence in his head was only slightly different than that of his master, disturbing him more than he would ever want to admit.

"Still," her voice returned to normal and went on, "time is moving on, and we are reaching a critical juncture. If we do not capture my first born in the next few months, the alignments will end, and we will have to wait another hundred years before we can bring the Master here, and," she looked at him, in a deeply scornful way, "quite frankly, you don't have that long left."

"I know that Hag," although, in fact, she was a statuesque, raven-haired, beauty. However, the insult bit home and she flicked her hair back, momentarily leaving her throat exposed, his hand shooting out and grasping it tightly. For a moment, she resisted choking, then his strength began to tell, and the grip started to close, until, the ring on his finger started to glow, causing him to suddenly let go, as though he'd just received a shock. He shook the hand, feeling a cramping pain in it.

"Ah! The ring still knows me," she rubbed her throat, then beamed a triumphal smile at the High Priest. "It still knows me, and, is protecting me. Think on that; and watch your back," she warned, starting out the room.

"Always, Harpy". She paused almost imperceptibly, but finally reached the doorway and stopped there and turned.

"I must return to the Other, to continue the training," her voice sounding unconcerned but he was. No human should be able to treat their own flesh and blood with such brutality and be unmoved by it. Even as High priest he had some human feelings. She seemed to either have lost most of them, or buried them with her late husband; Dark Queen indeed!

She finally left the room, and he stood, moving to the exit that lead to his office. He had things to do. He'd failed to get the girl by occult means, but, perhaps, he could use his other resources. He cast a basic illusion and entered his workplace. To all around him, it appeared as though he'd merely entered the operations room from his office.

"Evening sir," said the duty officer. "You want the daily reports?"

"Evening Sergeant. No. Can you get me Detective Inspector Browns, I need a private word with him," and he turned and went into his office and poured himself a coffee.

"Yes, Chief Inspector Blackmoore."

All those who had received Whisper's calling cards arrived at the location noted on it; 5 Cheapside Street and almost immediately recognised the building, in the middle of London, almost on top of the local underground station, right next to the Thames and well within sight of St. Paul's Cathedral.

John pulled into the building's small parking area and drew up smartly between the two yellow lines. The traffic around here was light, for Central London, but the pavement was packed with people, and in the crowd, John glimpsed the lanky forms of Simon and Jack struggling through the ordinary people, in his direction. He also noticed three other people, back some distance, with the usual large, and unsubtle long coats; characteristic of establishment tails.

As the two started into the building, the tails turned away slightly and stopped, assuming surveillance positions, in some shop doorways across the road. John sighed. Ah well, they had lost their own tails, only to gain another set. Perhaps their new taskmaster could do something about them. Or, maybe, they were their new master's tails, he was sure they would find out soon.

John stepped out and moved around the car. As he did, he caught the glint of someone else further back. Another tail, but this one was harder to spot and more skilled than the others. Only John's exceptional eyesight had spotted this one, and the fact that this one was not armed with standard issue equipment; no earpiece, no paper, and the bulge, in the long coat, was larger than any government issued sidearm; probably something more automatic. That spoke of someone more criminal, or professional; neither of which was good news for him or his charge. He opened the door and leaned his head into the car instead of letting Charlene out straight away, her own look becoming concerned.

"We have people watching us again, and an unwelcome presence further back as well. If I say run, just run into the building and keep going." He noticed a scared look forming in her eyes, "I don't think anything will happen yet, but just in case." She nodded but still looked a little pale. "You Ok?" There was still something wrong with her, she looked, off; but he could not identify what was actually wrong.

"I really need to get some equipment and do some tests. I'm not sure, but I might be having a bit of a reaction to something from the creatures," she replied her hand twitching uncharacteristically. "I definitely need an MRI scan too," she said uncertainly, looking him straight in his eyes. "I don't think it's the venom, but whatever it is it's affecting my nervous system and progressing rapidly".

"Perhaps we can get some help inside. Let's go," and he offered his hand, which unusually she took, smiling gratefully.

She slid out of the door and promptly sat right down on the ground. Charlene, ever graceful, suddenly looked a little panicky. John helped her up with the question in his eyes.

"I slipped," but the look in her eyes showed that to be a lie.

"Let's get you in, and find that help," he instructed grabbing her elbow and allowing her to lean into him.

She felt strange in doing so, but actually enjoying his masculine odour, and muscle, next to her. John kept his eyes open for movement from the tails, and the mysterious second follower, but they were either not paying attention, or they were not bothered as long as their marks went inside the building.

Once inside, she felt a little steadier and shook off John's help.

"I'm better now. Perhaps it was just all the excitement of the journey," she smiled, knowing the John would be scornful of such a bare face lie.

"Yeah right," John smiled back, knowing that she knew, he knew, it was not the case.

The lobby turned a corner and rounded to where the others waited with a man dressed in a Savile Row suit. His face was stern, middle-aged, robust but with, to Charlene's trained eyes, a bit of pallor to it.

"Ah, here are our missing pair," said the stranger, indicating for them to join him. "Greetings all. Allow me to introduce myself: I am Craig Starling, of Starling Enterprises." Everyone's eyes in the group shot up, they had all heard of Starling enterprises; it was an FTSE 100 company, with an international portfolio in science, manufacturing, transport, and defence. This was a man with resources, power, and connections with the highest places, and people, in Whitehall and not a few in the other seats of power in Europe.

"I am a businessman, entrepreneur, patriot and among other things a liaison to our more secretive citizens," he coughed delicately.

"You are here because you now know about them, and because my department deals with people like yourselves. I have looked at your files and found that you have a set of skills that I think might be, helpful, to my department and critically you were properly discrete with the police interviews, and M.I.X. need people like you."

The group looked perplexed by the acronym, and he nodded in response to the implicit question. "Military Intelligence, section Ten. A branch of the Intelligence service that is responsible for new weapons research and technical analysis of intelligence reports."

"I thought GCHQ dealt with that now," John interrupted, not hiding his confusion.

Craig smiled at that. "They are the public side of the department, the portion that is overseen and monitored, budgeted and do the bulk of the active intelligence work. We are the real secret part of the department, having different funding channels, a special oversight mechanism and we're not seen by the current government, per say." He indicated that they should move deeper inside. "A necessary precaution, should the politicians become, shall we say, less than loyal to the democratic spirit of the country," gesturing for Simon to proceed him down the corridor, "I have space in this building and, I would like you to make yourself at home here, while we deal with the police investigation, into the attack on the conference. However, first I would like to introduce you to some others that help me here sorting out problems. It will let you get to know me, and them, a little better, and give you a taste of the life that you are entering."

Simon moved down the corridor followed by Jack, John and finally Charlene.

As she passed him, Charlene looked at Starling, noticing occasional dark spots on his skin, then his eyes and noticed him looking at her, seeing her concerned look. He slightly shook his head and nodded for her to follow the others, acknowledging an unspoken issue between them. She turned her mouth slightly indicating she would like to speak to him about his problem later.

The corridor ended in a lift that could just about squeeze them all in. As Craig entered the top floor was selected, and the elevator speedily moved them to the penthouse suite, which turned out to be a spacious modern office with a feel of understated luxury.

As the door opened, the group stepped out into a luxurious open plan suite, with minimalistic furnishing, comprising a large oval glass coffee table, a pair of large white L-shaped leather sofas and a scattering of standing lamps. The whole suite bordered an open rooftop area that covered a full half the width of the building. A large wall box nearby, indicated that the roof could be closed, if necessary.

On one of the sofas, sat someone they knew; the magician from the conference's show, the woman with the wand.

Harry's face was a picture of astonishment. "You work for him?" His face changed to show his confusion and a little anger.

"For a few months now," she said a bit sheepishly. "I'm Helena Osgood, Craig's personal assistant," she said for the benefit of the new arrivals. Then to him, "It's not the first time my wand has become active recently, and Craig wanted to know if there was a pattern to the incidents. We are still working on that one." She looked questioningly to Craig, and he nodded for her to leave it at that.

"And, I, am Isabella White," came a youthful female voice, its' owner concealed behind part of the other sofa. A stunningly beautiful, young, raven-haired, girl's head poked out, from the side of the sofa. "I deal with web intelligence gathering." She waved a tablet over the arm of the sofa; miming tapping the keys, to the visitors, then vanishing back around the sofa's arm. "Lately, my task has been trying to keep you lot out of the public eye," She started tapping keys quickly. Craig motioned everyone to go over and see what she was doing.

The group surrounded the sofa, to see several laptops, all perched around the large coffee table. Each computer seemed to have several windows open, some running complex programs, others, showing U-tube clips; the common theme of the snippets being the attack at the conference.

The news clips covered the entire build-up to the chaos in the hotel, and the aftermath. However, several, displayed clips from the hotel's internal security camera feed; feeds of remarkably quality, showing the actions of each of the four newcomers in graphic, and detailed, slow motion, a neat trick, given that the displayed scenes could not possibly have been caught on the ageing hotel cameras.

The group watched for a few seconds, each of them registering incredulity at their supposed actions to look at the others. Charlene showed her suspicions about the videos first when one of the feeds showed her throwing a flask of acid directly at another member of the crowd. She frowned, trying to remember what had actually happened, and failed. She must have totally blacked out at that point; but another image on the feed shocked her into vocalising the thought she was having, when it showed John turning and shooting a fleeing woman, in the face; not accidentally, but deliberately and with malice in his eyes.

"That did not happen!" John barked in indignation, beating her to the words.

She tried to think what had actually happened at that point, but the whole thing was blank; not even just blurred.

"John would never do that," she regarded him, giving him her tacit support, although, to her surprise, his face was less sure than hers', his look similar to hers, doubting his recollection of the event, and his certainty that he had not actually deliberately killed an innocent. Then his eyes cleared and true recollection came, and her indignation was echoed by that look of certainty on his face. She relaxed, then had a thought of sympathy for the person who'd just incurred the wrath of one powerful and incandescently furious man.

Craig looked up, "we agree." Isabella looked up and smiled.

"It did not even cross our minds, that you could do such things. The doctoring is good; top notch in fact. Almost as good as I could do; but there are too many temporal inconsistencies in the files, feed timings and the frame rates produced for these events to be as presented on these feeds. Also, when you check the timings of the posts, they would have had to have been a live feed for all the camera shots to be possible." She shrugged, "still the people who watch these clips are not interested in that kind of thing; they just like to see the gore and violence."

Isabella took a sly glance at John, a sparkle in her eyes, for the big bodyguard, the returned look showed his gratitude and, perhaps, a hint of something more.

Only Charlene glimpsed the moment, and, to her surprise, felt a tinge of reaction at their obvious instant connection. Was that jealousy she was feeling? What the blazes was that? She was a scientist, he was her driver and bodyguard; Period. Charlene did a quick reality check. Why was she bothered what two virtual strangers felt for each other when they were in the middle of the most significant historical event any of them were likely to EVER be part of? She pursed her lips. She was not, although there was a niggling little feeling that, perhaps, she really was, even if there were more important things that demanded her attention at the moment. Charlene piped up. "So, what are you going to do about this?" She looked between Isabella and Craig.

"Well, I," Isabella emphasised the present tense, "am making sure that the doctored clips are being deleted, as fast as they are spawning on the web." Her fingers a blur on the currently held keyboard, before moving onto another; to initiate another set of programs. "Whoever is doing this, they are talented; and they are testing my abilities, big time." However, her face was calm and confident. "Unfortunately, they have made a big mistake," her audience leaning in, to hear the next few words, "although they are shifting the source of the signal, they are using part of the London phone network infrastructure to do it, I presume because they think they can hide the traffic that way." She suddenly looked a little smug, and she looked at John, "Unfortunately for them, I have web bots to detect such things, and they have tracked the signal down to a comm. towers in this area." She pointed to a small area of the map.

"I considered sending a team to deal with the problem, but, since it is in your best interest, I think you are the people to go check this out." Craig looked at the four people in front of him. They all looked back at him in shock.

"Us?" Simon squeaked, looking ready to bolt.

"I have it on good authority that you will be able to handle the situation." Craig sounded confident, as he raised his calling card to them, "but first, you'll need equipment. Fortunately, I have a goodly supply of such, a selection of the very best."

They were not investigators, well, except John, and they all continued to look at him as though he was crazy. He starred back for a few seconds thinking that perhaps he was, to even consider this, then bowed his head and muttered, "OK let's get this done," in a voice filled with resignation.

Simon was the first to speak up "We'll need a van, overalls, equipment, markings,"

"And fluffy dice," said Harry. Everyone looked around at him slowly, as though he'd suddenly gone, quietly, insane. "Never mind what the side of a vehicle looks like; just ask anyone who drives, or is a passenger, how they find their car. It's not what the car looks like, the make or the colour these days. There are so many cars the same it would take too long. It's the personal things in it; the car seat, the stickers, and the fluffy dice, so the absence of such things can stand out as much as their presence." After a few seconds, Harry could see that they understood, and after a wave of nods greeted the comment. He smiled; for professors and computer geeks, they were remarkably fast on the uptake.

"Ok," said John in his most business-like tone, "so let's get some equipment."

Craig stepped forward, "use this," he said handing them a gold credit card, "'its' access to a quiet account I use; Isabella's routines keep it off the grid. It should allow you to get the equipment you need without attracting any unwanted attention."

"I'll get a van that has some 'oomph'," said John, "I know what to look for; and I know a few people that I can trust, to get one that is both legit and untraceable."

"I'll get some tools and equipment capable of dealing with comms traffic," said Simon.

Charlene felt a bit of a fifth wheel here. The strange feeling tingling through her body was still present, if barely perceptible at the moment, so she moved over to Isabella, and had a look at what she was doing. Although Charlene used computers and programmed the software for her work, this youngster was using incredibly complex algorithms, way beyond her skill, although, she did recognise portions of the code. Perhaps in time, she could learn to get to that level. She'd have to have a talk with the young girl. Harry was looking about a little lost, and Charlene realised that he probably felt as superfluous as her. There was little call for illusions, escapology or sleight of hand around here. Then she had a notion.

"Harry, perhaps you could help bring a more personal feel to our new office," she smiled at him, but the look he returned was one of annoyance.

"Harry is my stage name, Dr. Klerk. My real name is Jack, Jack Somerfelt," he carried on looking around, "but you are right, this place does need a little re-design," and his demeanour softened a bit, "and if we are going to live here for a time, we might as well make ourselves at home." He looked at Craig who gave a little nod of ascent.

"I'll show you the rest of the place later, but for the moment plan what changes you want. I need to do a few things and get some other resources in place," and with that Craig started to walk back to the elevator; then stopped, doubling back, "oh and you might need these." He reached into his top pocket and produced four badges made of an unknown metal, handing one to each of them. They looked like police warrant card IDs, except they had the royal crown with three letters beneath it: M.I.X. They all looked at Craig, as each card had a blank space with the heading codename on it.

"You can decide your code names when they become necessary, just trace it in with your finger and it will be registered with your DNA in the database against your name. To be used in emergencies; and if there is no other option," he resumed his withdrawal to the lift.

Charlene intercepted him, pulling him around by his arm and nailing him with her eyes. "You have Cancer, don't you" she more stated than asked, daring him to lie, and saw he was about to refute the statement. "I can see it in your skin and pulmonary system. How bad is it?" She kept her voice low so that the others would not hear her.

Craig sighed and nodded imperceptibly, "bad, inoperable and terminal in a few months. Normally anyway." She saw a gleam in his eyes and understanding followed.

"Except that my work might be sufficiently advanced, to address it?" He nodded.

"I get reports from all the labs working on such things. And your lab reported in last week that you were making progress."

Her look was of a challenge accepted, but there was a worried edge to her voice. "However, I have only just managed to get the process started. I still need more time, and I cannot promise to get it in time for you, and I'd need the latest Nanites from A.G.E."

"That will not be a problem, and we can sort out equipment, in short order, to progress your work." He smiled at her, "I have every faith in your abilities, Dr. Klerk," he reassured, putting his hand on her shoulder, with a warm smile, "after all I know just how good you are. He went into the lift and left her pondering what to do next. That being answered as the others came through.

"The kit's been ordered and Isabella said that a van's ready downstairs," John informed everyone.

"Already?" Charlene was a little startled at the speed of things.

"Money allows you to obtain things fast in the business world; and Starling Enterprises netted near a quarter of a billion, last year alone. That makes their orders something that companies response to rapidly," John's explained, his eye's rolling at the figures involved.

"Let's pop to B&Q too and get the last items we need. Then let's see what we can find at the location Isabella gave us." Charlene could not believe she was now an agent of an intelligence agency, along with a group of strangers, and she needed something to calm her nerves. She usually meditated, but that couldn't be done while travelling, so the only thing available now was shopping.

"I'll come too," added Helena, "you'll need someone with some experience in this kind of work." She was looking directly at Charlene, who mouthed a silent thank you. The other woman winked cheekily and the group moved into the returned lift to go to the van.

As they left, Helena grabbed a clutch bag, with some company phones in, for use later.

Once they had left, Isabella looked up from her programming, as Craig returned.

"Is that them, then?" She asked although the answer was fairly clear.

"Has to be. You pulled their files, and this note was a little too specific to be a fake. I don't know how they knew, but it seems we need to get this lot up to speed, as fast as possible." He shook his head, holding a small folded square of writing paper, watermarked 'France'. "And god knows what they will find there if this is the result," he said, waving the paper at her. At least the little icons had given him their code names.

She did not know what the letter actually said, but it had him worried big time; enough to get him to get M.I.6 to dispatch a tactical team to Paris.

There was something big going on, and he did not like it when there was, and he did not know about it. Isabella had tried to find anything on the web, but this it seemed was something that only a ground team could investigate adequately. She may not have been here long, but she knew not a lot rattled that man, and he was seriously rattled.

The trip to B&Q was blissfully uneventful, netting a few chemicals and tools. Helena and Charlene even chatted a little, about trivial things. It was strange for Charlene that one could spend time with people and talk to them, about topics unrelated to work. She found the whole conversation like talking in a foreign language, and yet, she found it strangely appealing, almost natural. Her discipline, however, took over after a while and steered the conversation back to what was going to happen next.

Helena looked at her with a strange, almost pitiful look, for a second. "Charlene, you know, it's ok to actually have a social life. Millions of people do it all the time."

Charlene knew the tone; it was the one her father had used once when trying to get her to go out with her class, at the end of her school days. The problem was, the rest of the class were sixteen, and she was twelve, and substantially smarter, and taller, than most of them. He eventually gave up trying to talk her around; after all, she knew what he was trying to do, except, he'd been dead for many years then. Yet she remembered it so vividly; how strange. And the criticism made her a little touchy.

Helena's attempt at making friends with Charlene was a natural thing for her to do; unfortunately, she'd said exactly the wrong thing in precisely the wrong way.

"One point five million people die of Cancer, every year. All people can have fun, but only I can help the ones with Cancer, Helena." She was suddenly incensed that this stranger was intruding into her personal life, no matter how nice she was. "I need to do this Helena, and until I succeed, there is only one direction I really want my life to go; and I'll need all my discipline to succeed." She saw the effect on Helena, as the women's face showed her pain at such a hurtful rebuff, and was immediately sorry, causing her to bow her head a little, in shame, then tried to explain, "I made a promise to my father; that I would help all the people I could." Helena saw the effort that Charlene was making to calm down, and followed her lead in defusing the situation.

"I understand that you need to keep your promise Charlene, but I'm sure your father would not want you to live your life friendlessly."

With an effort, Charlene gathered her composure and realised that Helena was, of course, right. She took a deep breath, the kind that she started her meditation with, and looked at Helena eye to eye, then nodded; relieved when the woman smiled, in recognition of the implicit apology.

Isabella looked at Craig as they went through the files of their new recruits.

"You will have to tell her you know." She talked over her shoulder, as he moved to sit next to her.

"She is not ready for it yet, my dear." He looked at her, but her eyes were glued to the laptop screen, typing away.

"Is anyone ever ready to hear that the people they loved were not just lost but were murdered." A few paper cuttings landed on one side of the laptop," Isabella stopped typing and looked at Craig, spotting the tell-tale squint in his eye.

"Oh; It's one of those," she frowned. "Well, how much worse COULD it be?" Her voice projected a serious question. She was more experienced than the newbies, but even she was relatively new to the strange world that Craig had opened up to her.

"Much worse; much, much worse, I'm afraid," he paused a little, trying to decide just how much she needed to know.

"The tabloids mentioned cults and such, although the broadsheets were more matter of fact. The police were baffled, but would not release even the basic details." She frowned, "interesting. Many files are zipped up tighter than a gang member's hoodie," giving her boss a suspicious look. He nodded. She threw her hands up in the air in exasperation "I knew it; you sealed them." He sat, deciding some candour was in order.

"I had to. Charlene's father, John, was a member of M.I.X and was working on a gene he'd discovered, something he said could be the key to unlocking extraordinary powers; a hybrid of some kind, mostly human but with extra properties he could not identify."

"He called it Chimera. He never recorded its source, but I think I guessed when he took his daughter away from the mainland."

"Chimera is totally unique. When stimulated, the gene seems to alter the function of any organ in the body it is present in, augmenting its function or even adding new ones, with unknown capabilities," he shook his head, a little bewildered by the possibilities.

"The problem," he said in exasperation, "is that the gene rejects any form of control, reacting differently in any given host and environment. John managed to implant it into the Endocrine system, the cardiovascular system and most importantly into the pituitary gland of various test animals; but he could never get it to do anything the same way more than once, and he indicated that the results only scratched the surface of the gene's potential. In short, it was highly adaptive to control; almost like it treated control like a form of attack."

"Unfortunately, John, like his daughter, was a genius and he kept the more important research in his head" Craig stood up again. "John, and Sylvia, her mother, were both M.I.X., but Sylvia was found to be compromised, and John found out. After that, they never meshed well, finally breaking up, forcing John to move to a new location, in Scotland. He continued his work, but after he'd made one important discovery and tried to contact us, Sylvia must have intercepted the transmission and struck."

His eyes looked at the floor, and Isabella knew that he felt responsible for what had happened. "When we arrived, it was a bloody mess, in the literal sense. The reports from the tabloids were actually fairly accurate for a change. There was gore everywhere, even the ceiling was covered in it. What the reports don't say is that Charlene was actually there." Isabelle's eyebrows shot up. "Whatever happened, she saw it. However, afterwards she was totally catatonic; not really surprising given the fact she was covered in blood too. We had to take her to one of my covert people, who purged her memory, and replaced it with a trip to a neighbour's house that night."

Isabella heard something else in his' voice. "You don't know what happened?"

He shook his head, "no, well not the whole thing. The reports, however, gave us enough information to know that it was bad. The words, Demonic Cult, crept into the conversation, and when I mentioned it to the church people we normally deal with, they would not say anything more than, "God help us". It was the first time they had ever been reluctant to elaborate, almost like they wanted to spare me knowing about it at all," and for the first time, Isabella saw that Craig actually was glad. "The abbot said, quote, 'In the middle ages, people knew about such things, and it changed them, for the worse. They are not called the 'Dark Ages' for nothing. The simple knowledge of the creatures turned people crazy, or so it was said." He shuddered. "He also said that some things should never be brought into the light. Not even to put a child's mind at ease then escorted us out."

Isabella kept tapping, but she was seriously worried. "But can she deal with it? The first time Charlene saw whatever it was, she went into a catatonic state. Who's to say that she will not just do that again? Eh?" Isabella was feisty, thought Craig, and genuinely concerned about Charlene, even though she had only known her a few brief minutes.

"My dear Isabella, Charlene, as a child, would have had fallen back on the natural defence to protect her mind, as a matter of course. Charlene, as an adult, has developed a scientific mind of power, logic, and discipline. If she cannot withstand the knowledge that she will need to know, then I suspect no one earth can," he was emphatic, honest and thoroughly confident.

"No, the worry I have is the knowledge we are missing. We do not know much about her mother since her records were destroyed, how the demons are related; and whether what is going on now has to do with her past or her future." He sighed. "There is so little we actually know."

At A.G.E., the security door to Charlene's laboratory opened, without alarm, and a smartly suited man entered, accessing Charlene's terminal and inserting a small device into one of the USB ports.

The login screen appeared, and commands appeared on the screen without a hand touching the keyboard. The login screen disappeared, but instead of the expected desktop icons a little picture of Charlene was displayed; her voice came from the screen. The intruder drew back a little surprised.

"Well, we have a visitor, that's nice. However, this system and its data belong to the A.G.E. corporation, and they own the data you're trying to access. All data has now been encrypted, please enter the encryption cypher to continue," her face smiling sweetly, and disappeared.

The figure typed a few characters into the keyboard, the face reappearing.

"Thank you, Project Director. Would you like my latest report or the raw data uploaded to the site server?" The figure typed again. "Uploading data to specified server".

After a few minutes, the data transfer was complete and, with a few more taps, the terminal shutdown. With a smooth swipe of a hand, the device was removed, and the figure left, back the way he'd come, satisfied.

Chapter 4

A LITTLE INVESTIGATION ...

"Ok. We're here," Helena informed them, indicating that John should pull up on the left, while the group looked around the street. Sure enough, just up ahead on the left, there was a small communications tower, comprised of various dishes and wires. They contacted Isabella, on one of the company's burn phones.

"The tower there is transmitting the feed, while the others they are using are just dummies, relays or spoofs," she informed them.

Simon rummaged through the box of equipment they'd bought, and started to bolt, screw, and micro-weld together several seemingly random bit and pieces; turning them from spare parts, into a full-blown working device, in a matter of minutes. After he snapped the last item on and gave it a quick tweak, he flicked the switch, and the machine beeped into life; producing in genuine a smile of satisfaction from Simon.

"I'm getting the signal frequencies on the detector now, Isabella," he said, partially talking down his phone and mostly into mid-air; as he'd tied the device, he'd just constructed, into his phone's transmitter/receiver assembly. He was trying to point the device at the tower, at the same time as talking to the mouthpiece of the phone.

Helena pointed to the Bluetooth earpiece, and he switched his conversation to the Bluetooth microphone instead. "There appears to be another signal, being emitted locally, relayed from the same tower."

"We'd best take a look around; see if there are any clues as to what is happening around here," Jack offered. Before anyone else could say anything, he was up and out of the van. As he dropped out, he caught sight of a twitch in a curtain from a ground floor window of one of the terrace houses, in the square opposite the tower.

"Aha," he muttered to himself, then said out loud, "we have a neighbourhood watcher." He flicked his head in the direction of the twitching curtain, the others following his gaze, but seeing only the houses.

"I love cities! They have so many eyes, especially for those that want to acquire information. You go deal with the comms, and I'll go and have a little talk with our little spy." The others started to get out, wearing 'Mixer Enterprises' standard workmen overalls, as he trotted across the road to the indicated house.

Jack politely rapped on the door, which flew open, to reveal a mass of white hair, hawk eyes, vitriolic tongue, in the form of an old woman, dressed in a flower printed dress and slippers, carrying a fish slice like a rapier.

"Oh! Here we are, yet more workmen. How many of you does it take to fix the television aerials, and phone lines, around here?" her waspish voice was shrill and penetrating.

"Well, after the last lot reported the problem, we were dispatched immediately," Jack tried to get his prepared explanation in.

"Immediately, my backside," the woman interrupted sharply, "it's been two days since they were last there, fixing the thing. And after that, it got even worse!" Jacks face was a little perplexed. The current signal they were investigating, had been there since last night; yet the woman implied there had been problems before then, which did not add up.

"Hmm, my notes seem to be incomplete, on this incident, then. When exactly did your problems with the signals start?" He tried to sound concerned rather than confused.

"Blooming typical! Not nearly as smart, or efficient, as the ads would have us believe." She scythed into him, then poking her slice at his mid-rift, she continued. "In my day, they'd have sacked the lot of you, even before you got back to your office," she was obviously building to a full-blown monumental tirade.

With a flourish, Jack produced a pen in his left hand to make notes with. It was a simple trick, but it worked; the woman blinked, stopping mid-scold.

"Perhaps, if you gave me all the details, I can get the work completed faster," he said quickly, in a placating tone of voice. Reluctantly, the woman calmed down a degree or two.

"Well, it's been a bit dodgy for years, but got much worse a week or two back, well maybe three or four, just when that spate of murders happened on the soaps; made me miss who done it," her hackles rose again, and she looked about to start off again; Jack needed to head that off.

"So, was there anything happening about then; vandals, strangers, or anything like that?" He readied his pen; like a journalist, awaiting a Pulitzer prize story. The woman seemed flattered by the attentiveness and started talking as though she was delivering life-saving information.

"There were lots of those darn youngsters banging and breaking things late at night and a big crash over by the old station over there. The rapscallions around here keep taking things, and the police don't do anything about it. They even tried to take the wheels off Mrs. Green's mobility scooter, but I chased them off down the road." She did not seem that spritely, but then she was feisty enough, "then there was the incident," she went on and on.

While Jack carried on his interview, Charlene looked about the street, noticing a few broken items firstly, then a pattern in the locale; all having once contained metal. The metal had been snapped, prised or retched from their housings, and carried off. There were few drag marks, indicating that, whoever carried them was very strong; superhumanly strong.

Finally, Jack came back to Charlene and grabbed her elbow. "Let's get back to the others. There is more going on here than just those signals."

They walked back to the van, and, when they arrived, John and Simon were waiting for them; Jack brought them up to date with the woman's stories.

"We'd best try and triangulate the source of that second signal," Charlene and Jack said simultaneously; they looked each other and smiled. Simon nodded, and grabbed his detector, and made some adjustments to the controls.

"Ok; I can register direction, strength, and form now. We should be able to track, it down to about a hundred meters or so, depending on the strength." Simon's skill with devices was being tested, but he was proving his reputation. The rest of the team all fervently hope that he would continue to do so.

"Excellent work." Charlene was rewarded with a small smile of gratitude back. For some reason, she always seemed to get on better with professional people, especially scientists.

John started off. "We'll do a standard sweep pattern. That should give us at least a general idea of the direction, or distance if it's not local."

Jack shook his head, "I doubt it will be far. Something the old woman said about the big crash near the station," They moved around the streets, asking some more questions of a few residents, and the odd passer-by; during which time they took signal readings.

It was soon reasonably apparent that Jack was right. After only a few minutes they had a set of intersecting lines, almost directly at the local underground area.

"Ok, so we go underground," said John, with just a tad of annoyance in his voice. He disliked people who said I told you so; even if Jack had not actually said it.

Four of them collected hard hats from the van and headed for the local underground, while Helena stayed to guard the van, lest the erstwhile scrap collectors decided it was fair game.

Strangely, there were no passengers to be seen as the four went down the steps, causing them to become uneasy. Generally, during the day, the underground was crowded, and this was usually a fairly busy station. Of course, there were masses of improvement works in London currently, that were part of the expansion of the underground, but the work was not in this area, at least to their knowledge.

They leapt over the ticket barriers, still not seeing any people, not even guards that should have been there. The team looked at the boards, and the reason soon became apparent; the station seemed to have been shut down for some reason.

"Train stuck in the tube?", they all looked at each other in confusion.

"Power failure?" John asked.

Charlene looked up at the lights "if it is, then it's just the tracks. It's possible, I suppose," but her tone suggested she was sceptical of it being the cause.

Simon looked at the other boards, "No. Or if it is, then it's local only; then again, why no people? There is something else going on; it's like the people have been diverted from here, and what about that other signal?" They looked at Simon.

"The waveform is strange, the wavelength low and the carrier signal is short range; it could not possibly control the station equipment." He kind of shrugged indicating that he would need better equipment, more time, or both, to give a better answer.

"Well let's get down there then," said Charlene striding off.

They weaved down the usual multitude of public access tunnels until they finally reached tunnel nearest the source of the signal. As they entered the platform area, there was a tromp of feet, and a portly station guard came shambling towards them, a bit out of breath.

"No people allowed on the platform! There is a problem on the line. The police should have stopped you from coming down. I'm sorry, but you will have to leave." His voice was stern and rabbiting fast; as though expecting resistance.

John reached into his overalls and flashed his M.I.X. ID. The old guard squinted a little, and nodded; out of habit, John thought, rather than actually having seen the ID. For one thing, the old fellow had not put his, rather thick-lensed, spectacles on.

"We're here to deal with the situation," he informed the guard, projecting a calm air of authority. The guard seemed ill at ease, and willing to relinquish the handling of the situation.

"Wow; that was quick! I only just called the problem in and cleared the station of the early commuters. You some sort of fancy response team?" He seemed sceptical, looking at Charlene as though she seemed out of place. The look she returned was, at best, challenging, at worst frosty. He took a step back feeling threatened.

"Yes, we are a response team. We were actually near anyway," John wearing his authority with such a natural air that the rest of his team just let him deal with the guard.

"Well, I guess we know where to go next, don't we?" asked Jack, the others just nodding and all starting off towards the tunnel; however, Charlene suddenly halted and turned back towards the guard.

"Do you have any Torches down here?". He nodded, still a little dumbfounded by events. "Please can you go get one for each of us, if you have enough?" she smiled sweetly at him. "Sorry, what was your name?" she asked him.

"Bob, Ma'am," he replied carrying on into his office, and rummaging through a large steel locker, digging out some large, high powered inspection torches, used for checking the tunnels periodically. He returned slightly out of breath giving them each one.

Then Charlene had another thought. "Do you have a fire axe? In case we have to clear debris from the track." The man looked at her in an exasperated way, she could have asked before he came all the way back.

"Well, we would have Ma'am, but a few days ago the axe head was stolen. Vandals steal anything metal these days for resale." He paused, but he brightened a second, "I've still got the handle, however, and its stout enough to help." He toddled off to the office again and again dug around in the locker. He was back in a minute, with an elegant, oaken, axe handle. Charlene indicated that he should give it to Jack.

Jack looked at it and, with a showman's flare, spun it around in a circle with his fingers. "Hmmm, nice feel. I could use this in my act; it has class," he murmured.

The four investigators, torches in hand, moved into the track well, avoiding the power rail even with the power off, just in case, and, walking carefully into the dark, trying to find the source of the increasing strong signals. They moved slowly and cautiously; watching their step and scanning the walls of the tunnel for clues and the more unsavoury inhabitants of the underground. The scanning yielded little information until, about three hundred yards in, John spotted an unexpected, wide, circular hole in the left-hand side of the tunnel wall.

The hole was about twenty feet in diameter, angling down at about forty-five degrees. The intersecting tunnel's walls were perfectly smooth, as though sliced through by a beam, but there was no evidence of any such device in the main tunnel, so the source must have either been mobile or a natural phenomenon; both seemingly implausible. There was no matching hole on the other side of the tunnel however so it could not have been from outside; very strange.

Simon moved to the edge of the opening and ran his hand around the corner of it.

"Smooth as a baby's bottom. Sliced, but not by any mechanical tool; and no melting pattern either, so not a laser." He looked at the others, in the scattered light. "If I were to hazard a guess, I'd say that this was caused by powerful molecular level shearing forces."

John looked at him and nodded, although his face said that he did not understand what Simon was talking about. Charlene understood, partially; the forces he was talking about were unlikely to have been generated from anything that existed on the world they knew. Indeed, they did not yet; or at least they should not.

"Ok," Jack said out loud, clapping his hands, "who goes down first?" smiling, at the ridiculousness of their situation now. They were about to try and descend a perfectly smooth, forty-five-degree incline; even the world's greatest acrobat would find this distinctly challenging.

John, ever the pragmatist, suggested a rope. Simon had cabling that would help secure it, so they combined their efforts and slowly inched their way down the steep shaft, for several dozen yards, to reach the bottom. It ended in a sewer, a foot or two deep in contaminated water; the air thick with methane, and other more odorous gases.

Charlene had been feeling strange the past few days, choosing now to release that knotted sensation, in a spectacular act of recklessness; tumbling to the edge of the tunnel, leaping and sliding down the entire length of the slope, arms out, squealing with an exhilaration she'd never felt before as she did so. She landed perfectly on a small dry spot at the bottom of the channel, laughing. The release was cathartic; a sensation frightening for someone used to being in complete control. She suddenly looked both embarrassed and ashamed of her action; the 'Dark Queen' would never have approved. At that thought, she lifted her head in defiance. Who cared what she'd have thought? Certainly not Charlene; not anymore. It was time to start doing things for herself and not just for others.

John and Simon looked at each other, then at her and finally at each other again. There was something wrong with her, for sure. The real question was, was it just her, or was it something which had happened to her in the past couple of days.

Jack finally arrived using the rope to get down. Now all down and settled, they surveyed their new surroundings. The tunnel walls in this area were damaged too, but with less precision; large swathes of concrete, stone, and earth were gouged from of the centre line of the irregular walls. Rubble was underfoot, making progress slow and uncertain. The water was barely moving, though not quite stagnant, containing various, nasty, floating objects; the men wrinkling up their noses.

"Pheewww," complained Simon, looking at Charlene, for a similar reaction, but saw the other scientist seemed oblivious to the stench. She glanced at him and saw the revolted look on his face.

"What?" He wrinkled his nose, waiting for the response, "oh, the smell? Well once you've smelled some chemicals, this is not so bad," the shrug she gave dismissed it as irrelevant. Full of surprises this one, thought Simon. Just because she was blonde, some people would think she was a flimsy bimbo, well until she corrected them that is. He knew her reputation however and, for her years, she was the most respected scientist in her field.

Everyone continued looking around and moving away from the main tunnel. After a few minutes of advancing, a distinctly female scream of terror came echoing from the tunnel ahead, causing them to increase their pace to a careful run. After about half a minute, they entered a large, dimly lit, sewage collection tank. There, two people faced a creature, as strange as any of them had seen; including the ones from the conference.

About twenty feet in front of them, stood a nine-foot-tall, twisted giant of a creature, humanoid in shape, with an extremely muscular upper torso, topped by a head resembling that of a great ape; gorilla-like with huge double tusks protruding from its extended lower jaw. To their left, was an uninjured woman, wearing a long grey overcoat, backing up towards one of several ladders surrounding the area leading to a higher gallery. On the floor, just above the water-line, lay an unconscious man in bad shape with a large gash in his head, his hand still clutching a smashed video camera. It was fairly evident that this was a news team investigating the same events that they were.

While the others gawked, Jack had an idea and slipping a camera from his pocket, aiming it at the creature, he took a picture of the towering threat with a sudden flash of light, attracting the creature's attention. The shaggy creature bellowed as it started at the unexpected arrival of daylight, in its lovely dark home.

Charlene looked at the creature and decided that Jack had hit on the correct course of action, but that something more substantial was needed, if the brute was to be neutralised, instinct replacing fear with a calm assuredness of action.

From a collection of useful chemicals, she'd assemble in her pack, she quickly unwrapped a small lump of Phosphorous, about the size of a small flare, from its oily cloth, and threw it behind the creature. The idea was simple enough, the phosphorous would ignite in the air and blind the beast. However, Charlene, being ignorant of real-world mechanics, had not considered that flares actually only contained a fraction of the Phosphorous that she'd just thrown. The effect, in the methane-rich atmosphere, was less distraction, and more, to put it mildly, Catastrophic Overkill.

As the last of the oil evaporated from the small lump of phosphorous, it reacted with the oxygen and methane in the air and ignited, in a deep, thunderous, detonation; a brilliant flash of white light, and a wave of sound engulfing everyone in the local area.

Fortunately, the phosphorous had reached the water-line, the water absorbing the heat, but everyone was hit by the concussive force of the explosion, and a wave of warm water, slush and worse, as the wave propagated outwards flooring all in the room, which was blasted clean; much to the annoyance of the resident rats.

Simon and John shook their heads, trying to get the ringing out of their ears, while Jack and Charlene attempted to rub the glare from their eyes. Fortuitously, it had also had the desired effect on the floored creature, the blast stunning it, causing it to bellow, claw at its eyes and stagger to its feet.

"What, the blazes, was that?!" exclaimed the reporter, also looking around, to clear the flash's blue after image.

As the rest of them tried to gather their wits, the creature homed in on that exclamation. It was apparently still dazed but recovering quicker than the rest of those around it, and as the brute advanced on her, the reporter retreated, backing up towards the ladder again.

Simon skirted past the creature, and guided her hand to the rail, indicating she needed to be quiet, the pair moving quickly and quietly up the ladder; careful not to scrape the rusted iron rungs as they secured their footing on the way up. He settled the woman in a dark nook, there and checked down the ladder that they were not being followed, but they were safe as the creature was still flailing a little, starting to turn towards the centre of the room.

Then, from behind, Jack shouted, to get the creature's attention again, "Oi, ugly. This way!" the beast immediately turning, homing in on Jack's voice. It snarled advancing now able to see a target and quickly becoming steady and fully mobile again.

From the upper gallery, Simon surveyed the scene, everyone manoeuvring to avoid the creature's clawed hands and tusks while trying to rescue the cameraman.

From further in the complex, a sound like a slow train rumbled towards them reported through the air, and, with a startled glance, Simon regretted separating from the others. He quickly doubled back, while staying out of the way of the creature.

Charlene, after her initial blunder, tried to pull herself up one of the ladders, her initial attempt, while still semi-stunned, ended with her slipping on grease on the bottom rung and landing in six inches of mucky water up to her waist.

"Eeewwww," she said, slapping the water around her in frustration, getting her even wetter. Her face grew disgusted, but she pulled herself up, obviously still dazed, but determined to get moving.

John had finally cleared his head and pulled his stun gun from his overalls. "This should drop it," he thought firing, the barbs striking it directly at the base of its skull, tazing it for fifty thousand volts. There turned out to be just one problem, the thing turned towards him apparently un-phased by the jolt. John took a deep breath; obviously, fifty thousand volts was not enough. "Oh boy," John muttered. "A little help here!" he bellowed, as the hulking creature took a swipe at the new threat, just missing.

Jack came to the rescue, closing quickly, swinging his axe handle, and cracking the brute on the base of the skull. Still a bit confused, the hulking creature took the full brunt of the stroke; but was only staggered. Undeterred, Jack swung again with all his strength, and, this time, there was a distinct crunch. The creature's eyes rolled up into its skull, and its jaw dropped, as the goliath collapsed to the ground. Jack inched closer, giving it a final thwack, ensuring its unconsciousness while scrutinising the creature, whose bruises were rapidly disappearing; their opponent was obviously healing.

The others now rushed in to aid the cameraman, Charlene, kneeling beside him and quickly bandaging the worst of the gashes on his chest, and arms. Strangely, they did not seem to match the tusks, or claws, of the creature; something else had inflicted these wounds. She administered some adrenaline to try and get the man on his feet quickly.

"Who are you people, and what are you doing down here?" demanded the reporter coming down from the gallery.

John stepped forward, briefly flashing his M.I.X. Badge. "We are investigating this incident, Ma'am; and you are interfering in a British Transport Police operation."

"Bullshit," said the reporter, full of defiance. "You are not Transport Police any more than that is a wild animal", she pointed at the creature which started to stir.

Charlene, still dealing with the injured man piped up. "Who said it was a wild animal?" she asked in a curious tone, her previous indignations forgotten.

"The local papers, the police, and the tabloid journalists, at least, they did the day after the story broke, a few weeks back; they were all over it. Then it changed. It was pretty obvious they were told to back off and that the story was being buried." The reporter checked over the cameraman, who was slowly getting to his feet supported by Simon.

"Well whoever we are, we are here to help; unless you want to try and get answers out of the creature yourself," said John, in his most authoritarian tone. The reporter took one look at the creature, shaking her head and headed out the way the team had come in.

Soon, she and her cameraman, still dazed but now up and mobile, just, and supported by the reporter, had staggered out of sight.

"Nnnnnaaa", a guttural and slurred voice started, "'I uuu hit Glark?"

Charlene and the team turned, to see, the shaggy beast rolling onto its front, in the water, the colossal creature slowly raising to its' knees, then feet. It looked even larger close-up, but Charlene was hiding her shock at it being able, and intelligent enough, to talk.

"You were attacking the woman and man, when we arrived," Charlene said quickly, although, when she ran it through her head, she'd not actually seen that, "we heard her scream."

"I no attck. NO Attck!" He raised his fist, and slammed the ground; its arms were long enough to do that. Jack raised his stick again, and the creature subsided, backing up; a little. "No; I hear yell; see girl with 'urt man. I come to aid." The creature looked warily at Jack. "She yell' at me. You came, with ligh' and sound," shifting his gaze to Charlene, who looked a little guilty at that accusation.

"So you were here to help too?" said Jack understanding and lowering the makeshift club, to a less threatening position. The brute nodded emphatically.

"Es!" A great hairy arm raised a hand, and he pointed to himself, "Ghool, 'eaceful. No 'urt Sunlight 'eokle," his voice was loaded with a grievance that the sentiment was not reciprocated.

"There are more of you down here?" Charlene was surprised that anyone would want to live in this filth. Although, in truth, it did not bother her, so why should it bother people actually adapted to it. Her head was kind of fuzzy, perhaps from the blast, or probably from the past day or so. For whatever reason, she seemed to understand the creature better now.

"Lots! Live off Sunlight 'eokle's gunk's. If need, we take. An' we go out, Sunlight 'eokle scream and yell at us; drive us home if u see us."

"I wonder why?" muttered John sarcastically. Glark ignored him.

"So go at night, so you no out. You out more an' more." There was a sad, depressed, feel to this creature; as though it knew its peoples' (eokle's) days were numbered, despite its seemingly low intelligence.

"Our leader, Sciborn, say not hurt Sunlight 'eokle, else they come and hurt us too. So, Ghool leaves alone, not need a flood of angry 'eokle and other 'oes."

"What about you taking the metal from the streets above? Surely you know that the daylight people would be upset, and come for you," said Jack.

"Not us do that. Us have all us needs." The was a look in the creature's eye, a hurt apparent even to the strangers around him. "No. Taken ones take 'etal, commanded, by talking hats." The brute was apparently trying to explain something, it did not have the language for, or that was beyond its' intelligence.

"Perhaps your leader could explain the problem," suggested Jack, with a hopeful look at the others.

The creature brightened, suddenly. "Yes. Yes! Lord Sciborn s'art! He' aid you, save us," and with that he loped off at an astounding pace, pausing for the team to catch him up. With a shrug, Jack started off followed by the others.

Into the gloomy torchlight, they followed the creature down a series of sewer tunnels; finally ending up in an area about twice the size the one they had battled him in.

There stood a contingent of about twelve, much larger, Ghools, apparently waiting for something or someone. As Glark approached, they lowered their spears, pointing them at the four rather small humans, now before them. Glark lowered his head and spread his left arm out, to indicate the newcomers.

"These Sunlight 'eokle need talk with Lord or Ghool, to aid us." He said in a deferential manner, to the largest of the others.

"Greetings Glark. The Lord knows and comes as we speak. Return to your patrol now, Glark," the largest Ghool spoke excellent English, it was noted by the team.

The other Ghools stood still, and the team waited for a short time; getting a bit nervous, when a deep thudding was heard, approaching the area, from a side tunnel. After a few seconds of the sound getting progressively louder, in strode a huge Ghool, easily twice the size of the others, but unlike the others clothed in finery and calf length leather boots.

"Ahhhh. Here we have our little intruders. Eh?" His voice filled the chamber, and the team all knew that this Ghool ruled by might, though his eyes spoke of a keen intellect too, giving them hope that they might actually learn something about their problem.

"Yes, great Lord," said the largest of the others, "Glark said they had come to speak with you, to help us," his tone filled with deep scepticism.

"And when have the Sunlighters ever helped us? Did they help us build our realm?" the Lord swept a huge arm out, indicating the surrounding underground sewers, "no. Did they help us when we were attacked?" He looked down on the four, stunted creatures before him, "No, they did not."

"But we did help out the Eldarin in trouble, the other night," interrupted Charlene, "and, The one that saved us thought that we might help here too." She subsided, but held her ground, when the great Ghool fixed his eyes on her, "Great Lord Sciborn," she finished.

"Ah! Glark's accent is as thick as ever. I am Lord SkyBorn, greatest of the Ghools and I rule here not the Humans." bellowed the giant Ghool lord.

John stepped forward. "Perhaps, we could help, where others could not," his tone was one filled with possibilities rather than straight fact.

Charlene stood next to him and added, "We were sent to investigate the problems here. At least let us try," she appealed to its' intellect, rather than its Status, and it was not lost on the Ghool used to ruling people. His eyes narrowed, at someone attempting to manipulate him in that way, then they softened, at the appeal in her eyes. The two of them stood for a few seconds, eyes locked together, then he relaxed, obviously coming to a decision, as though something he'd been looking for had been just found.

"Ha-ha-ha-ha-ha-ha!" I like you little Sunlighter," his laughter genuine and loud. "You help us, where my best warriors have failed? Ha-ha-ha-ha-ha-ha," he slapped his thigh, then stopped, mid-laugh, and regarded the quartet steadily again. "Still, sometimes, a mouse may enter places where a lion cannot; and you are tiny mice indeed. Also, my warriors, mighty though they are, cannot withstand the power of the enemy we fight, with their metal helmets," his intelligence showing.

"Also, other strange things have been happening recently," he opened his large jacket to reveal a dagger, with a glowing golden yellow pommel stone. "This is a relic, from before the gates to the other realms were sealed shut, a mystic dagger whose power is signified by the magic light of the pommel stone." There was something in his voice that indicated it had greater powers. "When the gates were closed, it stopped working and should never have become active again. However, some days back, it came back to life. Its' full power has not come, but the simple fact that even this has occurred is cause for great concern. This is disturbing, even alarming," the leader's strange face, with its huge jaw, showed his inner disquiet.

"Someone has either re-opened a gate to the other realms, or they are trying to." There was genuine fear in the old, powerful, face, "Some things, from the other realms, are too terrible to imagine. They must not be allowed to come through the gateways here." He nodded to himself. "Very well, we will aid you," A great gong started sounding. "What?" He turned to his retinue. "Go. See what is happening." Two of the guards immediately ran up a side tunnel, to investigate.

"Probably another attack; they have been growing more frequent of late, as although our enemy is growing impatient, or desperate."

Skyborn looked at them thoughtfully. "Or even in response to your arrival here. Perhaps, they fear the help you bring", although Charlene doubted that; after all, her first attempts at helping had been more destructive than helpful.

A couple of minutes later, one of the dispatched guards arrived back breathless and whispered something into his Lord's ear. A pained look passed across the giant lord's face, and he looked at the team, "Come! We will have an end of this," and he strode out the room at full speed, making it difficult for the team to keep up. The group marched through several tunnels until they reached a wall, which had quite obviously been recently breached, blood pooling on the floor, from a dead Ghool. There lay Glark, stone dead, with a great steel axe embedded in his skull, another larger Ghool next to him, with a broken neck and a strange steel cap on its head.

Lord Skyborn roared, a bellowing cascade of pain, shaking the tunnel roof and depositing dust on every surface, kneeled and cradled the Ghool's head in a strangely tender way, then after a few seconds lay the body down gently, in peaceful repose.

"Glark! You will be avenged! No more of my people will fall before this menace."

He turned to look at the shaken humans. "You will stop this! You will find the Taken and return them, or see to it that they are not used against us again. You will find who is responsible, and you will stop them!" It was less an order, and more a statement of fact.

Charlene felt a particular responsibility towards Glark, even though she'd only known it, him, a few minutes, and she stepped forward and looked the Ghool Lord straight in the eye.

"This we will do," and she meant it. The look returned by Skyborn was a strange one, full of a meaning that Charlene could not fathom. There was a click inside her head; not a sound so much as a feeling of pure rightness. Whatever it took, Charlene was now fixed on a course; wherever it led her.

"So be it!".

The Ghools guided the team down a deeper series of tunnels below the sewers.

"Old tunnels, these are," said one of the guiding Ghools. "Older than our current home." He pointed at crystal formations, that seemed to glisten in the chambers they traversed. "These are ancient magical crystals, that guide light to the lower halls."

The team saw that the crystals now worked, speaking of a power source out there somewhere. The further they went, the more nervous the Ghools seemed until their guides indicated that they were turning back.

"No further can we go, lest we fall under the influence of the enemy," warned the lead Ghool.

"We'll take it from here," said John, unlimbering his gun, releasing the Ghools from their duty.

Seeing a bright pale blue light in the distance, casting large moving shadows down the tunnel walls, Charlene and the others switched off their torches. Clangs and loud thuds echoed down the tunnel ahead.

The humans slowed and crept as stealthily as possible down the clean, dry tunnel, almost sweet and fresh in marked contrast to the mustiness of the Ghool's homeland.

As they approached the opening ahead, they saw the source of the light and racket, simply the most extraordinary sight any of them had ever seen.

A vast cavern sprawled out before them, glowing with light from a roughly circular metallic vehicle, some thirty feet in diameter and twenty deep, propped on a pile of rubble, composed mainly of rock, supported by steel plates obviously once part of a train. It was an almost classical saucer shape, with a small ramp descending from the lower part of the disc, allowing the internal white light to radiate into the blue algae covered, cavern.

From the open side of the saucer, came several large, flexible, metal clad, ribbed, cables attached to an equal number of, peculiarly shaped, wall mounted, devices, at equidistant positions around the circumference of the cavern. All around the area shambled Ghools, with metal skullcaps attached, by a series of wires, directly into the base of their skulls.

Simon fished out his detector and pointed it at the saucer. Sure enough, the signal was strong, but, as he redirected it at the walls, the signal strength spiked.

"Looks like the ship generates the signal and the wall antennae re-transmit it," Simon informed the others.

"This is not going to be easy. As soon as we are seen, you can guarantee that those brutes will be directed to defend the ship," John whispered to the others. "At least, that's how I'd do it," he continued, unlimbering his stun gun, and un-latching his firearm's holster. He seemed in two minds on which he'd need in this situation.

"So, how about we try this?" came Charlene's voice, steady despite her obvious fear at the overmatch in numbers and size. "Simon, can you modify your scanner to become a Jammer; interrupt the signal, for a short period? That would allow the rest of us to get into the ship, and shut it down," she suggested. The others looked at her appreciatively. Despite her age and inexperience, it seemed like it was a sound plan;

Simon acknowledged he could, starting immediately and decisively.

John thought it over, and the hastily conceived plan seemed fine, "OK, let's try it. Simon, you try and create your jammer, and, when you're ready, we'll go in."

Jack looked around the cavern again, spotting a trio of huge rats sporting metal caps perched on various large rocks obviously from the ceiling.

"Lookouts," he said, pointing them out. "Just three; but covering the entire diameter of the saucer and therefore most of the cavern. Clever. Whoever is controlling them has a good strategic mind"

Charlene pulled a white container out of her pack, triggering nervous looks from the others. She sighed. "Acid; to burn through the power cables. If Simon's jammer fails, then, perhaps, melting through the power cables will achieve the same effect." The others' faces were not filled with an abundance of confidence.

"I'll be careful. Ok!" Charlene seemed hurt by the looks, but given her previous failure, they were not totally surprising. She even doubted herself a little at this point.

The others moved to covering positions, while Simon assembled a micro-transmitter, designed to interfere with the control signal sufficiently to neutralise the workers without killing them.

He signalled he was ready, activated the device, and the team rushed out of the shadows. He pointed his instrument at the nearest wall mounted device; the effect was immediate.

Ghools, and Rats alike, began to writhe around in agony, the rats squealing and rolling onto their backs, clearly trying to scrape the devices off, while the Ghools were bellowing in an incomprehensible series of growls and, either trying to rip the headpieces off, or just standing there spasming, and drooling, uncontrollably.

Seeing the chaos spreading amongst the enemy, John and Jack raced into the ship, dodging spasming Ghools and rats as they went.

Charlene's eyes located the nearest main power cable, and she too dived forward, straddling it and carefully opened the white PTFE container, pouring the contents onto it. To her amazement, the chemical, the most powerful corrosive she had, simply dribbled off the metal casing instead of ripping through its molecular structure like paper. Apparently, the housing was either protected by some sort of energy shielding or coated with an anti-corrosive; just her luck today.

There was nothing else to do but help the others in the ship, so she bolted after them locating them just up the ship's entry ramp, seeking a way past three Ghools; one struggling with its skullcap, while two others just stood there convulsing. The two men hesitated a second longer, then tried to assist the Ghool with the skullcap, Jack prising the horrendous thing off the Ghools' head, while John started cutting through the tough metal wires.

Charlene slipped past them and scanned the two rooms opening out from the main area. To the left, masses of heavy machinery, that could only be the ship's engine. To the right, was what must have been the control room, containing several things that caught Charlene's attention.

On a couch lay a Ghool, a larger version of the other's skullcap encasing its' head. The cap was linked to a metal hub in the ceiling, that glowed and pulsed, like the light of the saucer itself. To one side of the couch was a globe of silver metal, that shimmered with rainbow liquidity, undulating and glittering in a scintillating fractal scattering of metallic disco ball colours.

"We need Simon in here," she muttered to herself., raising a finger to her comms set. "Simon get in here; we need your electronics expertise," Charlene aimed her voice at the mic., as well as shouting it out loud.

"I cannot keep the signal up much longer," Simon warned simultaneously.

"Never mind. It got us inside, now come here. I've found the command console, I think, and I need you to shut it down," her voice getting a bit tense.

The Ghool on the ramp finally freed from its control cap, collapsed to the floor bleeding and exhausted from its struggle. Charlene spared the creature a brief glance, seeing the damage the device had done already being repaired by the brute's body. It must have an incredible regenerative system; she must get a blood sample, if possible.

Her eyes were searching for Simon, when he bolted past her, heading for the couch in the control room. Wow, he could move when he wanted to. As he stepped in and started to remove the helmet from the fixture, the silver sphere next to it rose rapidly into the air. Uh oh, thought Charlene, just as a wave of energy was discharged by it, arcing to each exposed team member in the area. Simon shielded by the couch was untouched, but John and Jack were hit full on; each being flung directly against the hull of the saucer, and while Charlene was catapulted back, she shot out into the central hub of the ship again, landing on the metal plates, at speed. Ouch. That hurt.

Jack shook his head, glancing down at his arm, the energy discharge continuing to lick around his arm like a white flame, but not giving off heat and quickly subsiding, sinking into him, rather than discharging off to the wall. The sensation was not, entirely, unpleasant. His entire body started to feel strange, like, like; he was not sure what it was like, but then, he'd never been exposed to energy like that before.

Undeterred by the attack, John drew his gun and fired off a shot, not at the Sphere, but at the controller chair; just over Simon's busily working fingers. The bullet struck home at a critical junction, and the power fed back into the poor creature on the couch. It convulsed, its eyes bulging and muscles straining for a few seconds until it finally collapsed in an unconscious heap. The power then discharged, rippling up through the skullcap and frying the controlling circuits, forever ending the possibility that they would be used again.

Simon looked in reproach at John, but John just shrugged and carried on firing aiming next at the Sphere. The bullet was just absorbed by the sphere, doing no apparent damage, however, as it hit, a nearby panel shorted out, and a low-pitched whine began, slowly increasing in volume.

"Not good," grated John. "Sounds like it's getting ready to power up its engines," he yelled, just as a bolt of lightning shot from the sphere, hitting the wall next to him.

Outside, a commotion began, growls and hoots of anger. Charlene peeked outside spotting a figure advancing on the saucer. Ghools were challenging it, trying to block its progress, while it ignored them, with a disdain that belied the size difference between them.

Jack glanced outside quickly, commenting, "that's the thing that attacked Simon and me, at the conference."

As he said that, a Ghool leapt from a rock ledge on top of the figure. Unexpectedly, it bounced off a barrier of some kind surrounding the being, which continued walking; oblivious, or contemptuous, of the creature's failure and its groans of pain.

"We have company," yelled Charlene. The Ghools seemed unable to stop the figure approaching, and the engines were now reaching a sustained high note; ready to engage.

Charlene made a snap decision; to try and shut the engines down, and rushed into the engine room, looking for an emergency-shutdown button or something similar. She'd seen computers and machines of various kinds in her science studies. However, this was entirely beyond her. Try as she might, she could make head nor tail of the design.

"Simon! Get in here. We need you to find the off switch of this damn thing."

"A moment; I'm trying to stop the computer, security guard, or whatever it is, from frying us all," he grated.

John fired again; missing the, now mobile, attacker. A second after that, the sphere was slammed to the ground by the supposedly unconscious Ghool from the couch.

"Hurt me? Hurt me! Ha! Me bash you, little ball," the enraged Ghool gibbered, and started to pound the liquid metal ball furiously, somehow finding something substantial inside to grip, freeing the team to act.

Looking out of the exit ramp, Jack saw the advancing figure nearing the ramp layered in Ghools still attempting to block its progress. In a strangely concerted attack, they piled on top of the figures shield, stopping it in its tracks through sheer numbers as the engines' noise continued to shriek,

Above the saucer, a large swirling darkness began to appear, the edges looking like a boiling mass of sparkling water.

Simon slipped past the fight between the Ghool and the sphere, a rather one-sided affair, as the Ghool seemed to be ignoring sphere's electrical attacks. He quickly reached the engine room, seeing Charlene rummaging around in her sample case on the floor. He ignored her, looking over the engine and the surrounding panels. It took him a few seconds to spot a set of symbols that he recognised from the scanner, and the other devices he'd seen in the alien saucer. The engine now started to thrum indicated it was at full power, the ship beginning to lift unsteadily, wobbling slightly, leaving behind the battling Ghools and their target outside. He saw that they were now lifting towards the dark mass that the ship was generating. Beyond that mass, the men saw, not the darkness of space, or rather not just the darkness of space, but also thousands of other similar vessels, including some much larger ones obviously part of a fleet. He desperately scanned the consoles and pulled out what he surmised was the field stabiliser and power flow regulators, expecting the safety systems to shut the engine down; the engine pitch dropped, and the portal started to collapse. However, neither he nor the others were prepared for what happened next.

A massive wave of brilliant white energy discharged from the engine rushing past him.

Simon caught a glancing blow that hurled him across the engine room against the ship's hull. He felt the discharge hit him, but also, a surge of adrenaline, leaving a pulsing throb in his head. The discharge lingered along his arm, as a warm, almost pleasant, sensation, like unfolding after sleeping for a long time. The cascade faded slowly, but the body that it had hit had already been radically, and irreversibly, changed. Strangely he barely felt the impact on the wall, and he landed on his feet.

Charlene caught the full brunt of the energy wave. She saw the discharge moving towards her, as though it was travelling at a thousandth of its speed, though she could not dodge it and seemed to be creeping in a dream-like sluggishness herself. She could see that the wave-front in advance of the blast formed a distinctly distorted but clean edge.

Initially, the wave struck her samples box; squeezing the Nanite samples from containers, like paste out of a tube, spreading it along the boundary of the blast. Then it touched her, as did the Nanites, coating and penetrating her skin, transferring the energy of the explosion along that dermal layer, creating a skin-tight Faraday cage around her. Miraculously, instead of plastering her against the wall, the blast wave flowed around her; deflected by the ultra-thin armoured skin that the Nanites had created about her.

While it protected her from the damaging effects of the ship's power discharge; it also allowed the Nanites to flow into her body through her skin, integrating into and merging with her body. There, they incorporated the alien fields and extrapolated that technology into their own structural matrix; strange patterns and programming flowing through them. Previously unprogrammed circuits were impressed by multiple layers of programming from Charlene's DNA, Alien technology and probability-fields from the engines discharge.

With the power to the engines cut, the Gravity field supporting the portal collapsed, and the ship fell back into normal space. Fortunately, the portal had only been momentarily active, and they found themselves, still on Earth, a scant few miles up above London, meaning they had air to breathe. That was the good news. The bad news was that the ship was now being affected by the most potent local force; Gravity! They were now falling to earth at high speed. Even worse with the power gone, there was no artificial gravity to keep them on the deck of the ship meaning Jack started to lift off the floor, and out of the open ship's ramp. A muscular arm shot out in reflex to save the magician.

"Gotcha," John called, as his quick reactions grabbed Jacks' leg by the ankle, even though Jack was still halfway out the door. Jack was genuinely terrified as he glimpsed the view down from the ship.

"Jump!" Shouted Jack,

"What?" said a slightly dazed Simon, trying to orientate himself in the conditions. Gripping the edge of a door frame and pulling himself closer to the exit.

"The River: coming up fast. Jump!" Jack shouted.

The team frantically clambered and crawled to the ramp and glanced down. Below them, the river Thames was coming up fast, as the ship dropped out of the sky. They all looked at each other, and as one, they launched themselves out of the door, a few instants before the ship slammed into the Thames, with a hull-jarring thud and the groan of buckling metal. Thankfully, the ship's impact threw up a wave of water that diminished their own impact. The fall itself was not painful, but each of them felt the landing despite the cushioning surge; except Charlene, still encased in her golden armour.

After a few seconds of recovery, they each swam to shore and Charlene, who was there already, turned to see the saucer disappear rapidly under the water. She was suspiciously dry, so quickly spread the dampness from her hair to her clothes, then pressed her earpiece.

"Helena, can you pick us up please?" she asked, with a slightly strained voice.

"Charlene? Where are you?" came a relieved Helena, "we lost your signals for a second or two there."

"We're," she looked around, reorienting herself for a second or two, "about 2 miles from where we were, next to the Thames. I'll explain later." Her voice calmed down a bit. "We have a much bigger problem to deal with than we first thought. Best get the boss in real' quick. I think he will want to know what we found. Oh, and bring some towels and fresh clothes."

CHAPTER 5

... OF BIGGER PROBLEMS

Helena hastily brought the van to the team, as they dried themselves off by the riverside. Once she'd found them, she listened to their report as they drove, at speed, to the Starling building, her face showing she wanted to disbelieve them. Halfway there, Isabella interrupted the debriefing and informed them that Craig wanted to see them, as soon as they arrived, causing Helena to speed up, going as fast as the limits, and busy London traffic, allowed.

Craig Starling was waiting just inside the building when they arrived, his eyes strangely alive, with both concern and urgent energy. Helena pointed to the injured, "we need to get them to the infirmary as soon as possible, Sir," her voice not concerned, just pointing out a fact to her boss.

He nodded, "yes, but let's debrief them there, and get them to where they can get started on this problem; as soon as they get back on their feet." He waved them forward, and they all moved into the building. However, instead of going to the main lift, Craig directed them to a larger side elevator, producing a key and inserting it into a lock on the control panel. As it activated, surprisingly they started to descend, and Craig added, "Welcome to the real M.I.X."

The lift carried on down, for a more few seconds, then stopped in front of a large circular steel door, with an electronic keypad. Craig input a long sequence of numbers placed his thumb on a plate next to the keypad and let the device scan his thumb. The team was a little surprised at all the security and Craig saw the looks.

"I like my privacy. The other M.I. departments may know about upstairs, but few people know about this place." They all frowned at the few, he smirked at them, "real secrets are few and far between in this business."

As the lock whirred and clicked, a large clanged reported that the door was opening, swinging into a well lite, if empty, section of, what appeared to be, Underground tunnel, several football fields long. The group looked to Craig for permission and he nodded his authorisation to enter.

"Yes, this is a part of the Underground, although it's uncharted and unused. It was designed for use by the government, should the houses of parliament be destroyed in WWII, but when I found the old plans, I had Isabella file them as derelict buildings. She's talented at that kind of thing," he smiled the smile of a proud mentor or father. Charlene caught the look and felt sad at the thought that she would never get the same look from her father ever again.

Craig spread his arm out, indicating the vast area, "this space can be whatever you need it to be," and was almost immediately bombarded by ideas;

"A Lab.," suggested Simon and Charlene simultaneously, looking at each other and nodding.

"Fair enough," said John, thinking for a moment then adding "we'll need a Gym and training area too."

Jack took a few seconds longer but then added "I'll just help with the living area for now. A materials workshop would help both that effort and fitting out the other areas."

"We'll put together a list," pondered Charlene, "but we'll need a workforce of some kind. The laboratory we are talking about is technical and, while I'm sure of Simon's knowledge and Jack's construction prowess, what we need is a research grade installation."

"Really? Do we need something on that scale?" Jack asked. The look she gave him was enough to wither a giant redwood.

"I know what I need to test the samples I've been gathering. This is pure genetic grade work, and you cannot analyse that with magic tricks, or robotics," Charlene looked at Simon. Reluctantly, he nodded at the others scratching his chin a little.

"I know a few people that might be able to provide us with a skilled discrete set of quiet mouths. He looked at Starling, "we'll need some serious capital."

"No problem. Get your friends on the line. I'll make sure that the incentive money is sufficient to keep their mouths shut; permanently." The others made no comment, and Starling knew they would not ask further, having other things on their mind.

As Simon went to make his call, the others also went upstairs to recuperate and get some food.

"Pizza for me, please," ordered Charlene, "I need a pizza," the others looking at her and wondering how she could say that, having had breakfast only a few hours ago. John was even more puzzled, as she only ever had healthy food when at the lab. Where had this sudden craving come from?

"They'll be here later with several lighter units," Simon informed the others when he returned to the rest, sat down on the couches, in the roof garden. "The heavy units will arrive as soon as they can haul it here, as one or two are slightly esoteric. The mass spectrometer is going to take a more significant effort; let alone setting it up."

Charlene shrugged, "the electron microscope is the most important anyway. As long as I can get my data from A.G.E. and download 'Chimera' from the web, we'll be in business."

Isabella's eyes shot up, "Chimera?"

"It's a standard global package for gene analysis and manipulation," Charlene dismissed it casually. "Its the only package that can do the sequencing at the speed we need. If you can access my files from A.G.E., then I can do a basic comparative analysis of the samples and get some idea of what we are dealing with."

She placed her backpack on the floor and retrieved her sample pack. She dropped a few small pieces of cloth into a line of test tubes, then added one of the samples from the conference to the line, sat down and waited.

"OK. Let's get down to business," said Craig. "What are we dealing with?".

"Jack, you tell him," said John, chomping on a particularly large and juicy burger. "I'll go to Helena and get this sorted," he said pointing to the burn marks on his muscular body.

As he left, Charlene caught Isabella looking after the bodyguard again, a slight look of concern on her face, which vanished as soon as she realised she was being watched by someone. However, when she realised it was Charlene, it changed into one of undisguised amusement, and she winked at her. Charlene smiled back and flicked her head at the bodyguard, tacit acknowledgement that he was not her concern. Isabella's smile grew even wider with the realisation that the bodyguard was fair game, her eyes narrowing as if planning something special. The poor soul, Charlene thought; he would not stand a chance, against such a predatory, and guileful, young lady.

Jack filled Craig in with the details of the team's meeting with the platform guard, the reporter, the Ghools and their mighty Lord, Skyborn. When the story moved on to the saucer, the strange globe and in particular the second encounter with the glowing-eyed menace, Simon took over, giving specific details of the ship, its technology and the dark portal it had opened. Finally, John, having been at the door the longest, gave a detailed description of the other ships they had seen in greater detail.

When the report was complete, Craig's face looked grim. He whispered into Isabella's ear, and she tapped a few last times then stopped.

"We need to find the source of the original signal as soon as possible," looking at the injured and exhausted group, "but first we need to get you fit enough to do so," he smiled, a suddenly wan smile. "Rest up, get what you can done, then we can sort out what we need to do about the signal." He nodded to Isabella, "she will adjust the news feeds, to make the press more positive, rather than blocking it. That should force our opponents to keep the signal going until we can get out there and deal with it, and them." He swayed a little. But then he merely strode off towards the lift and disappeared.

Simon looked at Jack, and he just shrugged, "the contractors should be here in a few hours. If we work until midnight, we might get the light work surfaces in here in, ready for simple installations tomorrow." He was talking more to Charlene than to the others.

"There are some blankets and things in the cupboards over there," pointed Isabelle. The others followed her arm and noticed Helena and John coming back into the room through a door, "there's a bathroom through there too," she added.

John looked a lot better. Helena whispered something as she passed Isabella, whose eyes went wide. Helena nodded and Isabella looked briefly towards John, then looked back. Then the two girls laughed, with contagious mirth, that made all the others, except John, smile.

Charlene felt a certain pity for him. It was apparent that this pair were pack hunters, and their target exhibited a certain discomfort in the role of Prey. For some reason, she was not upset at these newcomers taking an interest in her bodyguard. She thought that, perhaps, if she was not dedicated to her cause, she might be; but, somehow, she knew that he was not the one for her. He did not feel right. Yes, he was a fine figure of a man, indeed as fine as they came; fit, skilled and even intelligent for his type, but there was a tang, a feel, to him, that she found unsettling.

She was tired, if fact, although she did not mention it to others, she was more tired than she'd ever felt before; her evening routine so ingrained did not fell worth the effort, or even possible. Her skin felt strange, her eyes were gritty, her digestion was working overtime; either that or she'd accidentally swallowed a tiger, the way it was growling. She desperately needed sleep.

"I think I need to lie down," she whispered to Helena. The older woman looked at her, the question in her eyes obvious. She noticed Charlene did not look well at all. "Right now, though," the words coming slowly, "… I need sleep." Her eyes drooping and Helena caught her shoulder as it sloped off to the left.

"Wooow! Easy there, I got you." Helena waved her hand at Isabella, and the two of them supported the flagging girl, without the others seeing. They lay her on an unmade bed and saw that, even in the short time they took, she'd actually already dropped off into a deep sleep. Wow, they'd never seen anyone go to sleep that fast, even under sedatives.

"Poor thing. In three days, she has gone from supremely confident research scientist to homeless government agent," said Isabella, feeling a deep empathy with this new girl, having gone through a similar transition only a few months previously.

"You know she needs to be ready for bigger things than just the social change, Isabella," chided Helena.

"That does not mean I cannot feel sympathy for her," she said looking down at the girl, who was in such a deep sleep that their conversation did not penetrate it at all.

"No, it does not. But just remember your training. We may be the ones called on to deal with her if she proves unstable." Helena was trying to get Isabella to steel herself for the possibility that Craig had mentioned to both of them previously. Charlene, of all the group, had a family history of instability and disobedience, which had caused all sorts of problems before.

"What of the others?" Isabella tried to deflect the train of thought.

"Craig showed me the results of the research her father did, on the Chimera gene," Isabella nodded, she'd seen it too, although she'd not understood most of the implications. The older woman's voice tremored, in a way Isabella had never heard before. "Chimera's potential is beyond extraordinary. Some of the test animals developed fantastic abilities; from an armoured worm to lemur that could bend the cage's titanium bars. If she gets even a tenth of that kind of might and falls into

91

darkness, she could push us all aside with as little effort as you blow a feather out of your way."

"We will do what must be done; as M.I.X. always has," Isabella reassured her, with a calm confidence that her own face did not share. Looking at each other, they turned their attention to the girl breathing deeply on the bed next to them and silently prayed that she would endure the ordeal coming. Because if she did not, they doubted they would be able to stop her.

The child Charlene stood in a corridor dimly lit by sickly green fluorescent lights. She was walking hesitantly towards the hospital's operating theatre. The corridor was empty, and there was that persistent buzzing again, coming from ahead; somewhere beyond the doors.

She moved slowly, knowing that she had to go through those doors, but dreading what she was going to find beyond. Still, her father had said that she should never be afraid to move forward; so forward she went. She lifted her hand and leaned forward to open the door when the buzzing stopped. She hesitated, feeling her heart pounding and the breath in her ears deepening, like that of a wounded beast in its death throes. She had the sense of something behind her and without looking, knew it was advancing; tracking or hunting her, but unsure which. Its breath was hot around her, and the scrape of claws on the floor made her wince. Time seemed to slow as she knew that the next decision was crucial. At first, she hesitated, but then she moved forward resolving to face her fear, hearing distantly in her head a familiar voice, "that's my girl. Never be afraid".

In the glass of the door, she saw a reflection of the creature behind her. As sometimes happened in dreams, the shape was familiar, and yet she did not consciously recognise it.

The doors opened, and the scene she saw made her young eyes bulge, and her heart stutter; it could not be. It was totally impossible.

Before her was a larger-than-life version of her home in Brae except, all the rooms of the period cottage were mixed up, into one conglomerate arena. There were the main room's pictures of her, as she had grown up. On the left, was the furniture from her bedroom, chemical molecules and all. On the right, was the little shed that her father used for his experiments and finally, in the middle, was a massive black hole in the wall with a whirl of dark purple cloud spiralling around and around.

Before it lay a separate scene of horror; she felt herself pull air into her lungs, and suddenly the scene changed. She was somewhere else, although there was nothing really around her. It was totally grey, yet she felt something soft and downy under her feet.

"Be at ease," a gentle, but powerful, voice pulsed around her.

"Who is that?" she felt, rather than heard herself say.

"I'm one that wishes you well," came a was soft, feminine voice, "I was once like you, small, weak, uncertain. Do not rail against your destiny. All you need to do is trust your instincts, and grow into what you were meant to be." The voice was at once scary and soothing, but also, vaguely familiar, as the creature had been, but more, more … personal.

"And what is it that I have to do?" Charlene asked.

"What you have always known you would do. Save mankind from being devoured by a cancer; although the cancer you face is beyond anything you have ever imagined; and you will need to change in so many ways to excise it."

"How?" Charlene would be grateful for any help.

"I cannot say how, for this is your path, not mine. You must first learn to how to survive the many threats in your world, then discover how to locate your prey. Finally, you must learn the truth," the voice and environs started to fade from around her. Charlene was not reassured at all, but she fell into a deeper calmer sleep; all the while, her body changed.

John went out for a run, to get some kinks out of his legs and to give their tails a literal run around London so that the team could work in peace. It seemed that the tails were only interested in following them when they were moving; not realising that they might be accomplishing more by staying put, at the moment.

Simon's workers arrived at ten pm, and after Craig had talked to their boss, handing over a card of some kind, started to transfer a large number of frame sections, benches, re-enforced glass and light metal panels into the building. Isabella greeted and directed the teams to the lift, to move the more substantial items down to the underground area. Being dark outside, the few people still out saw what was being hauled into the office.

Simon and Jack wore standard white dust masks, so that they would not be recognised and, once inside, directed the different teams to layout the various sections of their embryonic base.

The first work team began constructing the pressurised biochemical laboratory that Charlene had insisted she needed, the "Analysis" area being the most complicated part of the proposed new complex, requiring many days work.

Simon had designed the lab's main support structure, having consulted with Charlene, before she'd gone to bed. Initially, an outer skin of light-weight, but incredibly strong, Titanium would be created inside the tunnel. Next, the air system would be securely bolted to that outer shell, allowing it to process both the tunnel air and the inner laboratory atmosphere. The inner shell, again of Titanium, but shaped in a re-enforcing honeycombed lattice, would be constructed to hold the laboratories various compartments. It was apparent to Craig, who watched via CCTV, that Simon had long adored the material, and he kept asking for a reserve of it, for future purposes, from the foreman.

Charlene had also specified a series of filters, both air, and chemical. A series of airlocks connect the lab to the main room, with lab windows that were six-inch thick, armoured, glass. John had argued about the necessity of that excessively complicated and intricate specification, especially the bulletproof glass. He knew something about ballistics, and he'd never seen such thick glass, even to protect the most powerful drug lords. Charlene had caustically replied he'd also never seen what happened when you neutralised gaseous Hydrogen Fluoride and had shown him a U-tube clip of the resulting explosion; it was spectacular and he'd conceded the argument after seeing the devastation involved.

The equipment was being delivered at one end of the tunnel; the different sections would then be sealed off, lab by lab, and layer by layer. The whole project was going to take several days; two days per section, then one to seal and pressurise the whole system. Of the whole base; the lab would take the longest to complete, but the smaller pieces of equipment would be usable immediately; for the initial tests.

In the meantime, team two was creating a machine shop for Simon, which would allow him to do his heavy work in peace, but also to provide the other teams with, much needed, industrial grade equipment; to do the work on Charlene's laboratory, outfit Jack with equipment and provide John with better armaments. With an area the size of a standard MOT facility, it was lined, with modern electronic equipment and gadgets. The "Machine Shop" included a fully fitted tool chest, per section, heavy machining tools: drills of various sizes, all machine, and voice, controlled; lathes, circular saws, welding kits, plasma cutters. In the centre; a hydraulic ram was positioned just under an impressive set of twelve robotic arms, designed to hold various sized pieces of whatever was being built. Unlike Charlene's area, his area was basically finished when the appropriate portions of equipment were plugged into their assigned slots, although the control systems needed tuning. Simon positively beamed when he was informed it was ready.

Team three had apparently the easiest job, creating the gymnasium, training and living areas. What they had not counted on was the two girls, who'd had little input on the designs of the rooftop office, and had felt somewhat superfluous to the current effort. Now they imposed their will on the aesthetics and decor in the new area, much to the chagrin of the foreman of the team. They seemed to have differing tastes in furniture, lighting, fittings, colour schemes and in fact just about everything. It rapidly became distinctly competitive, almost confrontational, and finally, the Forman appealed to a higher authority before the two girls came to blows.

"ENOUGH!" bellowed John, newly returned from his run, as the two girls faced off practically nose to nose, shouting their decisions at each other. Both turned at the interruption and started, their mouths open when he flipped out his stun gun aiming it at both of them, the shocked look on their faces stopping the argument dead. He stood there for a few seconds, then raised it and blew across the top of his gun, holstering it. Then he grinned at them both and walked off, with a casual word with the foreman as he passed. The foreman looked like he was ready to kiss the large man's feet, but instead went to his men and the decor was immediately chosen as standard office white.

The girls went off, to the kitchen, to sulk after that. John turned to Jack, who'd been helping rearrange the furniture, grinning from ear to ear. Jack did a double take. For the quiet one of the group, this was a strange turn of events.

"They thought they were pulling a fast one on me earlier. Now they both have to re-evaluate who's playing whom." The tone was so smug that Jack could not help but feel a swell of mirth building up inside himself. Jack look sternly at John, trying hard to be serious about it, looking at the man for a few seconds, unable to help himself any longer roared with laughter. John just smiled and winked at him, then set off towards the Kitchen. Jack wondered if he even knew that's where the two women had gone.

The three teams did about two hours of work, to get the areas set out for the following day, then departed; ready to return early the next day. The living quarters were the most complete, but they still had crates blocking off sections of it.

It was nearly twelve o'clock, and the group was setting out who was sleeping where. By agreement, Charlene was laid to rest in her lab, on the bed put to one side for installation in the labs later. It was just before twelve when the last of them turned in.

Beyond the walls of the building, a figure stood in a long coat, with a limp and bloody body lying at the figure's feet. He was wiping a blade, sheathing it when it was clean and removing a machine pistol from under the bodies' coat, holstering it in a spare holster under his own long waxed coat. The enemy had made a mistake this time, their agent not having reported in since M.I.X. had intervened, meaning that they were ignorant of Charlene's location.

He felt a light hand on his shoulder. He did not turn, "Hello, Craig."

"They are getting bold and powerful to try and follow her here," Craig said.

"Nah, this one just got over confident. He spotted the first tail and assumed it was one of two, instead of one of four. Sloppy," and gave the body a kick. "Listen, Craig, I know you sealed the files, but she has been exposed to a lot in a short time; shouldn't you give them a break and let another team carry this on."

"Nigel Klerk. You, of all people, know that molly codling people does not help them grow." Craig indicated the body and two men appeared, from behind him, dragging it into a waiting van, which immediately drove off to dispose of the enemy agent. He did not add that they did not have that luxury in this situation.

The man sighed "Yes. I know. Father tried to protect me; that just meant I could not save my brother, from his wife."

He remembered the scene of horror revealed when he'd opened the cottage door that night on Brae. Black and red mystic marking all over the cottage, pentagrams and magic circles entirely drawn in both human, and demonic, blood; chalk markings that blunted detection; salt to keep away other unnatural creatures. In the centre of it all, a catatonic child covered in Demon blood; totally unresponsive. He'd carried her to the ambulance and looked into eyes that saw nothing, or still saw too much.

"There was nothing you could have done," comforted Craig, "and I'm still glad it was you that found her, and not one of that bitch's goons, or worse."

Nigel remembered that it had been one in the morning when they had arrived at Glasgow hospital, the doctors and nurses having all been sworn to secrecy. The mess at the scene was cleaned up, and samples were taken of the blood covering her, and the cottage, for analysis, the results being terribly disturbing. The blood was hers', and from something else, yet when they checked for wounds, there was not a single mark on her. At first, they suspected a sexual assault, but when that had proved impossible, they were at a loss as to how the blood could be hers'. The other blood totally defied analysis.

It was the next night when they had been given the first inkling of what had actually happened. Initially, the monitor alarm had sounded, indicating that the patient was stirring, a nurse going to the room and noticing Charlene twitching slightly in bed. She'd made a note on the chart, and called for the on-call doctor, to check on her condition.

Nigel had been sleeping, in a relative's room, and was woken with the good news, and was halfway to the ward when it hit Midnight.

The screech that followed was inhumanly loud, windows vibrating and dogs outside howling in sympathy and pain. As it continued, people writhed on the floor, hands clamped to their ears to blot out the agony, and Nigel had found it increasingly difficult to advance on the room. There was no physical barrier, but he felt a terror he'd never known pulsing in his head, a dark and ancient dread, and it had a name, and form: Demon.

He'd girded himself, and pushed forward, noting nurses and doctors falling unconscious to the floor, but that Charlene was sat up, in bed, simply screaming, eyes staring off to who knew where. How she'd maintained the scream, he had never known, but he had known he had to stop her. He'd dragged himself up the bed frame, and took the expedient measure of clamping his hand over her mouth first to silence her. Her head snapped around, looking him deep in the eyes, then, that frail young girl grabbed his arm and FORCED it from her mouth, Nigel being truly astonished at her demonstrated strength.

"It came for me," she'd whispered, in contrast to the cacophony she'd unleashed seconds before. "The Demon came for me. It spoke my name. It knew me. It called me its' child," her eyes bulging at the memory of that pronouncement.

"Easy Charlene. It's gone now. It IS gone now," he'd reassured her. But she was shaking her head. He held her under her chin, "there was no one there but you when we arrived. They are all gone".

Charlene again locked eyes with him and when she next spoke his spine tingled.

"It has not gone. He only delayed it long enough for it to fail in its' task; it will be back, and it will be coming for me." The surety in her voice was genuinely terrifying. Somewhere, out there, there was a demon ready to snatch and slay this child; and he knew that there was nothing he could do to stop it.

As the clock ticked past one, Charlene had lapsed back into catatonia. Nigel never understood where all that time had gone.

Eventually, they had asked someone special to help her to forget the incident, something they'd said was possible; but that for some reason the treatment was only partially successful. They'd been forced to tell the girl that her parents had been lost on a mission; partially true. One of the doctors who'd treated Charlene in the hospital, Dr. Trafford, had volunteered to adopt her; giving her a familiar home life to aid in her convalescence. He'd gone on to study her mental condition and help her almost completely forget her troubled past. He'd gone on to found A.G.E. as a research company, with Craig's backing.

Her later engagement at A.G.E. had been a bonus, giving her a purpose, in a subject that would help M.I.X. and allowed her to be well guarded, and kept out of the public consciousness and anyone else's eye, twenty-four seven. Perfect. Later, a large conglomerate had acquired them, not realising the intelligence connection they had inherited.

Nigel came out of his reveille, finding Craig had obviously gone; ah well back to work. He started scanning the area again, as Midnight struck on Big Ben …

… the dream began again. The child Charlene stood in a corridor dimly lit by sickly green fluorescent lights. She was walking toward the hospital's operating theatre. The corridor was empty, and that buzzing was now loud, persistent and emanating from ahead; just beyond those doors.

She moved slowly, knowing that she had to go through those doors, but dreading what she was going to find there. Still, her father had said that she should never be afraid to move forward; so forward she went. She lifted her hand and leaned forward to open the door when the buzzing stopped. She hesitated, feeling her heart pounding and hearing the breath in her ears deepened, like that of a wounded beast in its death throes. She had the sense of something behind her. She did not look, but knew it was advancing; tracking or hunting her, just unsure which its' breath was hot around her, the scrape of claws on the floor making her wince.

Time seemed to slow as she knew that the next decision was crucial. At first, she hesitated, but then She moved forward resolving to face her fear, hearing distantly in her head a familiar voice, "that's my girl. Never be afraid".

She saw a reflection of the creature behind her in the glass of the door. As sometimes happened in dreams, the shape was familiar, and yet, she did not recognise it on a conscious level but knew that shape had been with her, her whole life.

Beyond the doors was a larger than life version of her home, in Brae; except, all the rooms of the period cottage were mixed up into one weird conglomerate arena. There were the main rooms wall pictures of her, as she had grown up. On the left, was the furniture from her bedroom, chemical molecules and all. On the right, was the little shed that her father used for his experiments and finally, in the middle, was a massive black hole in the wall with a whirl of dark purple cloud spiralling around and around.

She recognised the bits of the different rooms, but that is not what caught her attention this time. Superimposed over the whole scene, was another image of two people battling over the motionless form of her younger self; but not only that, but beyond them somehow, larger insubstantial figures fought above them; one, the almost familiar multi-headed creature, the other, a demon with a nightmarish aspect, that just could not be described.

Finally, the woman, with the demon behind her, plunged a dagger into the man. Charlene felt herself pull air into her lungs, sat bolt upright and screamed. As she screamed, and awoke, just for a fleeting second, she saw a face at the foot of her bed.

"Mother?" she gasped, half in amazement, half in fear, as the image faded from view and she collapsed back, unconscious. The shock to her system meant that, when Helena and Isabella arrived a few seconds later, Charlene was out cold again. The two women looked at each other.

"We did not imagine her screaming, did we?" the younger girl asked.

"No. Look!" Helena replied, pointing across the room.

The unpacked glassware over the other side of the room was crazed, more had cracks, and the one directly opposite Charlene was in a state that could not be faked; the top half of the cylinder reduced to sand.

"Helena. What do we do about her?"

"I don't know yet. At the moment all we can do is wait and see what she does."

They made Charlene comfortable again and left her to sleep it off.

The next morning, as soon as equipment started to arrive, the group flew into action. At least, most of them did. Charlene rose groggily, ate some breakfast and almost immediately bolted to the bathroom, making the rest of them wince, as the sound of her retching reached their ears through the solid walls, causing the rest to look at each other with distinctly worried expressions; but they carried on, as did the retching.

After a few minutes, the retching stopped and it went quiet. Helena strode over to the door, gently tapping on the door, "Dr. Klerk? you ok?" She waited a second.

"Fine," croaked Charlene, "can you get me some sample bottles and some rubber gloves. I need to analyse these samples," Helena blinked. Even while being sick, Charlene was trying to be the consummate professional.

Helena did as she was told and passed the sample tubes into Charlene. The smell that came out was worse than any stench that had come out of the sewer, still being boiled out of their other clothes.

"Grief Charlene. What the hell is that smell?" Helena was part serious, and part in awe of the power of the rank smell.

"I don't know Helena, and that's the problem," Charlene's voice was terribly serious. "Give me a few minutes to clean up; then I can start my analysis and answering your questions."

Quite a few minutes later, Charlene came out looking dreadful, her face a strange yellow colour, not jaundice, more TOWIE, a burnished gold. The look she gave Helena was a combination of embarrassment, annoyance, and confusion.

"Don't you think you ought to rest a little after that?" Helena was truly dumbstruck by the attitude of this girl, "your health ought to come first, you know."

"My dear Helena, I need to analyse these fast, before these are contaminated, and it's my health, my future health, I am worried about. Now, please let me get started," and the fireball ploughed past her towards the labs, slowing slightly to grab a tissue, to wipe her mouth, as a little more of the substance oozed out involuntarily. Helena trailed behind her, the two grabbing necessary items as they left for an unused section of the tunnels; the used tissue was popped into a sample tube at some point.

In the selected work area, the younger girl slowed and swayed a little as they approached the equipment she needed. Helena reached for Charlene's arm but found it had moved out of reach. She looked sideways and saw Charlene staring right at her.

"Not a good idea to touch me just now, silly," Charlene smiled a little, "I might be infectious, and since I don't know what it is," she left it hanging. The look was one of someone trying to protect those that she cared for; so young a Sheppard thought Helena. Charlene lined up the samples she'd collected in a semi-circular arrangement on a solitary bench before her.

"Can you get me crates five and six of my shipment, please?" Charlene's requested, kneeling down. "They have all that I need for the tests I need to do; for now," her voice steadier now, urging Helena to find the requested boxes.

Charlene flipped her legs around, sitting down and started to get out the first sample; the vial of what Whisper had described as weaponised Eldarin blood.

She smelt it, recognising the musky and tangy odour the were-creatures had exuded, causing her to feel light-headed, not the dizziness of nausea, of lost sleep or nightmares, but more like she was only partly there, the other part of her still dreaming; a fog of unreality refusing to relinquish her.

Helena returned to her with a small packing crate, and Charlene's arm shot up to grab a portable centrifuge; a powerful unit the size of a kitchen blender. Her new acquaintance was more than a little shocked at the change in the girl. When she'd first seen the girl at the conference, she'd been a little reticent and retiring; less than a week later she was suddenly more forward, almost aggressive and more than a little scary, despite her current condition.

As Helena went off to get the other crate, Charlene began processing the first sample. She was already centrifuging it when Helena returned with the mini-electron microscope; an economical new device many times more compact than previously available units, that gave a high resolution on cellular samples, using a fraction of the power. Hands whipped out to relieve Helena of the device and set it down, with a reverence that Helena thought was almost religious.

This time, Charlene's eyes caught Helena's and in a husky voice said, "Thanks for this Helena, you have no idea what this really means to me." The look in her eye was strange, almost as if it was not Charlene at all. Then the look was gone and Charlene started sorting through the other samples. Helena left her to it. The girl moved at an astonishing rate, faster even than Isabella on a web search, her hands a blur, switching the samples between the various pieces of apparatus like a hyped-up speed demon.

Charlene locked in the first sample into the microscope, zoomed right in on the sample and just blinked. That was impossible! Her hand reached for her tablet, and she started entering notes on this batch. Its full details, reference, and structure were typed in before the shock of the revealed image truly registered.

"I'll have to get Simon in on this, and Isabella too!" She said to Helena. When no reply came, she looked up realising Helena had returned to help the others. She shrugged. The comment was rhetorical anyway. The sample blood, plasma, and platelets all looked all ok, the T cells and other human structures looked normal too.

No, the thing, or rather things, which had triggered her shock and interest were the myriad Nanobots. The simple fact that they were there at all was astonishing, but there was something more; they looked strange, well stranger than the A.G.E Nanobots. They were smaller, but remarkably similar even considering the possibility of parallel development. There was something about them naggingly familiar, hovering on the edge of Charlene's consciousness. She ramped up the magnification, checking the tail end of one Nanobot; her suspicions confirmed.

A few months back at A.G.E, she had proposed a radical new propulsion section for the Nanites. Taking a cue from nature, she'd selected the whip-like flagella as the propulsion unit to replace the more ship-like propellers that the company was using at the time. Here, at the end of this strange Nanobot, was her exact design of the time. As it happened the design had a slight flaw, in the coupling section, that caused the Nanites' directional control to deteriorate rapidly; something she'd later corrected, but here was the original flawed design in its raw form, perfectly visible under the lens.

The conclusion was fairly obvious; someone at A.G.E. had passed, or was passing, on her research to an unknown agency, and they had used it in developing the serum, to create a weapon? Charlene tried to remain calm, but she felt her teeth grinding, and her hands were clasping and unclasping.

She moved to the second sample; the venom from the were-creature. The toxin itself had a nasty anti-coagulant in it, one that stopped wounds from healing, and a necrotising factor, that prevented cells from replicating properly; meaning the injuries would continue bleeding until the host died, Nasty! However, there, in the venom, were more Nanites. Here, however, the poison had attacked the flaw in the Nanites, and they had failed entirely.

Charlene did not know Eldarin physiology, perhaps she could ask Whisper for details, but she thought that, if the Nanites were better they could be spread by the venom to another host. She had to ask the question, what were they there to do? The design was familiar, but the micro-programming needed deciphering. From her own knowledge, the coding could either be molecular or micro-computer encoded. These looked too small for the latter so the function would need teasing from the physical design, a rather laborious task. But hold on a minute, hadn't Simon said that once one werewolf had changed, they all had? Or had it been John? Perhaps the Nanites allowed some form of biological control, and had a built-in transmission system; but how and for what reason? To control the other creatures? She looked carefully again. The nanites sported myriad claw-like protrusions, that could tap into the nervous system, and several spines that could be guide-conduits or transmitter antenna. She could study this for months though and still not know the actual functions. It would have to wait until she could spare the time to test the Nanites effect on various cellular structures and types.

The third sample was her own blood. So far, she'd had bad news on both samples, and she was not looking forward to this. She was a professional, but this was beyond anything she'd had to deal with before; her hand was trembling and even using her other hand, that prevented her from getting the sample into the narrow slot on the 'scope. Her breathing was getting ragged, and she felt a sweat coming on.

From behind her, a masculine hand gently grabbed her wrist to steady it. "Easy there miss. Let me help", John's voice soothed her. She'd been so caught up in the moment she'd not even heard him approach. Ever the support in her need, he provided the strength to place the glass slide under the focal array. She looked around, and he gave her a reassuring smile.

"Ok Professor. What information does this sample give us?" John was all business, and she smiled back her thanks, her hand steadier now and her breathing calmer. What was happening to her? She'd never been this, weak, before. Then her curiosity kicked in, and she looked at the sample; she would remember it for the rest of her life.

Nothing about the sample would have made any sense to anyone but her. The red blood cells were distorted by embedded nanobots, similar to the ones that she had in her case. They seemed to have been altered somehow, being smaller, more compact, but where the companies' Nanites would be one-to-one with the red blood cells, here, there were ten or more per cell. The white blood cells had an entirely different Nanite type embedded in, and surrounding them, yet seemed inactive; though still pulsing with energy. Weird.

These observations explained much of how she felt, as her whole body was going through some, somewhat radical, upheavals. Her blood cells were hyperactive, her plasma teamed with Nanites, and that meant her blood pressure was up; probably the cause of her slight dizziness.

Strangest of all the blood's component cells were the platelets. Naturally designed to seal injuries and surrounded by tiny filaments allowing them to interlock to form a protective barrier, these cells repaired damaged skin, like plasters, melting away when replaced by fresh skin cells. Charlene's were, now, much larger, looking more like honeycombed stacks of semi-metallic plates surrounded with filaments many times the regular length. In short, they were substantially stronger, more robust and more resilient. Given her experience on the alien ship, it seems that these new platelets now acted as a defence mechanism against perceived injuries before they occurred, and had the ability to pass through the pores of her skin, to interlock flexibly forming a protective coating. In effect, when attacked, she'd produce a nano-molecular armour resembling tiny metal scales.

"What we got doc.?" John muttered a semi-interested enquiry in her left ear.

She shook her head. The processes involved should not have been viable, except for one thing; the Chimera gene. She zoomed in the sample, to see it in greater detail and saw something else; the venom that she wore the Sheriff's bracelet against, was still in her bloodstream, though it seemed as though, when it attacked the un-converted cells in her body, a reaction, possible at the genetic level, repelled it. She did not need the bracelet at all and never had.

"I've found a few things here that I'd like to study further." What could she say? She sighed. She'd have to tell the others that all of their troubles were basically her fault, or did she? Well, the work was hers', but the truth was the blame lay elsewhere.

"It seems that someone at A.G.E. has stolen my work, perverted it and is using it for a purpose I can only guess at yet." John's face was grim, but, surprisingly, as she looked at him, her face was grimmer, "and when I find out who, I'm going to show him just how angry I can get." John started forward as if to try to calm her down, but that look stopped him. "If I find out anything else, I'll let you know," and she looked down again. The dismissal was implicit and absolute.

Chimaera had protected her again the venom. What else could it do? She needed to look at the samples from her, indigestion, this morning. She selected the clearest of the group of sample tubes, and centrifuged it, separating out the different layers she knew should be there. Her hands were steady and relaxed. She proceeded with her analysis. It seemed fury could power her effort, as well as Adrenaline, not seeing John leave.

John took a last, slightly sad, look and sauntered back to the others. He had a sudden and strange pity for the person responsible for this when Charlene caught up with them. He'd seen that same look before, in the eyes of hard and vicious men; it looked much more foreboding on a woman. He was just saddened by the change in Dr. Klerk in so few days; she'd matured, hardened and grown in determination, very quickly. He just hoped that he could direct that terrible inner rage, into something that she could live with; otherwise, she might do something that she would regret, for the rest of her life.

As Charlene looked at the final sample, it seemed to have more layers than it should. She'd expected four simple layers: Food residue, ejected cells, dead cells and finally a few healthy cells caught in the decay processes, here there were six. She chose the unexpected new layers to test first. The slightly greenish layer read as rejected were-venom; apparently, the body was expelling it, despite the venom's usual propensity for retention. The second new layer composition was disturbing; a soup of mucus, deactivated neurons and inter-cranial fluid. What were the Nanites doing in her head? It explained another aspect of the dizziness and the strange feelings, and images, she'd been experiencing. Even as she thought about it though, the explanation did not entirely account for everything. The imagery was too specific and too recurrent, but perhaps the changes had allowed her to experience the images somehow. The mind was a strange area, and even the neural experts did not know all its myriad intricacies.

After a little thought she, eventually, moved on to the other layers; not expecting them to hold any great surprises, given what she'd already found. She was wrong again. They too were not what she expected at all; for one thing, there was no waste food, it was all dead or destroyed cells of different types. And the dead cells told a story that horrified Charlene; she had not changed - she was changing. Whatever the little 'bots were doing, it was systemic, radical and continuing. There were lymphatic cells, bone, fragments of altered DNA and RNA, all apparently rejected by her system. The bulk of the cells were still being worked on by Nanites which had been caught in the ejection. Apparently, their power source was not as limited as the company's bio-electric induction motors.

She used the built-in digital cameras, to record the processes she was seeing; it would give her an insight into the Nanite programming. What was most disturbing of anything that she's seen in the past two hours, was that the Nanites rejected resembled nothing that she'd made or previously seen; which meant they'd been made inside her, within the last day, after the incident with the ship.

These new Nanites seemed partially self-energised, as they seemed to last a short time outside of her body. There were also glimpses of molecules that she did not recognise in their construction. Now, that might be explained by one of the following: interactions with the venom, the Nanites being contaminated by alien technology as it had phased during the activation of the engines or a combination of all of the above. It was hard to say and again would only be shown by the detailed analysis, which would have to wait.

All she did know, for the moment, was that she was hungry like a large pack of wolves. She smiled at the thought, given the creatures she'd seen recently, it invoked a little inappropriate mirth. The accompanying growl from her stomach only exacerbated the bark of laughter that escaped her lips. She tried to get a tight grip on herself; difficult when your own body was betraying you at every turn, and on every level.

"Can someone get me a Pizza?" She bellowed from the half-completed lab.

Somewhere down the other end of the office Helena and John, who'd been talking in worried tones about the 'fragile' girl, heard the yell and looked at each other.

"Perhaps I was mistaken," Helena questioned her observation of Dr. Klerk's illness.

"No. Make that two; and, the large family size ones," Charlene's bellow added, from down the far end of the base.

John looked at Helena. "No, you were not, but I guess that it will come and go. At the moment her work will fuel her," he grinned a little. "If I know her, and I do a little, she'll work till exactly four pm," looking at his watch, "three hours from now. Then she'll shower and try to do her kata and gymnastics. Hmmm, better get that mat down soon then. After that; study, chess and bed at exactly ten pm."

Helena's eyes looked dubious after last nights' events. "Don't let her fool you, Helena. That is one driven lady. If she says she is going to make someone pay for this, then get out of her way. I may be able to stop her physically, but, to be honest; I'm more likely just to back off and watch her do whatever she has in mind and pick up the pieces afterwards."

He was decidedly serious, and Helena remembered the conversation she'd had with Isabella the night before.

"John have you had any physical problems after the conference, like Charlene," she asked, hoping that she could get some clues, to determine if Charlene was the only one affected.

"Me? No. Besides the bracelet is supposed to keep us healthy isn't it?" John seemed totally unconcerned, letting Helena relax a little.

"Any of the others reported any problems, besides Jacks fading in and out and the weird lines and patterns, he said he was seeing?" She was trying to be casual about this, so as not to alert John of the possibilities implicit in the questions, and the reason she was asking him.

"No, not really. We have all been too busy getting our wounds tended and the equipment set up; but if you like, I'll keep my eyes open for you," he put his hand on her shoulder and smiled. "Relax Helena. I know what to do; well I know what I would do in your place, and just to say I don't envy you the role, is a distinct understatement."

He grinned slightly, as he realised that she would not be able to relax, knowing that he knew that.

"Thanks!" said Helena, with all the sarcasm she could muster.

He just grinned even more. "Sorry, but you do deserve that," and her answering tongue said it all.

That night, the dream came again. The young Charlene stood in a corridor, dimly lit by a pale green light, although the previous dream's sickliness was fading. She was walking towards the hospital's operating theatre, where the few other people in the corridor either ignored her or did not see her at all, seemingly busy with their own problems. There was that loud, persistent buzzing coming from ahead; somewhere beyond the doors. A nurse appeared next to her telling her that she needed to see her parents now and indicated the doors, as she nodded in agreement.

She moved slowly, knowing that she had to go through those doors, but dreading what she was going to find beyond. Still, her father had said that she should never be afraid to move forward; so forward she went. She lifted her hand and leaned forward to open the door when the buzzing stopped. She hesitated and turned to look at the nurse, but she'd gone.

She felt her heart pounding, and the breath in her ears deepened, like a hurricane. She had the sense of something behind her. She did not look but knew it was very close, almost touching her. Its breath was hot around her, and the scrape of claws on the floor made her wince. Two large, but indistinct shaped, heads moved into her peripheral vision, either side of her head. One had horns on its crown, and the other was covered in scales. Another loomed over her head, its fur tickling her forehead slightly.

Time seemed to slow as she knew that the next decision was crucial. At first, she hesitated, but then she moved forward resolving to face her fear, hearing distantly in her head a familiar voice, "that's my girl. Never be afraid".

In the glass of the door, she saw a reflection of the creature around her. She thought she knew that shape, it'd been with her subconsciously her whole life; it was who she would become soon; Chimera.

The doors opened, and the scene she saw made her eyes bulge and her heart stutter; it could not be. It was totally impossible.

Before her was a larger than life version of her home in Brae, except all the rooms of the cottage were mixed into one conglomerate area. She recognised the bits of the different rooms, but that is not what caught her attention this time. Superimposed over the whole scene was another image; two people battling over the sleeping form of her younger self. Beyond them somehow, larger figures fought; one of them was the Chimera, the other a demon with a nightmarish aspect all tooth, claw, spikes, and wings.

Finally, the person with the demon behind them plunged a dagger into the other one. She felt herself pull in air to her lungs, and the scene jumped. She was looking at the view from the small girl's perspective.

The dagger was embedded in her father's shoulder, forcing him to scream. He managed to throw the woman off, diving to regain his own dagger.

"Your insane Sylvia. I will die before I let you take her to your Master."

Sylvia laughed slightly, "easily arranged, my dear."

She flipped another dagger in his direction but, despite the wound, he side-stepped smoothly to avoid the deadly blade. In reply, he presented his weapon and flew across the girl, aiming for the woman's heart, missing by fractions, instead, landing next to her.

Time seemed to slow at that point; a bolt of energy arced from Sylvia's hands, but strangely curved around her Father.

"No! Daddy!" screamed Charlene, in a faint voice.

Sylvia reached for the girl, trying to snatch her away. The woman's hand, and by association, the demon she served, touched her.

A silent concussive force exploded from the girl; catapulting Sylvia out the door and defenestrating her father. The demonic image behind the woman shattered and the room was plastered in its inky, black blood. The other figure, strangely, remained totally unmoved and it turned in some fashion, looking directly at her.

Her perspective suddenly changed, and she found herself, as she was now, standing next to the girl she'd been, who looked blankly at the space where the demon had shattered. Time sped forward around her; the police and ambulance medics leading the traumatised youngster away to begin her new life, with her adoptive father, in boarding schools and university.

"And now you know what really happened. Seek out the deeper truth, once you have found your strength. Then and only then; for our enemy is strong," and the figure before her faded again, allowing Charlene to fall into a deep sleep and, for the first time in days, slept soundly.

Across the street, her uncle, watched the area intensely; as vigilant as ever.

CHAPTER 6

GOING SOUTH, FAST.

Seven days after the start of construction, the new base was fully installed; not fully completed, there was still plenty to do, but, all the equipment had been delivered, workers packed off and, the labs were now ready for the tasks ahead.

Each member of the team had managed to get their initial work completed: Charlene having sealed her more delicate samples, Simon having built some small esoteric devices, Jack had made a few beautiful pieces of suspiciously multipurpose furniture, although he'd not specify what their real functions were and lastly John had his Gym and firing ranges up and soundproofed. In short, they were ready to gear up and properly begin their new careers in M.I.X; well sort of.

The four newcomers had made themselves at home and soon found that they worked efficiently together, and had even starting to use each other's first names. John and Jack, after their initial brief meeting at the conference, found that they and the scientists tended to split into pairs, Jack only really enjoyed Simon and Charlene's company when he was practising his tricks.

"A fresh and un-cynical pair of eyes helps hone a trick," he'd pointed out to John afterwards, although John just thought that he enjoyed pulling the wool over the logical minds of the pair; even the thought that Jack could, made John smile. Perhaps the reason Jack and he got on so well. They had the same, slightly twisted, sense of humour.

Jack also suspected that John's habit of asking Isabella, rather than Helena, about the security protocols, was a bit more than professional interest. The two were always heads together tweaking the security algorithms, or, utilising ladders, adding new sensors here or there, when she was not with the other two women.

The three women quickly developed a genuine rapport, arranging both equipment and decor. Jack suspected that Charlene was included in the group so that the other two could monitor her illness too, but perhaps he was being a little overly suspicious there.

Jack being the least active of the group, when not practising on the scientists, started to see a pattern emerging in the group's interactions. They may not actually be a team yet, but the whole base building task smacked of someone's attempt to turn them into one.

One day he cornered the elusive Craig, who looked in on them infrequently and mentioned it.

"Guilty," he said, with surprising candour.

"Why?" Jack asked bluntly.

"Why, what?" Craig asked, with a semi-innocent expression covering his face.

"Why all of this! Why pick us in the first place? Why try to turn us into spies? Why waste time and money building a base for us here? Why?" Jack's voice rose gradually through the list of questions he'd slowly added to through the days.

"Are the problems you've seen not enough?" Craig looked at him, intensely.

"Maybe to calm the others, but I am more world-wise than others. What are you getting out of this, other than four more people to help out, and pay wages to."

"Ah, the cynic wants to know the real reason for my altruism," Craig smiled slightly. "Of all of them you were the one I'd have expected to come to me first. I doubt Dr. Klerk or Professor Caruthers ever will, but John might make it," he sat down. "I've had a long career, full of battles, Ok not on this scale, but all-important at the time. And if time has taught me anything, it is that one day you lose the battle. For me, that day will be soon. I've been riding my luck more and more, of late, and I'm getting slower."

"So you're after someone to take up the fight?"

"More. I'm looking for someone to take up my banner. The people in my employ are all fine people, but they have a jaded view of the world, even more so than you, my new friend. They are just far too suspicious. No, I need someone that will not be deceived, but that does not see shadows on a sunny public beach."

"I'm not looking for a new job, I just want a stage to play on and an audience to perform for," Jack said, cringing at the thought of the responsibility implicit in Craig's role. "John," he started,

"… is a good man," Craig interrupted, "but he would not have the eyes to do the job, and the two scientists are too 'specialist grade' to be considered." Craig leaned back a little, "to put your mind at ease, Helena has already been selected, but remember that in wars casualties happen, so I have to have contingencies in place." He took a deep breath, "but to answer your initial question, stopping whatever is going on is only the start. We also have to find out about this enemy, and for that, I will need experts on hand to do the work. Security, Electronics, Biology, Computers, and Medical."

"What about me?" Jack asked not understanding his role or seeing himself in the list.

"You are here to see what the others might miss while performing their specialisms. You have more real-world experience and can see beyond the obvious. That's what you're here for; to give them a grounded and unbiased view of the world."

Jack thought about it and nodded; that made sense. It was in his nature to question and cut through illusions, both entertainment and social. He started to leave.

"And something to think on," Jack half turned to see Craig having a quick drink of coffee. "If you really want to entertain people, you should consider using the world as a stage and give people a show they will never forget. Life."

Craig called them to the roof the morning after the workers left. Charlene had brought them all up to date on the results of her investigations, leaving out the tests she'd done on herself. They were on her own pad encrypted with a somewhat esoteric algorithm, Isabella had provided. She had no delusions that it could remain secret, if Isabella wanted, or was ordered, to access it; but it was safe from casual examination. Besides, only she really knew what the actual results really meant. To the casual reader, it was so much medical gibberish. Besides the conclusions were just in her head anyway.

The next thing to do, now that they were all in full health again, with the slight exception of Charlene's continuing heavy flu-like symptoms, was to track the other signal to its source and find their tormentors. Isabella assured them that the signal was still strong.

John piped up at that point. "They must know that someone is on to them, so why continue to transmit the fake videos onto the web? It'll be old news by now; already debunked."

Craig looked casual about it, "simply put, it's bait. Like a flare. They want to guide you to a location they control, to deal with you; so, they send out a signal to lure us in."

Charlene coughed, then added, "it's a Gambit. They know we know they exist now. So, they invite us in, so that they can find out what we really know and in the hope of stopping us before we stop them."

"But don't we just call the authorities and hand it over to the authorities and the military?" asked Isabella.

"We are the authorities in this case, besides if we handed it over to the military, they'd cause a global panic with the response? No," said Craig, "Dr. Klerk, is right. They are inviting us to play the game, and we will play." He paced a little, but said nothing, inviting someone else to take up the conversation.

Jack spoke plainly, "So we go to the tower, track the signal and find their base. Then we see who can play the game better; who has the better tricks up their sleeves," so saying, he produced a small fluffy hamster from thin air.

It almost looked real, but Charlene guessed, it was a toy one. Still why not play the game, she thought, smiling; then frowned a mock frown. "Is that the guinea pig from my lab?" Jack smiled again, and produced a second one, "No. Absolutely not," as he added a third and fourth.

John laughed, "I knew they reproduced quickly, but not that fast," he was shaking his head. Craig smiled too, "let's hope your tricks are that good in the field".

Jacks' smile was blissful, "trust me!".

John shook his head laughing, "not on my life, Jack".

Jack suddenly stopped and looked John right in the eye, saying earnestly, "I hope it does not come down to that John. I hope that, but somehow I have a feeling it really will."

The team stocked the van up with electrical spare parts and equipment for Simon. As they had was no idea on what they would find when they returned to the comms. tower, they packed as many high-frequency switches, cables, and electronic circuits as would fit in the van. The most disturbing things in the vehicle were brought by Charlene.

Hung on her belt, were three whips. Not simple training whips, these were Leather and wood, combination fighting whips.

John had looked her in the eyes when she turned up with them and saw not an iota of mercy in them. Boy, she really was taking this personally; he'd never seen anyone that angry. Cold, deliberate, fury shone forth incandescent from her eyes.

They retraced their route to the same parking space at the communication tower. Jack had scanned the houses down the road with his eyes, and that same curtain twitched over the way. He smiled, "I'll just go check with our eyes in the square, while you lot have a look at what our friends have been doing up there."

Helena checked out the tower with a pair of binoculars, plainly seeing that there were two boxes, where there should have only been one. The main signal box, apparently the legitimate aerial, looked undisturbed, while the other was tapped up in an almost haphazard and amateurish fashion, ironically, making it easier to spot as the enemy signal relay, but more difficult to actually adjust.

John and Simon unloaded a wide-based, insulated ladder, stable enough to allow Simon to get to the top of the tower, where he could examine the device. Looking at the tower, the professor seemed decidedly reluctant at the ladder, gulping several times before starting up. Helena sat in the van, monitoring the comms, with Charlene vigilantly scanning for signs of unwanted attention from any visitors turning up as the others worked, and the team needed to make a swift departure.

Simon had a selection of the most likely needed tools on an equipment belt, including a bag to put anything they could retrieve. He froze about halfway up the ladder, when it wobbled slightly, even if it was not really that windy; but the tower was narrow, and the ladder precariously balanced against the tower's side. He looked down at John holding the ladder, John just waving him up higher. Alright for him down there, but Simon hated heights.

Once he'd finally reached the right level, he started to detach the box, with an eye on the detector clipped to his overalls, monitoring for any signs that his tampering was causing problems with the signal, in a way perceptible to the enemy.

He sliced through the tape with a Stanley knife; snarling as the power went dead. The signal was gone and, now that he inspected the tape more carefully, he realised that tape had been placed over a wire of some kind.

"The signal's gone," he called down, "some kind of anti-tampering circuit." His heart sank; they had lost their chance.

"Wait!" called Charlene over the comms, "get it down here fast. If you can juice it up again quickly, they might simply think that there was a glitch, and keep the signal active," suggested Charlene. "Besides, if we're right, they will want us to find them, so they will keep it up no matter what."

Simon scrambled down the ladder, with a strange looking orb in his hand. It looked like a transparent Perspex bowling ball, with several parallel planes of differently patterned plastics inside.

Charlene examined it, and whispered in awe, "a Crystal Computer!"

John looked at her perplexed, as did Simon, "a what?" asked John.

"It's a concept an engineer from Cambridge came up, with a while back. Using Nano-construction techniques, you build a computer-based purely on light impulses; theoretically, many orders of magnitude faster than our current electronic computers."

"When did you hear about that?" demanded Jack, curious. "I thought you were into chemistry and biology?" he was looking confused, having just returned from talking to the old lady.

Charlene seemed animated at the discovery. "A few months back, I was talking to an expert on Nano-programming, and he mentioned it, and the production techniques they were going to use to try and create a few prototype circuits. Besides, what do you think controls my Nanites? They have Nano-level computer circuits in them; crystal lattices, to avoid shorting out in corrosive fluids." Jack just looked blankly at her. She turned to someone that would be more receptive, but Simon had started to talk to Isabella, over the phone link, and transmitted the encryption algorithms so that they could track the signals better. She gave up at that point.

Simon looked the device over, to allow him to try and construct a jammer. Strangely, as he looked at it, he found he could almost see how it was put together; allowing him to adjust his tracking device just a little. He looked at Charlene, with a peculiar look in his eye, "I think I have got it," the tone was slightly worried.

"Already?" Charlene sounded impressed, but that look spoke of something else. "Too easy?" Simons response was a nod accompanied by a large grimace.

John looked at the two and thought he understood, "you think it should have taken longer?" Simon nodded. "So, it's either more comparable to our technology than you expected, or they are making it easy for us, by using things we can decipher easily." Simon nodded again.

Charlene looked at Simon, "another Gambit?"

Simon shook his head, "more likely a test, designed to make sure the people that find it, are the ones they want; so that they don't waste their time with simple spies."

John shrugged. "Well we had kind of guessed it was to draw us in, so let's just make sure that we don't use the front gate."

Simon tried to put on a professional face but failed. "Well, we best get started then. I doubt that fleet will wait too long in space, and I'm eager to get hold of more of their technology." Indeed, he was almost drooling, at the thought; Scientists thought John.

The team replaced the transmitter part of the device, cleaned up after themselves and started to circle London, to triangulate the signal's origin. As they passed St. Pauls they picked up Isabella, giving them the added benefit of having her computer skills, on tap.

It was soon evident that they were heading out of London. As they cleared the M25, heading west down the M3, their destination seemed to be in line with Bournemouth.

Behind them, a small, unremarkable, vehicle followed the van, five cars back; further than the driver really liked; but he knew one of the suspects was an advanced driver, so he'd had to adopt a more surreptitious approach.

Detective Inspector was not in his usual police car because, officially, he was taking his, long overdue, leave. Actually, Chief Inspector Blackmoore had told him, in no uncertain terms, that he was not to pursue this case; under pain of full disciplinary action. The phrase, 'Obstructing an official investigation', was used and that meant the scrutiny of Internal Affairs, suspension, and possible Imprisonment if disobeyed. Dilock had looked at his friend of many years, D.I. Browns, for aid, and saw a strangers' eyes looking coldly at him. Apparently, Browns had been told to toe the line too.

He had pleaded that he'd leads, that he could crack the case. That only led him to be told that, perhaps, he was working too hard, or, maybe, he'd been overwhelmed by the initial incident. The tone left no doubt in his mind that; they wanted a scapegoat, they were covering something up, or they were in cahoots with those he was following.

But where ever they were going, he would follow them; then he would find out what was going on. He'd never been a conformist.

So, intent was he on his quarry, that he did not see that he too was someone's quarry, as a motorcycle continued to follow him. The figure was slight, dressed in full leathers, with a blood red demon motif was emblazoned across it. He addressed his helm microphone.

"Griffon to Falcon. Target sighted in plain sight, with an escort. Unable to engage at this time. Moving to plan B." A few seconds passed as the news was absorbed at the other end.

"Confirmed Griffon. Falcon will advise secondary operatives. Falcon out!" The line went dead. Secondary operatives? Well, little help was better than none, but since when did he ever need backup?

As the team drove along the last part of the motorway, Helena piped up, "we're following a lay line you know?"

"What? What is that?" asked Charlene, hoping it was relevant. Helena did tend to babble child-like sometimes, despite her age.

"In ancient times, the people believed that the land itself had power, and they mapped out areas that exhibited, what they thought of as power, like Stonehenge and lay lines connected them like power conduits." The others looked interested and listened, over the roar of the wheel noise and traffic, while Charlene just frowned.

Jack joined in, "Given what SkyLord said about magic once working, it may have been their equivalent of a national grid. If that is the case, we may find we're heading for a similar place to Stonehenge down here."

He looked at Helena, but it was John that replied, "actually there are several areas of interest down here with a history from that time."

The others turned back around, looking at him with interest, and incredulity.

"What! Just because I look like a weightlifter, does not mean I cannot have other interests? Yes, I know a bit about the occult, although the modern connotations are all a bit dark for my liking." The rest of them all looked at each other; well that was a turn up for the books. They turned off and headed towards the smaller roads. "It looks like we are heading for Poole rather than Bournemouth. There is a major convergence of lay lines somewhere around here, and a few places that might be of interest."

Gradually the roads grew narrower, small B roads and they pulled over to do a bit of scouting ahead, on the web. They consulted with Isabella, passing on their theory about the lay lines.

"We're on the A351 about four miles from the turnoff. Can you send us a detailed map of the local area and a list of the local lay sites that might be of interest?" John asked. "We'll do some triangulation and see if we can track down the exact location."

John set off up the road, the signal getting stronger. He knew that, for a ground location, only three points were needed to get an exact location; but to get a line only two. They were close. He asked Isabella for confirmation they were on the right track again, mainly because she could look up details on the move, but also because he was getting quite fond of listening to her seriously sexy voice.

"The signals originating from lat. one nine five, long. four. Anything down there on the maps?" His voice carrying a kind of dubious question, as there seemed little in the way of anything on the map, save a few scattered buildings.

"There is a property called Wytch Farm. The interesting thing is, more detailed maps show a comms tower on the land there." The team all suddenly looked intently at the map; the name in its own right invoked images of ancient powers and dark deeds, much like the ones they were investigating. "What's more, the land belongs to a corporation, Peerco. They bought the land up a few years back, along with an island, which lines up directly with the signal." Helena saw the connection immediately, and so did the others. They also saw the inherent dangers here.

John was the first to express the situation. "So, I guess, what we are supposed to do, from their perspective, is: follow the signal to the house, investigate it, get captured in the trap they have there for us and thus be neutralised." He looked at the others; they all nodded seeing it too. He smiled. For nerds, these people were pretty savvy; even Charlene, which he was slightly surprised at. He knew her, or so he thought, but, it seemed, she was not as innocent as he thought she was.

"I think not, however," said Simon. "I think we get to the comms tower, sabotage the array and get them to come to us. Then we force them to give us the location of their real base and go pay it a visit."

A few nodded, but Charlene was kind is looking into thin air for a second then she spoke. "I sort of agree. However, how about this; instead of completely sabotaging the array, we jam the signal again. They are used to having problems with the signal, so let's try jamming it remotely, but from close by." She turned to

Simon. "Can you jam the signal, using another signal from range, say a few hundred meters?" He nodded, having had a measure of success with the technology, he was getting quite confident in his abilities; more so than he'd ever been before.

"OK, so we jam the signal; then wait to see who turns up to repair the problem," Jack started to see the plan forming.

"Then we cut the jamming just before they arrive and they try and find the problem," Simon added.

"Then as they go away, we do it again," John caught on, "they come back, and the jamming stops again. They check again and find no real cause because the signal cannot be detected and the equipment has no fault. They report in, and their commander says to monitor the problem."

Helena chipped in, "then as they go again they find it is not working again, so they report in that they have a fault, and start to do a full mechanical service, thus disabling it and keeping the service engineers out the way as we investigate the other property; which is almost certainly their base." They all looked at one another and suddenly burst out laughing.

"If they knew who we were, and what we're about to do to them, they would hate us," said John, as he tried to stop laughing.

"Yes," said Charlene finally getting herself under control. "The only thing is that they probably already do hate us!" Everyone stopped laughing at that.

"Ok," Simon started seriously, "I just need a few more components if we're, I mean I'm, going to do this remotely; some switches, focusing dish and things." He started writing out a relatively long list.

"OK. We get some food, go shopping, then we go hunting us some bad guys." John said in an impatient tone. "They've been tormenting us long enough, time to turn the tables." He looked at Charlene, who gave a wane, but determined, little smile back.

"You ok?" She looked pallid, and a little listless again.

"I'm hot, and I have a little tinnitus." She remembered he was not the technical kind, "Ringing in my ears. I need a serious amount of sleep; I've been having problems with that recently, ever since the conference actually," she patted his arm.

The team went about their business, with simple efficiency. It was interesting, Helena noted, that once they all had goals, they moved with a surety of purpose; more efficient than some agents who had years more experience; they were shaping up nicely.

As they settled down for lunch, just outside a local pub, John started a little, then casually leaned forward and murmured to Isabella, in a low conspiratorial tone, "just smile at me, and laugh a little. As you do, look about, as if you're embarrassed by the laugh. Tell me what you've seen once you're done."

His tone caused her to give him a severe stare, but, as he just flicked his eyes for her to do it, please, she did as he requested giving her shoulders a little shrug and putting her hand to her mouth, looking around guiltily. As she did so, four people deliberately looked away, with a partially guilty look of getting caught. Gotcha! She looked back at John, patted his hand, as though in apology and leant forward to continue their conversation. Indeed, she did feel apologetic; she'd thought he was having fun with her. Apparently not!

"So?" whispered John curiously pulling her closer by her hands.

"Firstly, I'm sorry. I thought you were having a joke at my expense." He waved that away, with an impatient waft of his fingers, but kept hold of her with his other hand.

"Tell me!" Isabella was getting the feeling that he was getting impatient, so she described what she'd seen. He held on to her hands as she did, looking at her intently.

"Table 12, Front left; single male, with standard issue police radio, poorly concealed, under a long trench coat. The bulge is not too obvious, but the signal is," she nodded to her laptop on the table, which she'd obviously set scanning for such things, "so I'd say, experienced, but old-fashioned. At a guess, that's this detective that you told me about."

"Table 19, A young couple nice enough, none combatant; she's pregnant, but not showing, given her choice of food." John dismissed them, but noted their location should things go south.

"Table 4, Partially hidden Biker; drinking a totally inappropriate drink for his age, culture or for the weather. Watch him."

"Table 9, Non- descript businessman; nowadays that's a no-no. All businesses advertise at the drop of a hat, and he's not. Also, he's using a plain phone, meaning it's a burn phone, probably scrambled. Government, military or secret service; probably our new official tail."

"Table 15. Never mind she has just stood up and left," her voice was strangely monotone.

"All in all, a bad group of spectators to be having around us," John complained.

"None of them seems hostile, at the moment, and they cannot be anything to do with the current problem, other than Dilock; but he's no real threat,"

Isabella finally noticed that he was still holding her hand. She looked up and deeply into his eyes; his face was relatively young, and he was exceedingly strong. She looked at their hands and decided to leave them where they were. His smile was calm, and she felt a gentle pulse on his hand that meant he was relaxed too, well, about moving slowly with anything that might be developing here.

Then Charlene appeared, and the hands were quickly withdrawn.

Isabelle was a little annoyed at Charlene's timing; forcing her to let go of the bodyguard's hand, then looked at Charlene and suddenly became very concerned. She looked awful and was walking unusually slowly and deliberately. Isabella and John both stood up and moved quickly to her side.

"What's wrong? You weren't this bad a few minutes ago," John put his arm around her, Isabella supporting her on the other side.

"I administered myself a little pick me up," she admitted.

They both looked at each other, groaning silently. She saw the look and smiled slightly, "no, it did not go wrong, before you ask. It is keeping me on my feet. If I had not given myself something, I'd probably be out of it totally." Her voice was strong enough, it was just her legs that seemed suspect. "I just need a few more minutes for the stimulants to take hold and I'll be fine."

They sat down just inside a covered porch area and waited for John and Helena to return from their shopping trip. They kept an eye out for the tails they appeared to have dragged along from London, but they seemed content to stay in their current places.

As Charlene started to perk up, Isabella addressed her condition. "What is the matter with you?" She sounded genuinely concerned for the other girl, "any ideas?".

Charlene lifted her head up; the red flush on her face was more pronounced than before, but her voice was a little stronger when she answered. "I guess that, whatever the actual contaminant was at the conference, I managed to contract or make contact with it somehow. Apart from John, I'm the only one who had direct contact with the contaminants. It may be that because I had substantial exposure to the blood, rather than the venom, I am experiencing an allergic reaction to the antigens in it." She knew this was not the truth, but she had to make it convincing for the others.

"Could it spread?" Isabella could not help ask.

"I would not have come here if I thought it would," replied Charlene, a little hurt by the implied negligence on her part. "That's why I think it's a reaction, rather than an infection. If it were an infection, the infecting cells would be generating new pathogenic cells, with the infecting agent's DNA or RNA in them," she explained the processes in the simplest terms she could use.

"If anything, my cells are getting stronger. The only problem with that is that my system is under a great deal of stress at the moment, hence the temperature. The appetite I have developed will be sustained, until the reaction has run its course and, even then, I'll still probably be eating to restore my physical reserves." She did not add that she'd probably have a permanently higher metabolic rate, that would take time to explain, and she was not ready for them to know that yet.

Her stomach gave a particularly loud growl and her face became stern as she looked at the others with a kind of forced anger on her face. She tried desperately to stay like that, but then a second, louder, growl issued from the same spot and she wavered, then just collapsed in despairing howls of laughter.

John was shocked. He'd never seen her lose control of herself so completely. Her head was on the table and tears flowed onto the tabletop from beneath arms surrounding her bowed head. The laughter started to get to the two others, initially causing them to smile, but, as the laughter carried on, they eventually caught it too. After a few more seconds, they were all in hysterics. At that point, John's stomach growled as well, and the three simply dissolved again into an incoherent burble of laughter.

Finally, John was laughed-out, and he saw that Charlene was looking at him. Isabella was leaning against Charlene, still smirking, and chuckling.

"Driver," she said loudly enough to be heard by other customers, who all looked at the group like they had gone temporarily insane, "Please can you order some food and drinks for us. Water for me please." He smiled but got the message; business as usual when they were in public.

"Yes, Ma'am!"

She had not discussed it, but he guessed that she would need something simple and easy to digest. So, he ordered soups and buns, for the girls. He could not subsist off such light foods, so he ordered himself a bloody sixteen-ounce steak, with everything on, and, a large, side order of spare ribs.

The food took about twenty minutes, and while they waited, they chatted about Isabella's rather idyllic past, her middle-class family and a few snippets of the current news, until the barmaid arrived with the food.

"Steak?" She asked, looking around the group.

Charlene did not hesitate, her hands flashing to the plate like lightning and, before John could stop, her she tucked ravenously into the thick steak. The other two sat with mouths open, at both the speed she had moved at, and the appetite she was exhibiting. John had a quick word with the barmaid, and she set off to get additional items.

The speed, and intensity, with which Charlene attacked the food was bewildering, to both of her colleges. In three minutes, she had gone through a large portion of the meal and, was just finishing off the large steak, when the barmaid who'd served them came back with some soup and a large bowl of chips.

"Was everything, ok?" she looked at the nearly-empty plate, in astonishment.

"It was lovely. Can we have some desserts please?" Charlene looked up at John and Isabella, then realised what she had done. A small rumble then issued from her stomach. Her face was one of utter consternation. "Hmmm. On second thoughts, can we have the menu? I think I'll need to order a few more things." The barmaid's eyes went wide. "Quite a few more; Please?" her voice was small, apologetic and almost ashamed.

The others just covered their eyes and sighed. This was going to be a long afternoon. They sipped their soups slowly and waited for the next orders to come.

After about two hours the others returned from their shopping trip, to table covered in a heaped pile of plates; Charlene had just finished her fourth order. The others had gone from surprised to disbelieving, and finally to totally awed, as she made her way through the menu; going through protein, vitamins, carbohydrates, and fats, in vast quantities. The growling diminished; gradually.

Simon arrived back and looked at the other two's faces, begging the question.

"She's been at it for about two and a half hours; showing no signs of stopping," was all John said. Helena looked at Isabella with a question on her face; the younger girl shook her head, and the other smiled a little. John caught the look but did not understand it, so said nothing.

"You two stay with her," Simon nodded to John and Isabella, "if she carries on too much longer you might as well have tea down here too. Helena and I have some work to do in the van. Once we've finished, we'll join you back here."

They climbed into the van, to assemble a directional jammer of sufficient power to block the local signal from the tower. The work was simple enough; the only difficulty being the designing of the control unit. Simon studied the retrieved crystal sphere, duplicating its' functionality using a substantial number of modern computer circuits. The signal was of an unusually high frequency, limiting the potential range of the jammer to a few dozen meters; all they really needed.

It took about two hours more, then, finally, it was done. It was crude, wasteful of power and had a particularly narrow signal arc, but it would work, for as long as they needed. Packing it up, he locked the van and went with Helena to join the others.

When they arrived back, Charlene had finished her meal. The bill was staggering, but when she tried to pay for it, the owner himself came over.

A large and portly man with an anchor tattoo on his arm, he looked her in the eye and in a guttural Devonian accent "I don' know how you did that miss, but it's on the house; anyone who can eat all that, and not explode, either needs it, or deserves it. Either way, you have both my admiration and my sympathy," and he started to walk away.

"Sympathy?" asked John and Charlene in tandem.

"Aye miss! We heard the growls of your stomach, all the way over there," and he pointed to the bar nearly twenty feet away. "With that racket, you ain't going to get any sleep tonight." He beamed a smile at her and sauntered off. At that point, the whole group, bar Charlene, roared with laughter; pointing at her face, as a worried frown appeared there. Then she too understood the humour of the situation, and could not stop herself from laughing along with everybody there.

Fortunately, it appeared that her appetite had been put to bed. Indeed, she felt like going straight to bed; but she still needed to maintain her routine, if just to keep herself anchored in reality if anyone could call this reality.

Simon informed the team his device was ready, and that he would test it later. By common agreement, the group split up after the others had had a light snack. Some went upstairs to their rooms, while, ostensibly, John and Isabella went for a walk in the nearby woods. They were actually trying to get readings on their tails, to better identify them; of course, this also triggered the tails trying to follow them. The two of them played Cat and Mouse with the different tails for a few hours, while the others ploughed on with their tasks.

As the evening came, the team, bar Charlene, came down from their rooms, to discuss what had happened that afternoon.

"I've never seen anything that could come close to what that young girl put away," observed John, "Not even the chunkiest officer I've known, and they are some big guys, could tuck that away, and not be sick or have a wracking stomach ache after it."

"Truly astonishing," said Simon, "but then we have all been through extraordinary events recently, and, it would not surprise me, if she is not the only one that has had some side effects during all this," he looked at Jack, who was sitting in the corner of the pub, looking thoughtful. "What say you, Jack?"

"Hmmm, yes," came the kind of distant reply. "When I was at the conference, just for a few moments, I seemed to see things that I could not explain; my perception was altered in some manner."

The others, so busy with unfolding events, had not really discussed their experiences in detail before. With Charlene's blatantly obvious demonstration, now seemed the right moment.

"Helena's show, at the Conference, could be described as, what the Ghool Lord described as, magic," speculated Simon, trying to get the others to open up a little.

"Well, I don't believe in magic," chimed in Isabella, "it's all trickery and deception, no offence Jack," she added quickly.

"None taken; I'm an escapologist mainly," Jack seemed a bit preoccupied with something. "Normally, I would agree with you Isabella but, in the past few days, I have seen things that just could not be faked; at least in any way that I know of. Of course, that is the sign of a good magician." He now looked right at her, "however, I have been mulling over the history I know in my mind; I'm talking way back to the African homelands in South Africa. There are stories from there that suggest that magic may well have been used then, that it as real as anything we can see now."

Simon looked at him as if he'd just gone entirely do-lally.

"I'm serious, Simon," and indeed he was. "Folklore usually has some basis in fact, and the stories are just too specific and detailed to suffer from much distortion. Just look at the Eldarin. Are they not mythical creatures? Yet, they are, now, very real." He stood up and started to get another glass of juice.

When he came back, he continued, "our ancestors taught us that magic was the province of spirits; they called forth those spirits, to do tasks for them. The Eldarin's description matches that too; it seems that, with two entirely different cultures referencing the same thing, that magic may well have existed and exists now, in whatever guise it may be invoked, performed or expressed.

John looked at Helena, "what do you think of all this Helena?"

"Weeelll," she started, obviously reluctant to get into this too deeply. "I have been regaled by many stories, from my family's collective history. They always contain the wand I carry and end in something magical happening. My wand is a family heirloom and always proscribed mystic powers that I always doubted." She looked kinda guilty at her doubt now.

"At the conference, I felt a connection to the wand, and suddenly it worked, as described by my father, and his father and all the stories."

As the others carried on their discussion, Charlene had a long, steaming, soak, in the pubs' bathing room. Her stomach gradually settled down, and the pain in her joints calmed a little. She lay her head back, slowly sinking under the water and closing her eyes; just floating there, in a state of total relaxation.

For the first time in days, her body was calm, quiet and, almost, pain-free. She lost track of time just floating there; the sound of the water just sloshing over her, the warmth of the heat on her skin and the flow of the water over her face. After a few minutes, that fact registered and she suddenly sat bolt upright!

She looked at the bathroom clock. She'd been under the water for more than five minutes yet she'd not needed to breathe, and no water had entered her mouth. She tried to focus on what had happened, as she ducked under the water again; but whatever had happened, it did not happen again. Had she just imagined it?

It was no good, she could not relax again after that. She still needed to go see the others downstairs but was not up for it yet, and she still needed to do her

Gymnastics. There was nowhere here with space and, besides, her joints would not support the manoeuvres she usually did.

She changed into her mediation outfit, a red silk Kimono, that actually felt so much smoother and softer since her experience with the saucer. As her breathing settled, she started to fall into her regular breathing pattern, and her heart rate started to slow. She began to drift into a deep meditative state. Even with her body in a state of flux, her mind became calm, and she felt herself leaving her body and shifting from this world to another one; where she floated above an ocean of cloud.

With her mind in that state, she did not hear the intruder, black leather jacket and all, picking the lock and carefully opening the door. The intruder saw his mark, drew the dart gun and carefully inserted the dart into the breach of the weapon; the tranquiliser guaranteed to knock her out in seconds. He aimed precisely at her carotid artery, for maximum effect.

He was so intent that he failed to sense another's arm slowly reaching around his throat and when he did, he convulsively fired the dart, hitting the target in her left shoulder.

In her current state, all that she felt was a small backward shove on her left shoulder. She tried to open her eyes but the dart's drug was already affecting her accelerated system, and she simply slumped on the bed; returning peacefully to the sea of clouds again.

She did not see the two figures wrestling at the door; her attacker throwing the other forward over himself, using a clumsy judo throw. In return, the second figure, sporting a camouflaged army jacket, rolled back twice to get under the attacker; levering him into the air. As the camouflaged protagonist came down, he thrust up with a dagger, trying to catch the other if he'd followed up immedaitely.

The leather-jacketed attacker saw the dagger and managed to twist slightly; so that instead of getting gutted, he managed to deflect the blade to skitter off his ribs. His gasp of pain did not go unnoticed by his opposite number.

"Nice move Browns!" came Nigel Klerk's voice, and he stood up, finally coming into view, ready to finish the corrupt detective. "I must try that one some time. I know you need the practice, but, I'm sorry, you will not get the chance." He moved towards the policeman, but the attacker rolled over the bed and came up with a knife on the opposite side.

"I don't know who you are," panted D.I. Browns, "but I suggest you stay where you are; unless you want her to die, here and now!" The knife went to the throat of the now unconscious girl.

Nigel's eye narrowed but continued to advance. "I might even believe you if you had not come equipped with a dart gun. No; you came here to take her somewhere, and I think that, if you could, you'd call in your accomplices, to aid you." He put his finger to his earpiece. "All clear?" he asked loud enough for the Browns to hear.

"Taken care of, sir," came the, louder than usual, reply.

Browns eyes' went wide. "Who are you?" He moved his dagger; close to the nose of the unconscious Charlene.

"Someone who is going to make sure you don't get her," and with that, he made a prodigious leap. As Brown raised his dagger, Charlene received a small nick on her nose. The skin parted, and blood started to flow.

Meanwhile, the two men battled over her; flicking out dagger strokes left and right. Browns was younger than Nigel; but the older man was stronger and more experienced, and it finally told, as the older man's dagger caught the detective's eyes. He screamed for a fraction of a second, then stopped; as the agent thrust his blade into the other's throat. Nigel held him up for a few seconds, preventing the blood from dropping on the floor as he laid him down. He gently removed the dart from Charlene's shoulder, dragged the attacker out of the room, closed the room's door after him and knew she was safe for now.

He dragged the body of the dead man out via the fire escape, into a waiting van; where the others, who'd also been apprehended as they had waited for their leader, were also piled. He needed to get these to a discreet location; other agents could sort out the mess.

Charlene, was blissfully unaware of the activity around her; floating in a silent cloud-filled world. She was well practised in achieving a meditative state; but this appeared different, her dream body looking strange. Where her skin should be, there was a transparent membrane, rippling with a rainbow shimmer. In the underlying muscles, that teamed with Nanobots and other strange mechanical structures; her blood saturated with the Nanobots she'd seen in her tests, shimmering with an alien power.

Looking deeper, she saw tiny versions of the alien engine and other equipment, deep in her bones. What was that; an analogy of something, or an actuality? Was she seeing herself or some dream possibility? She did not know; this was a seriously bad trip or dream. Then the scene changed.

The sky darkened, and she stood before her mother, at one of their many training sessions in the mirrored studio they'd used when she was younger; except, she remained in her adult body.

"Charlene, you will obey!" One of her mothers' whips cracked, and there was a pain on her nose. "Do the move again! This time, get it right." Charlene remembered that she'd redone the complicated more easily; although her mother had not been in the mood for being mollified so easily. "Again!" and again the whip cracked, hitting its mark. Charlene repeated the manoeuvre faster and faster, till it seemed that she moved in a blur, actually disappearing between points. As the whip came again, something strange happened. Another whip, from Charlene's hand, intercepted the painful attack, and the two adults were locked eye to eye

"No more, mother," she heard herself say, in a strange voice. "No more punishments, no more pain, no more orders. No More!" The image of her mother faded, and she regarded herself in the studio's mirrors.

She looked like herself, except with gold skin.

Another figure appeared by her; it was her without her golden skin. "We are changing. We are becoming more," said the other." Then it became an unfamiliar man, almost like her, but with a serious face on, "We are so alike; yet we are so different."

The figure then changed again and slowly it became the figure from the dream and being of three heads; a goat, a lion, and a serpent peering over the others.

"We are three, yet we are one," said the lion head.

The serpent hissed, "I am you."

The others spoke in unison, "we are with you."

The male appeared again instead of the animal, "I am you."

Then the figure became her again, except she wore an evil visage and it grabbed her by the throat, "you will NOT become," and the two wrestled, until the mouth of the other opened; to reveal a massive set of teeth and a long tongue with venomous fangs on it.

But she stood up higher than the other and threw it into the mirror.

"I will become Chi'mera," she screamed out; into the clouds, that now returned beneath her. She had not noticed that her heart rate now beat incredibly fast and she was breathing as fast as a sprinter at full pelt; she gradually slowed both again, wakening and opening her eyes just as John rushed into the room. She realised she'd laid down at some point in her dream. That had never happened before.

"You ok?" John gasped. He looked out of breath like he'd been running. "You screamed!"

She looked confused.

"You did not know?" He looked exasperated.

"Honestly? No, I have been meditating. I," She stopped mid-sentence and put her hand to her nose; it was throbbing a little, almost like the trance-dream had been real. But the nose was unmarked still she remembered that she'd had to sit up. She just sat there looking confused and perplexed.

"Well, if you're ok, I'll go back to the others," he started out and heard a quiet, "thanks" from her. She was nice, but, since he'd seen Isabella, he had barely thought of her. He felt a little guilty about that, but he was a man, and Charlene barely thought of him in that way at all; give her a virus sample though, and she would go all gooey-eyed and drool over it. He shook his head. She was a strange one, for sure.

The following morning, the team met in John's room, sitting down to plan their next move, neither John nor Charlene mentioning Charlene's screaming to the others.

They gathered around an outside table to look at a map of the area, John taking the lead, pointing to a blown-up section it.

"Ok. So, we park-up here, out the way of the tower and hidden from the approach roads." The others nodded, as he described his idea, "then, Simon and I hide here, just in range of the tower but, out of sight of all but the most sharp-eyed hawk."

"Meanwhile," started Isabella, "Charlene and I will observe from Cleaval Point and alert you when there is activity on Furzey island; if that is their base of operations."

"Jack and I will guard the van, and act as pickup team, should anything go wrong," added Helena.

"Once the engineers are dispatched, we hunker down and jam the signal. They either stop and head back, or arrive and check it out and find there is no problem".

Simon could not help grinning. "Once they have returned, we jam it again. They come out again and, this time, we see who they are."

He looked at John, who added, "then we move out and make our plans."

"Ok sounds like a plan," said Helena. "Let's get to it."

John brought the van around the side of the pub, and the group all piled in. The actual comms tower was not far, but they dropped the observers up the coast, to check-out the maintenance crew approaching from the island. The two girls, armed with high powered binoculars and a comms system, hid out of sight; but close enough to the harbour to see the small spot of land clearly. The view was breath-taking; at least it would have been if they'd had the time to appreciate it.

The rest of them started out for the comms tower, stopping about a mile from the location. John and Simon leapt out with John packing the heavy duty signal jammer, even as Simon moved on ahead, revising the design to reduce its size for future use on route to their spot.

"Before we jam the signal, we'll just check that the signal is indeed being emitted from the island, rather than somewhere close by, like a ship, or a submarine," suggested Simon.

"Good idea," John was all for making sure they had the right target. No use in wasting time unnecessarily clearing out an enemy position, especially when it would almost certainly be more heavily armed than they were.

They walked around the tower, with the detector perched on John's shoulder. It did not take them long to get a beeline on the island. "That seems to confirm it then," murmured John, placing the jammer on a direct line with the tower, concealed on all sides by vegetation, barring the front, although even that had a fair amount of vegetation for concealment.

"We're all set. Is everyone else ready?" asked Simon down the comms.

"All set, Simon," the team replied in unison.

"Let's go," he said flicking the switch and activating the remote blocking signal relayed by the comms tower.

It took about five minutes for signs of activity to appear from the island. The two lookouts first noticing a patrol boat circling the island heading back, then tying up at the island's jetty, then coming out again, doing a rapid circuit of the island. It had taken about ten minutes to make a circuit of the island previously; this time it took half the time.

Observing the boat's occupants carefully, Helena distinguished black uniforms with some suspicious bulges probably concealing weaponry. Perhaps a local security group or a private company; she hoped they were local, rather than private. She had found, during previous operations, that private security could be more serious, and thus much more dangerous, than local security enforcement.

When the others were told about the boat, John piped up.

"Are they carrying guns?" enquired John quickly, as he waited for other news.

"How would I know from this distance?" Charlene retorted with exasperation and just a hint of trepidation.

"Good point. If you cannot see anything at that distance, they are probably unarmed, or just carrying sidearm's, rather than heavier calibre arms." John seemed to ignore her tone, or perhaps he just did not hear the slightly frightened quaver in her question over the comms. line.

Another three minutes passed, and a larger slower boat headed towards the coast near the comms tower. "Heads up people; we have a potential bite," reported Isabelle. "Looks like two engineers, with a three-man escort. The escorts are carrying rifles of some kind," she noted in a chill tone.

"I was afraid of that, "John's voice, however, was more determined than scared, "but it does not change the plan. And the fact that they think they need an escort means this is no normal operation."

Simon crouched by the jammer, tinkering with it, attempting to get more juice from its small power unit. He'd more than enough bits and pieces in his equipment bag to help in the job, which he used as a distraction to keep himself calm, although that was not the only reason. When he'd been hit by the discharge in the spaceship, it'd surged through his entire body; something he'd not discussed with the team. He had never been one for massive amounts of exercise, although his work with robotics tended to involve him moving large quantities of heavy equipment around, so he was not unfit. Now, however, he felt energised, almost giddy, and there was a feeling in his body, a kind of etherealness surrounding him, as though he was generating a static field. Indeed, he'd had to put on rubber shoes during his work on the jammer, as he'd produced the odd discharge that would have been disastrous to the delicate circuits in the device.

Dr. Klerk was experiencing a terrible physical reaction to her exposure to the portal energy, whereas he felt so much healthier. Strange that the same event had such markedly different outcomes, he thought.

Meanwhile, John heard the engine of an approaching van down the road to their current location, and tapped Simon on the shoulder, getting a spark in the process. He nodded in the direction of the sound, while starting at his finger, and Simon nodded, reducing the signal strength to zero. Simon looked at his teammate, "now, let's see what happens."

The Peerco engineers staggered out of the van, each lugging a toolbox and wearing utility belts packed with other equipment, accompanied by two stiff-faced guards. Just a few steps out, one put a finger to his ears for a second, giving the tower a disgusted glare. "We'll give it a once over anyway," growled the engineer in exasperation, obviously addressing someone in his dispatch office, "it's probably just a loose connection."

He signalled the guards to wait at the base of the tower, as the two engineers approached it and disappeared around the other side, presumably to inspect it and take measurements.

"Good job I set the output to zero. Otherwise, they'd be all over us by now," whispered Simon. John just put a finger to his lips, slowly moving his hand to his holster, as one of the guards started to move slightly away from the tower in their direction. Had he seen or heard something, even at this distance?

The guard was moving casually, however, not stealthily at all, and he soon turned to his left, then back towards the tower. Simon made a show of pretending to mope his brow, John replying with a cautiously relieved nod.

After fifteen minutes of measurements, the company team packed up their kit with disgusted looks, shut the gates around the tower, clattered back into their van and drove off.

"Tell me when the boat hits the island, and I'll pump up the signal again," whispered Simon, into the comms unit. Now would be the test of the plan. Depending on how good the opposition was, this would be the making, or the breaking, of their efforts here.

It took another ten minutes for the enemy team to get across the water to their landing jetty on the island.

"Now!" said Isabella, from inside the van, when she received the message from Helena. The jammer kicked in again, and the forward team awaited the response.

While she waited, Helena, the most experienced agent here, worked through the plan that the team had devised. In a short time and under pressure they had devised a fairly impressive, if simple strategy and started to work together as a coherent group: Charlene surprisingly provided the strategy; John provided the authority, and muscle; Simon the technical expertise and Jack was, quietly, providing scouting skills and a level of reality.

The plan had holes in it for sure, as the party had limited firepower; however, given their total novice status, they were handling the pressure well.

Sure enough, a few minutes later the engineers came out again. They took about five minutes to cross the river part of the journey this time, much faster than initially. And the van arrived at a screech, a few seconds after Simon had shut the Jammer down again.

The group coming out of the van was six this time, a senior guard appearing with them, possibly the leader of the group's guards.

"We'll recheck the units, but they were fine just a few minutes ago," the engineer was saying to the large guard, as he came out. "We'll set up a detector on site to see if we have, or have had, visitors."

The large guard pointed to the other three, "search the immediate area. See if you can spot anything out of the ordinary," and the guards started to fan out a little. Fortunately, they had no idea of the range of the device, and they stayed too close to find the two-man team.

"Glad we made this a remote device. Otherwise, we'd now have guns pointed at us."

The guard's search proved fruitless, and after ten minutes, the engineers packed up again, the guards continuing to scan the area until they climbed warily into the van, which finally drove off.

"Time to leave I think," said John, "We'll give them a quick burst as we go, to give that detector they installed a false direction, then we'll see about scouting the island out tomorrow."

Simon nodded with a small grin, "I've never had so much fun. It will drive them wild. The detector will show the wave signal and strength, and they'll know it's only short range, but they won't find it within range. It's a horrible thing to do to an engineer," he grinned again, and they were off.

They picked the girls up, changed the markings on the truck and drove casually towards the town. They did not want to exhibit too much haste.

"Let's head back to the inn. They will be alert for hours and have extra patrols on shore and on the island. We can do some sightseeing tomorrow and let them cool down a little before we go in later." John had had some experience of the waiting game; he knew how it was played. "They can only stay alert for so long before they lose the edge. That's when we'll go in."

"We'll find a boat that will take us around the harbour, to check out the patrols and the island's general terrain, from the other side," added Isabella, "then pick up a few bits of equipment, that will make the scouting easier."

Jack checked off on his fingers, "Night-vision Goggles, Cameras, Bolt cutters; your usual everyday items." They all grinned at that. It seemed that the best way to deal with the extraordinary nature of their new life was to make to as ordinary as possible."

"Let's try and get an early night," said Jack, noticing Charlene's frightened look when he said it, trying to settle the group down. "We will have a long day tomorrow, and we will need all our concentration to do what is necessary."

After, they settled in to have a relaxing evening as best they could, talking about anything but what they were there to do.

Charlene for the first time in her life found sleep entirely elusive. So far, since the conference, she'd had nightmares of differing kinds for nearly a week and a half; she was obviously screaming out loud every time she woke up, disturbing the others, especially John. She did not want to go to sleep, but, in her current state, she needed it more than ever.

In between the reluctance to sleep and the light day, her body conspired to keep her awake past her ridged ten o'clock bedtime.

When it hit eleven, she thought she heard movement outside her room, and she quickly stood up and peered out of the door. Nothing. Or was there? In the back of her mind, almost like a feather-light touch, a thought impinged on her consciousness, "there is something there, something is watching, something is spying on me." But strain as hard as she could, her eyes could not see anything, and her ears did not hear a whisper.

She switched off the light in her room and retrieved a set of night vision goggles, one of a box-full, which had been acquired during their shopping trip. She peered out at the spot where the feeling was the strongest, but again there was nothing there, except that nagging feeling. She put the goggles down and settled back down, trying to shake the mood, but only succeeding in making it even more pronounced. Maybe she was just going crazy.

As she settled down, she suddenly became extremely drowsy. Sleep overtook her, and she started to dream …

... except she sat bolt upright. At the end of her bed was a 'something'; a faint distortion in the air, but not actually in the air. It was, she struggled hard to identify what it could be. It was nothingness. An empty feeling, like a playroom without children, a kennel without a dog, or rather, where a dog had been and was no more. The problem with this feeling is that it was moving, slowly, deliberately and it was making a noise.

Much like its' actual presence, or rather lack of presence, the noise was not a true sound, but Charlene understood what it was; the sound of absolute void. Not the emptiness of space, or the vortex the ship had made, but the absence of anything and everything. Something else she understood, it was watching her, as though assessing her.

She found herself talking, but the voice was not hers, but a strange other self.

"Be gone from here! Your time is long over, never to return!" The voice spoke in a tone of command and authority, but the undertone was one of defiance.

The reply was strange, as the presence spoke using the air in the room. The atmosphere became tinged with the red of anger, and a black overtone of confrontation.

"Be gone I say, I am the Guardian of life. You will not be allowed dominion here."

The room grew redder and darker until finally, she could no longer see the thing. However, a second later she felt it right next to her and pulsing in a way that suggested it was about to attack. She raised her hands to ward it off, seeing them through the gloom ...

... then sat bolt upright. She was sweating profusely, and the nausea was terrible. She waited for John to come in, assuming she had screamed. But all was quiet, she lay back and pondered the fact. This time she'd not screamed. In actuality, despite the fact it was even stranger than her usual nightmares, she had not actually felt fear; what she'd felt was, a sense of fate and, a steely determination to make sure that her doom did not come to pass. So many different dreams and portents. Perhaps she was going crazy.

CHAPTER 7

A TRIP TO THE SEASIDE

Poole was lovely this time of year, it had to be noted. The sea was calm, the winds were light, and the sun was warm and comforting, which was just as well, as Charlene was not feeling well at all; nausea from the last few days was burning through her body and blistering her stomach. In fact, in all her life, she'd never felt so chronically unwell. Of course, she'd never really had any childhood diseases, that she could remember. The vaccines had never really taken, something that some doctors had commented on at the time. She'd become used to the sterile lab environment protecting her and subsequently had never needed any sick days.

She now knew that this was part of her heritage, what her father had called the Chimera gene. It had been his life's work to discover what it was and did, although he'd not succeeded in learning many of its secrets; but then, he never had the tools available to Charlene. She had found several chemical properties, but the genetic ones remained elusive. The way she felt at the moment, she would not have been surprised if she never discovered another secret before she died; in the next ten seconds.

At the moment did not she really care if she did survive; she felt wretched. Every smell was awful, every taste was like those blancmange deserts people hated from school. Her eyes itched, and the sounds were all too loud. In short, only her sense of touch was not amplified. It was as though her entire body was being rattled around a colossal drum and toasted on a roasting-spit simultaneously.

The team had gotten up early and packed their equipment into the van. Although they did not share it with one another, each of them had a strange intuition that this was going to be a momentous day. They drove into Poole, tails and all, and headed straight to the Harbour. While the others bought some food and drink for a day's sightseeing, John started checking the jetties for a boat they could hire suitable for their needs. He was busy trying to talk to a local boat captain when the others caught up. The captain was acting more like a pirate than the tour-guide the hoarding showed him to be, but John was patient. He had to be, this was the only guy within a mile even willing to talk about piloting his boat near the river mouth; near the island, they wanted to visit. To others had just shooed him away, locking up for the day after he'd gone.

"I don't care how much you want to go out there, or how much your offering," he was saying, "they don't like visitors, strangers or anyone not part of the company, even close to that island." The old, white-bearded, sea dog was chewing his lip, and squinting one eye. "And, if I were you, I would not goes a poking where they don't wants you to." Before John got a word in edgeways, the sailor, genuine tattoo and rank insignia to the effect, poked him with a large and well-used smoking pipe, "and don't think that anyone around here will help, because they have a police patrol boat out there too."

Now that did pique John's interest. "Really? You mean with police officers like this," and he flashed his warrant badge at the startled man. His attitude seemed to brighten a bit.

"Oh 'ere, why did you not say you were a bobby first off?" his tone became one of interested cooperation.

"I'm on an assignment," true of course, but probably not the way that the words invoked, "and I need to see the island to," the sailor put his hand up.

"Best not tell me, soney. What I don't hear, cannot be spoken or lied about; and I probably, really, don't want to know now, do I?" The tone was one of knowing the answer already. John shook his head, rather glad that he'd been silenced, as the guy was genuinely likeable and he didn't really want to lie to him. The old sailor seemed to think about something for a few seconds, then nodded, seeming to have come to a decision.

"Tell you what, soney. I'll sell you m' boat. That way I can say I sold it to you t' get a new one with all the mod-cons." the man looked hopeful, but when Isabella nodded the OK, John just nodded.

"Now then let's talk about the price," the two starting to haggle. Isabella listened in for a short time; then did the expedient thing and just doubled what the old pirate had initially asked for, giving him a credit card with the named sum on. John stopped mid-haggle and scowled at her; a look she chose to ignore.

"There. I think you'll find that the card will be accepted just about everywhere," was all she said.

The man beamed at her. "You're a good lass you are my deary."

"And you're a true pirate," she countered, his grin growing even wider; waving the card as he turned and sauntered away.

John looked shocked that she'd bypassed him and that she'd paid a small fortune for a decrepit old boat.

"Why you do that for? He'll just go and," he stopped, then looked at her with newfound respect.

She nodded. "He'll go and celebrate his good fortune and how clever he was, probably all night. And after he wakes up tomorrow and does it again, it will be all over; hopefully. He'll have earned the extra for his cooperation in our mission." John blinked.

"Isabella you are a genius!" he said, giving her a forehead a gentle prod.

"Smarter than most men, that's for sure," muttered Helena, nodding at John, to Charlene. Charlene just smiled, as Isabella and John shared the moment.

The team took a little time to look over their newly acquired transport, a small motor launch, that looked like it might make it around the harbour if they did it swiftly. The sea water in the bottom did not, however, inspire confidence, even though the team did not need it for long and they would all fit on; besides it was all they had.

"Well, now we have a boat," said Jack. "Anyone know how to pilot it?" He looked around the group as they all viewed the craft; they all looked at each other blankly.

John looked around again and sighed, shaking his head; then looking at the sky. "Ok, I'd do it. I mean how difficult can it be?" The rest looked back at the boat and immediately donned the old brown life jackets in the back of the relic.

The team embarked, unhooking the mooring ropes that kept the boat flush to the dock. The boat started to drift slightly, with the outgoing tide, and John started the engine. Despite its rickety appearance, the motor started first time, the wheel smooth and positive, allowing John to guide the vessel easily clear of the others moored nearby, and into the harbour.

Charlene sat near the rail, trying not to feel the undulation of waves, as the launch hit the river swell, the very thought making her queasy, causing her to clutch her stomach, in a battle to keep her breakfast, and everything else, down.

Jack watched the departing shore, while Isabella perched near the bow looking out to the opposite one. At the stern, Helena and Simon both leaned back with apparent unconcern. There was little room for them all to sit down, but standing was possible, if they ignored the faint sloshing of water around their feet, indicating a broken bilge pump. They had really overpaid for this little boat, but they had only a few minutes to contemplate that.

As they reached the river delta and a good hundred yards from the island, a fast speedboat angled out from its circling of the island to intercept them.

As the two boats approached one another, the team saw the other boat's occupants were wearing standard police uniforms.

John frowned, then quietly said over his shoulder, "Company, and they're armed," he'd already spotted the characteristic bulges of side arms, as he assumed they had spotted his; this might get tense.

"Ho there!" bellowed the large-shouldered sergeant, at the front of the launch. "These are privately owned waters, and we have orders to make sure that trespassers don't get too close to the island," flashing a genuine looking warrant card at John.

"I'm on protection duty," shouted John in reply, flashing his own warrant card and hoiking his thumb over at the obviously ill Charlene; who obligingly went even paler than normal now being the centre of discussion. "Her doc said some sea air might do her good, so we're off to the river mouth, to get her some. We don't want to go anywhere near the island, just need to get to the sea."

To John, the others' voice seemed strained; as though either he was lying, or, he was performing his duty reluctantly. This situation was also slightly strange for protection duty, especially if they were also armed; that meant either corruption higher up, or these were not real policemen.

"We have strict orders not to let anyone past the island, "reiterated the sergeant. The two other officers getting a bit fidgety, "but as long as you keep your distance, I suppose it is alright," the sergeant relented somewhat. This group was either no threat or one that the three of them could deal with.

"Much obliged," smiled John, glad to not to have to try and fight his way out of the situation. He could not help adding, "she has a loud voice when she gets upset," which of course he knew only too well. Charlene took this moment to eject her lunch, violently, over the side of the boat, the sound carrying to the shore.

The sergeant on the other boat actually smiled pityingly, "yes, she does seem the type, doesn't she. Go on, get her, her sea air. The trip might even give her some sea legs too if she's lucky," and with that, he indicated that his pilot should continue their patrol, which they did, but in a way that kept the group's little boat in sight as they passed the island.

As they started to get in line with the island, Jack suddenly averted his eyes from the island entirely. "What's the matter Jack?" asked Helena curiously, spotting him deliberately obscuring the island from view.

"Remember when I said that, at the conference, I thought I saw some strange lines around your staff and the room?" His voice was steady, but there was an element of doubt in it. Helena's head shook in the negative. "Well, the oil drilling tower on that island is emitting a bright, pulsing glow and number of lines, like magnetic emanations. I'm not looking at it because it is so bright and I don't want to get blinded. "The lines appeared to emanate from under the ground, quite a ways down.

"That kind of confirms that this is a place of interest to us, even if it's not their base," said Helena. "But it also means that we may be able to use some magic here. That could help us a lot."

She looked at Jack, and he nodded. The group discussed the general layout of the island from the map and decided that they would need about half a day preparing for the assault on the enemy base. This time they were facing an unknown number of assailants, with superior firepower that they would not hesitate to use. The team would need to use stealth to avoid detection, destroy or jam the transmitter in such a way as to render it useless and finally escape. Then they would have to decide what to do next.

This was not just dangerous; it would have been thought of as suicidal just a few days ago. However, they had all faced the impossible in the past few days; from fighting werewolf abominations and zombies to Ghools and even alien death machines. This would be no different, and as they headed back to the harbour, trailing their shadowing police escort until they were out of range of the island, they reflected on that fact in their own different ways.

As tea time came around, they headed back to the inn just outside Poole.

As they popped out of their van, a small car passed them, John recognising its driver immediately. "Oh boy," he muttered, as an irate detective Dilock charged out of his car and strode up to them at a startling pace.

"What are you lot up to? I have had a call from my boss demanding, Demanding! That I stop investigating this case," his face red from anger. "He threatened me, Me, with disciplinary action and, suggested, I take a holiday, or a leave of absence, until the case was resolved. Then, they set about doing absolutely nothing. No further surveillance, no tails, no nothing."

John looked at Charlene whose eyebrows were raised. If the tails were not his, who was tailing them?

"So why are you here Detective Dreadlock?" asked Simon, trying not to hide his, somewhat inappropriate, amusement.

"That's Detective Inspector. And it's Dilock, smartarse," corrected the detective trying to calm down, despite the comment from the overly amused scientist. "I know something is going on, something big and I want to know what it is. I know the internet video clips on the news cannot be true, it's too obviously implicating you." He scratched his head a little, "but I'm betting my pension, that, even if you are not responsible, you know what's going on." He looked at each of them in turn and locked eyes with Charlene. "Some sort of conspiracy; a distraction, to cover up a virus you let loose, or some technology that they don't want us knowing about?"

"In truth, we really don't know what is really going on, detective," Charlene replied with her most sincere eyes. Here, she saw an honest, if slightly stressed, ally that could potentially help them. "If you want, we can call you if we find out anything; we have a comms unit that can reach you with anywhere, in the UK." We'll she hoped it could; it might need to.

The others just spectated, giving Charlene her shot at getting him on board with them. A few silent seconds went by as Dilock absorbed her offer, device in hand. His eyes hardened slightly at first looking at the device, then softened, with her genuine attempt to help him. "Ok," he said, snatching the device, and looking it over suspiciously, "but, if you don't contact me in two days, you'll wish that tub you call a boat had sunk." He handed her a card, "here is my number. I'll be waiting."

"Thanks; Detective Hemlock," muttered Simon, dodging Helena's attempt to elbow him in the ribs, although John's heel did catch him in the shins, causing him to both wince and subside immediately.

"Don't worry detective," said John loudly, "I guarantee that you will hear from us as soon as we find anything." He did not need to add if they survived long enough, the look that the others gave him showed they all understood that.

The detective stomped off back into his car and drove off, heading back to town.

"Let's get some rest," suggested Isabella, looking at John and indicating he should follow her.

Jack and Helena walked away together, talking in a companionable manner, about magic, and what each thought it really was. Simon disappeared back into the van to work on his jamming devices; leaving Charlene to try to enjoy a warm afternoon, in the back garden of the pub.

"Lovely day eh?" came a vaguely familiar voice. To one side, on an adjoining table, sat a weatherworn man, in his fifties, sipping a long, cool glass of lemonade. Strangely, the smell did not upset her stomach as some had of late.

"Yes, I suppose it is," she replied, with more indifference than she intended after all the man was trying to be friendly.

"Suppose it is? You don't sound so sure," his tone was sincerely empathic, and she had the feeling he was deliberately reaching out to her. So, what he said next, hit her smack in the face. "What happened to make you so sad?" She froze.

It was a question her father had asked her many times after he and her mother had split up when she was feeling down.

Locked in position, she took a much closer look at the person. Yes, it was quite bright, but the features were almost familiar; older, more seasoned than her father's were when he'd died; and there was a strange scare on his face that her father had never had, but it could easily be an older version of him. She started to open her mouth, but her reaction had telegraphed what she was about to ask. He raised a finger to his lips and looked around quickly.

"I'm your uncle, Nigel," he leaned in closer, seeing disbelief, then shock take hold. "I know he never mentioned me because we had a falling out about your mother. We agreed not to tell you, 'til you'd grown up." He saw anger as well as understanding in her eyes, so he carried on quickly.

"I don't have much time, so I'll say this quickly. Craig has assigned me to keep an eye on you, not just because of this current situation, but because you are being targeted by people who wish you ill; people your mother got involved with. I just need to say that your mother is not actually as evil as you might remember her. I can guess what you think of her, what your father thought of her, but let me just say, she thought she had valid reasons for what she did. She might have gone about it differently if she did it again, but that's not relevant now; it has been done, and she will have to deal with that, should you see her again." Her eyes went wide, and her hands started to tremble. "Yes; she is alive, but that's all I can say at the moment." He suddenly put his finger to his ear, indicating that he had a comms unit like her own, and was receiving a message.

He held her hand for a few more moments, then whispered in her ear. "I must go now, but, quickly; don't worry about your tails, I'll deal with them before you depart. Good luck, and Be strong. I know you can do anything if you just put your talents to the task." And with that, he stood up and quickly disappeared out the back gate of the pub, followed, coincidentally of course by three people with sudden urgent business elsewhere.

Charlene was too shocked by the visit to do anything but stare at the gate. From being supposedly an orphan she now had at least two family members; and, if they had survived the night she'd dreamed of, what about her father? Belated she thought of following her newly discovered uncle, but decided against it, given that he was being followed himself.

She was confused and needed to rest, but it was nearly time for here exercises, and despite the aching and general feeling of malaise, her latest encounter seemed to have given her new energy. She was not a true orphan; although, if she and her mother met at the moment, she might well be without at least one parent once more.

Charlene went inside and took a quick shower; the inn frowning upon guests using all the hot water, which her usual shower probably would have done. Once she'd towelled herself dry, she went out through the inn's side gate to a secluded area she'd picked for training.

She had found a nearby scrub field where she could perform her exercise routine. She'd brought her travel bag with her red kimono, ribbons, and towel and she got changed and started her meditation. Half expecting to fall asleep, it seemed her body had other ideas. Although she was feeling down most of the day, she felt the meditation take hold as it had used to, her body pulsing gently, the world dimming and her pain and discomfort along with it. Her breathing slowed, her pulse dropped, and finally, she felt her heart relaxing after all its overexertions of the past days. After ten minutes like that, Charlene started to feel much better; indeed it was almost as if she'd never been hurt at all. She thought it strange that when people lived their lives, they only appreciated being pain-free when they were in pain. As she came out of her meditation and opened her eyes, the pain returned, although it was nowhere near as bad as before.

Charlene was so relieved, that she launched herself into her gymnastics routine with a renewed vigour. Out here, in the fresh air, the manoeuvres seemed so much easier to perform, and she managed to go through the entire series in about half the time; thus, she continued with another set, improvising some moves and found that they were successful too. Finally, with some doubts, she produced one of the whips she purchased, the twenty footer, and re-started her routine, finding almost immediately, that the extra weight caused problems. She definitely needed to train with these, rather than with her ribbons, as the tip of the whip had caught on her ankle, causing her to cart-wheeled in a spectacularly ungainly arc; landing in a dense clump of grass.

She took stock of the situation, saw what she was really doing, and just keeled over laughing. Here was Dr. Charlene Klerk, renown scientist, potential Nobel prize winner; playing hero and rolling around in a field, in the long grass. What on earth was she doing? She was no hero, she had no strength and no skill in combat. So far, her contributions to the team were a couple of ideas, an acid hit on an innocent civilian, who subsequently died, nearly blowing everyone out of the sewer system and crashing a spaceship into the Thames.

And in the past few days, she had barely done anything, except eat the inn's kitchen larder bare and eject it into the river. Her little pick me ups were getting more and more frequent, despite her attempts at moderation. Tonight would be the biggest yet, four times as strong as the first one, and she was getting the first worrying indication of an addictive reaction in her system. She tried to shrug the negative mood off by doing her Judo kata; but if she was honest with herself, her heart really was not in it, and, after her tumble with the whip, she was not in the mood. Still, she followed her routine, then went inside the inn to clean herself off. Tonight was going to be severely taxing.

The group gathered by the van as the inn started to empty for last orders. Another person was already waiting for them.

"Detective Inspector," John addressed him, recognising the smaller man's Mack.

"I thought about what you said and came up with a better idea. I'll escort you as far as the island you scoped out. That way, if you get seen, I can say you are helping me with my enquiries. That should get you past most ordinary problems."

"Not much ordinary around here the past few days," came Simon's quip which, surprisingly, he ignored.

"After I drop you off, I will wait on the opposite side of the river, with the comms on your frequency. If I hear any serious shooting or you call, I'll send SO19 your way."

The group looked at each other and John came to a quick decision.

"Sounds good," was all that John said, digging his elbow into Simon's ribs before he could add anything sarcastic, "thanks."

The group donned camouflage outfits before heading to their boat in the harbour, and loaded it up and squeezing themselves and Dilock in.

When they arrived at the launch, "Whoever sold you this boat, ripped you off," was all he said, padding his shoes in the water at his feet.

John started them off in the opposite direction to the island, to avoid suspicion, should anyone be watching the harbour. They timed the patrol boat circling the island and found it took twenty minutes at night. It was faster during the day, but there were several sandbanks on the far side that required careful navigation, especially when travelling at night.

Then, having built up some speed, they cut the motor and drifted towards the island, around the back side, using only their night vision goggles to see. The river was calm, and a new moon hovered darkly in the night sky, allowing a stealth approach and giving them a tactical advantage.

Once out of sight of the patrol, they paddled quickly to shore under a small overhang of trees; the only sheltered area on the facing side of the island, the trees providing concealment from casual observation. The imminent return of the patrol motivated them to throw themselves over the side of the boat, with only the equipment they needed. John helped the others off, but the rest of the group were surprised when Isabella disembarked too.

John looked at her with a question in his eyes, "Where do you think you are going?" John whispered, his voice more worried than stern.

"I need to get some field experience, and you might need my computer skills to help shut down the security systems." Her tone was defiant, but with a note of reluctance.

"This is not a picnic Isabella; these guys won't hesitate to kill you if you are a threat to them. The least that will happen is enslavement," John trying to dissuade her, despite her resolve.

John stepped forward and held her by the shoulder, "you sure?"

She looked at him, bit her lip but nodded. He smiled, "ok, but stay close." She nodded gratefully.

Dilock powered off quickly, and was well away from the island before the patrol boat came back into view. The team took cover behind the trees and waited to see if any alarm was raised. They all had low powered night vision goggles on, so the dark of night was actually quite bright, allowing them to see sufficiently to move around with ease.

The patrol boat chugged past with a seemingly empty deck, and Isabella whispered confirmation that there was no increase in comms traffic from ship to shore. All looked quiet.

The overgrown trees were leaf heavy and large branched, seemingly deliberately grown to increase the foliage density and making it difficult to push through. However, they had spotted a partially concealed, but reasonably well worn, trail moving off towards the oil tower. The intruders proceeded down the short trail, single file; keeping a lookout for wires, cameras, and patrols. They may not be commandoes, but they had some inkling on the potential threats they might face.

After five minutes, John raised a fist to indicate they should all stop, turning towards them slightly and the group shuffled up slowly to his position.

"We've reached the gate," he pointed just over his shoulder to a small metallic post sticking out of the ground beside a fence. "There is a code pad and a security video camera. No actual guard. No wait," he spotted a shadow just coming around a corner, fifty feet from the gate; "a one guard dog patrol," he whispered.

The compound they had reached was about fifty meters square, attached to a second compound twice as large again. Another compound lay behind them, but the oil tower there was dark, although Jack found he had to continue to avert his gaze from the central tower, despite using the goggles. The others saw only the powerful spotlights shining from the corners of the compound, into the buildings and containers. Fortunately, the lights were arrayed inwards, allowing the group to get within arm's length of the security keypad without having to worry about the camera. However, there was another much more significant problem that became apparent as they got nearer.

On the gate, a familiar black and yellow sign warned "Danger! Electric Fence! 50,000 volts. Danger of Death". Oh great, John groaned inwardly.

"Any ideas on how we can by-pass that?" John muttered into his headset.

"Well," started Simon "I could jury rig the keypad,"

"And the guards would see you and alert the entire compound," interrupted John.

Charlene gave the camera the once over, analysing the way it was set up. "We need to take a picture from the same angle as the camera, then pin it in place, so that the image covers our breaking in," the others turning to look at her. She shrugged. "I've been observed by cameras all my life. You get to understand how to work around them."

Jack nodded "I can get up there and do it."

"How, without being spotted?" asked Simon, just as Jack started to fade from view, startling the others around him.

"Oh. Ok, yes, that would do it, wouldn't it?" Jack reappeared.

"How long can you maintain that?" asked John and Helena simultaneously.

He shrugged, "It's a bit of a strain, so perhaps a few minutes; but long enough to get the job done."

"And if you can do that I can probably do this," said Helena as she produced her wand that, with a quietly whispered word, became a large iron bound oak staff," and this," at which point, she started to hover just above the path, making the others gawp in astonishment.

John shook his head, trying to come to grips with the demonstrations, thinking for a few seconds, thinking careful of how to bypass the gate in the safest manner.

"Ok, so Helena takes Jack up behind the camera, and he uses his trick to take a picture without getting in the shot. He then secures the new image in front of the camera, allowing us to work on the keypad; between the guard's rounds. Isabella and Simon should be able to get us past the keypad and close it after us; setting it up so that we can get out fast if we need to," John laid out the initial plan of action.

"Then we try and find a way into the control centre, disable the signal and call in the cavalry," added Charlene.

"We'll wait for the guard to round the corner, then go," finished John. They all nodded and waited quietly for the guard to finish his round.

The warm, almost humid, atmosphere of the spring night, was added to by a miasma of anticipation, trepidation, and adrenaline. The guard walked around with a large German Sheppard, big even for the pure breed. Given the smell of the group close by, Charlene was amazed that the dog did not detect them; although there was a small breeze blowing from the north-west animating the trees.

"He takes about ten minutes for a full sweep," said John, having measured the time from his first sighting, "meaning we have about seven clear minutes for the two phases. Let's move."

Helena took off and hovered near Jack, who grabbed the staff and nodded to her. The pair flew up, as quickly as they dared, manoeuvring above and behind the camera but, not high enough to be seen from the other compound due to the obscuring buildings.

Jack whipped out his camera, flashing a quick, brilliant, picture and praying silently, to his ancestors, that the guards were not paying too close attention to the night sky.

In the guards' control room, the camera's flash was not actually noticed at all, as the two operators starred at their cards; desperately trying to supplement their meagre wages with each-others'. Other cameras showed rooms full of equipment, including a laboratory that looked remarkably like A.G.E.'s. but the team's luck held.

Jack tapped the picture to a metal rod, placing it in front of the security camera, then signalled Helena to land them next to the others, which they did lightly, both with a slight grin on their faces.

"That was fun," was all the Jack whispered, as Simon and Isabella advanced to deal with the keypad.

"Looks like a straightforward electronic pad, with an RS232 connector," observed Simon, almost conversationally to Isabella, "so feeding to a standalone computer. That one's for you. Just block it, so their board shows the gate closed.

I'll pop the actually electro-mechanical mechanism." Isabella nodded not really needing the advice but carrying out the work anyway.

"Two minutes," counted John.

"Already done," replied Simon, as they returned to the tree line.

A minute later, the guard rounded the corner with the dog, which remained calm, just as the team needed it to be.

The patrol seemed entirely oblivious to the fact that six intruders were concealed not twenty yards from them. The group held their breath, and waited in frightened stillness, as the guard completed a quick loop of the smaller compound, before moving back into the main one.

As he disappeared for the third time, the group rushed forward through the gate, to reach the port-a-cabins in the compound quickly, flashing to the first cabin door, jimmying it and scurrying in en-mass.

There was little in the shadow-filled cabin outlined by the compounds light filtering through semi-clean windows, except the mining equipment expected for an oil-well. The question was, however, if the equipment was here, what was actually going on down in the well? The documents left carelessly on the desks were all well out of date, the last oil shipment being marked down as being weeks ago.

As they pondered that, they heard the guard approaching again, causing them to duck down, concealing themselves, in the event the guard looked in, however, his footsteps continued past the container, between them and the gate. The team remained frozen in place until the steps came from the other side of the prefab. two minutes later, carrying on past the cabin; the dog snuffling close, but apparently not detecting their scents. As the pair moved on, the group slunk out the other side of the cabin and sloped towards the main compound.

The sky started to get darker, with the few clouds hiding the bright stars above. The air in the compound began to feel closer, as the team skittered around looking for places of concealment between the compounds. Jack found a large space under the drilling tower, where he noted there was no actual sound of drilling, but instead heavy mechanical throbbing from below; the repetitive cycling of heavy-duty pumps.

As the guard passed by them again, the dog paused, looking in their direction, then carried on. They all breathed a sigh of relief, it was apparently too dark for it to see them, their camouflage probably also helping.

They frittered and scuttled into the main compound, but as they started in, the sound of a vehicle entering the compound came from the other side of it. The hidden team hesitated and watched from where they were, trying to see what was happening, as a large white van pulled up in the centre of the open yard area compound buildings.

Three people in handcuffs and other restraints were bundled out of van's side by two burly security guards; the team could not see who they were but, it was fairly evident that they would need help once the team entered the control centre.

They could not see where the three were taken from where they were, but shortly after the van left the site, just as the security guard returned on his next round. The group had to wait another eight minutes before they could investigate the inner compound and find a way into what they suspected was the enemy base.

The guard strode within inches of Jack but failed to see the illusionist and his ability either affected the dog's ability to smell him too, or the stink of the all-pervasive oil was masking their scent.

As the guard disappeared again, the whole group bolted forward into the central area. Unfortunately, as Jack rounded the corner of the first building, the magician failed to notice a pile of matt black metallic cans stacked against the wall and clipped them, causing them to collapse on top of him. He was forced to tumble left, rolling across the way, into the shadows created by a small standing tank there to avoid detection. The others scattered, around the corner of the building to hide in some haphazardly piled crates.

Barely seconds later, the guard came at a run, proceeded by the straining dog. He had his flashlight out and used it to scan the area, from the corner of the compound. He regarded the cans and ordered the dog to check them. The dog started forward only to sniff them and yelp; backing away rapidly. The guard cursed, taking a closer look at the cans. He swore, then laughed out loud, "cleaning fluid eh? No wonder you don't want to go near it." He stood there for a second glancing around, then started forward again.

John started to draw his stun gun, but Isabella rested a restraining hand lightly on his, slowly pushing it back in the holster. The guard stopped in the centre of the courtyard and scanned the building next to them, then finally turned back; pushing the cans to one side and resuming his interrupted lap of the other compound.

As he resumed his rounds again, Jack whispered to the others that they should investigate the other building, spotting another keypad there. Simon went straight to it and activated it, waiting for the others but starting as Charlene walked straight past him, went inside and, beckoned them immediately in, once she was in.

This was the notional control room for the oil drilling operation and should have contained several oil workers, charge hands, equipment and lots of noise, accompanied by orders being issued about whatever they were doing. Instead, there were a group of six large pumps and a small bank of equipment monitors. For the most part, the pumps and associated pipes were leading off landward; however, some of the equipment had clading that led straight down. They could sabotage the equipment quickly enough, but without knowing what they were doing, it might be wasted effort or even worse dangerous to the local population. No; they needed more information and some inkling as to the best course of action.

"Let's check the other buildings," muttered Helena.

"We'll find 'em." John tried to keep the mood optimistic. "There is a large door on the other side of the compound. I spotted it while we were waiting for the guard to leave; we'll try that next."

After a few minutes, they crossed the courtyard and examined the door.

It was almost ten feet high and solid metal, with a small catch securing it. Simon started to reach for crowbar from his equipment bag, to help open the door, then frowned. Instead, he pushed the door gently, its heavy section swinging in, on a smooth and well-balanced hinge. A two-day-old kitten could have opened the door, with a mew; his frown deepened.

"I'm getting a strange chill down my spine," Jack informed the others, as they entered a deserted, barn-sized, area. Although there was sound in here, it was produced from speakers all around the room, reverberating around the empty space, making it seem even louder. At the centre of the area was a metallic, circular platform, bordering a small podium, with a raised keypad, at hand level.

"Looks like we go down," John said drawing his sidearm.

"Yup. Looks like we do indeed go down," reiterated Simon.

"Not sure what we are going to find down there, so we best get as ready as we can before we go," John warned the others.

"Perhaps, but I'll keep the jammer in my pack so that it's not obvious," cautioned Simon.

Jack drew his club, and Helena kept tight hold of her staff. The others looked at each other and nodded. Charlene clutched her whip, not unfurling it, but holding onto it more for comfort.

When everyone indicated they were ready, Simon triggered the keypad and, with a loud, subterranean, whine of motors, the whole platform started descending.

It appeared that the Platform was one huge hydraulic ram and its descent was excruciatingly slow. The light above started to fade and below they could see a dim, blue, light, replacing it, coming up the deep shaft, through the gap between the platform and the precisely cut rock, which looked remarkably like the smooth tunnel from the underground.

After about thirty feet, the shaft gave way to the ceiling of a vast cavern, its' concrete re-enforced walls, supporting the underlying clay, covered in long thick metallic conduits and, transparent, liquid transport, pipes. A multitude of tubes, threaded through the walls at various points.

"Well that explains the drilling equipment, I suppose," whispered Isabella.

At one end of the cavern, there was a wide, circular, platform next to a shaft of pure, pale blue, light, flanked by a control console and a sizable bank of equipment that thrummed with the now familiar energy. At the other end, was an arc way into an adjacent cavern. The thing that surprised the group was that the whole area was empty; not a single person, robot or device moved in the entire cavern.

"My child is getting stronger," muttered Jack, registering his unease again.

"Trap then?" asked Charlene and saw John's emphatic nod in response.

"Well let's go spring the trap; everyone keep your eyes open. Simon, you know what to do, the rest of us will check out the rest of the complex." As the lift stopped, the group spread out.

Simon started visually scanning the cavern, for a place to conceal his jammer; so that it would take determined searching to locate the device. Once he'd found a likely spot, he tapped into the caverns power system, using an induction loop around a power conduit, to supply the mini jammer and ensure that its counter signal would be of sufficient amplitude to cause maximum disruption. As he continued his work, the others moved into the other room, switching off their night vision goggles as the light went from pale blue to brilliant white. The door arch, a generous ten feet wide, accessed a room that looked more familiar than the team, and Charlene in particular, thought coincidental.

It was a good fifty meters in diameter, with computer screens and various medical equipment positioned all the way around the area. It was almost an exact duplicate of one of the labs at A.G.E., except for the large central structure.

What drew all of their attention, was that central column, containing several man-sized cylinders, covered in a thin layer of frosting, displaying immobile, humanoid silhouettes. Could these be cryogenic freezers?

"I'll see if I can hack into their systems to try and find us another way out of here," Isabella informed John, slipping off to the left and grabbing a terminal, immediately tapping furiously on the consoles to break into the system. After that initial success, however, the battle was joined with the security protocols, and her swearing started. It was the first time that the team had heard her use that kind of language, and even John blanched at the phrases she was spewing.

The remaining four carried on, Charlene moving closer to one of the tubes, curious as to their contents. Clearing a patch of ice-water from in front of the face of the figure inside she did a double take. The visage was not only familiar, it was Dr. Trafford, except it was crisscrossed with a strange, almost delicate, metallic mesh; the face was mostly covered, but the mouth was free, and the lips moved slowly in a repeating message; "it hurts, it hurts. Help me." Over and over, he mouthed the same thing, before Charlene final unfroze and ripped the tube open.

"Charlene?" Simon whispered a protest loudly, forgetting his usual formality.

"Fa …, Dr. Trafford, what is it? What have they done to you?" she tried to get through to the person under the metal structure.

"Help me," was all he could manage to vocalise.

"Right on it, Dr!" She gestured to the others to have a look around. "I'll see if I can find a way to remove this, while you see what else you can find out about this place."

John and Jack started checking the cupboards and other furniture around the lab.

The metallic structure looked familiar to Charlene, like the nano-tubes from her own Nanites. Had they used her work to do this? This metallic mesh was a strange use for her work, but the structures strongly resembled those nano-tubes; the same lines, linkages, and building pattern. Another figure in an adjoining tube looked familiar too, so she wiped the surface of the tube and recognised the head of the A.G.E. facility, Dr. Matthew Rampton. His face was covered entirely in metal threads and, if she read the vital sign monitors on the tube, he was not doing too well. Well, if it was some form of her Nanites that were infesting these men, and causing the damage, then she should be able to take control of them and use them to repair that damage they had done to their hosts. She needed to get to one of the terminals, get access to the Nanites' command system and re-task the Nanites.

As she moved over to the computer screens, she spotted some nano-injectors; probably the ones used to infect her colleges. She'd used the same kind in her lab's cleanroom many times, although this area was not a clean area at all.

She managed to gain access to the computer, possibly a little too easily given Isabella's continuing battle and started to investigate the research that needed doing.

Several shocks hit her all at once. Firstly, it seemed that they were receiving not just intelligence from A.G.E., but intelligence about several other projects and whole programs, and not just haphazardly, but at regular intervals. Finally, and here was the biggy, the information included the most recent activities and discoveries, from before she left for the conference. There must be a mole, agent or spy in the company; the word traitor also came to mind.

As Charlene read the files, it became apparent that the enemy was doing work on mind control. Their Nanites, a slightly modified version of her own were designed to seek out the areas of the brain responsible for the higher brain functions, in the frontal lobe, and circumvent them; in effect redirecting the control chemicals, as her Nanites diverted cancer cell growth. At the same time, they created a Nano-receiver, to receive the signal that the team had detected, in effect, putting the enemy in control of the person.

They were, however, having problems. Their control of the Nanites was imperfect and currently, the Nanites over-whelmed the central cortex and either paralysed the person or killed them outright. Charlene now saw displayed the contents of a third tube, where the person therein had his hands to his face. He appeared to have been in the process of ripping the filaments from his head as he'd died, resulting in his hands now having invasive filaments threaded through them, binding his hands to his cheeks in a grisly tableaux-of-death.

She had to find the commands and structures they had used, replace them with ones that worked, and repair the mess the imbeciles had made of her work. She thought back to her own work, trying a pattern-matching algorithm for the control commands and recalling her detailed knowledge of brain chemistry to formulate a plan; not only to repair the damage and overcome the mind control but also to protect the person from future exposure to such technology and machinations.

She soon found the files on their work, displayed on multiple screens around the science station. The sheer scale of the results was staggering. Not dozens or hundreds of test subjects, but thousands; and so many died just to get them this far; even with the help of her work. The brain was not something to mess with, but it seemed that they had no thought of losses or partial successes; they were only interested in the rapid completion of their work, and getting the end product as fast as possible, heedless of the human suffering inflicted in the process.

She'd dwell on that later, for now, she had two patients that were, it seemed from the results, in the mid-stages of the procedure; and they desperately needed her help. She began running through her simulation programs on her tablet, testing possible solutions without actually using Nanites on her patients, saving time and potential problems, something the enemy had either failed to try or, more likely, just never considered.

She muttered to herself, as she began to get a feeling in the back of her neck like she was being watched. She looked around but could see no-one besides the team there, but the feeling persisted even as she continued to work to find a solution to the problem.

Meanwhile, Jack and John had finished their search, keeping an eye out for anything unusual, or any potential exit in the meantime. They too had that feeling of being observed, and both of them had frowns on their faces, accompanied by the expression of missing something important, until John suddenly twigged, asking aloud, "if these three were the people we saw coming in here; where are the guards that brought them?" He swung around and, after covering the whole room again, confirmed what he'd failed to see; a visible exit.

"Something we missed, or a concealed exit?" Offered Jack. Then he guessed what John was about to say, just as he said it.

"Or? They are still here, hidden," offered John, with his gun coming out, and slipped the safety off.

Jack now looked around again, using his unique sight, "nothing that I can see."

John huffed, "That's what's worrying me. We have no idea of their real capabilities," his frown deepened, then he suddenly became totally relaxed. The kind of studied relaxation of a gunslinger getting ready to draw, "ah well. No use really worrying about it. Just stay alert".

In the meantime, Isabella had managed to hack into the power control systems of the base, setting up a remote access override switch in the control sub-routines, so that she could control them, instead of the enemy, at any given moment. It was hard work, as the systems were using a language she was unfamiliar with; part grammatical, part numerical and part hieroglyphic. Their number system translated to a duo-octal form, in a strangely distorted way. Also, the algorithms were incredibly well protected; she'd used most of the tricks she'd learned trawling the internet, just to get through the initial security protocols. After that it had become harder still; the system seemed to have an active defence routine, that adapted to her attack style and it was getting harder to fool the darn thing to gain additional access levels.

Helena looked around the room and sensed that something was wrong. Like the others, she knew they had walked into a trap but, the feeling was growing that they were not alone here; but if they were not, where was the enemy. They were so vulnerable here, so ignorant of what was going on really and who they were up against.

Simon had managed to open up one of the power conduits and, using the equipment from his spares, had started to attach the power syphon to the casing of the internal power lines. He'd been feeling strange since they had entered the cave; the blue light had made him feel more awake than he usually did; more alive and energised than he'd ever felt. Also, he'd had a few sparks of, what he thought was, electricity discharging from him into the conduit, even though he was thoroughly grounded. He had visions of being successful, posthumously, with all this power buzzing around.

Charlene was at the terminal for about five minutes when she finally hit on a solution that cleared the alien Nanites and restored the person's control. She immediately snatched up a Nano-injector, pressed it against her wrist and drew out about a half vial full of blood; took the bottle and snapped it into a centrifuge, spinning out the red cells then injecting the remainder into a control tube. There, she downloaded the new control program into the Nanites, using an induction program feed and recombined the solution with a pseudo-plasma; to enable rapid absorption of the solution into the host's system. The real test, however, was using it on the subjects that the enemy had used.

"Got it!" she yelled, rushing to Dr. Rampton's, whose vital signs were falling rapidly.

"This should do it. If not, we'll know that it cannot be reversed." Her hand was unsteady, but then, it was a man's life in her hand, and it had been about as rushed a study as she'd ever done; it might cure him, but it might also just kill him. On the other hand, it was almost inevitable that if she did not, he would be dead within another few minutes.

As she pushed the injector to his neck, she gave herself over to her fate, feeling a strange sensation go straight through her spine as she did so. The hiss of the injector announced the delivery of the Nanites; his salvation, or execution.

After a few seconds, he started to convulse, and the monitors on the tube all started to go red. This was not necessarily bad yet, and Charlene's eyes went to his, currently hidden by metallic filaments, praying that they opened. If they did, she'd won her first battle. Seconds passed so slowly, then his eyes started to twitch, finally fluttering open, his mouth beginning to move.

"Dr. Klerk?" whispered Dr. Rampton; pain spasming through him.

"Easy there, you're going through a transition. Try to stay perfectly still until the treatment takes full effect." She understood his confusion, but could not help him recover any faster, nor ease his tortuous agony. Her own relief was reflected in his eyes.

She moved to her old friend and mentor and gave him a similar dose. One success did not prove a product, but two would say that initially anyway, it was safe. It would save their lives and get them free; the important thing at the moment.

Once the serum had started to take effect, Dr. Trafford tried to talk.

"They came for me as I arrived at the conference. Took me to one of their camps. After that, I don't remember much." His face started to clear of threads; the enemy's alien technology no match for Charlene's advanced Nanites and her better understanding of human physiology.

"Who came for you, Dr. Trafford?" She leaned forward.

"The Ghe'Dar did, Dr. Klerk," came a strangely familiar voice from behind her; turning around she understood why.

There stood Niles Wallice, C.E.O. of A.B.C, having appeared from nowhere; dressed in a sharp business suit, his voice smooth and relaxed. A man in control of the situation.

Beside him, someone fitting the description of Jack's assailant lurked, along with three uniformed security guards carrying automatic weapons.

John, Helena, and Jack put their hands up, slowly, so that the armed men were in no doubt that they were not going to do anything stupid, while Isabella tapped away at the console, behind a partition and a set of monitors, un-noticed by the new arrivals.

"You see, Dr. Klerk, they simply had to have your research to complete their mind control system," he pointed to the huge central column in the middle of the room, "to let them advance their grand scheme." He looked across at her terminal, "thank you for your help; it will make things so much easier." He saved the work and secured the data. "As you may have discovered, we have changed the primary function of your Nanites; that, by the way, offered them, and me, a neater and more efficient option to their initial rather brutal invasion plan of the Earth," he took a pace closer to the guards.

"As you may have gathered, the Ghe'Dar is not a gentle race of aliens,. Dr. Klerk; they are one of the top predators of the galaxy, as I understand it, and they have needs." He paced a little as he talked, betraying a slight uncertainty, "when I first met them, they demonstrated themselves to be too powerful to resist; so, I offered my services, for a small commission, to aid them to initiate their plan. They already have control of significant areas of the world, either using agents like Blavnic here," he hooked a thumb at the figure, with the hat and face mask, next to him, "controlled humans, or indirectly using the services of people and groups willing to overthrow their current government. Of course, the groups have no idea that they will be nothing more than cattle, for their new masters, but then they hardly care about that now do they," he smiled at the irony.

"Your cure will aid us in fixing the unpredictability of the controlling Nanites and allow much more complete control. Thank you!" he added grining at her. John saw the look of pure hatred that Charlene directed at the collaborator; he did not envy that man if she laid her hands on him.

"You won't be able to control it properly, you know; it's not designed for your purposes." She was desperately trying to persuade them not to do this. They were corrupting her entire life's work. "You cannot do this!" She shouted at him.

"I'm sorry, Dr. Klerk, but it was help the Ghe'Dar, or die; with the rest of the company bosses. I'm sure you understand."

Charlene ground her teeth. If she could get close enough, she'd inject her cure right where it would do the least good.

"Enough!" snapped Blavnic, in a guttural, slightly muffled, hiss.

"I'm sorry, I do witter on. Surrender and you will die quickly; resist and, well, let's just say that you will have the first-hand experience of the Ghe'Dars', less savoury, experimental techniques. They are, really, quite the experts on inflicting pain and suffering, and not the least bit merciful. It is for the best, you know; besides, you have no choice really."

Jack looked at John and kind of shrugged his shoulders; what else can they do?

Charlene was still clutching her Nano-injector and had started to inch towards one of the guards when the lights went out. Isabella had managed to get to the lighting circuit and shut it down.

The team suddenly erupted into action, each of them slamming down their night vision goggles, flicking them on and striking. John levelled his gun at the nearest guard, pumped three bullets into him and saw him dropped like a stone. Jack decided that his club was not really a proper weapon for a gunfight and instead grabbed a towel from the bench next to him; circling quietly around the back of the enemy, targeting their greatest threat, the Ghe'Dar agent Blavnic.

Hit by a surge of Adrenaline, Charlene, felt something strange happening to her skin. As had happened on the spaceship, her skin rippled and turned metallic in texture. She slopped towards the guard nearest her and slammed the Nano-injector onto his ankle. The effect was not what she expected, as the guard froze for a second, then started to grip his head and tremble violently in a similar fashion to the people in the cryo-tubes.

"The guards are controlled," she yelled out hoping that the sheer volume would protect her from location by the attackers.

Inevitably, the invaders responded. One of the guards tried his luck and sprayed the room with a magazine of bullets. Unfortunately, disoriented in the dark, he caught one of the other luckless guards, who collapsed in a heap. He also clipped the Ghe'Dar agent the bullet ricocheting off some form of shield around the creature, who then faded from view. It seemed it had some sort of invisibility field; which explained how they had remained undetected for so long inside the base. The accidental hit did not go down well with the Ghe'Dar; who lashed out with an attack of its own; a sizzling bolt of energy, aimed at the misguided guard. The bright bolt of energy momentarily light-up the room, revealing where both sides were, except for Jack who could not be seen at all. The bolt struck the guard who spasmed for a few seconds, before collapsing to the floor; unconscious or dead. The enemy was three down already. The team had hope now, but they still need to affect their escape.

Simon had almost completed his work when he heard the battle commence. He reached inactivate the device and started to move to the sounds of the battle when, with a loud whine, the lift began ascending. Uh oh, it was being recalled to allow others to come down, closing the trap. At the moment he could not do anything, other than conceal his work, as the comms were down; probably because of the power coming from the blue shaft of light.

"We've company coming," came the yell down the corridor, from Simon.

They needed to finish this quickly. Helena had witnessed the Ghe'Dar agent blast the guard, and, in reply, she levelled the crystal-topped end of her staff at the masked being, unleashing a cone of blazing white fire that bathed it in flickering white flames, forcing it to emit a muffled high pitch whistle of pain and anguish.

Jack was enough to see that the fire seemed to sear straight through the force field.

The second Helena's blast faded, Jack struck. He leapt directly behind the figure, whipped the towel over the creature's head and tied a formidable knot in it. He could feel the power and strength in the being, but in effect, he'd now blinded their primary opponent, except, despite the impairment, the enemy still managed to home in on its attackers, with uncanny accuracy. Firstly, it decided to deal with the blast from the powered human before it.

John fired at the final standing human enemy, Niles Wallice. Two shots rang out as one; John did not miss, but neither did Wallice. Wallice somehow managed to clip John, ricochet off a pillar, hitting the Ghe'Dar as well, the bullet bouncing off its surrounding force field. John felt the impact of Wallice's bullet, but even as he did, he saw Blavnik turn and blast the unfortunate human traitor, before performing an athletic dive to avoid the deflected blast, which struck a glancing blow to his arm; his leap saved him from taking the full brunt of it. Wallice was not so lucky as Blavnic hit him directly in the chest. Wallice's last sight was Blavnic ripping the towel from his head, and lashing John with its power again. John's acrobats saved him again from getting incinerated, but he was tiring and feeling distinctly the worse for wear now.

Isabella, seeing the chaos around her, decided to make a run for it, sprinting for the other room, only to see Simon looking up at the descending lift. He glanced at her a little helplessly as she entered, but she instead of freezing, she instinctively ran to the control panels.

"Do any of these control the lift?" she looked at him for guidance.

"No; the keypad is the control, and that's on the lift itself," he glanced at it, feeling like he could explode; remembering the laser attack at the conference, the figure raising its figure and blasting Jack. He frowned. Was that what he was feeling? No time to try anything else. Isabella was desperately punching the buttons on the console, in various sequences, in a vain effort to try and stop the lift.

Simon regarded the descending platform, eight figures, all armed with machine guns, on it. He raised his left arm as they came in line with him, and kind of pushed the strange feeling down his arm.

He was a little unprepared for the result, as a thick bolt of lightning shot across the room and connected the front line of guards in a single arc of electricity. The figures did not precisely react the way that he would have expected either. They did not jerk around, or drop their guns or even scream. Instead, they gurgled in place, convulsively gripped their weapons tighter, kneeling, then finally, just curling up and dying.

Isabella was astonished, not only at Simon's action but at the sheer power he'd displayed. He raised his other arm and the second row was dropped by another, slightly shorter, jolt of electricity. All the guards on the platform lay either dead or unconscious as it stopped at the floor level.

Simon's face showed more astonishment at the effect than horror at having just killed eight people. Isabella now regarded him with horrified eyes. The look he returned was one of cold indifference, both to her implied accusation and to the fate of the guards, controlled or not.

Having seen John injured, Charlene ran to the tubes and released the two captives from their restraints. "Get to the entrance; that way. Try to stay low and don't get hit by any of the energy flying around; I doubt you'd survive it for a second." The two men nodded at the golden figure before them, and frantically zigzagged, at desk level, towards the indicated exit.

The Ghe'Dar's true face was now exposed to the horrified combatants; looking bulbously squid-like, but with six, black-veined, blood red, eyes and a fearsome, twitching, saw-toothed mouth, splitting the short tentacles vertically into two writhing clusters. It finally locked on to Helena and blasted her with energy; or tried to. It seemed she'd a surprise for the creature as well. As it fired, she raised her staff before her, and the creature's energy impacted an impenetrable barrier.

She staggered as it hit but gritted her teeth in the effort and reached out to John, who was recovering from his encounter with that energy.

Charlene glimpsed one of the guard's guns nearby on the floor and twisted to grab it; not seeing, but feeling, Blavnic's rushing approach behind her. It did not blast her with energy, but instead, smashed its' large, armoured, appendage into her flank. Her dermal armour saved her from broken ribs; but the force lifted her physically, sending her flying across the room to land next to the opposite wall. She twisted acrobatically but still landed with a thud, making her decision to execute the better part of valour for her.

Rolling to one side, she leapt to her feet and sprinted towards the exit, her skin suddenly becoming normal. She'd no way to defend herself and no training in the weapons she had, well ones that would affect that thing anyway. Still, she had the gun now; perhaps John could teach her how to use it, or something like it, sometime. She had actually done more good with the injector and, honestly, the noise of firearms would put her off using them anyway.

"We need to get out," said John seeing Charlene's departure; Helena agreed, and the two followed the prisoners in running for it. Jack appeared in parallel to them. "We almost had him, it, whatever," he grumbled.

"Yeah. Maybe," grunted John, as the team disappeared out of view of the lab. "But did it think the same thing, I wonder? We simply don't know how tough those things are," he clutched his ribs. "He had energy weapons, force fields and a cloaking device of some kind. Who's to say what else he could do and you can bet, now that we're out of there, he is now calling in re-enforcements, informing his superiors and making sure that we don't escape."

"How do you know that?" asked Helena curiously. She reached out and guided him into the main room, to see the carnage on the elevator, and a hole in the air, showing a scene of blue sky and trees, starting to form on the platform, next to Isabella.

"Because I recognise a scout's behaviour when I see one, and, it's what I would do in its place. Besides its just common sense, and it's best to assume they are least that intelligent, and potentially a lot more so, than us."

"I think this is an exit of some kind, a transport portal, to somewhere else; the console says it's drifting a little, but anywhere is safer than here, at the moment." The others looked at him, saw the shadow of the Ghe'Dar moving down the corridor towards them and nodded. One by one they entered the blazing energy of the portal."

Blavnic saw the humans entering the portal, running to the controls and checking the destination, just seeing the first digit as the whole panel went blank. It tried to reactivate the portal, but to no avail, the humans had sabotaged it. Clever, for such a limited species. They must have uploaded a virus, or worm, of some kind to erase the control protocols; at least that's what it would have done. It'd download the remote security logs later and analyse their methods of disabling the protocols, then transmit them to the Motherships for neutralisation.

Having followed security protocol, it moved on to transmit his security report to the fleet, warning all outposts that there were some beings of power on this planet. Blavnic transmitted the estimation of their potential threat level; higher than expected on this rather primitive planet, but that it was easily containable. Still, they had managed to cause significant injury, incapacitated several guards and somehow managed to locally jam the mind control signal.

The technicians were recalled to locate the problem and get the equipment running again. Ah well, there were always plenty more humans they could use.

The computer indicated that some test subjects were now no longer detectable by the Ghe'Dar control program, meaning that they were now free to act on any knowledge they had of the Ghe'Dar, although Blavnic doubted they could cause little true damage to the Ghe'Dars' plans now. The Ghe'Dar third fleet was almost ready to invade; the scout force obtaining the scientist had only been needed to be thorough, eliminating the last obstacle to assuming complete control.

What could such a small group of minor beings possibly do against a Ghe'Dar fleet that controlled the critical people in virtually every major population centre on the planet?

Still, there was no point in risking even such minor interference. A couple of buttons were punched, indicating that its' task was complete and that the invasion could proceed immediately. In effect, Blavnic began tolling the planet's death knell.

CHAPTER 8

REBIRTH

Entering the portal gifted each escapee a different experience.

The two guinea pigs, Dr. Trafford and Dr. Rampton, experienced a disturbing few seconds as the Nanites, already adapted to this environment, formed a protective cocoon shielding the traumatised men from any harmful effects. They landed in a field of browning stubble, on top of a stack of hay bales.

For Isabella, who also had never been through a portal before, the experience was more like a psychedelic rollercoaster ride, lasting the same few seconds and ending in her flying through the air and landing, with a bone-jarring thud, in a rather strange orientation, about ten feet up a scrub tree. Struggling to decide which way was up, she realised that her leg was wedged in the fork, of a branch, above her head that dangled next to another, wedging her shoulder at forty-five degrees to the rest of her body. In short, she was seriously stuck in the tree.

Helena's transition was silent and calm. She drifted through the portal and floated gently down on the other side, to land on the other side of a hedge from the two civilian scientists.

John found his transition more like a bullet ride through the portal with a rush of dislocated images, most disturbing ones, from his police career. It catapulted him through a haystack, causing him to leave a long thin furrow in the grass, as he ploughed to a stop.

Simon almost tumbled out of the portal at zero speed. He fell onto a road and saw the others dropping, seemingly from thin air, out of the portal. Each came from different locations mid-air, following a line, from first to last, back to where a vehicle of some kind had crashed. Only Jack and Charlene had not emerged as he stood up, brushing himself off and picking his equipment pack.

Jack's experience was distinctly different from the others. As he moved through the portal, he seemed to see his family's history going back in time towards his ancestors; almost like a family portrait gallery. He saw his father's face, getting progressively younger, until it finally faded, changing into his grandfather's beginning a series of others both male and female, ancestors he could never have known. Each face spoke to him non-verbally; but he understood their message as if he was reading it from a book, "take our power, and use it wisely. We will fight for our lands against these new invaders, as we did in ages past. They will not succeed."

Unfortunately, as he tried to answer that implicit call to arms, he dropped like a stone out of the portal, and landed on a branch, in the same copse as Helena. She was just climbing out of the bush she'd arrived in, took one look at him, smirking ruefully.

Charlene stepped into the portal expecting to land on the other side immediately, however, as the field took effect, she started to hear a strange whining sound, inside her head and surrounding her. All motion seemed to stop, and the others faded from view, as her vision become blurred. Then the whole vortex turned white.

"Greetings," said a distinctly familiar voice. Charlene 'turned' to see an exact duplicate of herself some distance away smiling at her. Charlene opened her mouth but found she could not speak.

"Don't try to talk here, it's not real, as you define the term, or should I say, as we define the term." The other began shifted her form to that of herself with Golden skin. "I am you, or rather another you. Call me a Quantum Duplicate, if you like." She was exactly the same, but the aura of power she projected was phenomenal. Even if this was not real, the energy Charlene sensed was awesome in magnitude; in fact, it dwarfed the portal's power, like a giant redwood dwarfed a seedling.

"I cannot stay long. This trick takes up a fantastic amount of power, and my Simon is burning out several power stations to make it possible at all." She raised her arm and, tattooed, on it was the three-headed creature that Charlene had seen in her dreams.

"I know you have many questions, but they must all go begging. I am here to tell you what you REALLY need to know." The other looked away briefly, as if seeing something else behind her, then turned back to her other self.

"You have been, and will be, granted many powers. Needless to say, you have been gifted them for a reason." The face of the other screwed up as if trying to find the right words.

"You have a Destiny. That destiny is the most important one a human has ever been given. You don't need to save just the world, although that will be the start of it. You need to save reality itself. You must withstand the machinations of our dark mother, her allies and face their terrible master, in preparation, for the final enemy; the one I have failed to destroy and the one only you can."

She squinted a little, as though trying to pick the essential information to pass on. "Trust that people can change. Never give up. Sometimes going back can move you forward and," a distant, background, voice came, "ten seconds!"

The other started to fade, "I'm out of time. Farewell sister, for all our hopes, are with you. You must succeed, or all will be lost." As the other finally vanished she smiled, as if remembering something, "Oh and remember this above all: Trust your instincts."

The white background started to fade, but her eyes still did not to want to focus properly. She could see that she was descending into a field, near the two company men; but it was as if she were seeing it through a fuzzy, greased up, camera lens. Was she going blind? A buzzing filled her ears, and the pain increased; she was apparently having a reaction to the experience. When she finally touched down on the other side of the portal, her head was swimming, feeling like she'd been through a tumble drier. In addition, sounds started to register, but as though she was hearing them through a clogged-up grating.

They had arrived in a well-maintained grassy clearing, looking not unlike a golf course fairway; patches of smooth grass, rough, hedges, bunkers, a few shrubby hedges and the occasional water hazard within view.

There were, however, a few things in locale that did not fit the image of the peaceful and safe place that Isabella thought they might be entering. When Charlene finally got her bearings, she realised one thing almost immediately; they were not safe at all and were all in very immediate danger as the area was being patrolled in the air by strange unearthly craft and the area was enclosed by a massive forcefield.

A huge Pyramid- like structure sat in the centre of the area, walls made of a dark blue metallic-sheened material; an overlapping crystalline mosaic, strangely distorted by pulsing, rippling portal energy, magnified a million fold, flowing over the monolith.

Above it, the atmospheric distortion of a powerful energy field hanging like a canopy of boiling water; produced by four smaller pyramids, beyond the corners of the great machine. Surrounding those pyramids were constantly rotating machines that might be the Ghe'Dar's version of air defence batteries.

The team had arrived at the western side of the pyramid; spanning a road, that went north-south, where a crashed Ghe'Dar vehicle lay, looking much like an octopus; the bulb of the head being the cockpit and the arms being the landing struts of the strange contraption. Purple light pulsed dimly from a ribbed section underneath, and a peculiar, but efficiently made swivel mounted weapon protruded from the rear of the craft.

The sled, for that's what it resembled most, was apparently just settling from a recent crash; the very front of the vehicle was missing three of four feet, in its central axis. The pilot was severely injured, though still moving, while the gunner, or passenger, was motionless, seemingly out cold. Both wore strange armour, the bulbous head sporting four orb-like structures, a mouth with six small hole seals, broad shoulders connecting multi-segmented arms and a lower section that might have been a torso and legs, except that the chest and waist area seemed far too short and the legs were again multi-segmented, ending in a splayed multi-toed foot. In addition to the alien crew, there was an empty set of slightly damaged human-shaped armour. It lay powerless on the floor of the rear section.

Simon started quickly towards the sled, then noticed, between the hedges, another vehicle just landing, its engines beginning to idle. The occupants were in the process of disembarking and advancing purposefully along the road, to aid their fallen comrades and investigate the situation. In the sky, just above the treetops, other, Airsleds, circled the larger area slowly in a predetermined patrolling pattern.

It seemed, they were in the middle of, what amounted to, an enemy army camp. They needed to take cover and find out where they were in the world; if indeed they were still in their own world.

John stood up, brushing himself off, and was immediately spotted by a sled flying a little distance away. Unfortunately, it appeared, he was well within the range of the sled's rear-mounted heavy energy cannon, its gunner swinging the snub barrel around and firing in one smooth action, as the pilot applied more speed towards John. The blast narrowly missed, but still marked John's location for the advancing Ghe'Dar, who quickened their pace to a lumbering trot, while unlimbered their rifles. Their actions were not the sloth of guards; but more the focused regimentation of soldiers, showing the team they had somehow blundered into the spearhead of the invasion force.

John drew his gun and squeezed off a quick shot at the sled above him; impacting its shield and luckily, its propulsion system too, causing it to tilt mid-flight, making the occupants slide to the rear and forcing them to cling desperately onto anything to stop themselves from falling.

The invaders had been engaged.

Charlene saw her A.G.E. colleges huddling next to a nearby haystack and decided to check them over. Her medical kit was on her back, so she whipped the rucksack off, opened it and scuttled over to them, staying low.

"You ok?" She asked in a low, concerned voice.

"We're fine, thanks to you, my dear," said her mentor, with his usual warm and unconcerned banter.

"You really know how to have a coming out party, Charlene I'll give you that," said the other.

"Yeah well, all I can say is; I wish I were elsewhere." Her voice sounded so strange, grating slightly, in her own ears.

What could she do to help the others deal with these aliens? She had a gun, but did not know how to use it, besides she needed to get these two out of the way first. But How? Fighting was out of the question, as she'd had little practice with her whips certainly not enough for this, and she'd learned that her chemical knowledge was of little use without practical, weaponisation application, skills. The comms. were still a little fried, and the shield above them was probably adding to the static.

She tried to concentrate and clear her head when something appeared in her field of vision. At the bottom left of her eye-line, a cursor flashed casually, but insistently. There was no screen or monitor around, but there it was; a green cursor and a message in front of it that she'd seen so many times in the mornings when first entering her lab.

"Systems Booting." What the blazes?

Perhaps she could do something; at least, once whatever system it was coming online. It appeared her Nanites had been exceedingly busy inside her, and whatever it was they were doing was about to become active. As a scientist, she was fascinated, but as the host she was petrified. It explained so much, but the real answers would have to wait.

She wondered desperately, how long before the system was up?

Isabella was hiding in a sand bunker, trying to send a general distress message across the internet. She'd tried it as soon as she'd arrived but, to her consternation, she found all her regular connections were blocked; in fact, there were no connects available in this area, wherever it was, at all. Then, she'd had a crazy thought; perhaps she could link into the Ghe'Dar equivalent of a local data network.

Having found something she was furiously trying to hack into it, seeing if she could find out their location, what was happening and what she could do about it. In this rather, fraught, situation she'd fallen back on her computer skills as something to blot out the terror she felt. This was not how she'd imagined field work being; this was more like a war zone. At the thought she did a double take; this really **was** a war zone, the first in the battle for the earth.

Above Isabella, Helena was disentangling herself from her slightly awkward position, finally succeeding and dropping from the branch; to hover a few inches from the ground.

Nearby, Jack saw Helena floating mid-air and suddenly knew, that he could do that too. Indeed, he now felt the power of his ancestors within him; knew that, should he call forth their ability, he could do many things just by willing it. The first thing to do was try and see what was going on, so he willed himself higher than the surrounding trees and shrubs, feeling true astonishment when he felt himself slowly rise.

A quietness in his mind calmed him, letting him know that his people were with him. Honestly, the fact he was, in effect, hearing voices in his head, freaked him out, but he could scream loudly later; right now, he just accepted the situation, responding as best he could.

As he cleared the concealing foliage, he saw the situation and responded to the most immediate threat first; pointing to a sled which started to veer in Helena's direction.

Helena nodded and pointed her staff at the sled, unleashing a bolt of white fire; engulfing the vehicle, occupants and all. Their screams, high pitch burbling whistles were over almost immediately. Their craft did not fair very well either; as it started down and hit one of the AA turrets, causing it to explode, in a series of small cracks, followed by a louder flash of sparks that put it permanently out of action.

The Ghe'Dar from the landed sled moved carefully as they broke through the bushes, located their target, aimed and simultaneously blasted John. However, the bolts of blue energy missed him, as he dodged with incredible speed; faster than Charlene had ever seen anyone move. His response shocked the socks off her; afterwards, she'd see the next moments in slow motion.

John looked at the Ghe'Dar snarled, his limbs expanding both length and width wise, muscles bulging even more, and his face twisted into a fierce primal grimace. Charlene actually winced, at the pain, that the bones and joints expanding like that, must have inflicted on him. His body grew even more muscular, minimally taller and more-deadly. She could see he was denser, more highly strung and his skin taught over that tense frame.

Then he shot off; and Charlene's demeanour changed from jealous, to awe. His legs blurred as he charged at his attackers, almost immediately standing nose to nose with the squad leader, delivering a spectacular uppercut with his now clawed right hand, launching the target, armour and all, skywards.

Charlene did not follow the progress of the flying Ghe'Dar; but looked down at the other, who now took a desperate shot at John. The shot went a bit wild, but John's immediate counter-attack did not. Instead of punching the Ghe'Dar he grabbed the hapless creature and hurled it towards the force shield, causing it to rebound with such force that it lost its helmet; its body, wreathed in energy and plasma, crashing to the ground, apparently dead.

Finally, Charlene's vision and hearing began clearing, revealing strange symbols, interspaced with English words; like crazed spiders running riot across a computer screen trailing random letters in their wake, darting across her field of vision. Then, like a crazed kaleidoscope turning, the image folded in on itself and resolved itself into a desktop of icons, graphs and displays, with the real world as the wallpaper.

A list of available systems dropped down the left-hand side; Attack, Defence, Transport, Auxiliary and Internal. Most appeared in red, the subsystems labelled as offline, while the auxiliary systems reported as functional, but not fully powered. A single Defence system showed as already active, the rest indicated they were initialising.

She wondered if, like John, she could move faster; or perhaps, like Jack, she could fly? How wonderful if that were possible, the image flashing in her mind was that of herself soaring through the air; now what had prompted that? How strange.

Then, Charlene realised something else; the pain was gone. All of it; in fact, she'd never felt so good, almost euphoric; so much so that, when she saw the 'Transport' system light go green, she willed it to activate, getting ready to fly into the sky. What she did not notice, however, was the smaller red-light underneath it marked, "Guidance".

Charlene heard that low whining noise from her dream start and go up in tone for a fraction of a second, peak, and finally, experienced a slight pop; the world suddenly shifting and changing.

Almost instantaneously, she was a short distance, perhaps twenty feet or so, from where she'd been. Unfortunately, she was also a good thirty feet in the air; for all of the two-tenths of a second before she started to fall, as gravity took hold.

"Oh Shit!" was all she could say before she hit the ground chest first; she heard her ribs crack and her left ankle bones shatter, as fiery pain ripped across her battered chest and her bruised legs. Fortunately, she'd automatically shielded her head with her arms. She thought she might pass out, but she managed to remain conscious somehow.

On the display, one of the auxiliary systems suddenly lit up, reporting 'Repair systems activated', the pain almost immediately subsiding as Charlene heard bones straightening, snapping together, and skin re-knitting. Her body could heal itself?

She looked down, and, sure enough, there was a slick sheen covering the injured ankle; a film of microscopic Nanites rippling over the area, re-positioning her bones and growing her skin back to cover the wounds. The pain may have been blunted, but the sensation of bones moving back into place by themselves was not one that she would recommend experiencing; nor would she be able to describe it to any normal person.

It was beyond her wildest dreams as a scientist. Never mind cancer; with this kind of ability she could heal virtually any injury, fix deformities and; she stopped that thought. She needed to study this. The repercussions could be global, and the risks, in the wrong hands, could be catastrophic: she'd have to think this through, just as soon as they saved the world from the invaders.

Well, she could travel quickly, after a fashion, and recover from wounds, but she still had no abilities that would help her combat, let alone defeat, the Ghe'Dar. She started to think, really think. If this had been a chess game, then they were in the mid game, and she needed to plan out what was needed to get to the end game. She had battled with some clever players at chess, and she could think fast when she needed to. The odds were against them, and they needed to start to balance up those odds on the battle field. She tried moving and found that her ankle seemed ok again. Wow. That had been fast, even for a simple break. She ran towards Helena, Isabella and Jack, trusting John to keep the enemy busy at her rear, especially with the abilities he'd already demonstrated.

The strange pyramid suddenly began to rumble, the sides not only opening up but splitting and expanding; the whole building changing to resemble a vast, four-fingered, claw. A mechanical grinding and electrical buzzing filled the air, as the machine expanded, grasping the sky in its deadly grip. From each of its talons now arced dark purple energy; flowing in and around the base of the building, occasionally deigning to touch the control pylons. The air was filled with throbbing power, and a strange sense of dark anticipation filled all those seeing it; whether running towards or away from it. Above the area, there appeared a faint inky spot, like a snooker ball; occasionally impacted by the arching power, making it expand more each time.

Simon finally reached to the downed sled; noticing that the gunner, had started to recover. Its' helmet had been lost during the crash, and he could see its face for the first time. The head did not appear to have a real solid shape to it, being much like a four-eyed octopus. Where the front holes in the helmet were, six short tentacles writhed idly surrounding the mouth ringed with jagged needle-sharp teeth. The jaw could apparently open sideways, and a blood red tongue flicked around those teeth, almost subconsciously cleaning them all. It had no real neck with the body and upper tentacles starting just below the jaw.

Simon was not usually a violent man and his shocking of the guards, at the enemy base on Furzey, was still playing on his mind; but these creatures were about to invade the planet and, he'd plans of his own, that required that they did not succeed. So, he stepped up smartly to the waking Ghe'Dar and smashed it in the face, between the eyes, returning it to unconsciousness. He ignored the trickle of blood that flowed out of, what might have been, its ear gills and mouth.

He looked at the strange empty suit of armour. It was not Ghe'Dar; indeed, it was almost human, except that it looked more advanced. Could a human possibly use it? Did he really have a choice if he wanted to defeat this enemy? It looked like it might actually be used by both races; especially given its strange leg structure and overly large helmet. He stepped forward, dropping his equipment bag, turned around and carefully stepped back, plugging himself into the mechanical device. As his clothes touched the inner connections, the armour's front started to folding in, close up automatically, metal links wrapped around his arms and torso then, with a little discomfort, his legs. Finally, the helmet closed over his head, its HUD activating. However, there was already an issue; it only displayed a warning light indicator, in English, "Low power". The suit had apparently been damaged, or drained of power, needing a compatible power source. He frowned, then brightened. Perhaps he had something that might be suitable. The stone he'd found at the conference had proved to be capable of holding a high-frequency charge when he'd tested it back at base, and that stone was in his bag, on the floor. He crouched, difficult in the suit without much power, retrieved the small stone in the surprisingly delicate hands and pressed a button on the chest plate, ejecting a similar object onto the ground. He placed the power source into the slot, hoping it was of the same type and waited.

There was a quiet click, and a message appeared in front of him, "Initialising systems. Adjusting settings for new pilot." The leg joints on the armour shifted, panels and supports re-linked, motors slide into new alignments fitted better and supporting his legs properly. Then, finally the HUD was fully displayed, all systems showing green, and Simon had a suit of powered armour, ready to go. All he needed to do was learn what the hell to do with it. Well, he had an invading army to test it on, the next course of action seemed obvious.

As he looked around, trying to get a sense of what the armour could do, the area began to look vaguely familiar to Simon. Yes, the force field distorted the scene beyond it a little but wasn't that Lac Léman reflecting Geneva in the distance, meaning they were at CERN, the world's largest particle accelerator, the LHC; the one that they had been informed was experimenting with the new exotic matter, z443. If the invaders had control of that and were using it, any damage to the buildings in the area might be catastrophic.

He looked at a shield generator and selected a place to start, the team needing outside help, the best way being to break through the enemy force field and call in military assistance, as long as they were informed of the LHC's dangers.

He lifted his hand, and the suit's arm opened up in anticipation of what was about to happen. Simon's electrical bolt arced from him to fry the force field generator, opening a gap in the field surrounding the machine and silencing the interference field causing the problems with their communications. Now they could start to coordinate their efforts. It was a beginning. The first thing he did was tell Charlene where they were, and his suspicions about the aliens using z443.

Jack was worried. It was fairly obvious, even to him, that the machine must be a larger version of the engines that the Ghe'Dar used to move their ships through space. This must be the focus of the invasion, and it needed stopping, at any cost.

He made a decision to destroy the machine. It was powerful, but he doubted that, if anything went wrong, it would be worse than being cattle for the Ghe'Dar.

He summoned up as much will and courage he could muster directing it at the machine; in a silent plea for the power to destroy the machine. In answer, a powerful blast of mystic power hit the side of the machine, breaking through the force field surrounding it and causing a sizeable dent in the machine's metallic casing, but the flow of power around the top of the machine did not appear to have been interrupted, so he levelled his arm again to continue his barrage.

Charlene saw the blast hit the machine then heard the comms become active again. It was time to take command since no one else was. She visualised the building exploding, taking the planet with it, so she yelled down the comms.

"Stop! Don't Destroy the machine! We need to take control of it."

Jack froze in the act of summoning the second bolt of power. What did the scientist know? Yes, the explosion would be significant, but nothing could be worse than being obliterated by an invading army.

Jack put a finger to his ear, "Charlene, if we leave it intact, they will swarm us under," Jack shouted, still aiming with his arm, building up a devastating charge in his arm. "We'll literally be eaten alive; the whole world will."

Charlene looked across the distance, at the escape artist, and measured her words with care. "Jack. I know I've made a few mistakes recently, but if the Aliens are using z443 here, blowing the machine up may well obliterate the solar system, let alone the planet. We need to take control of it and, we need to do it fast."

Jack was a little startled with the tone of command in the young girl's voice; she meant it, and something told him she was right. Against his own judgement, he lowered his arm. "Ok, what do you want me to do?"

"Can you see everyone from where you are?" She started running towards the machine.

"Yup. Your moving towards the machine, John is taking care of a Ghe'Dar Airsled," and said, rattled off everyone's locations, the buildings proximity and enemy dispositions. One thing he noticed in particular, was that there was a heavily guarded saucer connected by cables to the machine.

"Everyone head towards the saucer, we'll see if we can control the machine from there," said Charlene loudly down the comms after being informed.

Jack considered the saucer's contingent of guards, checking where the others were and decided he was the best placed to deal with them. He silently prayed to his people to protect him and prepared to attack. As he did that, a fine mist flowed around him, and although it did not look substantial, he'd a feeling of being protected.

"Why not the machine itself?" John asked, "especially, as the saucer is guarded."

"No. They'd be forced to fight us, and again we'd potentially risk blowing the darn thing up." Charlene was thinking fast on her feet here. "No, we need to relocate any battle away from the machine itself, then, either use the saucers control systems to power down the machine or perhaps use the portal itself to stop the rest of the invasion fleet."

As the rest of the team approached the saucer, they caught their first glimpse of the large contingent of, very capable looking, guards positioned near the ship; fortunately, they were not actually blocking the access ramp.

John looked at the guards and started to slaver a little; at last, a real fight with opponents he could see. He felt his juices start to course.

"Ok, John, Jack, see if you can get their attention; Helena you protect Isabella. Simon and I will plough through, or dodge past, and see if we can get access to the saucer. Let's move."

As they started forward, an explosion erupted to their rear, just missing them all, the Airsled circling around behind them, taking aim once more. However, before it fired again, an air-to-air missile smacked into its shield, rocking the entire vehicle sideways off its suspensor field, causing it to drop out of the sky.

Through the gap in the shield, advanced two Tiger attack helicopters, which had apparently been outside the field awaiting a break in it to make an attack. The Tigers had French markings, which kind of made sense if they were where they thought they were straddling the French and Swiss border.

Jack saw several Ghe'Dar soldiers running towards some grounded Airsleds and pointed them out to the team, indicating that the battle was escalating rapidly.

"The 'copters will have to be a diversion, as I doubt they will actually get past the Ghe'Dar AA batteries," observed John, as he lined up his attack approach.

"I'm doing my best to get the AA batteries on our side, or at least off their side," came Isabella over the comms. "At the moment, I've managed to set them into maintenance mode, but I'm having problems with the twelfth firewall, it's a be'atch," added Isabella.

John was still high on the adrenaline in his system, took one look at the guards near the saucer, and charged full pelt straight at them. Unfortunately for him, they spotted the blur coming and deployed to block him.

Simon arced around right to flank them; flying low to take advantage of their military precision, to line them up.

Jack tried to approach from the same direction, but he'd to dodge past several bushes, reducing his speed and spoiling the otherwise coordinated attack.

Charlene was a little behind the rest, still trying to make head and tail out of her internal HUD settings and displays. There were lines, symbols of various colours and multiple layers of vision. Some displays had words, others just strange icons; some were in colours that she did not know the words for. In short, it was utterly bewildering, and behind it, all the real world was still slightly out of focus or just distorted.

As John neared the saucer, he hit a wave of energy blasts projected from the front row of soldiers; despite his incredible burst of speed, and spectacular evasive acrobatics, he crashed to the grass, tumbling to a stop, unconscious, having bought Simon time to get into position. The armoured figure unleashing a vivid bolt of lightning down the line of the enemy, hitting all eight. Though many of them remained standing, turning to retaliate, with another volley of energy, most of the bolts missed. Unphased and with military coordination they slung their rifles, each reaching for grenades.

Simon selected a new approach and landed in a crouch, his armour rippling, becoming encased in a darker, denser metal, in effect turning him into a static metallic statue. As the eight grenades landed around him, the comms seemed to go silent, as the team held their breath waiting to see the conclusion of the attack. As one, the grenades went off, energy blazing around the point, like a rainbow of deadly swirling power, lasting a few endless seconds, then clearing to reveal the tableaux of Simons' unscathed, invulnerable armour.

The Ghe'Dar looked at one another, perplexed at the lack of effect of their, normally irresistible, energy grenades walking up to the armour and giving it a long, puzzled, look. Then they seemed to dismiss it, returning to their vigil at the entrance, un-phased by their apparent failure.

Jack admired their military training, actually thankful for it as they were now line up again in perfect position for his attack. He rose up higher, then swooped, blasting all of them with a lance of Mystic power, the heavily armoured troops finding their armour useless against the mystic energy, as it passed through both their force shields and battle armour. Despite being struck by the powers of both Simon and Jack, all held firm, battling on.

From beneath trees, a larger Ghe'Dar, probably the other's commanding officer, advanced confidently. The burly creature took one look at Jack, unlimbered its' rifle, took aim and fired in a single fluid movement. The blast from its' weapon struck Jack full-on, piercing the translucent armour he'd previously felt so safe in, seemingly totally ineffectual against this new weapon.

Jack bracing himself for another blast, hoped he could withstand another blast from an opponent that he obviously could not deal with on his own. Surprisingly, another mist englobed him, this time it seemed thicker; almost solid. The new barrier dampened the energy hit, but it still caused him intense pain, weakening him, and causing him to feel dizzy. This was not going well, and as Jack's spirit quailed, he vanished from sight, as he headed towards the bushes seeking cover, getting ready to run.

Charlene finally reached the saucer and saw the carnage that the Ghe'Dar had wrought against her friends: Simon, sealed up in his armour, unmoving and, possibly, dead inside; John on the ground burned, bleeding and bruised, again, possibly dead, or dying; Jack was nowhere to be seen, only Isabella and Helena remaining in the fight.

"Helena; see if you can revive John. Isabella; keep trying to subvert the AA guns. I'm going in." The HUD was all green, one important phrase finally resolving itself into English "Weapons"; so she selected the "Attack" option and charged the Ghe'Dar; at least they'd go down fighting.

Her skin suddenly rippled into a golden armour, and she pumped her arms breaking into a head-long charge. As she approached the line of troops, she cocked her right arm as though to blast the troops, hoping that her new Nanites had given her some kind of fancy weaponry like Simon, Jack or the Ghe'Dar themselves.

The HUD displayed a set of crossed hairs, lining up with the two guards blocking her path and outlining them in thin red silhouettes.

As she closed the distance, she felt what John had felt when he first used his power, a massive surge of steroids being released into her system, making her stronger and faster.

But that was not the only event triggered, as, from beneath her armour, just below her wrists, two semi-organic tentacles, pulsing internally with a purple light, tipped with razor-sharp spearheads, launched themselves with tremendous force at the selected targets, piercing both their force fields and armour, embedding themselves in their helmets, finishing them off.

The shock, of the weapons produced, and the result just did not initially sink in. Charlene kept running forwards, flinging the two dead Ghe'Dar out of her way and targeting the next two in line. Two more felt her sting, however, this time, only one fell; the second staggering under the impact. The remainder levelled their rifles at her and fired off a volley; two bolts striking home. Her HUD announced the damage, but Charlene ploughed on relying on her healing ability, dodging a grenade, as she went past the troops and into the saucer; stripping off her clothes and equipment belt off as she did so. She did not exactly know why but there was something instinctive going on, and she let it happen. All her previous training and dreams had instructed her to trust her instincts; so, she did. She could pick up the kit later after all.

Simon was exploring the capabilities of the armour he'd acquired, as he hid within the protective armour cocoon. It seemed it was designed as a heavy-duty space repair unit; designed for manoeuvring, heavy lifting and protection. Once the grenades had finished discharging, he quickly disengaged the cocoon and manoeuvred behind the saucer, to use it as a weapon. The awesome hydraulic power of the suit would allow him to lift it up and crush the Ghe'Dar soldiers like bugs.

"Simon get in here! We need your technical skills to decipher the control systems," came Charlene's voice, over the comms, spoiling his initial plans; still, time enough to play Frisbee with the saucer another day.

Meanwhile, Helena had arrived at the blasted body of John, his skin, his body bleeding and grossly distorted, his muscles were massively bloated. She touched her staff to him, releasing a pale white light over his body, flowing over the flesh and sweeping away the burn marks. She leaned over him to see if he needed any more healing, when his eyes popped open, startling her a little.

"Thanks. See if you can help Charlene," he said in a slight groggy voice.

She nodded, "OK", but instead of moving, she planted her staff into the grass and starred through the crystal at one of the Ghe'Dar soldiers.

The soldiers near the ramp, ignoring the golden creature inside the ship, started towards John and Helena, the two of them raising their guns and firing, but instead of hitting the human pair they encountered Helena's Mystic shield.

Regarding the shield with some perplexity, one started re-tuning its' weapon, in the hope of penetrating it. However, the other turned to behold its' comrades with a mixture of confusion and loathing.

"Yuck, they're as ugly on the inside as they are on the outside," muttered Helena, focusing another of her powers on one of the soldiers.

"What are you doing? asked a confused, if stronger sounding, John.

"Fighting fire with fire," she said. "Watch!"

The second Ghe'Dar soldier started twitching strangely, then raised his gun, took aim at the others at almost point-blank range, and fired a volley of energy bolts. Those closest were hit, and one of them went down. Then, just for good measure, the guard stood right next to the survivor and dropped two grenades right next to his feet, the other looking down just in time to see the explosion. The detonation sent them both flying, in different directions. Incredibly, the one seemingly under Helena's sway, started to get up, while the other remained down, probably because its head was somewhere else, and the legs had gone walkabout, separately.

"Wow, remind me to NEVER get you angry, Helena," John muttered, respectful of her newly displayed talent, to which she replied with a grimace of concentration.

From behind them Isabella suddenly whooped, "Got 'em."

"Sorry?" asked John, as a whining noise started up from nearby. One of the AA guns was training itself on a Ghe'Dar Airsled, flying towards the breach in the force field, and fired. The Airsleds' shield held, but now they realised they had more to worry about than just the humans attacking from the breach; they were in danger of finding themselves in a deadly crossfire.

"Good work, dear," Helena praised the younger girl, who beamed back at her, John smiling too, Isabella winking back at him.

The Ghe'Dar did not fear the human air attack from the meagre forces coming through the breach, but the AA batteries were tipping the balance in the human's favour, and that could not be allowed.

The Ghe'Dar commander completed the remote command initiation sequence for the invasion portal knowing that, with a mothership on station, the humans would not stand a chance. While its' elite guards were all but gone, and the Airsleds were all engaged or destroyed, re-enforcements were barely a moment away, on the other side of the portal, it had little to worry about, except for that gold creature in the command saucer. What was it doing? Also, it seemed that one of its' elite troops had suddenly gone insane, slaying its' own comrades.

Gorranar would deal with that traitor itself. It advanced on the traitor, lifting the hapless soldier into the air and smashing a fist in the faceplate, causing it to go limp, falling to the ground dead.

Charlene balanced unsteadily on the entry ramp looking around, in a state of bewilderment, trying to adjust to yet another mind-blowing and systemic shock.

She had entered the ship afraid that there would be more soldiers inside or an automated defence system of some kind. Her system provided an instinctive reaction and solution to that; camouflage. Not Jack's invisibility, or the elegant Chameleon's colour changing, but a far more potent, and potentially, much more useful camouflage.

Her body had changed form; shifting skin and bone, pigment and muscles to mimic a Ghe'Dar, and an armoured one at that. The transformation had not been slow and gradual, as one might have thought, but a bone cracking and jointing popping explosion of biological activity, like being hit by a car. It was not perfect, after all, she'd only seen one before today and, she had barely seen the multitude outside, but, for all intents and purposes, she now looked like one of the alien invaders of her home planet, her body protesting the new configuration with every breath and twitch.

She looked into what should be the control room and saw that this ship was either exactly the same as the one lost in the Thames, or as close to it as made no difference. The Ghe'Dar it seemed had a great many of this type of ship.

To the right of the control room stood three immobile humans, staring into space, as if waiting for something. She glanced behind herself and saw the engine compartment, the area which had changed her so radically in the previous ship. Finally, to her left she saw the third section containing what resembled a map or briefing room just as Simon finally arrived inside the saucer, to see her standing there. He started to raise his hand, but she raised hers, then pointed into the control room, "it's me, Simon," sounding almost like Charlene; slightly muffled by six tentacles, unfamiliar teeth, and a faceplate. His face froze. "See if you can access their systems and what you can find out about the machine,"

His eyes went exceedingly wide. ".Dr. Klerk?"

The figure nodded clumsily, "hurry, we don't have time for explanations."

Charlene moved slowly into the engine area, on unfamiliar legs, if that's what you actually called them, though they were more like segmented tentacles, and had a look around; partially, to check for crew and, partially, to see if she could understand this area any better than before. The answer to both questions in her head was no, mainly because of the strange optical arrangement in her new form, even if the HUD remained the same.

Simon was doing much the same as her, but in the control room, when one of the dazed humans wondered up. "You are not of this ship. Only the master can authorise you to help with the task at hand!"

Simon pointed to the engine room, "she is in there, go ask her. I'm busy." The dazed human took Simon's statement literally, shambling past the entry ramp, where a few troops were starting to head up, entered the engine room and, seeing Charlene, in her Ghe'Dar form, bowed and asked in reverent tones, "what is your will master?"

Charlene had never really had someone ask her what to do before, so she was at a loss as what to say. Perhaps, Simon had some idea. "This one thinks I'm its master and asking me what my will is. What do I say? Any ideas?"

"Ask it where the combat systems are," was the reply from a perplexed Simon, who was desperately looking for the machine controls, or a weapon system, that they could use against the Ghe'Dar.

"Where are the combat systems for the ship?" The human looked confused.

"The master honours us by using our own language. All praise the masters." Then the human remembered the question, "The master should know the controls for the ship are in the control room, I do not know more," Charlene tried to grind her teeth in frustration; the Ghe'Dar equivalent sounded absolutely disgusting; a squelchy, rasping parp of a sound.

The portal generator gave a great metallic heave; energy curling from each of the four corners of the pyramid to strike the now sizeable black spot in the sky. As they smashed it apart, a rent appeared in the sky, a purple disc, with pink and purple swirls rippling and flowing around the periphery, giving the hard edge a three-dimensional aspect. The air did not whoosh out like the plug hole that it looked like, more it made the air around it thrum; as though more space was being pumped into an already full container, giving the impression that the world might shatter if it remained open. The scout ship started to vibrate, even on the ground; as though reality itself felt challenged by the appearance, in this world, of such a phenomenon.

Through that wound in the sky appeared a massive saucer, many times larger than the scout ship on the ground; a Ghe'Dar Mothership, boasting Ghe'Dar commandos by the thousand, ready to overwhelm the pitiful few human defenders, and, even as the ship arrived in the atmosphere, its external turrets began acquiring lock on the visible targets. Inside, Airsleds by the dozen prepared for launch; the full-scale invasion of Earth had begun and Humanity's time was running out; fast.

Jack looked up and felt a wave of despair, but strangely he also felt an overwhelming sense that all was not lost; there was still a moment to turn the tide. He quickly scanned the area to see if there was anything that looked like it could do so.

The Ghe'Dar had started to home in on the primary source of their troubles with the AA batteries, advancing towards the bunker where Helena and Isabella were hiding.

John had started to stand, and the whole group outside looked up to see what was happening, regarding the new threat in the sky. The AA batteries, being short ranged, could not help with the Mothership, being so high up; but they could help with any Airsleds that came low enough to fight the Helicopters. There were even a few human troops advancing through the gap in the Ghe'Dar force field, not many, but anyone that made it in would distract the increased Ghe'Dar force.

The leader of the Ghe'Dar ground forces; seeing that the machine was now active, ceased being worried about the human troops on the ground. Soon they would be crushed. Now he could focus on the invaders in the control ship and ordered the remaining Elite to slay all those within the Saucer, even, or especially, the slaves.

"Come in here and see if you can shut the damn machine down," yelled Charlene, over the noise of the engine, and the roar of the machine outside.

Simon clanged into the compartment and examined the engine, immediately locating and following the command sequencers to a shutoff switch and nodded; that should do it. He stabbed it confidently, frowning when there was no change in the sound of the machine. Instead, the saucer's control field, started to collapse, its gradually diminishing sound causing Simon to desperately look around for a restart sequencer or anything familiar, as his confidence dropped to the floor, and faded out the ship.

Charlene saw the look through his faceplate, "wrong switch?"

He turned with fear on his face, "and, from the look of the control signals now, we have little hope of reinitialising the system before the damn thing starts going critical," Simon added. "I cannot see the re-initialisation sequence control. It must be in the machine."

Her face stayed surprisingly calm, not panicking, but thinking "what will happen?" she asked.

"No idea, but the Ghe'Dar will have a bad time of it too. If we can disable the machine, rather than blow it up, we might still stop it. This ship is not big enough, but the mothership might be. I'll see what I can do."

They both looked around the room for ideas and saw only Ghe'Dar gibberish.

With John still severely wounded, Helena decided to get him under cover.

"Grab Hold!" She said presenting her staff, activating its power and began flying them both, out of physical range of the Ghe'Dar, towards the ship; skimming over the enemy and their commanding officer, who tried getting a bead on them as they flew by.

However, Helena was moving too erratically for it to get a good line on her, or her passenger and the three remaining Elites were still reeling from the other attacks. She zipped, at rather reckless speed, zigzagging to the saucer entrance and up the ramp, managing to narrowly avoid a multitude of bolts from the powerful Ghe'Dar rifles.

Having entered the saucer, they went straight across the central area, into the briefing room, not even seeing the others inside as they went by. Although they landed somewhat awkwardly, Helena started to healing John as fast as she could, both needing to get back into the fight.

All the traffic into the ship left only Isabella and Jack outside, Jack starting to think this was a bad idea, especially now that the Ghe'Dar were redirecting their forces towards Isabella and him. While maintaining her control of the Ghe'Dar AA batteries, she needed protecting at all costs, so he willed himself into invisibility and flew, straight line, to rescue her.

"Is there any way to translate the controls for us to use?" Charlene had pretty early on realised that these humans were not really as intelligent as other humans were. They were given the absolute minimum information to perform their duties and no more, everything else being erased or blocked somehow; the ultimate slave race.

After a few moments hard thought, the slave replied. "The master can do anything from the control chair," he replied. Finally, something they could use.

"Stay there," she instructed the slave, striding out, almost casually noticing that he bowed and froze on the spot. However, as she passed the ramp, she saw two Ghe'Dar Elite cautiously advancing up the ramp, rifles ready. Her tentacles lashed out; not at the soldiers, but at several controls on the hull, next to the ramp, that should control the external door. As her tentacles stabbed at four buttons, several things happened; a force field was erected across the entrance to the saucer, the doors to the engine room and the briefing room was closed, and finally, the air intake fans started. The Ghe'Dar on the ramp paused and did a double take; why had that Ghe'Dar in the saucer started a pre-flight sequence, with them on the ramp?

Charlene slithered into the command area and sat in the control seat, her Ghe'Dar body feeling wonderfully comfortable in it, despite the armour, and indeed as she settled down it was almost as if the seat welcomed her into its embrace. Her flexible arms rested palms down on, on to what looked like, flight control pads; designed especially for the strange, lateral, joints on the end of the Ghe'Dar's gauntlets. As she relaxed, Wrist clamps secured her to the chair arms, and, at her eye-line, two bars slid to position themselves just in front of her helmet's frontal lobes. As they did so, she felt her eyes start to close, and the ship's engines started up; the ship immediately starting to hover fractionally above the ground. The ship's interface linked with Charlene's mind and her view of the world opened up.

She saw, superimposed over her own HUD, a display that showed the entire area: The scout ship, whose designation was now known to her, the mothership creeping through the portal, Jack (fully visible), Isabella, the Airsleds battling the French helicopters, the ground battle; everything. To one side, away from the primary engagement, several black-clad commandos had managed to sneak into the shielded area and seemed to be going for the AA turrets. All was clear. However, the images were projected in a strange form of 3D with a purple colour shift and overlaid with Ghe'Dar markings and other unfamiliar symbologies.

Charlene thought as concisely as she could, commanding the computer to translate the ship's controls into English. As one, all the onboard consoles, as well as the HUD became translated into the Queens' English, even if her own was not. Then, another thought occurred to her, looking at one of the helicopters being displayed; she willed the computer system to send the imaged helicopter a targeting reference and guided it towards the large machine's shield generators. She also pinpointed other priority targets and, in effect, identified where the information was coming from. She did not know why she used the code she did, it just seemed right.

One of the Tiger attack helicopters, listening in on the secure M.I.X. frequency, received an open transmission from one of the enemy ships.

"Echo One to base. Receiving enemy transmission as expected. Authentication code: Chi'mera," said the navigator, as the pilot tried to evade a Ghe'Dar energy bolt. It clipped the rotors slightly, but it did not shear it off as it might have done.

"Code Confirmed, Echo one. Transmit target coordinates to Bravo Two and proceed to initial targets."

Below the helicopters, the commandoes were still advancing spreading out. Heavier groups were moving in behind them; with some AA further back.

"Bravo Two to command, deploying for phase two," came another communication, as the commandoes had split into three squads; one going left under cover of a hedge, two staying in the centre and three flanking right in a wide arc, all three forming a crescent of troops protecting the perimeter. The left group were moving right inside the edge of the shield, skirting away from the centre of the conflict, the main strike team of four. The centre group of four started unpacking light AA missile launchers, grenades and ammunition, acting as a forward command position. The final group seemed to scatter into the bushes, trees and scrub, which started sprouting laser lights, as the special forces started lighting up their targets with high-intensity laser designators.

"Bravo Three to command, Christmas lights in place, call Santa to deliver the presents." There was no reply, except the distant roar of jets approaching.

Back in the ship, Charlene battled to get as much done as possible, vaguely aware that Simon was trying to activate the scout ship's small turret weapons, intending to do as much damage as he could to the alien Mothership. Then she had a stroke of genius, instructing the computer to download both the Ghe'Dar language and as much of their general knowledge and history as possible into her own memory. The computer acknowledged the request, but, just as the initial download of the language completed, the system started receiving an external encrypted signal, up-linking to the Ghe'Dar computer system from somewhere within the ship.

Simon suddenly released his purloined armour was transmitting data to a wireless network, and immediately got a bad feeling, trying to shut the connection down, but not before Charlene screamed in mental agony, her brain on fire; the walls of the ship vibrating dissonantly.

John heard the scream and flipped to his feet, briefly thanking Helena, then flexing his newly enhanced muscles, to bolt out to help Charlene and teach these monsters a lesson they would never forget, once he'd got past the closed door. He stopped and looked at the door wondering how to get it open, then realised he was still thinking like an average person and a weak one at that. He was no longer someone to be stopped by doors, or aliens, no, he was a fighting machine; something to knock these creatures to the ground and drive them six feet under, a piledriver. He liked the sound of that; from now on, that's what he would be Piledriver. So, he took one look at the door again and attacked it with all his augmented strength, ripping it clean out its guide rails. Then he was free of the room and heading towards the exit, except, he spotted an armoured creature, in the control seat to his left, probably attempting to take off and attack the others. Seeing the Ghe'Dar in the control chair, he did what his instinct told him to do; he rushed to the Chair and smashed the Ghe'Dar full in the faceplate, for all the people who'd died or been controlled and those that might still be.

Charlene was vaguely aware of the fact that John and Helena were on the ship as the requested information, and the virus attack ripped like razors through her brain. She was rooted to the seat, as a virus tried to re-write her mind when another pain exploded unexpectedly in her face.

No one was prepared for the reaction of John's misguided attack on the saucer either. Locked into the ships control system as she was, anything that affected her, affected the ship, thus responding to the sudden impulse to her body, the ship responded with emergency thrusters to evade whatever the pilot had just seen, shooting evasively ten metres away from the portal machine, tilting at a forty-five-degree angle to port.

While Charlene, as the pilot, was secured in the control chair, everyone else found themselves thrown around like rag dolls. John, Simon and the human slaves were catapulted across the control room and landed in a heap on the floor. Helena, still flying, was pinned against the wall as the saucer zoomed against her, while the two Ghe'Dar soldiers from the ramp suddenly found the floor disappearing from beneath their feet, tumbling against the wall underneath her.

Helena realised that they must have come through the force field; it must have been unidirectional, only stopping things going out.

As Charlene recovered from the blow, she swivelled her helmeted head to look piercingly at John and said in a forced steady tone, "If you do that again, I'll take it REAL personally, Driver. Now go deal with the Ghe'Dar!" John blinked, on hearing Charlene's distorted voice coming from the Ghe'Dar armour. Only she called him Driver. Oops!

Another effect of the ship moving violently, was that the control cables to the Portal machine were ripped from their sockets, severing their connection to the machine.

Jagged streaks of energy started to flick between the tips of the machine's 'claw' and down the sides of it. The thrumming in the air grew louder and, occasionally, parts of the building seemed to fade, driving the screech up an octave or two. Worse still, the power was arcing to, and impacting on, the ground directly in front of Isabella.

Jack was nearing Isabella, seeing her desperately looking about her for an escape route, as the advancing Ghe'Dar spotted her. He cursed that he could not fly faster, that he'd not had much chance to use his powers and that fate had even chosen him for this role. Finally, after agonising seconds, he was close enough to reach out to her.

"Isabella, it's Jack. Hold up your hand; I'll get us to the ship, I think they might need us in there."

"Jack? Ok. Get us out of here. I've had enough field work," she said lifting her hand and Jack grasping it as hard as he could, willing both of them invisible. Unfortunately, this time, his needs went unmet, causing him to grit his teeth when he realised, she could still be seen, making them both vulnerable to the Ghe'Dar, who'd had a hard time trying to locate the ghostly warrior who'd been plaguing them; indeed, he'd eluded their best tracker. Now they aimed their rifles at the empty space above the human female, preparing to fire.

At that moment, a sizzling bolt of power leapt from the open pyramid, striking the ground barely five meters from Isabella and, like a rock thrown in a lake, reality shattered around it, rippling outwards with soundless chaos; the exotic energy from the machine unleashing its' full potential. As if in response, similar bolts wound out from the other corners of the machine, striking the sky, causing the veil of the world to peel back, with the pyramid as the centre point, in a riotous kaleidoscope of otherworldly images and colours.

One quarter of the atmosphere was wreathed in dark fire, jagged sheets of it rippling across a blood red sky; strange flying creatures circling around the rent seemingly unable to cross; no earthly animal could replicate the horror of these fanged and burning forms, with six wings four arms, two bulky legs and fanged mouths that emitted cries of despair and suffering.

Another portion of the shattered sky pulsed with absolute blackness; not the dark of the night sky or the blackness of space, but the absence of light; any light. And from that darkness radiated a malevolent pull on the viewer's soul, a conscious hunger and absolute evil.

Opposite the machine, the ground gave way, revealing a world covered in plants; or rather semi-organic plants moving and swaying in a different disturbing motion. The animals in that strange jungle also moved disjointedly, almost mechanically; as though they were cybernetic in nature. A feeling radiating beyond them, one of unity, but with a strange sense of emptiness too, as though something was missing.

Then the ground underneath Isabella opened up or rather faded away. Far beneath her writhed a world covered in strange, mouthed worms, or threads, cities drowning in wave after wave of black, slick, vermicular, life forms; devouring everything in their path with their saw-toothed maws. Buildings crumbled under their weight, seas boiled with their feeding frenzy, and birds that feed on the horrors, dropping from the skies, as the hunters found they were the prey of this apparently unstoppable menace.

Isabella dangled helplessly from Jack's hand, starting to slip. "No! Don't let go. Don't let me fall," she screamed at him. Other horrified screams filled the air as the Ghe'Dar ground troops, without any support, started falling that great distance to be absorbed into the worms, to disappear under their mass, as they landed.

Jack tried to hold on, but knew he was not strong enough, looking into her eyes, and gasping, "I'm sorry. I cannot hold you."

She misunderstood and yelled, "no! Don't let me go!" gripping even tighter, making his grip fail even faster as her desperation stopped the blood flow to his hand and, as his wrist went numb, the grip failed totally, and Isabella fell screaming after the Ghe'Dar. The last thing he saw, was Isabella falling towards that grizzly mass. After a few seconds, he closed his eyes and silently prayed for her; that she would not suffer too much. Jack did not really know Isabella, as John did, but no one, not even the Ghe'Dar, deserved the fate that awaited below. When he opened his eyes again, the rents had closed and reality was back to normal; for now.

But he'd little time for mourning or recrimination. He had a world to save. He resumed his flight and girded himself to meet the others; knowing he would have to tell John sooner rather than later. He could imagine his reaction and was truly scared that John might lose himself to grief, remembering the brusque officer really cared for the younger girl; had cared for the young girl, he corrected himself. It was not a task he relished, but it would have to wait.

First, he had to reach them, as they were now moving off at a speed he could not hope to match, in the, erratically flying, saucer. Perhaps, he could do something about the machine instead, so he changed direction and headed towards it instead. The ground looked stable enough now, although the fresh memory his feet seemed to have was that the land was not there, so he continued to fly and looked for a way inside.

John was shocked by Charlene's voice issuing from the Ghe'Dar armour, he'd just slammed his fist into. He tried to process what had just happened and saw the shocked look on Simon's face; realising what he'd done. Had Charlene managed to steal a suit of armour from the enemy? No, it would not fit, so what had happened? He had no idea. That would have to wait. As if reading John's thought Simon just shook his head and pointed to the other room.

"Help! Someone! Ghe'Dar in the briefing room," came Helena's voice, over the comms. John did not hesitate, he shot back through the central room to aid Helena; but as he started out, a diminutive human slave, blocked his path.

"You attacked the master. You will pay," and the man attacked.

Such was John's surprise, that the man struck a blow, that even the best fighter had never struck him before, managing to smash his surprising solid foot on the side of John's knee. Agony rippled through him staggering him. Shocked, at the unexpectedly effective attack, John's new reflexes replied with unnaturally augmented power, the attacker being hit with a blow that made him bounce messily off the wall, into sweet oblivion.

Angry with himself, John continued into the briefing room to exact retribution on the Ghe'Dar, hobbling badly. How had that strip of a man so completely gotten the drop on him? He guessed that he was so pumped up, that his normal defensive reflexes were not functioning; or perhaps the element of surprise had confounded his otherwise excellent training. He'd have to train in this strange new form and come to a decision on whether either of those reasons was the case, or whether it was something else.

As he advanced into the room, he found his first Ghe'Dar, just through the door; staggering to get up. The figure received a huge blow to the head that caused him to simply collapse like a puppet having its strings cut. The second turned to face him, struggling to get its' gun into position. John grabbed the gun's strap and smacked the Ghe'Dar over the head with its own rifle causing the alien's head to explode, reacting much like a melon being hit by a demolition ball; Helena winced, gagging a little at the gore.

"You ok?" He asked her, trying not to think about what he'd just done. She nodded gagging again, trying to hold it in, but failing and losing control, splashing her dinner on to the floor to her right. He honestly did not blame her having been excessive, mainly because he was still unused to his augmented strength but also because he was very, very angry.

"John," It was Jacks voice, softer than he'd ever heard it. John did not respond until it was repeated in that same soft voice. Something was up.

"I'm sorry, Jack, I did not recognise your voice, I,"

"John, I'm sorry, it's Isabella," Jack stopped, as John interrupted.

"What about Isabella?" He called her name, on the comm. "Isabella?"

"I'm so sorry, John," came Jack's voice. "The ground; it dropped away beneath us; I could not hold her." John froze, his face going ridged like granite, his body deathly cold.

Helena saw the look on his face and stepped forward and put her hand on his shoulder, as he suddenly grasped for hope shrugging her hand off. "Perhaps she landed on a ledge?" He asked desperately.

"The portal opened a rift in space, John. She fell from the sky into a mass of creatures, there is no chance. I'm sorry," coming from Jack, it was literally a death sentence.

Jack's face dropped, and he felt a terrible rage building in him; the Ghe'Dar would pay. They would all pay with their Blood, every drop from every one of them. They would PAY!

He moved slightly and looked at Helena, who recoiled at the ferocity displayed on his eyes. "They will Pay!" He growled, in animalistic fury. At that moment she knew what real fear was. It stood in front of her, born in vengeance: awaiting its' time.

In the sky, the mothership was attempting to contact the scout ship controlling the machine. When there was no coded reply, it became apparent that the vessel was either under attack or already under the control of the enemy.

"Tactical:" ordered the captain. A display showed it the situation from their superior altitude. A subordinate moved up and gave it a brief overview.

"Area Shield is breached, but the Airsleds are holding off a small force of human aircraft. There are enemy ground troops inbound to this location, and an advance force taking up positions within the shield area," came the report.

"Scout one is not responding to hails, and the machine appears to only be running at 90% power, hence the problems with the confinement beam," reported the tactical officer. "The rest of the fleet has been signalled; they are assuming their assigned transport positions at the terminus."

"Deploy secondary armaments. Target the enemy ground troops. Port' a squad of troops over to the scout ship to eliminate any invaders, then the crew. Such incompetence cannot be tolerated. And Port' a tech unit to bring the machine up to full power again."

"Sir!" The tactical officer saluted across its' chest, relaying the orders to the various groups. On the outside of the ship, turret domes opened and targeted the humans.

Simon saw the mothership activating, what he assumed were, weapons.

".Dr. Klerk, we need to stop that mothership from taking us out," he said, rapidly considering at the options, few as they were. The human re-enforcements were nowhere near strong enough to take it out, and the ship's weapons were pitiful in comparison.

"We need to ram it!" He concluded.

"But we need to shut the machine down," Charlene disagreed.

"We don't have time to argue. Ram it!" He glared at her and she, reluctantly, directed the required thought at the computer; it complied immediately. Raising defensive shields, the scout ship lurched towards the much more massive Mothership

"Hold on everyone," she shouted just as the two ships ricocheted off one another. For the second time in the battle, everyone either grabbed onto the nearest solid object or fell to the floor. The impact did not appear spectacular from a distance, but the people inside the saucer were rattled around like marbles in a jar.

The scout ships' shields were up, but the Motherships' were not, and the damage was substantial, not from the actual impact, but from the fact that the collision had forced the larger ship back, against the portal's aperture.

The contact sliced through the top deck, across half of the ship, while the mid decks were unevenly penetrated; some lost completely, others barely scraped.

Fortunately, for the crew, the lower engineering decks remained intact, meaning that the ship was still a reasonably sizeable if severely damaged, threat; the command staff having been lost.

The other side effect of the impact was that the scout ship ricocheted off the mothership, tumbling uncontrollably into the portal aperture, with damaged engines and failing systems; falling into a vortex that would soon be packed with Ghe'Dar warships.

Charlene tried to make sense of the alarms and blinking information, reminding the command interface that it needed to display the data in English, as the download had not been completed, but she was not getting much of an intelligible response. She was struggling to get the machine to repair itself, and the ship was moving in the wrong direction.

Jack had seen the collision, his teammates disappearing into the portal, and perhaps from existence judging by the state of the larger craft. As far as he knew, he was the last hope for the planet. The Mothership had completed emerging, more of its' turrets remaining un-deployed, while others were halfway out and others just stayed nestled next to the hull; not in a position to shoot at anything. However, two of them looked like they were still being deployed. One sent out a laser targeting beam, aiming somewhere near the gap in the protective force, which suddenly sprouted a guided missile bloom, the turret erupting in flame. The damage was not visible for a few seconds, then, as the smoke cleared, Jack saw the blast was virtually ineffective. Whatever the alloy was, it was either, too strong for such light ordinance or protected by a field of some kind; probably the former given the damage to the mothership already.

Jack knew he had to enter the machine and attempt to shut it off, although he could really have done with Simon to do it. Perhaps it would be easier to understand than the other Ghe'Dar technology. He looked at the entrance, spotting a keypad with just a single button for entry; well finally a break.

He ran forward, pressing it and entered quickly, only to look around in bewilderment.

Bank upon bank of heavy machinery, computers and huge electrical relays pumped power towards the 'claw' currently rending the sky apart. Jack understand the basics, but he did not know where to begin shutting this thing down. Also, there were several obstacles in his way: firstly, the machine had red lights flashing all over the place and a voice, probably in Ghe'Dar, booming out for someone to do something; secondly, the power was also jumping from the external relays along the internal framework, making moving through the machine virtually impossible without getting vaporised. He had his mystic shield for sure, but he doubted even that that would protect him from that magnitude of these discharges.

He looked the area over several times, then spotted a portal unit, partially obscured by shielding, in the corner. It was a small, single person unit and, again, there was just a single activation button. Perhaps it could send him back to the base in England, where he could get some help, or somewhere safer; anywhere but here.

He ran towards the portal, raising his hand and smacking the button; being transported, he prayed his instinct was right.

The ground force saw the effect of their standard ordinance and started to unpack a new weapon, more substantial than the missile launcher, requiring two people to use it on the mothership. Once in position, the commander aimed and depressed the trigger; the thing whining a little, before emitting a bolt of purple, Gravitronic energy at the already damaged ship. The effect was instantaneous; the turret and a portion of the vessel broke free from the rest of the hull, landing on the ground milliseconds later.

"Bravo Two to command; lights are green, repeat, lights are green."

"Command to Bravo Two; engage at will. Command to Bravo One. Proceed!" The nearest squad started to move towards the machine.

The others were desperately trying to get the saucer back through the portal; but the ship was slow, damaged and they knew they still had the mothership to deal with.

As Helena took stock, she noticed that there was a portal pad in the corner of the map room. Perhaps they could transport back to the machine and stop all this back there. She pointed it out to John, and he made a snap decision, waving the others to the device.

"Charlene, we are leaving!" yelled John, as the others gathered near the unit. Helena tried to activate it, but the machine just whirred a little, a red light flashing on the panel.

Simon frowned, "er, possibly a short-range device? Otherwise, it would not show any signs of activity. We'll probably need to manoeuvre closer to the portal aperture."

Charlene opened her eyes, getting ready to leave, the interface shutting down, with the course set and locked. The requested download was incomplete, so she partly understood the language and had some knowledge of the Ghe'Dar. They were creatures of the void and empowered by nexus energy. Like an army of trapdoor spiders, they emerged from the void to feed on planets then return with their spoils. They had done it for so long that it was ingrained into their culture and would never stop attacking unless they were wiped out.

She ran into the map room and waited for the portal unit to either repair itself, or to get in range. Finally, as the ship reached the edge of the portal vortex; the light on the panel went green. However, as soon as it went green, the portal machine activated, receiving an incoming traveller. The blaze of light revealed Jack stepping forward into the map room. The rest saw him with relief that he was alive, and they were together for the first time since the start of this insanity.

"Jack we need to get off this thing before we crash back into the Mothership," said Simon.

"You get no arguments from me. This leads to the machine, so perhaps Simon can switch the damn thing off when we get back." He turned around and with the team stepped into the Portal Generator.

Simon suddenly had an alarming thought, a theory he'd read about concurrent energy streams causing unusual quantum effects, "Ah guys, we might have to wait until we're out of the portal's aperture before,"

"No time!" was all John said, as he pressed the button.

As the button was pressed, the world exploded around them; energy ripping through the ship, blasting outwards. The ship's machine worked for a fraction of a second catapulting them elsewhere, then vaporised, as the unexpected, and unstable, energies unleashed by the machine's initiation inside an already active portal, rippled outwards.

The concussive force cascaded outwards in both directions, ripping the mothership apart, which thankfully shielded the machine below it. Now the way was clear for the invading fleet, even if bolts of energy still flashed at irregular intervals form the machine to the portal's edges. A scout ship exited the portal, then another, but as a third came through, it was sliced in half by a bolt of unstable energy, then vanish to who knows where.

But of the M.I.X. team and their ship, there was no sign.

CHAPTER 9

PARADOX

It was dark, cramped and the air was already stale as Charlene woke and tried to move, finding she was pinned under something, or rather someone, given that it was soft and fleshy, explaining her cramped space. She nudged up, the body above her grunting, "Hey! Cut it out, I'm trying to get the door off me," peeved John's unmistakable voice, his body having the not entirely unpleasant musky smell of his exertions, Charlene noted. His full weight was uncomfortable, as it shifted onto her, until he rose slightly, the movement accompanied by a loud metallic thunk, as the door hit the matching metallic floor of the saucer.

"Careful where your chucking that," complained Jack, from behind them and to the right. "Some people cannot throw things around like you, and we'll get hurt if it hits us."

"Sorry," came the partially apologetic reply, as John's voice shifted, along with his weight, as he clambered off Charlene, edging around the room, judging by the sounds and curses as he stumbled over and around fallen chairs.

"Unnn," came a feminine moan, from Charlene's left.

"Helena, you ok?" queried Jack. There was a sound of switches being used, and light bloomed, focusing where Helena's groan had issued from.

The map room was more or less level, although the furniture and other items were in two clumps, where they had slid during the impact with the Ghe'Dar Mothership. Occasional sparks could be heard from a nearby area, but there was little in the way of powered mechanical, or electrical, noise entering the room, and little indication of external conditions.

Helena was slumped against the wall, with a few of the strangely shaped chairs scattered around her. John leant against the outer wall of the room, blinking at the sudden illumination. The door that he'd heaved off himself with his newfound ease was lying behind Charlene, who's feet were against the central map table, where Jack was poised semi-crouched; in case there was something dangerous nearby.

Simon, who had not made a sound so far, was completely out of it, with a pool of freshly drying blood surrounding his head. However, even in the light of the torch, they could see that the gash on his head was starting to heal, little sparks of electricity arcing between the edges of the wound; stopping the bleeding and re-knitting the skin. He began to stir but looked terribly groggy, his eyes rolling around and the mouth working, but not speaking. Strangely, before the crash, he was in the armour, yet now it seemed that the armour was not there. What had happened to that?

With the arrival of the light, people started to extricate themselves from their current locations, stand, get their bearings and switch on their own torches.

Helena, moved over to Simon, pulling her wand from under a slightly crushed chair in the way, light blooming brighter in the room, as her wand, once again, became the large staff she wielded in the battle. The crystal light was bright, pure white and illuminated the whole area.

"Well, the good news is, that still works," she said, more to herself than the others as they started to tidy the room; stacking the chairs out the way and propping the door out of the way. John seemed to still be a little bewildered about his ability to do it so casually.

Helena touched the staff to Simon, and the healing was immediate; so was the way his eyes cleared.

"Thank you, my dear," was all he said, sitting upright, looking around and feeling his head, shaking it slightly as he felt the dried blood from the now healed wound.

"It looks like you have developed certain abilities that you did not share with us Simon," John's slightly gravelly voice accused.

"It looks like we have all undergone changes," Charlene leapt to Simon's defence. "We have been exposed to multiple pathogens, energies and environments that seem to have caused us to develop new and unusual abilities and, while I have been trying to analyse my own metamorphosis, none of us has had the time to either assess or process everything that has happened to us." The others stopped a moment to absorb the meaning of her words. "I suggest that we get out of our current predicament, where ever we are, then sit down and try to evaluate our own changes; perhaps even pool them so that we can be better prepared for the war to come."

"War?" said a sickened Helena.

"One can assume that the machine is still allowing the Ghe'Dar to bring their fleet through," Charlene said authoritatively. "Before I left the machine, I managed to get some information about them out of their main computer. This is no minor incursion, they mean to suck our planet dry, then move on to the next." The others looked at her in horror, "and little of our technology can stand against them. Our only hope is to try and get back there, with as many re-enforcements as possible, and shut down that machine."

"Firstly, let's find out where we are," John started, after a moments silence. "Helena, Simon. See if you can get us some power, light, computers; anything to give us some idea on what is going on. Jack can you see if you can look,"

"I know 'for anything else we can use,'" they all started to move out the room when they heard a groan from the left.

"Unhh? Wha? What is? Where? AHHHHH!" the human scream was followed by a thud. The others quickened their pace to see a human on his knees, clutching his head and feeling around the wires implanted there. The team had forgotten the two converted humans in the command room. "What have you done to me," he looked up at them, his eyes pleading for information.

Helena leaned her stave against the wall and stooped in front of the man.

"Easy there, we are here to help." The man looked dubiously at the group. She gently turned his head from side to side to get a better view of the control apparatus, the wires crudely implanted into the skull inside a metal cap, some only partially attached and others sparking occasionally. It seemed that the Ghe'Dar either had no surgeons amongst their numbers, or they did just the required work and no more; of course, in the ethos of a race that were conquerors, why bother expending effort on slaves or food?

Charlene came over and looked the man over. "It looks like the system was damaged during either the battle or the crash." She reached downed and with a pair of pliers snipped a few of the wires. "There, that should make sure that the damned thing won't work again." She looked at the man. "We'll try and get you sorted out properly when we get to a hospital if we can," she added to the others.

"Simon, where are the engines?" John asked.

The scientist nodded to indicate the direction, touching Helena on the shoulder, to suggest that she should follow. The two went to the back of the group and looked at the closed engine room door.

"Er, John. Your assistance please?" He said pointing at the firmly shut metal door.

John strode over to the door and lifted the door with ease, the metal grinding against its stationary motor. He held it up as the two went into the room to make sure, then jammed the door in place by twisting its' edge slightly and returned to the control room.

Jack was looking at the closed entrance door and started to move into the control room, spotting Simon's armour motionless near the right of the entrance, linked into the control system of the saucer. Why was it plugged into the ship? He went to the engine room telling Simon, who was totally relieved that his armour had been found.

Simon checked the circuits in the engine room and found them to be functional, if powerless. Perhaps, if he channelled the armour's power into the modules, he could jump-start the engines, or at least get the emergency power online. He assumed there was some sort of power surge when the engines were damaged. That thought stopped him on the way to his armour, which had apparently tried to do something just before the crash; what? He tried to remember. A virus of some kind had been deployed. The armour was a Trojan horse, designed to shut down the systems of the spaceship and thereby neutralising any threat is posed. Clever; except for the fact that it was one of the thousands of such ships.

He climbed into his suit, which activated remarkably fast, despite a few new items on the UI, indicating package delivery status of one hundred per cent. It must have ejected its' pilot, him, and completed its' mission without him; charming! He'd have to delete that feature from the system. He wanted complete control of this armour, not have it pulling fast ones on him whenever he was unconscious. The thought that it might do things without him was genuinely scary, and just a little thrilling, for someone who had imagined the evolution of cybernetics and robotics. He disengaged the cybernetic link to the ship and started towards the engine room, startling the, still cowering, human as he clanged past; Helena trying to keep the man calm at the sight of an armoured being walking past him.

Charlene was now in the control room, with John, looking around it. The internal damage from the impact with the Mothership was negligible, but whatever had happened when they had activated the portal had ripped through the power systems en-mass. Many panels had blown, and they were still trying to understand which systems remained usable.

"What about this one," John pointed to one, behind the position that the humans were standing in.

"Astrogation," she translated the markings above the panel. "We won't need that unless we are in a different part of the galaxy." He tried to see if she was joking when she said it. It was hard to tell in the available torchlight, but it looked like she was serious; exceedingly serious.

"Just how far away from Earth can we be, given that we only travelled for a few seconds?" He was trying to understand why she seemed so concerned.

"How much do you know about current Quantum Physics or Wormhole theory?" her voice was not hopeful of a useful answer.

"If I say I've heard of them, does that answer the question?" he replied sincerely.

She sighed. "OK. What sci-fi films or programmes have you seen?"

"Saw Horizon once, about the space probes. It was when I was on nights, and I fell asleep halfway through," he apologised, lifting his hands up.

"Great. Ok, let's try a different tack." She thought carefully. "Right. Imagine you're a snail. You can only travel slowly. Then a bird snatches you and drops you right across a garden. It would seem to you like you had travelled instantly," John nodded, understanding the analogy at least. "That's what the engine of this ship can do, but on a galactic scale, maybe even universal; travel between any two points in the universe, instantaneously. Now, do you understand the problem?" John nodded, then thought about it a little, and his face became concerned; he'd finally twigged.

"We need power," she'd begun, when the lights started to flicker on, the pair looking up. It seemed Simon was having some success with the engines.

In the engine room, Simon ran a power bypass from his armour to a power conduit on the engine control panel, allowing him to reboot the engine subsystems, and get emergency power active. He'd looked at the transaction logs for his suit, noting that the viral program, activated during their attack on the mothership, had not been logged; confirming that there was a set of hidden programs in his suit's onboard computer. He quickly programmed in a fail-safe program to block external access, before running the power line to the console. Then he began adjusting the suits outputs to match the ships frequency to get the consoles active, with which he could get the emergency power up too, getting the ship's computer systems online. The console gradually started to pulse with its fake electrical life. The displays confirmed that the virus had done a fair amount of systemic damage, then shut the ship down totally; ironically that had probably saved them from feedback as they had exited the portal. Simon started to purge the damaged systems of the viruses' commands and implant several safeguards against the ship doing anything against the human occupants. After a few minutes, lights started to come on, along with a few of the consoles, including the doors, air vents and the internal force fields.

As the light came on, he noticed that behind him was the body of a human stretched out across two of the power bars. It was blackened entirely from prolonged electrical shorting going through it. Another victim added to the tally against the Ghe'Dar, thought Simon; a little shocked at his highly unprofessional thought.

"Ok, we've got as much power as we can without the engines; I'm sorry but looking at them, they are beyond my ability to repair," he said over the team's comms system. He noticed that the scanners were not active, but that the navigation system was; at last, a break. "Charlene, we have navigation up. See if you can figure out where we are."

In the command centre, the command chair started to show signs of activity, even if the control sphere was well and truly wedged into its housing. Once again Charlene stepped forward and sat in the seat, focusing ahead; but nothing happened. John looked at her with a question in his eyes.

"It's ok I just need to do this before it works," she concentrated on herself, and before John's eyes, a beautiful girl changed into one of the nightmarish Ghe'Dar; his face betraying his anger and disgust at the form she clothed herself in. It was the first time he'd seen one on the flesh.

"That really makes my blood boil you know, and gives me the chills at the same time," he said straight out, in a tightly controlled voice.

"It really is only skin deep you know. Well apart from the weird joints; they are terribly strange and uncomfortable." Her voice was distorted by the tentacles again, but if he focused really hard, he could understand the weird squelching sounds. She closed her eyes.

The control chair activated again, and the interface came up; overlaying her own, however, there was little displayed as active; auto-repair was active, whatever that did, although the percentage efficiency was exceedingly low, a mere four per cent. Scanners were not powered but there, sure enough, was the navigation and tracking system.

The current date and coordinates, Ghe'Dar reference for the planet, solar system and galaxy all showed up along with a warning that the transceiver was locked, whatever that meant. Charlene referred to the downloaded language details, allowing her, with a little mental effort to translate the words into English, since it was displayed in their language.

"Well, the good news is that I know where we are, at least, I think I do. However, I think we best discuss it before we do anything else. Simon. I'll need you up here, we'll need your expertise again I'm afraid."

"Be right there," he said clanging in. "Oh," he said, as he saw her in the chair, "I thought I'd misremembered that," he indicated Charlene's form. The shrug she gave was as much as an apology he was going to get, and it looked more like a shudder in her current form.

"so, what's the problem, Charlene?" Jack and Helena came in, trailing a bewildered human slave; who gasped and fell to his knees, upon seeing the Ghe'Dar in the command chair.

"As far as I can tell, we are in, no, sorry, under London," she saw the hope and incredulity flash through their faces, then they grew suspicious.

"So, what's the thing that needs an engineer, or cybernetics expert," came Simon's question, in confusion, "why don't we just head out and get Craig?.

"Well, it's a rather strange situation and a big problem and one I don't know how to get us out of, but you may," she said, opening her eyes, the control panel shutting down and flowed back into her real form, to the amazement of the cowering human.

"From the information from the panel: we are back in the original spaceship we found in the underground."

The others look perplexed, but Simon's eyes widened, and he groaned shaking his head, Charlene nodding, the others looking at them, waiting for an explanation of the problem. Charlene flicked her eyes from Simon to the others, he frowned, but reluctantly turned to the others.

"God; I hate temporal mechanics. Right, so we found a Ghe'Dar ship almost repaired in the underground in London; we sabotaged it and escaped." The others nodded, still waiting for the problem to be explained.

"But, now, here we are back in that ship; at the point in time when it originally crashed." He saw realisation dawning in their eyes.

John bowed his head, getting the picture, if not the actual problem. "We were sent to investigate our own crash," he shook his head, and Simon nodded.

"The **problem** we have is that we now have to decide which of the two main temporal theories we are going to believe and follow the appropriate course of action."

"Either: events are pre-determined, and we have to set up events so that, we leave the ship how we found it before, else the universe ends. Alternatively, we can do what we want, potentially changing events; and time will compensate around us. At least, that's how we will see it, because we might now be on a new timeline, unlikely, but not impossible."

Charlene thought back to all the things which had happened in her past, and immediately came to a decision. "The former." The others looked at her, begging the answer this time.

"Why so certain?" asked Simon.

"Certain. Something has been guiding us, and others, this way for a long time now. There have been a few things that did not add up before, that now start to make sense if the former case is true."

"What if you're wrong?" Jack asked the obvious question.

"Then at least we will take the Ghe'Dar with us," said Charlene, with grim finality. "But I am not wrong," she looked at them again and they all nodded. "I think we now have a timescale too. The auto repair system is saying repairs would be complete in about three weeks."

"That matches up with the timings that the woman from the square above gave us. We appear to be the cause of her problems with her television," thought Jack out loud, and he rubbed his head slightly.

"That means we now have three weeks to devise some sort of counter to the Ghe'Dar invasion," John said.

"That won't destroy our space-time continuum," added Simon.

"Or getting us caught by the Ghe'Dar," chimed in Helena.

"Yes, we have to get out of here, back to where we can do some good and make sure that contingencies are put in place to stop the Ghe'Dar; even if we fail."

Charlene started to say something but stopped before the words came out. Then, because of everything that had happened recently, she just sat down in the seat again and shook her head.

Simon came up and patted her arm, "there, there. It's a lot to take in."

"It's not that Simon," she muttered, "we need to do all this without popping up on the official grid either. That means we cannot call in M.I.X., the police and we cannot call in the military either," her spirit failed her for a moment.

"Not necessarily a problem, "Jack looked at her, and the others looked at him. "The authorities can be called to an incident. It does not necessarily need to be the one we're dealing with; but we can arrange it so we will have an effective diversionary force, to allow us to get in and do what is needed." Charlene and the others brightened. "The advantage of being a magician is that you are used to creating diversions and knowing when to do it. This is that time," the team nodded.

John suddenly frowned. "I think we need to get out of here. The longer we're here, the more likely we'll get caught here," the others nodding. As one, the group went to the door, opened it and went out into the dark rubble fill cavern that would later become a busy hive of activity. They took the only other natural exit from that cavern, noticing as they did so several large rats. They too would become victims of the Ghe'Dar eventually, but the group had larger concerns at the moment.

Helena was walking and sliding along with the captive they had rescued. "So, who are you?" she looked at him wafting torchlight in his direction, her shoulder under his arm.

"I am Henry Stewart-Denns, Ma'am, N.Y.P.D. police. I was investigating the disappearance of a scientist when I, erm, I think, I found a clue pointing to a location downtown." His voice was weak, uncertain and hesitant; not surprising given what had been done to him. "When me and m' partner went to investigate the location, against orders I may add," the others moved close and slowed to hear the story, "we were intercepted by a S.W.A.T. team and taken to the location, apparently having been expected. Then they did this to us," he flipped his hand at his head, looking at her and found, not incredulity, as he'd half expected, but simple acceptance. "How did you get in there?" It looked like he was starting to recover his faculties. Then he stopped. "Who are you people anyway? Where are we going?" and he started to resist Helena's helping arm.

"We are the people that saved you from the people that captured you," said John with his air of authority well in evidence. "We are British police," well it was nearly true, "and we require your help, as much as you need ours." Charlene was impressed by the way he had turned that around.

"Why do you need my help?" asked Henry, calming down and starting forward again.

"We have been investigating certain incidents here too, and we need to know what you found out about your disappearances." The statement was more an order than a request; the other policeman, however, recognised the tone and the need.

"Well, as I said," he stumbled a little, but continued, "we were intercepted, and the S.W.A.T. team took us to a warehouse in the docks area. When they removed their helmets, they all looked pretty much as I did when you found me. My partner tried to make a break for it, but someone shot him with a strange kind of tazer; he did not get up again." His head bowed remembering what for him was a recent event.

"What happened then," encouraged Helena, acting as a friend to the lost American.

"Well, they took me to a ship much like that one, inside the warehouse. Goodness knows how it got in there, but then virtually everything is a blur. I vaguely saw something that looked like a man with a squid on his head; no wait, a squid as a head. But that cannot be right," his voice faltered. Then he looked back towards Charlene. She looked a right at him, so saw as his eyes rolled up in his head, as he sagged in Helena's arms.

"Helena? What is it?" Charlene lifted the man, startling Helena so that Helena could look at him, without him sinking in the filth of the sewer around their feet.

"I cannot tell without proper equipment, "Helena complained. "I guess that the damage he has sustained is too much for him, even with our help." She lifted her staff to him, not only for light but also to try to give him some healing.

Instead, when she saw his face, she used another power to scan his mind; probing to sense the problem with the officer. The images were confused, but there was a fierce pain in the back of his head, and it was moving. Her head jerked back, felling his agony as the link broke.

"I think there is a failsafe in the device, design to kill the host after a fixed time without the control signal, and it's killing him right now." The shock on Charlene's face was apparent, but that did not stop her taking immediate action.

"Guide my hand," from beneath her wrist a slim metallic tendril came out. The others were as shocked as Helena, but she applied the hand and her power to guide the thing over the man's head.

"Easy, easy," Helena measured with her fingers the length Charlene needed to go into the skull to get the lethal device; Charlene nodded. "Now!" The tendril punched drown, and a crunch sounded. Little sparks flew up the tendril, and Charlene gritted her teeth.

"Little bastard doesn't know when to quit," she snarled, pulling hard and with a distinct pop out came a writhing, metallic, worm caught in a tiny set of jaws. Helena immediately applied some healing, as well as a bandage; but it was fairly evident that they would need to get serious help for the man soon.

"Simon, see if you can deal with this," requested Charlene, holding out the worm, its' large head thrashing around, glaring with eight eyes surrounding a circular mouth, filled with rotating saws for teeth.

"Wow, that's a seriously nasty fail-safe," he observed, lifting it and applied a hefty voltage to it, stopping the little monstrosity's movements dead. He then popped it into his hand and looked at it, with his HUD active.

"Can you look at it on the move?" asked John from the front.

Simon looked down and popped it into a belt container; it could wait.

"We are losing Henry. We need to get him help," Helena informed the others, getting quite anxious.

Charlene looked at her, then at John. "John, try and find us a way out of here, fast. Once we get out, Jack, we'll need an ambulance. See if you can either call or acquire one." John started to object, but Helena stopped him.

"He's got minutes to live unless we can get him some expert medical treatment. Just do it!" He stared hard at her, then nodded curtly and bolted off at incredible speed, arriving back a minute later, in a wave of sewer water and other debris.

"About two hundred yards, left, then another hundred right there is a manhole cover, coming out into a small alley, off the main street." He gasped, his chest heaving; he'd never used his speed for so long before, and he now knew what Charlene's hunger was like. He would kill for a good sixteen, no, thirty-two, or sixty-four, ounce steak right now. "Oh, and I called in a fake nine-nine-nine call to an address across the street. The ambulance should be here in about two minutes, give or take heavy traffic."

Helena was using her power to sustain Henry, but the look on her face said that his system was failing faster than she was healing him. As a Doctor, there was nothing worse than knowing you were doomed to failure when dealing with a patient. Jack, having had a similar feeling recently sympathised entirely. John lifted the man, and they hurried to the exit he'd located. The group moved quickly behind sombrely, but strangely not panicking; a man's life was in their hands, but then so were the lives of everyone in the world, panicking would not help.

As they arrived at the manhole, Jack went ahead, disappearing, as he left the hole, to go find the ambulance, returning a minute later, to see Henry starting to have difficulty breathing and his colour becoming jaundiced.

"Dammit we're going to lose him," Helena gritted, straining to pour more healing into her rapidly failing patient.

"The ambulance is just over the street," came Jack's voice, as he appeared halfway up the ladder. "The driver and responders are, sleeping, in the back," he said brandishing a hypospray. "They'll be out for an hour or two. Their call sign is

Charley One-Five. I've told their control that they are dealing with a situation in the locale. It will give us about thirty minutes free time."

Helena's look of relief and gratitude more than made up for Charlene's brusque attitude towards him as she focused on the patient. Well at least one of them was grateful.

"I'll back the vehicle up here, and you can put him straight in," John said, climbing the ladder carefully. "Then we can take him to a location I know, near a hospital. It will have to do for the moment until we can get him stable."

Lifting Henry into the large ambulance was easy but getting him onto the bed and treating him was harder, with the other two people in the back. Simon took the expedient course; simply dumping them out the back, onto some rubbish bags. Jack was outraged.

Simon saw the look and laughed briefly, "What?"

Jack looked at the scientist, "and what if they tell their superiors about the incident?"

"And what will they say? That someone drugged them, stole their ambulance, then abandoned it without taking the equipment, or the drugs." The scientist looked at Jack very seriously. "I don't think so. They will report it stolen, unless they want to go through disciplinary procedures for not being on duty, or worse, being asleep on duty. It will be recovered, and the reason for the theft will be left a mystery; one more in old London town." Simon's response did not placate the irate Jack's sense of mortality.

Meanwhile, John had put on the blues and twos and screeched off, for their destination; the Sat Nav showing that they were near North Clapham.

Helena yelled from the back. "The best place is King College Hospital. The Oval Ambulance station is only a mile from there so they won't ask too many questions about receiving an unannounced arrival. We'll say he's a homeless person, make up some mummery about him being a veteran, that'll explain the skull plate." John was impressed by her improvisation. He hit an unusually large bump in the road, as he swerved to avoid an oblivious pizza scooter.

"Easy there, Driver," came Charlene's voice, "it's hard enough keeping him with us, without all the bumps."

"Feel free to come up here and drive if you like!" He yelled back. She was going to reply, but Helena called for more Adrenaline.

"The Morphine has blocked the pain and de-stressed his system, the fluids and plasma have slowed the deterioration of his vitals, but he still needs surgery urgently."

"Getting there!" came the voice from the front.

"How are you going to explain to me when we get out?" Simon, in armour, was wedged in tightly against the driver's cab, in the back.

"Ah, well, we don't. You stay there while the girls wheel him out. Charlene can change her appearance, and Jack can be invisible so they will get someone out here somehow, then we'll leave him to their mercies, while we get out of here, dump the ambulance, and get undercover again. "Jack thought about it a second, then come up with a better idea.

"How about this instead. I go invisible and get the name of a doctor, then Charlene can tell the admissions people, that he's a transfer for that doctor." Charlene believed that Jack was actually enjoying the theatrics of this bizarre situation. "Then, we come back, and we're off. Once they have operated on him, we can come back and get the info. If he survives."

"Seems sound," John complimented them. "Thirty seconds. We're almost there," as he swerved past another ambulance, carrying on past the hospital, to get into the entrance. The other ambulance had blocked the CCTV camera's view of their vehicle.

Charlene looked out the window, as a male paramedic walked away from the entrance; either off shift or having a lunchtime break.

She studied him then quickly shifted to look like him, well almost, and popped the ambulance door open. Jack was already invisible, out the ambulance and through the reception's automatic entry door. Helena, as a doctor, had a face mask on and pulled the stretcher out of the ambulance with Charlene catching the other end.

The whole place bustled with patients, porters, and doctors, with that antiseptic smell that seemed all-pervading in hospitals, along with the old lights, worn fittings and the air of obsolescence. The girls wheeled the patient to the emergency entrance and, as the doors opened a voice reached Charlene's ear,

"Doctor Shavine Chakra; neurology. He arrived about thirty minutes ago and is on floor two. See you in the van," and Jack's voice went silent.

The patient and his carers pulled up to the reception area, "Patient for Doctor Chakra. Transfer from Lambert. They said it was urgent."

The receptionist was a middle-aged woman, short-haired, lean, stern but not severely so. "Signs?"

Helena rattled off the very low vital signs, indicating the patient was borderline.

"Doctor?"

"Paramedic," replied Helena, pointing to her purloined jacket from the ambulance.

"David?" the receptionist asked. Dam, how had she missed that? She'd only looked at the surname.

"Her hubby. They sometimes swop shifts," Charlene bailed her out.

"The doctor will be down soon, put him in bay five and I'll send the resident to you as soon as he's out of the one he's in at the moment." she indicated bay three.

"He needs urgent," started Helena, the receptionist putting up a hand to stay her next request.

"This is A&E dear. They are all urgent." The mixture of pity and resignation on her face was unmistakable. "We know that we can save some. He will have to wait his turn for examination." She pointed to curtains. "Bay five, please."

Charlene nodded and pushed him to the bay then closed the curtain, carefully guiding Helena out and into the Ambulance; which departed immediately.

"Well?" Simon said.

"My best guess is that he'll not pull through, but if he does it will take some time, and it will most likely be all over by the time he does," Helena had to be content with that.

John sighed. "All for nothing then."

Helena looked at him sharply. "It was not all for nothing. A man's life is not nothing John Brickman. You of all people should know that."

The grinding of teeth at the front told Charlene that the retort had hit home, and hard.

"I'm sorry," was all he muttered a few seconds later.

"We are ALL sorry," consoled Helena, and John realised she was not talking about the stranger they had just tried to save. "She was a vibrant, beautiful, young girl John, and a friend. I miss her too, you know, but don't let her passing stop you from living, or saving the rest of the girls, and the men, on this planet. Focus your anger on the Ghe'Dar, not on what might have been; then we can stop them from causing more deaths like Isabelle."

An emphatic nod was all the sign he showed that he'd heard her. Helena turned to Charlene, who mouthed a "thank you," for her words. John was grieving, in his own tight-lipped and secluded fashion, and it had made him waspish. Now perhaps Helena had focused him where he could unleash that grief and the anger it generated, against the real enemy, rather than the closest targets; his team.

The ambulance was parked in a bay furthest from the ambulance station, not a mile from the hospital. The station cameras did not see the driver, or the passenger, leave the vehicle, and the person that opened the back seemed to accidentally discharge a fire extinguisher, causing a great billow of mist from the rear. By the time it had cleared, there was no one in sight. On the remaining stretcher was a note. "Sorry about borrowing the ambulance but it was an emergency. Don't discipline the crew."

"What if they do fingerprint analysis?" Simon asked.

Charlene shrugged. "Good luck to them. I randomised my fingerprints patterning. If they can match it, it would be a remarkable coincidence. You might even say fated."

Simon laughed at that, "Charlene, you could say that about just about anything really."

Then he stopped laughing, as she looked him right in the eyes and said earnestly, "actually I really could." Their eyes stayed locked for a long time before she released him with a severe nod; then, Charlene just crumpled forward unconscious. The rest looked at her and wondered what had just happened.

Charlene started to come around, with the sky looking blue-grey and the rest in a huddle to her right, discussing something causing it to get pretty heated.

"And you never thought to tell us?" growled Helena, gesticulating at John.

"We had a mission to plan and an invasion to stop; we still do. It still may be nothing but the hysteria brought on by her condition," John replied, trying to control his anger.

"There have been the nightmares and the screaming fits, but we ascribed to exhaustion caused by her past," Simon added.

Charlene had heard enough. "I was going to say something," they all turned to look at her, "when we had time." She turned and put her legs on the pavement, dangling them from the wall they had lain her down on.

"John here said you'd made pronouncements like this before," Helena approached her, with staff in hand, in an uncharacteristically belligerent manner.

"Easy there Helena," Jack's diffident voice tried to sooth the tensions that were obviously boiling over, "she is still recovering from her faint. Remember, she is almost totally inexperienced, with the outside world, and has in the past few days undergone a series of traumatic changes." Jack's voice of reason, seemed to penetrate the anger Helena felt.

Charlene nodded. "When I was ill, I remembered a lot about the night my parents died," the other's faces shifted in surprise. "I mean when they were supposed to have died.

Helena's face froze at that, "supposed to have?"

Charlene continued. "I remembered that they had fought over me and that something else was there too. A Demon." Simon's face became pure sceptic at that point. "I saw it as I see you all now. As real as this wall; perhaps even more so." Her hands started to wring, and her voice was getting higher. "It spoke to me if you can call its' language speaking." She started to shake, and Helena now regretted her words as the poor girl was actually trembling almost uncontrollably. "And, do you know what it said, it said to me."

Suddenly the trembling stopped and a terrible voice issued from her mouth, enough to stop everyone in their tracks. "I am coming for you, my child. Nothing can stop me. I will be back for you, Charlene Klerk," then she sparked out again.

The second time she came around, the others were all gone; bar Helena. They were in, what appeared to be a dusty old shell of a warehouse, or factory.

"Easy there. I did a quick medical assessment, you're fine." The voice was Helena's soothing bedside manner, but Charlene was feeling confused; her HUD was skittering from green to red all over the place. What was happening?

"Helena we need to talk," Helena's hand restrained her.

"Easy there. I'm sorry about before, I had not realised that Isabella's loss would have such an effect on me," Helena shifted uncomfortably. "I believe I know why you're having problems. It seems you're suffering from Hypoglycaemia, amongst other things," Helena's voice contained a huge amount of certainty. "You're exhibiting all the classic symptoms; hunger, dizziness, tiredness, blurred vision, trembling, pallid skin and palpitations." The 'other' things they'd have to look at another time.

"Yes, but that is not all." Charlene tried to push past the hand, but was too weak and listless, probably because of the shapeshifting, requiring her to lay back again, as Helena reached for a cup.

"Here drink this, it's a sports drink Jack acquired for me." She pointed to a line of them. "He's becoming quite a good Quartermaster," she smiled a little. "He might not like the roll, but his new powers are perfectly suited for it."

She pointed to some rather non-descript clothes. Fresh clothes. Ah. It was the little luxuries that one missed first; a change of clothes, a bit on the large size, but then she could literally, make them fit. She'd never been the self-conscious type, having been too busy, now she just had no need. If she did not like her body, she could literally change it. The thought made her smile a little at the vanity of it in the midst of such a critical time. Besides her real body was the default for her and she would never change that; not for anything in the world.

"Where are the others?" Charlene asked, turning her head to the side to slurp the drink. It did make the systems alerts in her head quiet down a little, most going amber, rather than red. Note for the future; have glucose drinks on hand for emergency recharging.

"They are trying to acquire another vehicle as transport; something less high profile, that no one will miss too much. I did not ask for the details. John and Simon seem to have contacts that, perhaps, I don't want to, officially, know about. Jack said he was going to get a few things; again, I thought it was best not to ask, and he did not seem happy about it. I think the others were asking him to get some ready cash and you know how strict his upbringing was.

Charlene had not, but filled it for future reference. "Helena, we really need to talk about what has been happening to me."

Helena sighed, "yes, we probably do my dear." She stood up slightly, and Charlene sat up, not feeling nearly as dizzy as she had before, the drink having worked its' magic.

"I read your files before you arrived at M.I.X. Your parents' deaths were unexplained in the papers and official reports, precisely the thing M.I.X. relates to; the fact that both your father and your uncle worked for them already kind of made it personal for Craig."

Charlene blinked. "He knew? About my family; Dad, Nigel, and my mother."

Helena lifted her hand and wagged it a little, then blinked, "You know about Nigel?"

The girl nodded, "he visited me briefly during our stay in Poole."

Helena huffed a little, then sighed. "I sort of guessed he might be around. John worked on the science development arm of M.I. then, but Nigel was an actual M.I.X field operative. It was Nigel that introduced Sylvia to John." Helena frowned, "We all wish he hadn't now of course; nothing personal my dear, but it would have saved us so much trouble." It was Charlene's turn to frown. "Oh, not because of you, but because of Sylvia. You see, although she was an excellent Agent, and nice enough to talk to, it turned out she'd had her own agenda." Helena sat down next to the girl, reached out and put her hands on top of the other girl's own; they were surprisingly warm given how chill this large open plan area was.

"You see when M.I.X. recruited Sylvia, she was given a high-security clearance; fair enough you say. But after a few months, things started to go wrong. She lost two or three people during a particularly easy assignment. They just vanished according to her and, with no-one to gainsay that, it was filed under the, rather substantial, unexplained files section. Isabella would have been able to dig it out for us given time but," she shrugged, and the younger girl could see the hurt in her eyes. Charlene reversed the hands on her lap, comforting the other this time. Helena looked up, and her eyes were slightly red. She coughed to clear her throat and carried on.

"Anyway, things progressed, and Sylvia continued to make inroads in the cases we had. She had an aptitude for weapons, gathering information and special knowledge of the occult; one that allowed us to break a large coven in Cambridge that was using women as spirit conduits. She offered to sort through their records to try and break the Coven, once and for all. She ploughed into the recovered documents and put her other assignments on the back burner." Helena smiled, a rueful twist on her lips, "we should have guessed at that point; but hindsight is a truly wonderful thing." She stood up at that point.

"She met your father about that time, introduced by your uncle, Nigel. At first, it was just work, hitting it off well enough while rifling through the records. Then it got more serious, and John fell for her big time according to Nigel, who was, of course, furious, as he'd been seeing Sylvia for months. While Sylvia and John were not together long, because of his work and her reviewing of the material from the Coven, they grew close, and you were conceived.

For a short time, they were blissfully happy, and their work continued, mainly at A.G.E, or its, precursor actually; until she grew too large to do fieldwork. Then she was put to working on deciphering some obscure writings, discovered in the occult books which were located in the aftermath of a raid in Lancashire." She turned her back on Charlene and walked a little. "She found what she'd needed M.I.X. to find in those books." She turned back, angry with Sylvia. "She was trying to find a way to channel spirits alright; Demonic ones."

"How did M.I.X. find out about that?" Charlene was starting to feel strange again; like the life, she thought she knew was a lie, a figment created to hide the truth.

"The M.I.X. records office burned down; we suspect now that Sylvia organised that, but we cannot be certain; if she was though, she slipped up. The office was virtually obliterated, the fire was so hot that even the steal re-enforced girders melted. So M.I.X. had to conduct a review of security clearances. It turned out that the person who'd cleared her had falsified her references and referees; we never found out why, as during the course of the investigations he died under mysterious circumstances. It started to get messy at that point. You don't need to know the full details but basically the M.I. sections had a purge, of sorts, clearing out infiltrators, trying to recover lost records, that kind of thing. They attempted to restore Sylvia's reference records from the original immigration records, but they came up blank there too; all lost during transfer from paper to computer records at immigration. In the confusion, Sylvia escaped. So, John took you to a section safe house."

"What about her visits?" Charlene objected, at which point Helena stopped and stared at her. "She used to come to Brae and take me to visit her house and train me."

"That's, impossible," Helena looked at Charlene with incredulity.

Charlene shook her head, "every few weeks, she'd come; telling me that Daddy had said she could, to train me in specific things. We used to train in Gymnastics, Martial Arts and the like, using whips," she managed to control her voice as she said it, "I remember 'them' all too well."

Helena shook her head slowly, still bewildered by the information. "John reported into the mainland every month. I guess that she monitored him, then visited you during those visits." Helena was getting more worried by the look on her face. "The question is why? If she really wanted you for sacrifice to her Demon, as you say, then she could have just taken you. The guards planted in Brae obviously could not stop her; even your dad would have been vulnerable to her abilities."

"In my dream, the demon was opposed by something behind Dad; another creature. Perhaps that stopped her?"

Helena shrugged, "possibly," sitting next to her, "perhaps we'll find out eventually, but for now we have other worries."

"What about my mother?" She was trying hard to tell Helena that she'd seen her recently, but the words would not come out.

"Ongoing investigations have attempted to locate her, by using her maiden name, via Interpol. They suggested the name is Eastern European in origin, but that's as far as we got."

Helena looked at Charlene, who was now looking healthier, if more confused. "The real question is what does your past have to do with what's happening to you at the moment? Not being a psychiatric doctor, it would be a guess, but I'd have to say multiple personality disorder brought on by acute childhood trauma". Charlene looked at her shocked until she realised Helena was using a fake Freudian accent, which caused her to smile. Then the smile dropped. "Seriously though, having been what you have been through, I would not be surprised if you had developed those kinds of problems. Hell, I've had problems with all of this," she admitted candidly, "who would not. Our entire world has been shaken up and rattled until even our past is suspect." She paused a second. "At least I'm less worried about you now."

Charlene turned her head slightly begging the question.

"If you were under the power of Sylvia or that of the demon, you would not have told me about the training she gave you," Charlene's eyes suddenly went very around.

Helena saw it and smiled, "You were worried?" Charlene nodded, then shook her head.

Helena looked at her harder, not understanding the mixed signal. "You are worried?"

Charlene nodded vigorously and looked at Helena wand. Helena's eyes showed a growing suspicion. "Oh, no. She would have at that wouldn't she," She drew the wand and whisked it slightly. Once again, she held a large staff, but not only that she now wore a costume of white robe, embossed with golden runes. Charlene had never seen someone look so radiant in her life; not even her mother on her wedding photos.

"Now we discover the truth,'" her voice was vibrant, commanding and the words that followed did not register to Charlene's hearing. She seemed to float in the clouds again for a few seconds, then Helena fell quiet. Light surrounded Charlene, Helena starring deep into her eyes; as if looking beyond her.

Then the world 'blinked' and they were sat back down again, and everything was back to normal. With the exception that Helena now leant against her staff in her regular clothes.

She looked exhausted. "My poor, dear, Charlene, I had no idea." She sat and fell against the girl, her breath ragged.

"What happened?".

Helena looked at her and shook her head, "I cannot say really. The answers would only confuse you at the moment."

"I'm not a child Helena," Charlene bristled.

"I know dear, but magic is, complicated and I don't understand some things I just saw." She thought a second. "You've had a spell cast on you, literally. It's complex and powerful, but in essence, it's guarding you against certain things." Helena then shrugged, "me finding out what it is, is apparently one of them. I'd never even heard of magic that protects itself before, and it took all my effort to save myself from insanity."

Charlene passed her a sports drink which was gulped down in seconds.

"I don't have all the answers, Charlene. All we can say now is that we know part of what is happening to you. I imagine that your changes have also influenced, if not exacerbated, your nightmares and general condition." Helena shook her head again. "It's a wonder you can function at all. You're stronger than you look, apparently. Not surprising though, given you parents nature; no matter how your mother ended up, although I suspect we don't know the whole story with that yet." Helena stood.

"Let's leave it there for the moment. Perhaps we can come up with something to remove the effects in time; once we have found and sorted out this Demon of yours."

"You sound so sure we can," Charlene was genuinely scared they could not.

"Did you mention that you had seen yourself saying that the Demon was your final test for your real challenge?"

"Yes," although she could not exactly remember when she'd told her that.

"There you go then. You think you could do it, don't you!" Helena cracked a peculiar smile at her, and Charlene understood the rather strange joke.

She gave up and laughed a little "I suppose so, at least part of me does," and they both laughed. Then they started to discuss other things, for no other reason other than they were not world shattering. They discussed many things; Charlene's schooling, Helena's training in medicine, then onto less familiar ground for Charlene; the men in Helena's life, her nights out and what university life was like for the thousands of 'normal' people. Charlene learned about true friendship in that time, and her view of Helena changed from a teammate to that of a sister that she'd never had.

After another thirty minutes, the boys returned to find the two women huddled together, talking quietly to one another, as they approached. The girls looked at the three returning men and whispered again, laughing at something. The men's faces said it all.

"So is it a private joke?" said Simon a bit grumpily.

"We were just saying that you all looked like three naughty schoolboys," said Helena, in a perfectly straight face.

"I was under orders," said an even grumpier Jack. Although he was more-guilty for actually having enjoyed his little crime spree, rather than actually committing the crimes. He'd only targeted those that he saw as overly wealthy, or in one case, a group of criminals who'd been about to rob a bank. The irony is that he'd manage to steal the keys from their getaway car too so that when they came out from their heist, they would find that they could not get away. Since he'd also filched one of their phones and made a 999 call, they would also probably find a group of police cars waiting for them too. It was almost poetic in its symmetry; shame no-one had actually seen him do it.

Simon had had to un-suit to go with John to make a call from an out of the way pay phone; one of a few remaining still operational. They had arranged with their contacts for a vehicle delivery at a nearby location, cash on delivery.

John informed the rest about the vehicle. "They said it will be a large van; probably a square back kind; large enough for Simon anyway." His face was a little tense though. "There may be a slight problem, however, "everyone became alert. More problems were the last thing they needed. "They asked for more money than we have at present and,"

"… we still need the van," finished Simon.

"We could just steal one," offered Helena. It was the obvious solution.

"And risk getting the police involved, and changing the timeline?" Simon asked, Helena, sagging a little. That did make things harder. "It might be a good solution," Helena perked up, "but why take the risk. Besides we had a specific requirement, that a random van will not fill; an extra internal power system."

"The money is no problem," said Charlene. She seemed much stronger than before, John noted. Whatever Helena had done seemed to have worked wonders. "We use knockout gas on them then," Charlene suggested. The others looked around, and there were no complaints, so she continued.

"Simon can your suit, and bits and pieces, run up a little computer interface for me?"

He nodded, frowning at her, wondering where this was going.

"I need to start using my chemistry skills, to create us some non-lethal weapons for humane enemy suppression." Her voice was filled with frustration, at not being able to apply the simple solution.

Jack passed Simon a small box. "Picked this up in a second-hand shop. Might help."

The box contained a load of circuit boards of varying ages, causing Simon to purse his lips, but instead of complaining all he replied was, "yup, almost certainly will. I already have the other electronics in my bag".

Charlene started towards the line of drinks, turning her head to Jack. "Sorry Jack, but we'll need quite a few more of those drinks bottles, and something larger, to produce enough knockout gas."

John was looking at Charlene, with a certain amount of curiosity. She saw the look and nodded for him to ask the question she saw in his eyes. He shrugged "OK. How are you going to create knockout gas with those plastic bottles and some high sugar sports drinks? There I asked it!" He said in exasperation.

She smiled, a pure white, almost beatific one; pointing at Simon. "Actually, he's going to produce it, all I need the interface for is it add a little control to my tentacles, and my HUD; it's fritzing slightly." She pointed at the bottles. "Under certain circumstances, the plastic in the bottles breaks down, producing chemicals that can be used as an anaesthetic. Simon can create those conditions with his electrical powers; we just capture the resultant in the other bottles."

She frowned a little, "it will be messy, wasteful and dangerous close-up; but I'll be stood several meters away, and Simon will be in his armour, so it should be safe enough."

"How fast will it act?" Helena asked.

Charlene shrugged a little, "a few seconds, probably, in the concentrations we'll be making." Helena turned her head slightly, and Charlene shrugged again, "best I can do, with the equipment at hand." Helena slipped her wand into her pocket.

"It will have to do. I suppose I can always control them a little; to muddy the water."

John turned to her. "You could just control them and get the van that way."

Helena shook her head. "The stronger the mind, the more likely someone will get shot. Best not risk it. Besides, I need line-of-sight; by the time I managed that, we may well already dead. It's why I did not suggest it." She chided. John looked disappointed but shrugged to indicate it had still been worth asking.

The next hour or two was spent creating a make-shift, laboratory and generating the knock-out gas, seemingly petty compared to saving the world, but they had to start somewhere. As they neared the end of their little experiment, Jack appeared from outside, where he'd been keeping guard, reporting calmly, "we've got company!" Oh great; they just did not catch a break.

Helena started towards the entrance, "Jack and me will deal with this." She showed the man outside. "What we got?" She asked, trying to understand the situation.

"Looks like someone saw the fumes, thought it was smoke and called in the Fire Brigade. There is a fire engine deploying out front. They have breathing apparatus, and there are two coming down the alley."

Jack took off and vanished, drifting above the scene. "Looks like a senior guy and someone with a measuring unit of some kind. Probably checking for noxious fumes," came his assessment down the comms.

Helena switched frequencies. "How long do you lot need to complete and tidy up?"

"Too long for either," came Charlene's voice, "and neither Simon nor I can help. Plus, if we leave now, we won't have the gear for our meeting in an hour."

Then the simple answer can to John. "Time to test it!" The silence was stunning, then a snigger came down the comms.

"John, you're a true genius," coming from Charlene it was a real compliment.

"With the senior man down, the scanner in situ and increasing volumes of gas coming down the alley, they will have to declare a major incident; meaning a COBRA liaison, police, ambulance, more fire units. By the time they mobilise all that we will have enough and be out of here."

"What about the cordon, CCTV and getting the police involved?" Helena was getting a little alarmed by the way this was escalating. "And didn't we want to avoid corrupting the timeline?"

"Sometimes to hide a small op, you pull a big one," said John, "but in this case, there is another reason. If the enemy has infiltrated the local government, and services; this will give them something to occupy them, while we slip through to get to Geneva."

"John, sometimes you're too smart for your own good," and she gave a little bow in his direction, even though he could not see it.

"Ok," said Jack, "but if they are wearing breathing apparatus how do we knock 'em out."

"Guess!" said John, with a certain satisfaction.

Jack groaned, "my mother would disown me if she knew what I have been doing today."

The fire supervisor, Ashley, walked down the narrow, cluttered alley slowly and carefully, the other access route blocked by building support work. He could see the white smoke billowing from the build to his left, but he could not see any flames, nor feel any of the expected heat yet. "Foxtrot Bravo One proceeding in, at twenty metres. No signs of combustion yet, moving on."

"Confirmed Foxtrot Bravo one," replied his Control, monitoring their progress.

His operational buddy, Bob, was right behind him with a gas probe; a new piece of kit they had received just for this kind of thing. He was nearly as experienced as Ashley, and they'd been working together for years, gaining a sixth sense for when trouble was near, a something that he felt right now with great urgency.

Suddenly from the open warehouse doors ahead came a blast of white fumes, rolling up almost right in front of them. "Not getting any monoxide. Something though," came the buddies report, which died halfway through, followed by a choking sound.

Ashley turned to see his second trying to get his respirator back on. It seemed to have come off, possibly caught against a nearby fire escape ladder somehow, but strangely, he seemed to be experiencing an awful lot of trouble refitting the respirator; almost like he was unable to get it back on. He stepped forward to help when he was shoved from behind, and his own respirator popped off, unseen hands blocking his attempts to get it on, and felt himself slipping into unconsciousness. He tried to call for help, but another invisible hand clamped itself over his mouth, stopping him from uttering the plea for assistance; the whole scene going dark as he slumped to the floor.

Jack grabbed the second respirator and caught some fresh air. "Ok. they are out."

"Right, get them out of the gas, then call it in," instructed John.

Two tentacles came through the smoke and lifted the bodies out of sight, while Jack floated up again, with the super's radio. Knowing that the receiver would distort his voice anyway, he made the call simple.

"Foxtrot Bravo One to Control. Situation Report. We have a chemical release at grid Delta Seven Five, reading as toxic, possibly, Di-ethyl ether. Requesting three respirator crews to attend, as well as local evacuation to about five hundred meters." Then in a more conversational mode, he added, "the residents beyond the cordon will need to close their windows and keep their pets indoors, and the police need to evacuate beyond the cordon before they set it up; this gas will knock them out too. Foxtrot Bravo One Out"

"Confirmed Foxtrot Bravo One. Three engines Chemical incident. Police and Ambulance to been alerted. Out." Jack smiled; by making sure that the police evacuated first, they made sure that they could escape as soon as they were ready. As he came down from his vantage point, he saw one of the vehicles in the building site next door and suddenly had an idea.

When Jack rolled into the warehouse through the back entrance with a large yellow truck, the others were startled.

"Well, I guess the plan changed," said John scowling.

"What happened to your strong moral sense, Jack?" asked Charlene, as she loaded up the containers into the back. The smoke was now just some rubbish they were burning to replace the chemicals they had finished collecting.

"I figured that it's Ok to have a strong moral sense; but only if you're alive and have a planet to practice it on." He shrugged, and the others just smiled. "Besides I'm just borrowing it. I'm sure they'll get it back. Well fairly sure."

"What about you're contacts? And their truck?" Helena asked.

Simon looked a little sheepish. "Well they may be a little disappointed, but they get to keep a rather nice truck." He was eyeing up the power generator truck Jack had delivered with avarice.

The whole team drove out under cover of the evacuation, about two minutes ahead of the second fire team, Simon hooking his armour up to the generator almost immediately.

They drove the truck to an area sparse in CCTV, and concealed it, much to Simon's disgust; or rather, John drove it to that location, then ran back to where he'd dropped the rest of them off.

Another warehouse area, this time in Woolwich, near the docks. The building was more intact and modern, requiring greater care to enter. Jack guided John in, shorting out substations near the warehouse complex, and the team moved in, Jack and Simon disabling cameras and power relays as they progressed. Once a couple of local substations fell prey to their sabotage, the team finally reached a warehouse near a docked ship at the quay and, coincidentally, near the other thing they might need; an airport.

"You realise the damage we are causing?" asked Helena.

"Of course I do," said Jack, almost casually, "I checked the power grid specs in the truck on the way here. The women from the square told me all about the problems they'd had with the electricity and television signals, both in the square and, in the local area. I'm, specifically, targeting power systems that she mentioned, as well as the security systems."

Helena blinked. "Sorry I did not link those to us, but of course." Her problem was that he was quiet and rarely gave suggestions, but when things needed doing, he was the one to just do them. Perhaps because unlike the scientists, he did not need to confirm it was the right course of action.

"No problem. Most people think their power comes directly from a local sub-station. But actually, they come from rather around about places in London. This is the source of the transmitter's power for that area; as well as that underground system," his pride seemingly fully justified. Some people thought he was a simple illusionist; he thought there was no such thing.

"Now all we need to do is plan our next steps. I think we'll have about a day before we have to start dodging again," said Jack.

"Why a day?" said John, "why not sooner."

"Few engineers other than those for the power grid come out on Sundays; it's Sunday today, and we have the power grid's truck." They'd been running so fast these past hours that they had not even thought of the day. Sure enough, the calendar clock on the wall said, it was Sunday, the sixth of April, twelve days before the conference attack which had started it all.

"Ok," John started, "Let's plan." Then he stopped, "but first we sleep. We've been through a lot, and we cannot keep going without at least a few hours."

"Where?" Helena asked, looking around and just seeing some containers with bubble wrap around them. John saw the glace and indicated them to her.

"You're not serious?" He nodded. "You are serious," she shook her head.

"It's those or the floor." He settled down near a pile of rubble; he'd needed the ability to sleep anywhere on stakeouts. Jack wrapped his stage cloak about himself and knotted a couple of handkerchiefs together as a pillow, passing some to Helena and Charlene.

Simon just sighed and lay back against the floor. "Thank goodness it's Spring and not Winter," was all he muttered. Having padding in the armour, meant he was the only one with a ready-made bed.

Charlene thought about changing, then realised that even if she changed form, her skin would still be right next to the cold hard floor. So, she just settled down for the most uncomfortable night's sleep she'd ever had.

The next morning, they started to plan in earnest.

Chapter 10

PLANS WITHIN PLANS

It took them a few hours of contentious planning and vociferous counter planning before they had a course of action that they all reluctantly agreed on, also settling on the code names they would use for communications, none's really being a surprise to the others. However, they decided that they should continue to use first names until the use of code names was needed.

The plan would allow them to safely get to where they needed to be at the correct time, they hoped. The whole team had argued heatedly about that time: should it be when they had vanished from the vortex, or when they arrived at the machine the first time before Isabelle fell; allowing them to save her, or even before they came to CERN to allow them to prepare for it.

John insisted, quite vocally, that the team be there in time to save Isabella; but the fact that Jack had seen her fall so far had put pay to that idea.

"Charlene, could we not try," his voice hoarse with emotion, when he argued the point. The look she gave him was full of regret, but also steely resolve.

"John. I'm sorry, but the risk is too great, and I have a feeling that her sacrifice was one of the necessities of this event," her head bowed, missing the red-faced rage erupting on his visage, directed at her.

"What makes your idea of right and wrong so much better than mine?" he'd yelled, starting forward at her. She'd stood ready to protect herself, but Simon had stepped in, shaking his head in regret, his eyes locking on John's like a restraining hand. John had turned his back on them, then parked himself silently next to the wall; even John could not be so blinded by rage, as to fight that massive metallic figure.

"I have had a sense of such things since my change, John," she addressed him, even with his back was towards her. "It is not a logical thing. It just is. She is not supposed to be here. Yet,"

"Perhaps you are wrong," he'd snarled, and walked into the warehouse office.

"Could he be right Charlene?" opened Helena and flinched at the fierce look she received back.

"We are trying to save the world. One person, no matter how precious to us, is not worth losing that for," growled Charlene. The others, bar John, had finally agreed.

The group split up, some making detailed notes on what they needed to do, others getting food; Charlene and Jack were all for that. While they found a local place to get a take away incognito, Helena wandered into the office to see how John was doing. He was sat in the corner his head in his hands.

"You OK?" she asked quietly, not wanting to startle him.

"What do you think?" he said through gritted teeth, remorse dripping from a trembling, deathly quiet, voice. "I know I had only just met her really, but I've got, had, feelings for her, and we were getting close when I lost her. Now we have a chance to save her, and it's denied me; how do you really think I feel?" He lifted his head, and it was pretty obvious he'd been crying; the claw marks on his palms said he'd also been clenching his fists. Unlike Simon and Charlene, his body did not seem to repair itself, only the bruising around it vanishing quickly, unlike his grief.

"Simon told me about the various theories; they are pretty sketchy, but they all agree that paradoxes are not something we want to mess with," Helena consoled him. His face started to go slightly redder, but she quickly carried on. "They are also not something we have dealt with before, at least not knowingly," she checked they were alone, "it may be that, as we get nearer to the time, we see something; an opportunity, a, let's say for the sake of it a get out that may allow us to save Isabella." His eyes locked onto hers, hers showing she was obviously willing to try, given an opportunity, "we cannot know what will happen. Despite what they say," she flicked a semi-dismissive, thumb in the scientist's direction, "it may be that we can save her without any issues, but, if we do, she must come with us. If she tries to do something separately, she must be stopped, understood!"

His eyes brightened, and he nodded. Where before there was only rebellion and grief, now there was hope and determination. Just what they needed to succeed. "Oh, and one other thing John."

"Yes?" he seemed lighter now, or at least less down.

"Don't tell the others yet; at the moment they will not understand. Let me work on them" Helena stared at him until he nodded, this would be for Isabella, not the rest of the world.

Charlene and Jack were on their way back to the warehouse, when a police car flew past them, probably on the way to the incident' they had caused. She looked like a tall, teenage boy in a tracksuit and jeans; the face she was using did not look exactly right, looking quite effeminate. Jack was in a hoodie, looking non-descript, unlike his stage outfit. They were carrying a sizable portion of chicken and chips, fish and chips plus snacks in a bag. Charlene had already eaten a fair portion, but even so, most of the food was still earmarked for her.

"Charlene, can I ask you a question?" asked Jack, seeming a little reticent about whatever he was about to ask, so Charlene slowed a little, leaning closer to allow him to talk quieter.

"Jack I think we have been through enough to call us at least colleges, if not friends. You can ask anything you like."

"It's kind of personal, so I want to know you're ok with discussing it," he glanced sideways. "It's about your parents."

"Ah. Well, what can I say? If I can remember, I'll tell you," although she was a little less sure of what she knew about her parents these days.

"What do you remember about them?" His voice was less questioning about them and more questioning what Charlene knew.

"From what I remember my dad was kind if totally distracted by his work. He was into his chemistry but liked to play games and do puzzles with me. Before my parents broke up, they took me to places in the country; parks and forests, although usually to do science things and collect herbs. My mother," Jack noted the bitterness and painful undertone when Charlene said the M word, "really liked to get fresh herbs. I bet she picked other things there too though."

"Other things?" Jack frowned, wondering what else there could be.

"In the woods and wild places of the country, some plants are used for darker purposes than just feeding people. Poisons from Berries, Mushrooms that yield addictive drugs and plants that can kill at a touch." She looked at him sideways too, "it is the kind of thing she would collect. I never told daddy, she made sure of that." She carried on walking, but her head dropped a little, "even before they split-up, she'd started training me. The Gymnastics was the worst. You'd probably think that the Martial Arts would have been worse with the throws and block, but at least they had proper instructors. The Gymnastics, she taught me herself and used whips; whips, on her own daughter, so that I would be, motivated, to get the moves correct."

Jack winced, that would really hurt a girl with no real muscle or fat to protect her bones from the stings.

"How did she get away with it; what about the marks?" Jack objected.

"She was always good at controlling people. Dad was under her spell for a while, although he did not know it. It was uncle Nigel; apparently, that broke that, and even then, daddy fell out with him over it, or so Helena says," her voice dropping and becoming almost child-like, as she started feeling sad talking about her father. "She'd cover the marks with either makeup I suppose, or the people that visited were under her spell too," she finished.

"Hello sonny!" said a figure in front of her, one of about ten.

Ordinarily exceedingly observant, the two of them were so wrapped up in Charlene's reminiscing that they had failed to notice a group of ten people slowly surrounding them.

"We're famished, can we have some?" said one only semi-jokingly.

"Well actually we'll have it all of it if that's all right," came a voice from behind.

A tall, leathery-skinned man, mid-thirties with short cropped hair and a southern European accent, sauntered towards the two, while four slightly smaller men flicked out lock knives to emphasise the request.

Jack looked at Charlene and cringed, as the look on her face meant only one thing; this was going to get ugly rapidly. She touched her ear, and he heard the comms channel going to Open; the others could now hear everything.

"Well since we are only two blocks over from where we were going, I think that perhaps you might want to leave us alone." Her voice was almost her natural voice. What was she doing?

"What have we here?" said the man, stepping closer, close enough that he sniffed her, "he thinks he's a she." He laughed, and the others laughed a little. Jack could see her hands slowly curling up and stepped back a little giving her room, should she start to act.

"Hey Frederico, is this you' boyfriend?" he laughed at Jack, who actually smiled, quite affably back.

"Boyfriend? No. He's a friend though, just like his bodyguard, who is about to hand you all your butts," Jack had heard the noisy arrival of John behind himself.

"Call for help?" asked John quietly, arriving at speed.

"Me? Nah I think he," pointing at Charlene, "wanted an audience."

The gang leader looked shocked by the speed of John's arrival, though not nearly as shocked as when the strip of a lad suddenly hoisted him effortlessly into the air.

Charlene's male form greeted John, "oh high there," before pulling the gang leader nose to nose. "Always wise to check who you are dealing with, wouldn't you say?" the young man snarled at the, suddenly subdued, older man.

"Ok. You keep the pizza then, friend," the Greek, grinned pleadingly, with a quavering voice, his gang just watching in amazement at the unfolding scene.

Charlene was seriously trying hard to make a point, but the man was actually quite charming; in a gangster kind of way. She could not help herself, breaking into a smile too. "That's good cause I'm ravenous; you might have ended up on the menu otherwise." She looked around the gang who also laughed at the joke, but when she looked at the boss again, her eyes told him that she was only half joking. She put him down.

"You' very strong for a skinny boy/young man," the boss dusted himself off a little and corrected his description.

She shrugged, "I work out lots. On the docks, you need a certain physic." Jack was a bit worried that she would start making up a story they could fall foul of later. "We'll be going now. If that's ok?" she dropped her nose slightly; a final challenge.

"Sure. We just like to make sure there is no trouble around here is all." He shooed his gang away. "There have been problems with strangers recently is all, we just want to make sure it's not someone muscling in on our turf," he explained, ignoring the attempted robbery.

Charlene froze with a chill running down her spine, looking at John with worried eyes, John nodding that he'd check it out.

"Problems? What kind of problems?" asked John putting on his authoritative voice, which the gang leader recognised immediately, and started backing away slowly.

"Just problems," he started to turn, to find himself facing John again.

"What kind of problems?" John started to reach for him, but a hand stopped him, and Jack nodded to Charlene.

"Leave it to him. He's got it covered." Jack smiled at Charlene, who put a hand on the man's shoulder and gently guided him to one side.

"I apologise for our gruff manner, my friend. We have lost someone close to us recently, and that can cause anyone to lose their manners." The voice was soft and persuasive, "it's just that we have had problems too, recently and we thought that they may be related. Mr?" Inviting him to introduce himself.

The leader sat on a low wall, "Karello; they," indicating the group in the shadows, "all call me 'Cap-i-tan.'" Charlene nodded for him to continue.

"It started a few months back. Little things; a shipment lost here, a few new arrivals that never made it here to expectant families. The families could not all tell the authorities, and those that did never received any help, like they were not bothered."

"Or they knew, and they were covering it up," Charlene finished for him.

Karello's eyes went wide, "exactly!" his hands springing up in front of him in exasperation, "I mean what were we supposed to do; complain?" He threw his hands up into the air, "to who?" He stood up. "They are the ones that are supposed to protect us, they are the ones that get paid to stop others from hurting us."

"But, then, it got worse. At night, my people glimpsed missing people working at the docks; at night, when even the normal Dockers were not." His voice started to drop into conspiratorial tones. "The places even warned those checking off, with Armed guards.

"So, one night, we had a look. We sneak onto the docks and sees," he shook his head in disbelief, "the missing, with strange things on their heads. Walking around like the living dead; helping to load heavy machinery, and crates of people. I swear on my mother's grave. Crates of slaves, in these days," He slumped with relief, glad to have finally unloaded his burden on someone. Charlene patted him on the back; she thought she knew what kind of man he was now, and knew the team now had something else to do.

"Charlene, you cannot be serious," John starred at her with total bewilderment. They had returned from their little gangland encounter, having gotten a contact number, should they get any news about little Greece's missing people.

"I'm serious John. We need to get a look at those crates, and the equipment, to check if the Ghe'Dar are responsible, or not, before we leave here."

Simon looked at her and hated himself for asking, "Why? It has to be them, doesn't it? I mean getting two races invading at the same time would just be, insane."

"And getting one at all is not?" She shook her head, "no, what I'm thinking is, what if they are building another portal, or something worse," the others faces dropped. "Exactly; at least 'that' threat is known. What if we sort out one, only to find that it was a feint, or, even worse, one of many." The people in the room suddenly became an awful lot grimmer.

"What else could there be?" asked Helena. "They are practically in control as it is, according to our late mister Wallace."

Simon mused a little on that, then snapped his fingers. "A transmitter; one sufficiently powerful to cover the earth; or even one to override satellites signals, to use them, as secondary transmitters, for the mind control signal."

"That would cancel out any hope of blocking or jamming the signal." John was aghast, "they'd have global signal coverage; no one would escape it," Charlene nodded.

"Also we have only seen one base. They may be building more, in case there is a sustained and effective resistance. I know I would," came John next.

"Then we are agreed; we have to find out what they are doing in there," Charlene concluded, as one by one, the others reluctantly agreed.

"Heaven help us all," was all that Jack said.

The docks comprised mostly of open, concrete areas, filled with stacks of containers, forklift trucks, and cranes, surrounded by security gates and fences, especially around the actual unloading areas to stop casual theft and immigration. At ten feet, the barriers were high enough to stop ordinary people. But the team were not ordinary people, and their only problem was avoiding being seen, the consequences of which they did not want to ever find out.

Jack was the obvious scout as, if there were anything out in the open, he would be able to see it by flying invisibly above the area. So, sporting the night vision goggles, he quickly scouted the nearby docks; this took a while even travelling in a straight line. With it already being Sunday, looking for any place wherever there was excessive activity.

As he returned, Simon and Charlene were in a huddle; taking the time to program something into the interface they had been designing, to access her internal network and improve her HUD system.

"Let's try that," Simon was saying, as Jack popped into view a few feet away, Charlene casually looked around and smiled, her HUD seemingly more understandable now.

"Ok guys, good news; I found the locations we need to investigate," Jack informed, the others.

John did not miss the plural. He just shook his head. "Busy little aliens. How many?" John asked.

"Four." Jack's voice dropped a little.

"Four? Bloody hell." John's expletive summed up the group's reaction, but Jack raised his hand.

"There is some good news, however. I overheard one of the supervisors talking; looked like a collaborator, rather than a convert, saying that their shipment would be complete in two days, meaning we have a day to stop it."

Charlene and Simon joined the group, "We can't stop it!" Simon commented, causing them all to look at Simon, shocked. "If we stop it, they'll know someone is on to them, and they'll increase their security, and vigilance," everyone's face became thoughtful, then a little down.

Charlene sighed, "he's right, but there are some things we can do." She hefted a few bottles in a string bag. "I managed to get some cleaning fluids and WD40. We'll apply these in small quantities to any delicate components; it will look like production damage and force them to get more in and make repairs. In short, it will slow them down and make sure that they are not looking for saboteurs."

"Good thinking," said John, looking impressed by the suggestion and the subtle approach, until Charlene pointed to Simon, who shook his head sheepishly.

"I just remembered how frustrating it was to get a new component, only to find that the dam thing won't power up because it has a micro short in it," he grinned more. "It's a terrible thing to do to an engineer, but then these lot deserve everything they get." The rest smiled at that, almost hearing the howls of frustration already.

"OK let's mark up the map and see if we can visit these areas as efficiently as possible. Once we have that sorted, we need to find a way to get to Switzerland; preferably without going through the usual channels." John knew that those channels would be monitored minutely, at that point one of them was bound to be seen, identified and then things would turn very messy. The airport was the closest bet, but also the most problematical.

Jack started by marking a cluster of three areas about a half mile apart, then the final smaller one, in a quiet location, right at the end of the docks. John looked at Charlene, then at Simon.

"Well?" asked Jack who'd seen the strange look the others were sharing.

"Look at the power station next door to this area," said Simon, nodding to the others.

"It's a possibility only but, I think we're all thinking; portal, right?" John and Simon nodded, Jack's eyes brightening, then he frowned as a thought hit him.

"Then why not just send through all the equipment?" Simon frowned at that, but Helena piped up.

"Power, and, possibly, electrical damage. Creating these portals probably requires vast amounts of power; enough that they cannot generate the required magnitudes here, and they're possibly unidirectional too, forcing them to send people through to transport the equipment by more conventional means," postulated Simon.

"Wouldn't they just put it anywhere?" Jack was playing devil's advocate.

"They would probably still require a huge amount of power to stabilise the exit portal. Hence locating it as close to the sub-station as possible." Simon sounding more and more convinced.

"So, we check out the other areas first, do what we can, then stake out the other area for activity that will allow us through." Helena vocalised the thought percolating through all of them.

"And if there are problems?" Charlene suddenly asked.

John's face grew stern, "we deal with them!" And that was that.

It was late. Two hours past midnight precisely, as Big Ben's chimes sounded; covering the sound of Simon's armour landing in the first area; it was not as if his landing was actually loud, but it did make some noise, echoing a little in the still night. It was apparent what had attracted Jack's attention here. A conveyor belt shifted goods, automatically and unsupervised, from an unloading area, covered with cameras, to huge hydraulically opened cargo warehouse door, which was not.

From the external view, the entrance to the offices must be inside the cargo area; a strange design for a building in the docks, but a secure one. Fortunately for the team, the designer had not counted on anyone being able to lift the two-tonne door.

As Simon lifted the door, with his armour, with he'd called Titanium, there was no protest of metal, as it glided up smoothly, quietly allowing the team in, seeing no cameras at all. Perhaps they had thought that there was no need to worry about cameras here; why would they be needed when no one could open the door to get in; still it was a strange omission in an otherwise secure operation.

Once through the door, the team was in the cargo area and looking around, the interior lit from above by dim blue lights, revealing a simply horrific scene.

Row upon row of human-filled machines, the mechanisms drilling slowly into their victim's skulls, feeding wires into the holes, then sealing them with a sickly yellow organic sealant, that seemed to act as a combined anaesthetic, antiseptic and super-glue. A few of the humans twitched in pain, others were silently screaming; probably because they had had their tongues removed.

It looked like the whole operation was automated. However, a familiar small sphere floated over the top of the automated lines. It did not seem to spot their intrusion, possibly because it was in the process of fixing the power systems, the humans had damaged, the whole place apparently running on backup power.

"That's mine," whispered Jack as he floated up invisibly.

"Wait, if you damage it they'll know we were here," whispered John hoarsely.

"He'll be fine. His mystic blast is probably not something detectable by them," commented Helena, John shrugging at that; how would he have known that?

"The Ghe'Dar, being fairly logical, would find the device damaged next to a power conduit, and assume a simple power surge," added Simon, John letting it go at that.

There were a few blasts of power, the battle quickly over, the rest looking around, to determine if there were any other automated defences. Strangely, they could not see any.

"Maybe they think that they are so close to victory that they don't need to guard against anyone," Jack seemed genuinely relieved that they had finally caught a break.

"No. They are an army. They would never just assume such things; my best bet is that we simply have not triggered anything yet. Let's just keep our eyes open and stay together, it's likely to get nasty rapidly if they detect us. Let's just hope they did not anticipate people just wanting to look around," cautioned John.

"Jack, can you stay up near the ceiling and use your sight? It might pinpoint something we might want to have a look at," Charlene suggested.

"Gotcha," he turned on his mystic sight, and rotated in place, not seeing any mystic lines or nexus energy readings anywhere here. "Not much to see on that level. Anything down there?"

"No," the others just saw the machines, and little else.

"It looks like it's fully automated," replied Helena, "using those cages to ship the people out, probably" pointing out some cages stacked on one side of the warehouse wall. "The vehicle that collects them probably just shoves about five of them into a container; then moves on to the next truck. I doubt the drivers even know what they are carrying, or they get paid too much to ask questions," she sighed.

"Probably true," Charlene sighed in return. It was a depressing thought; they were fighting not only the Ghe'Dar but also the worse parts of humanity, the thought causing her to straightened her shoulders; well if that's what was required, she'd do it, just another Cancer to battle, even if she'd never imagined that she would be literally battling a Cancer. The idea was weird, but her resolve was firm, having promised daddy that she'd be true to her nature, and determined that she would, no matter what.

"Found something," came John's voice, "up on the second level. You all need to see this," everyone converging on him.

John was looking at a pile of thin plastic films, with more Ghe'Dar writing on it, on the single desk.

"It looks like a list of items in Ghe'Dar," Simon observed.

"Charlene?" John saw her mouthing words as she looked at the sheet of plastic with the details on it.

"It is a shipping manifest; although the interface is having trouble translating some of the words, the general information is split into three sections: people converted, number and location; base locations and timetable for the invasion," everyone looked at her. What luck. "The only problem is that it is a fake." She looked at Simon.

"Why do you say it's a fake?" Helena was less alarmed and more simply curious.

"The Ghe'Dar rarely make hard copies of things; no tactical maps on the soldiers," she was ticking items off her hand using her fingers, "The number of people converted is massively more than even a dozen of these facilities could convert in months at the rate we have seen," she looked at each of the team members in turn. "The clincher is the invasion date though. It six months from today; yet we know that they are almost ready that means,"

"Either we've been made, and this is a trap, or it's disinformation for spies," concluded John and started looking around.

Charlene looked at the sheets again checking at a subtler level. "This is freshly printed. I mean within the last few minutes." The others all suddenly became tense, ready for action.

"The sphere! Its' destruction probably acted as a trigger for the security system."

"Rats. Time to go?" asked Jack.

"Is there a way out the roof?" asked Simon, hopefully.

"Nope. No, wait. There is an emergency ventilation system, although it's too narrow for your armour Simon, the rest can probably get through."

"And Simon?" asked Charlene.

"I have an idea," said Jack.

Less than a minute later, Commander Khlerack entered the security code into the keypad, his squad of troops waiting outside using their camouflage systems to remain hidden. There was a blip as the security system warned him that a security lockdown was in effect, something he already knew. Intruders had broken the command link to the building's security drone. He entered the release code and signalled the troops to ready their weapons. The door started to open and stopped barely five inches up, causing him to frown as the system began shorting; which ended in a loud pop as the keypad died.

Khlerack swore a guttural Ghe'Dar oath, which was surprisingly answered.

"No need for that commander," came a slightly metallic voice from inside.

If Ghe'Dar could be said to frown, he frowned; a strange pushing together of the tentacles on his head.

"Show yourself intruder or die!" yelled the commander in passable English, swinging his own rifle into a frontal position.

"Intruder? I am the med tech for this facility. We have been having power problems," a metallic hand lifted the door, with ease, to reveal Simon's armour, mostly closed but with a Ghe'Dar head poking out of it.

"Identify yourself!" demanded the Commander, not recalling a med tech unit in this area, although of all the casts they were most likely to do things without orders, usually because they needed to, so they were given a certain amount of latitude; still.

As inferior casts were only identified by family and service number, Charlene trawled through the download information, coming up with a common lesser Ghe'Dar name.

"Chortchal'ish 4513," she saw the commander's attitude change, hoping that her cast and the command's current position would stop him from pursuing the matter. After a few seconds of silence, while he digested the reply, the commander waved his troopers forward, the previously hidden creatures rushing past the armoured figure, trying to locate any intruders.

"Why did you not activate the communicator and call for aid? That is standard procedure. Other units are still working," demanded the incensed commander; Charlene getting a feeling he was more brawn than brain.

"I tried commander, but the auxiliary units failed too. We think that the humans managed to overload a power unit nearby, causing a surge in our powerband; an unusual occurrence but not totally unheard of," she shrugged visibly, an impressive feat in the armour.

The squad leader came back, "no sign of intruders, sir. The security unit indicated that some strange kind of power hit it, but nothing anything that humans could generate." The soldier looked at the armour with a strange look.

The commander nodded for the troops to return to their positions. "What unit are you using there, med tech 4513?"

Charlene tried to act as if it was nothing exceptional, "latest lifting system from the tech systems core, Commander. Its designed to emulate human physical appearance, a kind of social camouflage. I was instructed to test it. Our place is not to question," quoting the mantra for the Ghe'Darian science corps, indicating the med tech didn't actually know the armour's source.

"... just to Serve," finished the Commander. "Very well. Fix the security system and return to the advanced tech corps with your report; I'll open the portal in five Kretchens and report your situation in the meantime." Uh oh; that meant they could not stay around much longer. On the other hand, in five, damn what did Kretchens mean? Minutes, hours, days? Blast her partial understanding of the language.

"Sir!" she acknowledged.

The Ghe'Dar started towards the east, then put his hand to his head, listening to something. He turned back after a few seconds, "Humans," it swore, like a curse.

"Sir?"

"Another alert. Natives causing trouble at the gates. What I would give to just be able to kill them all? We never had this much trouble with the Nordeth, and they were far more advanced, if less spirited."

"Sir," Charlene had never seen the Nordeth mentioned in the download, so she filed the comment and closed the door, as the troops took off in the opposite direction.

Once the sound of troops leaving diminished, Charlene lifted the door again and exited the warehouse. Jack appeared next to her, making her jump a little.

"Dam Jack. Don't do that again, I might have hit you," she snapped.

"Easy there. Looks like the locals decided to take a little unilateral action, organising a protest at the gate, causing a mini-riot down there. The police have been called in, so we don't think the Ghe'Dar will use their weapons for it, but the locals are blocking lorries getting in or out," Jack smirked.

"Perfect. It delays the Ghe'Dar in a way that will cause maximum delay while being untraceable to its source. I'll give Karello a kiss later," she said facetiously, but then realised that the idea was not too far from what she impulsively wanted.

She shook her head; stop that she thought to herself, having more important things to do than getting involved in adolescent games and pastimes. Still, he was quite nice. Grrr, she was doing it again. What was happening? She was usually not interested in such things as a scientist; she was a questioner, an explorer not an adolescent romanticist, so where had her objectivity suddenly vanished to?

As she postulated on that something started catching her eye in the HUD, a faint red light in the background, a low-level alert somewhere down in her lymphatic system, hardly registering at all. She tried to clear away all the other information, clogging the display, that she'd not really had the time to figure out yet. When it was all shoved to the side, she tried to understand what it was saying, as it was partly in Ghe'Dar.

Two of the molecules displayed she recognised, caused her to examine the details of the alert and becoming more alarmed; especially when a strangely familiar Nanite showed up on the sidebar display. How had one of her old Nanites managed to get into her system?

As she thought about it more, she realised what had and was happening. Her system was contaminated by another form of Nanite, and they were causing contention within both her system and the HUD. Damn. Why had her systems had not warned her? She used her new interface to run a check, in parallel with her own internal HUD. Sure enough, there was a set of reading that did not match up. Yet where had it come from and why had her new Nanites not cleared them out?

"Everyone. Listen up. We have a problem that we need to deal with, now. Meet up back at the warehouse." She heard a few angry and alarmed mutters down the comms. "Yes, I know it's dangerous, but this absolutely will not wait."

Once they were back at the lab, Charlene brought them up to date, explaining the problem as concisely as she could.

"We've all been infected by some sort of Ghe'Dar pathogen that's affecting our judgement, and I need a lab of some kind to identify it properly, figure out what it is actually doing to us, stop it, and this is the closest one."

"So what makes you think we have been infected by a Ghe'Dar pathogen," asked Helena.

"Well, unless you know of anyone else, besides me, that can put something like this little bugger in your blood," she displayed a Nanobot on her tablet, "I'd say I was right."

"Ok, so why do you think we picked it up here. Could it not just be something we picked up in the last few weeks.?" John was getting a little tired of all the surprises coming at him recently, "perhaps you let it loose on use from your stockpile of nasties!"

"John was that really necessary? We have all," started Simon.

"Yes, it was bloody necessary, she has sat around, mewing that she is ill, stopping us from," he stopped dead. What was he saying?

"I think we should all just stop there," Helena, the team's voice of reason suddenly realised what was happening, as did John.

"Shit. Sorry Char," she raised her hand, showing she already knew what he was going to say.

"Damn," John was trying hard to fight the temperature rising in him. "Helena, I need to get out of here."

"That won't help John," Charlene was regarding him carefully, assessing how far gone he was, "we have to deal with this now, treatment or cure, but whatever we do, it must be immediately, or we'll end up killing each other, or worse other people."

"So what is it, and can you help?" John realised this was her area.

"My guess, at the moment, is that it is a prototype for their new mind control." She shrugged a little, "from observed effects it's tied itself into the emotional control systems of the brain, hence John's anger and my, ahem, daydreaming," the others looked a little curious at that, "never mind. All we need to know is, can we use the same cure I applied at the Poole Lab, or do I need to do more work?"

She produced an injector, one of the ones by the machines, probably for the regular maintenance team. Taking a sample of her own blood she, applied the adjustments which had worked in the original base and before anyone could stop her re-injected them into herself.

Simon had his hand half up to stop her but just froze as the blood went in. "Er. I wish you'd have used someone else, Dr. Klerk. What if it does not work?"

"Then, my internal systems will warn me in short order, and I'll know to make other adjustments," she replied, stopping to recheck her systems, the warning lights remained, though the foreign Nanite levels began diminishing, their signature subsiding. The others waited, while she'd that slightly distant, almost dazed look, of someone listening to something else. Finally, her eyes refocused on them and their expectant faces.

"Darn, that helped, but it needs more work; still it will help buy us time to get a permanent fix." Then she snapped her fingers as she had an idea, "I bet this is the work of that A.B.C. guy. My work early work was on limiting the addictive properties of anti-depressants chemical by limiting their ability to bind with the brain's larger molecules. I bet he suggested reversing the work, the stupid bloody amateur; the binding does not work that way. If you try to get my Nanites to link that way, they'd affect addictive behaviours and overload the sensory nerve, hence the sudden lack of control in our emotional centres; electrical feedback, in effect."

"Ok, give me a few minutes; I can sort this. It will be slightly disorienting and may make us all lose our dinners, but it should remove the effects without any damage."

"Just like that?" Simon questioned.

"No, not just like that Simon," snarled Charlene, then restrained herself. "The bastards are making me ill more times than I have ever been in my life and I'm trying my hardest not to strangle you all at the moment, so just Shut up!" She stomped off in mid-conversation, grabbing some plastic containers filled with liquids from the surrounding machines.

"Best leave her Simon," John's hands were clenching and unclenching.

"Perhaps if we could find some sedatives," Helena suggested.

"NO!" came a command from behind a line of converters. "No other drugs in your system. This will be messy enough with the ones I'm using. Let's not add to that mixture. Please," yelled an exasperated Charlene.

About five minutes later, she came back; sweating a little, as though she'd just run a mile.

"This will do it, but let's do it one at a time and can someone get lots of water and an empty container to catch the residue." She motioned for the others to step back.

"Simon, you've demonstrated a certain healing factor recently, let's do you first. If it goes wrong you should survive," she speculated, motioning him forward.

"Charlene you are not filling me with confidence here," he hesitated in moving forward.

"Stop being such a wuss. I know what I'm doing here; it's those idiots of A.B.C. that don't. Now get here, unless you prefer a more direct approach." She raised her eyebrows, as she looked at him eye-to-eye.

"Hmmph," he stepped forward, "here," pushing his arm aggressively forward.

"Neck silly," she indicated using her free hand.

He moved closer, presenting his left side. She gently pushed the injector to his skin, only a slight hiss indicating it had been done; he'd felt nothing. He backed off a little and pursed his lips; well that didn't do anything.

"Ha, nothing to it, or perhaps I was not affected, or perhaps, er," he suddenly felt light-headed.

"Simon?" Jack grabbed the other man, as he started to lean alarmingly.

"Oh, Jack. Er, what was I? Umph," his stomach cramped suddenly, causing him to make a muffled gagging sound.

"Get him over the container," guided Helena, just as the first liquid load gushed from his mouth. The solution did not appear as you'd generally expected from such ejections. It was almost totally clear, with a slight silver sparkle to it, and the occasional orangey food residue.

"Well about what I expected, although having just had pizza I would have," Charlene stopped as the second expulsion occurred, containing the expected result, "Ah there it is, my mistake." She looked at Helena, who's mouth twitched with amusement; the look she received in return was one that told her that her amusement was totally uncalled for. She shrugged.

After the third set of material had finished being expelled, Simon's eyes looked clearer, and he stood up, sipping the water provided.

"Next, John." Charlene stepped in front of him and raised the injector. He just nodded and presented his neck. In the background, Simon leaned against one of the machines to try and recover from the loss of all his day's meals.

The hiss occurred, and John started to move towards the container when the door alert started. The door was being opened from outside using the access code, that meant …

… Khlerack was infuriated that the med tech had kept it waiting at the Portal. Lessers should know their place in the Ghe'Dar, especially the Med-Techs.

The door lifted smartly taking a few seconds to get past its height. There, near the back, was the med tech with its' back to those entering leaning over something it could not quite make out. It strode forward to administer a heavy rebuke.

"Chortchal'ish 4513. Explain immediately why you did not come to the western portal as ordered or face termination?"

The metallic voice replied instantly, "Another technical issue commander. One of the converts is having an adverse reaction to the process. I have interrupted the conversion cycle to assess this interesting development." The armour turned around and indicated the prone form of John, depositing the latest batch of residue on the floor. Simon looked past the commander and saw no soldiers, only the commander having returned. Careless.

"Sir, I would have called you, but you said that you had business elsewhere?"

"I delegated that to my second in command; It will meet us at headquarters. I have a security code for the transport portal to take us there as soon as you have dealt with this."

The armour nodded. "Deal with it. Yes, sir" Titanium dealt with it right then, reaching out and lifting the unfortunate commander into the air and slamming it into the machine right next to him, head first; knocking the unfortunate Ghe'Dar out straight away, despite its' force field being on.

"Wow," was all the wane John added, as he continued retching and filling another container, Charlene appearing from behind the other machines, followed by Helena.

"What do we do with it?" Helena asked, Charlene, grinning.

"Good question. We cannot hand it over to the authorities, and we cannot exactly leave it here," Charlene started

"Perhaps we can." Jack was looking at the automated facility. Then pointed to a line of figures awaiting full conversion.

"You cannot be serious. Leave it here?" Helena was a little shocked.

"What has it seen? It encountered a strange med tech repairing some damage who then caught it unawares and unshielded and knocked it out cold. From what I know of these people, that will be seen as a sign of weakness. Yes, they'll check into it but, with no actual sabotage and no signs of real tampering, it will remain a mystery; one it'll probably try to hide, rather than report. After all, it is in charge here. If it reports that it had a problem here that it could not fix, it might mean demotion, or worse, execution."

Charlene absently nodded as she finished, dosing the last team member. John thought about it, having had work colleges that worked on that principle; bad eggs all. He grinned at the thought and Simon caught the look. "It could be the worst thing we could do to it; worse than death." John stood up. "Better now!"

He looked at Charlene, "thanks." She just nodded.

It took a few more minutes to adequately sedate and place the alien into the conversion container. The security code was on a small metallic wafer that only showed when a Ghe'Dar touched it; but since that mechanism had been contained in the Ghe'Dar download, and Charlene could change form, it was not an obstacle.

Now the only question was; where? The officer had mentioned the western portal, that kind of implied that there were others. The western one was the obvious one, but what about checking the other areas. Did they dare and did they have the time? Did they dare not?

"Well?" John was looking at her again, this time with a strangely demanding intensity for some guidance.

"Give me a minute," said Charlene, there was something else; something playing on her mind but in her subconscious. A vague idea, something she was missing; she almost had it, when Jack piped up.

"Charlene," it was Jack, "where are they getting all these people from?" He was looking over the ones in the machines, as well as the ones in the crates. They were a varied bunch; ranging from young Africans to elderly Chinese. "I mean I know the Greeks had spotted that people were going missing, but there are others here, and there are an awful lot of them." He turned to the others.

Then it dawned on her, the question they had not answered; where had they really picked up the pathogen?

"Oh no. I'm so stupid," Charlene tapped her head. The others looked at her with the question in their eyes. "When I did the analysis at the lab, I did it on the people who'd been exposed to the werewolf venom."

"So?" asked Jack.

"I never thought to test if anyone else had Nanites already in their system," The groups' eyes went wide. "The old type of Nanites had an inefficient propulsion system that frequently failed. That meant that it took a long time to travel around the host's system; the substance that you ejected has probably been building up for weeks, gradually affecting your emotions and judgement." She bowed her head, "It's all my fault. All my fault."

Helena moved over to her and wrapped her in her arms, "easy there."

John shook his head, "I don't think you are to blame. What was it that that guy from the lab said. Your work offered them an alternative to conquest; I think you slowed them down, stopped them from whole-scale destruction and," Charlene's head coming up slowly, "you have given us a chance to stop them."

"Indeed, my dear Charlene," Simon came up to her and put his metallic hand on her shoulder, "Your work had also enabled our teams' creation. By creating your devices, you guided us all to this point, and given us the powers that may be the downfall of their scheme." The use of her familiar name made more of an impact than anything else.

John took on a severe tone used for his lectures to recalcitrant children, "far from being to blame, it is more likely that you have given us our one chance to stop them."

He tried to get the others back on track. "So, what do we do?"

"We check the other sites; let's see if they are more people or equipment. But let's make it fast. John, South; Jack, North and the rest of us will meet you at the west most. I'll use his form to get us past security then we find out where it leads."

She shook her head, "and from there, we will begin to make these creatures pay for their invasion. Pay dearly."

It took about ten minutes for Charlene, Simon, and Helena to find a location they could safely view the dock warehouses from, John only a minute behind them.

"Anything?" Simon asked John, as the late arrival skidded to a stop barely panting.

John bobbed his head a little, "Equipment only. Looks like heavy-duty equipment for high powered electronics, marked up for travel to Switzerland, robots being used for loading and unloading; our tech rather than theirs."

"What is it with the crude conversions, Charlene?" Simon asked, pointing at the group they were looking at. "If they had this pathogen, why do they still use the other ones?"

"It must be simply that the pathogen has not been out there long enough to actually work. That explains why the Ghe'Dar were watching me; waiting for me to fix their problem, which of course I will, in a fortnight or so. Charlene flicked her hair, "I'll deal with them first though," she said through gritted teeth.

"Ah, that's my girl," muttered John, just as Jack arrived.

Jack arrived swearing colourfully.

"My, my," chided Helena, wide-eyed at the language, "what's got you so riled?"

"I found out what the Ghe'Dar do to failed conversions," he said in a tight-lipped fashion, still enraged, his face had a slightly sickly caste to it.

"I'm probably going to regret this, but, how do they dispose of them," John asked.

"They don't let them go to waste that's for sure, they really do treat humans just like cattle," said Jack, still being particularly evasive.

Helena looked at Jack, a rather dreadful thought dawning on her, "Oh, no" she looked away, but Jack was nodding.

"The other site is their food store." he finally reported, "people are, processed, there," he heard Helena wretch. It had been a bad day for her and the rest.

"Another reason to hate them," was all that John muttered.

"Right we are all here; let's see if we can get back to the real battle and stop this before it gets any further." Charlene tried to focus their anger and sound optimistic about their chances.

They looked at the portal site, trying to determine the best approach; for Jack, it would be easy enough, but for the rest, it would be substantially more difficult.

The portal was set up in another warehouse, but there were significant differences from the ones that were part of the main docks. This one was behind a fifteen-foot-high combination wall; brick at the bottom and closely packed metal slats in the middle, topped with, what looked like, a high powered electric fence. Behind that, armed guards were patrolling; looking like private security rather than actual Ghe'Dar, and there were dogs too, for good measure.

"The dogs will make this harder," muttered Jack.

"Look over there," whispers Helena, using a pair of binoculars. She was pointing at a crane tower. The others view swung around, and as they focused in on the tower, it became apparent that the crane was not the only thing on the tower.

Instead of a driver, there was an automation unit of some kind, topped with a silver sphere. Unless you really looked, you could not see it from the ground.

"Security drone?" asked Jack.

"Yes, that's what nearly caught us last time. It either spots us, or we deal with it, and they investigate the drone's failure. It's a sweet security arrangement. Damned if you do, eaten if you don't."

"Any ideas?" Charlene was at a loss. Simon kind of shrugged. The area was too open, and there were too many guards.

"Charlene," it was Jack, "what would happen if there was a spillage of a chemical compound in that area?" A strange question coming from him.

"Depends on what it was and what it mixed with," she nudged over to where he was and started scanning the nearby docks, "but if," she locked onto the area he'd been studying so intently; a large selection of heavy duty plastic drums, set away from the others.

She mouthed a few of the names then stopped, "but if there were a spillage of that Fumigant, a brown cloud would fill the area, forcing them to at least evacuate their human allies. It would cause enough confusion to give us a shot, and block the drone's view," She half turned to look at him, with a tightly vicious smile on her face. After seeing it, Jack was glad she was on his side.

They scanned the area again and spotted some forklift trucks in a useful spot. The two updated the others with what they'd found, and the team started to move with purpose.

The guard was getting tired, he'd been on duty all day without relief; but, hey, he was used to that, knowing it was the boredom that made him tired. He shifted his position in the guard house, although guardhouse was a bit of a misnomer; it was actually an old dock shed which had had few comforts added. Moving to one of the windows he looked away from the docks towards the now disbanding demonstration. His shift was nearly over, and he wanted to go spend his rather generous pay. The demo would be fun to sort out, but he was getting too old to get involved in that kind of fun anymore and had thought better of it. As the guardhouse door swung open, he turned to greet the other guard, being surprised when there was no one there, starting forward to close the door when he saw a bright light, followed by stars, dropping to the floor; out cold.

Jack's mystic blast was designed to knock the guard clean out, and he doubted the old guy would wake up for half an hour, or more. Plenty of time to get the next phase done. He went around the small post and efficiently loosening as many electrical relays as he could; bar one that stubbornly refused to play along. Jack thought a second, then casually sprawled the guard's arm across the table 'accidentally' knocking a half cup of coffee in the required direction; sparks and a dark screen announcing the success of the stratagem.

He also sprinkled a little of the spillage near the foot of the old guard to make it look like the guard had been electrocuted by the coffee spillage.

He looked at his work, smiled and was off to signal the rest.

John selected a forklift truck near the warehouse that apparently housed the portal, heavy-duty power lines converging on the huge hanger sized building. The front was an open, shallow affair that displayed little of the cacophony of work going on inside. Huge spotlight towers lit the entire loading area where real employees stacked boxes into containers, which were then lifted onto the back of a converted articulated lorry; pushing them into the building through an airlock, the front occasionally opening, revealing the rear airlock mechanism.

Strange place to put one thought Charlene unless there was a second one beyond. What was it required for? As the outer door closed the team, and a few of the workers glanced at the lights at the flickering of the lights. There was a drain on the power grid, or some kind of local interference, as the container entered the building.

"There's an entrance at the side," commented Jack, straining slightly because they were at the wrong angle to actually see it.

"Let's take a peek," Charlene started.

"No. Wait," Simon was holding his armoured hand out. "Let's just slow down a little. We have been running around a lot recently; reacting when we need to be planning." He saw them start to object, but his hand remained up. "Let's try to apply brains to this."

"Jack can you use your sight to see if there is any exotic power being used here, to tell us if there is anything like a portal in there."

They all looked at Jack, who looked up at the sky and slowly lowered his sight to just above the building, then shut his eyes and shook his head as he'd just had a flashlight shone in them, re-opened them and nodding, "lit-up like a Christmas tree!"

"OK! So, there is a power source in there, that could be a portal. That's not to say it could not be the transmitter or some machine we don't know the function for. So now we do a few other things." He produced his signal detector and frowned a little. "OK, not the transmitter we feared, but it's pumping out some distinctly strange frequencies, hmm. Charlene what do you think?".

Charlene moved a little closer and examined the display, her HUD processing the signal waveform too, in a flurry of analysis and waveform pattern-matching. Damn, she wished her interface was more advanced and readable; the result appearing half in English, the other half undecipherable. She ground her teeth in frustration, but the displayed information actually made some sense.

"Well, I can tell there's a portal in there." They looked at her enquiringly. She shrugged. "My HUD's giving me a positive teleport signal, which I've never had before. However, the coordinates are all in Ghe'Dar, so I have no way of telling you where it's going to, although, because there are only four values, I postulate it's an Earth coordinate, rather than an astronomical one."

Simon nodded, "Yes, it would require at least six values for a point to point in a 3D grid. Using a standard lat/long grid, you could cut that down to two per point, hence four."

"OK, so it's somewhere on Earth, probably; any way to determine where?" asked John.

"I don't know their units of measure, at least relative to our own, and that would throw off any guess or calculation." Charlene was obviously frustrated by her limitations, her hand clasping and unclasping at being so close to real information, and not entirely being able to decypher it.

"What if, you assume that one set of coordinates is this site, as a point of origin?" speculated Simon, throwing her a challenge, "think best-fit probabilities." He looked at her, and there was a look in his eye; one she'd not seen before, a kind of aggressive get your brain moving sort of look. It was the first time he'd reminded her of her dad; genuinely weird to see that look on else, especially someone she thought of as quiet, almost timid.

She nodded her head. "OK, let me think," She turned her back on the group and sat on a small stool, put her head in her hands and thought. Thought about the mapping system, the Ghe'Dar language, and all the tests that she'd done in mathematics; mapping out the body for her Nanites and their guidance system. Her mind jumped. That was it; they used a Ghe'Dar guidance system. The others watched Charlene, and it looked as if she were dozing except for the slight tilting of the head, this way and that. Then she slammed her hand down on the desk in front of her.

"Got it! My teleport system must be able to translate my brain's visual targeting information from English to the Ghe'Dar distance measures to perform the teleport, as it uses Ghe'Dar technology, so," She grinned triumphantly at Simon, passing the test.

"There must be a translation algorithm in there somewhere!" He smiled at her, but the others were looking at the pair of them as if they needed translators themselves.

"Teleport system?" asked Jack and John together, while Helena just looked confused.

Simon, who'd been the only one around when she'd teleported before, smacked his head, looking from Charlene and back to the others, "they never saw you. John was going one way and Jack the other." Jack and John looked at each other, then back at the pair.

"I can teleport apparently. I've not used it since the machine, because I had problems with it and I've not had the chance to experiment with it much; no real need. But it's locked on to another compatible signal in there so we can assume there is one."

"Could you teleport inside then back again? Tell us what's there.?" John was suddenly animated.

"It does not work like that, at least that I know of. I need to see where I'm going; and the internal mechanism seems to use body fuel, glucose, and fats so I cannot go far without it burning up lots of that, plus it hurts big time." John's face fell, "but if I can see inside somehow, I can probably make it inside from here."

Simon's face was intensely interested. "We're nearly two hundred feet from the wall here, you sure." To his surprise, she nodded, changed into what looked like a worker from a distance, pointed at a non-overlooked area behind them, then, with a slight pop of air, disappeared.

They all looked at the area nearly seventy meters away and there stood the worker swaying slightly, but on her feet, rubbing her head slightly. "Not as much of a strain as I remembered," came her voice over their comms units, "just give me a second or two."

She took a deep breath and seemed to steady herself, and after a few seconds, that pop occurred again, and she returned, looking pallid, cold and wobbling slightly. Jack handed her a glucose drink he'd saved from the warehouse, Charlene gratefully gulping the whole thing down in ten seconds flat, steadying up, the colour returning to her cheeks.

"Umph, I'd not like to try long jumps, without getting the system more power efficient, or even an external power supply. Simon, if we ever get out of this, we'll need to work on that together."

"How long do you need?" Helena was looking Charlene over, her professional and personal concerns in evidence.

Charlene took a few deep breaths, then a few more, finally looking reassuringly at Helena, speaking in a much steadier tone, "no time at all really, it was just a little strain." But there was something else in her voice, something like worry.

"You sure?" Helena stood close and touched her cheek, Charlene did not flinch, and she gazed into Helena's eyes.

"I'm fine," Charlene's voice clear and growing stronger, "Now let's see. I've run the jump I did through my system, and I think I've calculated a relative set of values for coordinates my systems locked onto in the warehouse." The rest waited patiently as she did a little mental calculation, "it's not going to Switzerland," the other's faces falling. That blew their previous theories about the Ghe'Dar portals; they were far more prevalent and required less power than they had hoped. "It's about halfway there, give or take a dozen or so kilometres. Near Paris, probably somewhere near Soleil Synchrotron; there are a few large labs there that could probably handle the power and technical requirements."

The others looked at her questioningly.

"What? I deal with them occasionally; they have some interesting projects on the go there; in all sorts of things." She looked at Simon, pointedly, "I'd have thought you'd have had some dealings."

He shook his head. "I'm engineering mainly, not theoretical physics," she looked disappointed.

John ignored them as he thought, "well, it would get us halfway there. Besides, if we popped straight into the middle of the main staging area, we'd probably be mown down by guards, before we could get into a defensible position, as nearly happened last time, as I recall. Now, all we have to do is figure out how to get through their portal."

Jack looked pleased with himself and lifted a finger. "They have personnel portals. They had one for the technical staff, scientists and mechanics in the machine."

Simon nodded. "So, we are, what? Techies and you are dumb humans?"

Charlene did a little reassessment, "Possible, but more likely you are the techie, I'll patch in a few phrases of Ghe'Dar, to your systems, to get us past any encounters."

She started to tap in a few instructions into her interface, "and we will be three subjects," she pointed to herself, Helena and John, "of interest to the Command.

"What about me? asked Jack.

"You're our Guardian Angel," Charlene pointed up. "You'll be above us, invisible, as we move through the enemy, watching our backs. If anything goes wrong, you can get to the authorities and, at least try to get them to listen."

"Great!" Jack muttered.

"Ok. Do we wear those cap thingies?" John asked. "That would make it obvious that we were under control, so to speak."

"No, standard converted humans will be of no interest to the Command, but humans that have been converted by the new Nanites might."

She considered it. The more she thought about it, the better this approach seemed.

"It has its' risks. If they already have lots of specimens, then we are of no value again. If they have none, then we might be considered, suspicious." She kind of shrugged at that point. "I think it's our best option."

Chapter 11

ACROSS THE CHANNEL

The team scanned the perimeter of the building, for a place to join the workers and general building area, while Jack lined up a forklift truck to create the diversion when the team made their move. They had spotted a third entrance to the building behind a guard room, in the full glare of the warehouse lights, sealing the need for their diversion.

Charlene waited with Helena, as the others grabbed some worker's overalls.

"I know we are doing this because we have to, but if you'd have told me a few weeks ago I'd be raiding a guarded alien military installation, to try and save the world from an invasion of squid creatures, I'd have thought you were totally insane." Helena turned her head slightly and whispered back, smiling,

"and I'd have agreed with you. This IS total insanity. Unfortunately, it's also true, and only we can do it." Helena smirked a little, "at least I think so," she looked at Charlene and received an answering nod,

"Well, if not, we both need to be sectioned," a pain shooting through her head, causing her winced.

"Still hurts?" Helena had noticed the eye movement.

"I have to get myself scanned and see what they did, are doing, in there," Charlene rolled her eyes. "The HUD is weird enough, part English, part Ghe'Dar, but it has so many layers to it, and not all responsive to me. It's like watching a 3D image with the glasses only working on some of the layers to resolve them, then you have 'real' life in the background."

"You tried doing it like that? like a 3D image, focusing on different sections?"

The taller girl nodded, "it sort of works, but then other areas are not visible at all." She shook her head. "I think it's arranged for the way a Ghe'Dar would process information. Their senses are different, and they have different processing priorities. Even with the interface, it's difficult to rationalise the two biologies; it will take time and some modifications.

The others returned with some workers uniforms for the girls, but Charlene just looked at hers' and changed appropriately.

Helena looked at her, "well that works well enough."

"Yeah; but it's all instinctive, rather than me planning it. I hate it," Charlene did not hide her frustrations with the current situation.

"Are we all ready, then?" John was just as frustrated with all the delays in getting away from here. They all nodded.

"OK. Let's go to war!" He nodded to Jack, who promptly vanished.

The mercenaries guarding the transport facility wore the supplied dock guard's uniforms and batons, but their real tools rested readily to hand; MP5s, grenades. There were also a few switches that the employer had set up and said were for use should any authorities turn up, they had not asked, as they were not paid to ask questions; and the pay was excellent. Still, the boss and his six crew had looked the place over and marked where the heavy weapon systems were so that they could keep out the kill zones.

Cameras covered the full 360-degree perimeter, although the cameras had been fritzing recently, so Red One kept his eyes on those areas, in particular, just in case someone took advantage of the occasional lapses in coverage; indeed he had men positioned in those areas just in case.

He did not see the careening forklift at first, nor the slight trail of brownish liquid streaming from the barrels on the palate, until the workers started getting knocked over and the brown cloud bloomed in a line towards the warehouse. The scene on the camera was almost comical, but through the window horror and panic spread like a wave on the forecourt. People bowled over, with injuries to either their arms or heads depending on how they were impacted, the noxious fumes causing them to fall to their knees coughing and choking; some staggering to try to escape, others just dropping and vomiting.

He hit the alarm, although some workers were already running to help the affected.

People, in strange environmental suits, arrived from within the warehouse, passing behind him, striding with exaggerated steps towards the incident; in a hurry to get the spillage sorted out. He left them to it, resuming his scanning of the monitors; it was not his business, and he did not think it strange that another suited person appeared from the other side of the compound.

The distraction had worked, not only on the control staff, but also on the perimeter guards; a bit hard on the workers involved, but necessary, the team moving steadily towards the main entrance, behind the guard room, avoiding the worst of the drifting plumes of nauseating gases. The three supposed controlled humans moved forward ahead of the larger armoured figure; not running, nor moving slowly, just acting slightly out of it, ignoring the mayhem around them. Simon's armoured form looking much like the other armoured suits around; each different depending on its function.

As they strode past the disturbance, they noticed that the people that were injured were not actually being helped. As the suited figures approached them, they drew slim, wicked looking, blades and efficiently slide them up into the skull of each of the injured people, then started to drag them off, probably for processing.

Simon saw both John and Charlene tense up as if to stop the cull. "Stay focused," he whispered sternly into the comms units, "if we make a move now, we'll all be dead in minutes, and the world will be doomed. They'll pay in time."

He saw their shoulders slump a little, but they seemed to accept that they could not help these people. They had all assumed that the workers would be taken to medical facilities, as losing workers would slow things down. Apparently, the Ghe'Dar had more than enough workers, so they just repurposed those that could not function.

Just outside the building, the team was intercepted by two larger armoured figures coming from the left of the warehouse, carrying Ghe'Dar weapons and on their guard.

"Halt and identify," ordered a synthesised English voice, sounding much like Simon's through their suits. One guard was in a heavily armoured version of the suit. The other trained his gun on Simon and activated a laser sight.

"Chortchal'ish 4513, med tech, West facility." He raised his hand to indicate the other, "Taking medical samples to the main facility for detailed analysis," his suits' voice modulator hiding his nervousness under pressure.

The large Ghe'Dar raised his left arm and started to tap on a keypad on the forearm of the armour. Uh oh, was he checking to see if the ID was correct, that could mean big trouble. Wait, perhaps there was something he could do. Very quietly, he whispered to the suit, "Computer, initiate foreign virus targeted on suit indicated." A green light indicated his instruction had been received and a download started, finishing a few seconds later, the Ghe'Dar beginning to tap harder on his suit.

"$*$*$*$*$*!" had the creature just sworn? It was hard to tell as its words were now interspersed with static, followed by a waterfall of sparks from the back of its armour, forcing the creature to one knee. A cascade of sparks raced around the suits power systems, and as a climax of the pyrotechnics, the suit bleeped, went dark, and the figure collapsed to the ground with a solid and final clang; the other following in short order, giving Simon an idea.

"Commander are you alright, here let me help you," Simon reaching forward to ostensibly help, his armoured gauntlet opening to reveal his hand and deliver a massive electrical jolt to their power systems, knocking both ridged and unconscious. Having dealt with them, his hand disappeared, and Simon addressed the two as though they were still awake, just in case others were listening on the frequency.

"I'll get help commander; it's probably the human power systems interfering with your internal transformers." Well mostly true. Simon looked at the others who were still in their roles. "Move Humans. Forward!"

"I think he likes the role too much," muttered Jack from above them.

"Hush," said Simon, in a worried voice, casting a glance at the display showing his ID did not exist but also showing the ID of the officer, Kelnarth 8964. Well, that incident had been useful. Now he had a valid ID for the next Ghe'Dar encounter.

The mercenary leader looked at the cameras and saw the fall of the two armoured figures, experience recognising the pattern immediately; diversion, then infiltration.

"Red One to Red's Two and Three," he called his second.

"Reading you loud and clear boss!" deep voices answered.

"Crank you ass up here. We got visitors," he said, in his usual clipped tone

"Great. It was getting boring babysitting these zombies anyway," said one, referring to the pale workers that walked like the undead.

"We'll meet them in the main zone, and bring the 'Cracker,' one of them is in armour."

"Always wanted to try getting through that stuff," the other mercenary growled.

Simon's armour had a bit of trouble with the human-sized steps up to the main level of the warehouse; the rest awaiting him at the top, looking concerned, because of the security guard staring at them rather than his monitors. Charlene was looking at the guard in a kind of vacant stare, her systems displaying useless details in Ghe'Dar on him.

As Simon finally place his armoured foot on the last step, the guard exited the room, carrying a submachine gun and waving for the armoured figure to approach. Did the guards really know what they were working for? He doubted it, and he also questioned that they had the kind of authority here that they thought they did. He decided to take a gamble and bull his way through.

"What is it, human?" he used a voice with an air of superiority he did not really feel.

"Nice try," the guard laughed, raising his weapon to point at one of the others. "I've pulled enough ops in my time to spot you lot a mile off." Simon blinked but did not raise his hands, his mind working furiously. The door to the main hanger opened up, and three more guards came out wielding heavy machine guns and wearing body armour.

"The armour won't help you again us," said one of the new arrivals, exposing the grenades under his jacket. "We got you covered and," he never got any further

From a standing start, John bulleted into the mercenary and catapulted him into the noxious cloud a full thirty feet away, turning to face the other mercs and dropping the grenade pins he'd pulled as he'd struck. Meanwhile, Charlene had vanished from her position, reappearing behind the other mercenary relieving him of his grenade pins too, along with one of his guns, as she flicked back gasping for breath with the others, as the guards fumbled to get the grenades free of their harnesses. One succeeded, throwing the weapon at the three humans, only for it to hit something mid-air, and bounce back at him.

All the grenades exploded as one, taking out all three guards, their commander and igniting the toxic cloud scattering people, armoured and un-armoured, all over the concourse; chaos, screams and moans filling the air. In the confusion, the team rushed inside, trying to ignore the shattered bodies of the guards as they passed through the security perimeter.

"So much for the element of surprise," cursed John, "they are going to know someone has discovered them now."

"Let's hope we can still make it," answered Jack from above them.

"Go on ahead, see if you can find what we're looking for," John instructed.

Charlene changed, from her worker form, to appear just like the, now deceased, head of security. She, he, nodded at John.

"Good thinking," He complemented in a, grudgingly, impressed tone.

"Thanks, now let's move," and she lumbered off, at a trot.

Jack was flying around the busiest area when he spotted on the right side of the warehouse the main power cables, the rest looking like B&Q on a Saturday afternoon, filled with people trying to stack the warehouse with various boxes, items and crates. However, the roof was covered in power units, air conduits and sets of ultraviolet lights that gave him cause for concern. It was then he saw the spheres zeroing in on him.

"****." John heard Jack's curse through the comms. "Their spheres have spotted me somehow," a sizzling sound affirming that over the comms.

"Jack, you ok?" John asked, picking up the pace to try and get to Jack as he dodged another sphere's blast. Fortunately, the way they were detecting Jack was obviously not visual; they always a fraction off.

Air currents? No. Dust? More likely. The UV must be illuminating the dust as he swirled by and if that were the case, it was time to kick up some real dust. He reached into his pocket and fished out a small hand full of his show's flash bangs, scattering them in an arc against the edge of a nearby wall and the ceiling, then clapping his hands over his ears, as he spun away.

The result was; spectacular. As each hit the surface it exploded with a metallic retort, the sound ricocheting off the other metal surfaces of the warehouse walls; showering vast amounts of dust from every girder, support and conduit in the ceiling, and especially off the lights, obviously too high to ever be cleaned, sounding like a giant banging a bell with a hammer. Even the controlled humans flinched at the sound as it went off, armoured figures holding their helm as the effect overwhelmed their acoustic sensors, others just dropping, knocked out cold by the sensory overload.

"Well that was a bonus," was all he muttered, lowering his hands.

The sphere drones stopped shooting; their sensors confused by the multiple new inputs and returned to seeking the intruder they had detected throughout the warehouse.

Jack went lower and spotted his objective, an operational Portal in the centre of the warehouse, in a large roofless cubical, with surrounding metal partitioning walls. Easy enough to see from his position; however, there was a slight problem in getting to the portal itself.

There was a platoon of Ghe'Dar soldiers stationed around it, plus several spheres.

"Holy ****." His mother would have had a fit if she'd have heard him mouthing profanities like that at home.

"What's up?" John was just relieved to hear Jack's voice after the huge detonation the team had heard ahead of them.

"We have a dozen Ghe'Dar and six spheres guarding the gate," complained Jack, "Hope you have a plan, 'cause we cannot fight through that lot. Turn left at the next junction, and you'll see them."

The others stopped; they had thought that this would be a simple walkthrough. Of course, their luck was such that, that idea had been a forlorn hope.

"Wait," said Helena, with a thoughtful look on her face, "I have an idea."

Sub-commander Yethlor 854 had heard the explosions outside, and the detonations inside; and was keeping its many eyes open both for intruders, and someone to give it an explanation. This posting was a punishment detail, of little importance, but a battle might give it a chance of recognition, a chance to return to the fleet; and true honour

It was a little started when a commander marched in with the motley entourage of a strangely armoured med tech and two subdued humans.

"Halt and identify," came the standard challenge. Commander, or not, it had to follow protocols; not doing so was the reason it'd been assigned to this wretched installation in the first place.

"Kelnarth 8964, sub-commander!" came the reply in Ghe'Dar, and the inflexion was strained, which it interpreted as rage.

"What is happening out there?" it asked, curious more than suspicious.

"Some sort of computer malfunction has affected the spheres, they seem to have a targeting error, firing at anything and everything," Charlene tried to sound as confused as possible.

The guard started to wave through the team when it did a double take; swinging his gun to block the progress of the group. "Why are you not using the translator?"

"The system was infected with a virus; one perhaps that infected the spheres too." The sub-commander nodding his understanding, realising it would explain their erratic behaviour. "I'm heading back to get my system flushed, the idiot med-techs do not have the correct equipment here," the guard looking at Simon's armoured form with the same contempt as the other soldiers.

The sub-commander was visibly disappointed, ah, well, back to routine matters. It'd let the techs sort out the spheres. That was their task, and they were welcome to it.

"Security code." The Ghe'Dar raised his hand to accept the document.

Charlene handed the one they'd taken from the other Ghe'Dar officer and prayed to God that it would be enough.

Yethlor checked the code; sliding the card into the security slot. It came up as valid, although the time indicator was only just in the right zone.

"You only just made it. Another few Helts and it would have had required renewal." Damn, there were those Ghe'Dar time measures again.

"Honour to your family. Serve Well," Charlene used a formal leaving phase, hoping that the respect that it entailed would help alley the guard's inquisitiveness. The effect was immediate and quite startling. The Sub Commander stood to attention and saluted the group as the portal power kicked in, the lights in the ceiling fluctuating, and, as the group went through the portal, they again felt that strange sensation of being in two places at once.

Charlene felt herself being energised again. Strangely, her HUD showed her to actually be in two places at once, then resumed being as confusing as before, or did it; more of the symbols were now recognisable, not English, but more of the Ghe'Dar ones. Interesting. It seemed that the more she was exposed to Ghe'Dar technology the more she understood it, something that Simon had casually commented on during their time building his detectors; only with him it was the electronics and machines, for her, it was their portal systems. Perhaps there was a connection somehow, she'd have to think on that.

As the team exited the portal and saw the other Ghe'Dar base on the other side, they could not have been more surprised. On the English side, there was massive security and equipment; squads, guards and soldiers plus a group of spheres, as though to withstand a full-scale assault.

On this side, in an almost entirely empty laboratory, there was a lone human guard who looked both startled and unprepared for their arrival, so much so that he just waved them through. Perhaps the guards from here had gone through with the start of their diversion. Worrying; if true, it meant that they were reacting to every incident with maximum force. Not really surprising given their naturally hostile nature.

"Passer par," said the guard eyes half-lidded, appearing converted, half asleep or just ignoring the presence of the Ghe'Dar in their number.

The group carefully glanced around moving past the guard, who was almost immediately back dosing, having probably been awakened by the whining of the portal generators coming to life. The building seemed practically brand new but totally empty; perhaps one which was built for a future project, with a hollow feel to it that only the absence of humans can produce, one that would always be there, if the Ghe'Dar succeeded, Simon thought coolly.

The French signs were translated for him, by his suit, and the team moved to a set of double doors, covered outside by tape, which did not cover the actual gap between the doors, having been obviously sliced through with a sharp blade.

"You wait here," came Jack's voice, from above John, "I'll scout around and see if the security is as lax outside," drifting slowly off ahead of them.

Simon lowered the two he'd been carrying, John in particularly being grateful as he'd been underneath Helena, although, in all honesty, it had not been entirely without its' perks.

Helena looked at him, with a glint in her eye, but leaned forward and just in front of his nose said, "not a word! Not ever".

John looked at Simon, who grinned at the man's wide-eyed innocent expression. He started to open his mouth to protest when a finger was shoved across it at speed.

"I wouldn't if I were you," it was Charlene, "she's not in the mood for it."

Indeed Helena, stood behind the imposing armour of Titanium, looking like she was ready to explode.

"What's her problem?" asked John curiously, "We've made it to France at last, and with minimal problems."

"Men!" Charlene exclaimed now warming up herself, "it was all the people we maimed and killed to get us here; that's what has her riled. She thinks that perhaps there was a better way."

John looked down, "sorry I did not understand. But I don't see how we could have done it another way. We," Charlene's finger came up again.

"I know, but that she is a doctor, sensitive to the loss of life. Just leave her alone, and she'll reconcile it in her own time. We tried both the obvious ways in and, still had to fight it out. The Ghe'Dar had all the bases covered, so we had to blast through, rather than do it the straightforward way. Against beings who have fought like this all their lives we are bound to," she stopped and looked around.

"What is it?" John looking at Charlene's worried face.

"Why no security?" Her face looked panicked.

"Simon, scan the area, I think we are in trouble." Charlene, suddenly became golden; deploying her Nano-armour.

Helena reacted too, her shield going up, in response to Charlene's actions.

"Guys, run," came Jack's voice, sounding out of breath, down the comms, "there are about two dozen French police and Military units heading down the road in your direction."

"Some sensors we missed, or an alarm from London?" Charlene was beginning to think they would never get a break.

"How long we got?" John said starting to run.

"Twenty seconds tops before they can see the exit."

"Go! Switch to coded comms, NOW!" John yelled urgently, indicating they should switch frequency and use their code names, running to the nearest emergency exit at full speed, nearly shattering the plastic and glass doors, the hinges straining as they slammed open. He emerged next to a road that went between building, followed by Simon, who flew up, along with Helena, shimmering with a force field around them; almost dazzling in the sunlight. Charlene appeared for a second, then disappeared; reappearing on the low roof of the building opposite. Good enough, scattering would confuse the enemy, for a short time, before they got organised, then the real searching would start. John was vulnerable at the moment out in the open, speed being his best defence, so he bolted at full pelt; leaping to join Charlene on the roof, faster than he remembered he could run or was it just the adrenaline?

"Nice of you to join us! PileDriver" Somehow her voice was gruffer and less soft, in this form; he could not think of her a Charlene when she looked, and sounded, like this.

"Nice to see you too Chi'mera".

From this vantage point, they could see the police cars and vans, accompanied by soldiers running down the road, about a hundred meters away. A police helicopter flew in, from the west, skimming the rooftops.

"We are sitting ducks out here. We need to move," John observed, inviting suggestions.

"CERN is to the East, but we still have a few days before we need to get there," said Charlene trying to establish their general orientation, while trying to adjust to her codename.

"Let's concentrate on losing these guys first, then we can worry about everything else later," prompted John. "WitchFire, Titanium stay out of sight of the helicopter. If it spots you, lead them away south; let's worry about recognition another time."

"Chi'mera and I will give the ground troops the slip."

"GhostKnight, we need you to find us a path through the local area. Locate somewhere to lay up safely, until we need to get to our target location."

"Got it!"

"Chi'mera?" she looked at him.

"Aren't you?" he nodded to her current form, before setting off.

"Not quite yet," she muttered, giving herself over to her new name, "but I'm getting there," and she was off after him.

From the air, the two flyers staying together could see the Eiffel tower to the North, looking beautiful in the sunlight, a truly phenomenal product of human engineering and something to be protected at all costs.

"We cannot outrun the helicopter, so perhaps we can knock it down," he looked at her and saw the reply in her eyes, "not blow it up, I mean, this," his hand opened up.

"No! We do it another way," she squinted and turned to face the helicopter, adjusting her grip on her stave. Rolling on her back mid-flight, she looked through the crystal adornment and sent her mind out, towards the pilot's, locking eyes with him and struggling briefly for control. The pilot was intelligent, pilots had to be, but his determination was no match for her mystically enhanced willpower, and she commanded him to land the helicopter, it immediately started to slowly descend.

"Impressive," Simon muttered

Simon was indeed impressed. Sometime she'd have to show him how she did that. Perhaps he could replicate the effect of stunning or controlling enemies, then stopped himself. Wasn't that precisely what the Ghe'Dar were doing? Best not go down that path he thought, shuddering a little. Once the helicopter was safely down, and the pilot napping, they started to fly east, towards their common goal.

Jack saw the two other flyers weaving through the buildings at roof level, avoiding being spotted from below as best they could. Of course, being a lab complex, few people were actually around outside or looking out the window, being too busy with their experiments. A few non-lab staff looked up as the two sped past, wondering at the shadow as it passed by, but the lack of any sound meant that the Flyers were barely noticed and those that did mostly mistook them for a reflection off a window, or a passing pair of birds.

Of course, Jack had no such problem, being invisible, and was actually ahead of them to their right, giving the grounded pair directions, as they did their dance with the security forces. The troops were moving in as though they had a specific destination, rather than following the fleeing pairs. Interesting.

"Guys' I don't think they actually know we're here. They're heading for the Portal, they must be here for something, or someone else. They are in a hurry though."

As soldiers started to get closer to John and Charlene, she casually reached out a hand to hold John's, both of them disappearing.

Jack blinked amazed; he'd not known she could do that.

The soldiers and the police had missed them, and Jack thought that it was an excellent trick. From his vantage point, he saw the two reappear on the roof of one of the other nearby buildings, next to a startled smoker. John's casual strike rendered him unconscious instantly, while Charlene shaking her head for a second or two, tried to clear the fog of the fatigue. Then the two of them vanished again and appeared on another rooftop well away from the advancing army line. However, as they re-appeared, Charlene dropped to her knees, utterly spent, John, picking her up and heading off running at full speed.

Jack, invisible, started after them again, but could not keep up with John in a straight-line run, that man could really move, if only for short periods.

"PileDriver, head South East, right at 45 degrees, or with the tower at your back, as fast as you can, for about an hour, I'll catch up. I'll hang back here and see the aftermath. It might tell us more about what we are up against here."

"GhostKnight to WitchFire. Adjust course right twenty degrees and head to the mountains."

"Copy GhostKnight," came Helena's voice.

"Why are we suddenly using our code names?" asked Simon, flying low over a series of terrace houses.

"I'll guess that he's worried that our comms. are no longer secure."

"Fair enough; WitchFire." Simon tried to shrug but flying in armour it only translated into a slight wiggle in the air.

"You're welcome, Titanium."

Meanwhile, GhostKnight hovered near the army line as they continued to search the area. They had radar tracking, infra-red detectors and microphones; all to no avail. The flyers were too low for the radar, the buildings blocking the infra-red, while the microphones were only for quiet areas; which Paris most definitely was not.

He hovered within earshot of the commander, hiding in the spring foliage of a tree.

Strangely, he was talking to the men surrounding him in English, who wore different uniforms and demeanours.

"I do not understand why the military, and non-French military at that, were called, to, what is obviously, a French civilian incident."

"Our colleges in DRM, via the DCRI, received intelligence that there was a possible terrorist cell here; a plot to destroy Paris by sabotaging experiments as this facility," said one of the others around the commander, "we were, asked, to provide tactical assistance the other day. When the alert channels indicated that there was an alarm here, we naturally feared the worst. It was orders, you understand."

His voice had a slight acrimonious edge to it, not lost on the commander.

"You were close?" this obviously disturbed the commander in some manner.

"We were on campus, talking to the staff," added the subordinate, although his scanning his eyes were saying other things, Jack just did not know what.

"Well whatever the alert was, it is over now, with no trace of whatever triggered it,"

"We can check the CCTV from the labs," offered the still scanning subordinate.

"We are not in England here, Colonel; we do not have CCTV everywhere, and the laboratories only have cameras in specifically equipped experimental rooms."

An Officer came running in from the direction the team had arrived from, whispering in the commander's ear then dashed off again, the commanding officer nodded absently.

"I'm told, that they cannot find anyone, that the alarm went off in an empty, non-operational lab, so there will be no footage viewable, as power is not wasted here."

Jack heard a slight change in the commanders' voice, a strain, indicating he was pushing to get the others away. Two of the others started to go back to a camouflaged truck, as the other three conferred. He went invisible again and drifted to the back of the truck with them, where he spotted military transport containers covered by a tarpaulin; interesting.

"Whatever he found, he's gone silent again. We'll need to debrief him when he gets off his shift," whispered one.

"Agreed, we dare not push it, else they'll get suspicious, even if they swallowed the terrorist plotline; but this commander's smart and it definitely won't wash if we press it without further evidence," said the other.

The colonel nodded, and they went back to the local French police officer.

"You're right Commander, I guess we'll have to await your full report, as always," the words seemed genuine enough, with a weary sigh that indicated that the soldiers awaited the local authority's help far too many times, with little to show for it.

The commanders' eyes narrowed a little, but he let the comment slip.

As the two English officers returned to the truck, the Colonel looked meaningfully at the other, "Ok back to H.Q. Let's wait and see if our man can tell us anything when he meets up with us at the usual place. I've a funny feeling that all hell is about to break loose."

"Yeah, I'll send a report off when we get back too. We might need more people out here. You notice the arms they turned up with?"

The other nodded, "not standard issue; more heavy-duty weaponry; as though they were expecting more than just a few thieves." They climbed into their truck and drove off, not realising they now had a passenger along with them.

Jack thought for a few moments. OK, he was strictly going in the wrong direction, towards Paris, but he was getting such great Intel. here, that he did not want to waste the opportunity to meet people who might prove to be potential allies, so he settled down for the ride under the tarpaulin.

Charlene woke in PileDriver's arms, with a slight ripple in her skin; he was still running, faster than ever, along a dirt track, apparently no longer in the city. "Can we stop please?" She was her normal self again if there really was such a thing anymore. He did not seem to hear her at first. "John? Please?"

He looked down, then seemed to come to himself again, "what? oh, sorry." Slowing down he headed for a large cherry tree. "The rhythm of travelling so fast can be kind of hypnotic, I … I'm sorry."

Finally coming to a stop, he gently put her down and shook himself.

"I did not realise you could get so fast," she noted.

"I think it was that second pass through the portal; it kicked me up a gear. I imagine it did the same to you; that trick dragging me past the security line was something," Charlene smiled, but John was leaning forward. "Don't do it again. It bloody hurts."

She sighed; he was still touchy. "You think it hurt you! You should try initiating it! Yes, it does bloody hurt, that's why I've been out of it for so long," she stopped, and looking at him, saw him grinning slightly; he'd been teasing her.

"uuwww," she stamped her foot, then with a strange look, grabbed his ears and kissed him, full on. He struggled a little, but just as he was about to pull her to him, she vanished, and he found a foot playfully kicking his backside.

"Humph," Charlene flounced away, looking around the tree to see where they were.

John was a little bewildered by the kiss. He'd never thought of Charlene like that and was pretty sure that she'd never thought about him like that either. At least, not that he recalled; still it had felt rather nice. She was probably just teasing him, as little sisters did; but somehow, he'd never really thought of her as a little sister either. It was perhaps the after-effects of the past few weeks making her act-up, but then, he'd not known her that long. Then, of course, there had been Isabella, and thinking that he suddenly felt his anger at Charlene rising again, and ask himself the same question again; why couldn't the team try to save Isabella? Then he remembered that kiss, getting all confused. He liked Charlene, it was Chi'mera he had issues with, it was just that they were the same person, or were they?

Then he realised that she was getting him as messed up as she was. No, he was not going down that road. She may still be his charge, and now his teammate, but he could not risk her becoming anything more. He would have to remain professionally detached, else fall into the trap that others he'd buried in the past had; mixing work with play. That never ended well for either side; perhaps explaining why Chi'mera was so anti-Isabella.

Jack's curiosity having been peaked by the soldier's conversations, he was hitching a ride in their three-ton truck, and once they'd left the immediate vicinity of the labs, the discussion quickly become much more interesting.

"So it looks like they had a security breach of some kind, meaning that perhaps others are onto them. I thought that there might be others in play, especially once we'd confirmed the number of missing people reports. They were just too numerous to be isolated to this region."

"What I don't get is why there is so little actual investigation going on. I mean the information is out there, from what I gathered from the professors. They have all had someone in their departments fail to come in or call in sick. Perhaps the others are doing what we are; being exceedingly quiet about it, until they figure out just how far the situation has spread, and what the purpose is," speculated the other.

They pulled into a side road, leading to the small consular zone near the British Embassy; a little surprising, but then it figured, given that they were speaking English.

The vehicle occupants showed their IDs, and the guards inspected the inside the truck, front and back, forcing Jack to briefly go invisible, but quickly being waved through. Jack relaxed a bit, realising he'd just casually bypassed all their security thinking that, once this was all over, he might find a cushy job as a security consultant, or even a spy, here. Getting out might be harder, but he knew that this was an essential part of what was happening, and he needed to know things that these people knew, potentially being resources that might need utilising in the forthcoming battle.

The truck pulled up next to a rather grand ambassadorial building, protected by bollards, heavy iron gratings across the windows and armed police. Jack did not know Paris that well, and he could not see the Eiffel tower from here, but he gathered they were right in the centre. He hoped he would be able to get to CERN from here, not knowing for sure where here was.

The two officers climbed out and walked past a formal armed French police guard, into an open lobby area, where they turned right almost immediately, towards the area marked 'Authorised Personnel only'. Jack, floating close behind them, strained hard to maintain his invisibility long enough to get him past this new security perimeter. The two seemed to clam up in the open areas, but then they probably expected this area to be bugged; by the French, if not by other governments.

"So," said one of them as they started to scan their security tags at a large steel door, "what do you make of him using the priority one code?" The larger of the two appeared to address the wall.

"Voice pattern match. Enter Commander Haines" He nodded as the door slid open.

Strange, Jack thought, the French officer had addressed him as Colonel.

Inside there was revealed a small office, with half a dozen desks surrounded by a large number of large display screens. As the commander walked in, Jack wafted in just above his head, a tight squeeze, even with his wiry physic, to fit in without alerting his unwitting hosts. As the second officer entered, Jack hovered in a position where he could overlook the office, which seemed a compact operation, four other officers tapping away at either laptops, tablets or utilising computer monitors on the walls, slicker than the M.I.X. setup, but then this was the professional military intelligence, he'd expect that.

"Commander, we are detecting a foreign signal within the perimeter. We'll need to scan you for bugs."

Blazes! They had picked up on the comms signal from his headset? He'd not even thought about it until now, but of course, they would be alert to such things. What to do? Hide? He could not stay invisible much longer; it was a strain at the best of times. Flee? The whole point was to get information, that idea was out. Fight? Against six of them? Besides, they were potential allies, and he did not want to miss that opportunity if they were engaged in the same investigation of disappearances. The team would need help from others at some point. He made his decision quickly, as another officer stepped up, with what looked like a smaller version of a scanner that Titanium had used to find the Ghe'Dar signal.

He landed quietly, putting on a handkerchief as a face mask, before moving quickly behind a cabinet. Then he made himself visible and stepped out, slowly; speaking quietly, so as not to startle the room into a, potentially fatal, rash action.

"No need for the scan," the people in the room tensed up, some reaching for weapons, as he appeared, "it's my comms. signal."

Commander Haines started to reach for his holster, then saw the intruder was empty-handed and relaxed slightly. How he'd penetrated their security could be dealt with later since he'd revealed himself and was apparently unarmed.

"And you are?" the commander was not complacent, but then he was smarter than the average agent, and not therefore stressed.

"I'm GhostKnight," the two soldiers looking at one another at the pretentious name, although the way he'd actually sneaked in did lend some credence to that appellation.

"I'm here to give you some information and answer your questions," he tried to sound casual about it.

"Oh are you?" Jack could see the officer mulling over the statement, calculating how to proceed. Who was this intruder? How much did the strange figure know? Could they gain more knowledge without giving their situation away?

Jack smiled, although it was kind of lost on his audience. "I know what you are thinking. What does he want? What do I know that you don't? etc." The look they gave him was one of how did he know what they were thinking. He indicated the seat; asking implicitly if he could sit, "and more importantly can he be trusted?"

The name-badged, Commander Ricks, nodded, both to the request and the question.

"Well, let me tell you a story, then you can be the judges." He settled himself a little under the watchful eyes of those in the room.

"Firstly, much like you, I've had to make a judgement call. I have decided to trust you," he nodded at the two commanders, "the real question however is, can you trust the others in the room? Because if you have any doubts, now is the time to get them out of the room. What I am about to tell you is classified beyond TS; 'For your ears only'. "It was a little dramatic, but he doubted this could be described as over dramatic; after all, getting it wrong here really could mean the end of their world.

Both officers both looked at each other, then around the room. Did they have anyone that might be part of the conspiracy? The look they shared said they'd better play it safe.

"Clear the room. Leave the tracker," the others looking slightly hurt at the request.

"Nothing personal people, and if there is a problem, we'll call. We need to check security anyway, as his presence shows." One woman showed a particular reluctance to go, but she was waved away too until just the three of them were sat in the room.

"So, where to start," Jack asked mostly to himself, knowing they would not talk first, the beginning, seemed best.

"Well, first of all, I'm Military Intelligence, although not like you," he flashed his M.I.X. badge at them, their eyebrows going up in surprise.

"I thought section ten was shut down decades ago," muttered Ricks.

"It figures though," Haines added. "Secrets within secrets. It's the job," he shrugged and indicated that Jack should continue.

"We were sent to investigate certain disappearances," he continued carefully, balancing trying to convince them with not giving too much information should they prove untrustworthy. If these two were converts or infiltrators, they would like nothing more than to know who they were dealing with. It required him to be persuasive enough to get their trust and be believed, but not reveal too much, should they prove to be collaborators, a delicate balancing act.

"We detected a set of radio signals, leading us to a remote location," nothing the enemy did not know already; no wait, that hadn't happened yet, so there would be no connection. That was fine, he hoped the Ghe'Dar if they did learn about it, would probably assume he was referring to something else.

"You are keeping a lot back," Haines pointed out, rather than asked.

"Out of necessity. To say too much would endanger too many people. Well, actually, all of them."

"Just how bad are we talking," Ricks chimed in; he'd never been that diplomatic.

Something was telling Jack that he could trust these two, but dare he risk it? They looked sincere, but then they were the professionals; they could probably say black was white, and still look sincere. At that point, he made a leap of faith.

"I'm only an amateur here, but we're talking about ELE here."

The two agents looked incredulous. E.L.E., or Extinction Level Events, meant not only the end of civilisation but of everything. He was telling them plainly that all life on earth was threatened.

"You're not serious," Rick's voice was low and disbelieving.

"I think he is." Haines looked around, getting out a small device from his pocket and setting it down on the table. Ricks looked at it and nodded. Jack just frowned.

"Jammer. If our friends are listening, they'll just hear static. Talk fast. We'll consider what you tell us when we leave. We'll decide if we believe you later."

"You simply would not believe me, if I told you it all, so let's just say it this way. We need a sizeable military force at CERN in," he did some mental calculation, "eighteen days. It needs inserting slowly, quietly, and piecemeal, so that official channels cannot highlight it." He could see the others thinking very fast. They obviously did not like where this was taking them. After a few seconds, they aired their conclusions.

"You're talking about whole-scale infiltration," Ricks was the fastest of the two.

"Virtually full. You need to use only those you absolutely trust. Most of the enemy are obvious, others have little choice, but the others will not be conspicuous at all."

"You're asking an awful lot, with nothing to show for it." Haines stood up.

"Look, I heard what you were talking about on the way from the lab," the men started again.

"How? A bug?" Haines asked.

"I was right there with you, you just did not see me," the two looked at one another with a question still in their eyes.

"It does not matter. You investigated disappearances, right?" They just nodded slightly, frowning.

"Scientists, right?" they looked at him a bit more intently, then grudging nodded.

"Well, I happen to know why," they leaned forwards. Ah, now he had their full attention; great.

"Our targets are developing a biological weapon, one that will affect virtually one hundred per cent of the world's population. It's almost ready, but it needs an active ingredient that can only be produced at CERN." It was mostly true and close enough that they would do what was required.

"The problem is that they're a powerful group, with friends in the highest places," well space was very high, "and, they've the power to cover up their activities," those bloody cloaking fields, "so we need to dig them out, rather than just confront them."

"Then why not just inform," Haines started, then stopped and thought about it a second, putting hand-to-head. "Ah!"

"Now you see the problem. With the authorities infiltrated, we cannot alert any to the danger. It would tip the enemy off. Also, if we try to stop them now, we just alert them to the fact that we know. They would just vanish, and we never find them. We'd just have to wait for their next scheme. If we wait until they are ready to go, we'll at least get a shot at catching all them."

"But who are they?" Ricks asked in frustration.

"That comes under the 'you would not believe me' category.

"Look we've been in intelligence a long time, we've seen everything under the sun."

Jack looked at him, and he made his eyes wide. "And if I were to say that would not even scratch the surface?" Rick rocked on the tabletop, turning his head slightly.

"Haines is this going where I think it's going? You've had dealings with some strange people before, what you think?" Haines looked at Jack and slowly moved to the window.

"I think we need more than just your word," Haines looked out the window, seeing more than the two police outside the Embassy that there should be. "And that means our time is up. We have company coming." Ricks jumping up and glancing at the security monitors. Jack looked around, not seeing anything until one showed a small group of 'men in suits' heading their way. The others saw them too, starting making ready to leave.

"We'll contact you on one point five nine Megahertz at six am, on the day. Codename GhostKnight." Jack looked at the two men, wondering if all this was in vain.

"We'll be listening, but how do we know what to bring?"

"Everything you can get your hands on if they have infiltrated the military as well. We'll send a message here with my 'Father's' phone number on it, nearer the time. Call him, it's an untraceable line, and he'll send more help. He'll know what's needed."

"Out the back?" Ricks asked.

"Only chance. What about you?" Haines nodded at GhostKnight.

"I'll come with you. At some point I'll disappear; don't worry about it."

The men shrugged, opening a concealed door, hidden behind one of the enormous wall monitors, opposite the main entrance, leading to a poorly lit lift shaft and an old thirties style service elevator. The two agents stepped through the door and turned to check on their guest, only to find he was already gone.

"How?" Ricks asked.

"Probably best not to ask. You know the rules." It was a standard phrase they all used. But the question was in his eyes too; who was this guy that he could do that trick, the door closing behind them.

In actuality, Jack was still right where they had last seen him; watching the approaching group with interest on the monitors. One of the staff who'd been sent out, surreptitiously pointed to the office, allowing the entering group to pass, suddenly collapsed to the floor, blood pouring from their neck. The Patriots had assassinated the collaborator in their group without the thought that they might have been under duress; the professionals it seemed were far less forgiving than his own team.

As the Ghe'Dar agents entered an empty office with the provided security code, they swept the room, for the enemy their agent had described, claiming he'd important information; but there was no-one, not even the two officers who'd been investigating the disappearances. This was bad. In situ, they were controllable, a known quantity, one that could be dealt with by simple means. Now, they potentially had information that might compromise the operation; that did not mean it was a big problem, but it meant they needed finding, and dealing with, one way or another.

The leader looked at the computers and other equipment, primitive by Ghe'Dar standards. Their agent had already given them access to; unknowingly, passing on all they needed to know. Still, a small tapping device like a thin button was carefully placed, in one of the office organisers, to relay any information and communications that they might find useful, should the appropriate keywords be detected in the data streams. And with that, they swept out.

"Come. We need to go to London and check on security there, as well as our gate here." If the two agents were spotted, they would be dealt with by their human allies.

As a top operative, it had more important things to deal with, like the apparent security breach at the London locations recently reported by a sub-commander. It would have to use the Paris gate, where it could check out the reports that were coming through from there too.

Jack smiled, from his vantage point, almost able to see what was going to happen next. The Agent was going to investigate the team's trail but in the wrong direction. By starting here, he would end up back at London, follow an increasingly cold trail and find a dead end at the crashed ship, rather than at CERN. Wait, was that the same agent that they'd initially met? Perhaps, but from this end of history it was too late now, he'd had his chance. The way it'd said it, it was evident that it was viewing these incidents as separate events, rather than as a connected chain. If it had thought of them in that light, it would have searched the office more careful and taken more time. That view made the assumption that the enemy, Jack, in this case, knew about CERN and its' link to London. A top-notch agent might have made that connection, or at least considered it, thankfully, this one did not.

He carefully lifted the bug and carried it with him, leaving through the same door he'd entered by, as the others started to filter back in, minus two; the fallen double agent and obviously one to take care of the disposal. He looked around and saw a slight trail on the carefully polished marble floor, off to one side of the main hall, deciding to follow it and using one of his scarves to obliterate the trail. He caught a glimpse of a woman ahead of him dragging the body out of sight, dipping into a room marked Library. He flew, exiting the door arch just before the person closing it, having lain the body on a table within.

As she locked the door, Jack quickly riffled through the pockets for clues. He did not have much time, but he managed to get the wallet before the other turned around.

The room was large, with huge, thick velvet curtains covering the original windows. It was gloomy, but not dark; allowing Jack to become visible while remaining unseen. The Décor was old-empire; deep reds and rich browns, on the thick aged carpets, walls and unlit lamps.

The woman moved over the body and repeated Jack's search of the body; just a bit more thoroughly. Producing two extra items he'd not found; a small, thin, metallic device from the shoe lining and an earring.

"I did warn you not to take the job, Sally," the woman muttered to someone she'd obviously known well, given the sniffs that she was making as she riffled through the clothes to check for anything that she might have missed.

"I bet it was that bloody Club you went to eh? Did they recruit you there?" The woman seemed genuinely upset, but also angry. "Oh hello, what's this?" She lifted a fine wire with a little nodal on it. As she pulled it, the line went up to the head and stopped near the base of the neck. "What the?" As she pulled, the whole head moved.

Jack recognised it as the same kind of wiring that he and the team had seen in London, used to control the Ghe'Dar slaves, although this exhibited much finer construction, apparently designed to be less conspicuous.

Jack decided to leave her to it, but as he did something caught his eye, on the far wall, in a huge bookcase; a book shining with a faint light. At least he assumed it was light, but one that strangely did not cast any shadows in the rest of the room. As he turned to look at it, there was a faint whispering in his ears; too indistinct to make out the words, but obviously directed at him, as the woman apparently could not hear it. Was the book calling to him?

Helena had discussed with him how he might develop his powers, alluding to studying mystic books, when possible, yet here was one apparently reaching out to him. She'd shared a few dos and don'ts with him, but this was beyond his experience and their conversations. He started towards it, the light getting brighter, and the whispering becoming more distinct, although still not comprehensible, music beginning to back the whispers. Again, the woman did not see it or even notice him as he moved past her, almost against his will.

He reached out for the book, his finger touching it and the room shimmered and changed, bright daylight flooding through the windows, the decor becoming newer, a less dusty, beautiful wood room, with open curtains.

"Ah, hello there," came a very English voice, from behind him, Jack whipping around, to see a white-haired man, in his early fifties, sat in a plush chair, behind a large oak table, by a roaring fire. The man was smoking a pipe and had a small glass of port to hand.

"What? Sorry?" Jack was not at all articulate in his confusion, looking for any sign of the woman and the body which had been on a table, and seeing none.

"Confused? I'm not really surprised. Magic has that effect on some people."

The man was observing Jack's reaction to the words he used.

"Magic?" Jack retorted, trying to rationalise what had just happened.

"Yes, Magic. That which brought you here."

"And here is?"

"Well, You're in Oxford, England. The University to be precise, although you obviously are not from your attire and accent."

"Impossible. I was in," Jack was starting to look around for more clues as to the real location.

"Oh, I assure you that you are really in Oxford. For some reason your power triggered a spell I placed on the tomb, a long time ago," the man standing and flicking his fingers, the door opening, admitting a suited butler to the room.

"Sir?" the butler addressed the man, eyeing up Jack in his camouflaged outfit.

The man looked at Jack, "Coffee, black sir?"

Jack blinked, "Right!"

"The usual for me, Gregor," the man said, the port is his hand vanishing, along with the pipe, forcing Jack to blink again.

"I am Boran, Dr. Charles Boran. I am the leader of the Magic Circle; a coven of people, magicians and witches; although I actually dislike that term myself. It's as good a descriptive as any to the uninitiated, and inexperienced people, like yourself.

"I thought the Magic circle were a group of magical entertainers," Jack interjected.

"What better way to remove the fear that our powers would engender? Use it to entertain the people that do not have that gift and protect them from the darker uses of it that others might enact upon them," he gestured for Jack to sit on another chair at the desk.

"Let me give you some history to help you understand. Magic was here long before humanity and civilisation and will survive long after us, that is for sure, and there are beings in the universe that try to drain it, divert it, and others that try to subvert it and control it. We of the Circle try to utilise it, guiding others in its use and its dangers. Even when the gates to other worlds were closed some magic lingered in this world, like your friend Helena's Staff." He smiled at the shock in Jack's eyes, with the realisation that others already knew.

"Don't worry, she was one of us before she left for her other duties." He lifted his hand to intercept the next question, "have no fear. We are not tracking her as we do not interfere with human affairs. Our considerations are larger, more exotic, and expansive than such considerations. That is why you are here." That piqued Jack's interest.

"Your power has triggered a spell designed to summon such beings here. You have a specific connection with us, or will do in the future."

"I had not even known you existed till now," Jack shrugged.

"Ah, but you are working with Helena at the moment,"

"Well yes," Jack could not hide that point really.

"And you are magically gifted, that much is obvious," the man's logic was direct.

"Yes."

"Then let us examine why the book has brought you here."

"I,"

"Do not need to speak about your current situation, let us just discuss your powers, and how they may be used," he stood, and blurred across the room, to stand next to the startled Jack with his leathery hands poised over Jack's head, murmuring a few words that Jack almost understood. Jack tried to adjust his sight to look at the old man's mystic aura and almost immediately jammed his eyes shut, the man's power blazing like a giant star.

"Hmm yes, I see, your name says it all, doesn't it," the man murmured a little.

"Name?" he had not said anything.

"The codename you chose," Jack stayed tight-lipped. "You are not a believer then." Jack shook his head almost involuntarily. "That will not help, but it is not insurmountable."

"Listen well then, GhostKnight. Your chosen name is written all over you, in a mystic sense, and that name is both your power and your fate," his voice became deeper more resonant, the very air speaking of this man's power. "Your power comes from the spirits of fallen warriors; any fallen warriors, no matter who they fought against. Your power is derived from them; armour, shield, weapon, and transport. I don't know how or why this power has come to you, but what is obvious it that is has done so for a purpose."

"Know also that the powers of the Knight are as protector of the weak, and as an arbiter of justice. I sense that in your life up to now, you have striven to avoid injustice and survive. Now you have the power to go beyond this to protect others and bring true justice," Jack saw the man's face radiate trust, his eyes glowing with light and power, "do these things, and you shall grow to become what others need you to be, and what your deepest heart desires; a true hero." Then the light dimmed, and the man smiled sardonically, "who knows you might even make a fair magician too," he chuckled.

"Does Helena know about my powers?" But the man immediately shook his head, "I am the Psychic, not her. She can only see what is in the mind of the person; my power is more, diverse."

"How can I gain control of my powers, I mean,"

"I know what you really mean. Hold onto, and read, the book that brought you here. It will guide you, guiding you in the path that you seek," and, with that final pronouncement, the man made a wafting motion, returning Jack to the original gloomy room, the woman had gone, along with the body; he'd not thought he'd been talking for so long.

He looked at the title of the book and laughed silently to himself. "Search for the Inner Light, by Dr. Charles Boran". Even as he picked it up, he sensed the change within himself; so, some of his powers were granted by warriors long gone, yet others were from another source. He wondered who else had an interest in him.

He found a fire exit, quickly disabled the alarm, then, book in hand, he slipped from the Embassy. The surrounding guards did not see him, but two people moving down a nearby street, saw the door open, then close, and questions filled their minds, but answers would have to wait. Escape was the priority now.

Charlene looked around the building they had taken refuge in; a large barn, with sturdy walls despite the large knot holes in its timbers, the rafters about fifteen feet above her, suggesting it was used as a hay store, amongst other things; she'd never really studied French farming techniques, so she did not know, nor did she really care. The smell was tolerable, and the darkness outside showed that it was still night, perhaps dawn was near, as spring nights were substantially shorter.

She was trying to analyse why she'd so impulsively kissed John. Yes, he was a fine figure of a man; but he was not really her type. Of course, she was so busy, over her teenage years, that she had never really developed a type, so the point was moot. It was not as if he'd not teased her a little previously, nor was it the pressure of the situation. She could blame the residual infectious Nanites in her blood, altering her emotions slowly; but somehow, she knew it was not. He was a nice guy, always there to save her, always ready to help; even if he'd been paid to do that. Yes, he argued with her, but that just made him more of a match rather than a problem. No, the simple fact was that she was not interested in anyone at all. Even if she were, she would be competing against a ghost. Isabella, for all her brief passage through John's life, had taken his heart with her; in one way, making him an impossible match for her, in another, making him, subconsciously perhaps, a more significant challenge, and Charlene had never backed down from a challenge, as exhibited from their current situation.

She shook her hair and ruffled it a little and started to take a step back to John, when Jack appeared in front of her, startling her.

"Jack, please don't do that, or at least warn me next time," she snapped in exasperation.

He had changed somehow, and he was carrying a book, which did not register on her scanners at all; but for some reason, she reached out to touch its dusty cover. She suddenly felt another personality rushing forward in her mind, along with an overwhelming urge to take the book and destroy it.

As her hand touched the beautiful leather bindings, there was a flash of light, and suddenly all her systems went totally haywire, as a jolt knocked it away. She tried grasping the book, again but it refused her touch still, remaining firmly in Jack's grasp.

"Don't, Charlene," his eyes fixed on hers', and hers' suddenly went very wide.

"How dare you tell me what to do?" the voice snarling from her lips was most definitely not hers. Jack's eyes narrowed, and he vanished, book and all, as a crushing fist flew through the air he'd just occupied.

"What's the matter, not used to not getting what you want," Jack's voice taunted her, somewhere above.

Two tentacles lashed out and whipped around mid-air, wrapping around the invisible GhostKnight. John looked around shocked to see Charlene, no Chi'mera wrestling with something mid-air.

"You insipid little magician," snarled the enraged woman, taking on the face of an old woman, so like Charlene it had to be Sylvia, "let me show you just how easily I can get my own way," one of the tentacles retracted briefly then came out needle sharp, aiming for the space where the other appendage held Jack.

A heavyweight descended on her back. "Let him go Chi'mera," huge hands wrapping around her throat, as PileDriver joined the fray. "Release him! Or you'll hear your neck snap. Try regenerating from that!"

The tentacles released their target and retracted, followed by a thud, as Jack reappeared on the ground a few feet away, looking shaken and dishevelled.

Chi'mera's face changed again this time to a male face, one who'd a vague, masculine, resemblance to Charlene. "Easy there PileDriver, Sylvia's gone for the moment. Charlene is young and vulnerable right now, no need to go any further."

"What's to say this is not just another trick?" he asked.

Then he was gone from beneath his hands.

"Because, if it was," said the man, his face becoming more distinct, only a few feet away behind him, "and with her training; you would already be out cold. Or dead."

"You're her father, right?" John noticed the family resemblance; the figure nodding first, then shrugging.

"A shadow of him; her memory of him," the man took a step to the side. "I try to guide her as best I can from within. But what the Demon and Sylvia, her mother, did to her, that is part of her now, and I can only do what he would have."

"What did they actually do?" Jack asked.

"The Demon fractured her mind; hence Sylvia and me," his face seemed to struggle with the concept of being both real and unreal at the same time.

"And Sylvia?" John trying to coax an answer from the apparition in human form.

"Sylvia, started out simply training Charlene, as I did, I suppose. But, as the Demon influent took over, she became crueller, more demanding. I do not believe that she truly meant Charlene to become a sacrifice, as others did. She had something else in mind, even if I don't know exactly what. She always was secretive, especially about her past, and family. Anyway, I must go now," and saying those words, his face melted away, to be replaced by Charlene's.

She whispered, "I'm sorry," as she slowly collapsed in a heap on the floor. They waited a few minutes, but she did not get up, she almost seemed asleep.

"What is wrong with her?" Jack asked John, as they sat her up next to the tree, waiting for her to come around. "I've seen her get hit for six, then get straight up and go at it again. Every time she has one of these episodes, however, she seems to shut down totally, almost like an off switch has been pulled."

Helena came around the corner, with some bags in her hands. Various boxes and bottles filled the bags. She looked at the unconscious Charlene and shook her head.

"What this time?" her eyes combing the slightly guilty looking faces before her.

"She attacked Jack, nothing serious really, the usual," came from both men. They looked at her, and each other, then they just shrugged.

"She may be a tadge unstable Helena, but she's been through a lot, and all this hopping around is taking its toll on her system; systems," John chimed up defending the girl.

"We need to rest up for a while and let her recover. I think we could all do with a rest; especially as I think that the last gate triggered further changes in us. Whatever is happening to us all is not complete. We have not been changed: we are changing."

Helena nodded. "Charlene is the most obvious indicator of that fact. I think that the more she evolves, the more 'out' time she is libel to require; as all her systems upgrade to match." She shook her head and walked over to the sleeping form of Charlene. "It could be worse I suppose; she could have taken the Caterpillar model, rather than the bear."

The others looked at her waiting on an explanation. She let out a sigh, "She could have created a cocoon, instead of hibernating when she changes." She saw the understanding appear in their eyes, and they sighed a little, almost in relief.

"I suppose that is true," Simon said entering the barn. "Although I think that would be less troublesome than her fighting everyone each time," he looked meaningfully at Helena.

"I doubt she'd take kindly to sedation until we get to the machine, Simon," Helena looked at her lithe form.

"Besides, I also doubt that we could safely administer the amount of sedative needed for someone like her. Indeed, she might even be immune to the effects anyway; we simply have no way of knowing." Simon sighed. They all looked at her, then made themselves comfortable.

"What about the farmer?" John asked, indicating the farmhouse they were inhabiting.

"Oh, I persuaded him to take his family on a trip for a few days," Helena shrugged. "I only pushed him a little. I know workaholics, and it only takes a little logic to change the 'I must work' to 'I must live', and as soon as I added that we'd keep an eye on the place for a few days, his resistance collapsed," she shrugged, smiling.

She saw the others relax with the realisation that they had a place to recuperate until Charlene awoke, and they could move on. Most importantly, they were now out of the enemy's stronghold, able to move freely, and that meant that they could soon start to act, rather than just react.

Simon looked at Charlene, then at John and decided it was time to gather some information on his other team members, amongst other things; a simple exercise in resource assessment would be a good cover for a more comprehensive assessment of them and their capabilities. He was not the chess player that Charlene was but, as an engineer, he did like to know the tools available.

"John, a word if I may," indicating that he wanted some words in private.

"What? Oh, sure," started to walk away from the others, with Simon.

"We have seen what Charlene is capable of," Simon started, "and I was just wondering if we should pool the knowledge of our talents so that we can understand our teams' strengths and limitations."

"Good thinking, well I," and the two of them walked off towards the farmhouse.

Helena started looking through the cupboards and making a note of their food and other essentials, keeping Charlene firmly in her field of vision, Jack standing up and moving quickly to help.

"What do you think is actually wrong with her?" Jack asked Helena, as they lined up drinking water and food for a few days stay.

"Hard to tell. From what she has displayed and intimated, her physiology is different now, so my best guess is, exhaustion and the effects of her metamorphic transition. I doubt any of my skills will diagnose her true condition, so we'll just have to trust her recuperative powers to sort out her current physiological, and psychological, problems."

"And if they don't?" He saw the reply before she voiced it.

"Then I have my orders. We deal with her," the tone in Helena's voice intimated that she did not relish the prospect at all. Or, was that fear in her voice? She had doubts they could stop her.

"You have discussed this with the others?"

"No, but we all know that, if she is loosed, out of control, we would all be in trouble."

Jack nodded. How do you find someone that could change into anyone? Even worse, even if you knew who she was, she could teleport away and be someone else before you even caught sight of her. The more he thought about it, the more he realised that most ways of tracking her just would not work, Sight, Automatic Facial recognition, Scent; all useless.

Stopping her would probably require all of them to deal with her, given her power and intelligence. The Good Lord knew that he'd nearly been skewered by her, and the way she'd dealt with the Ghe'Dar had been exceedingly clinical. He suspected that, if she lost herself to this Sylvia, then she would become both less merciful, and far deadlier.

John left Simon and, as he came back into the main barn area, he strode over to Helena. "Simon would like to talk to you about your powers, so that he, we, know what the team is capable of," Helena nodded.

"I was wondering when he'd start doing his cataloguing thing," whispered Helena. "Could you have a look about the rest of the farm and see if there are any resources we can use, that won't be missed too much?" He gave her a pert little salute, as she walked out of the barn door, and was a little shocked when her middle finger was the last thing he saw leaving the building.

Simon was eyeing up a full-sized mirror which had a large crack in it, from the doorway of the outhouse, when he spotted Helena, and waved for her to come over.

"Ah, Helena, our mysterious wand wielder. John passed on my request then?" Helena nodding in reply.

"I'm surprised it took you so long," she grinned at him.

Simon frowned then just nodded slowly, "I keep forgetting that you probably have files on us and our habits. I bet you probably catalogued our powers as they were revealed, and probably know more about this then you have let on so far. I'm betting you know most of it, right up to when we disappeared, correct?" He smiled at her dismay, which was quickly hidden, with a control few of the others had.

"Well some of them were pretty obvious," her voice trailed off as he gave her a demanding look.

"Oh ok, a bit pointless trying to hide it from you I suppose, although I'm surprised Charlene has not twigged too. Craig had an anonymous message to keep his eyes out for you four, sent to him, not naming you, but listing specialisations that indicated each of you, as potential recruits," her voice slowing as Simon unfolded a piece of paper in front of her.

"It carried a code phrase," she snatched the paper from him and looked at it.

There was the paper minus the code phrase, with the address of their London base.

"That's not possible. Wait. Did you just change something?" Her brow furrowing.

Simon smiled at her, "don't try to think about the paradox. It was pretty obvious that, when we arrived at the base in London, Craig already knew about us, the big giveaway was the speed at which the specialist orders were fulfilled; it was just too convenient. Once we were transported back here, the answer became obvious, well to me anyway. Someone had told him what was required, who we were, and our capabilities and needs."

"But what if the Ghe'Dar intercept this?" Helena was bewildered at the possibilities and aghast at the consequences of a mistake, with the whole world was at stake.

"That's simple enough. We send it to Jack's mother, as she is exactly the type of person the Ghe'Dar are least interested in at the moment, with her lack of official standing. With her strict morals and sense of duty, she will not open it, and we'll put a note in to pass it on to the required authorities."

"Still," Simon put his hand on her arm.

"Trust me, Helena, this is the only way. I did a statistical analysis of the other methods, and this has the highest probability of success available. And don't worry, because if it fails no one will know, there will not be anyone left to blame us either." His face belied the seriousness of the statement, and when it hit Helena, she just nodded mutely, added the code phrase and gave it back for Simon to send the letter. This was mad, but it might just be crazy enough to succeed.

Upon his return, Simon started to work on the mirror, scoring it and breaking it up, casually acknowledging Jacks arrival, when he walked in regarding the small sections of mirror that were rapidly stacking up on the makeshift workbench, nodding with approvingly.

"Camouflage right?" Jack half asked.

Simon nodded this time, "it was the way you just waltzed through their defensive perimeter. Being invisible is a great tactical advantage, especially when the odds and numbers are against you, and although this will not be true invisibility, it should allow me to get within targeting range before they can knock me out of the sky with their energy weapons."

"Did you really want to list my powers, or did you want to just talk to each of us?" Jack not being fooled by the stated intent, as someone like Simon would already have catalogued their powers; he was up to something else. At first, Jack had thought Simon a dull and, relatively, simple Scientist type; but as they had gone on, Simon had shown himself far more complicated than that; so, what was he up to?

Simon looked at Jack appraisingly, then became conspiratorial, leaning closer, "it's John and Charlene." The eldest of the group, he knew Jack's type well enough that the truth was the best option, as when you lived by deception you could smell it on people, like an overripe banana. "I'm worried that they are getting too, err, now it's hard to explain".

"Entrenched in their combativeness?" Jack suggested.

"Yes and no," Simon having trouble explaining what he saw developing. "As their powers stabilise, they are beginning to vie for leadership, and while Helena is senior, she is standing in the wings, acting as a guide rather than a commander." Simon tilted his head slightly, "John's police training gives him the authority and, I think, he should indeed be the leader because of his experience, but Charlene's powers are growing. She's a teenager, and she sees herself as the obvious choice; logical, from her point of view anyway."

"And you're wondering where I stand?" Simon nodded and gave him a slight sideways glance. "I noticed that you did not think to consider me," he put on a fake frown.

Simon waved his hand impatiently, "you know you are not a leader any more than I am. The others know your street background and, for all your confidence, they know you are a survivor. Survivors do not make good leaders and much as I respect your upbringing, I know that illusionists are trained in deception, and that does not engender the trust that leaders must engender."

Acknowledging the logic, Jack thought. "Very well. I think John, as the most trustworthy, should be the leader; I just hope we can get Chi'mera to see that."

Simon's head turned to face the tall magician, "Charlene will see the logic in it."

Jack frowned, for a smart person Simon could be tremendously thick.

"That may be, but Charlene and Chi'mera have subtlety different outlooks. Don't tell me you have not noticed that Chi'mera can be more, savage, when in combat? More powerful yes, but she falls back on primitive instincts, and it's not just the other personalities; I doubt she even notices the change, but in the heat of battle she becomes more primal, more reckless and more arrogant. So, I restate the point, I hope Chi'mera views John as the logical leader."

Simon seemed to look off into the distance a little, then shuddered, "I hope so too, because, otherwise, we may end up having PileDriver and Chi'mera fighting each other for leadership, in the middle of a battlefield full of Ghe'Dar Elite troops."

CHAPTER 12

IПΠER CALΠ

"Dare we move her?" John was saying to Helena.

"It should be ok. Whatever is affecting her is psychological, or technical, now rather than physical, I think. She is in a coma, possibly self-induced." Helena was holding Charlene's wrist counting, "it's fairly deep, but not dangerously so. She is barely breathing at all, strange given her high metabolic rate, judging by the amount of food she's been putting away". She shook her head as she rechecked the pulse, "her heart rate is three beats per minute; anyone else checking her would probably think she was dead," looking down at Charlene, then reaching into her mind, deeper and deeper she went, but all she saw or heard was a kind of strange, electronic static, background noise.

"She has withdrawn so far that I cannot reach her mind at all." Helena touched the girl's forehead, then just shook her head, "I cannot do anything for her, but she's stable in all the usual life signs, so I don't think we need to worry too much. If that changes, then I'll try to bring her out of the coma by chemical means, even though she will probably resist, if she thinks she is not ready so it might do more damage than it's worth."

Downstairs a few minutes later, most of those awake met in the living, "ok, what next?" John looking around, noting that Simon was missing. No, wait, what was that in the doorway; a faint, broken, outline blocked it in the gathering light, "Simon?"

"Damn!" came Simon's exclamation from the doorway, the outline shimmering to reveal the armoured form of Titanium. "guess it needs some work?"

"I only saw you because you were outlined in the doorway, even Jack has some problems with that," John noted.

"So the camouflage works?" Simon's metallic voice was hopeful.

"I did have to look twice, so in flight, it should be able to keep you from being spotted."

"Great, that means we can now fly everyone to CERN without having to dodge ground patrols and obstacles." His relief was almost palpable, even though the armour.

"As long as we stay out of RADAR and IR tracking. You able to detect and avoid them?"

In his armour, Simon's face dropped. "No! I would need more time to block that kind of thing. Of course, then there is ECM to think of too." Simon nodded and started muttering under his breath, "let's see, wavelength, output, amplitude," the voice trailing off towards the barn again.

"Our RADAR signatures should be very faint, and we will be flying virtually at ground level anyway, so don't worry too much about it," John called out the room.

Chi'mera listened to their conversation, as though they were at the other end of a long tunnel. Her eyes shut, surrounded by darkness a huge version of her HUD hovering like a giant screen before her,

"Right," her mental voice echoed in the vaults of her own mind, "now we start to try and understand what the blazes is going on in here. Let there be light!" imagining a blaze of light and willing it to fill the area to reveal the mental landscape, only partially succeeding.

She stood, in what appeared as a vast hangar, with dim lighting all around now, rather than darkness. Screens appeared before her, shimmering slightly, more revealed, in the form of an outer ring, displaying incomprehensible data flows, from another ring, hidden in a kind of grey fog around the screen, "well, it's a start."

She realised that this was not real, probably being a mental construct that her mind was using to portray the HUD systems processes and her internal Nanites. The Main HUD was what she saw with her eyes; the next ring was probably the messaging systems between the Nanites and the HUD, including the translation matrices, like the targeting systems. The outer fog was, in most likelihood, the actual sensor data and other programming for the Nanites, which was probably what she needed access to, to allow her full control of her body. In effect, she was about to reprogram herself, creating internal interfaces she needed to match the external one she and Simon had created.

There were however a few fundamental differences, as here she was on her own, at least as alone as she could get, with the other personalities that kept emerging. They might not take too kindly to what she was about to do.

"No, I don't suppose we will!" came a stern voice from behind her, causing her to whip around to confront five figures standing there.

Sylvia, at least one of them, was dressed all in black, whips ready, but standing as if to attention. A second Sylvia, looking radiant in white, as she had been when Charlene was a small child; Charlene had not even realised that she still had memories of her mother like that before the training had started. Her father stood there, dressed in full military uniform holding the second Sylvia's hand. The fourth figure looked like Charlene, but with a strange snarling, almost animalistic, look on her face, while the fifth figure was indistinct, wavering, insubstantial. She did not understand what that meant, in this context, but then all of this was a bit surreal.

"What now?" She addressed the line of figures, a bit disconcerted.

"That my dear is up to you; this is your mind after all," replied the second Sylvia.

"Just give yourself to me," snapped the first, glaring at the second.

"Trust your instincts!" instructed the other Charlene.

"Trust your training," guided her father.

The final figure remained silent.

"Great!" she said sarcastically, but she thought she understood the replies. This was not about her personal demons, it was an interpretation of her request by her own mind, each part of that mind answering according to its nature to the query, and she needed to translate the answers into actions.

"Hmmm. Ok. I'll need a computer interface," one immediately appearing at her figure tips, seemingly suspended in mid-air; at last, some progress.

"Right, now," she tapped in a couple of commands, one of the figures, the darker Sylvia, seeming to fade a little. "fair enough, but she has her uses if she is what I think she is." A few more taps and the dark Sylvia seemed to have changed subtly again, more relaxed, trimmer, less evil but more commanding.

"An excellent choice my dear. Just let me take full command, and you could move the heavens themselves," but the tone in the voice belied the sentiment. Charlene did not respond, having just increased the availability of her muscle memory from her training. Interesting that the system had interpreted the commands by altering the figure in that way.

"Hmmm, let's try this now," she muttered, entering more commands; attempting to gain full conscious access to her teleportation systems. The indistinct figure on the right seemed to twitch and writhe a little, then started to become distinctly more human in outline.

"Command sequence confirmed," came a synthesised mechanical voice from the figure, indicating it was the technological aspect of her, appropriately amorphous, not being fully defined yet. On the HUD, yet more Ghe'Dar symbols disappeared and were replaced with English words. A new section, marked Teleportation subsystems appeared, although the remaining words were blurred; the work continued. This would take quite some time; after all, she was no Isabella.

Jack sat with his book, watching the comatose Charlene, the thick leather, gold leaf embossed and lovingly illustrated volume laying on his lap. Although the person who'd given him the book said that reading the book would help, and he'd a passion for certain types of books, this book was dry and dusty. It mainly described the practice of the different philosophies that allowed access to the different parts of the mind.

All well and good knowing such things, but it hardly helped him gain access to, refine or grow, his supposedly mystical powers. Perhaps there was something deeper required, so, instead of reading the book, he started to flick through it, looking to see if anything dropped out of it. He flicked through it till he neared the final page, when a loose leaf of paper, dropped out. In an archaic script, but in a modern language, three questions were neatly written on the paper. Why had someone written this and put it in this book? A book on enlightenment. He scanned them and frowned.

The first one asked; "What is Power?"

The second read; "Why would you seek it out?"

The final question; "How much Power is enough?"

Intrigued, Jack picked up the paper, setting the book down next to him, pondering the questions. The more he studied them, the more obvious the answers became, namely because they were part of the path to enlightenment. So, was it that you needed to answer the questions to reach enlightenment? Or perhaps they merely allowed you start to seek enlightenment.

Ok, so what was power? There were various types of power, but in its' simplest form, it was the ability to perform tasks. So that answered the second question; you sought out power to complete a task. Indeed, that gave him the answer to the third question; enough power, was power enough to successfully complete the task.

Well, that had been easy enough. Or had it? It had been easy enough for him but would some like Sylvia have answered differently and thus missed the point. Probably.

He looked down at the paper, and the questions had gone. Or rather they had been replaced with one more; "How much power is too much power?"

The question was disturbing; more so than the other three combined. Jack and the others had power now, but would it be enough? Indeed, it had already hurt some, despite their best efforts, and Charlene's was still growing, with no end in sight; yet, they were struggling to get to CERN, the place they needed to get to. That last thought started to get to the point. They might not make it, but if they had more power, they might cause more damage than they prevented.

"How much power is too much? I don't know; but if we have enough power to do the job, to save the world, I'll be happy," he said out loud, "because if we fail, then what's the point?"

He looked down, and his hands were empty, the paper gone. On the bench next to him the book was opened back at page one. Strangely though, the words seemed different; they were the same words but, their meaning now seemed cleared more, right.

And so it began, as he picked it up and began to mouth the words as he read.

Helena looked over at John, who was packing up equipment into a rucksack, getting things ready in case they needed to depart in a hurry; as they had had to at least twice in the past few days. She wondered about the former policeman. Of all the people there, he was the one with the most unambiguous past, officially speaking, but the one that talked the least, and that bothered Helena. It was almost as if he was isolated; not deliberately by the others, but almost surely deliberately by himself.

"John?" he ignored her query as she started over to him. "John, can I have a moment?" He turned around with his gun in pieces in his hands, apparently in the process of being cleaned.

"Helena?" His tone casual, but he was clearly annoyed at the interruption. She reached out with a hand and gently pushed his full hands to the table.

"Can we talk?" she said gently.

His face turning into a scowl,

"I'm not in the talking mood," he snapped, shaking her off, her hand returning and grabbing his more firmly.

"It's important, and it's time," her voice becoming firmer, his eyes flicking a second, as though he was going to shake her off again. Was that fear she'd seen?

"John, you need to talk," they both knew what about.

"Look I know you liked her, and the fact the others are against attempting to save her hurts. But if you let that get between you and them, we will fail. If we do see an opportunity, it would be better if they were not at loggerheads with us. Ok?"

John let the words sink in, having been thinking about the problem a lot lately, especially with Chi'mera's newly revealed talent to teleport others along with herself. She could perform the rescue, if she were close enough at the time of Isabella's fall, she could do it; where he could not.

"Helena," he looked down a little, "I understand. Really, I do, but, Ok, I'll try. I've never really been the talkative type, but I'll try." She looked at him and saw the sincerity in his voice. She nodded, then went on to more mundane matters. "How's the packing doing?"

"Ready, as best I can make it," he gave a wane little smile for her benefit, "and if Titanium can conjure up an improved flying speed, we'd have our own personal jet."

"I guess that he has about ten dozen upgrades in mind; if we ever get the time."

"Probably more, given all the drawings he's been doing; including a size upgrade."

They both heard the Cockcrow announcing the dawn, and, as the sun peeked over the horizon, they both saw the most beautiful sunrise; purple-orange with wisps of silvery cloud spreading a fan of sunlight across the otherwise pale blue sky, the first sign of the real world they had seen actually worth saving. They both savoured the moment like people lost in the desert savouring the first water in days. Then, across the sky, vapour trails started to appear; aircraft travelling to their destinations, causing both of them to sigh and resume their conversation.

"Any idea how long we need to stay here?" John asked, making Helena look back across at Charlene.

"Until Charlene has had enough time to sort herself out, or until we run out of time."

Helena shrugged. "When it comes to Charlene there is no telling."

"I hope she does not take too long. We have a few days, but we still have a few hundred miles to cross, and I don't like staying too long in one place either, as the Ghe'Dar agents are bound to start making connections. If they do, they may well begin guessing our destination, or at least our line."

"Maybe, but our trail is in the future, so they don't have much to go on."

"We did not either, to start with. But we made it here." He looked at her with concern in his eyes.

"True. But this time we know who they are and, more importantly, where they are. At this end of history, that is not information that they have of us. We have the element of surprise and that, plus a few tricks from Craig, may well be enough," she saw his look. "Yes, I hope so too."

Charlene had managed to clear up a few things, in the hours she'd been at work in the strange environs of her mind; gaining access to other teleportation functions, while other systems remained obscured by layers of code, or as represented in this place, fog.

Still, the core area was lighter, and now she could see other displays that filled this area. It was no longer just the main screen, there were lots of other smaller monitors all over the place. Some at a distance, others close enough that she could see their titles; one, marked 'Interfaces,' looking promising, while another entitled 'Analysis' was enormous but virtually inactive.

She was getting the idea that the more she stayed here, the more she could achieve. She also knew that she needed to come out of the coma creating this environment had caused. She'd be hungry, she knew; famished would be a better description, given the growling of her virtual stomach.

This whole exercise had allowed her to get an inkling of her real potential. The fusion of her nanobots, the Ghe'Dar tech, and the strange Chimera gene seemed to have broken through so many limits, that ordinary people took for granted. She just needed time, the one thing which had enabled her arrival here; the one commodety in short supply.

Perhaps, after they had defeated the Ghe'Dar she would, then she stopped. When had she started believing that they could overcome this seemingly unstoppable force? She tried to recall the moment, but she could not. She was reasonably sure that they would do so though; it was, ironically, just a matter of time.

She had done enough, she decided. All the internal interfaces that she needed were in place; all the figures now looked as she expected them to be, the final one looking almost like a smaller, more clipped version of herself with dark gold-flecked eyes.

"Ok let's see if we can control what I just did," she muttered to her virtual self. "System," she addressed her technological self, "initiate reboot."

Everything went black. Then all the alarms went off at once!

Out of the corner of Jack's left eye, he saw Charlene's body convulse; arching her back clean off the table she'd been laid on, then thudding down again. The others were frozen for a second; then they all sprinted to her side.

"What's wrong with her?" asked a straining John, trying to hold her down.

"Seizure of some kind," as Charlene went still Helena reached over her, to get a sense what was going on. After a few seconds, she looked alarmed, "heart attack, by the looks of it," looking around, then at the farmhouse door, yelling, "Simon!".

Almost immediately, Titanium stomped into the room, bits of armour hanging off the main frames; trailing wires, like a mummy trailing bandages, apparently in the middle of modifying the external plating.

"Simon, over here. She needs a de-fib charge," Helena pointed, beckoning him over to where she needed it to go. He ran, with great thumping steps, to the spot indicated.

"Clear!" he bellowed, Charlene heaving again, this time lifted by the electricity from his hand. At full arch, the body suddenly snapped back down, thudding into the table with a sickening crunch of bone, then remaining still for a couple of seconds. He prepared to deliver another electrical pulse when Charlene's eye shot open, Titanium suddenly finding himself lifted into the air; about ten feet into the air, by a pair of tentacles.

"That's enough Titanium. I'm fine now," said a surprising calm Charlene.

The rest of them heard another crunch, as bone slipped back into place, while Titanium was lowered carefully to the ground. Unlike previously, her eyes were clear, and her demeanour was calm, despite having just been electrocuted.

"You're, OK?" Helena looked at her and, for the first time in over a week or so, the girl actually looked like the old Charlene; a little mischief on her face, rather than just pain, sickness or another person looking out of those gold-flecked eyes.

"Yes. I have," her leg twitched a little, as another crunch resounded through her frame, "managed to do some work, technical adjustments, that should give me greater control now.

"What about your other selves?" John asked, just as surprised by the change in her as the others; she seemed almost pleasant.

"They are silent for the moment; not gone, just, in balance," the others looking both relieved, and a little dubious.

"Hey. Trust me!" Charlene could almost see the rest of the team all grind their teeth at that request. "Does anyone have some serious food handy?" She just could not resist saying it and smiled when they all groaned, relaxing visibly.

John looked at the others, "Yup, she's back folks," and John smiled a little at Charlene, and winked.

"The farmhouse has a fully stocked kitchen, and I guess it's time for breakfast," Helena pointed out, leading them all into the courtyard; the sun streaming into it over the barn roof.

"Great, but I think Helena should cook. Simon's diet, of electricity, was a real pain."

The rest laughed, but he just grumbled, as he got outside the back door and climbed out of his suit.

"Typical. Do the girl a favour and what you get?" he muttered, still not thoroughly practised in getting out of the cumbersome suit. It was especially tricky with wires dangling from the legs, where he was still attaching the reflective tiles for his camouflage.

"A cold breakfast, if you take much longer getting out of your tank," came Charlene's tart reply. He moved into the old farmhouse kitchen, not noticing, as he did so, that the armour was not actually powering down.

Deep within the armour, lights started to turn green, power systems cycling up and the onboard computer displaying messages on the HUD.

"Auxiliary protocols enabled. System repair required. Overriding safety systems. Primary objective: Seek out enemy signal, infiltrate and neutralise. Locating nearest enemy signal."

On the HUD a series of locations scrolled down the screen until a site was selected, its' coordinates appearing on the screen, its GPS location being locked into the navigational computer.

The suit silently re-sealed itself, ripped off the dangling wires, then slowly started to exit the farmyard, fading from view, only a few small tiles visible.

As the team sat down for breakfast in the farmhouse, Jack had a sudden strange feeling as if something was wrong, as though someone that should be there was missing.

"Hey guys, did you," they all looked at him, "never mind," but Charlene nudged him.

"What?" She asked as she tried to get the first spoonful of a rather lovely tasting muesli into her mouth, at the same time as a piece of banana.

"It was a feeling of emptiness, almost like I was suddenly missing someone."

"Yes," John said quietly; only Helena hearing him.

"Well, you did leave your book in the Barn, and you've been getting quite attached to that," laughed John out load, trying to lighten his own mood.

Jack gave him a withering look, but started to out head towards the door anyway, almost like he was being tugged on a string and more than a little reluctantly, the others following out of curiosity, Charlene carrying her bowl.

As he reached the courtyard and looked about, the feeling immediately vanished. "Er, Simon, where's your armour?"

"What? It's just out," as he exited the door, he could see the courtyard was empty apart from a few strands of wire and reflective mirror tiles.

"Oh great. We just get Charlene under control, and suddenly Titanium develops 'zombie headless chicken' syndrome." John was looking distinctly un-amused, while Simon looked at him angrily.

"Where is it's going?" He yelled, pointing to a reflective speck in the distance.

"Never mind that. How do we get it back?" said Helena, who looked at Simon.

He thought a second or two, then nodded, "It must be that virus function, that tried to download to the Ghe'Dar mothership, kicking in again after my latest series of modifications. I thought I'd purged it all, but it must have had a second redundant backup store somewhere in the power systems," Simon mused.

"I'll go get it!" John was getting ready to run, but Charlene put a hand on his arm.

"You cannot fly, and if you attack it from the ground, you may force it up into RADAR controlled space. Titanium is the one thing that will show up on their screens, then we'll have massive damage to the timeline on our hands, may be too much to repair." She was referring to their need to remain hidden, rather than the electronics.

Jack piped up, "Perhaps if we three worked together we could force it back," bobbing his head back and forth, weighing up the options.

"OK, Magician, let's hear your plan," John was in no mood to be patient. The more they planned and waited, the further the armour got, and it looked like it was heading for a local town, Troyes.

"OK," Jack mimicking John's comment, "You pick us up, run and get ahead of it since it cannot fly that fast. Then I fly up and force it down, from above, allowing Chi'mera to can wrap it up, while PileDriver pummels it, and my blasts penetrate its armour, to shut it down and since it does not auto-repair like Simon we can get it

251

back here." He checked with Simon, "It can't repair itself, right?" Simon was looking alarmed at the plans they were making.

"What? No, no, that's in the new designs, but it needs a full rebuild for anything like that. Although," he paused before giving them the bad news, "I did install a secondary power system so that the suit could channel my electrical bolts, I'm guessing that is what allowed it to up and fly off by itself." He looked around guiltily, though the others did not appear too surprised.

"Does that mean it can fire bolts at us, at point blank range?" Charlene was looking a little hopeful until he nodded sheepishly.

John just threw his hands up in the air, "oh, great!"

"He did not know, John," Helena defended Simon, "how could he know that the damn thing could get a mind of its own."

"My armour can deflect some damage, and if we get it the ground, I can use a trick to avoid those blasts, I hope," Charlene turned gold, "but we don't really have time to debate the plan, and not much more after that before it gets to where it's going."

John snarled a little, his muscles rippling.

Jack calmly stepped next to the impatient PileDriver, and Chi'mera looked at the face of her Bodyguard, extending a tentacle to form a kind of rucksack-like fitting for her and her fellow passenger.

"Drive carefully!" she requested; then both she and Jack yelped, as the strange living vehicle bolted off after the armour. Simon stepped back into the Barn to see if he could put something together in the way of equipment, should the team fail. He was like that; solve from one problem, then try to answer the next.

Helena looked after them, then continued to make her breakfast. This was a strange turn of events. She wondered what Craig was doing at the moment. She tried to remember what they had been up to before all of this had started. Ah yes, they had been receiving reports of strange events in the London underground and deciding what to do about them.

Craig had been correlating reports from the various intelligence agencies in the area for a few days at that point trying to determine what was happening and whether it was within the M.I.X. remit, and jurisdiction. The reports ranged from electricity companies reporting power surges, police reports of vandalism and weird animals, public nuisances including missing people, sewage company reports of large-scale damage to their network caused by strangely localised earthquakes in areas not undergoing tunnel work activities. All the reports were examined and correlated by his small team.

It had taken a few days to complete the work, as she remembered, but the bombshell had hit the office a few days later. A package was delivered, from a local M.I. Office in London, containing a padded box and a coded letter that just could not be a coincidence.

"How did you receive the package?" Craig had asked the young lad, through the intercom, actually a junior M.I. agent place in the post office to track specific items and ensure a secure postal service to all M.I. facilities; just another drop for him.

"It arrived from a small-town post office, sir, no way to trace it from there. No CCTV, no traffic cameras, no nothing, whoever sent it made sure that there was no evidence to trace it back."

Craig looked the man over, noting he seemed a little nervous, standing to attention as the military types always seemed to do here, while the civilian recruits always seemed to deal with it better; that seemed the wrong way around to him.

"We did a standard fingerprint, DNA and chemical screening. The results were deemed classified above my level, but the station chief just said that you would understand the implications," and with that, he deposited the package containing the letter in the night safe transfer box.

After getting it up to his office, he and Helena looked the package over.

"I know the office is new; but do we have a UV scanner in here?" Craig looked at Helena, who pointed to the other office area.

"I'll get it," Isabella rolled off the sofa, and bolted across the office to go fetch it.

"She's fitted in well," Craig muttered to Helena, who just nodded, saying 'I told you so.'

When she returned, she dropped the scanner next to Craig, who was sat in his corner of the other sofa, not being as young as he used to be. He ran it over the outside and spotted three things that immediately set his alarm bells ringing.

Firstly there was a distinct fingerprint on it, that the others would not recognise, but he did; it was his. He KNEW that he'd not sent this package, so how in the hell had it gotten there? Ok, so whoever had posted it now had his attention.

Point two was even stranger, spotted under a UV lamp, a blood spot on the stamp, well the franking actually. Almost imperceptible to normal vision, but glowing like a beacon under the light, which he guessed was the point and drawing his attention to it. He'd have to check the markers in the blood, but he'd hazard a guess that it would be familiar too.

The third one was the clincher. The delivery address was the exact office they were sat in; not just the building, but the unit and floor, of a supposedly empty office suite. This had been sent by someone that knew they had moved in and had access to knowledge and material that they potentially had no right to have.

Now for the letter, he thought, carefully pinching the package opening using forensic gloves and large tweezers, while Helena took the tiny blood sample off for analysis at the M.I.X. labs elsewhere in the City. Carefully extricating the regular white A4 letter, noting the watermark was French, he read the letter, realising the words were full of means that only he might understand, reading as follows: -

"Hi there, Bossy Boots. Firstly, you don't know me," Craig blinked, "secondly, yes, I'm going to be cryptic, so I hope you are smart as you say you are. I'm also hoping that the credentials I sent will prove it's real."

Ok. Craig had seen some strange messages before and thought he was ready.

"1. Seek out experts in Biology, Cybernetics, and Security, then order some equipment for them; they will be coming to stay."

"2. **E**verything you are about to do has already happened for us." What?

"**3**. We will need help, but you must not use the regular channels." Oh great.

"**4**. I cannot tell you much, but big trouble is coming, and you need to get ready."

"**5**. Trust no one outside your office," apparently the layout was part of the message.

"I have asked your girl with us to give you an appropriate signature I could not know otherwise," now then, this would be interesting.

"Finally thanks for listening, the fate of the world is in your hands." Ah, what?

The signature was a code word or phrase, that would give him an idea of the scale of the event they were talking about. The next words were in a familiar scrawl, Helena's, "Love ELE" with nine kisses under it.

Craig's was not usually the emotional kind, but this time hand started to tremble. A level nine was terrible enough, but it was saying, as the letter had intimated, that they were talking about, not just a simple terrorist or security threat, but an E.L.E. or Extinction Level Event, and one he could not take this to anyone else. It took him a short time to assimilate the connotations.

Before he'd become ill, he'd battled terrorists and criminals for years, in a suit of special armour, codenamed Gravitron. It seemed that he might need to do so again, but he had to do something now, so he started to tweak out as much information as he could from the letter.

It had come from France, so whatever was happening he needed to get in touch with someone over there or send a resource over there that could be in position. The problem was they had not said where the focus was.

Or had they? They were obviously clever, whoever they were, and they had one of his team with them, apparently. But how would you tell someone where you were without telling people outright. The credentials were on the package, what about the letter? He looked at it again, nothing else showed up on U.V., and there were no more visible spots or watermarks, wait; if you were in France, how would you tell where you were, in such flat land.

As he pondered the possibilities, he realised something else, vaguely impinging on his consciousness a faint whiff of something familiar. Craig looked at the watermark a bit harder, then sniffed the paper; ah, you clever, clever person; Wine. Most people knew Craig was a wine connoisseur, but few people knew how good he really was; Helena one of them as they had shared the odd bottle recently. He sniffed again letting the aroma fill his nostrils and admiring the cunning to use this as a communication method. Even if the letter was intercepted, the enemy had read the contents and done a chemical analysis; only the best of the best could track down exact location by the aroma.

Now the grapes were drier than the southern area's wines produced, so they were talking the mid-France, Champagne route, the Aube region? No, too full-bodied, something a bit more rural, a local wine, not the mainstream ones. Another sniff detected a hint of local tree pollen, Troyes? Possibly but that to was mainstream, he should know having an archaeological unit near there. Maybe a bit further down, Auxerre. Yes, that was nearer still. Crémant de Bourgogne.

Ok, what was down there? Well plenty of wine, that was for sure, but nothing in the way of technology, that would require the skills suggested; Troyes was the closest for that, and yet there must be some logic to it. He thought harder, perhaps the message was not so much a fixed location, as a line or destination. Yet where could that be?

Craig stood up and looked at the tone of the letter, logical, serious, methodical.

The writer was evidently a scientist, one that did things by the numbers. Wait, the initial characters were bolder than the others, perhaps that was the reasoning. By the numbers it read; SE 345. Ok, Craig thought, assuming that Auxerre was the primary location that they were talking about, then assume that the letters were a direction and the numbers were a distance from the starting point, and that would give, South East 345 miles?

He displayed a map, trying to find something in Italy near Piacenza. Nothing of great note in the way of science facilities. No wait, this was from France, perhaps he should use kilometres. He recalculated and found it was placing him somewhere near the Switzerland border, Geneva and, just north of there, something jumped out at him: CERN; the one place on the planet dealing with high energy particles and new forms of matter, like his own Fusion core generator. If something were to go wrong there, it could be catastrophic.

A chill went down his spine, one he'd learned to trust; that was the target for sure.

He knew he'd need to get there at some point, but at the moment he continued to check the letter for more clues. There was an implicit tone in the message, that he and the writer'd met, "Hi there, Bossy Boots", was just too familiar, and too casual to be random, but couple with the "We have not met" set his mind working again and the only conclusion he came up with both thrilled and terrified him. This person knew they were going to meet because they had already met him; how he hated quantum time theory, even if an engineer and physicist himself, he did know the assumptions behind it.

He would have to start getting the equipment he thought he'd need and started ordering a few sets of gear for delivery to a warehouse in Geneva. He had personal resources he could get in situ plus a few agents in Europe that could be mobilised at short notice and, while M.I.6 could probably do it better, he could probably call in a few favours to getting military units in place. He'd have to rely on Helena, to get the connections rolling, unless he went direct and a few carefully placed words would have a team in Paris within a day, without alerting anyone to the real magnitude of the problem.

Well, the message had been received, plans put in place, yet there was still one thing that he could do. He could polish it up his old armour and do a few upgrades. Indeed, he had an older set too, that he'd not used it in quite some time, but could be set up as a failsafe; a trap to catch the enemy even if M.I.X. fell. With that in place even if they did not succeed, they might still save the world. It was a long shot, but he set his own genius to work envisaging the enemy requiring the professions he knew would be present, plus Helena.

Helen shook her head. Remembering the day that they'd received the message was all well and good, but getting things done was another, and she shook herself looking for things to do, and saw Jack's book lying there, having a sudden twinge of curiosity. She had her staff it was true, but she wondered what was so important in the book that GhostKnight had received it, when she had not, especially as, from Jack's description, the person who'd directed it to him was obviously her master in Oxford.

Well, Helena knew the pitfalls of having too much power, Sylvia being a prime example, but there were enough over the history of magic that the lesson should be obvious to all. Perhaps the book was not suitable for her, or it just did not contain anything she needed. Still, there was that slight tug, faint but she could see a soft light coming from it, a pale blue enticing her in, like a star guiding her to something she'd always wanted. She tried to shake the feeling off, but a small voice in her head keep saying perhaps the book was calling to her, it's actual owner. It was not unheard of that a magic source was usable by more than one practitioner; unusual, but not unheard of, and she found herself moving towards the book without really thinking about it.

That simple act stopped her feet. "Nice try," she said to no one in particular, "but you are not dealing with some initiate here," she muttered, stopping very still, then deliberately stepping away from the book, which actually required quite an effort; like swimming against a rip tide, but she was easily up to this task. Gathering her will, she forced her legs to move and tore her eyes away from the light.

When she looked back at the book, the light was gone, and it became merely an interesting book, even if she now knew it was also a dangerous one. A subtle form of test perhaps, probably one created by her mentor to test those around the owner. She'd passed that one and hoped she was up to passing the one life had thrown at her. She sat down to ponder that and wondered how the others were doing.

PileDriver landed on the hard ground, a heavy "Umph", his breath exploding from his lungs; that blow had hurt, powerful even for Titanium. He looked at his chest where the armoured fist had hit him; bruised certainly, ribs were broken, possibly.

Jack was still staggering after them, after being hit by a surprise electrical discharge, which had caught him unawares at the start of the battle. Beside him, Charlene was seemingly out cold, from the jolt channelled through her tentacles. Whoever had programmed this thing had been thorough; it seemed to have a response for all the powers that they had demonstrated so far, probably having catalogued them and formulated counter strategy as they had travelled.

The damned armour had twisted around before they could initiate their attack plan with a sneak attack of its own. It had apparently reconfigured its power system to replace Simon's biologically generated electrical bolts, with hull channelled electrical discharges. Not as powerful or accurate, but just as dangerous, and painful. The result was the current situation.

The armour advanced, measuring the distance between it and PileDriver, and leapt, landing barely three feet from him. He did not hesitate, having seen Chi'mera pull this routine before, and threw a blow aimed at the faceplate to obscure its vision, to deal with it. His first stab at the trick had earned him the ribs, this time he tried another manoeuvre; something entirely new. He dropped to his knees and smashed into the suits knee joints; the most heavily armoured part of the leg, something only an idiot, or someone with a trick up their sleeve, would do.

The armour rocked a little taking a step back to steady itself and found a tentacle wrapping around its ankle, pulling it further back than was adequately balanced. The armour's head spun around to see the supposedly unconscious Chi'mera heaving at the leg from the ground with all her might.

Seeing the tableau, GhostKnight fired a mystic bolt at the armour, causing it to tip over and its camouflage to fail entirely. It was damaged, but still operational enough to put up a stiff fight, and, it showed it was not so quickly put down as it started flying at virtually ground level, dragging Chi'mera with it, whipping around, her back to the ground, disoriented and unable to gain any purchase.

Sparks started appearing along a ridge down the armour's back. "It's getting ready to shock me again," she called to PileDriver, still recovering from the previous knuckle cracking blow, "I can hear the cycling ramp up." PileDriver nodded, bolting ahead of the pair, in a desperate burst of speed, GhostKnight also fading out, ready to initiate another hit and run strike which, for this battle suited him more, than it did the two brawlers.

Then, as she continued to be dragged Chi'mera saw an opportunity, a telephone pole in the line of the armour's flight, with wires descending into the ground. Useful! Firing out her other tentacle, she grabbed the pole, anchoring herself and the armour to the spot and yanking with the last of her rapidly failing strength, bringing the whole procession to an abrupt stop; PileDriver adding a stunning blow to the suit's cranial unit. Of course, machines are incapable of actually being stunned, in the proper sense of the word, but the overall effect was just as good as the helmet flew off, landing several feet away in a ditch by the road. Fortunately, there was no traffic here, something they could be grateful for.

At least, they might have been grateful, if it were not for the fact that Chi'mera was still holding the suit, that continued to fight, sending another jolt of electricity through her tentacles, triggering a shudder from her. This time however she did not feign unconsciousness, simply looping the shock back through a conductive layer in her tentacles, and using the telegraph pole as a transformer, her tentacle acting as a solenoid to step-up the returning voltage. The effect was much more satisfying than the removal of the head, as the armour sparked, then blinked and jerked for a few seconds, then went limp. Chi'mera looked at the suit, running a quick scan with one of her newly created internal monitors.

"It's lost its' main power now," she sighed, and GhostKnight appeared behind her.

"We'd best get it back to Simon before it loses all its power; otherwise he'll be without his suit for the final battle, and that would never work," said Jack.

"Yeah," puffed John, "And I'll need to see Helena about these ribs of mine, and my knuckles." Chi'mera started to change back into Charlene again, then looked at him, scanning him too. His vital signs were good but the ribs were showing some signs of being cracked, and while her vision was not X-ray, they showed gaps and twists in his ribcage.

"Looks broken alright," she announced, before realising the effect it would have on the others. They both regarded her carefully, in that infuriatingly questioning look that they both had.

"And you know that how?" came Jack's pointed question.

"I, well, I can see it. Some type of scanner that's appeared on my HUD. It's not precisely MRI, but the output and display are similar. Only works on people though; machines are just solid lumps to it.

"Something else you forgot to tell us?" asked John, incensed that his body had been probed without his permission, grinding his teeth again.

"Saves you having to ask Helena for a diagnosis, right?" She said defensively.

"You keep your beady little eyes to yourself missy, or you'll find them full of my fists; understood," he ordered, stomping off without waiting for a reply.

"We'd best walk back ourselves," said Jack in her ear, coming up beside her. She nodded. "It will give him time to cool off."

"Any idea why he so touchy?" Charlene was perplexed and concerned, but she'd never admitted the reason for that, even to herself.

"My Guess?" Charlene nodded for him to proceed, "he saw you lying there on the grass, and saw Isabella all over again." And there it was again, Isabella reaching out from the grave to hurt John, even though Isabella would probably have been the last person wanting John being sad at her passing. He was getting more and more obsessed by her departure, Charlene hoping there was some way to get John to reconcile her death before they actually had to face it again; as they all knew they were going to have to.

Helena heard the group arriving again several hours after their departure, having seriously considered following them with Simon, but discounted the idea since it would leave all their equipment unattended. She was going to ask them what had taken so long, but thought better of it when she saw the look on John's and Charlene's faces, the state of the suit, both singed and battered, probably during their attempts to immobilise it and Jack's weary walk.

"What happened?" she muttered to Jack, as he passed by.

"Later," was all he said, meaning something significant had happened which had affected all of them.

Simon came out of the barn with a small electronic unit of some kind, groaning as he saw the burnt state of the suit, frantically waving the device over it, determining the extent of the damage. After a few minutes of frantic assessment and tutting, he looked at Charlene and John. "Did you really have to blow out the main power relays and the transformation matrix?" He groaned again and, before they could say anything, or apologise, he put his hand up to them, with a small plain looking black box, "these things are rare, and we'll have a devil of a time replacing them. We'll need to locate a source of heavy-duty industrial parts."

Helena pursed her lips, "in the middle of rural France? yeah right."

Charlene looked up at John, who was deliberately looking down at the ground, introspecting. Simon glared at the others with indignation at the damage inflicted on his precious suit, including a very quiet Jack.

"John could go to a" Simon started, halting as John looked up sharply, anger shining fiercely from his eyes. Helena touched the strong man's arm casually, but causing him to wince a little.

"It would probably be best if Jack went," Helena interrupting Simon's request. "He could not travel as fast, but he could do it more, surreptitiously." John's hand tried to flick hers' off, but, surprisingly, she resisted him doing it. He did not attempt to remove it again, and his head dropped, and his feet shuffled a little.

For once, Charlene stood tall and move right up in front of Simon, who was also, for the first time, undaunted by her manner, "well, it needed doing, and personally I don't think we could have done anything else unless you wanted it totally trashed! Come on John let's see if we can get some food around here," and with that, she grabbed the arm of her bodyguard, almost dragging him into the farmhouse. Surprisingly he did not resist.

Simon looked a little stunned. "What did I say?" looking a little hurt.

Helena opened her mouth, then snapped it shut. Jack gingerly stepped up to Simon, looking at him slightly sideways, pointed his foot slightly towards Simon and just shook his head. For someone so smart, Simon had suddenly come down with a severe case of Stupid. "Simon. They both could have been killed getting that armour back. Sometimes, show a little gratitude, before you tell them off, ok?"

Simon blinked. Jack wondered whether he'd actually heard him, because, instead of replying, he merely stomped off, muttering about the carelessness nature of people and how he'd need to make Jack a parts list.

Jack looked at the farmhouse and, for once, decided the Charlene had the right idea. It was time for food, giving Simon time to cool off before someone told him that he'd need either Charlene or John to move his armour into the Barn to start work on it. Simon, at the moment, was in a world of his own, planning repairs and upgrades, and the others would probably not be welcome there.

Ricks took another quick look out of the narrow loft window overlooking the roof, "still clear," he confirmed to Haines, who was on a small burn phone, "Ok, you're clear," he relayed quietly.

A figure suddenly burst from cover a few buildings over, racing across the rooftops at breakneck speed, hugging the chimney breasts and crenulations of the old city skyline. In a light grey jacket, the figure moved with control and purpose, still managing to keep eyes looking everywhere, evidenced by the fact that, as he landed on the roof next to the observer, he suddenly ducked down, reacting to a helicopter in the distance. It flew low at a forty-five degrees to the building; close enough that a running figure might attract attention. Once it was out of sight, the runner continued to move, more slowly now, trying to keep at least one chimney between himself and where the helicopter had gone. Even at this distance, Ricks could sense the concern of the figure.

"He's jittery, even for him. Whatever he thinks he's found, it's hot," Ricks observed.

"Given what GhostKnight said, I'd not be surprised," Haines agreed, sounding as though he was still considering the strange masked agent's message.

"You're not really taking that seriously, are you?" Now that they had moved out, his natural suspiciousness began reasserting itself, "it must be mummery, a ploy to distract us from something else."

"I'm not so sure. True we could only see his eyes, but he thought he was telling the truth, of that I'm positive. People don't throw the phrase E.L.E. around unless they have been talking to scientists, one of the few groups of people that use it, along with disaster planning teams. It's too scary a word for budgets and government circles, and he did not seem the sort to frequent ANY of those circles, which means,"

"… someone discussed it with him, in a context that convinced him that it was true," Ricks finished, the two of them always were in tune, when it came to their thinking. It had kept them alive for a long time; well a long time for the intelligence business.

"I believe he believes it, let's see what Gareth thinks."

The roof door rattled twice paused and once again, Haines reaching across and unlatching it, allowing the figure to come in at speed and roll around the door frame, closing and locking it, in one fluid action.

"You took your time," Haines started but stopped dead when the figure whipped around and placed a finger on his lips, lifting a small bug in his other hand.

Haines eyes bulged and raised his jammer, activating it quickly, then exploded, "are you insane bring that here. They will know about this place now, and we have a few other places,"

"Shut up. We don't have the time. Listen, carefully, and grab your gear as you do," the figure was collecting equipment and moved around the room at speed.

"This is no simple terrorist group. They have infiltrated both the government and the military, probably even our unit," he starred at a monitor briefly, and slammed his elbow into it, shattering the screen.

"Yeah we," Ricks started, grabbing a rucksack and filling it too.

"I said, shut up and listen. They're combing the various agencies and comm. channels using kit like I've never seen before; overriding security protocols that should be airtight, cutting straight through firewalls; you name it. Perhaps even through, oh rats," he looked at Haines's jammer. Haines looked up, and the apology in Gareth's eyes was plain to see. It was Haines' turn to hold his hand up.

"We know!" Haines expleted.

The figure stopped dead, "how?"

"We'll tell you en-route," Haines said, grabbing the last of the equipment they had there and shouldering a heavy metal framed carry all; packed with electronics and weapons.

"Where to now?" Ricks started.

Haines looked at Gareth meaningfully, who shrugged and hurled the bug out the window, into the gutter of an old house.

"Good shot," applauded Ricks facetiously.

"He was always good at throwing things," Haines muttered.

All three of them were out the door, carrying heavy rucksacks full of gear before they heard sirens and helicopters approaching in the distance.

"Their response times are getting faster," Gareth complained.

"Yes. We'll head for S4 this time," Haines saw objections start on both men's' faces, but he continued, "yes it's in the sticks, but it's on the way to the target site." Gareth's eyebrows lifted a little at that; but he said nothing, "and we can swing past the labs, to see if we can pick anything up from there."

Gareth piped up at that, "best not. I left a few loose ends around there that would make answering questions awkward," he actually managed to look a little sheepish.

"That's not like you. What happened? I mean we received your code one alert until it was cut off,"

Gareth looked back a little wide-eyed, as they dodged through Paris's narrow alleyways, startling one beggar who yelped as the three went past him at speed, Gareth flipping a Euro coin into the bowl by the dark-bearded man's side, finger to his lips.

"Well," he started, still running smoothly, the strain of running and talking starting to show, it was one trick he'd always had problems with, "I discovered that the missing people were being captured and processed in the labs." He continued, skip-hopping over a small metallic box in his way, "so, I tried to infiltrate the compound and see if I could find out what they were doing to them."

The group took a left through a small abandoned house but carried on running. "I hit a brick wall with trying to discover that as, apparently, they were using the area as a transfer point," his voice becoming more strained.

As they turned into the next street, they slowed a little, trying to blend in with the few people strolling down the road, especially as running people tended to draw attention. The trio carried on a bit more sedately now, while overhead they heard the sounds of helicopters flying back towards their original location. As they walked undercover of a shop awning, a police helicopter passed overhead, moving in a tight search pattern with a few others, failing to see the agents deep in the awning's shadow the aircraft too high to effectively see them.

As the 'copter circled, Gareth continued his story. "Anyway, I managed to get into the compound, despite the security being tighter than it should be for a civilian science lab and the local police turning a blind eye to the security arrangements."

"The same with the Embassy security and the squad that came for us," Haines interjected. Gareth turned to his superior, bit Haines indicated it was a story for another time, so Gareth continued.

"Anyway, I entered their computer hub and started to hack it, when I noticed that a section of the establishment was marked in red on a sitemap. It was away from the main complex, marked as under construction."

Gareth, taking a quick look out of the shade, indicated that the nearest helicopter had gone, and started them off again, at a casual stroll.

"It sparked my curiosity, so I concentrated my searches in that area. Strangely, they were all negative, no signs, no cameras, not even construction records. So, I went in slowly with triggers set, expecting heavy duty opposition. Nothing! Well,

OK there was a small silver sphere; a drone of a type I'd never seen before. I tazered it, and that was that." He shrugged, indicating he'd thought that'd be the end of it.

"When I reached the centre of the red area, there was a strange doorway to nowhere, standing at the end of one room, a seat and a desk with a bowl-like receptacle, that suggested it was the charging station for the drone."

"I was just about to investigate the door when the damn thing started powering up, so I grabbed the seat and just waved the new arrivals through. It was like something from a science fiction show, as they just arrived out of thin air. Not like teleportation but more like, well we can hand it over to the scientists after this is over."

The two officers looked at Gareth like head just gone slightly over the edge.

"Anyway, some arrivals came through, and this is where it gets really weird," Gareth's voice dropped to a barely audible level, "one was armoured, like one of those heavy lifting units, but larger and weird looking, carrying two human bodies like they were cargo, or for the morgue, a bodybuilder, and a worker of some kind. The strangest thing though was an alien looking thing, armoured similarly to the other, without the opposable knee joints and with a freaky head like a four-eyed cuttlefish, but meaner."

The all stopped near a small blue door, in a side street. "You sure it was real, not a disguise, some sort of sci-fi costume?" Ricks asked seriously.

"Been trying to figure that out, but it looked real enough, besides the doorway, gateway thingy was real enough. I mean, why have something like that without an audience otherwise; besides the next thing was what really mattered."

They moved into the hallway of the house and bolted the door behind them, looking around the was mouldy, and poorly lit, place ignoring the peeling paintwork and broken balustrade slates on the narrow staircase. The three agents ran upstairs to a ground floor flat, sat down on a long, ragged, couch and relaxed a little; they'd made it.

"So what happened next? We did not see anything outside when we were there, and given that the person we spoke to at HQ pulled a disappearing act practically right next to us, there is at least one clever operative at work around here."

"What I saw was phenomenally different," the man leaned back, and closed his eyes, trying to remember the details. "After the arrivals had gone through the doors, one of them changed, not clothing, or style but their skin, to appear human. Now I know octopi can change colour, but this, thing, changed into a human," the alarm on the others' face became suddenly real.

"They can change shape?" Haines' voice dropped, Gareth nodding. Haines' hand came to his head, his finger tapping his temple, a sign that he was thinking furiously; who else could be one of these shapechangers? How could they possibly tell? He looked genuinely scared, for the first time that Gareth had known him.

Gareth held up his hand, "It might have been some sort of camouflage, or projection. I don't know, but then it seemed like they became alarmed themselves, smashing their way out of the building, and split up." His voice becoming kind of distracted at that point, describing how some had started to fly, to evade the incoming security forces, that he must have triggered when he entered the lab, another running off at incredible speed, and finally he described the way the shapechanger had disappeared.

"But they were evading the security?" Haines pressed.

"Yes. It may have been staged, but we may have missed an opportunity there," the agent semi-shrugged, indicating that it happened sometimes.

"Maybe not. We encounter someone at HQ, that managed to get past all our security," Gareth's eyes shot up, "and gave us information that could not really be ignored. He said that the authorities were completely infiltrated. Implausible then, but very believable now that you have seen at least one can shape change, or take on the appearance of anyone. It means they really could be everywhere, exactly as he suggested, lending credence to his assertion that they were working on a biological weapon."

Gareth face was getting tense, "What else?"

"He mentioned the phrase E.L.E., in the techno-babble," Ricks added.

"Bloody hell. What are they up to?" Gareth queried.

"Well, let's just have a think," he put on the kettle.

"Let's assume it's all real, best bet, given the severity of the warnings, what actually happened and take it from there," he started off, sipping his tea, not really believing that he was about to say this.

"One, we have been invaded by aliens, that are bent on our destruction. What is the evidence to support, and what contradicts this assertion?" Haines passed it over to the others. Ricks started, being closely followed by Gareth and, as time went by, Haines joined in too. By the end of the afternoon, they were pretty convinced that the world was in deep shit; but that there was an opportunity to stop the enemy. There were others out there that were on it, and they needed any help they could provide. The real question became; what guidance could they provide, given that they were in the dark and being hunted as well?

That evening was spent planning a way to show the enemy that people backed into a corner can be much more dangerous than any animal.

CHAPTER 13

THOUGHTS AND EMOTIONS

Simon pulled the strange plastic circuit board from deep within the back of the suit, the first time he'd needed to get to the guts of this advanced armour, which he now realised was, for all its exotic programming and materials, still vulnerable to basic brute force and overloading attacks that other, less sophisticated, units were.

The advanced light circuitry had large fracture marks crazed all over them although, interestingly enough, the material they were made from seemed capable of repairing a nominal amount of such structural damage, making it more resilient to physical punishment. The worse damage, naturally done by Chi'mera, who seemed to have an innate ability to exacerbate any situation, had come from the electrical overload; not from the actual electricity, or magnetic induction damage, but from the heat produced when the excessive charge passed through the circuits. It had merely melted the plastic, although there was some other damage which had occurred, he could not account for. Some circuits had degraded somehow, suffering premature ageing, in a fashion that confused him. How the blazes could plastic oxidise in that way; perhaps Charlene could explain it, when she and John had calmed down.

The pair were so touchy sometimes, usually with each other, although today they had decided that Simon was the target, and they were currently in the farmhouse, stuffing their faces. They at least shared that pass time, and both the metabolism to burn it off; he envied them that, but not the associated temperament.

He put down a circuit he deduced was the power regulator, and picked up one of the blown power relays, turning it over and over, finally spotting the fine line crack straight through the whole wafer. How had they managed that feat of vandalism? Usually, a wafer broke across the thinnest part of the plane of the material, yet here, incredibly, they had managed to break it along the plane of the wafer. Fortunately for him, a light coating on both broken wafers, and some creative use of a UV lamp he'd rigged fixed that particular piece, allowing it to be usable again, with only minor degradation of performance.

The barn was actually surprisingly dry, warm and well light, although not as good as a full-blown workshop, of course. The farmer parked his tractor, plus some other farm equipment in here; he'd have dreaded to work here otherwise. He'd had a preconceived idea that all French farms were of the small, traditional, kind, one that he'd been pleasantly surprised was wrong when he spotted that there was a power supply in the wooden building and an industrially rated one at that.

The building looked like this had once been a milking shed, but had since been converted into a vehicle storage building instead, and he thanked whichever family members made that choice, though its' current state did not help with the advanced electronics. He had to do that himself; but then he'd been brought up with 'fix this,' 'fix that' and other similar phrases early on in his life, as his dad had been a REME, not the role his family had wanted, but one that he suited perfectly. The British army trained their mechanics well and, as his father's son, he'd absorbed the explanations fully and so often that, by the age of ten, he'd been helping as a full worker; at least in their own garage.

He remembered his first and, it turned out, only motorbike had required many months of repairs, just to get it running. Apparently, his dad had found it in some scrap yard and bought it for a few dozen quid. After using a few borrowed spares and some serious electrical tweaking, the thing purred like a kitten, something his father not been happy about and had commented on at length. When Simon had given him the explanation of how he'd changed the cycling of the engine to reduce the standard bike noise, his father had not been the wiser and had stomped off angrily, muttering something about the nose being part of the biking experience. He'd never let Simon near a motorbike again.

But since he'd done his apprenticeship, he'd been ready to move on to the serious work. He'd asked his father, who was around a surprising amount for a soldier, to introduce him to his friends so he could offer his services to them too. At first, his father had been reluctant but relented at the insistence of his mother. She had been a teacher, then eventually a professor, and had seen the gleam in Simon's eye whenever anything mechanical, or electrical, was mentioned. So, the following day he'd been taken to the barrack's open day and introduced to his father's colleges.

He still remembered that day vividly, as the mechanics showed the people their work, he'd watched as one of the more junior mechanics had started a faulty engine. Simon had tried to warn the poor man who'd been sent flying as the thing overloaded. Fortunately, Simon had managed to by-pass the overload, shutting the engine down, before the arcing current had killed the poor soldier.

The other REME attending commended him for his bravery and common sense during the incident but being honest with himself that day caution became his middle name. Others might think his slow, deliberate and hesitant nature was cowardice, but since that day he saw it as a logical approach, to an unpredictable world. Why go deliberately into danger, when a little thought might eliminate the threat altogether?

Still, there were things to do and, this daydreaming would never get anything done.

Strangely, even though he'd felt part of something bigger than just himself of late, he'd found that the damage to his suit was much more interesting. It was not that he did not like the people in the team; as people went, they were pleasant enough, and their banter was a pleasant counterpoint to the running, and danger all around. It was just that, as a preference, he preferred the company of other engineers and machines.

Now, Charlene might appreciate his position. She was pretty, smart and with her, how should he put it, her, transformation? Amalgamation? Hybridisation? Hmmm, perhaps a new word was needed, but anyway, because she'd, in effect, become part machine herself, he felt more comfortable when talking to her than with any of the others.

Ok, she had a tendency to lose emotional control, not surprising when others were trying to take control of her mind all the time, and she had a seriously bad habit of playing the hero; although he doubted, she realised she was. Perhaps her dad's less-subtle influence on her. Otherwise, she was a good conversationalist and, occasionally, her tiny machines, and insights were useful.

There, he was doing it again. He put down the circuit, rubbed his eyes and wiped off the WD40 from the plane of the circuit. It turned out that some high-tech circuits could be repaired with a screwdriver and WD40; his old college pals would have laughed at such a suggestion; his classmates always being so rigid in their methodologies.

Grrr, this was getting him nowhere, he thought as he laid out the remaining broken pieces, and thought about what he needed to fix them. It seemed that there were remarkably few items that did not have a workaround or an actual fix. However, three rather large pieces, as such things went in his armour; the frequency modulator, the transformation matrix harmoniser, and the photoelectric converter, needed some top tech to get them operational again; and the optical guide prism system was a right off, just needed replacing, if another existed.

The last was the stopper. Without that, none of the suit's computer systems would receive command signals. Worse, the team would have to get it from a science facility that used lasers, since there was nowhere else that he could possibly think that would have such components, outside of a military base and that would be worse, risking losing the equipment altogether, making the job even harder.

He wrote out a list on a piece of writing paper, for Jack, as it would be up to GhostKnight, and his formidable stealth skills, to obtain the items; except for the prisms, they were all light enough that he could just carry them in his costume. He'd need a rucksack, with padding, for the prisms and their associated circuits, Simon making a mental note to tell Jack to get those too, as they would give vital alignment and wavelength data for the prisms, that Simon could use to tune and re-structure them for use in his armour. Even after the parts were obtained, it would be a push to get the suit up and running and get to the machine in time to stop the invasion.

Ga, he would do it somehow, but when this was all over, boy he would just love to get back to the bay, and retro-engineer all this into a new Shell; Ramp up the flight systems, get the suit to channel his powers properly, self-repair systems; now that would be something else. Between him and Charlene he was sure they could figure something out; after all nature had invented regeneration, and now that she bridged the technological and biological boundaries, he was sure that she would have some fascinating insights into the subject.

He put his head down and added item descriptions, manufacturers, specifications and serial numbers that he knew, then put it to one side and started repairing the first of the other modules. This was going to take hours.

John too was reminiscing, having decided that it was the place itself that forced one to think a lot. Since they were not farmers and did not all have work to do, they had time on their hands, although he suspected that Helena was actually doing the farm work; collecting eggs, feeding the animals and milk cows.

With all that time, you began to introspect, thinking on things that sometimes you were reluctant to address. They had been moving so fast, with so much happening, that they had barely had time to reconcile their feelings and emotions about their situation. Now he was getting all that thought, and reaction, crashing in on him and was having problems with the reconciliation.

He went through everything that had happened; the conference, the conscription into M.I.X., the discovery of the Eldarin, his subsequent transformation into PileDriver, the Battle at the Base and the incident at the Machine. It was all so beyond anything he'd experienced in his police career, that it overloaded his emotions. Now, as he thought about it all, he was surprised to realise he felt little, although he knew why.

He had noticed that, during his reminiscing, he his thoughts stopped at the battle for the machine at CERN. He still remembered how cold he'd felt when Jack had told him of Isabella's fall into the other realm. He pictured her screaming, imagining her being devoured by the, no, best not go there, although even as he thought it, he imagined her screaming his name as she was ripped to pieces by venomous saw-toothed monstrosities. His blood started to heat again, Charlene having warned them that the Ghe'Dar Nanites were still slightly active, that they should not trust their emotions until she could find a permanent cure, but, somehow, he knew, this was him and his passion alone causing his blood to heat up.

Why couldn't Jack have held on just a little longer? Why had it been him and not Simon; who had the strength, now, to hold onto a tank, and not let it fall? Why had it been Isabella and not Helena or Charlene? Why? Why? Why?

He started to rise, to go talk to Jack, and thought better of it, knowing that, in this mood, things could get real ugly fast.

Calm down, John. Where is your professional detachment? He remembered the words of his police instructors; lose your cool, lose your job, a mantra that they had drilled into his head, day in, day out until it became a part of him. He needed that right now, and he'd thought that he would always have it after those lessons. Perhaps that was where the Ghe'Dar had scored their first victory against him; stealing bits of his past. The thought started making his blood pressure begin to rise again, forcing him to go for a walk, as he had in his cadet days.

He thought about his days in the police cadets, the good days and the bad, the discipline, the instructors, the lessons in first aid, drill, self-defence, and the law. He smiled as he remembered the drill instructor; an otherwise light-hearted and cheerful soul that turned into a dragon on the parade ground. Eagle-eyed and hypercritical he either broke you or turned you into someone that could spot things out of place at fifty feet, could march in your sleep and ignored all adversity to get the job done. He'd actually managed to get to know that instructor quite well, and he'd been taught so much more than mere policing; people skills, detection and, finally, friendship, ah, he missed his patience wisdom still. All his class had been at the funeral when he'd died of cancer.

Something he shared with Charlene; a need to see cancer eradicated. At the thought of her, he felt calm, that he'd started to feel, dissipate.

Charlene. Yes, at some point he would have to deal with her. Even though Helena had kind of come around, Charlene and Simon were vehemently against him trying to save Isabella. He knew their objections, but given that they had already survived nearly a week here, and the universe had not come to an end, he was of the opinion that they were wrong. Besides Isabella was worth saving just like the rest of the human race, and he was going to try to do it no matter who said what.

He even had a plan to do it in a way that the others might possibly allow, as no one had seen anything after Isabella had fallen, so no one had seen anyone trying to rescue Isabella. There was at least one person that could go invisible in the team, although he was probably not strong enough to save her. However, Simons' camouflage would allow him to catch her after Jack had lost sight of her, return her to the team after Jack had left the scene, but before the walls of reality closed. He needed to talk to Simon about that, assuming Simon managed to get his armour repaired.

As John, subconsciously, walked towards the farmhouse, there was a faint buzzing in his ears, like a sound not quite in range, or being distorted. He strained his ears, trying harder to hear what it was pricking his ear's attention. Nothing. In the distance, he heard planes going overhead, towards Paris, and a train or two going west, but nothing that he'd usually be bothered with. He shook his head and entered the building.

Jack was in the corner, reading his book, in an old, and slightly worn, high-backed leather chair; Helena being further back, judging by the rattling of the pans in the kitchen, probably still cooking. She was rather good at it if her meals at the base were anything to judge by. Strange that, although they were planning to save the world, everyone had fallen back to doing their normal everyday routine when they could not actually make any progress.

Thankfully, Charlene was not about, "Charlene?" he queried.

Jack looked up, "upstairs somewhere, said it was time for her lunchtime wash."

"What is that you're reading?" He was not actually bothered, just making conversation.

Jack did not bother looking up this time. "It's a book on focusing your thought. I think it's one of those books that Helena talks about all the time; a Tomb."

"A Tomb?" John had never heard the phrase, but it sounded as dusty as the book looked. In fact, the book seemed like it might fall to bits if it was caught in a puff of wind. The more he looked at it, the less it looked like a book and more it looked like a slab of leather.

"So is it any good?" getting curious, given that it was absorbing Jack's attention more and more.

"I'm not sure that you'd say it was good, or bad; it is hard to explain. I understand from Helena that it has powers, apparently having warned her off." John's eyes went wide.

"It warned her off? It's alive?" John was disbelieving.

"Not exactly, but it has an 'awareness,' a 'purpose.' I did not fully understand what she said," he shrugged, starting to read again, and thus did not notice the strange look in John's eye.

John did not really believe any of what he'd heard, but he needed to convert Jack to his cause if he was to save Isabella.

"Can we talk?" Jack did not look up, "Jack?"

"Sure," came the response in a kind of half-hearted voice, "just need to finish this paragraph," John ground his teeth.

"While the others are not around?" Jack still did not look up, and John felt his impatience rising. A life was at stake. It was almost like he could hear that imploring wail in his head again.

He moved across the room, "Jack?"

"Just one sec," oh for heaven's sake!

John grabbed the book, lifting it clean up above his head, attempting to get Jack's attention.

"NO!" came a yell from the doorway, as Helena came in from the kitchen, with some sandwiches for the team. The look of horror on her face was a picture, and John was about to come out with a suitably witty retort, when he was catapulted across the room wreathed in purple energy from the book, pulsing through his arms and across his body. To Jack's ears, the book was making a snarling sound, like that of a threatened wolf, apparently offended at being grabbed in such a brutal fashion; but not only that. It seemed to be reacting against something much more fundamental within John.

"John!" Helena dropped the plate she was holding, sandwiches and all, running to him, as he writhed in agony. Jack had leapt up too but stood back uncertain of what to do.

"How can we help him?" Jack had never seen John so helpless, his hands locked onto the book, his body contorting in agony, teeth peeled back, and eyes slammed shut. It was as if he was wrestling with a bear ripping into his stomach, having trouble breathing because of that rigour.

"I don't know," she panted, "… we need to break contact with the book, with something that won't channel its' power." She cast about for anything then stopped, "get Charlene! She might be able to do it."

Jack bolted like a half-boiled rabbit, up the stairs, yelling Charlene's name.

John writhed back and forth, a pallor spreading over him, as all his blood was drawn to his head and back. Charlene came thundering downstairs, saw John and was at his side in a blink.

"Jack said something about his book," she looked imploringly at Helena, then back at the energy encased John. The more he grasped the book, the more power cascaded over him, almost like it was weaving a cocoon around him.

"We need to get it off him," Helena informed Charlene, "but without touching the book,"

"Or him" added Jack, shrugging at the impossibility of the request.

Charlene sighed and screwed up her face, then she cocked her head slightly and leaned forwards over John while focusing hard on the book. For a second, she emitted a faint high-pitched whine, the air around the book turning an even darker shade of purple, then popped from sight, reappearing on the chair that Jack had been reading it in.

Charlene let out a gasp of air and slumped to the floor, faint wisps of that purple energy licking around her like a thin swirling cloud. Helena, and Jack, both gave out little gasps of relief that John was now relieved from direct contact; however, John was still convulsing, and without the Book to grip his nails were now deeply embedded into his palms.

"Helena," was all Charlene could gasp, as she let her powers restore her from the effort, and she was hungry like a pack of hyenas.

Helena produced her wand and used her healing powers, trying to restore the still writhing PileDriver; for there was little of their teammate in the wildly thrashing figure on the floor. He kicked a stout coffee table, and, the heavy object, went crashing through an internal wall into an anti-room. Finally, as the healing energy took hold, his convulsions started to subside.

Jack watched how Helena used her power, remembering something the book had been instructing him, that even the destructive energies could be directed towards healing. He took note, thinking that his own powers could be used in such a fashion, or other ways. With insight, he realised he could now be considered Helena's apprentice; though he doubted the appellation 'Mistress' would sit well with her. Still, the thought was there.

As John's body stopped its thrashing, more of 'John' returning, Helena slowing the flow of power, looking quite exhausted. She took a moment to rest, then reached across and touched his throat, counting the pulses for a minute or two.

Jack was about to ask her how John was when she started to open John's shirt.

"Helena?"

"Not now Jack," her voice was full of professional concern.

"John? John? Can you hear me?" Her voice started to get louder. "John?"

Charlene stood slowly, starting to approach, seeing Jack's look of concerned.

"John?" She put her ear to his chest.

"What's the matter with him," Charlene asked, Helena's hand going up for silence.

She was listening intently, pressing her ear against John's chest, which was now barely moving. Then they saw her relax, "he's still breathing, but his pulse is way low, and his heart rate is also below normal. Charlene, any chance that you can do anything?"

Charlene looked through her HUD, which showed her own vital signs, and wondered if she could make it register his too. Perhaps tie in the targeting scanners, from the teleport system? "On it," was all she said as seemingly standing still, except for furiously typing fingers, on the interface pad on her left arm. After a few minutes, she came up for air, noticing that a sports drink had appeared on a table next to her.

"Ok, I've kind of done a rough and ready patch through some systems, and I can detect his vitals now. You're right, they are weak but regular. If I hazard a guess, from my own experiences, he's in a coma, as I was."

Jack looked concerned, but Helena seemed a bit more relaxed about it.

"Any thoughts?" Charlene passed it back to Helena.

"Well, it could be one of two things; a reaction to the attack, or self-induced to allow him to heal better. Either is plausible, but I think the former."

"What do we do about it?" Jack interjected.

"Do?" Helena looked surprised, "we do nothing until we see which way he is going to go. Charlene can monitor his signs and, if he gets worse, we can try and resuscitate him, but the coma is pretty deep, and it's probably better to leave him in and let his body sort itself out. As we did with Charlene."

"And if we run out of time?" Jack, playing devil's advocate.

"Then it starts to get more dangerous, and we try and pull him out before he's ready," Charlene said sternly. "I imagine I'll have my work cut out for me then," she did not seem so concerned, now that he was confirmed alive and breathing.

"John?" the voice was barely a whisper in his head. He looked around, seeing he occupied a pitch-black room, with nothing visible around him. He took a step and the thinnest thread of light, the merest glimmer, appeared illuminating a tight circle of black floor around him. He sat up, and heard the whisper again, "John," so faint that he could not even distinguish whose voice it was.

"Hello?" he tried to shout out, but his voice seemed weak, tenuous.

"John, help me, John!" the voice grew slightly louder, but remained unidentifiable, so he started visually scanning the area, the illumination level rising to reveal close cut grass at his feet, and within reach small shrubs and trees, that seemed vaguely familiar. He listened hard, trying to hear that voice again, thinking its' owner might be somewhere up ahead moving away. He began to jog, fighting a resisting force to do so.

Then more light flooded into the area, and with horror recognised, he stood at the edge of an enormous gap in the world. There ahead of him was Jack desperately holding onto Isabella, trying to keep a grip on her, her slight weight seemingly too much for him, as she started to slip. Looking down she, and John, saw the masses of devouring worms in that other world, where she' fallen to her death.

He tried to reach for them but the opposing force was too strong, and he was too far away. As he fought, he looked down to see one of Chi'mera's tentacles wrapped around his arms and legs restraining him. He looked around, struggling,

"I have to save her,"

Her reply was firm, "we cannot save her. It will destroy everything we know."

He did not care and fought harder to free himself, Chi'mera holding fast, stronger than he remembered.

Then Isabella fell again, as he screamed out in anguish, the scene again going dark.

John moaned, fell to his knees and wept for a long time, a very long time.

"It need not be so," came a strange, resonant, voice from the gloom.

"Who's there?" John called out, eyes red and bleary.

"I have no name as you use them, so you may call me, Male'on," light blossoming around him to reveal a small room, almost like a shrine, where stood figure, barely four feet tall clothed in white, and draped in a shaft of pure lavender light.

"But who are you and what do you want?" the creature remaining silent, perhaps giving John time to adjust to its' presence.

"Where am I anyway?" John looked around, almost as if he should know this place.

"The place where your power comes from; the deepest part of your soul. The part of your being that your kind has almost forgotten; hidden by years and years of training, discipline, and professionalism." Male'on arced his arm around the room, and John remembered it now, it was his families old church, although there was something disturbingly different about it, almost like it was being used for something darker these days.

"Your old haunting grounds are not what they used to be eh? Well, that's not at all surprising really." The figure glided as it moved towards John. John thought it was a male, from the timber of the voice. "But remembering your past is not why I'm here. The figure suddenly appeared right next to John causing him to jump slightly, even with his trained reflexes. "No. I'm here today because of what you want for your future."

John's eyes narrowed, desperately trying to clear his mind of his desires. That that had been expected was confirmed by the ironic laugh that came from the entity.

"Now, seriously, did you expect that to work? Here? Don't you think you're deceiving yourself a little, if you think I don't know what you really want."

John had to admit that it was probably true. Self-deception was one thing he'd been guilty of in the past; he could see it in others he just could not always see it in himself.

The figure pointed, and John saw the tableau, that he'd seen previously, but in slow motion. "You want to be able to save her; don't you? And you don't really care if it means that the world or time is broken."

John thought of either not replying, or lying again, but he found himself telling the truth anyway, "no. No, I don't. After all, it may well already be broken."

"So true. Well now, that's where I come in. I can give you a shot at saving your beloved; just a shot mind you, nothing guaranteed." The figure seemed a little uncertain at this point, as though there was a possible problem.

"But?" John was used to picking up on nuances in speech, and this one was projecting all the signs of being unsure of being able to deliver.

"There is a slight problem. Other forces are involved," the figure admitted, "potent forces that are focused on this event, and they have their own players in the arena. If they were to get too close, they might stop what must be," the figure wrung its' hands slightly, and John saw that they were humanoid, though covered in scars. He had miscalculated, having thought this might be a demon or devil, but seemly it was at least partially human; or perhaps it was a shapeshifter, like Chi'mera.

"So you need my help to keep them out of the arena?" John suggested. Now what had made him say that? It seemed obvious. He was acting as though he was going to go along with this, being, although, it was probably not the best course of action. The best thing was to leave this place and forget the offer, but something stopped him from doing that.

"Not exactly. We need to ensure events proceed as fate dictates rather than in the way they plan, then the invasion can be stopped, you'll have saved Isabella, and you can be happy with her." The tone seemed so reasonable, but common sense said there was a catch. No one ever did something like this for nothing, and when it came to deals, there was only one group renown for reneging on them.

"So what is it that must be?" again the question was out before he could stop it.

"An important thing that you do not need to know about. You need to try to save Isabella, that much is certain. You do want to try, don't you?"

"So, you want me to save Isabella, and you will give me the power to do it?"

"Well not exactly," John frowned. It was not the answer he'd been expecting. If this creature really was a devil or demon, it was not the best or most experienced negotiator. In fact, it seemed like it was almost trying to put him off the deal.

"Not exactly?" Johns' voice seemed angry even within this strange room.

"We require you to do a deed. We will then give you the power you require, a special word I will implant within your mind, you won't understand it, or be able to speak it until the deed is done; but once it is spoken, you will have a chance to save the girl you love. Once done, what must happen, will happen and the deal will be complete. Deal?"

John did not hesitate, "Deal!"

The figure stumped off into the light. "Excellent. The deed we require is simple; you must keep Helena from entering the battleground again. If she enters there again, the forces of darkness and chaos will surely slay her. Once her safety is assured you can go try to save your girlfriend, and we can go our separate ways."

"But, I thought you were, never mind," John had thought himself dealing with dark forces. Perhaps he was wrong. "What's so important about Helena?"

But the figure was gone, and he suddenly had a feeling that he had severely misjudged what was going on here. Then the darkness crowded in on him again.

As he looked into the darkness, he saw again the girl falling into the sprawling worms and heard her screams, his resolve hardening. He thought that he would wake up soon, but the scene repeated itself over and over again, getting more and more visceral, and louder in his ears. As it continued, his own screams were added to the cries of the girl, as his mind started to turn in on itself under the strain. After a couple of minutes, his mind fled to the only place it knew where to go, inwards, towards madness.

After four hours of almost continuous scanning, Charlene decided that bed was probably the best and safest place for John's, somewhat cold, body. She lifted him, placing him in the farmer's bed, and she sat in the bed next to him. Strange that after all the problems that she'd caused him, she was now the one looking after him.

She looked down, and she wondered what was going through his mind. She had virtually ignored him when they were just Driver and charge because she'd thought that he had a low opinion of her; which of course he had, though not in the way she'd suspected. Then, when they were inducted into the team, they had been busy setting up opposite sides of the base. Where he applied skill and experience, she countered with youthful zest, intelligence, and strategy. They were polar opposites, yet they could have been good friends if it had not been for the incident with Isabella.

If it were not for the timeline and the necessity that drove her, she would have been the first person to propose a rescue. But with such dire consequences if they triggered a paradox, she, and Simon, could not accept the risk.

"You know that if you try, I'll have to stop you right?" She muttered to the comatose John. There was no reply; but then she'd hardly thought there would be, "just so you know, is all." She slid under the sheets of her own bed, comfortable enough that, for the first time in what seemed like ages, she fell straight asleep. Whether it was the proximity of the two, the fact that she'd had to target the book to save him or some other factor; Charlene's dream was even stranger, but whatever it was she did not remember it when she awoke.

When she did wake, just before dawn, she found that she was holding John's hand. Not like a lover's grip, more like she'd been trying to haul him out of where ever he was at the moment.

As Charlene tended to John, and Simon was doing whatever engineers did when they had broken things to fix, Jack and Helena sat down to discuss what had happened with John and the Book.

"I don't understand why the book would react so strongly to John," Helena was saying. "It tested me, yes, but he has no mystic power that I can detect and he'd no interest in it, other than you were reading it and you said he was trying to get your attention."

She was passing in front of the log fire, in the open plan area that served as main living room, kitchen, and dinner, the central part of the kitchen a little around the corner.

"It seemed almost like repulsion, except he could not let go," Jack observed, in truth as baffled as Helena. "I don't begin to understand these things, but I had a feeling like it was angry. I cannot explain it more than that," he said, putting the book and covering it with a tea towel, hiding it from sight.

"Angry?" Helena looked at Jack in a peculiar way, "how could a book, even one with a spell on it, be angry?" She had seen many strange things in her time with the Circle, and this ranked well up there amongst the most bizarre of them.

"Well, I heard a kind of sound, like a growling, when John touched the book. Afterwards, it was also almost like it whimpered? Yelped? like it was in pain or hurt." He was almost talking to himself, trying to explain something that he was too inexperienced to actually describe.

Helena smiled gently, knowing what he was going through, having been through it herself several times, trying to explain the inexplicable to Craig. She reached out and placed her hand on his, "here let me help." He looked down at her hand as if it were slightly out of place, "I can see and hear what you heard if you let me look into your memory."

Jack pulled his hand away, "err, have you in my mind? No thanks," he looked slightly shocked that she would suggest such a thing and worried she might see things he did not want her to see or know that he was feeling either.

"It's not dangerous, and I would not see anything that you did not want me to see, and if you focus on the event I will be able to observe through your eyes, and ears, perhaps drawing information from it you could not. It might even help me to understand how to help John recover from his current imposed isolation." Jack did not seem convinced.

"Pleeease!" Helena knew it was a little silly, but she put on her best wheedling voice and threw those big brown eyes of hers at him.

His face changed from shocked, to overtly amused, that she would even attempt to pull a fast one on him. Then he recognised it for what it really was, an appeal to his sense of the ridiculous, that someone, with mind control powers, would actually try to persuade him like that. The smile he gave was gleaming with all the laughter she needed, given the situation.

"Oh, go on then, all great mistress; yea of overwhelming dark powers," at that her face dropped, "Helena I'm sorry I did not mean," the look on her face was one of thinking rather than anger.

"Dark powers? Yes, perhaps that's it," she muttered.

"What? I did not mean," a finger was planted on his lips.

"It's a book, with a white magic spell on it. If somehow, it is reacting to what has happened to John, as though his power was from a dark power, it would try to repel it; because it would genuinely interfere with the spell, cause it pain, if you like." Her face was set as though trying to balance out the probability of this, against other, even more far-fetched, ideas, her head bobbing a little.

"I, but he is not evil," was all that Jack could add, muttering past the finger.

"Sylvia Klerk did not initially do evil, but that does not mean that she was not to start with. Besides I'm not saying that John is, what I'm saying is that perhaps, what gave him his powers could be mistaken for evil by a spell, or an item with a limited perception of the world," she started for the book, then stopped as she remembered its' reaction to her.

"Indeed, it might not even be that. It might not be reacting to power, but rather just being loyal to you," she glanced back at him. "Perhaps, because the owner gave it to you, only you are allowed to touch it," her head went from side to side, and her body bounced, from right to left foot. "In that case, John might be totally innocent, but his touch triggered a reaction, designed to keep the book out of anyone's hands but yours. That's probably it," having convinced herself. "This is your book now, so it warned me off, I imagine I'd be out cold if I'd have failed its' test."

"Not a good area for experimentation," Jack muttered under his breath. Her logic was possibly flawed, but it did make a certain sense.

"But with John, he directly made a grab for the book, so the book shocked him to drive him off. Normally, people are not strong enough to hold on if you channel a spell through them; John's very strength acted against him, turning a mild jolt into a punishment, or a lesson not to do that again. I imagine that he will avoid the book like the plague, after he wakes up," seemingly settling down to the idea now.

"So we don't look inside my head then?" his eyes lit up, grinning like a Cheshire cat at her. She smiled back, shaking her head slowly, patting his hand and starting to walk off. He starred at her back as she smoothly walked out of the main area into the kitchen. As she reached the door frame, she hung on to it slightly and looked over her shoulder at him, Jack still watching her. There was a disturbing look in her eyes, her face suddenly mysterious and almost a little wicked, "not that I wouldn't mind rummaging around in your mind sometime, perhaps," and with that, she whipped into the kitchen.

Jacks face was frozen slightly for a second, then took a deep breath. "Oh boy," he felt his chest and his heart rate rocketing up alarmingly, "perhaps I should call a doctor," he smiled at the thought, although the next one was that if he did call the doctor, his heart rate would probably go up much higher and faster than if he just settled down to a good book.

"Another time perhaps," a thought, just a thought, but one that made his heart skip again. Right now, they had to concentrate on saving the world. Still, that other thought was what they were saving the world for, so he would keep it safe, and make sure he acted on it when this was all over. "Definitely, another time."

He'd been muttering to himself a lot; lately. He'd have to try and break himself of the habit, especially with a woman like Helena around, to hear everything he vocalised during those bouts of talkativeness.

Helena was having similar thoughts, not really liking where they were leading. She led this team, supposedly, providing them with healing and guidance. She should not be falling for any of them, let alone the least know of them. But darn it, it was his aura of mystery that caused the attraction to him; that and their matching powers.

He was tall, dark, quiet, and brave; as the scout of the party, he had to be. Look at how he'd gone into the embassy, where he might have been caught, tortured or converted if it had been a Ghe'Dar trap. She thought that and shivered.

Oh come on, she thought to herself, they had barely even talked together, let alone done anything else, her left cheek screwing itself up and, as she started to roll out some dough to form a pie, she began to frown. Why was she so concerned about him anyway and why think about him, so much? He was not loud, or even present most of the time, yet she did seem to be focused on him, perhaps, because he was not the apparent hero of the group. He was not tremendously strong, fast or bright; although he was street smart; or could it be his thoughtfulness, the kindness he showed.

Grrr, she was doing it again. Think professional. Baking would take her mind off it. She started the pie, making it as exquisitely as ever, almost immediately falling back to her contemplation of Jack and the problems he was causing her.

John stood on the battlefield, near the gaping maw of the rift to other realities, the scene frozen, stopped at the moment Jack had lost sight of Isabella. John had not seen it, but somehow the scene was displayed in glorious colour for his, edification. It must be because he'd asked Jack to describe the scene in-tote that he now saw it in such vivid detail.

Ghe'Dar troops falling mid-stride, in the area below Isabella, as she began to fall, the look of horror on Jack's face, showing that he was truly remorseful at his inability to save Isabelle. But all John could do was look at the girl's face, the way her eyes reacted to the scene below her, the way her hair was framing her face, the way her hands seemed to reach out for something to hold; almost reaching towards his vantage point in the middle of this unreality. He drank in the scene, but he knew he could not do anything.

Why? He asked himself, why had it been her, with all her talents and skills, why did the universe have to take her. He had never understood, as a policeman, why the innocent, and the good, were the ones that fell before evil every time; while the old war dogs, those who'd already been through hell, were the ones that survived. He assumed that the reason the warriors survived was that they were tougher than the rest.

He wondered why he was trapped here, in this immobile scene, stopped at the moment she fell. Why? Probably because he'd replayed it so often in his mind, that it had stuck there; or was there another reason? He pondered this as his eyes wandered over her face again. Was there a specific reason for him being here? Perhaps he should assume there was and look for it if he could. Since it seemed, he was rooted here until he could figure a way out, or the others managed to get him out. Ok, where to start? He tried to shift his point of view and found that, with a great deal of effort, he could tear his eyes away from Isabella, and look elsewhere.

Above the machine, the mothership had already started to come through the machine-generated portal, while in the distance, Airsleds held off the few human helicopters. The portal itself was a roiling mass of energy spinning over and around the portal's edge; blues and purples rippled around the circular aperture, only being interrupted by bolts of energy from the machine. Beyond the first Mothership, other ships, large and small, could be seen travelling through the vortex, from where ever they originated from in space, across the dimensional barriers. It looked like space, except for the swirling energies of purple, and azure blue surrounding the ships.

John turned his attention to the ground, not to Isabella; it took a great deal of effort not to do that, despite using his police skills to try and stay focused. He looked at the Ghe'Dar ground troops, the Airsleds and the human troops trying to get to the machine, facing off against the Ghe'Dar with their high-tech weapons and shields. What could these troops do against that kind of firepower, especially with the Ghe'Dar having almost complete air superiority?

It seemed hopeless. The human commanders should see that, but there was something in the set of the human troops that was nagging at him. He tried to will-himself closer to that peripheral battle. Again, it took a considerable effort as he felt himself tiring, but after a few seconds, he succeeded.

With his analytical eyes on, he noted the formations, the setup of the artillery, light as it was, the look on their faces. There was something in that look that reminded him of a film he'd seen. They were setting up overlapping fields of fire and taking cover; all too necessary given the Ghe'Dar weapons' lethal force. But there was something strange about that. What was it? He started to go through the war films he'd seen with his dad, his mind was trying to recall names of films he'd seen and what had happened in each of them. Somehow, call it instinct if you like, he knew that this was important. He was here to sort out a puzzle, and this was part of it. He ground his mental teeth, as dozens of films flashed past his recall, stopping at one particular D-Day film. The Germans had created an overlapping field of fire on the beaches. Yes, it was a sound military tactic, kill as many of the enemy as possible before they landed. So why was he getting fixated on it? He thought harder, trying to tie down what it was his subconscious was trying to tell him.

Wait! Go back to D-Day, there was something else he remembered. The overlapping fields had not just been hailed as sound military tactics; they were sound, Defensive, tactics. That was what made no sense. If the humans knew they were being invaded, the logical course of action was to attack the machine and stop the invasion there and then; especially with hundreds more ships just minutes away. Yet, here they were wasting time to set up a defensive position; something, to hold the breach in the force field open but not let the enemy get out. Why? There was something else going on here.

Then it hit him; they were stalling for time, that was it, but what for?

They could hardly Nuke the area, and the force field would probably withstand anything they could throw at it anyway unless they managed to get it through the breach. Ok, that was a possibility. He'd seen enough of NATO firepower to know that cruise missiles could probably be deployed, but he guessed that it would probably not be considered because of CERN, and the possible explosion from a reaction with the exotic matter.

More troops? He doubted that. The Ghe'Dar had probably thought of that and planned against it, controlling key people in the available armies. Even if re-enforcements were on the way, by the time they reached the location the Ghe'Dar would have a beachhead established that would be impossible to break.

Then it became so obvious, he was surprised it did not immediately suggest itself. Diversion! It was all a diversion. Somehow, the military had been tipped-off, knowing there was a team in position to allow them entry; though he doubted that the troops would know who was inside. They knew someone was there and were laying down their lives to buy them time; time to take their shot at closing the gate with the minimum of damage.

The irony was great, thought John. The military, apparently, had not been told that the team did not know how to shut the machine down, or even if it would seal the portal, let alone stop the Ghe'Dar from just creating another one. So, if this was a diversion, where were the commandoes, marines or whoever they were buying their time for. This now became a simple matter of hide and seek.

John went back to training, looking again at where the humans had set their defences, seeing a pattern that suggested it was deliberate, screaming 'Attack here!'. So, they wanted the enemy to look there, and yet that too was slightly off. So, John took a leap of faith, that the planner of this attack was brilliant. He would assume that the enemy would also do the analysis and set the real offensive line in a blind spot.

Yes! That was it, on the line between normal vision and periphery vision, where the two contested. He examined the Ghe'Dars' eyes; predator's eyes, but large for the type. Given that, if he was right, the team was going, there.

The line of shrubs going away from the breach, only slightly towards the machine, but curling around to the back part of the conflict, where they had originally-downed an Airsled.

Was that? He tried to view the area closer but found he was too exhausted. He thought he could see something there, but the whole scene was starting to fade, perhaps because he'd seen all that he needed. He now knew what to do and where to go. Now all they needed to do was to find a way to shut that infernal machine down and stop the Ghe'Dar from ever being a threat again. He knew he was fading and all he could think was that it was a shame Isabella was not there to see it. Then he sank even deeper into his mind; into dark places, few ever reach.

In the morning, Simon, having been at it all night, came out of the Barn with a small, well thought through list of parts for Jack to obtain. He'd carefully added on the note that Chi'mera should go to move the heavy equipment as he couldn't and John was indisposed.

As he approached the house, it seemed almost idyllic with the sun just rising, and the cock crowing, to attest to the fact that Dawn had come and invited everyone else, whether they wanted to or not, to join it in welcoming the day. Yes, it was most people's idea of idyllic, as Simon was sure that the farmer and his family would avow.

He sighed as he opened the farm house's front door; then inhaled the smell of freshly baked bread. Wow, now that, was something else. He had not smelled that kind of homemade bread since, well, ever. He was already salivating at the thought of a slice with lashings of butter, and proper farm churned butter at that; none of that pre-packaged paste.

On the chair in the corner, Jack was sleeping with the book which had caused so much chaos wrapped safely in his arms; like a sleeping child, safe and sound. Well whatever took your fancy. Some people had once called him a bit of a bookworm. He wished they could see Jack now; they'd have split their sides laughing.

From the sounds in the Kitchen, Helena was up and baking the bread.

"In here, Simon," she called out, and while he'd not exactly been trying to tiptoe, he was still surprised she'd heard him, he'd not been making that much noise.

A head popped around the corner, looking straight at him and smiling. "Surprised? I used to live in the country, during summer terms. Most noises, no matter how small, can be heard in the country; when there is peace and quiet, you can hear a pin drop."

"How do you do that?" It was a question he'd meant to ask for some time. Now was as good as any.

"What?" her face suddenly went all innocent, something that made him immediately suspicious.

"Seem to know what we are all thinking," his face scanned her for any sign of duplicity; but he almost immediately gave up the idea, because he suddenly came up with the answer to his own question. He stopped moving his face and was rewarded with a smiled, and a nod.

"Reading body language then?" Having some proper confirmation would be nice.

"Yeah, as much as I can control minds, actually reading them is another thing entirely. I can do a few tricks, but nothing on the full reading scale. We did at one time have someone that could do that, not sure what happened to them. Isabella," and her voice dropped a little when she mentioned the name, and there was a catch in her voice, "… Isabella found references to them, but most of the data had been erased; beyond even her talents to recover. Only the code name remained, and a few references to Craig having had to deal with them," she straightened up and came around the corner to lean against it.

"As I understand it, controlling is just a battle of wills, one mind reaching out and subduing the other, then using that mind remotely. Reading another's mind is more, delicate. You have to understand them, know how they think, know how they view the world," she could see that Simon was having trouble with the concept.

"Ok, think of it like this: with mind control, you're the Driver; You can steer the car, you can start the music, and you can use the sat nav.; Mind reading, you're the mechanic; you can repair the engine, you can talk to the onboard computer and see what's wrong and you can re-programme the sat. nav.," She saw understanding enter his eyes. She'd always had a way with words, it was part of what she'd done for Craig, at least when it did not involve social media and the like.

Jack started to stir in the corner. "Is that freshly baked bread I smell?" came a sleepy, but eager, voice.

"Sure is. Come and get it while it's still hot," Helena throwing Simon an invitational smile too.

"Absolutely," and Jack was suddenly wide awake, and on his feet, having been listening to Helena's explanation too. He'd also been disturbed by Simon's entry into the otherwise cosy house, the drought sending chills straight to his toes.

"Where is Dr. Klerk?" Simon asked, looking around as he shambled, quickly, into the dining area. Somehow, they had all relied on John to know where she was since he knew her routine. Without him, and because of their previous concerns about her, they had grown nervous not knowing her whereabouts. Helena pointed up.

"She's in the bath, I think, or the bathroom anyway, complaining that the farm did not have a shower. I pointed out that showers are for clean people to stay clean, while baths are for dirty people, like farmers that have been feeding pigs, to get clean." Her face betrayed Charlene's reaction to that statement.

"She did not take the explanation well, I see" Jack caught the 'swallowed a sour grape' look too.

"She was less than lady-like in her description of what she thought of farmers at that point, yes," Helena looking up and grinning like a cat who'd just won Cat of the Year and got a bathtub of cream.

"You enjoyed telling her, didn't you?" Simon asked, but already knew the answer.

"Now who's the mind reader?" Helena chuckled. "Yes. She can sometimes be a bit stuck in her ways and taking her down a peg, or two did feel good." Then her face became more serious. "Isabella was the same, the young are always like that," then her face brightened. "But Charlene has been through so much that she is growing out of it, extremely fast." Helena shuddered, "any way let's eat, don't know about you, but I'm starving."

The others just nodded and tucked into the steaming hot loaf, butter and some slices of cured ham and cheese, strangely, a nicely matured Cheddar.

Charlene languished in the tub upstairs, missing her regular shower in the morning, because she had work to do, and regularly did her bathing in the evening.

Today, for the first time in many years, she did not actually have any work to do, or rather, there was no real work that she could do; a strange feeling, even more, outlandish than shape-changing. It had been a great realisation that, for the first time in weeks, she did not need to run, hide, sneak or teleport anywhere, and she was in full control of herself, as much as, or even more so than, most people.

Now she lay in the hot bath, just relaxing, finding, to her surprise, that when she was so relaxed, her HUD faded into virtual non-existence, giving her eyes some downtime. Also, it was with delight, she found that her new body made the water feel almost like silk when she entered it. Every ripple was a stroke on her soft skin, and the pleasure was so intense that she had trouble not actually moaning, something the others might misinterpret if they heard it downstairs, while both she and John were up. The thought was so funny that it made her giggle; not the idea of her and John, but that people might so misinterpret the sound.

She supposed it would be natural for her and John to have that kind of relationship, especially given their similarities, but she did not see him like that, despite the ongoing corruption of her emotional systems by the Ghe'Dar Nanites.

The others were cured, now. She'd not told them, but they were. The changes that she'd developed were fine, it was just her stuck with the problem. She'd not told them that, because that would make them worry about her motivations, and that would just not do.

The problem was, that when she was changed, she'd already been infected by the Ghe'Dar Mind Control Nanites, the energy hitting her, had impacted both sets of Nanites, merging them and her DNA, to form new hybrid Nanites, to become an integral part of her now. No simple fix to remove the other Nanites, as they were not separate; and their Ghe'Dar instructions were deeply embedded into the new hybrid operating system.

It might be possible to alter the instructions slightly or mitigate the problems caused by those instructions, but getting rid of them might cause more problems, or worse, make her normal again; something that, at the moment, would not be a good idea. Even if she could remove them, she was Chi'mera now, for better or worse and, remembering the warning of her other self that there was worse to come, she did not dare become normal again. At least, until she had dealt with the threats, she'd been warned of.

She lifted her hand out the water and extended a tentacle; a thing of beauty, from a biological point of view, as well as useful. It arced across the room to the towel rack and grasped a towel. She could control them well now, after only a few days; that might be instinct or just computer control, although her mini-computer systems were almost entirely dormant at the moment. She had tried to understand what had happened to her in those first few moments of transformation and failed. Genius she may be, but even genii need information to work with, and she just did not have enough to formulate the answers that she'd tried to find.

She stood and dried herself off, a tentacle being a godsend for doing that, effortlessly reach any part of her body, while the other reached for her clothes on the side, as she stepped out of the bath, dried herself and dressed in one fluid motion. She could definitely get used to this, and, now that the sickness, dizziness and all the pain had gone, she was going to enjoy every sensation, move and moment of her new life.

At that thought, she kind of did a double take; her new life, not her old one. But she had unfinished business with her past life.

As she opened the door, she smelt the freshly baked bread and her stomach growled. "Oh, for heaven's sake!" it growled again, and she thought she was in control; she smiled, nope her stomach was in control. The darn thing commanded her to eat, she ate. It commanded her to sleep, she slept. The next thing she would do, given half a chance; was to try and get control of her internal energy requirements and get rid of the necessity to eat everything in sight just to keep going. If she'd been in a desert, she suspected that she would now be starving to death.

She walked casually down the narrow hallway to the stairs, when her stomach growled again, exceedingly loudly, "will you stop that?" she snarled at the greedy thing.

Helena heard the very audible hunger pangs and could not help call out, "Charlene! Get your pet tiger down here, and get it fed".

Charlene appeared right next to her, "not funny Helena," she snarled through gritted teeth, the others trying to keep their faces straight, and failing miserably.

"A bit silly to teleport, using more energy, just for a few seconds," Helena chided, at the same time stacking a massive pile of food designed for about six people onto the platter. She lifted it in front of Charlene's face, who looked down at it in annoyance, trying to have a sensible conversation, the food distracting her.

"This is not over," she said, but there was little point in hiding her desperate interest in the platter. "Rats!" she muttered grabbing the plate, slammed herself down and ploughed into the ham and cheese sandwiches, and cold chicken wings.

The others watched for a few seconds, then, as she looked up, suddenly found other things to do, like clean their plates away or go back to the barn; anything else!

"Easy dear, you'll choke, or get a stomach ache," Charlene found Helena holding her arm tightly, trying to stop her from cramming both a sandwich and a pork pie into her mouth at the same time.

Charlene looked at her in serious annoyance, then stopped. "Helena?"

"Yes, dear?" sounding like a mother answering a young child.

"What am I going to go about my food requirements. I cannot keep stuffing my face like this, and those sports drinks are only a short-term answer."

"In truth, I am no nutritionist, but I bet Craig knows one or two experts that can help. After all, this is over, perhaps they can set you a special diet that will help. It will probably require you to get a full medical, but they should be able to help even you. Or maybe you will find something to help yourself."

"Mmrph, the problem is," she said through a mouthful of crust, "that I cannot think very well when I'm hungry; and I'm constantly hungry at the moment."

Helena's face split in a huge grin, "that is a problem. I tell you what, I'll go out and get a side of beef from the ladder, and I'll cook a stew that will make even your sides bulge. Then you can do your thinking, and we can all have some peace and quiet from that monster you call a stomach," she said gently poking Charlene's, now quiet, belly. As she did so, she frowned.

Charlene saw the look, and with a questioning glance said, "What?"

Helena looked at the table, trying to avoid looking at Charlene suddenly, "nothing."

"Helena," in a demanding tone, "What is it?"

Helena raised her eyes, "Charlene have you had any problems with your stomach or such since your change."

"Helena you have been around me for the past two weeks since my change, you know the problems I've been having," Charlene sounded as exasperated as she could be.

"That's not what I'm on about," Helena gesturing for her to stand, Charlene standing, with the platter in her left hand.

"May I?" Helena requested in a definitely professional tone, opening the central portion Charlene's jumpsuit. Curious, Charlene indicated she should continue. Helena reached up and started counting Charlene's ribs. There was something strange about the ribs too, they seemed narrower than usual but less flexible than bone should be.

"Ten, eleven, twelve, thirteen," eep! Had she counted that right?

"Thirteen? What?" Charlene almost dropped the platter.

Charlene pushed Helena away and did the count herself, "ten, eleven, twelve … what the blazes," she rarely swore, but honestly this classified as the right time to do it, "thirteen." Her eyes slowly raised to Helena's.

"That's not right, but when I prodded you, Charlene, I felt something else."

"Helena, what else could possibly as disturbing as the fact that I now have an extra set of ribs," She threw her hands up in disbelief.

"Perhaps it's a hangover from the change into a Ghe'Dar?" She moved closer again. "Just move your hands," Helena reached into the suit and, gingerly, moved her hands over Charlene's stomach, a large frown developing as she continued.

"What? What are you doing?" Charlene tried to feel what was there, but it all felt normal to her; her muscles had always made her stomach tight and solid.

"Charlene, is there something you're not telling us?" The question bit home; had she somehow guessed about the Ghe'Dar Nanites, no, this was closer to her heart, so to speak.

"What do you mean?" Charlene was trying to understand the context of the question.

"I mean about you and John."

"What about John and me?"

The girl genuinely seemed not to understand the question, so Helena dropped the issue. What could that be? The was something in there, but it could not be what she'd initially thought, given Charlene's confusion.

"Charlene, I think you might have to get yourself scanned, real soon. There's a mass of some sort in your stomach, possibly a tumour of some kind, and it's pretty big. That might explain your sickness and food cravings too, beyond your other changes."

Charlene looked genuinely shocked. "No. The systems show nothing wrong they,"

"… would not know what to look for, "Helena finished. "They have only just come into existence. How would they know that it's not supposed to be there?"

"They would, I," Charlene could not express her shock.

She felt the edges of her stomach, then moved her fingers slowly towards the middle. On her right-hand side, only moving her fingers a little, there it was a large solid lump. She shifted her fingers around it, detecting little of the expected softness there, it was hard, but not tight like muscle more like cartilage or bone. She looked down, and now that she pressed down hard, she could see the outline of the lump. "No," she let her hands drop, Helena seeing the shock ripple through her, and was about to offer more advice when she saw Charlene's face raise up and lock itself in a fixed grimace.

"Jack!" Charlene bellowed. Helena had never heard such a sound. A rather awed face poked through the doorway.

"Get the tractor, we're going to get Simon his equipment; we are leaving now!" He saw the look on her face, nodded and bolted back out the door. Smart man.

Helena started to raise her hand to try and stop Charlene, "that's really not wise Char," her voice faltered when she looked at the girl. The face that swung down to look at her was hardly Charlene's at all.

The voice that came out too, was not Charlene's either, "I will find out what is happening, WitchFire," using Helena's codename, her way of saying that the conversation was over, "and I will fix it," the gritted teeth silencing any further objections as she strode out the building without looking back.

"Yes, I'm sure you will, Chi'mera!" Helena knew better than to argue with that one.

Jack, was trying to keep his eyes front, driving the tractor towards the main road.

They had found the rickety old thing in the back of the barn, hidden under a tarpaulin. Under Chi'mera's exceedingly daunting gaze, Simon had quickly checked it over, managed to get the under oiled engine running and packed them fearfully off. There was something in Chi'mera's eyes that said she was not in the mood for no's, or talking; so, the others just did as they were told and got out of her way, Jack's position being the hardest, directly in the line of fire.

As they had left, Helena had quickly rushed out and whispered something to Jack, and he was now wondering if he should even make an attempt to talk to the obviously very upset Chi'mera. The problem was he was sure that he could talk to Charlene, but when she was in this kind of mood, he simply was not talking to her; he would be talking to Chi'mera, and the difference was more pronounced now than when she had just received her powers.

He was not sure she'd noticed, par say, but when she was Chi'mera, Charlene's face changed subtly, even in her original form. There were harder edges to her features. Her eyes did not change colour or anything so obvious to a stranger, but they were harder, more angular, more intense, her eyebrows dropped a little, making her look sterner, more determined. Lastly, her nose was ever so slightly narrower and sharper, more, what was the word? Fierce. She looked predatory, as though hunting prey.

He started to open his mouth uncertainly, when she saved him the effort, "don't!" she ordered, his mouth snapping shut again. He thought about it for a second and decided it really was time to have words. Everyone was pussyfooting around her. He'd seen the Prima Dona types before, usually running gangs, trying to get everyone to do their bidding. In no time the power went to their heads, and they started to make bad decisions because there was no one there that thought to stop them.

Now was the time to head this off; what they were doing was too important.

He slowed the tractor and turned off the ignition.

"We talk now, whether you want to or not," turning to see that fierce look again; this time he returned it with a stare of stony resolution, matching in strength. He'd had to avoid, face down or just out talk, many gang thugs before; this would be little different, at least he hoped so.

"What are you doing? I said let's go," she grated at him.

"Yes you did, didn't you, but I want to know what this really all about," his voice had turned cold and calculating. "You're a scientist. You know about Cancer, Biology and you know that this can be dealt with, so why suddenly the hissy fit, and theatrics?"

The words struck Chi'mera like a slap across the face, her harshness dropping a little, although not entirely. She'd not really been together with Jack awfully long over the weeks and had kind of thought of him as just a joker who'd helped them out. Here it seemed there was someone different, someone, who'd an insight, even though they had not talked much.

"Helena had no right to tell you. She,"

"Told me nothing except that you had a problem, and needed a friend to talk to," the harshness dropping another notch, her eyes going softer.

285

"I can be that friend for you, Charlene," he hoped that he'd not used the name too soon, but she did not react so negatively, so it seemed safe. He saw her bottom lip start to tremble.

"You would be my friend; really?" from somewhere deep in her throat, a catch sounded. Jack was astonished to see her hands trembling, it was almost like she was Charlene, but not the one he knew, her voice suddenly sounding very young.

"Of course! We," he never got that far, as Charlene suddenly engulfed him in a crushing embrace, of tears and sobs. He'd not expected such an extreme reaction, gently returning the embrace, Charlene continuing to sob her heart out.

"I've never had a friend before," the tears did not seem to want to stop. Jack had an idea where this had all come from, the book having given him insights into the mind, heart and what is referred to as the soul.

He now had tremendous empathy for her; losing her parents, then never having a true friendship before. The trauma's she'd been through must have built up a thick wall of self-reliance and confidence, that she'd depended on over the years, to guard her against those heartaches. The past few weeks had relentlessly battered at that wall until finally, this last incident had broken through it. He hoped this was a good thing.

Perhaps the alien Nanites had done the work too. Ironic that they should be a threat to the world, but a cure for Charlene's lonely heart, and while he may not believe in God, if he did, this would have been a good score for him.

He let the storm wash over him. He'd seen other women cry, but this girl was making them all seem tame. Finally, he reached into his costume and handed her a cotton hanky; his silk ones would just not cut the mustard with this flood of tears. After a few more minutes, her crying subsided, and instead, she started shaking as if she was suddenly freezing. He just held on to her, trying desperately not to fall off the seat.

Ten minutes later, it all stopped suddenly, and she sat back on the seat her eyes averted from his like she was totally embarrassed with the outburst. Jack hoped that that did not mean that it had been a waste of time. She started to hand him his hanky back; but he smiled a little smile and quietly said, "er, Charlene. It's totally soaked. Just let the poor thing die, ok?"

Charlene looked at him, then it and suddenly barked a laugh at the assessment, Jack making a motion like he was shooting it, putting it out of its misery and Charlene's face lit up, laughing again, a more open, warm and genuine laugh.

"I suppose. Perhaps I should analyse it?" she saw the look on his face, and they both laughed at that.

"Ha, even a layman like me knows that it's dead!" They both laughed again.

"Thank you," Charlene started, but Jack put his hand up.

"You needed the release, and you need a friend, not just a doctor, a mentor or a bodyguard; not ones that speak your language or help with work, but a friend that can help in the matters that hurt you." He was speaking from experience too, as he'd had few friends either. He looked her in the eye, and she knew that he was also talking about himself.

"Friends then?" Charlene asked.

"Ha, until next time Chi'mera turns up?" only half joking.

"I think you could even be friends with her too; on a good day," she smiled, then Chi'mera was there, that look reappeared, but with subtle differences. That hawkish look appeared more for others rather than for everyone. "I think I really would like a friend like you, GhostKnight."

"Chi'mera, I really was always your friend. Perhaps it took Charlene to let you know that." It was strange, but the two voices seemed almost the same again, as though Charlene and Chi'mera were merging back into the girl he'd had first met.

Good deed done, he thought to himself; but somehow, he knew, it was more than that. With his jaded view of the world, Charlene represented the innocence that the world had lost, while Chi'mera showed him what that loss of innocence resulted in. In just offering his friendship he'd restored some innocence to the world, and in doing so, restoring a portion of his own faith that the world was worth saving.

"We'd best be going?" Charlene's voice now softer and more human.

"Yes. This old thing won't do more than thirty kilometres per hour, and France is considerably bigger than England. If we are to get Simon's parts, we'd best keep moving." He re-started the engine, and the pair were off again driving past the fields towards the nearest big town, Troyes.

They talked in a much more companionable way now; commenting on the flatness of the surrounding fields, the occasional farmhouses, that must be their neighbours and the scenery in general. For hours they travelled until the finally reached civilisation.

They were coming in on the Saint Germaine side of the town heading for the University of Technology of Troyes.

"Why this town, Charlene?"

"You mean other than it's close and has a university?" She looked at him with a kind of innocent, dreamy look on her face, a big giveaway that she was hiding something.

"Save the doey-eyed look for those that can be fooled by it, Charlene," but the voice was soft, and he kind of knew the joke.

Charlene smiled, suddenly feeling emotionally close to this strange magician, who was so mysterious on the outside, and yet a simple, no-nonsense, man, on the inside who just wanted a clear direction. She gave in.

"Oh ok. Troyes University is an International University; I've had conversations with a few of their people. They have two main departments that I want items from, besides the equipment that Simon needs: LNIO, their Nanotechnology, and Optical Instrumentation department and GAMMA3, Advanced Automatic Mesh Generation Techniques. In LNIO, their new DynaCam system is small enough to scan my internal structures and see what is happening in there, that's not appearing on my HUD. The GAMMA3 research could help me get better control of my shapeshifting abilities, and of course, Simon wants the power systems research from LASMIS, the Mechanical Systems, and Concurrent Engineering."

Jack detected a slight note of trepidation in her voice, a hint that she was nervous about coming here. "Ok, so it has all the latest gadgets. Why is it that you're so wound up about getting it?" And when he looked at her, the look she returned was one of guilt.

"Well the Ghe'Dar are after scientists, and they may already be there," but her face gave away something else, something was reluctant to speak about.

"Charlene, we're friends now right?" she still seemed a little reluctant, but then she seemed to come to a decision.

She sighed. "One of the people I talked to here had a bit of a crush on me." She really seemed uncomfortable with this. "I am hoping not to bump into him. He was nice enough but, well, I don't want that kind of thing, especially not now." There was more, but whatever it was she did not add it. Some things just were not for public consumption, so Jack did not press it; but it seemed that being cooped up in a lab, all your life did not stop you from having baggage, no matter how hard you tried. Jack's opinion of Charlene's naivety suddenly shifted; ok so she'd not physically been out in the word, but it was evident that, via the internet, she did have some contacts that she really did not want, especially now.

As they approached the city, they made the decision not to take the tractor too close and found a small country road next to the main highway past the university, leaving it hidden there, in a shaded area under a stand of elms. They would have to take the tractor back, but it was hardly a getaway vehicle, so leaving it there seemed the best bet idea. Besides, despite the extra petrol can, they doubted they could have taken it much further.

The university was made up a series of large, distinctive, buildings separated each from each other by pleasant avenues of green trees and small clearings. This allowed them to avoid the main population of the university, as they acquired the equipment and, even better, the security, who were nowhere near as good here as they were in the other places they had been to recently. So they just walked into the campus.

"Jack," Charlene started.

"I know, check it out. On it, oh and Charlene," he said fading from view,

"What?" she whispered.

"It's GhostKnight," and the voice faded off into the distance.

She smiled, doubting he would not admit it, but she thought that she understood. Jack was as much an invention as Harry Hidden was. He thought of himself as GhostKnight now, and he was beginning to realise this, enjoying the freedoms he now had, and the responsibility that they entailed. He did not even think of it as power, but rather as a means to escape his past and begin a new future. It was a good way, but it was not her way.

She checked she was not being observed then changed into a smaller female body, someone that looked more professor, than student. The wrinkles were something she found, strange, and the form, being more thought out than instinctual, felt, distinctly uncomfortable. At first, she thought about just picking someone around to copy, but that would cause more problems than she really wanted at the moment. Next, she tried to shape a face herself, looking at a window and trying different parameters in her Interface. It was difficult, like trying to draw a straight freehand line, with a bandage on. At first, the face was old but smooth;

that looked like a film star, with lots of Botox; too angular and airbrushed. She frowned, except the face it did not show it; most peculiar.

After that, she tried a slightly modified copy of someone else; a student who'd passed by, at a distance. This had resulted in them giving, the somewhat strange looking person on the bench, a second glance, before trying to get to their lesson. The results were less than encouraging, as even the slightest change in the parameters she was using resulted in the face changing in a way that just made it look, wrong.

She was glad that the first time she'd used her shape-changing, she'd not had to pass inspection by another of the Ghe'Dar; she imagined she's have stood out like a sore thumb, and that would have been the end of the entire team. Things were never as easy in practice as they were in real life, although to say that the past few weeks had been real life was stretching that definition beyond the six sigma limits, and probably to the limit of any boundaries she'd once believed in.

Then she had an idea. She stopped putting parameters in and imagined a look she wanted to adopt. It was funny for her because she was not a fashion follower or a celebrity fan. She had few 'icons' to follow but she'd more imagined herself like Marie-curie; a pioneer into the unknown. That thought made her chuckle; into the unknown all right. Marie-curie would have fainted if she'd have realised just how far the unknown actually went.

She looked in the window, and there stared out at her an image of the great woman, complete with clothes and hair; whoops, the clothes needed a modern makeover. Fortunately, no-one was looking directly at her, and she quickly changed into a stylish casual suit. Phew, that could have been very hard to explain.

"Having problems?" She whipped around but saw no one, the voice different from any she knew. The panicked look on her face faded almost immediately. Instead, her cheeks went bright red, a change that she immediately tried to reverse.

"Damn it, GhostKnight, don't do that. You nearly made me jump out my skin." The chuckling in mid-air showed that he'd enjoyed it, and funnily enough, she started chuckling too. "Yeah, alright, I'm having trouble. Doing things by instinct is good in a squeeze, but it seems that trying to controlling the finer nuances of the human face and body is considerably more difficult than I would have imagined. Doing a copy of a random face is one thing, going for a specific 'look' is like aiming at an atom using a needle."

"The nose is wrong," he commented.

Her head whipped around and she looked carefully, eliciting another chuckle came from behind her. "Oh, very funny," she muttered, he had her there. "You're not helping," she complained.

"Ok keep still. I'll critic you," the voice moving around causing a slight draught, "umm, yup." Another sounded a second or two later, then another. "Your fine Char…, Chi'mera," appearing beside her, in a slightly small t-shirt and baggy jeans. He looked around and casually wink at her, looking so at home as the mature student, that she envied his confidence.

"How do you do that?" She asked.

"What? Get the clothes, oh I just borrowed some money for a meal, then took the clothes, and left the money behind as payment." She'd not meant that, but the description of his methods was heartening. He was being honestly dishonest, a strange combination that only an illusionist would come up with.

"Who did you borrow the money from?" She was sure this was going to be complicated.

"Well, let's see I did a little magic show just over there, while you were practising your makeup; hence no one around here to bother you; I thought a diversion would help. Then I just topped it up by asking the church to help, let's face it, students are not the most generous people in the world." There was something in his voice at that comment, and something in the way he ducked a little.

"And they just gave you. No, wait," she looked at him sternly.

"Well they do call it the Poor box, and we are poor at the moment," he shrugged, palms up slightly.

"Jack!" Charlene was genuinely shocked this time.

"Oh come off it, Charlene. They want to save the world. If we fail there will be no world to save, so it's only fair that we give them a chance to pitch in, right?"

Damn his mouth could weave logic into knots sometimes, but she had to admit his argument rang true. "Ok. But once this is over, we come back and sort this out Ok?"

"I knew you'd see it my way," he beamed at her.

"I do not, and neither do you, but I'll let it go this time," flipping her hair and walking off. They started to meander through the campus.

"Engineering, is that way," he nodded to the left ahead, ignoring the sign that followed a path branching, back and to the left, "the other departments you mentioned are that way," off to the left, where some large, two storey, buildings, substantially more modern than the Paris labs rose prominently.

"Engineering labs first, so we can get Titanium up and running."

Jack realised the impulse she was fighting within herself, to scan herself first and find out what was happening in her body, "then, the Imaging department," Jack placed a hand on her shoulder reassuringly.

"If there is any trouble, we meet up back at the tractor, right?" She added tightly.

"Right," Jack nodded emphatically, "because we must save the tractor for the farmer, right?"

"Right. It's no use saving the world if we don't save the people on it."

Jack considered that then slowed a little and nailed her with his eyes, "we cannot save everyone, Charlene," a sad inevitability in his eyes, and she knew he was not just talking about the farmer and his tractor.

The look she returned was pure Chi'mera, "I'm fully aware of that, GhostKnight, but we will save as many as we can," he slowly nodding at that. Jack realised that their friendship was new and not cemented full yet, so he left it at that for the moment.

He looked at the name of the road next to them and nudged Charlene.

"Oh," was all she said, "Rue Marie Curie" and they grinned, moving on.

"Let's get Simon his parts. He must be desperate by now," Jack diverted the conversation to something less potentially volatile.

"It's only been a few hours Jack, surely he's not that worried yet."

Jack side from the side of his mouth, "You don't know Simon that well yet Charlene. Without his suit he feels much like that first time you met him; weak, vulnerable, I suppose mainly because he is. He needs his suit so much more than we need our clothes."

Charlene wondered how he was handling things back at the farm.

CHAPTER 14

INNER DEMONS

John was deep in darkness, not even a glimmer of light to be seen in this place, feeling his way down a long corridor, perhaps of a hospital, as voices in the distance, beyond these walls, kept calling out for nurses and doctors; for anyone that could help.

"Hello?" he called out as he staggered along, although he did not remember having been injured, and it was unlike Helena to leave a patient unattended; unless the team was forced to move on.

A funny clammy feeling permeated his body, being both cold, and overly warm at the same time, and although he could not really see his flesh, it felt weird, like he'd been in the bath too long, loose, wrinkled and baggy.

"Hello?" His teeth ached too, like someone had punched him in the mouth and rattled them, some feeling loose, others missing. What had happened to those lovely gleaming white sparklers he'd always had?

He moved around a corner and was engulfed in a breeze rushing down the hallway, from his left, coming through a swing door. Ah, an open window. Perhaps, if he saw outside, he could see where he was, and from that, figure out what was happening, he thought as he pushed through.

The light was better in this section of the building, the darkness occasionally broken by briefly flickering neon lights, that might have been the strip lights of a hospital corridor. Of course, this might have been anywhere that used those dim, unreliable, things; but at least the wind gave him a direction to travel.

Behind him, a door slammed, and he whipped around but saw nothing that could have made the noise. Then something moved by his foot, skittering away when he peered down. He tried to follow the fleeing sound, and spot it when the light flashed on, but again there was nothing close when the flickering light revelled where the critter should have been.

He leaned against the wall, felling a slick, slow trickle of an oily substance dribbling down it. When the light flashed on, a pale, sickly green mottled light; the liquid did indeed look black, and when he raised his fingers to his face, it looked the same, although smell disclosed, it had the tangy iron smell of blood; human blood.

He snatched his hand back and rubbed it against his clothes, but the damn goop would not come off; and in the light he now noticed that he was covered in it too, causing him to breath faster. What was going on? He looked around and called out again, his voice seeming quieter than he remembered, "Hello, is there anyone there?" The voices stopped.

He staggered forward, clipping his toes on something on the floor. He paused, cursing the lack of light and dropped to his knees, his muscles creaking and groaning as he did so. Feeling around near his feet, he could find nothing at first, strange as he'd almost tripped over whatever it was, realising it must have moved. He strained his senses in the gloom and started trying to identify outlines moving nearby.

As the light came on again the shape of a crawling person appeared indistinctly, just on the other side of the corridor, dragging itself along, away from him. He bounced to his feet again, despite his discomfort, and moved towards it. "Wait! Stop please. Where are we? Perhaps I can help," he could not run fast, something ringing alarm bells in his head, but he tried to focus on the needs of the moment. The figure, scrapped nails on the dirty floor, still trying to escape from him, or something else, down the corridor.

He reached for the figure, when the light flickered on, brighter this time. The face that looked back at him was one he knew intimately.

Isabella faced him, dishevelled, bleeding from multiple bites and covered in still feasting worms, looked at him and, in a vastly augmented voice, screamed at him; a scream filled with hated and rage, suffering and strangely, pleasure, at her current state.

She raised her hands, also filled with voracious worms and looked at them; then deliberately crammed them into her mouth, not for her to eat them, but to help them devour her. Her eyes rolled, then, with her mouth empty again, she spoke in a warped version of her old voice.

"You? Help?" The figure now turned to face him fully. "You abandoned me when I needed your help. The light grew brighter, but the light turned a vibrant red now, accentuating the blood on the walls and floor of the hospital.

The figure was obviously getting stronger, as it stood, its' legs, however, were either covered in worms or were part worm themselves, as they undulated and writhed in a paradox of large motions and small advances.

"You warned me not to come, told me it was dangerous, then did nothing to protect me." The voice was filled with a venom Isabella had never used, but the apparition moved forward, advancing on a John, who now began backing away.

"I could not. We needed to stop the Ghe'Dar. We,"

"But you did not, did you," spat the girl, or whatever it was, "and, you knew, didn't you, that you and the others, had little chance of success? Yet, you all still ploughed on, in your ignorance." Literal venom was dripping from her mouth, sizzling when it hit the floor.

"I," He found his voice faltering because her accusation was true. They had known, and they had continued, not only putting their lives on the line but also that of the entire planet; and perhaps even more.

"You left me in the hands of a bumbling fool, who did not have the strength to hold on, for even a few seconds." She strode to within a few feet of him, the ruin of her face clearly visible now. Although he shied away from seeing it, he knew he was guilty.

A hand touched his cheek; soft and delicate, "Do you want to see what they did to me?" The voice was suddenly soft, seductive and, lured in by it, he turned, expecting to suddenly see Isabella, as she had been.

Instead, the horror before him loomed closer, distorted, as though he was viewing it through frosted glass. Then darkness descended on him again.

John sat up in bed, the low light of evening coming in through the farm window.

"Easy there, soldier," said Helena's voice, while Simon looked at him with concern.

"What the, what happened? I," he looked around wildly, expecting himself to be covered in blood. Nothing.

"You don't remember?" Simon's voice was curious, rather than comforting, but then he was just Simon. "Helena said there might be some short-term memory loss from the blow to the head you received as you fell."

"How long have I been out?" He was still a little groggy.

"It's been a good day or so. Charlene said the shock might cause you problems too," Helena leaned in to look at his eye, her skin shifted slightly, like a muscle twitching a bit. "You had us all worried for a while," the twitch became more pronounced, the movement catching his eye, even more, when another area of her face developed a similar twitch.

"Isabella wants to see you after," she said leaning back a bit.

"Isabella?" He was even more confused.

"Yes. Isabella," the voice, coming from Helena, was distorted by a strange rage and vibrating noise. "The one you abandoned to her own fate," Helena's form ripped apart and Isabella, all covered in worms, burst out of the husk. "The one who will rip you to pieces. Grwwwwrrrr," and she reached for him darkness swallowed him again, pain following, as he felt his flesh ripped from him piece by piece.

John writhed on the bed, and against the restraints, placed on him, just in case. Helena looked down at him. It looked like he was in REM sleep, having a nightmare; but his heart was racing, and his pulse was beyond human norms. Yet he was not responding to the environment at all, as if he was dreaming at a much lower level than people usually did, his body reacting appropriately. The restraints, made by Charlene and Simon, based on what they knew of his strength, were being tested.

Helena's healing powers could be used on physical injuries, but, whatever was up with John, was beyond her ability to influence. All she could do was keep his body safe, and fed, and hope that he could sort out whatever was going on inside his head himself.

A head popped around the corner of the bedroom door, Simon looking through.

"You want some food?"

"Er, Simon, if it's ok with you can I do the food?" Simon's face perked up.

"Well if you insist," he grinned at her.

"I've had food that has been cooked by people like you," she said as she passed him, with one last look at John before she escaped the room.

"And?" Simon said innocently.

"I don't think we have time for a trip to the local hospital just now," his face fell, but there was a slight smirk on the scientist's face, "oh, can you keep an eye on him while I'm doing that food you wanted?" This time his face really fell, and the grin sprouted on her face.

He shrugged, "OK," and the voice betrayed the knowledge that she'd won that round, the laughter that came from the kitchen afterwards indicated that she knew too. He sighed, for someone as smart as he was, he seemed particularly vulnerable to getting lampooned by the others a lot, when it came to the little jokes, they all had with one another.

He sat down next to John and watched the tortured writhing of the ex-policeman, feeling like a fifth wheel without his armour, not that he did not have his own ideas on what to do, it was just that he'd seen the wonders of the advanced tech in the suit and he was totally distracted by it. He'd invested a vast amount of his intellect into trying to bridge the gap between what he knew and the technologies that the suit was packed with. It was not even the current functions that the suit itself had; but rather the fundamental science of the components and a little time could yield. The computer system alone was astonishing, both in form and potential, add to that the circuits and materials, plus a little knowledge gifted by Charlene, and the armour promised a whole new family of technologies for human science.

Indeed, if he and Charlene put their heads together, there seemed limitless possibilities to the things they could achieve. The only limit he could see was the nano-to-macro interface; partially bridged by Charlene's interface already; he'd obtained the specs for that and to her higher-level control systems.

He had the feeling though that there was something that she'd not placed in the specifications, from the fact that he'd tried to extrapolate a robotic interface of the same design. It had failed after a few seconds through lack of power, perhaps there was something different in Charlene that enabled the interface for her. Of course, most things about Charlene were different, things that screamed, alien; almost more so than the Ghe'Dar. Of course, he imagined that his interest in machines made most of the others feel exactly the same way about him. He shrugged again and settled down to watch John, trying to work out the power requirements for the independent interface system.

He hoped that Helena would not be long, he was starving. Besides, there was something particularly disturbing about the way John wiggled, and writhed, on the bed. It was like he'd become one great big worm.

Charlene picked up a piece of equipment, some kind of microvoltmeter, turning it over and over, trying to find any numbering on it, "wrong serial number," she muttered.

The search for the equipment was not going quite as fast as they had wanted.

They had entered, well, broken in, easily enough as lab security was nothing against their combined skills, in fact, it might as well not have been there at all. Once in, it was just a matter of finding the right items, except for the fact that there were dozens of types of each of the required things, and just ploughing through a room, this large took time.

Jack pointed to another candidate unit, Charlene pointing the flashlight at it, and giving it a quick scan, her HUD indicator going green, "yup, that's one. Just the micro-electron pulse generator and the prism system to get, and Titanium's order is up."

Charlene was glad. It had taken them too many hours so far, and while the night was probably best for what they were doing, because they'd taken so long it would most likely be morning again before they returned, time ticking by too fast for her liking.

"What does this one look like?" Jack asked from up near the ceiling.

"It's a small black box," Jack groaned, "like the waveform regulators, but it should have a magnet-coil assembly on one end, and it should be heavier, I think."

Charlene agreed with Jack's frustrations. Everything that Simon had requested was either a circuit, a little black box or switches; and this area had masses of them in various forms and size, meaning they needed to painstaking search by hand, rather than eye, through draws, cupboards, and sometimes even folders, to find the required items.

They'd spotted the prism assembly which had been requested, straight off, in the small side room, under keypad lock and encrypted security key, which might have been a problem if the room had not also had bulletproof glass. Typically, the armoured glass would have stopped them too; but with Charlene's teleport ability being line-of-sight it became a simple matter of her going in and getting the device, not even needing to hack the security as there were no camera feeds to worry about.

The search went on. "Do we really need this micro electro thingy?" Jack muttered down the comms.

"It's a must have, sorry," apologised Charlene, for about the tenth time that night. She opened up a draw and saw something that caught her eye, a small sheet of plastic, that looked familiar. Oh shit.

"Damn," she swore looking around.

"What is it?" Jack was still rummaging through the draw as he said it.

"We may not be the only ones interested in this facility, GhostKnight," his head shot up as she used his codename, meaning they had a bigger problem than they thought.

"Intelligence? Or the others?" He shifted to Knight form; glowing eerily as his name suggested, Chi'mera deploying her armour too.

"The others. I just found a manifest like the one we found in the warehouse," she turned it over and scanned the contents. Not good.

"But I thought that they never printed anything out," Jack complained.

"Not for themselves. But, what if, the Ghe'Dar use it for their converted people?" she'd not considered that in London, but it seemed logical.

"That means they have people here or slaves," he speculated looking around and spotting a piece of paper which had some similar strange diagrams on it, hanging off a side cupboard. He flew closer and squinting, brought up his flashlight to see it more clearly.

"Cha …, Chi'mera, look at this," he heard a pop, and she was right there.

"What is this?" He asked, passing her the paper with the scrawl on it.

Charlene looked at it, then tried parsing it through her HUD, blinking at the result.

"I think it's Ghe'Dar, but it's like nothing else I've seen," the HUD was weirdly still trying to translate it. It should have been able to do that instantly given it had a Ghe'Dar translation matrix. Finally, the HUD gave the writing a red light and an error message: "UNKNOWN."

"Let's make a copy, then leave this for now. Either my HUD is glitching, or it's not Ghe'Dar at all," both dropping their armour in relief.

"Oh great! Something else to worry about," Jack looked down and spotted something; the missing equipment piece. "Got the micro-electron what-u-ma-call-it" Jack whispered triumphantly. It was not black, but green, but the serial number matched when Charlene checked it.

"Right. Let's off to the LNIO," and she was out the door faster than a jackrabbit being chased by a den full of foxes. Jack was about to protest that they did not have the Prism, when he rechecked the room, realising that Charlene must already have taken it. Jack smiled. She was in a right royal rush this time, and nothing was going to get in her way.

"How long can he last like that?" Simon said, through a mouthful of chicken and bacon baguette, that he was thoroughly enjoying, despite the human suffering before him. Helena had left her food downstairs, to eat later, if she could.

"As long as we give him water every so often, and can get food into him every few days, a long time. I'm more worried what he'll be like when he comes out. This kind of stress can do serious damage both to the body and mind."

Simon seemed to be, almost, indifferent to the contortions and moans coming from their teammate. As a doctor, Helena had been called on to do some pretty hard things; deciding when to turn off life supports, helping those that did not deserve it and refusing care to those that asked not to receive it. When doing that, you developed a reasonably thick skin; not insensitivity, just the ability to not let it hurt you. But the way that Simon seemed to barely notice it seemed just; cold, almost frosty.

"I'll just go have mine. I'll be back in about ten minutes," Helena turned, half bolting down the stairs, even as Simon nodded acknowledgement. He still did not understand her, even if he liked her as a friend; she was an excellent cook though.

The LNIO was at the eastern side of the complex, in an even less populated section of the campus and had one thing that the other area did not, CCTV; strange considering the storage room held a great deal of expensive kit.

Charlene had the Prism assembly under her arm but put it down when she saw the extra security. They were across a small plaza area from the main building, looking at the monitoring cameras and the guard on the door.

"Not good!" Jack muttered.

Charlene looked at him and nodded. He knew what she wanted and how to do this. The lab was reasonably close to the countryside and so had little in the way of lighting except at ground level, so Jack went high to see what was happening.

A few minutes later, he drifted down and made a gentle landing just next to her.

"You're going to love this," the tone of his voice was one of wicked pleasure.

"Go on, hit me with it," after he'd paused for effect, her voice sounding slightly sick.

"It seems that yonder building, is a company funded annexe; hence the hired corporate security group. It is apparently open twenty-four hours a day, unlike the rest of the university." There was something else, and it was amusing Jack immensely.

"Well; what is it?" Charlene began to get exasperated.

Jack's face tried to look innocent, but finally, he could not contain himself any longer.

"Owned by, Starling industries," Jack barked in laughter.

Her face split into a massive grin.

"Even given the possible issues, we can walk right into this one." Jack laughed, Charlene smiling. This time, just this once, they had an easy job.

"Follow me in," she ordered, shifting into a rather bland looking, nondescript person and retrieving her M.I.X. pass, making sure that Jack did not see what she was about to do, as the image on the card now matched the form she'd taken, a layer of Nanites covering the card. These would also re-program the reader to give a positive ID reading, thanks to an inductive substance in the Nanites. It was a trick that the interface allowed her to pull, but not one that the others knew about. After all, what they did not know, they could not reveal. She also thought it best to keep Simon from knowing about this trick, as it would also allow her to perform some reasonably interesting tricks with his suit too, that he might consider, potentially threatening. Best keep it to herself.

The security guard saw a stranger walking up to the door.

"Can I help you miss?" She was about five-foot-six, brown hair, carrying a strange piece of equipment that caught his attention. When she did not answer immediately, he thought she was French, he was used to that, especially when her head moved to one side.

"I have the prism equipment, for the LNIO," her voice quiet, and almost hesitant; perhaps a lab assistant. Not French then, judging by the slight, Devonian accent.

"I'm sorry miss this building is for pass holders only," pointing to his own, from an International security firm.

"Oh sorry. How thoughtless of me? Here is my pass." A ripple passed across the card as she handed it over, and as he read it, it read as a Starling Enterprises, executive level, card." The guard looked at it and passed it through the reader, which burped, turning red for a second.

"Hmmm, the reader's having a problem with this card miss," he said trying again, Charlene guessing the Nanites needed time to infiltrate the reader's system fully.

The reader burped again, "damn technology," the guard muttered, then looked up, realising who was watching, "excuse me miss, but this thing has been playing up all week."

He made one more pass, initiating a beep, indicating that the card had been accepted.

"There you go miss," he said very relievedly, handing the card back.

"Thank you," she flashed him a smile and took it, palming it rather than putting it away, allowing the Nanites to reintegrate into her system, Charlene finding that some strange data was coming back from them.

"The LNIO is up the stairs to the right," the guard added, as she passed.

"Thanks," she gushed trotting up the stairs, Jack appearing by her side when they were out of sight of the guard, and the cameras.

"What took it so long?" Jack asked slowly, trying to catch his breath, his power usage taking its toll on him.

"They took so long because someone else similarly bypassed the security recently," Jack stole a glance at her, showing she was thinking furiously.

"Not Ghe'Dar, they would have just replaced the guard or controlled him. No this is something else, something advanced but," she paused, "ah, our mysterious scribbler has been here too."

"Why?" Jack was getting more puzzled by this trip by the minute.

"Don't know, but let's do what we need to do and puzzle that out later. We are on a schedule here, and it's getting tighter."

They hustled down the corridor and entered the LNIO through a set of swing doors. The lights were on, but there really was no one home; excluding the one cleaner, using a buffing machine in the hallway, but he paid no head, listening to "Sounds of the ocean."

As they entered the imager lab, Charlene took a deep breath. Having waited many long days to know what was going on inside her, she was about to find out. Her hand started to tremble, as her nerves began to kick in, despite her control.

Jack saw the terrible transformation from calm agent to a frightened teenager, and for once did not envy her. This must be truly terrifying for her; knowing the possible outcomes only too well, so he slipped his hand into hers, and smiled; a carefully contrived smile of reassurance and hope. Seeing it, she smiled one of gratitude back.

"Well Chi'mera?" He saw the effect of her codename take hold, as he tried to instil her with the required bravery and stoicism. He knew she knew it, her chin going up as she moved towards the scanner controls, even though her foot hesitated a little, Charlene glaring at it, forcing it to obey.

"I'll need to run several section scans to get the full picture of what is going on in there. Keep an eye out; the last thing we want right now is unwanted visitors."

She began programming a series of scans into the scanner, using her own interface. The damn controls were in French, but thankfully her interface just ignored that and went directly into the logic circuits. Thank God for USBs.

Deep within the imager's computer, a small green device activated, lights flashing briefly, sending its report, then going dormant again.

In a nearby building, a man ran through a list of people on his computer, the lights on the device stopping the scrolling and displaying a brief series of strange symbols on his screen, much like the discovered scribbling. He leaned back against the chair and typed a few commands into his terminal, which the computer acknowledged, then went back to listing all the registered scientists who'd the required level of Nano-technological expertise on this organic planet. As the list ended, there were a few that met his entered criteria including a certain. Dr. Charlene Klerk, who topped the list with an impossible 100% match.

He ran his finger over the image, "interesting," came the strangely modulated voice. Not quite human; but certainly not Ghe'Dar.

Helena sat down in front of the fire and started to relax. It was getting late, and it seemed that the others were not going to make it back till morning now. She started upstairs to the bedroom when Simon came out of John's room.

"How's he doing?" She asked automatically.

"The same," he said closing the door. "He had a quiet spell for a few minutes, so I sponged some water into him, which he tried to spit out, though we got there in the end. It triggered another bout of nightmares though; at least, he immediately started to moan and writhe again." He shrugged, indicating that he did not really know what it all meant.

"Guess we'll just keep going until he breaks out of it, or until we can think of something to help him," Helena decided. "I don't like to interact with outsiders at this point, but there may be some people that can help; once we get nearer to the time."

Simon's eyebrows raised slightly, "holding out on us, Helena?" Simon was surprised. She'd always seemed the open kind, but then, he remembered she'd been in M.I.X. before they first arrived. She was by definition a spy, and they all had secrets; which he realised now included himself, even though he'd never really thought of himself like that. Still, things had changed, that was part of life. Nature kept secrets, people did, and science did. It was just a matter of time before all his teammates would do it.

He shook his head before she replied, "never mind. When do we decide on whether to call these people in?" She looked a little surprised at his acceptance, but then he was a scientist; they were practical people.

"Not until we are officially missing from the battlefield at CERN; a few more days."

"But that will be when we need to arrive AT the battlefield," he protested vehemently.

"Don't worry. The people I can call in can handle things and get us there quickly if necessary. But I cannot do it yet, it would,"

"I know, cause complications," she nodded. Simon hated cutting things too fine, his engineering background, meant he always tried to leave a safety margin to make sure things worked correctly. It looked like this time he might not be able to do that. Some things did not let you build that factor in, and life was one of them, so he went downstairs, and settled in for a night of guard duty, trusting Helena to keep an ear open for any changes in John.

The scans took about thirty minutes, during which time, Charlene had just laid back, forcing herself not to jump up after every scan, and just let the series run. When the final scan had finished, she slowly swung herself off the table and, with hesitant steps, approached the control console, genuinely terrified what the scans might reveal.

Jack, having seen the machine stop, entered the room from an office across the hall, that provided an excellent view down the corridor.

Charlene moved around the end of the console, starting to run the processing systems on the scanned images.

"How long will it take to refine that much data?" Jack asked, trying to get her to think scientist, rather than a panicked teenager. The team often forgot that she really was just a teenager and an inexperienced one at that. Well, inexperienced in dealing with anything like this, though to be honest they all were. He automatically excluded her parents' death, as she barely remembered that.

"A few minutes," she tapped at her interface, running the results through to a monitor on her left. They waited. Strange how time seemed to stretch out while you waited, for these minutes, Charlene thought, it was time's way of punishing them for breaking its' laws.

Finally, after an interminable wait, the console beeped, indicating the processing was complete and the data available. When Charlene did not move to retrieve the data, Jack gave her hand a squeeze, making her looked at him, with pleading in her eyes.

"It will be fine," somehow, he knew that, but could not say how. It was another of those hunches of his, "I know it will," he squeezed her hand again.

With a great deal of reluctance, she disengaged his hand, displaying the results on the monitor, displaying a 3D model of Charlene, rotating from head to foot, then horizontally.

The outer skin all looked strangely symmetrical for a human, and her stomach seemed a little larger than she remembered it being before all this happened. A frown appeared on her face as she zoomed in on her ribs and abdomen. It was strange, not at all as she'd expect it to be, with her intestinal tract seeming longer, and thinner, than expected, taking up less than half of the area it should. Her heart was slim-lined to, while the heart rate was three times faster than usual, though strangely she felt it to be perfectly normal.

The lower area was the one that caught her eye. For a man, this would merely have comprised his bowl and bladder, but for a female, it held the most important thing of all; her womb. It appeared the Nanites had been terribly busy in this area, as what should be a virtually empty area on the screen, was filled with hard echoes of solid objects and structures; not tumours, since they would have been around and dark. No. There were a whole array of small cubes, angular ghosts, and lattices comprised of nano-machines which had apparently found a space not being used and made themselves right at home.

She could not help but gasp and put her hand to the area, her bottom lip trembling, despite her not really being the mothering kind, well certainly not yet; but to be denied even the choice of being a mother, before she'd had a chance to think about it, was too much. She looked at Jack, with anguish in her eyes, starting to tremble uncontrollably and feeling her legs start to go, Jack grabbing her, as she sloped to the floor, "easy there. Easy."

She tried to say something, but all that came out was blubbering, tears rapidly following, her HUD fading and disappearing, and her muscles failing utterly; she just dropped onto Jack's shoulder and wailed.

For the second time that day, science and technology were overcome by a simple human emotion. Jack wondered as he comforted the distraught girl if that would always be the case and if indeed, that might be a good thing meaning that, no matter how powerful the technology, human emotion would overcome it. Perhaps Love really did conquer all, whether human love of each other, or love of life.

It took nearly a quarter of an hour for Charlene's tears to subside, and even more for her to start to let go of Jack. "I'm s," Jack shrugged her off, to forestall the apology.

"So what now?" He asked, "it's not a tumour?"

She tried to speak but was finding it difficult.

"Chi'mera! What now?" He asked more firmly, trying to get through her shock.

She shook herself, trying to relax, using her meditative skills to become calmer.

"No. All the shapes are nano-machines and structures, the large one at the centre is probably the 'mainframe' nano-hub; the primary controlling interlink. The rest probably control the other systems, like my healing and teleport. I had supposed they'd be distributed throughout my body, as Nano-systems tend to be de-centralised, perhaps they are as well, although it's hard to tell as the image is full of a strange kind of interference. But it seems that they merely saw this as an ideal location; not in use, with plentiful blood supply to transport the Nanites quickly throughout the body, and access to a pure genetic pattern from the eggs. I doubt I could get them to move, as there is just too much there to relocate."

She was starting to talk more like the scientist now, the image she liked to portray to others, showing just how much this discovery had hurt her, beginning to build those walls up again. He put his hand on her shoulder; the answering hand reassured him that they were still ok, hoping that was true.

"See this," she pointed to a barely visible shadow across the rest of the area, "across it all, appears to be a nano-tube re-enforced internal cage, to protect it from damage, supported by this extra pair of ribs," two structures spanned the entire stomach top and bottom.

"Wow," Jack was really none the wiser, except to realise that Charlene was now a real tough cookie; hitting her stomach now would probably hurt the attacker more than her.

"It also means that all my work on the interface, and internal reorganisation, was the tip of the iceberg. The scale of the structures there indicates that I'll need weeks, perhaps months to explore what they have done, are doing, in there."

"Well. I don't know about you, but I'm hungry. I also know we don't have much more time free here. Eventually, someone will come to see how we are doing; then there will be problems, one way or another." Jack looked at her.

She nodded, drying her eyes one more time, "but not a word to the others." When Jack started to object, she pleaded with her eyes, "I'll get some wisdom from Helena, but the others don't need to know about this. Right?" when he seemed to object, she added, "Please?" His face took on an appearance of shock, that she would use that tactic on him. Her eyes all wide and sorrowful again like she was about to cry. He threw his hands up in the air, his face becoming resigned.

"OK! But talk to Helena. She can help you as she did me. Mother knows best." The moment he said it he regretted it and saw more tears welling up on Charlene's face.

"I'm sorry, truly I am, Charlene," his hand coming up to show his genuine regret; intercepted by hers.

"It's not your fault, nor the Nanites," her face suddenly turning very hard, almost literally. "This is all the fault of the bloody aliens, and I'm going to make sure that they pay!"

"Easy there," the words stopping as he now faced Chi'mera once again. With a sad little purse of the lips, he just nodded. "Let's get this equipment to Simon and start on that debt recovery plan."

Charlene downloaded the data from her scan into her internal systems and wiped the data, leaving some Nanites to continue erasing the records properly. She also left a message for Craig, should he get there.

The trip out was quiet and uneventful. Travelling by tractor at night, down the back roads of France, was apparently the safest place that they had ever been. After all, it was not exactly where you expected to find British Military Intelligence Agents.

"What are they doing?" asked Ricks.

Haines answered, looking at the feed from the remote camera they had planted at the Troyes University, "looks like they are packing some equipment into a ten tonner."

Gareth looked up, "the main tower is definitely capable of receiving the signal frequency GhostKnight gave us." He produced a signal scanner, "though not a trace of other headsets, so they're not here at the moment. But hacking into the local comms cell tower shows traces that they have been here recently. Two together and another, that tried to mask their signature," he grinned a little grin to the others.

"A third one?" a shake of the head indicating not. "An enemy?"

"I don't think so, just another party, perhaps someone more experienced at covering their tracks than the others. They were pretty good too, just not good enough to fool me."

Gareth was using a small tablet-like device, "hello, what's this?" he asked rhetorically, the others stopping what they were doing at the tone and coming over.

"There is a message encrypted into the residual signal code logs. I take it back this guy is good. It's designed to activate on my analysis frequency only."

"This is not a trace; this was transmitted separately directly to the tower logs. Impressive; anyone else would have mistaken this for a normal log."

The others looked at the screen as Gareth ran the message through a decryption algorithm, "my guess he's M.I. too, possibly the super."

"Here it comes. Bloody hell. It's a compressed file too, this guy knows his comms. Ok, finally." They all looked on in perplexity, as the message read as follows: -

"To all Military Intelligence units, Western Europe Region: Reaper 9. Gravitron and friendlies are active in the area. Proceed to CERN with all readily available resources, using stealth approach; date and time on subchannel five. Priority One."

Ricks and Gareth both looked at Haines.

"What does it even mean?" Gareth being too junior to understand the full enormity of the message.

"It means my dear Gareth that GhostKnight was most likely telling the truth," said Haines. "Gravitron is the code name of the highest operative in the M.I. network. When he issues a call to arms, you don't refuse it; unless you want to retire early."

"He was the one that neutralised the Kal-de-Nar terrorists A-bomb plot in '87," Ricks added, starring at Haines, who nodded. "CERN it is then. No more trying to find out by ourselves. We just hope they know what they are doing and pray we can help in some way."

"What does the subchannel say is the schedule?" Gareth asked.

"We have eighteen days," Haines looking on thoughtful, followed by a brief flicker of pain. Ricks had seen that look before

"You thinking about Selena?" Ricks stated rather than asked., Haines wincing at the use of her name.

"Well, he said bring everything. She'd be the one to get things at short a notice around here," the faraway look appearing again.

"She won't thank you for this if it goes pear-shaped," Ricks warned.

"And if I did not, I'd never hear the last of it," Haines pointed out.

"True. But you do remember she tried to kill you last time?" Haines shrugged.

"All lovers have tiffs. It was just one of those things. She has forgiven me since, by text anyway."

"You sure she remembers that?" Gareth added.

"No, but then that's what keeps things exciting. Besides if it is really Reaper 9, there is no one else I'd like to share the end of the world with," grinned Haines, and headed out.

The other two looked at each other and shrugged too, "he's crazy you know; she'll more likely slice his gizzard open," came one voice drifting off into the night.

"My bet is on, she kisses him first; then tries for his gizzard," came the other.

"Nah; she tried that in Algiers. I should know, she nearly skewered me then, too."

"I remember." They did not see a large, black metallic, suited, figure silently descending from the sky, where the truck was being loaded.

"Evening sir!" said the guard, greeting Craig Starling, heavy raincoat on, and lifting his ID to the scanner, the scanner still fritzing a little. He looked down then at the guard.

"Couldn't I just," he mimed going through the large load gate.

"No, sir. I cannot pass you without the system registering you; fire regs. you understand." The guard tapped the scanner a few times, running his own card through to clear the reader. "The girl with the kit for the LNIO was patient with such things," the guard had seen Craig before, but he knew his job was to be a stickler.

Craig's face remained still, but he became more alert, "ah yes, the new machinery. Is she still there?" He asked carefully.

"No. She left, oh, about ten minutes ago, muttering that the new units were all installed. She took a box of junk out to the bins, around the back," gesturing in the opposite direction from the loading area. Craig tried not to look disappointed.

"A bit tight-lipped, but pleasant enough," the guard commented, as the scanner finally let the card scan. "There you go, sir!" Go right in."

Craig strode in, opening his coat at the top of the stairs and activating his own armour, becoming, Gravitron.

He stopped at the LNIO doors, and cautiously entered, the lights coming on in response to his presence. He cast about for anything that might be missing, or things that might have been added, pulling up his internal HUD and scanning for foreign, non-French, DNA and particles disturbed within the last half hour. The colour of the particles swirled around him using IR light, while a few strange fingerprints appeared, under UV light, on the scanner and its control mechanism. Someone had indeed used the scanner.

He looked at those fingerprints, but the lines were distorted, not by the way they had been left, but by design. They were obviously false because the lines formed a distinctive pattern; the outline of France, with an arrow crossing it towards Switzerland. At least it looked like that when you analysed it under UV light, as he was doing. Ah, the mystery message writer; a girl? Somehow that seemed less likely, but then he had two exceedingly capable women in his employ, so, why not?

He disengaged his armour, the plates vanishing under his heavy coat, as he turned his attention to the console, which was in standby mode. There was a particular pattern on the side of the console too, a hole in the panel, and while his scans had not detected any dangerous chemicals in the vicinity and he felt safe to proceed, he approached it cautiously.

As he hit the start button, and the system started to warm up, he speculated as to who these people he was chasing were. They seemed bright, knew him well, but seemed not to have the normal security codes to contact him directly. It smacked of terrorist thinking, but then, they had his DNA, and the trust of his aid; even though she'd denied any knowledge of them. That and the fact that the message had suggested that all this had already happened for them, was scarcely credible.

As the main screen came up the usual menu was displayed; except a new setting, marked 'Update report.' He selected it.

A face appeared on the screen; a young plain faced girl holding the imaging scanner.

"Hello, Craig. I tied the message into your DNA signature, so only you can get this; as proof that we are on your side."

"The fate of the world depends on our next moves. My instincts tell me I cannot say much without causing greater problems so I'll keep it brief. We are trying to stop an invasion, and almost all of the command structure is compromised. I hope that is enough. Also, we need a few things from you. Your special equipment; serial number 121/245552/123-Theta with the software package TY56-4; use the attached interface protocols to make it effective."

He did not know how they knew about these things, but future knowledge would be a reasonable guess at this point. Temporal physics was not really his strong point, but there were some theoretical ways it was possible.

"Oh, and you need to get back to England soon, certainly within the next few days. There's an incident about to happen that requires your attention," now that really did smack of foreknowledge.

"One final thing. Please get Isabella to run up a program with the following parameters, and the second attached file. I've rigged it so that only she can access it, so no peaking." Craig shook his head trying to register all this. "See you at the party, if you can find any 'clean' people, get them to bring their biggest toys. We may be delayed, but we will be there. As to who to expect, 'All for One' and all that,"

He looked a bit bewildered for a time after the message finished.

Whoever they were, he guessed he really was going to help them. After all, they seemed to know his most secret equipment, what he needed to do and when.

He uploaded the files, shut down the machine and walked out of the building, waving to the guard as he left, barely turning the corner before becoming airborne.

He pondered the messages last comment, thinking it was exceedingly strange, then twigged. It was saying that there was four of them; three plus one being the exact reference. He initiated a secure call to his HQ.

"Helena, can you get Isabella up and start her on monitoring the security forces frequencies."

"Sir, she's only had a few hours; it is three am," Helena complained.

"I know. I'm inbound, about thirty minutes out. We are now on Reaper 9 alert, and we are all going to get extremely tired before this is over" The startled silence over the comms channel spoke volumes.

"Yes, sir. I'll get right on it," Helena suddenly sounding all professional, and Craig knew she'd see to it that resources would be in place by the time he arrived at the tower. The question really was; could it be a hoax in any way? There was a part of him that desperately hoped so, but something in his gut was telling him it was not.

Jack was getting tired but using a trick the book had taught him to put off the effects. He'd an exhausted Chi'mera, next to him. Although she seemed to be able to maintain a form indefinitely, something about it that drained her. Perhaps, it was just the after-effects of the stress she'd been under in the past few weeks catching up with her, but whatever it was, they had barely started out when she'd leaned forward, her breathing becoming slower and slower, until he knew she was fast asleep when she changed back into her original form.

She really should keep her regular clothes on in that form. He covered her and carried on.

The lights on the tractor were not tremendously bright, but they were safe enough out here, with so little traffic moving in this region at night. Jack estimated they'd hit the farmhouse about dawn.

John ran. He ran and ran and ran, but seemed unable to outpace the worm-infested Isabella, who stayed just a few steps behind him or just behind the next building.

"But don't you want me, sweetheart? You still love me, don't you? Come to me; feed me," she repeated, over and over again, as they ran, through worm infested streets. The worms were black, oily creatures about a foot long, with sharp jagged teeth, which he had to shake from his legs as he went, as some attempted to burrow into him, those which he did shake then fell back into the masses, although, strangely, where they had been on his legs showed no signs of the inflicted wounds.

He turned suddenly and hid in a house, the girl missing the move, running past. He breathed a sigh of relief and gasped for breath, turned his head to see if there was another way out of the building. There she was leaning against the wall, watching him, then reaching for him with clawed hands, dripping worms. He bolted again.

"You cannot escape me, just as I could not escape the fall. There was no help then, and there will be no help now, or ever," she laughed, in a distorted version of her voice and continued her horrific pursuit.

CHAPTER 15

THE CALM BEFORE THE STORM

Jack and an extremely drowsy Charlene arrived just before morning, the light from the sun just starting to colour the distant horizon, with a pale pink-blue fan of thin cloud. Jack nudged Charlene, the sleepy girl groaning, trying to stay asleep.

"Come on Char, I'm tired too. Once we get this to Simon, we can sleep for a week if necessary," speaking only half in jest. He knew that the others had had a rough time of it these past days, but he'd used his powers a lot last night, taking it right out of him.

"Mmmm? Sh … sure," she murmured leaping out of the tractor, landing on her feet only after a mid-air adjustment, the crunch as she landed speaking of breaking bones, which did wake her up, "Ooowww," the following sound of bone re-knitting, audible from the cab.

"Careful Char," Jack said, with concern in his voice.

"It's ok, I'm awake now! Pain does that you know," Charlene indeed now fully awake, her repair systems protesting at the sudden requirement.

"Not the best way to do it though," her scowl telling him she knew.

"I'll get them into the barn," she looked in that direction but saw no light in there. Not at all like Simon. "You go tell Simon. He must be in the house."

"Sure," Jack mimicked Charlene's sleepy tone.

He tried the door and found it locked, the remaining pair having obviously secured the place for the night, assuming that they would not get back before dawn. He smiled, producing a small pick, quickly entering the farmhouse, seeing that there was no sign of anyone up at the moment.

He heard someone, probably Helena, moving around upstairs, in all likely hood just getting up, being the get up at the crack of dawn kind of person. He thought he might surprise her and start getting breakfast ready but thought better of it. It was one thing to enjoy the company of someone, it was another to usurp their position in a house, especially a woman. He'd tried that once, when his mum had been ill, and his ears still rang from her vitriolic recriminations.

"You think I'm incapable of cooking my own breakfast, boy? I ain't no layabout just 'cause my ankle ain't working properly, unlike your brothers and their friends. They may sit around listening to their pods and discs, but I work hard to keep this place shaped up. Now get out of my kitchen. Besides, you burnt the toast and used too much marg."

And that had been that. Strangely, he thought he really could still hear her charged vocal reprimand; his mum had a powerful voice alright, with an attitude to match. Who knew, after this, he might even be able to send her some money, something that would make her shout for sure; with pure joy, for a change.

He stopped and suddenly felt weird, realising that none of them had really considered, when they had started out on this mission to save the world, what would happen afterwards. It was all well and good to say that, if they did not, it would not matter, but if they did, did they get paid for it? He smiled at himself, of course not; but perhaps they might actually live to draw an M.I.X. wage packet that he could send home to his mother.

The simple thought that he might be the first person in their family to earn a real wage in three generations, short of their dad's conscription pay, made him puff his chest out slightly. He might not be immensely strong like the others, but he suddenly felt a mile tall.

"Well the rooster might not be up, but you seem to be," came a voice from the stairs, Jack suddenly embarrassed, Helena padding down the steps in bare feet.

"I didn't hear you coming down," Jack half complained.

"They train you to step quietly, even in creaky old houses. Eventually, if we survive this, you'll probably go on those courses too, in fact, I even think that Craig has already booked you all in for the whole set of them. Enjoy," the slightly sadistic tone in her voice indicated strongly that she had not.

"So you don't like the whole sneaking around thing really," he stated rather than asked, the look she threw at him confirmed that assessment, "so why?" He indicated the house.

"Orders are Orders with Craig," she pulled a packet of flour out of the cabinet, frowning when she saw that it was nearly empty, relaxing when she saw a massive bag near the back door.

"You needed a field medic, and a supervising officer," she twisted the left side of her mouth, "Yeah, that went south. He obviously thought I could step up as a field commander," her tone indicating that that had not happened. "I'd told him that it just was not me; if anyone would have stepped up, I'd have thought it would have been Isabella, that did not work out well. Sometimes when you throw people in the deep end, they just drown," she looked away, her eyes obviously having some flour in them.

He could appreciate that sometimes things just did not work out, his brothers constantly trying for jobs, but, in all honesty, they were not the brightest people in the world. Strange that he did not think of them much, but his mother was always in his thoughts; they were all family, but only his mother made time for him. The rest seemed to ignore him, and he them; rivalry perhaps, or just an acknowledgement that they lived in different worlds. Ironic now, that, that statement, meant so much more to him than to them.

"Anyway; where's Simon? We've brought his precious equipment, and thought he'd be down here, eager to fix up his suit."

"He's upstairs in the room," the statement was so bland that it took him a few seconds to process it.

"The room you were in?"

She turned and smiled, "no. He may think he runs on atomic power, but when it comes down to it, we're all human," she stopped and tilted her head slightly, "well maybe. Anyway, he flaked out in a rather small cot bed in the side room. Must be still there."

Charlene entered, "no Simon?"

Jack pursed his lips, "we were just saying he's not up yet," he indicated Helena, who had started to knead the dough for the day's bread.

"It's early yet, let's give him a lay-in," Charlene thought about it quickly, "he'll have a long few days ahead of him fixing that thing outside, genius or no; and I'm positive he'll have damn little sleep during that. I know how that works," which in all fairness she probably did.

"Speaking of sleep. You two upstairs, sleep, now," Helena ordered looking at them sternly, and they were about to obey, when Charlene's stomach gave a rather imperious growl.

The three of them all looked at Charlene's stomach, Helena was trepidation, but then all three burst out in hoots of laughter, trying to contain it after a few seconds so they would not disturb the still sleeping Simon.

"Oh, Ok," Helena conceded, "after breakfast. But then sleep until you are refreshed."

The command was absolute, and neither of them was really in the state to argue.

Simon woke up, feeling that he'd just missed something, his limbs leaden, but he immediately perked up when the smell of baking bread grabbed his nose; wafting in through the bedroom's open door. He looked around confused, realising he'd slept in his clothes and on an undersized bed; his arms draping over a side of a four-footer, feet dangling just above the floor. He must have been so tired last night, that he just found the nearest empty bed and collapsed on it. He remembered checking in on John last thing and seeing him still tossing about, although not as violently as during the day, having given up on trying to put a blanket on him.

He heard other voices coming from downstairs, meaning the others had returned causing him to become suddenly excited, bolting upright, and earning a dizzying rebuke from his head. He staggered a little, adjusted his clothes, then headed for the door, remembering to check John before he disappeared as he reached the door.

He looked in on John, still there, sleeping almost peacefully, having stopped tossing altogether. He started to head down when Simon realised that indeed John HAD stopped moving altogether, and darting forward put his fingers to John's throat, as he'd seen Helena do. He pressed a bit harder, then bellowed, "Helena, get up here. I cannot find John's pulse."

"He's still with us, but he's slipped into a much deeper coma," Helena said drawing a blanket across him. "His pulse is way below the norm, his breathing barely registers, but he's still there."

"Would a hospital help?" Jack asked.

"We dare not move him. He's just too subject to the environment at the moment." She seemed less desperate, more resigned, "we just have to wait it out. If we run out of time, we can call Craig to come to pick him up, but let's hope it does not come to that," and she ushered the others out of the room, closing the door behind her.

"Our best bet is to prepare for what is to come, so that, when he recovers, he has a world to come back to."

"What if there is a problem?" Jack asked.

"I've rigged his comm. system to act as a kind of baby monitor," Simon replied for her, "if there is any change in his pulse, heart rate or breathing pattern the sound system on the comms unit will register a modulation and alert us." Charlene nodded her approval of the improvised system; he was a genius, she'd thought it before and, no doubt, she'd probably say it too, sometime.

"Clever," was all she actually said.

"Why, thank you,. Dr. Klerk," Simon said in mock thanks, bowing slightly. "Now, if you'll all excuse me, I have some serious work to do."

Grabbing a blanket on the way out, he was heard, stampeding, across the wooden floor, towards the barn, to start his repairs'.

"That man can be very," Helena waved her hand slightly, trying to illicit a descriptive for the dismissive manner, despite his friendly nature.

"Cold?" Jack supplied, but received a shake of the head,

"So, so," Helena, was building up a head of steam to find the right word.

"Infuriating!" Charlene, seeing Helena's reaction, had found the right word.

"Damn right. Infuriating!" Helena burst out, releasing the head of steam, in one, huge, expletive.

Jack and Charlene looked at each other, and replied simultaneously, "we know!"

Simon was cataloguing the equipment his scavengers had returned, which appeared to include additional microcircuits, chips, and organics that Charlene had thought might be useful. Well-intentioned he supposed, but some of them were just too delicate for him unless she had some ideas; he'd need to check back with her after he'd started on the few calibrations that could be set off testing.

Firstly, the power grid had had a damaging polarised magnetic pulse sent through it, which he needed to reset, by normalising the potential differentials, to allow the suit to work at all. He built a mini substation, using some thin magnets and spool of copper wire which, once functional, would produce a counter field that would gently drain the offending magnetism, allowing the suit's power to flow again. It would take a few days, but they had the time; at this end of history anyway.

Charlene was awake at seven on the dot, her HUD coming up with the time, date and an all systems green. She shook her head, finding she was fully refreshed, if a little disoriented because, over the past weeks, she'd woken up on sofas, walls, floors and in a crashed spaceship. Now she'd been in a bed for an hour, it just did not seem real at all. How strange that that simple pleasure now seemed so, alien, to her. What was it they said? Given enough time and you can get used to anything. Well, she'd no intention of getting used to waking up in derelict warehouses, old houses, or anywhere else other than a nice bed in future. She made a mental note to herself to talk to Craig about having bed rolls included in agent's equipment packs in future; the thought was funny, but after a second or two, she thought that perhaps it was possible given the Nano construction techniques of today.

"Who am I kidding," she muttered to herself, sitting up, and noticing Jack in the other room, flaked out on the cot bed, suddenly feeling a great deal of sympathy for him. Of all the team, she subconsciously excluded Helena, Jack was the least resilient, though able to push himself physically; he must really have been struggling recently. She sent out her tentacles, grabbing some clothes from a nearby wardrobe, sliding silently out of bed, and realising that when she'd fallen unconscious, she had reverted to her original form; naked.

This did not hit home until she'd finished getting into real some clothes. Every time she had been unconscious previously, after the transformation, she must have reverted to being a naked human, the others not having said a word! Suddenly, she was outraged, and, gently closing the door behind her, leapt down the stairs to confront the others in the kitchen, however, only Helena was there.

"You could have told me!" She snapped at Helena, who was busy slicing up some cured ham for lunch, while everyone else was busy.

"Oh hello, Charlene. Could have told you what?" her voice so unstrained, that Charlene suspected that this was Helena's version of humour.

"That I revert to human form when I'm asleep," her voice sounding so like her original voice now that she even recognised the petulance in it.

"Oh that," Helena glanced up, hardly paying attention, "we were all a little distracted with all the screaming and fighting, that we had 'barely' noticed." Now that had been an attempt at humour.

"Ah, well I didn't, I mean," she stopped, realising Helena was trying to deflect her, and succeeding quite well. She looked harder at Helena's face and realised that the woman was silently laughing under her breath.

"OOOwww," she stamped her foot, as Helena's face came up.

"Ah ha! Now there is the old Charlene again. Welcome back," Helena grinned broadly and laughing more openly.

"You, you, you're as bad as any of them," she accused her, still laughing, woman. The woman seemed to be unable to stop laughing and, the problem was it was getting infectious. Charlene tried, so hard to remain angry, to not to join in, but it was hopeless. Eventually, the pair of them were leaning against the kitchen worktops, crying with laughter. It was so ridiculous really. They were getting ready to save the world and here she was complaining that the others had seen her without her clothes.

After a few minutes, Charlene was brought back to reality with a growling stomach.

"Oh for heaven's sake Charlene. Can you make your next upgrade a silent stomach? Especially if you need to go on any reconnaissance missions," she asked, only half in jest.

"Yes Ma'am," she laughed again give a little salute, but then leaning forward and grabbed one of the sandwiches, wolfing an addition the large slab of cheese straight down, silencing her loud and seemingly bottomless stomach.

Helena's face turned serious. "What did the scans show?" She indicated Charlene's lower body.

The knowledge was still a little raw, but the initial shock was fading slightly. "It seems I'm fine, other than my Nanites, and their new home," her tone level; quite a feat considering the circumstances.

"New home?" Helena strained to understand, "they are in your stomach? That would explain the constant growling," relief filling Helena's voice.

"Oh no," Charlene's voice was starting to fill with bitter sarcasm, "my dear little friends decided that I had some space spare just above my bladder, so they moved in and made themselves right at home, even re-enforced the body to protect their new digs," she felt tears forming in her eyes again. Helena saw the tears, her own eyes going extremely wide. She rushed to embrace the obviously distraught girl.

"Oh, my dear. Oh no," Helena's manner radiating genuine sorrow. Charlene had endured so much and now this; how much more could she take?

"It's, just, not, fair!" sobbed the girl, clinging to the older woman and, for the second time in less than a day, sobbed her heart out.

"No dear, it is not," Helena's voice tried to sooth the poor girl's distress.

"My parents, my job, my career and now any future family. All lost," her tears turning hot and bitter.

"No my dear, not all lost," Helena needed to head that off, Charlene's tears slowing, her face came up.

"Not lost?"

"We know that Sylvia still lives, and as Jack's mother might say, the Lord always forgives those who seek repentance," seeing that idea bound off Charlene's armoured exterior.

"Redeem? My mother? You are insane," Charlene pulling away from Helena quickly, "and even if, by some miracle, and it really would be a miracle the Lord forgave her, I would not. Never, ever, ever, ever," she almost chanted.

"Well you have an uncle, and you still have a career," Helena put her hand on the shoulder of the now settling girl.

"Oh yes, Charlene the spy!" Charlene said sarcastically.

"Hey," Helena became stern and put her hand on Charlene's shoulder, squeezing a little harder than she intended, making Charlene quiet down. "This career may not be what you intended, but just remember, your parents were spies, for want of a better phrase, and they had a good life."

"Until they tried to kill one another!" Charlene blurted.

Helena froze. "What?"

"Oh, did I not tell you? Must have slipped my mind," the vitriol and sarcasm came out at full strength, like hammer blows.

"I remembered a whole saga of details during my, transformation into Chi'mera," her eyes drying up and her voice dropped dangerously. "When my mother was trying to sacrifice me to the Demon, she and dad had a little spat," she turned her back, then whipped back around. "They were trying to kill each other with knives; she stabbed him as the Demon tried to claim me," she closed her eyes, the tears restrained by force of will.

"The only person that really bothered about it all was my uncle. He came to collect me after the battle; even he left after that, placing me in care. Of course, I was only there for a few days before my Mentor decided that he could place me in a special apprenticeship scheme. After that only he took any care of me."

Helena frowned, that had not been in the reports they'd received, "but, what about social services, the reports said you did not enter the program until later." Oops.

"The reports?" Charlene's voice dropped even lower; her head tilted dangerously. "Reports?"

"Ah, hmm, Craig said that it was M.I.X. that put you into care, with the shock and all; and your contact with the supernatural, he requested regular," Charlene's face was going dark red, then suddenly went pink again.

"Yeah, not the first time he's been wrong," the voice was now normal again; suspiciously so. "I think, I think I will have 'words' with him after this," striding out of the house towards the Barn.

"Rats! I'd best warn Craig about that conversation before she starts it," Helena muttered, imagining the conversation deteriorating quickly, given Charlene's currently volatile nature; the images that came up were not pretty, not pretty at all.

"Hi, Char, what's up?" Simon saw her red eyes and generally agitated demeanour.

"Nothing!" She barked.

Simon knew he was not the most sensitive of people, but even he could see the barely concealed distress. He also knew however that he was not the best at dealing with people when they were upset. Still, there was something that he suspected might work, especially for Charlene. He could deflect that distress.

"Good. Then perhaps you could give me a hand here. I need our expertise on these things you brought back," calmly pointing out the extras she'd brought back. Charlene was a little surprised at the number; there were dozens of them, and her distress was suddenly lost in the complexity of a scientific problem.

"Hmmm. I remember them, but," there was a group of small green ones," I don't remember them."

"Oh? How'd they get in there then? Magic?" he asked casually, suddenly remembering who was with her at the time, his mouth turning down.

Charlene was about to snap back but saw his face. "No," she started to lose the severity in her face, "I don't think Jack would have known what to add, although he might have added a few things that might have some unexpected effects. Handkerchief production, opening locks, etc."

At that, even Simon smiled, "best check them all out, just in case they're useful."

She looked at one of the small green things; a mini-circuit board, about the size of a USB interface, by eye, then through her HUD interface. It looked like one of the needed parts, except it had no serial number on it, just some microscopic scratches, probably from being carried on the bag with the other devices. Wait. Hadn't she seen the number before?

"Looks fine. I'll run it over the pad and see if it can hold a charge."

She placed the chip on the pad borrowed from the university, and ran a scan, using a program from her interface. All the stats looked fine, but there was a strange energy signature spike from it, and while she was no electronics expert, it seemed functional. If Simon had seen it, he'd probably have spotted something was strange about it, but he was busy actually putting the equipment in the suit. "All Ok," she reported, passing the chip across to Simon and in it went as part of the comms system; there were a few slight positional issues, then it was in, and the cover was closed.

"Ok. Let's move on to the distribution units." Simon instructed.

Deep in the comms section, the green unit seemed to glow slightly and produce a few extra strands of wire, linking itself to other parts of the unit; the activity only lasting the briefest instant, then it was over. The unit was ready to fulfil its function; even having repaired a hairline crack in the casing that Simon had not noticed and improved the efficiency by one point three five nine one four, approximately, per cent.

Jack woke at about mid-day. He'd never really been one to sleep in frequently, but recently sleep had been an optional extra. Listening carefully, the others had returned and were apparently starting to get lunch ready; Simon and Charlene's voices echoing upstairs.

He peeked in at John but saw there was no change, risking going in and wetting his college's lips with some water. Someone had obviously been giving him something earlier, a damp sponge laying on the bedside table, with a glass of liquid, which he risked a smell of, causing his eyes watered.

"It's a concoction of my own devising."

Jack jumped, at the voice, from the doorway.

"Chi'mera, do you have to do that?" hearing a wicked little chuckle burbling from just inside the door.

"Oh? When you appear out of nowhere, it's funny, but, when I do it, you complain?"

He pulled his mouth a little, thinking it over then started to justify it, "don't." Charlene suggested, quite firmly. He tugged again. She seemed more cheerful now, better not spoil it.

"What is it?" pointing to the tear-inducing liquid.

"Energy Drink concentrate, with a relaxant," He face assuming a worried look at that point, "don't worry, Helena cleared it. The chemical formula would blow your mind, so I'll not tell you exactly what it is, and the technical name, would stretch your linguistic capabilities anyway." She kind of pursed her lips, "even I have to take a deep breath, before having a go." She looked down at him, and suddenly he realised, she was not smiling at him, or to him, but for him.

"I'm, sorry," her head slightly bowed. He realised that she was apologising, not just for the latest issues, but for all she had done before, and, that she wanted to clear the air, of everything.

He really did not know what to say. For Charlene, this would be like the queen bowing before one of her subjects, and if anything, it showed she really wanted his friendship, not just now, but as a lasting thing.

He put on his most serious face, "my friend, we," and he waved his hand between them, "have been through so much, and endured so much in the past weeks; You most of all." He bowed his head to their hands. "Do not be sorry for your part in making us what we are, or will be," and with that, a small, fresh yellow, rose appeared in their linked hands.

Her eyes began to fill, as he pushed it to her, but the smile on her face was worth it, the strangest thing was; he'd no idea on how the rose had actually appeared there.

"Come," she said to him trying to get herself under control again blaming the alien Nanites, for still messing up her systems; anyone else might have admitted it being repressed feelings coming out, having been suppressed for far too long; she would not.

Helena and Simon were busy discussing the pros, and cons, of a healthy diet when Jack and Charlene came down, the conversation faltering as the two of them reach the kitchen, as it was pretty evident by the looks on their faces that something significant had just happened.

"John, ok?" Helena looked concerned.

"What? Oh fine, he's quiet," Charlene sniffed, blowing her nose on one of Jack's handkerchiefs, rose in hand. Helena looked at Jack, questioningly, but he deferred to his new friend, a looking saying it was something positive for a change.

"Charlene can tell you when she's ready," he said looking at her, her nod saying she'd address them all, in time. Helena looked at Jack suspiciously, but she'd seen the nod from Charlene and took it to mean all was well.

Jack sat next to Simon, and filched a piece of bread, as Simon tried to catch Charlene's attention, from the rose she was finding a vase for. Helena brought over some more food, replacing Simon's bread before he actually noticed it had gone. Her look of reproach did not phase Jack, causing him to simply grin at her, "got to keep in practice. Otherwise, I get sloppy."

Charlene sat beside Simon, having seen his attempts to catch her eye, her plate heaped with masses of meat and cheese, banana's and pineapple, which she started on immediately. Simon looked at it and sighed, "I'd hoped to get an early start after lunch but," he indicated the meal for ten before her. Helena looked again at Jack, using eye contact to ask the question again.

Charlene caught the look, "the answer is no," the tone was not snappy, just so neutral that it almost seemed like she was hiding something. Charlene put her cutlery down and sigh, more at the necessity of clearing the air before eating as anything else, a little note of exasperation creeping into her voice.

"We talked a lot last night is all and, I," she hesitated, chewing her lip a little, "apologised to Jack for everything," ending the sentence in a rush, Helena's eyes shooting up. Charlene missed that, as she'd already started to plough through the food. The others seemed to take that as a signal to clear up their dishes and go to the kitchen, Charlene not looking up, being thoroughly embarrassed by it all.

Jack came past Helena, and she grabbed his arm, "she OK? You know she did not need to apologise for anything."

Jack smiled, glancing at Charlene, then back, "you know that and I know that, but she felt that she needed to. For all her toughness on the outside, that is one hurt young girl. She needed to express it in a way that allowed her to purge it from her system somehow."

"And has she?" the look was direct, and Jack's return look was cool, but sincere,

"Yes, a little bit. As her friend, "and he stressed the word emphatically; leaving Helena in no doubt that he was saying just that, "I will help her through getting the rest of it out of her system, as best I can."

Helena let him go, "you do that," and she went back to the dishes.

An hour, or two, later, Charlene finally did her dishes, then walked out to the barn, where Simon was trying to perform three calibrations at once, although when he saw Charlene coming across the courtyard, he breathed a sigh of relief.

"Ah, at last; the cavalry has arrived," he breathed, pointed to some meters on the back of the bench. "Could you grab those and see if the amperage is right in the optical sub-processer units?" proceeding to continue to do the three other calibrations himself without waiting for a reply.

"Yes, Sir!" she said, in a good-humoured, if sarcastic tone.

"With your help, we might actually be able to get this unit up and running within two weeks," he commented to no one in particular.

"That's great, but if we don't, you may have to provide support, rather than going in with the team," Charlene warned throwing him a sideways glance.

"Um hu," Simon either not actually hearing her, or choosing not to.

"After all, I know how much you hate combat," she adjusted a small power sensor.

Simon put down the circuit he'd been carefully adjusting, and moved a small power cable connected to a micro-generator; casually placed it close to Charlene's leg and switched the generator on, unleashing a bolt of electricity to arc between them. Power surged through Charlene, not enough to damage, just enough to make her jump back seriously; about five feet.

"Yowww," Charlene landing with a yelp, her hands out, ready to use her tentacles if necessary, although Simon's look was so bland that she did not know how to read it really.

"Do not mistake my Prudence and Caution, for Cowardice, Chi'mera," his voice deliberately neutral, with underlying tone of umbrage, then moving the power sensor that he'd just activated, via the shock, linked it to the circuit he'd been working on seemingly oblivious to anything out of the ordinary.

"What was that?" she demanded, a little wounded, metaphorically, by the jolt.

"Charlene?" He seemed unsure what she was asking, picking up an arm section, adding the circuit into an open compartment and closed it up.

She started forward, almost aggressively, and Simons' arm came up, the suit arm fully active, aimed right at her face.

"When the time comes, Charlene, I'll be ready; if it comes to a fight." He looked down the length of his arm at her eyes. There was something really disturbing about the look he gave her. Was he talking about the fight with the Ghe'Dar, or someone else?

Then he smiled, so warmly that she did a double take. "Well. That's the arm weaponry, altered. I don't need to open the suit up now, to channel my electric bolts; and I did an upgrade on the power amperage too. I'll be able to recharge my batteries using the solar photoelectric transfer from the camouflage system; at least, once that is up and running."

For once, it was Charlene who felt nervous around Simon, rather than the other way around. They had not really talked much, even though they had much in common; yet now that she had, it was apparent that there was a vast gulf in their attitudes, although they still had to get on, so she lifted her hand ready for the next circuit, while stepping further away when it was handed to her; just in case. Perhaps she should just ignore his busk attitude towards people and get on with the work.

Simon looked at the equipment, and the readings he'd just, surreptitiously, taken from Charlene. The potentiometer was in the high tens of thousands, meaning he just could not stun her with his power, which also meant, that if they needed to get to the machine, as described by Jack, Charlene was the perfect candidate. He certainly could not, since his armour would act as a lightning rod, much like Helena's staff, and John just had no protection from the discharges. Jack might have been the obvious answer, but Simon was of the opinion that since he'd been in the machine before, he'd be too close to his other self for comfort. Besides, he did not have the knowledge of the Alien machines that Charlene did. No: it required Charlene, much as he suspected that she would insist on fighting the Ghe'Dar there. Normally, John would be making these decisions, but with him out of play, Simon knew that he was the best chance of getting the job done. John and Charlene were good planners and intelligent, but they were both too close to this battle with the Ghe'Dar.

They were not the real enemy here; the machine was, and he needed to crack the problem, modify and redirect the power matrix, so that when they arrived at CERN, he could send a massive electro-kinetic pulse into the portal, collapsing this end of the portal, 'squeezing' all the ships in transit back out through the other end. Should any of the ships' engines go critical, the shock waves would amplify the effect at the other end, destroying the enemy fleet and everything else in a large radius.

He casually calculated the radius of the blast, based on the exotic matter potential, the amount available and the engine size, and found it would be about nought point nought one AUs, or about one million miles, assuming only one unit went critical. Most likely it would be far in excess of that; perhaps even enough to vaporise their home planet. He considered this possibility, bearing it with great fortitude. They would have felt no remorse, compassion or sympathy, nothing, about doing the same, if it were necessary and, although the others might have relented on this, he could not; besides there was little else he could do. If they just shut the machine off, the Ghe'Dar would only find another way to come to their world, or another just like it, and ravage it. No; they had to be stopped here.

He almost found it fitting that they were providing the means for their own destruction; just as they had tried to use Charlene's work to try to conquer humanity. It seemed that, even in human affairs and trials, there was a balance of nature; one that Charlene was probably quite in tune with. Poetic Justice? Well yes; but the simple fact that the Ghe'Dar would probably not even know what poetry showed just how much they needed to be eradicated from the Cosmos. Bah. He did not need to justify their eradication any more than Charlene needed to justify killing cancer cells. It just needed doing for the universe to survive.

He ploughed on. So many circuits needed adjusting, not just for the battle damage, but to recalibrate the suit for his newly incorporated systems, and, his own personal comfort. Besides, several systems just would not come up yet. He did not know what they did, but there were tantalising hints, here and there, that the suit could integrate with other systems; access ports, with no equipment that matched up internally, redundant security protocols, that were so heavily encrypted they were in effect in a different language. Lots of things. But no matter what they were or how deeply hidden they might be, he would find out what they did. He would make it his life's work if necessary; on the days he was not saving the world of course.

He'd best tell Charlene his plan later. She seemed to get a little touchy when he sprang surprises on her; not a good idea, without his suit on anyway. Still, it had been a little fun to pull that one on her.

Haines pulled up, to a small restaurant in the outskirts of Dijon, in a 'borrowed' Citroen. The cathedral city lit by cascades of rich golden lamps in the twilight and, the distant burble of city noises balanced by the local wildlife signalling the end of the day, giving it an air of rural civilisation, that larger cities tended to drown out.

"I remember this place," commented Ricks, pulling on some black gloves and turning to Haines with a slightly sardonic look.

"Yeah. Five one five zero nine zero," Haines pursed his lips.

"Strange text number," Gareth looked puzzled.

The others snorted in derisory laughter, "it's the scores we had in the three fights we had here," the two un-holstering their guns, flicking off the safeties, and opened the doors of the car.

"She might say hello first," Ricks suggested, palming a stun grenade.

"Nah, you know her, besides even if, by some miracle, she did forgive me for messing up her plan last time, she'd kill any security she had if they let people like us near her without a fight." The other semi-nodded, acknowledging the point.

"Legs and wrists, then" Haines nodded.

"I'd almost rather kill them; that'll put them out of business." Ricks not liking to cripple people like this, thinking the alternative was cleaner.

Haines shrugged, "consider it a simple way of them getting early retirement."

Gareth was listening to these two with growing horror. Yes, he was a seasoned agent, but these two sounded so heartless. Haines caught the look.

"You get used to it," he looked at the younger man.

Ricks looked at him. "Well it's that, or you retire or get retired," he said lifting his gun. Gareth set his face and un-holstered his weapon, then smiled putting it behind his back, instead producing a strange looking semi-automatic pistol, with a small-bore barrel, from the back seat.

"I brought just the thing. Latest thing from R&D," the two pros looking at it dubiously.

"Leave the guards to me," Gareth strode forward a confidently, "you find Selena."

The two looked at one another then shrugged, starting around the back.

Gareth opened the door to the restaurant with a gun hidden under his long coat, hand in pocket; on the trigger guard.

"Welcome Sir, how many will the table be for?" a smart, efficient waiter, pounced on the new customer, as he shuffled through the door, "will it be smoking or non-smoking?"

Gareth smiled at the waiter, flicking his gun out, "Non-smoking."

The waiter's face was shocked, but his hand started to reach for the suspicious bulge in his own jacket, stepping a fraction closer, before Gareth shot him, the thin dart hitting the waiter in the neck, firing a brief, but powerful, shock into the nervous system, along with a short-term nerve toxin. The effect was simple, the man dropping like a lead weight on a plumb line.

Gareth swept his eyes and weapon around the room, dropping staff packing side arms, and customers in droves. Other people in the room, customers, and visitors started standing, swearing or screaming in consternation.

A waitress came through the door, saw the commotion and started back into the kitchen, receiving a glancing blow from a dart as she went, collapsing through the door; plates clattering alarms into the tiled room beyond, her unconscious body keeping the swing door open.

"Blast," swore Gareth leaping forward, dodging past customers and ducking down past those trying to grab him or sprinting out the building. Those that tried to grab him, from a misguided sense of public spirit, received a swift clout, from his free hand, at the base of the jaw; rendering them unconscious and thus out of the way. He slunk through the doors, keeping low, and feeling a volley of small arms fire passing just above his head, probably from the cook and his assistant. In his experience, cooks really hated being disturbed, but this pair was taking the biscuit. So be it he thought, unclipping a couple of stun grenades and lobbing them in a low arc in the direction the shots were pinging from, then quickly clamped his eyes and ears shut, knowing the mark six stun grenade was more effective than the usual flashbangs.

The detonation, amongst the pots and pans, resounded around the kitchen like a truck dropping off a cliff, continuing as pans cascaded off shattered shelves, impacting with steel cutlery and shattered pottery. After the cacophony subsided, he poked his hand out from behind the bench he'd been using as cover, and since no one shot at it, he peeked carefully out, then moved up. There were actually four shooters, all spark out. He twitched a little, "Well I'll have to give the R&D boys four out of four for that."

He started upstairs; a path of the unconscious and incapacitated trailing in his wake.

Haines and Ricks had decided that coming across from the next building was probably the safest route, and while Gareth may not be as experienced as them, he was considerably more skilful and accurate, so when he said he'd take care of it, they knew he would.

The pair entered through the, suspiciously open, roof access door.

"Ah here you are," came an impatient female voice through a hidden speaker, "you might have knocked."

"We thought about it, but having you shoot us as we waited, would just be unprofessional now wouldn't it?" Haines looked around, spotting the wall-mounted camera, smiling winningly at it.

"Oh! So, we're professional now?" the voice casting sarcasm like a net over him, making him wince; asking so many questions, in that short sentence.

"We tried it other ways before, remember?" Haines tone was slightly sad, if partly nostalgic.

"Yes. We did at that. Good days though," and there was a note of longing for a return to those 'simpler' days.

"We are here on important business," Ricks interrupted the pair, trying to break the mood of nostalgia, that might drag the couple into something they did not have time for.

"Important enough to kill all my security?" Selena was watching Gareth moving through to the second floor now. Boy, he was top class, maybe even better than Haines.

"Selena," Haines face, cleared of the nostalgia now, looked up at the camera, "M.I. are on full alert. I need your help." Ricks looked as if Haines had just committed a cardinal sin, Haines lifting his hand, and nodding at the camera.

"I'm not M.I. any more, you know that" Haines' eyes were pained, but Ricks' shot up, not having known Selena was M.I. at all, "you made sure that I was 'removed' from active service."

"No histrionics Selena. I'm field officer here, and I can make sure you are heard out in full, this time," his look turning professionally serious, indicating he was being genuine.

"An amnesty?" Was that hope in her voice?

The pair were eyeing up the doors; one on the left and one ahead of them. She could be behind either.

"A fair trial is all I can offer," Haines words held a note of pain.

"We all know where that would leave me, don't we?" Selena's voice hardened with cynicism again. "Perhaps I should take my chances."

"This is no political threat, Selena, we're talking about the real end of the world scenario," he raised his voice slightly, "it's a Reaper 9, and the world is counting on your help."

Ricks indicated left, and Haines marginally shook his head, arguing patience.

"You're not serious," Selena's voice seeming shocked. For all her cynicism, she'd never really thought that she'd hear that level of code from anyone.

"People are dying as we speak," strictly speaking true, "it's in its' final stages, and we are the last line of defence," he was appealing to her family history, as members of the French resistance during WWII, her parents having aided the allies as the Germans invaded France, and later when they had tried to repel the D-Day landings.

"But, why you?" There was hurt all over the question.

"Because we are the professionals!" He was not only including the team he was with but her too. The door ahead clicked, and swung open, revealing a middle-aged woman, years older than Haines, with scraggly hair, in an ugly brown dress. Ricks frowned, it was not what he was expecting; Haines had always described Selena as a great beauty.

Haines saw a vibrant young woman, dressed as richly as a princess, her eyes a little raw, as though she'd been crying, or was extremely tired.

"Hello," he looked at her, speaking softly.

She looked at him, then whipped out a gun from her dress.

He looked at her sadly, not reacting, "I'm sorry," he looked at her again.

"Sorry? SORRY!" she released the safety, "your little witch hunt lost me my career, my family and all my friends; you were very 'professional' then."

"Your family was trafficking people across Africa and Europe, while you turned a blind eye to it all, at best, or worse, helped them. Either way, running did not help, and that's what lost you your friends, not me," he stepped forward, but she thrust forward with her gun.

"Well I may not be able to get my friends back, but I can avenge my family."

"You tried that last time, remember; you could not bring yourself to pull the trigger."

"I've had time to think about it since then, and you deserve to pay!" and she started to squeeze the trigger.

He closed his eyes, a faint 'phut' sounded in the room, as Gareth dropped her.

Ricks saw Selena drop, "GREAT! What now?" he exclaimed, more with relief than with surprise. Gareth really was indeed, very good.

"Now we try hacking her kit until she wakes up and tells us the codes," Haines shrugged, taking her gun, and lifting her carefully on a sturdy wooden chair, hands cuffed behind her back through, rather than around, the chair back.

"She won't you know," Ricks was merely stating a fact, rather than asking.

"Give us the codes?" Haines tried to get her balanced on the chair so that she did not fall off while unconscious.

"Be convinced that is all happening," Gareth agreed with Ricks.

"Let me worry about that. So far, I've played fair. Later I might cheat," Haines looked at Ricks, who glanced sideways at Gareth, nodding.

"OooK."

Selena woke up slowly, feeling like she'd been drinking heavily, and while she knew what that felt like, did not remember having done it recently. Then she remembered Haines, trying to sit upright and failing, and noticing the handcuffs and Haines sat in front of her.

She sat back, "this won't work, mon amie, I'm not falling for this trick."

Haines just sat there, staring at her for a while with her returning the stare harder. After a few minutes, she bit, "well are you going to say anything?"

He flipped his head at the other two, who looked at each other nervously, knowing they did not have much time before the police arrived, sirens in the distance saying minutes at most. They nodded and headed out, "Pizza?" Ricks asked,

"Yeah, the one just down the road. We'll see you there soon," Ricks and Gareth glanced at one another again, then dashed off.

"You want me to do this the easy way, or are we back to recriminations?" Haines turned to Selena.

"Ah, poor, Davey boy, you were always one for the dramatic," She drawled, rolling her eyes in amused ridicule.

"I don't have time for this, I need you to get your network to make a delivery in two weeks; men, weapons, machines, and support."

"What you going to do, Davey? You know I can take as good as you give."

"Cut the Davey out Selena. I know your weak points, just like you know mine, or did."

"You cannot hurt my family anymore Davey, but yours; they can still get hurt," strangely the words came across more as a concern, than a threat.

His eyes locked on hers, "your contacts have been holding out on you Selena; you cannot hurt them anymore," the pain in his voice was palpable. His eyes dropped to his left hand, the inscription on the ring was hidden since he'd received the news.

Selena stopped and followed his gaze, eyes going wide, "no," her attitude changed markedly, her eyes softening, her voice subdued.

He nodded, "air crash, a few months back. At least," he paused breathing heavy, "at least it was quick. They said that" his professional edge dulled slightly, he coughed, "they said that it was too sudden for the pilot to recover."

Selena was suddenly filled with a little remorse, and she rattled her cuffs, "let's go. You can tell me on the way." He looked up, with suspicion in his eyes, but he knew her well enough that the look she returned was genuine. He pulled out the key and undid her cuffs.

She laid a hand on his shoulder, "they did not deserve it."

"I know, and when I find out who sabotaged the nav. system," he left it hanging, but the shock on her face was so sudden that he now knew it had not been her. Well, one less to check after, though that still left quite a list. They moved silently out the window, down the fire escape and left the side ally as the police and ambulance arrived.

"You'll need to get better security," he said trying to get back on safer ground between them, now that he'd managed to get her onboard.

"Perhaps I should go elsewhere. They were the best I could get from around here."

"Perhaps. If any of us survive this," she was looking at him in a peculiar way.

"When and where?" was all she said, and he knew what she was asking.

"They were flying in from the islands, along the highland route when an unexpected storm hit. The vis. was low and the nav. system failed at the crucial point, causing them to hit a peak. They hit at nearly three hundred mph, something even I would not survive. That was four weeks ago."

So, fresh for him, Selena realised. "How'd you figure it was sabotage?" She linked arms with him, making it look like they were a couple, which they had been once, in a strange kind of way; old memories of a desperate race from enemy agents filled her mind.

"They made the mistake of leaving someone behind that knew," the memory of the fate of that one still burned on his mind.

"I mean how did you know to even look into it like that," She clarified softly.

"I used to fly, remember? I know how those planes work and how well trained the pilots are. When the black box was recovered, I had it hacked and did the maths. Even with bad weather, the pilot would have had three systems yelling at him before he ploughed into the ground. There were no bullet holes, explosives or toxins, so, sabotage."

They walked for a little way, then entered the pizzeria, where the other two looked strangely at them, when they entered arm-in-arm, Gareth handing Ricks a ten euro note. Haines shook his head in apology to Gareth but did not relinquish Selena's arm, something Ricks raised his eyebrows at.

"So, mon amie, you want me to start a revolution? Or was your code phrase real?"

As there was no-one else in the place, he leaned forward, "Yes it was real, but we have sketchy intel. on what is required. The source just said bring everything we could, time and place. That suggested you," Selena rolling her eyes, in mock gratitude.

"Think it's time to call his father?" Ricks added.

"He said nearer the time. It's only been a day or so."

"His Father?" Selena frowned.

"He gave us a phone, company special, to contact them nearer the time," Haines indicating it was not time yet.

"Perhaps I could have a look and get some more info. from it," Selena said casually, at which point both men shook their heads.

She smiled guiltily, "cannot fault a girl for trying."

Haines looked around casually and produced two things from under his jacket. His spare gun and a phone. She looked a little startled, "you're serious about this being big, aren't you."

"The more I think about what Gareth here told me, the more I think we are in deep water, and the sharks are closing in." Selena was more worried now. Haines had been in many scrapes, many prisons, and many life and death situations. This was the first time he seemed unsure and, scared, genuinely scared, in turn making her nervous; he was never afraid, sometimes even when he should have been.

Selena looked down for a moment, making her decision. "Ok, I have a few calls to make, and some very old family debts to call in. You'll get the best, and a few more that can get the vehicles," she promised, tipping her hand this way and that. "The aircraft we can get here by truck, using the airport as a staging ground once whatever is happening has begun."

Haines looked at her, "we'll stake out the target location; carefully. This is no training mission. This is the end game. Our end, if we mess this up; and I still have lots to do, before I retire," he slipped a glance at Selena, "or I am retired," who pursed her lips, but did not a response to the challenge implicit in the look.

"We'll wait until four days before the date until we contact the others," Ricks just shrugging at the random number, "that way we can always alert you to any change in plans, but still give our contact time to get things in place."

Haines slipped Selena something, which she palmed and slid into her jacket pocket.

They all nodded agreement, then split up, set about trying to get a small army ready to face an unknown alien onslaught.

"You told her, didn't you," Ricks caught up with Haines, as they piled into the car.

"Yes, most of it" he sighed, "it was the only way. She'd never have done it otherwise. If she believes they are dead then she will think she has a chance at me," he said without conceit.

"They might still be you know, given that information the Gareth and GhostKnight gave us," Ricks said it quietly, to try and discount the possibility.

"They said that the scientists were disappearing, developing some kind of bio-weapon, something Jas had expertise in."

"It would explain why they were not found amongst the wreckage," stated Ricks.

"If they took her, there is still hope. Otherwise," he stopped, starting the engine and driving off.

Ricks starred after him, "otherwise, someone will find a certain agent starring down at them, and wishing that they were the ones who'd died."

The comms. crackled a little, "Alpha One, Alpha one. Come in," Gareth's voice seemed relaxed enough, if urgent.

"Alpha One. Report. Over," Haines was not in the mood for talking.

"Alpha One, have details of the local police report of the incident at the previous location. Over," Gareth's voice sounded excited.

"Incident? Over," Haines was interested but hardly enthused.

"Alpha One, I'm en-route. Meet me there. Over and Out." Haines scowled at the diversion.

"This had better be good," Haines growled, teeth grinding.

"So, what we got?" Haines came into the campus grounds, just outside a police cordon, all impatience, and irritation.

"Robbery, from two of the labs," Gareth was looking at a notepad, as though he was a detective.

"So? That's what local police are for. I know we were interested in certain scientists, but surely not everything that happens to them?" rolling his eyes at Ricks, who seemed to share his opinion.

Gareth liked his lips, "unless someone happens to be stealing micro-electronics and nano-tech scanners," the other suddenly becoming more interested.

"Hmmm; the kind that might be used in creating a biotech weapon?" Haines made a great leap to get there, but then that's why he was the top dog.

"Possibly. I managed to get to the server with the CCTV footage," the others looking around the campus frowning, no cameras in sight.

"What footage?"

Gareth grinned, pointing to the tops of the building where there were IR communication arrays between the labs. deep in the shadows, amongst all the metal was a large black dome. "Yeah, I did not see them for what they are either; but apparently one of the companies insisted on having them installed before they would build their office here. Their buildings swarming with them, but out here that's the only one."

Haines grinned too, "if you missed it, that means,"

"Ahead of you, boss," producing a tablet from under his coat, starting a video clip.

"Most of the footage is just wandering students, but this is what I wanted to show you," pressing play and there, clear as day was Charlene, practising her shapeshifting, the faces on the different agents speaking volumes.

"Here it comes," Jack appearing beside her, the pair heading off in the direction of the Engineering labs, where the theft had been discovered.

"Ah! Our amateur M.I. Agent and the shapeshifter from the Paris lab," Haines thinking rapidly.

"Oh, there is more!" Gareth added, fast forwarding the video, while making sure they were still out of sight of others. The camera number changed and the time index was slightly later. The Starling enterprises building was shown in the background, the guard letting in a girl. As they watched, the girl went in and up the stairs with equipment; the man appearing again when they were out of sight of the guard. He fast forwarded again and about ten minutes after the girl left, still carrying the box, another visitor arrived.

"Is that?" Haines asked.

"Craig Starling? Yup, the great man himself. Entrepreneur, Recluse and, it seems, International Traveller," Gareth confirmed.

"When did his plane arrive?" Ricks queried.

"That's the rub; it did not. He did not get here, by plane."

"Hmmm," Haines was still thinking. Was this all connected?

"Ok, here comes the delicious bit," Gareth really enjoying this, putting to rest so many questions. Starling walked out of the building at speed, followed five seconds later, by a blur of dim movement from the back of the building. Haines frowned. "What was that?"

Gareth rewound the image, then zoomed in on the blur, enhancing the image using a personal algorithm. As the picture cleared, there appeared, in all his majesty, "Gravitron," Haines sounded almost sick, rather than surprised, the others looking at him, showing theirs, "I saw him fight a group of terrorists once; they did not really stand a chance." He said in answer to their question. "It's all true then," Haines' voice was not precisely panicky, almost like he'd hoped that it was all something else, anything else; a lesser problem, or a fake.

"But, Starling?" Ricks questioned.

"Who better than a recluse?" Ricks nodded slightly, putting together the pieces.

"Never mind that," Gareth diverted them, "what about our thieves?"

"Well, yes," Haines thought a second. "Two main possibilities. Either they had become turncoats, and are helping the enemy, including trying to delay any action being taken before they were ready, or, they are trying to help, and are taking countermeasures against the bioweapon." He did an imaginary toss of a coin, it comes down on the 'they were helping' side.

"We carry on as before, but I think I should lay a little groundwork with Starling. It appears we may be working on the same case, and that needs a little inter-departmental cooperation."

"Also a good way to confirm what has been passed to us, right?"

"Absolutely!" Haines did not like working in the dark, it was time to turn on the lights.

Craig Starling was perusing the latest set of unusual incident reports, nothing too startling for the most part. The shipments he'd sent to Switzerland had taken a detour to avoid an accident and were stuck driving through bad weather in the north, making heavy going of it. The southern vehicles were laid over for a day, in Annecy, using a more central tac to their actual destination. The mech unit had reported that they'd secured a hangar at the airport, though they had some concerns about the local security, always a problem. A few other reports from the region suggested that they were not the only ones encountering problems; some containers were lost en-route, a whole vehicle had disappeared, crew and all coming north; no alarm and the GPS going suddenly quiet, perhaps unrelated, but maybe not.

In his business, paranoia was a prerequisite.

"Mr. Starling?" Helena's voice on the intercom was loud and clear, as always.

"You have a call on line two. He's calling about an appointment he says you made with his office; something about a future operation?" Her voice was slightly surprised.

Craig knew the code protocol. Talking about the future was a tarot reading, of which The Grim Reaper was one. Someone out there had picked up his localised message and was asking for clarification. Not unusual, except for the fact that they were directly calling his HQ, meaning either his security was compromised, or the caller was remarkably good, something which needed establishing, before he talked to the man.

"Helena, tell Isabella, we have a hot call," meaning his hacker should be tracing it. Helena made sure Isabella was on the case immediately. He reached for the phone and picked it up after the trace light showed green.

"Afternoon Starling Enterprises, Craig Starling speaking."

"This is the Zodiac Clinic, I am ringing to confirm your appointment date, is that line clear on the document?"

"Yes, the documentation is perfectly clear," he waited for another green light on his screen that showed up seconds later.

"We're secure sir," came Isabella's voice on the line, "however, there is a sniffer worm in the system. I'll keep you free, as long as I can," for the first time since he'd recruited her she sounded uncertain.

"Codename?" Craig challenged.

"Foxtrot, Romeo, Zero, One. Paris. Alpha One," Craig waited, until another green light come up, accompanied by a face on an active M.I. 6 service record, the experience displayed was impressive, explaining how he'd managed to call the office directly.

"Evening, what can I do for you," he did not want to use names even now.

"We have been given a Reaper 9 imperative, can you confirm?"

"Confirmed," he kept his voice level, even though his own surety was less than one hundred per cent.

"We have been told that channels have static. Can you confirm?" meaning official lines were compromised; that explained why they were calling directly.

"Confirmed," given that Isabella was fighting a trace worm at the moment, it was reasonably obviously true too.

"We are currently working on a missing persons case; it appears it may be related, can you confirm."

"Sir the worm is starting to peel through the encryption, you have twenty seconds tops," Isabella voice sounding strained, and incredulous.

"Confirmed. Alpha One, proceed with mission as per message," and he put down the receiver, cutting the line before it went red.

The three agents were all sat in a car, on the side of the dark, empty road in the outskirts of the town.

"Confirmed," Haines finished, but the line was already dead.

"Well, that's that. We go where we're told and do what we need to do."

"So where next?" Ricks and Gareth asked in unison.

"I think we need to get a closer look at CERN," he said almost to himself.

"A bit soon, isn't it?" Gareth disliked disobeying instructions.

"I don't like surprises," muttered Haines.

"Especially ones involving bad intel," Ricks added.

"Especially those. They can get a great many people killed," Haines muttered, starting the engine, and driving towards Switzerland. He especially disliked being led around by the nose.

"Isabella?" Craig called out in the office.

"Sorry, lost it. As soon as the phone went down, the code vanished; erasing the signal trace logs with some sort of smart code. It's using a type of weird logic I've never seen before; almost like a different language."

Craig smiled indulgently. Sometimes, it was like speaking to a Junior school girl, the way her sentences were so clipped and precise, and virtually incomprehensible to anyone who did not speak 'computerese.' He looked at her for a few seconds bemused, but she did not look up to clarify anything she'd said. He decided to let the first sentence be the answer; he doubted that if she did try and clarify it at all, that he'd understand that either.

"Something he said was of interest," Craig sat near the furiously typing girl. "He mentioned that they were working on a missing person case, which is usually the province of the local or national police, not military intelligence." He thought a moment, then something clicked, "I want you to access the SOC, Interpol and PNC databases, and run a correlation program on missing persons," Craig knew this was a herculean request, and saw on her face it would take time.

"Oh, not urgent I hope, but let's see if any missing persons matching the following criteria," and he rattled off the subjects from the letter.

"Is that all the detail you have?" she asked. "In the old days that would have been a small community, now-a-days there are lots of them."

"Well, not on the missing person's database," he countered.

"True, assuming people have been reported missing," her mind had leapt at a possibility he'd not considered. He must be getting slow.

"Oh," he sounded a bit crestfallen, "yes, what if they are missing, but, no one has reported them missing," knowing at least one in that category, but not saying. He was glad he'd caught her talent before others had, else his job now would be near impossible.

"I'll do a pattern matching 'bot. It'll take a couple of hours to set up the code and the links via the net to the databases, but I'll get it done," her supreme confidence back after the battle with the worm, so he left her to it.

329

Chapter 16

STORM CLOUDS GATHERING

It had been four days, since the recovery of the equipment, and Simon was getting a little uptight about Titanium's onboard power systems. Charlene and him, had initially had a great deal of success in integrating, both the repaired items and new circuits; the arm modifications having been slotted in quickly, the power monitors and regulators had all taken a few hours at most, in fact, the items that still required installing was remarkably few; below a dozen.

However, even with Charlene's, oops, he meant, Chi'mera's aid, he was having a devil of a time balancing the systems power requirements. It was, almost, as if there was a certain amount of impedance, throughout the system, that should not be there. When he measured all the electrical components individually, using calibrated meters, they were fine. Start them up together, and they started screaming that they lacked enough power. Something was either wrong with the system, or there was a significant power drain on the units from an external source; the problem was driving him absolutely berk!

"Two one five?" he called over to Charlene, who was monitoring the module they had just recently pulled to re-check, focusing on its power usage, hoping for some indication of the problem. "Two one five, check." She glanced at the module then flicked back to the reading.

Simon adjusting the setting again, "two, two five?"

"Two, two five, check," the current problem was the switching voltages fluctuated wildly.

"Two-thirty?" he asked hopefully.

"Nope. It just jumped to two, seventy-five," causing Simon to slam his fist onto the table.

"Damn it," Charlene tried to say something, but Simon started to curse and swear.

"All right, Simon," Charlene said looking at the circuit again. Why did she keep inspecting the damn things; they had all checked out at the university, yet, she found her eyes drawn to them, more and more; weird.

"There were no other spikes that might indicate a short?" She shook her head.

"Nope nothing, it was so smooth, you might want to patent this circuit for military use; they always like the good kit." The comment was supposed to elicit some laughter, but he was in no mood for joviality. He stomped around, looking at a colossal circuit diagram on the board, that Charlene barely understood, except the parts he'd explained.

She looked at the circuit again, frowning, "doing it again girl," came the thought, so like one of Jack's that she laughed, and even as she did that, she had another.

"Simon?" She looked at him or rather turned her head towards him, while still looking at the circuit.

"Hmm?" He was turning the circuit over for the twentieth time.

"Has Jack had a look at these circuits?" She did not really understand why she was asking, but there was definitely something niggling at her subconscious, "I mean since we got them online."

"Hmm. No. Him and Helena have been watching John, and discussing Magic," he stopped his deliberations, and with only a slight interest asked, "why?"

"Because he can 'see' things that we cannot. Perhaps it's time for a new set of eyes."

"He won't understand this," he started, with no small amount of contempt in the voice; only partially deliberate.

"He won't need to. All he'll need to do is have a look at these circuits and see if there is something amiss from his point of view."

Simon frowned, looking at the circuit again, "suppose it cannot hurt," putting the circuit down, and shaking his head, not believing that he was about to do this; a top scientist asking someone to use magic to help him, feeling such a hypocrite. But then, was there anything in this whole situation, that he should really be surprised at anymore? It could not really hurt anything, except his pride.

Jack walked in and saw the tremendous amount of work that the two had achieved in just four days, the suit looking almost complete, even the little mirror panels of, what Simon had called, the camouflage system, were all in place, give or take a few imperfections.

"Charlene asked me to take a look around, said you were having some kind of power problem," he said with comical nonchalance, Charlene walking in behind him, coughing pointedly, "spoilsport," he muttered. She flicked her head scowling, indicating that this was serious. He paused then nodded more seriously, "OK, I'll have a look at the suit and see if there is anything I can see when you power it up."

Jacks eyes shifted slightly, and he started looking at the suit, Simon going over to the external power relays, activating the various sections, and waiting for Jack's verdict. Jack tried shifting his vision, as people might change the focus on a camera, finding that he had a new set of muscles that, with effort, helped him alter the type of things he could see. Its' effect would be hard to explain to someone without the same power, but he 'shifted' his vision different ways, trying to see if anything grabbed his attention, taking a few minutes starting from the top to the bottom, walking around the suit propped against the frame of the broken mirror Simon had used for the reflective panels. Trust Jack to make this theatrical, thought Charlene, as he moved up and down, humming and squinting occasionally, but apparently not spotting anything.

After about ten minutes, he'd almost exhausted all the options, when something impinged on his vision, or rather some things, tiny specks of light, barely visible even to him.

"There is something there. There, there, and there," he pointed, the others suddenly perking up from their sense of frustration, following the pointing finger.

"It's way, way, low on the range, barely perceptible as a power reading, more an electronic flicker than anything."

Charlene looked at the places he was pointing to and spotted the green units they had added to the suit, grabbing an energy meter, and ran it over the area; nothing. Simon was suddenly next to her, "what does it look like?" frowning as Charlene showed him the meter.

"It's a pinprick of green light, fluctuating slightly, like a star in the sky," Jack put his hand to his aching head, "I have to stop, or I'll strain my eyes. Never used it for this long before."

"Sure Jack, thanks," Simon acknowledged him absently, as Jack staggered away to the farmhouse, the two scientists going into a huddle around the indicated spots.

"Does not look any different other than its green."

"Perhaps the material is different somehow, causing a Piezoelectric effect," Simon muttered to himself, as much to Charlene.

She pouted a little, "or it has different circuits in it, that are doing something we don't know about?"

Simon tilted his head slightly. "Perhaps, an electronic micro-pulse. Perhaps if we," he grabbed the optical system manual; flicking through it rapidly.

"Aha!" Simon found the page he was looking for, "we take a second image, and put it through the image systems; but using the prism, we should be able to see the material spectrum and compare it with the elemental spectrum." He looked at Charlene, smiling, and saw her blank look, becoming exasperated; but he was so excited that Charlene smiled back. The phrase 'child in a sweet shop' sprang to mind. "It means we can do a material analysis without using a mass spectrometer!" She nodded, but still did not understand what he was on about, entirely, as he ran around, gathering lots of pieces of equipment and plugging them all together, the contraption forming looking like nothing short of a giant microscope.

He looked down the eyepiece expectantly, and his face dropped; Charlene, saw it and her heart sank. Nothing?

"Er, Charlene. You might want to have a look at this," as she realised Simon's face was more perplexed than disappointed; Charlene's became intrigued.

The eyepiece was big enough that she could put her whole eye to it, seeing that under the microscope, the surface was not a single material plane, but a landscape of different materials, almost like an orbital planetary map. "What the hell is that?" the surface should have been smooth at this magnification, as she read it.

"Piezoelectric effect for sure," he muttered. "Whatever that is, it ain't going to work in this suit; we'll need to use the black ones and figure out what that is another time."

"We did not get any black ones of those circuits, that's why we picked up the green ones, and they had the right numbers on them."

Simon tried to remove one of them from a circuit just to the imager and found it would not come off, "what, the blazes, is going on?" using the extractor but still failing to budge it.

"Charlene, ramp up the magnification on this one will you," he placed the circuit into the image, taking a long look. There, all around the part were small metallic tethers to the circuit board, as well as connections to other components, fine wire conduits.

"It's been bonded to the circuit, changing the configuration; no wonder it does not work as specified. Did you do this?" Simon was suspicious.

"Why me?" Charlene defended herself.

"This is not just electronics; this is Nano-tech, and you're the expert in that. Certainly not Jack, and no one else could," Simon accused.

"The Ghe'Dar?" Charlene suggested.

"This is so advanced that, if it were theirs, they wouldn't have needed your Nanites," he pointed out.

"Right!" She thought for a moment, then remembered something, "well, we did find some writing," she produced the paper they had found in the lab, Simon looking at it impatiently, then again, harder. He blinked, his face contorting like someone had hold of his ears and was trying to screw his face up. He placed the paper on the table, placing the circuit diagrams he had against it, and gave a low moan, touching a small portion of the scribble. "What is it?" Charlene had not heard that sound from Simon before but had made it herself once or twice. It was a realisation that they suddenly had so much more work to do.

"Where did you find this?" Simon was suddenly intensely interested in, what looked like a doodle to Charlene.

"I said. It was in the lab just hanging from a partition. It was not Ghe'Dar, as far as I knew, but it looked out of place so I thought I'd take it. So what is it?"

"It's part of a quantum mechanical formula," he said one eye slightly contorted in thought, "sort of. The symbology is slightly strange, but the structure is apparent. This is a fragment of, well, I don't know what, exactly; but whoever put it there knows the advanced quantum structure. Who knows, it might even be the mathematical formula for the portals. It has the look of the dimensional set theorem; sorry," as Charlene slowly shook her head to indicate he was talking 'nerd' again; a ridiculous accusation from her, "portal creation maths. The constants are missing though, "then he did a strange twitch, "no, wait, they are not. This is using a variable," he drifted off. Charlene needed to get him back on the problem at hand.

"Perhaps this explains the problem with the circuits?" she asked hopefully

"What? No? But it seems that we might have inadvertently picked up the tech from whoever wrote this," Simon said absently.

"Inadvertently? No, we were checking the numbers and the specifications," Charlene objected.

"Perhaps," Simon was thinking about both problems at once, "but more likely, you were scanned, and it changed to match your needs; well, as best it could."

"You're saying that this equipment is, what, adaptive?" Charlene was confused, sceptical and, perhaps, a little awed by the required technology.

"Probably. Do you find that so hard, given what your Nanites can do to your body? Just imagine if a machine could do that," she did that and shuddered a little at the possibilities.

"So how can we get this thing to work with us.?"

Simon was scanning the paper, only half listening. "What? Oh. Hmmm, perhaps it needs to reboot or something." He looked at the circuit and concentrating really hard raised his hand above the chip, as an almost imperceptible spark of electricity leapt from his had to one of the capacitors next to the chip in question. A tiny flicker in the lights all around announced what he'd just done.

"You can EMP circuits?" Charlene astonished, not really believing it was possible.

"First time, but then sometimes we learn by experimenting," apparently did not realise the enormity of his action. The potential implicit in the act was either something he'd not recognised, or he just did not care.

Charlene shook her head, looking at the circuit again, seeing as she watched the circuit's surface flowing with barely perceptible changes, even at this level. The material smoothed, though still undulated slightly with contours and valleys. She just blinked and stood up.

Simon, finally, put the paper down and tried the circuit again, the system registering a green light, and the meters showing green.

"Now all I have to do is reset all the green circuits," Simon muttered, "without frying the others. We will have to pull out all the green circuits so I can operate on them," Simon directing the comment at a slightly bewildered Charlene. She wondered if the others had even felt like this when dealing with her, and kind of knew the answer.

"Sure," Charlene started on the operation, realising this would probably require another few days to extract them all again, and readjust the suit for the altered properties.

She sighed.

In an office, in Troyes, one by one a set of lights went out on a display.

"Ah, you found them," came the strange voice again, sounding unsurprised, the figure standing up and moving to a box full of similar green devices. He picked one out and stroked it lightly, little arcs of electricity cascading across the surface. With a pop, a small set of wings flipped out of the device, a head appeared, the final form looking part spider, part ant, and all weird; finally, a set of two pairs of mechanical multi-jointed arms, ending in a four-way grasping claw, extended from the front.

"Keep an eye on these ones please, they show promise," he said tapping a set of numbers into the computer, addressing the newly created micro-drone. It beeped a few responsorial notes, "no, no, avoid direct contact with them. Focus on any scientists; and if our troublesome neighbours get interested, signal 01101001 and I'll take the necessary steps to discourage them." The device beeped a long series of notes in query, "well let's just say that they are talented enough for later utilisation. I need to find out if they are what we need, or just another false lead."

The little device pattered to the window sill, and started buzzing is wings. It started out the window, then hesitated when it spotted was raining, beeping a faintly complaining series of notes, as it left. The figure laughed, a semi-metallic laugh, and talked to himself, "they really don't like the liquids here. Still, better than the acid rains of some worlds," and wandered over to a small table on the other side of the large room.

".Dr. Sayers?" came a voice from an intercom.

There was a moment of quiet, a slight electronic zing being the only sound.

"Yes, Karena?" the voice suddenly that of a middle-aged human man.

"The lab has rung. Apparently, there has been a break in, your labs have been accessed and equipment removed," his PA sounded like this was a catastrophe. His own state was complete ambivalence to the old news. "The French police, Gendarme, are here, wanting to talk to you about it, to see if you know what was taken and why."

"Well now, I'm sure we can accommodate that. Tell them to come on up," he switched off the intercom and picked up another green block and ran his hand over it as he had with the other. This time it did not really change except, on his monitor, a small symbol appeared on the sidebar.

"Sorry my little friend, but you are to stay asleep. For now," the door buzzing and two officers being escorted in by the human PA.

"Gentleman, how may I help you?" He asked sitting and placing the device on the desk in front of him.

Helena and Jack sat on opposite sides of the table, having been looking at the book together, although strictly speaking, they were contemplating the outer cover. They had noticed that when Jack looked at the book, it had one title, while Helena saw another.

"It's an illusion, they're usually used to safeguard the most powerful of artefacts and a magician's Tomb," explained Helena.

"Do we have to use that term?" Jack complained, "It makes me sound like David Copperfield or Yuri Geller. Hey not that I would not love both their reputations, and their wealth, but," he left it hanging.

"They, stole the true name for people with our powers, not the other way around," Helena sounded quite passionate about that, so Jack backed off; Magician it was then.

"Strictly speaking, since this seems to only allow you near it, so far, this should be called a Grimoire." Jack opened his mouth to speak, but her finger indicated she needed to continue before any questions, Jack's mouth snapping shut again.

"I know it sounds sinister, but it's just the traditional name. Grimoire, differ from ordinary tombs in two significant ways: firstly, they are less reading material and more instruction, tailored to the magician who owns it," she emphasised the word, for Jacks' benefit, at that point he rolled his eyes, "secondly, they are not fixed text. They change, to focus the owner's power, to their will." She looked at Jack to see if he understood, the returned look was less a lack of understanding and more needing clarification.

"Ok. Say you, deep down, were more after, say, the ability to build a castle," Jack smiling at that, but accepting the premise. Helena continued, "then the book would probably be telling you how to shape stones, how to create mortar and how to lift heavy objects using spells," she lifted her hand, an image of Jack levitating stones appeared in his mind.

"Wow, that's a clever trick," Jack shaking his head, making the image vanish.

"It's a minor thing, not at all like mind control, something I can only do it with a willing subject, who is relaxed and comfortable with me do it," she explained, looking into his eyes, and speaking with a strange inflexion.

Jack smiled, "so, that must mean I am relaxed and comfortable you around."

Helena, tilted her head slightly as if trying to gauge if he'd answered her, in the way she'd actually been projecting the statement. She stood up and moved around the table, Jack obligingly moving his chair over, allowing her room next to him, to view the book together.

He smiled at her, and she at him, both looking at the book as it went totally blank.

"Hmmm, you look first, so that it is in tune with you," she instructed, turning to see him looking at her. "Ahem," She nodded sideways towards the book, and his head started to turn. She looked to see what the page they were on said, and it was still blank. "Jack?"

"Yes?" He said absently; still looking at her, just sideways.

"Look at the book, Jack!" She instructed sounding slightly cross, although the amusement at his interest was getting the better of her, coming out in her tone of voice.

"Yes Ma'am," came the snide little chuckle. Helena looked away, the other side then looked back again, the page still blank.

"Jack!" she looked straight at him, and he was about two inches from her face.

"Let's read later," he saw her looking deep into his eyes.

The book slammed shut, without either of them touching it, making them both jump and breaking that special kind of spell that only certain people can cast on one another.

Jack looked at the book and snapped, "Spoilsport!"

Helena giggled; a girly little giggle, that spoke more volumes than anything else they'd said so far today, Jack throwing his hands in the air loudly pronouncing,

"Fine! We do it your way then, lessons first," looking at the book, which obligingly opened at the page that he'd started on, now entitled, 'Controlling the Heart.'

Helena saw the title, her face contorting in amusement, while Jack's was a bit crestfallen, though he started to snigger too. Neither noticed that they were actually reading the same words now, rather than different ones. After a few minutes of reading the book's instructions, sitting close together, they ended up hand-in-hand, neither of them remembering how they had done so.

Later still, the others came in for tea, finding the book put to one side and both of them in one corner, heads close in in-depth discussion, tea un-made for the first time since they'd arrived at the farm. Simon and Charlene shared a look, "it's a kind of magic," was all she said, and coughed, to let the other know they had company.

Helena looked up, then at the clock and muttered something to Jack, causing them both to laugh and rise, heading for the kitchen. Jack was still smiling when he greeted the others.

"Share the joke?" Simon said, a bit surly after his hard day's work.

"She said as time travellers, we really should keep a better track of it," he continued to chuckle as he went upstairs to check on John again. The others just smiled; yes, there was a special kind of magic going on with those two alright.

"Let's just leave them to it," Charlene commented, Simon just nodding.

The next day, once breakfast was over, the two magicians started their huddle around the book again, the others wandering off to the Barn, from which occasional expletives came.

"So, although you have a way to channel magic; it is raw magic, not shaped by your will," Helena explained, as they tried to understand, and direct, his powers.

"What about yours?" Jack asked, "Yours expresses itself as fire, but not flame."

Helena thought about it for a few minutes, "when I was younger," Jack started to protest, that she was still young, but she placed a gentle finger on his mouth, to stop him,

"I was a bit more, fiery, and my focus was more 'elemental,'" she remembered the first day she'd learned she could use magic. "The fire brigade managed to save the school," but it was her mother who'd saved her from making the real mistake she omitted.

"A group of girls was bullying me," she continued, "there were about twelve of them. They carried on, and on, and on until I finally lost control." She looked angrier with herself than with them, "the result was not pretty; the magic just flowed from me and would have incinerated all of them, if my mother had not shielded them," Jack looked shocked.

"Oh, they were unharmed, but the incident scared me enough to never do it again," now she sounded slightly smug, although it was tempered with regret. "Mum had to wipe their memories but left the fear intact," rather subtle guilt in her voice.

"Hey, I know that feeling. I've had to do things I'm not particularly proud of, usually when gang thugs have threatened me, or someone else and I've been there." He put his hand on her shoulder, his look being one of sharing rather than anything more intimate. She looked up, her eyes expressing gratitude for both his understanding and his manner.

"Sometimes others don't give us a choice. I imagine that is why, when I tried to fend off the Ghe'Dar, my power expressed itself as a destructive force, rather than just repelling them," the conversation getting back on to safer ground, both of them sitting back a little, though still close.

"Yes, that would stand to reason, as when attacked, our most primal thought processes; self-preservation or flight, tend to guide our powers rather than conscious thought."

"So how can I do something more like you? I'd like to guide my powers towards healing, letting the power flow from me to cure those that need it."

Helena raised her eyebrows, "You just need to listen to your calmer emotions, then see what the book shows you, as I doubt the way I do it would work. As a doctor I tend to heal those I am attuned too; it's a very personal kind of healing. What you're suggesting, is actually quite different," she indicated the book and placed her hand over his eyes for a second. "Now, Calm!"

Jack closed his eyes, starting to employ the mind-calming exercise he'd first seen in the book before he'd tried to consciously direct his thought into it. He felt strange, as he started to stretch out and guide his magic to do what he wanted.

When he opened his eyes, the book was open showing him words unlike any he had ever seen before. Helena started to speak, but this time, he stopped her by trying to say the words. They sounded strange on his tongue, but he managed to enuciate them correctly as the words disappeared from the page once he'd spoken them. Once he'd reached the end of the paragraph, the book closed.

Helena looked at him and nodded, "pretty good for a first time."

Jack shook his head. "What did I just do?" Nothing had actually happened, other than the book closing.

A look came across her face, one he'd never seen before; "Helena?"

"What, sorry, it's just I don't have the words to explain what is, an intensely personal experience. Er," she seemed to come to a decision on how to explain it. "Right, ok it's like this," she stood, retrieving a pen from one of the kitchen draws, and put it on the table, with a blank piece of paper.

"Write the word for your mother," her phraseology was peculiar, but he took the pen, thought a second and wrote down 'Mother' then he put the pen down.

"Ok, now why did you use that word?" she asked intently.

"Er, well that is what I call her," he floundered a little at the simplicity of the question.

"Why Mother? Why not mom, Ma'am, mum or her name?" Helena looked questioningly into his eyes.

"It's what I have always called her," it was almost a verbal shrug.

"Ok let me put it another way. If I said 'think of your mother,' what image would it bring to your mind," for some reason this seemed important, so he thought it through.

"Well, it brings to mind the strict religious practice, the discipline she taught my brothers and me when we were brought up, and hard work" and pondered what he'd just said.

"Exactly!" Helena leapt on the sentence. "You were not just thinking of the person, but how they behaved, what they did with you and, of everything about them. When you say 'mother' it is not just a word, it is a whole lifetime of living with them, that you're expressing."

Jack nodded slowly indicating, he understood. "So, when I say the words from the book, I'm expressing a concept that goes beyond those words?"

It was Helena's turn to nod, "also, it is turning your power in the direction you want to express it; as in how you write the words." She wrote something down, "this, for instance, is 'Mother' for me," the scrawl itself did not look like a word, and Jack was frowning, when she took his hand and guided it to the book. As he touched it, the word changed and seemed to expand, as understanding came.

"You never knew yours'," he almost gasped, "but you said you had an idyllic childhood?" a welling of empathy sprang up from his soul.

"She died in labour. My Auntie brought me up with my father," there was only a little sadness in her voice, but also joy and other things, that hinted that she was not really worse off for the happenstance. "The point is, for people like us, magic is an experience, not art or science, it just is." She folded his hand in hers, then brushed it lightly with her lips; then dropped it.

"If that is the case, why do I need the book?" Jack understood some ideas, but others seemed contradictory.

"It's a focus, and sometimes an aid in understanding, where the human mind has not been before. It can give you second-hand experience of a place or concept, to help you train your mind for the real thing, without endangering yourself, experiencing it without going there. Like doing a guillotine act, without needing to put your head under the blade," using an example he was more familiar with.

"But sometimes doing something without experience can be more thrilling," suddenly pulling her near, to half-heartedly resistance.

"And sometimes you lose your head," she smiled and snapped the book closed, onto his resting hand on the page. She grinned at his yelp; even half the tomb was heavy.

"Oww, what was that for?" Jack complained, fishing his hand out of the pages.

"Just making sure that you don't' lose your head," she said dancing out of his reach. "Enough talk. You need to practice on your own, now that you understand so much more," she smiled, to soften the sarcasm. "Besides, I have to check on Simon and John."

The last word was more serious. There was something in Helena's voice that betrayed that she was concerned about the continued lack of progress there. The first few hours and days of John's coma had not been a problem really but, as time went by, everyone was getting more and more worried.

When she reached John, he had a pallor to him which had not been there before.

Moving closer, she took his pulse which was slower now, occasionally missing a beat. Whatever was going on in his head, he was getting weaker. Looking around careful she made sure she was alone, then she lifted her hands and poured her power into him, bolstering his system by giving his body extra energy.

She sighed, "master," she muttered, "his spirit is sinking too deep into the darkness. We will lose him."

"Fear not daughter," a voice responded from thin air, "he is much stronger than you understand, indeed more so than anyone understands, even himself. He will need to be as strong as any here. Be at ease, he will pull through eventually", and the voice was gone.

She wet his lips, dripping water onto them so that he'd not choke. Later she'd need to try feeding him again, else she'd have to start thinking about intravenous drips, meaning a trip to a local hospital for them all.

Simon was a little surprised, at lunch, when Helena pulled him aside, as Jack and Charlene caught up, "how's it going?" she asked trying to remember what his last update had said.

Simon's face was calm, "it's improving. I've managed to get the power up to seventy-five per cent, the armour can power up and down without sparking, and the systems stay up for nearly fifteen minutes before they start cascade failing, the last part being the current sticking point."

"How long?" It was a standard question throughout the whole repair job.

He looked at her as if to say 'really.' "As long as it takes; but in this case, the armour just needs a bit of grounding, in key areas. A few more hours today, and a bit of tomorrow and we'll be ready," meaning himself and the armour.

"Will, that get it fully operational?" Helena thought it through, if it were ready tomorrow, the team would need to start off in a few days. It would take days to get to CERN from here, a few days at least; and they would need to make contact with the M.I. team on the ground.

"Not one hundred per cent, but enough to get the job done, and that's the requirement," Simon sounded defensive.

"Easy there. I'm sure you're doing your utmost," she soothed. "How's Chi'mera doing?" She frowned. Now, why had she used her code name with Simon?

"She's fine. She's even learning a few things, which I assure you is a first for most of the people I've worked with," the tone being one of a professor teaching a student.

"I've meant to ask you something," She stepped outside into a fresh breeze, heading towards the barn, Simon following, slightly curious at the sudden change in the look on Helena's face; almost secretive.

"Some time ago, John asked me if we could try to save Isabella, although given that Jack saw her fall, Chi'mera slammed the door on that idea," she looked around carefully.

Simon kept his face neutral, waiting to see where she was going with this.

"But, with your addition of the camouflage on your armour, there may be a chance for you to save her," Simon's look was dubious. She raised her hand and, pleaded with her eyes for him to have an open mind. "The timing would be close, but if you were positioned near Isabella when she drops, you could catch her, just after Jack goes to the machine. Then you could put on full power and climb out of the portal before it closes."

Simon's face started to contort in thought, "I'd need to get the thrusters power up higher for that kind of manoeuvre, perhaps even replace the thrusters totally to get out in time," he looked unconvinced of its possibility, but at least he was considering the idea.

"Would you be able to do it in the time we have?" Helena asked eagerly.

"Possibly. We'll see. I'll spec it out and tell you nearer the time whether I can get it done," it was not the firm positive that she'd have liked, "It's a valuable upgrade anyway, so I'll put serious effort into it," he added more positively.

"Thank you!" She said, in genuine gratitude.

"So we are going to try and rescue Isabella eh?"

"That's the plan," She said absently.

Simon gave her a shrewd look. "Well good luck explaining that to Chi'mera," seeing the look of trepidation appear on her face. "I know her, and she has a rather fixed opinion on how this should play out," he put a consoling hand on her shoulder."

She pursed her lips, "You may be right, but she has to see that this is possible now."

Simon smiled, "like I said, good luck with that," and went off muttering to himself about thrust to weight ratios, air resistance, and fuel and energy coefficients.

Charlene was fascinated by Jack's description of the lessons he'd had with Helena, but the concepts were a little strange. After a short time, she noticed that Helena and Simon were no longer in the room and she wanted to talk to Helena too, so she excused herself, and went in search of the older woman, while Jack went to reading his book. She'd not told him that the book seemed to have a much different title for her. She'd not really seen the book before, but the title leapt out her when she did see it; "Rise of the Chi'mera." The title meant something to her of course, but there was an implication in it too, a feeling that rippled through her when she saw it, which translated directly as 'not yet.' She'd tried to say something to the others, but the feeling silenced her whenever they were around. She desperately needed to talk to Helena, to see if she could do something about this strange emanation from the book.

She met Helena in the courtyard, just heading back into the farmhouse.

"Ah Charlene, just the person," the comment stopping her initial question straight away. How was the book doing that? Or was it something else?

"I was just saying to Simon that his new modifications were interesting."

"I suggested them, you know," the girl was proud of her role, as a think tank. Perhaps an approach to use.

"Really? Clever trying to adapt a natural ability to mechanical technology; but then you are considerably smarter than most people, with the experiences of someone many times your age," projecting flattery, something Charlene was not really used to, causing the younger girl flushed a little.

"It is about that I had an idea too," carefully now, she thought.

"It was about the machine, and how we can get to shut it down, without blowing the planet up," the younger girl remaining calm, "we can get close enough, using Simon and Jacks' powers, then you can get into shut the machine down. We might even have enough time to save Isabella," now a strange look crossed Charlene's face, "what?"

"Helena, it's not possible," the words were out of Charlene's mouth before she could censor them.

"You sound so certain? Why" Helena was stunned that the girl had just dismissed the idea out of hand. "With Simon's camouflage and Jack's invisibility they could catch her, just after Jack saw her falling. Between them, they could get her to safety." Charlene was listening, but something in the set of her body spoke of her listening to other things too.

"Sorry. I don't know," Charlene's face said she was thinking it through. The idea seemed sound, but deep down in her gut, she knew it was doomed. The very thought that Isabella should be here now rang out in her head, heart, and soul, as wrong.

"But we can save her!" Helena said intensely, prompting both Jack and Simon to pop their heads out of their respective buildings.

"I'm sorry Helena, my instincts are telling me we must not save her, and I must follow those instincts, else everything we do will come to nothing." And with that, Charlene walked off into the farmhouse, the pronouncement seemingly final.

Helena started off after her, followed by Simon's unhelpful comment, "warned you," The look she threw at him was sufficiently venomous to shut even him up. Charlene walked past Jack and headed out the back, probably to practice; she'd replaced her lab time with gymnastics and combat practice. Helena walked past him closely after her, obviously going to have it out with the younger girl.

"I wouldn't," Jack said seeing the determination on her face. Helena slowed, then stopped and looked at him, with daggers in her eyes. "You know we need to work as a team to save her. If you do this, all that will happen is she'll dig her heels in, and you'll never get her to help."

"It's beginning to look that way already," Helena snapped.

"You, might be able to talk her around," soothed Jack, as he came closer and tried to steady her a bit.

"She seems pretty set," Helena said, calming a little, her face still flushed.

"We just need to work on her more that's all," he said smiling at her, and she saw that he would help her do this too.

"You're in?" There was gratitude in her voice.

"Let's just say that I don't want to see you upset, and, my mother always said; if I could help, I should help, if it was possible." Helena's face lit up, although Jack had his own doubts about their ability to save Isabella.

Charlene had been training hard on her kata recently, she could even use her tentacles now, instead of the much lighter ribbons. She'd managed to, separately, develop another routine using the whips that she'd bought before her change. She'd decided that there could be some fights that would just not either require the tentacles nor be advisable to show them. Undercover, undercover; the thought bringing a smile to her lips.

The issue of Isabella occupied a significant part in her thoughts though. Helena was technically right, given the newer abilities of herself, and the others, it might now be possible to achieve the rescue of their lost computer hacker. Even given that Jack saw her fall, he'd not seen her impact, or engulfed, in that other world, and they had a few usable seconds to recover the girl from the rip in reality before it closed.

Yet, somewhere, deep down in her being, there was a feeling that saving Isabella was the wrong thing to do. It was more than it could not be done; it was that it must not be done. She did not know where this certitude came from but hazarded a guess that it came from the other Chi'mera. At least she hoped it was.

Her main problem was that she really liked Isabella, and only her instincts were stopping her from saving her. Once again, people, other than herself, were guiding or controlling, her actions, all be it with her consent this time.

In her head, her mother had said 'trust your instincts,' and of course, her father had said 'trust your training,' having trained her to think logically, the two seemingly contradictory, making it difficult to know the real direction to take. It was all very confusing.

Having completed her kata, she sat down and looked at the timing of the rescue, if she became involved, based on what Jack had said happened. Of course, she'd been on the ship at the time with the others; so, it was only Jack's perception that needed consideration.

The timings were listed out; the opening of the rift, in reality, the Ghe'Dar soldiers, falling, a precious few seconds of holding on, then the drop, the wailing fall, Jack getting out of the way and the rift closing.

She whipped her borrowed tablet out again and started running an analysis. Her training gave her a uniquely independent approach to the problem; 'x' seconds here, 'y' seconds there even then the calculational model was involved, though nothing she could not handle. Looking at the result a few minutes later the scenario was marginal at best, disastrous at worst. Her best result meant they had about a three-second margin. In the worst case, all the team except Helena was lost. It really was not a good model to start with, and of course, that would have been the ideal, let alone in the middle of a war zone. No. Her instincts were right, they must not even attempt this, as much as they might like to save their college and friend. Tea time and evening that day was frosty, to say the least.

The following day was strange for the team.

Helena was in the kitchen early, making toast with the freshly made bread. Whether it was the cool discussions of the evening or just something about the day, only Helena was up before nine. For Charlene, this was highly unusual, and Helena looked in on the girl sleeping in one of the small bedrooms, seeing her tossing and turning in her bed, eyes closed, but restless; the others were in a similar state, even John, who was otherwise profoundly comatose.

Helena made the connection almost immediately. This was the eighteenth of April; the day, weeks ago for them, that they had first encountered one another. In twelve days they would jump back in time to get here. They had twelve days left, and things were starting to converge. Subconsciously, they all knew that somehow feeling the connection. She knew she would have to keep them busy today.

Fortunately, they all still had things to do; Titanium suffering a minor power outage forcing Simon to pull them all in to aid in the dousing of the fire it started and repair the shorts and overloads in the local area. It took them all day to completely smother the fire, and effect damage repairs. In near total exhaustion, the team hit the beds late-evening, after a hectic and non-stop kind of day, broken only by short meal breaks and Simon's occasional bouts of frustration.

Craig Starling had spent the bulk of the day trying to correlate reports on several events which had happened, very close to home, recently. He'd been asked, by his superiors, to look into problems in some areas of the underground, and sewers, that were deemed to be in his purview, rather than that of the local departments.

He was amazed at the number which had come in, just during the night he'd been away. From the electricity companies reports of unexplained power surges, police reports of selective vandalism and recent missing people alerts, to sewage company reports of large-scale damage to sections of the network and strange seismic events in parts of the city recently; they were all assessed and correlated. There were even reports on weird animal activities in the local parks.

He'd given up trying to find out all he could about the theft at the labs in Troyes and the strange message that he'd received there. The subsequent query from the M.I.'s top operatives gave several starting pointers, but most of them disappeared after a few false turns.

Then, late on, he received a visit from an old acquaintance, Whisper, saying she'd had a problem at a science conference, and that Craig might be interested in the people it concerned; as she left, he'd a nagging feeling that he would.

He'd started to call Helena, when he remembered that she was off, helping out at a magic show, to keep up her cover in the magic circles intact. He found that her pager was also off, against standing orders; strange for her. He'd have a talk to her about that later. Isabella was quickly woken, with lots of complaints about the time, and lots of coffee was drunk, till well into the morning.

When he looked closer at the people from the conference, he sensed an inevitable fate in the air. There they were in the reports, and news reports; experts in Nanotechnology, Cybernetics and Security just as the previous messages had required. The strange thing was, there was a fourth person too; a performer, illusionist, that did not really seem to fit as part of the group. The images of him were slightly, well, fuzzy, unlike the others that were crystal clear. But he'd been there too, and there was something in Craig's mind that kept whispering that he should also be included. Not only that but there was Helena right in the middle of the carnage, and electrical chaos; that explained the pager being off.

As the sun came over the skyline, he decided enough had been learned about the experts, to get them inducted into M.I.X. He probably needed his rest before they came in.

He was slightly worried about the Klerk girl though, as she was known to M.I.X., an asset that would require careful handling, especially as her mother was considered a rogue agent, after the incident with the lost team.

Still, perhaps he could keep it in the family, since her uncle was an agent too, and could keep an eye on her. Besides, he was an old friend, and he trusted him with his life. Given the signs, he might well be entrusting them all with his, and everyone else's too.

CHAPTER 17

BATTLE LINES

The next day, was the second-day people were up late; even Helena. The whole situation was taking its toll on everyone, but it was not the only thing that was weighing heavy on their minds. John seemed to show no signs of recovery, despite Helen's ministration and treatments.

"We need to get some more nourishment into him," Helena has noted after breakfast. "I can create a cocktail of nutrients, but we'll need some medical kit to get it into him."

"No, we don't" Charlene, disagreed, "all we need is a funnel and pour it down his throat," she snapped angrily.

"Charlene, I'm the doctor here. We do it the modern way, not the medieval way."

Charlene glared at her and stomped out towards the barn.

"She's moody again," Helena complained, the others just nodding.

Jack stood up, "I'll go talk to her. Something's on her mind when she comes out with that kind of statement."

"Can you do a run to the local hospital and get some things for us?" Helena asked carefully, Jack nodding as he stood up, "I'll write out a list," she added, as he followed the girl to the barn.

Charlene was sitting next to Titanium's armour when Jack came in.

"You alright?" The question seemed ridiculous, even as he said it.

Charlene looked up, ready to start a fight, then saw it was Jack and bit her tongue; quite literally. The blood seemed to soothe her a little, and of course, the Nanites did their job and healed her up again. Even that fact annoyed her today.

"I'm, well I'd like to say I'm ok," she started,

"But you're not, right?" She nodded, "tight feeling here," he pointed to the temple of his head, "and here," right at the base of the skull. She frowned, but nodded, acknowledging, he was right. How had he known?

"Me too," he smiled a little at the questioning look. "I got it when I went up on stage that first time" He sat next to and facing her, but not to close. "It's that feeling of nerves, just before you do your thing." He popped a piece of rope from his hands, then disappeared it with a slick flick of his fingers.

"Why am I getting it now? We still have two weeks before we can do anything about it?" She complained.

"Because, my friend, as I understand it, you have never needed to just sit down and wait before. You are used to controlling your life; well as much as any of us can, and now that you are forced to wait, your mind is complaining that it cannot do what it desperately wants to do." She considered this and saw the plausibility of the idea.

"I imagine you might have gone ballistic, if, in your lab, you'd have had a day where you could not actually work, or the system failed,"

She agreed with that, remembered the day the system had been down for five hours. She'd been uptight for the entire time, discipline notwithstanding. She just was not a waiter; she was a doer.

Jack could see that just talking was not enough, her face still looking down.

"So how is it doing?" he pointed at Titanium standing in front of them.

"'It is doing fine, we activated," she started.

"Titanium active," Jack jumping out of his skin, as the suit responded to 'activate.'

"Oh sorry," Charlene, briefly smiled at Jacks reaction and turning to get her tablet from the table. "We had it on maintenance mode, all yesterday, getting all the shorts fixed."

She tapped the tablet a few times, and the status changed to passive, the funny thing was that when Jack looked at her after, she seemed a little brighter. Perhaps playing the clown a bit would help.

Surprisingly Simon came racing in, "What's going on? I heard the suit," he looked a little haggard, and concerned about the suit; more so than he'd ever been about the others in the team.

"It's ok Simon," Charlene calming him, "we just forgot to switch modes when we hit the sack last night. It was late," the response seemed to settle him down, and he turned to head back to the open farm door.

"I thought for a second the damn thing was activating by itself and walking off again."

"Now, you know we removed all that coding," she looked at Jack and saw the amusement in the attitude of Simon, as he winked at her.

"I have a feeling we will never truly get rid of everything that Craig put in there. He has a certain devious way of thinking that I cannot hope match." His annoyance contained a certain amount of respect, for the amount of hidden code throughout the suit.

"I, for one, am glad you're more straight-forward thinking than Craig. It means you're more trustworthy," Charlene complemented him, making Simon feel a little guilty, about his involvement in the rescue plan for Isabella.

Simon regarded the armour, then Charlene. "You know, I don't really need your help with the rest of the work Charlene," her face dropped. Jack had hoped that working on the armour would keep her busy and help with the apparent bout of melancholy.

"Perhaps you should work on your equipment," he said pointing to her head. She immediately perked up, a wry smile appearing on her face.

"Should have thought of that myself," Jack frowned, then smiled.

"Yeah, you should have. For smart people, sometimes you lot are really dumb," a complaint he'd used before; causing the three of them to laugh a little.

Jack saw that Charlene was a bit brighter now, so he let the two get on with their separate day's work, and decided to have a day off from the book. Besides the last few days, he had not really practised his tricks, and magic, much.

He decided to find a quiet spot near the farm and try something, having had an idea. The others, except the unconscious John, could tweak and upgrade their equipment, he just needed to guide his powers in the right direction, and for that he needed practice.

Jack was busy concentrating, not actually meditating, but trying to focus on his power, primarily the energy he could directly channel through his hands. He imagined his magic to be a marshmallow; soft and malleable his hand, though never quite the right shape for what he wanted to do.

"Will is the primary ingredient in using your power," Helena had instructed, "mould the power, then direct it. The more you envisage the idea you are trying to express, the clearer the thought and the more precisely the magic will do exactly as you command."

He looked at a twisted tree he'd spotted, where a branch had been hit by lightning recently splitting it, looked at his hands and envisaged the branch, binding together and being made whole again. He felt the power start to flow around the wood, like a white mist obscuring it for a few seconds, then relinquishing it to the daylight. The result was strange; a twisted groaning filled the air, as wood knitted and twisted together, the bark around it warped to take the shape it had initially been. However, when it finished with a sharp retort, the tree now looked like the branch was too thick for the rest of the tree.

As soon as he saw it, he realised what had happened and felt particularly disheartened. He'd 'repaired' the tree in the physical sense, but the tree had not been 'healed.' The form of the branch was right, but its' internal structure had not been restored, because he had not really envisaged what was required. This was going to be much harder than he thought.

It was then that he saw the fox limping across the path. He loved animals, especially the urban foxes he'd sometimes disturbed, in his flight from gangs, in Birmingham. To see one in the wild was beautiful, but this one limped because it had a strangely malformed leg, a birth defect, perhaps, causing him to wonder how it had survived this long.

Perhaps, perhaps, he could heal it. He might not know about trees, but he could use his sight to see how to help the fox. He stood and slowly approached the animal, causing it to started to move to run, although it probably knew it could not escape a healthy human.

"Easy there, little one," he used a low tone, to try and sooth the skittish little animal, as it regarded him cowering. He adjusted his sight, to see if it could see the deformity properly, and as he did so, received a shock, the creature was radiating a kind of energy he'd never seen before; not magic, as such, but similar.

"My! What are you?" The animal quivering even more, not moving or responding. That could be explored another time, for the moment he could see the problem with the creature's leg. The hip was out of joint, and the bone in the leg was longer than the others.

He formed the image, of the corrected leg, in his mind and, before unleashing his power, made a comparison against what he saw. The correction would balance it up, allow the hip to slide back into place and get the creature moving; so, he willed that the leg to be as he visualised it, and fully functional. He sensed a building power in his hands, as his mind focused on the fox and its deformity then, with a silent rush, it surrounded the animal, taking effect. Unlike the tree, there was little sound except for a slight pop, the fox yelping as the hip was forced back into place.

The creature looked at the leg quickly then dashed out of the clearing, apparently at full pelt. Jack heaved a huge sigh of relief having seen the leg was functioning correctly before the animal, obviously startled by the change in its body, bolted.

Well, it had worked. He could channel his power into healing energies. He'd thought it would take too much time to do it, but it seemed he had a knack for it. Then, he thought about the tree and frowned. Yes, he could do it, but it would require careful thought each time. So, healing in battle would still require Helena, but, if he practised, he could help her out and perhaps, with her guidance, he could get sufficiently good enough to do it, on the fly, as it were. So, practice he would; perhaps the healing the tree could be improved; then he laughed suddenly realising he was practising, 'tree-ag.'

After the induced laughter subsided, he went back to the tree and envisaged the internal structures of the tree, and tried again.

In a small yard, just off the main one, Charlene was sitting looking at the sky. Well, that's what it looked at to the casual eye. In fact, she was exploring her HUD again, finding that even during their short stay here it had changed.

She really needed to make it a part of her routine, to highlight new areas of the HUD each day, and to catalogue the functions for future use. Even the interface was different.

Enough was enough, she started writing a cataloguing program. One step at a time she would get this machine, her body, with all its intricacies, under control.

Firstly; she needed control of her ability to exude her tentacles in an appropriate length and form to suit her needs. It was all well and good being able to fling them out in battle, but she might need something different if they were to become more useful, and if she needed her hands free at the time it meant another interface. It might take months to get it all done; but she would and then; well she did not know what. Firstly, she'd test out her capabilities on the Ghe'Dar, then consider what to do, if they succeeded.

As she was re-programming the interface, creating a new one she could use with her tongue, like a mouse pad, on the roof of her mouth; she thought of the possibilities. For herself, given what she could do now, there appeared no real limits although one thing impinged on those thoughts again and again; her mother.

Sylvia was devious, powerful, dangerous and she needed to be captured and neutralised. Bringing Sylvia to justice, along with the others who'd tried to have Charlene sacrificed would be her first goal. It was something she could not do on her own, but with the help of the others, and the resources of M.I.X., she was sure she could hunt her and them down, and make them pay, for everything they had inflicted on her, and others.

As her programs took shape, so did her plans for the future, with the usual provisos.

After a couple of hours, she had her catalogue. Most of it was under sub-headings of sub-headings, and the rest was pure gibberish, her HUD still could not decipher the full Ghe'Dar language. Another thing to add to the list, at some point.

She sorted through the mass of functions, over a thousand or more and, tried, to search on the HUD. She had an idea in mind and needed a specific set of functions for it to work. Ah ha; there they were. She tried using the new interface in her mouth. It was a little strange, but it worked; slowly. Still slow was better than not at all.

There down at about level fifteen was a menu marked 'extrusion parameters'; no, she did not really need. She explored further, to the area around functions, until she found what she needed.

It was in shape changing systems under 'utility usage.' When she saw the options she just gasped, the number of permutations was simply staggering. She'd need a whole new way of controlling this function, just for manageability. There were so many combinations of parameters that they filled her whole field of view. A standard interface would just not hack it. She'd have to discuss its' design with Simon, and perhaps others too; although she'd keep the specifics to herself. In the meantime, she had more adjustments to make, to a small portion of her vast array of abilities.

In the afternoon, a small ambulance trundled into the courtyard, much to the surprise of just about everyone, a French-speaking medic, leaping out of it, looking around for someone. Simon came out of the barn, with a small pad in his hand, pointing to the house, and the team, who heard Simon explaining, "I've called the local emergency service out." Helena's vociferous expletive masked a few words, "I told them that the man upstairs has been injured, but that the rest of you only speak English. I suggest Helena uses her mind control to make sure that he sets up the medical kit John needs, then leave thinking that the call was successful, requiring no further action."

"You could have warned us?" snarled Helena, grabbing her wand quickly and turning it into her staff; just as the medic knocked on the door. Charlene changed her face and pulled the door open, staying behind it out of sight and resisting the urge to speak; waving the man towards Helena, who was standing behind the staff directing her power at him, the medic's eyes almost immediately glazing over.

"Right. Got him," Helena directing the man back out to the ambulance to get the necessary equipment. Fortunately, he was on his own and, although he did not have the stands for the IV drips, he did have the rest of the equipment they needed.

After a few minutes, John was set up with a full IV drip, Helena directing the hanging of the IV drips on the walls, using hooks and wires, while Charlene used her tentacles to reach everything from the bedroom doorway, remaining out of sight.

It took half an hour in all, and for once the team saw the benefits of not trying to do it all themselves; especially Jack, who was grateful not to have to do any more stealing and creeping around.

As the man drove off, coming out Helena's control, he remembered that the man at the farm had actually had a diabetic episode and just collapsed. He'd had to use the appropriate medications, and fluids to stabilise him and the patient had rallied well. Finally, he'd been advised to go to the Hospital, although he'd declined, but agreed to see his local practitioner the next day.

Once gone, Helena, gently, guided Simon into the barn; the others pointedly ignoring that and going into the farmhouse, leaving Simon to get a little lecture about teamwork from 'Ma'am' Helena. The strange thing was, there was no discussion between Charlene and Jack as they walked, they knew automatically that Simon needed the talking to and leaving Helena to do it. At least now John was getting what he needed they could relax a little.

Once Simon had received a little word about telling people what he was doing and keeping people informed, Helena checked on John. The others, including the rather 'out of sorts' Simon, waited impatiently in the farmhouse for her assessment. When she came down, she looked thoughtful.

"There is no overall positive change," the others did not seem surprised, "but he is not as pale, and the drops in his heart rate and breathing have stopped. I'd say he'd stabilising rather than improving," well it was something.

In the evening, when Charlene checked the feeds, she noticed something. The packs were empty, which she commented about to Helena, who remained unconcerned.

"It may well be a good thing. It means that his body is absorbing nutrients to replace those he's lost over the last few days. We need to run him up a nutrient feed, similar to yours, and use it in the IV bags." Charlene nodded, and for the rest of the evening that is what they did.

The next day Jack went back to his rapidly improving tree. Each time he used his power, the wood complained, but it got a little healthier. There was new growth on the end of the branches now, and, he thought that the plant was recovering nicely. The bulge, where the break had occurred, was now barely visible, Jack using it as a guide to his progress.

Just before tea time, there was a great whoop from the barn, loud enough to reach the farmhouse, both women looking at each.

"His toy is working fully again! Has to be," Charlene smiled.

"Yup. Boys and their toys. He'll be happier now," smiled Helena, in relief.

"And he'll get his appetite back too," Charlene observed.

Helena pursed her lips at that, "we're not all like you, my dear. We eat to enjoy the food, not just fuel our bodies," Charlene looking hurt at that.

"I enjoy my food too; especially when it's fresh," she looked at Helena.

"Yes, it's nice to be able to do the cooking, but we'll have to go back to normal soon."

Charlene looked sad at that, "I've really enjoyed it here, I,"

"Me too," Helena interrupted. Charlene's look said that she was trying to say something important, so Helena fell quiet.

"I have enjoyed this quiet time, but I need to start doing things again," she was severely stressed out, not dealing with the teams' real problems.

"What do you think we can do, especially with John?"

"I've thought about introducing repair Nanites into John, to try and get his system running normally again," Charlene dropping the bombshell immediately.

Helena stopped and put the last bag of nutrient for John down.

"Do you think that is wise Charlene? You don't exactly know what will happen if you introduce your Nanites into his body."

"Actually, I've been working on my systems, and I have a fair appreciation of what my Nanites actually do now," there was a certainty in her statement that Helena had not heard since before her change.

"I doubt that John would want me to allow you to do this," Helena set her face against Charlene's confidence. Charlene saw the look and for the first time in her life stood her full height and looked down on Helena with an authoritative air.

"He also would not want to die," the two facing each other, not two feet apart.

"You sure?" Helena said very quietly, looking at him quickly.

Charlene's face dropped at that. "What?" she looked at him too.

"Isabella's loss was a hard blow, and his subsequent obsession with it may have dragged him down a lot. He might just not want to live with the guilt," there was something in her voice, almost like she knew how he felt.

"But it was not his fault!" Charlene raised her tone a little.

"No. It was mine," Helena muttered.

"You cannot say that she wanted to come along on the boat," Charlene complained,

"I suggested it," Charlene stopped at that.

"What! Why?" this was news to Charlene.

"I just did," Helena could not tell her the real reason, that she was under instructions to do so, and suddenly the guilt showed fully on her face.

"But," Charlene started,

"I was the one responsible, as team leader, if nothing else."

"So, you think you know how John feels; that does not mean that is what is actually happening," Charlene protested.

"True. But it would explain his decline," Helena regarded him in sorrow.

Charlene straightened again, "I don't accept that, and team leader or no, I'm going to try. If nothing else to bring him around enough so that he can make a choice."

Helena stood in front of John, but Charlene directly ported to the other side of the bed.

"Charlene don't," Helena raised her hand to stop her,

"It's already done: when I 'ported I placed them in his gut. Only target big enough to try that."

Helena was suddenly infuriated. "How dare you do that against my explicit order?" Her face was bright red, and she started to lift her wand.

Charlene did not flinch. "You did not order me not to, you simply said you did not think it was a good idea, and that John would probably not want it."

Helena refused to be mollified, and her staff appeared before her, "and what if they cause more damage and actually cause his decline or even death?" she said through gritted teeth.

"Helena, at some point you and the others are going to have to start trusting me and my skills, it might as well be now." Helena standing rigid, as though she was fighting the urge to smack the younger girl, around the head with her staff.

"Take them out," Helena grated.

"It's too late; they will already be in different locations than I placed them. They are designed to increase the oxygen supply in the blood and clear any blockages in the arteries.

Helena calmed a little, "that's all? What happens if they malfunction, get out of control or cause an immune response in his system? There a hundred and one things they might mess up," Helena still both angry, and concerned.

Charlene looked down at him, "they have limited functionality, Helena, not at all like the ones that changed me, and are biological, not technological, so they can only do what they are made to do. They are not programmable, and, once they have fulfilled their functions, they will be killed off by the bodies normal immune system. There is damn little that can go wrong," she could see the other woman slowly relaxing.

"But it still might," Helena insisted.

"If it does, then I will take the responsibility and do my time," she was as sincere as Helena had ever heard her be, her own look still showing her disapproval.

Helena looked at her and finally sighed, "Ok. Well, it's done now. How long before they take effect?"

Charlene looked down at the pale form in front of her, "they have already done their job; it's all up to John now. If the boost I've given to his system does not help, I really don't think there is anything else we can do for him."

They went to bed that night, finding it hard to get to sleep; the night passing slowly.

Deep down, in John's mind, things changed equally as slowly, but finally the balance shift, and he started to rise from the depths. Then the real battle began.

He was exhausted, but his chase through the town continued.

Then was a jolt, like an earthquake, in his system and things changed; the scene shifted, and a portal opened above him like a thunderclap, turning the dark sky to one wreathed in fire. From the centre of the gateway, came a terrible noise;

screeching, like the anguish of gulls, being torn apart; creatures of razor fang and claw, blazing eyes and despairing screams, descended on the worms, devouring the devourers.

At first, John watched on in horror, then in relief, as he realised that the creatures were clearing a path to him, seeing from the corner of his eye the worm-wriddled form of Isabella rushing to do battle with these new horrors.

The nightmarish battle that ensued seemed one-sided, as the girl leapt upon the demonic monstrosities, tearing them to pieces in defence of the realm she appeared to have claimed as her own. The fiery bird-demons seemed outmatched entirely, and flocked in to do battle with this impossible threat, a ball of fury rising into the air, as the struggle intensified. Fascinated, by the clash he failed to notice another, horrendous, form descending from the sky, to land a dozen or so feet from him.

"Ah, I had not counted on such resistance," the monstrosity said in an ordinary conversational voice, turning to face the shocked John, it's voice smooth and silky, like a feather drifting across an ice-topped lake.

"The girl has spirit, has she not, to defend you, even as she torment's you?" John tried to step back, away from it, but there was a compulsion in that voice to stay that his feet obeyed, ignoring his own commands.

"But is that not always the way of women? They implore you to stay, even as they steal everything you have, everything you are. They expect everything of you and give nothing in return, and finally, they torment you until you depart the world, then, just for good measure live off their ill-gotten gains."

John thought about the way his mother had constantly badgered his father, who had been a career policeman his entire life. John had watched him die, so slowly, gradually hen-pecked to death; his spirit drained away day-by-day, through thirty years of marriage to his mother, finally dying in his sleep, his will sapped and once great strength was gone. His life at the end was entirely subservient to his mother, and John had joined the police, as much to escape her as to have a career. She had tried to control him and his life, but he'd firmly put a stop to that; when she'd decided to switch her attention to him, he just moved out and left her to herself. His other family members were slightly shocked by that move, but those who'd seen his father's decline knew it was for the best.

The creature was right. His mother was still alive, living off his father's pension; ill-gotten gains indeed. If he'd married someone less domineering, he'd probably still be alive. John shook his head. This creature looked demonic but spoke smoothly, and there was that compulsion. His instincts screamed against it, but he stepped closer.

"Who, no, what are you?" he looked at the horrific visage.

"Ha ha ha ha ha ha," the creature's laugh was loud and daunting, but when it actually spoke the voice was smooth again.

"Surely you know what I am. As to who I am; that is another matter. My name, as my race speak it is unpronounceable to you and your kind, and even if you could, it would give you power over me, as of old; and that I cannot allow."

The creature bent a little, to look at the man, "however, you can call me Stranarack."

It reached towards John, who backed up a little. However the clawed hand simply opened up and left a small bracelet behind, "and I come to offer you a gift." It was hard to use his body reading skills on a demon, but John knew that there was more to it than the creature gifting him the bracelet; after all modern culture was full of Faustian mythology, and he'd read some books on the price men paid for accepting gifts from Demons and Devils.

"Why would I want a bracelet? And since we are not really here, why would it matter if I just left it there. I'll wake up without it then get on with my tasks."

"Ah, ha, ha, ha, ha," the demon seemed genuinely amused.

"So, you do not understand the real peril that you face here?" The certainty in the behemoths' voice was more convincing than any words it could have used.

"Peril? From a dream? There is none. When I wake up, I will be hungry that is all," his own voice seemed less sure.

The creature laughed again, but this time it was even louder than before.

"Oh, little man; how wrong you are. Tell me this then, how long have you been asleep?" John frowned. He knew dreams distorted time, but he could not remember how many times he'd run down that same part of the street in this nightmare.

"A few hours. Nothing more than that," he sounded uncertain even to himself now.

"No, my little friend, you have been here the best part of a week, and you will remain here until you find a way to escape, or your body gives out. And you have little hope of escaping that one," the creature pointed at the battle still going on, above them, "ever."

The battle, instead of diminishing, was getting fiercer and fiercer. Indeed worms now launched themselves from the ground, joining the growing ball of fire and black ichor.

"The longer we talk, the stronger she becomes. My forces, although powerful elsewhere, are subject to the rules of this realm; and she, it seems, controls this realm in some fashion. Even now she learns her powers, destroying my minions and subverting the vermin. Soon she will be powerful enough to break free, and you will be held here, at her leisure, probably until you die." The demon did not seem overly alarmed by this, it was just describing the predicament that John was in. It looked at him, and John realised it was up to him to make the next move.

"So, how can the bracelet stop her?" He instinctively knew the question to ask, probably because the demon had introduced the bracelet first.

"The bracelet has been infused with a small portion of my essence. It is a bridge, of sorts, between my realm and the realm of dreams. It will allow me to disrupt her control over you, and, allow you to escape to your world."

The demon looked at the battle again, the girl seeming to have grown, huge arms now gathering whole bird demons and crush them, leaving parts of herself free. From the ground larger worms arrived, reaching the battle directly; the rescuing forces seemed to be losing ground, the flames in the sky starting to waver and fade, the scene changing back to be a dark grey, rather than fiery red.

"You are running out of time, mortal. All you need to do, is put the bracelet on and you will be free of her, and this ensnaring nightmare," the tone of impatience was not lost on John, but did he believe any of this? No, but what if, by some mischance, this was his brain telling him a way out of the madness around here. Now that made more sense.

"And the price?" John did not honestly believe this was happening, but he would hear the creature out.

"Ahhhhh. Well, the bracelet is fashion out of a very rare essence, requiring something equally as rare to replace it," the demon looking John in the eyes.

"Let me guess; my soul," the words were out before he could stop them, but the sarcasm was not lost on the demon, it just ignored it.

"I am not a greedy creature; I do not require your whole soul, for such a small thing, just as much of it as replaces the essence will do. Say this much." It opened up its hand and showed John. It was a small, even for John, a palm full of wispy nothingness. "Hardly a significant fraction, you will agree."

John presented an air of indecisiveness, but the battle was starting to wind down, and he knew he was running out of time. Did it really matter anyway? Perhaps not, but if it did, he could deal with the consequences, with Helena's help, maybe, later."

"Our time is almost up," the demon was not wrong at Isabella's apparition exploded from the, remaining bird demons and started towards them, the demon turning to face the girl.

"Do you truly think you can stand against me here, Demon Lord, or no?" boomed Isabella, now matching him easily, inch for inch.

The Demon raised his hand, and she staggered as though hit by a mighty blow, John watching in a kind of mesmerised haze. Isabella brushed the attack off and continued towards him, almost contemptuous of the Demon lord's efforts.

John looked at the bracelet that, somehow, he'd picked up. It was barely anything, he thought, and all he needed to do, to stop all this, was to put it on. After it was over, he could probably pull it off again and get rid of the pesky thing.

The Demon Lord raised his hands higher and brought them smashing down, causing green energy to rip from the sky and burst all around Isabella, who was again staggered, but, still advanced. It seemed the demon was correct, in this realm she really was too powerful, and if the demon could not seriously affect her, he'd little chance. John snapped the bracelet on.

The effect was immediate. Isabella, or rather what appeared to been her, screamed and started to shrink, the Demon bellowing in triumph, causing John to sink to his knees as the Demons lord's bellow sent shockwaves through his entire body and mind.

Isabella started to dissolve and change, from being a horror, she shrank quickly to be the girl he'd seen on that first day after the conference. Her eyes come to his, looking in horror at him, and, in a faint whisper, she asked, "What have you done?" Then she vanished.

"The deal is done," roared a triumphant demon lord, "You are free to return to your life, but first I'll collect the agreed fee," reaching out and swiping its claw through John, who screamed, as an agony he'd never known swept through him. Looking down, he saw great gashes had appeared on his stomach and groin; although they were semi-transparent.

"Now you will return. But know this; part of you is mine now, and when next we meet, you will know who your master truly is."

A few seconds later, the scream of agony woke Simon and the rest. They piled into the room to see John writhing on the bed, his arms raised, fending off imaginary attackers, his eyes rolling in his head, the IV lines wrapping around his arms in the struggle.

"Hold him," commanded Helena, bolting forward, looking accusingly across at Charlene.

"Got it," tentacles restraining his wrists, her hands untangling the IV lines.

"Get off. I'll kill you. Arrrgghh," snarled John, his eyes not focusing on Charlene, but on someone above him.

"John? John!" Helena called to him, appealing to his sense of reality.

His head snapped this way and that, seeking the source of the sound, his fighting lessening dramatically, "Helena?"

"We're right here, John," she said waving a hand in front of his face, Charlene still wrestling with his strength as it started to subside at the sound of Helena's familiar voice.

"All I see is darkness, where is here? and what is holding me?"

Helena waved for Charlene to release him, the girl, reluctantly lowered his arms and retracted her tentacles. "We are all here, at the farmhouse," she was trying to assess how much he remembered and how disoriented he was.

"Right. Yeah. That's right. Oh! I, the book. It hit me with, something," he started to settle heaving himself up in the bed."

"That's right," she was looking at his eyes, looking bloodshot, stained with thin dark purple streaks. She crooked her finger at Charlene, indicating the eyes. She watched, a chill running down her spine; had she done that? She considered it but knew that the Nanites were too far away to effect that change, merely oxygenating his blood, and that colour change did not fit with anything they could have done, forcing her to shrug in denial.

"Why don't you sleep a bit more. I guess that the shock caused a lesion on your brain, that has now dissipated; your body needs of time to recover. Your eyes probably just need to heal and rehydrate to function again," pursing her lips to the others, indicating it was actually a possibility.

"What if they don't?" John asked, his voicing cold uncertainty.

"We'll cross that bridge later if we need to. The important thing is that we have you back and there's still time for you to recover before we need you at peak health again."

"How long have I been under?" he asked, remembering what the creature in his dream had said.

"About six days," Charlene, replied, putting a great deal of relief into her voice.

"Six days? Wow, that was a hell of a jolt that book hit me with," John shocked at the duration, although, the IV lines, were a clue.

"Yes," Jack had remained silent, feeling responsible for John's condition.

"Ok, Jack, next time, can you remind me not to mess with magic?" John said a bit more calmly.

"Next time?" Jack was a little shocked at the question, then realised that John had given a wane little smile, the rest chuckling a little at the forced joke, but Helena raised her hand.

"We'd best leave him to sleep now. Hopefully, your own recuperative powers will now allow you to get you back on your feet, soon," they started to file out slowly.

"Can I have some food? I'm as hungry as Chi'mera," Charlene rolled her eyes.

"I'll bring some up," laughed Helena, guiding Charlene away from the others as they went back to bed.

"Did you see his eyes?" it was more an accusation, than a question.

"Nothing to do with my Nanites. If they'd have affected his eyes they would be more red or blue, not dark purple, no, that is something else," Charlene was adamant.

"So what do we do about his sight?" Helena worried.

"I don't think it will be a problem. The over oxygenation of his blood probably just put pressure on the optic nerve, which his own powers should stabilise. He should be fine in the morning, apart from a residual headache."

"I hope so," Helena headed down to fetch the patient a substantial meal.

"Me too," muttered Charlene in trepidation filled tones.

John still felt a little woozy. Most of what had happened was fading, as dreams did. His head felt like he'd been hit with a tube maul, his chest and arms were bruised from his wrestling with Chi'mera, and his wrist was saw. He opened his eyes, and they let in the dim light from the hallway, under the door, although the view was impossible to make sense of; just a big blur. His ears worked fine though, and he heard footsteps coming up the stairs.

"John? It's me, Helena," he barely recognised the voice.

"Hi Helena, your voice sounds weird, and all I can see is a blur," his voice sounded weird too, kind of gravelly.

"Well, better than a few minutes ago," she observed, almost cheerfully.

"I'm parched," he complained.

"Yeah, you will be, and you'll be hungry too, for a time," he heard her putting something down. "I've brought you soup for your first meal," hushing him up when he started to complain.

"I know it's not what you want, but your stomach will have shrunk considerably while you were unconscious, so soup is probably the only thing it will keep down."

"But, I'm starving," he growled, getting properly angry now.

"And you'll stay starving if you try eating normally, as you'll either be sick or have a seizure," she pointed out, being deliberately heartless about it, to get the point across. John subsided.

"I have some news later that might interest you; if you eat up nicely," she offered, dangling the titbit to gain his cooperation.

John's stomach growled, and he sighed, "ok. I give in," he sat up and wiggled a little to get comfortable, his face full of resignation. "Feed me your damn soup!"

She smiled, "sure!" proceeding to spoon feed the convalescing man.

Afterwards, she settled into a chair across the room. "So, what's this news then; that you think you can bribe me with." John was straight down to business. No change there then; at least his mind was not as damaged as might have been the case.

"I've talked with the others about a plan to save Isabella," she saw his reaction, him leaning forward eagerly, but his face betrayed another emotion with a tremor of his lips. Was that fear on his face? Her face obviously revealed her understanding, at which point John nodded and confessed his fear openly.

"I had a terrible dream about her when I was unconscious," his voice trembling a little. "She was transformed into a monstrosity, in the world that Jack described, and she chased me around the city," the weariness he felt reflected in his voice.

"That's over now. Simon's agreed to try and use his suit to rescue her. I'll check up on that tomorrow, I mean later today." She could see hope appearing in his eyes, replacing the fear.

"Can you check with him?" She stopped him.

"They need their sleep, and it's nearly dawn here," getting closer and gently pushing him back. "You need more sleep too. Your body is exhausted, and the more sleep you have over the next few days, the better. Especially for your eyes to recover."

She yawned loudly, "besides I'm knackered too." He still grumbled a little.

"Just sleep, mister. Consider that an order," she growled.

"Yes Ma'am," he said sarcastically but felt sleep grab hold of him like a pike grabbing a minnow. He dropped off into a deep, but this time, dreamless sleep, not noticing his wrist now bore the imprint of the bracelet he'd picked up in his nightmare.

For the third day, they all rose late, though for a good reason this time, Helena beating Charlene up by a few minutes, the noise of their moving around, slight as it was, waking the others; especially when the smell of the fresh baking drifted upstairs shortly after.

When there was a loud thud and cursing from John's room, Helena motioned for Charlene to investigate, as she waited for the toast to finish, Jack looking half asleep walking past her in the hallway, as Charlene put her head through the bedroom doorway, spotting John flailing around on the floor, trying unsuccessfully to get up.

"What do you think you're doing?" asked the astonished Charlene.

"Getting dressed," John replied with a significant amount of exasperation in his voice.

"You've been out of it for nearly a week, with little food or water. You need to take today easy," she informed, starting towards him to get him back into bed.

"Easy my backside, I need exercise, and to get training," he said gripping the footboard and attempting to haul himself back onto the bed, gritting his teeth and straining for all he was worth. What had happened to his strength?

"Yes you do, but after you have regained your strength, that you have just found you don't have. Correct?" She asked. He hated her being right.

"Right!" he sighed, agreeing reluctantly.

He gave up, and let her lift his shoulder onto hers, and hoisting him up on to the mattress, inviting him to lay down. He gave her a sharp look that she chose to ignore, but he lay down and relaxed.

"There now, satisfied," he grumped at her.

"It's,"

"Yeah, yeah, I know, it's for my own good," he said spraying sarcasm over the edge of the bed, at her.

"I was going to say it's only for a day or two. Until your system's healing kicks in properly. Then you should be healthy again," she could see his eyes following her as she moved around to sit in the chair, showing his eyesight was returning.

"How is your eyesight now?" She quizzed him.

"Well enough. I can see you, although you don't have your natural body on. Not tall enough," he observed. Oops. Now she'd got control of her form shifting, partially, she'd forgot to reset to her Charlene form, which she did immediately.

"The medic we got in, might have seen me and was local, so I used a picture of the family here as a template," she explained. "Simon got him in without telling us, so I had to think fast."

"Hmm, sounds like him, so at least that has not changed," sounding a little preoccupied, worrying Charlene based on her conversation with Helena the night before.

"What's the matter, John?" Charlene leant forward and looked in those strangely coloured eyes again, which were truly disturbing close up.

"Why have you constantly resisted the idea of saving Isabella?" He went direct to the heart of the matter, as usual, and leaned forward, until they were facing off nose-to-nose.

He was relentless, Charlene sighed; time to put her cards on the table.

"When we first went through the portal to the machine at CERN, I did not get through directly." She tried to phrase her encounter in the portal with her other self, in terms that would not make her appear totally crazy, even if the situation was, "I had a message, from someone that looked like me, but was not me." Ok, that did sound a bit crazy.

"What? Telling you to let Isabella die?" John was understandably sceptical.

"Not exactly," she twisted her face in concentration, "it was more a warning; that this was only the first of many battles that we might face, and that I need to be able to trust my feelings," she got the words out in a rush.

Strangely, when she said those words, he suddenly got a truly horrible feeling in his stomach; if something else were guiding her to make this decision, then she would not deviate from the course she'd decided on. He also had a feeling they would remain on opposite sides on this matter. What did he care? As long as he saved Isabella, it did not matter if Charlene disapproved.

"And your feelings say don't save her? Fine leave it to us!" He was getting angry now and strangely as he did so, his eyesight started to get better.

"It's not just that I should not help save her John. The feeling is that she should not be saved at all; that her being here is 'wrong' somehow." She saw the anger building in him, but she needed to tell him her reasons, not wanting to be on the wrong side of him, not realising that it was already too late.

"Well I will try, and the others have agreed to help if they can. Just don't try and stop me," he finished almost growling the words out, leaving her in no doubts as to what would happen if she did.

She stood up and backed off. "I'm sorry you feel that way. I think it best if I just leave now. We can discuss this between us all when you're better. Perhaps then you'll see that we need to do it my way."

"Don't count on it Chi'mera," he snarled.

Charlene closed the door behind her and panted a little, her heart rate way up. She'd never really seen that side of John before, or instead, she'd never been on the receiving end of that kind of attitude from him before; it was quite, what was the word, ah yes; Intense!

When she got back downstairs, Helena was on her way up with breakfast for the convalescent.

"How is he?" Helena asked casually and stopped concerned when she saw Charlene's look.

"Very angry that I won't help him with Isabella."

"Ah, yes. I had hoped to talk to you again about that before we got to CERN."

"You all want to try and help her he said?" it was a seriously angry accusation, "despite my concerns, and premonitions."

"I talked to Simon, and he's working out if he can increase the power of his thrusters to make it possible," Helena had hoped that this news might sway Charlene.

"The possibility is not the issue, Helena, it never was," although she did not totally believe that, she did not want to weaken her case by admitting that. "The point is that my instincts tell me that we must not save her, and I must trust them."

"I'm sorry Charlene, but as team leader, I'm giving John his shot," Helena put her foot down.

Charlene exuded defiance, "and what happens if, during your little rescue mission, Simon is lost and you still fail to save her?" She could see all sorts of issues that Simon could deal with but she could not, especially with the alien machine.

"Then at least we will have tried, and I have to try; else I would never forgive myself, and nor would John." She passed Charlene and as a parting comment asked, "Could you?"

Charlene considered that. No, she supposed she'd never forgive herself either, but then with the world at stake, and perhaps more, she'd at least try. The others seemed set on this course, and it now appeared that not only the entire world was against her, but also, most of the team. It was time to come up with a plan, against this eventuality, and fast. Charlene went outside and started to write a new program on her system.

She'd seen the specs. of Simon's armour, worked on the power systems and the communications array. Now it was time to put that knowledge to the test and devise a little failsafe of her own. She'd have to set aside her other projects and see if she'd digested Isabella's unintentional lessons in computing better than Simon had. The cruel irony was not lost on her; she would be using the girl's own lessons, to stop everyone else from saving her. Sometimes, life had some exceeding harsh lessons to teach, and, it seemed, that to save all of life on earth, she now had to learn it; and quickly.

When the others came to the table, in the kitchen, at tea time, there was no sign of Charlene. "Simon, have you seen Charlene?" Helena asked as he came through the door.

"Nope. I told her yesterday that I could manage without her aid, besides I wanted to try getting my thrusters up to spec."

"Any luck?" Helena forgot about Charlene for the moment.

"As it turns out the systems were only working on about fifty per cent capacity. I assumed there was a reason for it, but it seems that's only because it was still partially in 'storage' mode. They can put out an awful lot more thrust if asked to. Of course, whether or not that translates into speed or actual lifting power, I cannot really say, as I dare not test it out here in the open. If it is speed, I'll ping up on RADAR fast. We need to get somewhere more rugged to test that one out, and now that John's getting better, we can think about starting to move towards the mountains. If we can get there a few days early, I can run a series of tests, and get the power rating balanced in time for our appointment."

"Good news." Perhaps that would give Charlene's feelings a bit of a stir? Somehow Helena did not think so, but there was always hope.

Jack came in through the back door, from his latest session with his tree.

"Jack, have you seen Charlene?" Helena remembered to ask him.

"I think I saw her doing some work on her interface, around the back of the barn earlier," he shrugged a little, indicating that he'd no idea what she was actually doing.

Helena started to put down her implements to go get her, when in the girl walked, looking slightly out of breath.

"Sorry about that, got kind of wrapped up in a new program I thought of," she said sliding onto a seat at the table, wondering if she looked as guilty as she felt. They were her friends, and she was about to pull a fast one each of them. She wondered if her mother had felt this way, before becoming the high priestess to a demon. She shuddered at the comparison and hoped it was not prophetic, desperately hoping it was not.

"Hey there you lot!" came a cocky sounding John, from the top of the stairs, dressed, and looking ready to take on the world again, except that when he took his first step down the stairs, he started to tilt radically. Fortunately, before anyone could react to catch him, he managed to grab the rail, landing his foot safely.

"Easy there," Charlene teleported just below him, before he moved again, to support him, as he made his way down the stairs. Much as they were at loggerheads, he was still someone she cared for.

"Did not think you'd be bothered with me," he commented under his breath, a slight inflexion in his words that did not quite ring true, causing Charlene to frown, sounding like they were not really his words.

"Well I don't want to have to keep feeding you and being nurse-maid to a convalescent, which you would be if you broke your leg, or other bones, again," she replied.

"When you two have finished your usual sparing, get down here so we can eat." Simon intervened. "You may not be as eager as normal, but I'm hungry."

Charlene dumped John onto a chair, then 'ported to her seat, in eagerness, looking at Simon, the thin smile he threw at her making her grin a little too. If he wanted eager, she could do that in Spades.

"So, now that we are all together again, healthy," Helena nodded at John, who was still frowning at Charlene, "repaired," and she looked at Simon, "catalogued," glancing at Charlene, who was trying to reach for the roast meal Helena had been cooking most of the afternoon, "and instructed," Jack smiling warmly at her, "we can catch-up."

She passed around the plates and, for the first time in over a week, they talked about other things; the food, the weather, the beds and the farm in general. They deliberately avoided discussing anything to do with John; his illness, his dispute with Charlene, and everyone else's' plans to save Helena. They talked amicably for hours until it was fully dark outside.

However, before they went up for the night, Helena stopped them, and deliberately addressed the main issue laying between them.

"Tomorrow we start to make our plans on what to do when we get to CERN."

They went to bed subdued after that; some still not asleep when midnight sounded. That night, it was John who had nightmares, though, each time he woke up, he could not remember what he'd been dreaming about, only that he'd been running, and running, and running, and strangely each time he woke his stomach hurt where the demon had wounded him in his previous nightmare. So did his wrist, where the mark, looking like a child's braided luck charm, started to change colour; from pink to inflamed red.

The five were up early, John wearing a baggy tracksuit with a sweatband around his right wrist, Charlene in a utility suit or at least what looked like one. Jack was in, what looked like a farmers' outfit, while Simon, in contrast, was in the same camouflaged clothes he'd been in since they'd all left England several days ago. Helena was using the clothes of the farmers' wife, although they were a little big for her around the waist, pulled together by a piece of rope from the barn, acting as a belt.

They hardly looked like a group of secret agents about to save the world, Jack, with a fine eye for the ridiculous commenting on that.

Charlene smiled, "actually," she started, pulling a rucksack from under the table, and opening it to reveal five matt black outfits, each having a little insignia on it, "I ran these up yesterday."

The others looked over the suits, apparently made of an incredibly thin, but flexible material, feeling almost like silk, and each coming with a hood and half face mask, with a little suspicion, and not a little confusion. How had she managed to produce these? When and where had she got the material or the design?

"They are a nano-weave utility suit, that will allow you to channel your powers through the weave while retaining its integrity. I've channelled our comms systems into them, so we don't need to keep pressing silly buttons to talk. When you need to talk, just name the person and the appropriate comm. unit will be activated. Without a name first, we all hear it."

"Handy," commented Simon, "what do I need one for?".

"It fits under your armour," she explained, nodding when understanding hit him.

"Anything else?" John was looking it over suspiciously.

"Well there are a few other things; but the main thing is that both Simon's HUD, and mine, can track these suits so that we will know where you are. That should help with the coordination of the battle; and if you're insisting on doing it," her disapproval was obvious in her tone, but equally as obviously ignored, "it will help coordinate your rescue of Isabella."

The others all looked at her in surprise, that, despite her opposition, she was helping. She looked at all their faces, with a slightly overly innocent look, "they may help you to at least survive your attempt."

"What else?" Jack was the first to air his immediate suspicions.

"Well," she seemed suddenly shy about her work.

"Spit it out," John barked not wanting any surprises.

"I put in vital sign monitors too," she added. "like the NASA suits."

Helena raised her eyebrows in surprise, "Good idea. Anything else"

"That's it," Charlene lied.

She passed the suits around, "Try them on. I think I got the sizes right but,"

A few minutes later, with everyone in their new suits, the meetings reconvened.

"What's with the symbols on them?" Simon asked, the others barely noticing, but each one had a different symbol, on the left-hand breast.

"They represent your code names," they rolled their eyes at that, she lifted her hand.

"Simon's Atom is that of Titanium," he humphed at that, even if it was appropriate.

"John's is a PileDriver," John looked at it feigning indifference.

"Mine's the Chimera, of Legend, of course," she smiled at the conceit.

"Mine's blank" complained Jack.

"Rub it!" Charlene instructed, and as he did so, a pale white knight appeared.

"So, what is mine?" asked Helena, a little curious. It was a serpent bodied woman, with two tails., surrounded by fire.

"Echidna, the witch mother of us all, WitchFire," Charlene having planned out this little charade to distract them from the real purpose of the badges, which were her safety net, should things go totally wrong.

"I suppose they are very nice, but why bother with them," Simon asked.

Charlene had planted electronics within the badges, but the actual question flummoxed her. She had no idea why she'd used those symbols, it had just seemed right.

"Watch." She whispered, "Titanium!" and his badge illuminated with her symbol and he heard her loud and clear, in his ear.

"I see, it amplifies, even the quietest voice. Why did you not just say?"

"Easier to show you, and it was for,"

"Dramatic effect," whispered Jack, all the suits showing his knight symbol because he had not specified a specific person.

Helena pursed her lips, "an effective demonstration, thank you, Chi'mera," Charlene nodding an acknowledgement.

"Ok. Let's get back to our original purpose here. Planning!"

"So, let's discuss what's next," and they sat down, and the planning began in earnest.

They were sitting at the table for several hours, going into details about who was doing what, but there were several sticking points; mainly about the timing of the rescue, what they needed to do about the machine and any Ghe'Dar that got through the portal.

"The main problem is that we don't know what kind of forces the other M.I. agents are bringing, only that they have been warned, that they turn up, and that our sneaky little Chi'mera, will get a message to them," Helena summed the situation up as they saw it, using a piecemeal battlefield map on the table, drawn out using sheets of paper, showing what they had been able to see. Stones from the courtyard represented the various forces there. They had been at it for some time when a thought occurred to Charlene.

"Helena, you can create images in peoples head right?"

"If I have a clear enough picture of what I'm showing, yes," Charlene twisted her lips.

"When I was tapped into the ship during the battle, I did see everything. The ship pumped it into my mind. Could you?" she made a twisting motion.

"Sorry Charlene, my power does not work like that," Helena smiled, "good idea but I'm not actually a mind reader."

"But," Simon interrupted, "you can probably feed the data into my HUD, our systems being compatible, then Helena can then see it for herself and do her thing," the three of them started to discuss the possibilities coming up for air after a few minutes, resulting in a workable plan.

So about five minutes later, Helena was sat in Titanium, as though it was a control seat; her head in the helmet, but her hands on her staff. Charlene, had a tentacle wrapped around the helmet, holding her interface to its' visor, the others looking on at the peculiar arrangement.

"This looks so surreal," John commented.

"Yeah, but I think we left 'real' and 'normal' a-ways back," Jack muttered, "I'm sorry John, but I think we just better get used to these kinds of things from them," and he chuckled, "and from ourselves in the future." He saw that they were nearly ready. "One more weird experience, in a weird world," John grimaced.

"Ok. I think we can try it now," announced Simon, standing next to the armour, accessing a panel, on the side of it.

"Beginning reply," said Charlene.

"I can see it," said Helena reported. "Get ready, steady, projecting."

Each person, simultaneous, saw the images of the battle, as seen from the Saucer's advanced tactical sensor array. For the first time, except for Charlene, they could appreciate the Ghe'Dar technology. In 3D, in their heads, they saw the portal machine, the mothership, the scout ship they had been in, the breach in the forcefield surrounding the scene; and the battle going on for it.

"Wow!" Jack said quietly.

"That's something else," John was surprised at the resolution and clarity of it all.

Simon gulped, "the scanning tech. required for this is way in advance of our own. If we don't stop them here, our forces won't stand a cat in hell's chance."

Helena recovered from the awe first, "ok, what do we look at first. I cannot maintain this forever."

John took up the gauntlet, "three things: The Breach, The Machine and our placements."

"Breach first," Helena instructed sounding strained, and bringing the mental images to focus there, "this is just after the machine malfunctioned."

There was a mass of two dozen Airsleds, rising to attack a small group of about eight helicopters. On the ground, several squads of soldiers, a mix of uniformed, black-clad and irregular civilian, or perhaps mercenary personnel, were entrenching themselves around the breach.

"Just like the dream," John muttered.

"What is?" Jack's sharp ears picking up the comment.

"While I was out, I had a dream. I could see all this, kind of frozen, like a picture, but in 3D," the playback stopping, as Charlene heard him speaking up.

"Like this?"

Pain, like fire, ripped through John's head and he staggered, but the images were there. A woman screaming at him, "What have you done?", The Demon, the bargain. Pain ripped through his stomach and wrist,

"Ahhh!" he screamed bringing his hands to his head, his eyes snapping shut automatically; though neither the view nor the pain changed, the pain forcing him to his knees.

"Easy there," soothed Helena, stopping the projection of the image.

"I, I don't know what happened," John lied. "Perhaps I'm still not strong enough to do this," he tried standing; failing as the pain in his stomach ripped like razors through him. Helena started to heal him, the pain only increasing, making him bat her hand away.

"I'll be fine. I think I just need rest. I'll go get some sleep," the pain starting to subside, although Helena looked dubiously at him, beginning to follow.

"I'll be ok, I said," he grunted loudly, waving her back.

The rest watched him stagger up the stairs, concern showing on all their faces, with the except of Helena. Jack saw her look, "what is it?"

"I'm not sure, there is something in the way that happened that is vaguely familiar."

"Serious?" Jack was suddenly concerned too.

"Not sure until I recall what it is that is so familiar," Helena's face was contorted into a gurn of attempted recollection.

"I'm sure it will come to you," he said, projecting confidence at her, her face relaxing a little, as she recognised his support.

"Thanks," and impulsively she leaned forward and kissed him, an electric thrill going through them as their lips touched. Time seemed to slow, and each put a hand to the others cheek, the moment appearing to last, and last, and last; both would remember it for their entire lifetime.

At that moment, as John disappeared upstairs, Charlene had briefly glanced in their direction, slightly embarrassed by their show of mutual affection. However, as they touched, the pair glowed slightly, or more correctly, Helena glowed slightly, that light flowing from her, to Jack, Charlene experiencing a sudden, almost familiarly, flush of warmth. She was going to speak, but somehow the moment kept her silent; and the second after, it had passed, she felt that perhaps it was better to remain silent. Maybe she had imagined it, and they all had enough on their plate as it was. As the pair broke apart, their looks of astonishment were truly a picture, Charlene looking away, with the sneaking suspicion she'd probably seen more than they had.

"I'm sorry," Helena saw the strange look on Jack's face, mistaking it for puzzlement.

He did not say anything, he just kissed her back.

A hand descended on Charlene's shoulder making her jump.

"Let's give them some privacy," Simon whispered.

"I," he started her moving, guiding her out, quietly, knowing that they needed to be alone and leaving as unobtrusively as possible.

When Helena and Jack broke the second time, they seemed to come to their senses looking around apologetically, to find that the room was already empty. They looked at each other, grinning like naughty school kids who'd just been caught out.

"I think they got embarrassed," Jack chuckled.

"I would be," her arm winding around his waist. "You know that they'll never let us live this down," she said.

"Would not want them to," Jacks' hand was under her arm.

"We only have a few days before the end of the world, you know?" She half-joked.

"Well let's make sure we have longer," he said pulling her to arm's length, "just for you, I'll save the world," his extravagantly romantic statement making her smile sincerely.

"Only because you live on it too," she contradicted.

"No. Only because YOU live on it," he corrected, pulling her close again.

"It's early yet," she murmured.

Jack frowned, but then let her go, "I suppose," he pouted a little, looking so much like the truant schoolboy, who'd just been told to go to school, that she laughed loudly.

"Let's go gather them again," he said, sounding extremely reluctant.

"Let's leave John, for the moment. He really should rest after experiencing pain like that again," he nodded and headed off to the barn.

About thirty minutes later, John came downstairs, feeling little better, seeing the others gathered around the table again, apparently staring into space, "what's this, planning without me?"

"We thought you were out of it," Jack countered.

"Seen anything of interest," he said in a slightly surly tone, his head still pounding.

"I could show you," Helena prompted.

John did actually consider saying no, but he needed to have input; for Isabella's sake, so with great reluctance, he nodded.

Once again he was there, but, strangely, this time there was no pain, the image almost the same, but with labels against everything.

Helena was looking at him, concern for him apparent, "I'm fine! No pain this time," he reassured her with a forced smile, despite the residual pain from the first session.

She pursed her lips, shrugged, then smiled, "Good. Then we can have your input then," John closing his eyes and, as he had in the dream, saw the pattern of the attack and human forces defensive stance.

"The humans are creating a diversion; probably arranged beforehand," the others looking at him awaiting an explanation, as to how he knew that.

"The setup is designed to draw the enemy forces this way," he swept his hand towards the breach, "they're not trying to overwhelm the Ghe'Dar, they are trying to get them out of the way of the attacking force, over here," he indicated an area on the other side of the machine. "Zoom here," he pointed to the hedge area; the place he'd failed to see in his dream. There, four shadowy images were crouched low, one fairly obviously Titanium, not really that low. The team all looked at the figures, trying to understand what was shown.

"Only four, and unclear," muttered Helena. "What time frame are we on?"

"Just before the temporal jump," noted Simon.

"Can we improve the resolution?" John asked.

"No. Sorry. The image is only as good as the Ghe'Dar scanners provide," Simon replied, making sure the others knew who to blame.

"So how come, with such advanced scanners, they could not see us properly," Charlene asked, frustrated at seeing important clues in so tantalising a fashion.

"My Guess?" Simon thought hard, "It's probably some form of temporal interference, either actual or conscious."

"Sorry?" Jack was perplexed by the statement.

Simons forehead furrowed, as though he was trying to formulate an explanation that the others might actually understand. "It might be that their science cannot deal with temporal energies. So, when an entity resonates with that energy, the scanner cannot process the image correctly, leaving it in a lower resolution."

"And the other possibility?" Jack asked as he thought the first answer though.

"Time does not want us to see," his voice trailed off.

"You're talking like time might be sentient?" Helena a little disturbed by both the thought and the fact that it was Simon, of all people, who'd proposed it.

Simon looked at her, amused by her face's projected puzzlement.

"Hey, I've read science fiction too, you know. Besides, with what we have been through even I have to open my mind to new possibilities sometime.

"But," she started.

"I don't know for sure, but there may be another possibility," said Charlene, the others looking at her this time.

"When I was coming through the portal I saw another version of me, a different possible me, I mean," She left it open.

"Yuck, Quantum-Temporal physics," Simon shaking his head in disgust; the others looking bewildered again. He took a deep breath. "Ok. She's suggesting, basically, that the images are not clear, because the people there have not been decided yet; so the system cannot determine what to show, because it changes, based on our decisions.

"They just show four there though, and there are five of us," pointed out Helena.

"Which might be significant, or might just mean that one of us is in the group at the gate, directing fire," John added.

"Well at least we know the route to take, and that Titanium will be there for guidance," Jack noted.

"It still does not answer the question on what to do about the machine," Helena pointed out.

Simon shuffled a little, "Chi'mera and I have come up with something, during our ruminations, and trials, with my power system," he nodded to Charlene.

"We noticed, that when I had my armour deployed, during our first experience with Ghe'Dar portal technology, I was saved from the effects of the portal energy, that caught our dear Simon in its grasp."

"So, she will go into the machine, and, using the comms. system, I will guide her through redirecting the power systems using her tentacles."

"What about me?" Jack asked.

The image shifted and showing the interior of the machine, a model that the others had seen for the first time. "This highlighted area shows the area that Jack could see; remembering that he was mainly looking at the discharges, the mothership above him, and the portal generator," Simon continued. "We have here," he pointed to a purple line, from another entrance to the rear of the one Jack had used, "the path, that Chi'mera can use to get to the control system." The image changed, showing power flows; and the cables coming in from the scout ship to a panel, opposite the small portal generator in the machine.

"We think, that, utilising her knowledge of the Ghe'Dar language, and with my engineering knowledge, we can regain control of the power, re-directing it through the portal in such a manner as to collapse the portal this end, destroy the invading fleet en-route, the remaining ships at the other end and, hopefully, the entrance to the portal as well."

"Ok, how convinced are you that you can do this?" Helena pressed.

The two scientists looked at one another, Simon shrugging and Charlene tilting her head, "90%", "95%", they said simultaneously.

The others looked unconvinced.

"Pretty good then?"

"The Ghe'Dar language is all about power, and my HUD is almost wholly translated, in that area. So yeah, pretty good," Charlene put her authority into the statement.

"While she does that, we'll try and rescue Isabella," although Charlene gave him a fierce look when he said it, "and try and get her back here," he pointed at the hedges to the rear of the machine.

"Meanwhile, the rest of us will coordinate the attack against the remaining Ghe'Dar forces, attempting to capture them and their equipment."

"And after that?" John asked, clearly eager to depart.

"After that, we go hunting down the remaining Ghe'Dar, their converts and anyone that helped them for gain," added Charlene, feeling angry that the others had assumed that the discussion about Isabella's rescue was over, while she did not think so.

"And we finish this," Jack said emphatically, everyone nodding in agreement of that.

The rest of the day was spent in ironing out the details, timings, ideas, and concerns. But during that time John had started to hear faint laughter in his head, gradually getting louder and louder. Finally, he'd had enough, "please excuse me, I guess I'm still a little tired after all. See you all in the morning," and, without waiting for a response, he went back upstairs.

"He seemed better when he came down," commented Jack, looking around the others and seeing agreement in their eyes.

"Perhaps, an early night would help all of us," suggested Helena, with a slight side glance at Jack.

It was Simon that replied first, "it most certainly would. Then perhaps we can discuss; how the hell we are going to get to CERN?" He moved up the stairs to grab a room.

"Good point," Charlene stated and started going upstairs too, deliberately leaving the other two behind. She made sure all the doors were closed upstairs when she went to bed.

Chapter 18

RACE TO THE FINISH LINE

Ricks used his binoculars to view the target site in detail, he preferred to look down on targets, but being well concealed, close up, came a close second. Fortunately, CERN was a well-documented and oft frequented site, and the web maps were sufficiently visited, that one more enquiry on a public computer should not cause suspicion he was sure. What he was also convinced of, was that the building he was looking at did not appear on any of them.

Where there should have been greenfield site next to the road, in the north of the laboratories, stood a strange new blue-purple building, looking like it belonged in a space opera, rather than standing next to a modern-day scientific research facility. At nearly fifty meters across and the same high, it dwarfed the other CERN structures; but that wasn't what Ricks was really looking at. No, he was checking the extremely well-armed guards, strange flying vehicles and armoured troops, as well as the workers and equipment being brought in.

"Wow. I think we have a big problem here guys," he muttered.

"You think?" whispered Gareth, from right next to him, even though there was no way that the people on the site could hear them over the noise of diggers, earth movers, armoured suits and Airsleds.

"I'm not thinking Bio-weapon here," came a from comment behind them, Haines sweeping the scene, spotting a few strange armoured figures clustered together, one without its' helmet being quickly disciplined, and putting it straight back on.

"Not unless you count bio-engineer creatures or aliens," the others turned at that,

"what?" they asked simultaneously.

"Check out eleven o'clock, there," he pointed to a saucer-shaped vehicle carefully obscured by bush and scrub, an armoured figure nearby, with a group of people wearing strange helms, clearing the brush in the area, towards which some diggers trundled up.

Supervising the workers was, a large un-armoured being, surveying the area with its four inhuman eyes; its' strange squid-like head tilting this way and that, scoping out the lay of the land. He looked at one of the smaller armoured creatures next to him and gestured, in a broad stroke, at the foliage the humans had started on.

"I guess he just ordered them to clear it all, so there is a clear field of fire."

"Wow, you're making a big leap there," Ricks complained, then turned, "but somehow I think your right. This is no terrorist bio-weapon plant," his voice sinking.

"It's a bridgehead," Gareth finished

"They are digging in and fortifying, the fact that CERN is here prohibits a nuclear strike really," Haines was leaping ahead.

"They would if it would stop an invasion," Gareth pointed out.

"I don't think so. If you think the A-bomb is powerful, imagine what a fusion bomb, fuelled by all the exotics held here would do?" Gareth cringed.

"Ok, so we crack the bridgehead. They have advanced vehicles, so probably advanced weapons too?"

"Check out that structure at three, there," Ricks pointed out a small pyramid and dome combination. They were just lowering the pyramid into the ground; but the dome had a small slit in it, like a mini-observatory.

"Tracking system?" Gareth postulated.

"Or AA battery," Haines surmised, "whatever it is it probably ain't going to aid us. I'm more worried about the armoured troops, let the air force worry about the AA and those sleds. They aren't fast, so easy enough to knock down, but the armoured troops will require grenades or RPGs, and armour-piercing rounds to take out, and there are too many of them for a small unit to neutralise in time.

"How many of them do you think there are here?" Haines asked, relying on their younger eyes to spot those he could not.

"Looks like in the order of a hundred; lots of workers; but about two platoons of actual troops, which are armed with heavier weapons, so I'd say one unit of light infantry, the other armoured infantry," Ricks estimated.

"Hmmm. Not a lot for a bridgehead, so either they are tougher than they look, or it was all they could get here, I'm hoping the later, but we need to assume the worst," Haines tugged his chin; a sure sign that he was thinking hard.

"That ship could not possibly fit all those troops, so there must be others. Let's think this through."

"There is a ship here. There are not masses of them, and there are no bigger ships that we know of. So, it's either a scout that has only recently found us or, there is a reason that others have not come," Haines' head started to hurt at the multitude of possibilities.

"The machine is hardly a small-scale endeavour; so that rules out having recently found us, that means there is a reason that the others have not come," he threw it open to the others.

"They are too far away yet, but are on their way," Ricks suggested, the others rolled their eyes with thanks for that, kind of grimace.

"The other cannot make it, or at least they need something to help them," Gareth said pointing to the machine. The others nodded, almost liking that option; thinking it was the most likely.

"They could also be doing this on their own, for reasons that we cannot guess," Gareth added, "although their military demeanour almost precludes that," he finished.

"So, to sum up, it looks like this is a bridgehead, they are trying to create some kind of machine that will bring others, and we need to stop them."

"How long did Selena say she'd take to get here?" Ricks asked

Haines frowned, "She said a week tops, but the people she needed were engaged with other matters at the moment and might be delayed."

"I wonder why no-one has noticed this, after all, it's pretty big, and there is satellite coverage of the region," Ricks wondered.

"They are probably the ones under their influence, or they just don't know what they are seeing. Let's face it, here, who would notice one more strange building, or piece of equipment here?" They all looked at each other at that and shrugged.

Ricks looked at the site again, "how did they get here?"

Haines looked at the humans, zooming in on them, seeing the wires into their skulls for the first time. "Who knows? Perhaps just a random flight path close by, perhaps they caught a radio show and followed it here, or perhaps someone decided they wanted world domination and invited them. However, they actually got here, we'd better stop them."

"Speaking of which, boss; we were told that we'd be needed in about a week and a half right?" Ricks asked.

"That's right?" He looked back towards the area where the pyramid and dome were placed, seeing that they had already been completed.

"Well, by my estimation, unless they have some pretty major problems, which they don't seem to have had so far, that contraption will be completed in less than three days." Ricks looked at Haines, Gareth catching it too.

"Well we aren't doing anything but waiting, at the moment," they all looked at each other and shrugged, then they all grinned, "let's go play!"

The other started to unlimber packs of weapons, but Haines shook his head. "No. They must think the problems are with their machinery or human error; else they will beef up security and the others will never gain entry."

The others objected noisily but got out electronic kit instead, tool pouches and belts.

"What about those helmets?" Ricks added.

"They look like some kind of implants, control units, at a guess," Haines decided. He got out a regular hard-hat, got some wires and, with a little pain, pushed them into his neck.

"That's not going to pass close inspection." Ricks pointed out.

"Well then we'll have to act normal enough to not get inspected," Haines winced as he tried to turn his head, the wires pulling at him a little but staying in, just.

"Wait, got an idea." Gareth took out a makeup kit that he usually used for disguises. He dabbed some glue, then a skin piece, making the join both secure and looking like a poorly healed scare.

Ricks looked at it for a few moments, then pulled his lip, "pretty good," he admired the effect with grudging respect.

"Hey makeup can save your life," Gareth rechecked his work, then dabbed again.

"Selena said exactly the same thing," Haines added, making Ricks chuckle. Gareth's cheeks flushed a little at that.

"Ok," Gareth signalled to Ricks, in a little huffy tone, "your next."

Annecy, France.

Selena ducked, as the huge fist went over her head, sliding to her left as she flicked out a hand to the ankle of her attacker; pulling up and back.

The huge man, not correctly balanced, tilted back and landed, with a massive crunch, head first on the wooden floor. A brief waft of air, above her, indicated the person trying to land on her back had missed. She rolled backwards, targeting the second attacker as she popped up into the air, leaving clean air between her and the punch that the attacker had thrown at where she should have been.

In mid-air, as she directed a heel to the temple of the second attacker, Selena spared a glance for the third, who was standing back a little. Smarter than the other two then.

The heel hit home, knocking the second attacker clean out, even before he landed.

"So, you are Selena then," commented the third person conversationally.

She landed, seeing a large weapon pointed at her forehead. She slowly put her hands up, realising that he was just out of range of any non-weapon attack.

"Relax, mon amie. They," and he pointed to those on the ground, "were just to confirm you're ID."

"You could have just asked!" she complained, dusting herself off.

"Hey, if you're coming to see the boss, you know that that is not true," he replied pointing out the door in the back of the room. He waved his gun and, carefully, guided her, from the small room they were in, up a small flight of stairs; staying a safe distance from her at all times. The corridor turned right and opened out into a larger room.

The room was well appointed with tables, chairs, bookcases, and a large real fireplace, its roaring log fire belting its heat out into the room, lighting that around the hearth, additional lighting, subdued candlelight; with a single crystal chandelier light, the main area. A fully lit Menorah took pride of place, under the portrait of a handsome couple on the mantle. In one of the half dozen chairs, relaxed a gentleman, great in both stature and girth, his face different from most in her business, being both friendly and cheerful.

"Ah, my little Selena! What a pleasure!" He waved her in, signalling for the other man to put away his gun.

"Pappa! The receptionists were a little rough today," the tone was slightly frosty, causing the man to wince a little.

"Of necessity, my dear," he indicated a chair close to him, but still with the other man between them, indicating a carafe of wine on the table, freshly started.

"We have heard strange things recently: People we have paid off for decades, not answering their phones; old friends acting strangely and people disappearing."

"I too have heard strange things," she replied carefully.

"Yes, your call was intriguing, hence our meeting," he poured a glass of wine for each of them, adding water to hers.

"Pappa," she chided, "I have been an adult for many years," she looked pointedly at the glass.

"Trust me, my dear, you'll appreciate this," surprising her, he took a deep gulp from his glass, not even smelling it first. He was usually quite appreciative of wines subtleties.

"The 'water' is actually a counter agent, to a substance we found in the mainstream wines, that I'm sure you have been drinking for weeks." Her eyes shot up, her hand hovering near the glass, but not moving it to her lips.

"It appears to be a kind of will suppressant, a very subtle one and, much as I miss your company at home, I would not like you to fall prey to someone with this in your system."

He pressed a button on the table, and a screen appeared on the clear wall, displaying a chemical formula, and an electronic device. "They appear to work in tandem, but we don't know who has laced the wines of France with them, nor their real goals."

Selena was sceptical, but if it was a trick, why display it when she was already in their power; besides this was Pappa. She looked at the glass again, lifted it in salute and took a large swig, as a sign of trust if nothing else, the man smiling reassuringly. "You were always braver than most," he complimented her, his smile broadening.

"What now?" She said, feeling a little light headed.

"Now? Well, you'll probably be sick," he said with a winsome little smile, signalling to his bodyguard, who grabbed a bucket from under the table.

Her eyes went wide at the pronouncement, but a rumble in her stomach indicated he was not joking, "you could have," the reaction taking effect, causing her to convulse.

"Easy there," said the guard, guiding her head to the bucket as a clear fluid came out through mouth, nose and even a trickle from her ears. "It will take a few goes to clear it all," he explained as she heaved again.

"While you're not talking, let me explain," the large man stood.

"For a few weeks, we'd been getting reports of spies, not unlike yourself, being spotted openly in various halls of power," he waddled over to a cabinet, getting out a large cigar. "At first, I thought the government was going through a purge, or a clampdown, on people like myself. However, as we looked into it, it appeared that they were in the same position. Then after a few days, things changed, the powers started to help this new interest, and the focus turned to us."

Selena, tried to speak, but her third convulsion included her breakfast; and she gave up trying to stop them.

"They shut down old Cherdal, taking all his workers somewhere up north, while they simply assassinated Herwell and all his partners, and I was next on their lists, apparently. Fortunately, my men were always better than Herwell's, even if I have fewer of them," he indicated his guard, who was looking at Selena's face, judging if she'd emptied herself fully.

"Renee, here got me out, just in time, before the police arrived with our new friends in tow," puffing thoughtfully on the cigar. "Their actions forced me to go deeper into the shadows and concentrate my forces here, just to keep them at bay," he glanced at her.

"Of course, I still have others in place to guard my assets, but they are in effect sealed up tight and losing business."

"Better losing business, than losing your life," croaked Selena.

"Exactly my dear," he said waving his cigar at her. "Feeling better now?" He looked at her, with genuine concern in his eyes.

"Well, not better, but nothing else is coming out," her throat was a little saw. "Was that really necessary though?"

"Unless you fancy working for the enemy, yes," he looked at her pointedly.

"Let's get back to you having your people close by," she said sitting up straight, looking at the guard, who saw the 'business' look coming into her eyes.

"Yes. I had them take up a few spots locally," he informed her cagily, trying not to give her too much information.

"That's good because I happen to have information on where our new friends are and what they are trying to do if you want to know."

The large man suddenly looked at her intensely, and put his cigar down, sitting opposite her. "My, I thought you were here for information, not giving it out," he smiled a particularly broad smile.

"Oh, I'm not giving out presents," the smile fell off his face, "I've come here to ask for your people, so that we can go and stop them," his face turning a little suspicious and, incredulous.

"You've come here to ask me for my people," he partially laughed, partially choking.

"You are a dear daughter to me, but you could not afford to hire out all my people from me, and even a dear daughter, will not get them free," the finality of the tone did not dissuade her.

"I'll bet you that I can!" She smiled a supremely confident, smile; and produced a large card from her pocket; hiding it from him under the table, the guard frowning but remained still.

"Ah, you want to play for it?" He reached for a pack of cards, slightly hidden by a couple of books.

"Oh, that's ok. I already have the winning card," and she flipped the card on to the table.

The man's face fell. "Your joking, right?" then he saw the Tarot card, his face going pale. There, the Grim Reaper sat in front of him. He looked at his guard who started to reach for his gun again, a brief shake of the head stopping him, but he did not relax.

"Is this a threat?" He pointed at the card.

"No. It's a call to arms," his face went even paler, a hint of fear entering his eyes.

"My former colleges are marshalling forces again for an operation. They need your help."

"Ha, then they can pay for my services like you, only more," he started.

"Pappa. It's a Reaper 9 alert. You know what that means. You above all, know what that means." Her eyes pleaded for understanding and cooperation.

His reaction was, to say the least unexpected, as he virtually threw the card away, as tears streaking his face with misery. "You. You bring this to me! Why?" He looked at a picture on the wall bearing the family name. "Did we not suffer enough before? 'Never again,' we said when we found out about the camps. 'Never again!'" his fist pounding the table, jarring everything on it.

"I'm sorry Pappa; you were the only one I could trust," she reached across to him trying to steady the man's hand, instead his grabbing hers' in a crushing grip. He looked deep into her eyes, his own flooded with bitter tears of remembered suffering.

"You find these people, who would do this thing. You find them, and, you end them. For me. For our people. Especially for your grandfather and mother," he glanced again at the picture over the fire; the caption read "In memory of those who Fell at Belsen."

"I will Pappa," she said in relief.

"Yes. Renee will give you the names and call them in," he dismissed them both with a wave, the sobs that came from the room did not stop even after the door closed behind them.

Renee grabbed a small object from a side room on the way out, handing her a diary. "Here are the names you need. Will a dozen men be enough? Or should I call others."

"They will have to be. We cannot spare the time to vet others." She stopped and looked at him, "take care of Pappa. It would be, a favour, for me," there was a wealth of meaning in the words, both gratitude and pleading.

"I will Selena, as my parents did before me; you are, family," and with that he bowed and went back upstairs, leaving her to let herself out.

She looked at the names and addresses. They were few, but she knew some by reputation. They were, perhaps, enough. This was emotionally draining, even more so than leaving Haines, the first time.

"Ok, Haines, you'd better have something for them after all this; cause if you don't, my father will kill you, even if I don't," she snarled, and went off to find her troops.

Titanium was standing at his full seven-foot height, impressive, even with PileDriver and Chi'mera next to him, who were not small. Even GhostKnight, with his armour on, looked small in comparison.

The team had spent another day debating, planning and counter-planning, and had all put in ideas and plans; Charlene had even given suggestions on the rescue of Isabella. Now they were getting down to the logistics.

"We need transport. Something big enough to transport Titanium, that won't attract too much attention from officialdom," Helena looking at where they were and scanning for an appropriate route. "Here we are, just south of Montargis, and here, is where we need to get to, CERN, right on the France Swiss Border." She looked at the roads "We'll travel by night, to the main roads and hitch a ride. Chi'mera can go as anyone she likes, but the rest of us will have to stay hidden or disguise ourselves as something other than who we are."

"An articulated lorry will serve us well. Chi'mera can get the lift, then, before it starts off, Jack, me and John can get inside. Titanium can stay up top, making sure he doesn't go to sleep near any low bridges." Helena nodded, but there were frowns from John and Simon.

"What about breaks and food?" John asked.

"Just call Chi'mera, and she'll ask the driver," Helena pointed out.

"I'm sure I can be persuasive enough," Charlene looked at John, who she knew was still trying to figure out why she'd helped with the plans to save Isabelle, even though she was dead set against it.

"Yeah, whatever," he growled.

"What about the border controls?" Simon asked. "Switzerland is not in the Euro-zone, they will have a fully functional border.

"Good point," Helena put a finger to her lips, "but as I remember it, the machine is on the French side of the border, on the other side of CERN so we won't need to cross it."

"That saves at least one problem anyway," commented Jack.

"As if the ones we have are not enough," John countered.

"Hey now, stop that," Helena ordered getting a bit cross with the way John was so negative. "We are doing what we can, the faster we do it, the sooner this will be over."

"One way or another," muttered John, under his breath. The laughter was still bouncing around in his head, like a severe bout of Tinnitus.

Helena's exasperation was growing, but she continued.

"Shut up John!" Charlene stepped closer to him, but Jack sidestepped to block her.

"Hey. Enough!" Helena raised her voice, something had not heard her do, triggering surprise on their faces.

"Let's try and remain calm. I know you have all had a rough time, but now is definitely not the time to have it out. John, Charlene. Settled down. That is an order." She did not use her authority often, but when she did, she could wield it well. They all looked a little stunned for a second, then moved around so that various people were not stood next to one another, all looking expectantly at Helena, like naughty school children.

"Let's discuss the rescue. Do we all understand our positioning to get this done?"

There were nods, but mostly they glanced at Charlene, the primary dissenter, though she remained silent, anything having made her position perfectly clear. There was no need to create any more discord, by restating it. She looked up, saw the faces turned towards her, nodding abruptly.

"Ok. Then let's review the approach," she wanted confirmation of their understanding as to what was required. The timing was critical, and they all needed crystal clear focus.

"We approach from the west, where the breach in the force field will appear," started Simon, remembering that the armour he now wore, would be found there. "We wait until Charlene has moved to take control of the machine, moving under cover of the hedge. Then we wait until Isabella," there was a catch in John's voice throat he said her name, "has disabled the AA batteries, to move down the rest of the hedge so that we are out of sight of our other selves before the main battle begins and the M.I. forces appear at the breach."

"Then I go camouflaged and get ready to power dive to save Isabella; when the machine control is lost," continued Simon. "When Jack drops her, I'll position myself under where she will be when he moves away. Then I powerclimb, at max thrust, to escape the Dimensional closure, depositing her with John," he looked at John, seeing the intensity of his attention, as he made sure everyone knew their part in this desperate attempt.

"Then we all aid either Charlene," Helena nodded at Simon, "or the attack forces," she nodded at John and Jack, "to stop the aliens from interfering with Charlene and Simon. Sound good to everyone?" everyone nodding, even Charlene who thought back to her first portal transit, "trust your instincts," which were screaming at her at the moment. She rather hesitantly asked the obvious question, "what happens if something goes wrong?"

They all stopped, especially John, "then we deal with it as best we can, and we go on," Helena said finally, although John's face suggested he'd rather not.

"Simon?" Charlene approached him.

"Yes, Charlene?" carrying on putting together a sizable piece of equipment. It seemed he'd managed to balance his power sufficiently to create small electrical induction fields, now being capable of moving small items without frying them, looking almost like magic to Charlene.

"Can you guide me through the reset sequence for the Ghe'Dar machine and the restructuring we need to cause the feedback pulse?"

"Ah, I decided not to worry you with that my dear, the device is a hardwired, self-grounded power interface," he indicated the equipment on the bench, causing her to regard it, wondering what new marvel the electronic wizard had produced.

"All you need to do," the irony of the statement was not lost on her, Simon smiling sardonically as he said it, "is get inside, find a power interface, bolt this on, securely, find the interrupt breaker and throw it." She raised her eyebrows with an inquiring look.

"This will then re-route the power, as the circuit reinitialises and goes through the transformer, sending a power surge through the whole system at once, locking the re-directed energy and fusing the control, to stop the Ghe'Dar from fixing it without replacing the whole machine. It will also cause a security lockdown on the building, so you should be safe inside from the Ghe'Dar outside.

"Once that is done, and Isabella is safe, I'll be free to fly in and get you out."

Charlene was indeed impressed with how much he'd thought it through, unlike the others, who'd been fixated on Isabella. She patted him on his armoured shoulder, forgetting about the mirror pieces. A slight cut on her fingers was her reward, although neither she nor Simon noticed it. The blood dribbled behind the tiles and into a tight joint in the armour. There the Nanites in the blood started to analyse the new environment and begin repairing the damage.

"I've left our hosts a little currency in their usual hiding place, that I picked up to pay for stores and parts," Jack was saying to Helena, who just shook her head.

"Yes, they should be back soon, I've been keeping up with the household choirs, so they will not be too suspicious.

Jack moved closer, and she looked around, making sure no one else was about.

"What happens afterwards?" he asked. She looked both relaxed and calm about their relationship.

"Well, we tell Craig, firstly; he should be ok with it, but we might find that we are given different assignments once we do." She did not seem too happy about that but was more philosophical than Jack, who had demonstrated a genuine attachment to her.

"I mean what happens to us," he was asking a different question she knew.

She smiled and leaned forward to flick his hair, and placed her palm against his cheek, "well that will be entirely up to you, love," him leaning against her hand and she brushed his other cheek with a faint kiss, then danced away laughing, not in a mocking way, but playfully. He was going to follow her, but an intense John walked through the door having been outside for some reason.

"John?" The man ignored him and ploughed straight upstairs.

"You'd think that he'd be little happier now that we are nearer to saving Isabella."

John had just been for a walk, trying to quiet the voice in his head, repeating a word, that strange word that he could not pronounce, or even visualise and saying over and over "don't forget the deal." The pain was no worse, but it was no better either, requiring him to find a supply of painkillers from the farm's bathroom cabinet, taking them without telling the others, but already using most of them.

He found himself upstairs starring at the bed where he'd been comatose and wondering if he'd done the right thing. It had only been a dream initially, but now he seemed to experience the effects, as though it was real. He looked at that bed once more, then started out of the room, when a faint voice caught his ears.

"Why did you leave me John?" a faint image appearing, of a pale Isabella reaching up from the bed, trying to grasp his hand. He reached out too, but the bed seemed to drop away into a pit of writhing maggots. He dived forward to catch her, landing on the bed, the image gone. He shook his head vigorously, something strange was going on, but he dared not tell the others, lest they thought he was cracking up. This would all be finished soon, he was sure: he'd get his girl, find a cure for his pains, and it would all be over. He had to keep that in mind if he could get over the pain and voices.

The real question was, how was he going to keep Helena away from the fight? Every time he thought that perhaps he should just leave it, the voice came to remind him of the deal. Sometimes the nagging worse than the pain from the wounds.

"What did you actually make that from?" Charlene asked, when she inspected the heavy piece of equipment, rapidly taking the form of a giant beetle.

"Oh, I, er, well, I used the pieces from the old tractor, and I took a walk in the area to acquire a few heavy transformers, that were in abandoned farms in the area. Well, a farm up for sale actually."

Charlene looked at him, not thinking he was the type to do that? Ah well, it was to save the world, so she'd manage somehow. "How heavy is it?"

"It's about the same as a small engine. Well within your capabilities," he answered, still adjusting the coils on one side, and putting the grounding shield on its back. "When you press it against the casing of the power unit, these magnets will activate to clamp it in place. I'd rather you use these points," indicating four large circular holes on the edge of the shield, "to place clamping restraints to the device, to ensure power surges do not detach it from the panel before the reset."

"I'll do my best," she murmured, not pointing out that without her steroid boosts she was not really that strong. God; she'd be starving after this.

It was a late evening at CERN, evening shadows hiding the M.I. agents next visit to the site. "Well?" Haines asked.

"They are guarding it like a father guards his daughter's virginity," Ricks cursed, "the perimeter has a two hundred per cent coverage, and those bloody guards don't rotate, nor do they seem to sleep, relax or even take a toilet break."

"Robots?" Haines conjectured.

"Possibly, or I missed when they went. I'm getting bloody tired."

"Oh come on, you went three days without sleep in Canada," Haines reminded him.

"Being chased by wild hunters is a bit of an incentive," Ricks pointed out.

"So saving the world should be a better one. Suck it up and check."

Gareth came bombing into their hide, "ok, I've arranged a little delay for them."

Ricks looked astonished, "you got through their perimeter?" He knew Gareth was better than him, but this was incredible.

"Not exactly. Watch!" He pointed to a truck on the Swiss side of the border, which looked like a local government repair truck. Gareth lifted a small remote and pressed the trigger, the vehicle starting to roll.

"A bomb?" Haines asked confused.

"Much better. Just watch and check the perimeter," he pointed to an area just in front of the truck. Some controlled engineers had finished their work, and a field appeared over the machine, blocking out any sign of the building, while still showing the golf course.

"Impressive. How did you find out about that?" Ricks asked, interested.

"I didn't. It's impressive for sure, but all I saw was a display on a terminal, as they were testing the perimeter defences," he shrugged, "this will work better if they are channelling power through that, whatever it is. Forcefield?" He looked at Haines, who just looked bewildered at him.

"Probably."

The truck was getting near the line in the grass, that demarked the defence perimeter, "best turn off your electronic kit now," Gareth added belatedly.

"You're not serious?" Ricks said, Haines eyes going wide too, but Gareth just grinned and nodded.

As the truck hit the perimeter field, the truck glowed for a few seconds as power arced around it frying the main engine and stopping the vehicle at that point. What it also did was send out a massive EMP: lights, the force field, and all the power in the local area, for nearly three miles around dropped. Even the lights on the saucer disappeared; for all of about ten seconds, at which point they came on slightly dimmer.

Gareth's face fell, "rats, they have backups that don't require fixing after that."

Haines looked around the area. "Look," a few workers were on the floor, either unconscious or dead, others seemed were clawing at their helmets and the armoured suits seemed to be acting strangely like their guidance systems were out. They all looked at one another. "Let's go. While they are like this, we can get some work done. They'll assume it's a product of the EMP," and they set off, staying low, but at speed, to use the time they'd bought to good effect.

The next day, after a quick breakfast, the team moved out, deciding on an older articulated lorry as transport. Helena tidied up the farm, removing as many clues that they had been there as possible, setting up explanations for those that they could not.

The rest waited until Helena spotted the family arriving, to make sure there was no visible sign that their visit had been noticed; then they strolled out, down one of the back routes, towards the main road.

The land was hedgerows and small houses, so when they spotted a lorry, with a Swiss number plate, it was a simple matter for Charlene to wave it down, and ask for a lift.

"Where are you heading?" asked the obviously German driver, the clipped phrases giving it away.

"Geneva. You?" her current body like her original, but slightly more muscled, and with an array of highly visible Tattoos as camouflage.

"Turin. Geneva is on the way, though I try to avoid the centre."

"Not a problem, I'll probably be getting off before the actual border," she smiled.

"Hey now, I'm legit," he warned her, thinking she might be trying to border hop.

"Nothing like that, just want to get to the French side of the town and walk in from there, the view from the hills nearby is exquisite, I hear."

The driver relaxed but still seemed a little wary, humming a little.

"Well, ok," Charlene saw Titanium fly up, quietly settling on the trailer's roof, as the others had disappeared around the back. The Driver opened the door, and she climbed in making a bit of a racket, to cover the sound of the trailer's back doors being opened. Then, with a loud slam, both her door and the rear door were closed.

Her HUD said that the others were aboard, so she relaxed and decided to enjoy the ride. "So, how long does it usually take you to get to Turin from here."

"Usually a day. I have to stop in a few hours; Bloody Tachographs. But honestly, on an empty run, I try to explain that I had a second driver with me, to cover the extra time I drive. Most bosses understand, and I do have a friend that sometimes comes with me to make it more believable, although he tends to only cover the German side of things, as his English is not that good," he explained, seeming quite open about his business dealings.

"Yours' is very good though," she complimented him.

"Thank you. I started to study at Hull, but my family called me back to help with the transport business," he did not seem too worried about it.

They chatted on amiably for a few minutes, then they went quiet, Charlene drinking in the view, and drifting off. After an hour or two, they were well on their way.

The driver eye's, generally on the road, casually looked across at his passenger, finding her was particularly alluring, it had been a long time since he'd seen anyone quite so attractive. He was a bachelor and had been alone for a long time, so was tempted to try his luck. It was not apparent whether she was open for a liaison, but he had a certain amount of juice that would help her feel more relaxed if she was not. He liked his lips deciding to go for it.

"There is some juice in the back, in the green water bottle, if you're feeling thirsty," he commented casually. "If you get some, can you pass me a soda from the fridge?"

Charlene had never been in long-distance transport, so it took a few seconds for her to figure out what he was talking about. As she went in the back, the driver stole a glimpse of her slightly muscular rump. Very nice he thought, he'd like some of that.

As she came back and handed him a can, she slid back into the seat and took a deep swig, as he opened his can, taking a deep swig too, hiding his sly smile.

As she took the second swig of the liquid, her HUD popped up an alert, with the system's analysis of the foreign substance. Hmmm, she recognised the chemical family; a relaxant used, in certain circles, to pacify aggressive prisoners. She yawned a little, for dramatic effect and slowly slid down on the seat. As the driver saw this, he looked at her, "you ok there?" the voice was drawling a little, almost dripping fake concern.

"Just a little tired." She tried not to sound bothered. However she'd heard of people like this on the news; and she hated them, deciding to teach him a real lesson. The simple fact that he would think about doing this made her feel sick. She'd lived a sheltered life, but this would have been something she'd have hoped to have avoided entirely.

As she slipped further down the seat, the driver started to slow down and pull over.

As the driver pulled to a stop, he started to lean over her to undo her seatbelt. She knew now was the time to grab his attention, and as he got within inches of her face, she gave him a scare he would never forget; with his lips' inches from hers, she changed form.

There were few she could do at such short notice, except the one she was really sure she knew would do. In a flash ripple of flesh, she changed into the Ghe'Dar form she'd copied at CERN. The tentacles around her mouth seemed to respond to the presence of meat nearby and shot out and wrapping around the head of the driver. He did not so much lean forward now, as much as get dragged on top of the now armoured figure and start to scream incoherently in terror. He got an exceedingly close view of the razor-shape teeth and suckered tentacles. He desperately tried to pull away; a futile endeavour with the strength that Charlene was using.

She tried to talk, but the strange language of the aliens came out as a peculiar growling, burbling snarl; the effect, with the mouth so close, was to further terrify the driver. Charlene decided that she'd done enough. Flipping back to human form, she released him. The driver, under his own effort, was catapulted back into his seat. She snapped into her former position and casually enquired, "you OK? You look like you just saw a ghost,"

"What the f*** was that?" the driver demanded hysterically, rapidly backing away from her, almost trying to claw through the steel door of the cab, his hand trying unsuccessfully to find the handle behind him.

"What you're talking about," she said playing the innocent. "Did you see something?" She looked around as if trying to see what he was talking about.

"You," he was still wide-eyed, but starting to think that maybe he'd been daydreaming. "I, hmm, sorry, I thought I saw something outside," he lied, tried to cover his attitude. Too many long hours perhaps, he was thinking, or a guilty conscience.

"Oh. Did you need to go?" Indicating that fact that they had stopped.

"What? Oh yeah. I think I will at that," he did have a slight wet patch on his crotch area, which he finally noticed, "damn. Could you do me a favour and get me my clean pants, from the back under the covers?"

"Sure!" she said sweetly. That shock might keep him honest, in future.

"Good move my dear," came a voice over the intercom, "the others needed that. You ok?" Charlene smiled at that.

"I'm fine. Romeo, up here, will behave himself and we'll probably make good time now that I've introduced him to the real me."

"Charlene," Helena moaned, "what did you do?"

"He thought he was going to have fun with me; I showed him his future, if he continued; he thought better of his actions after that," the smug tone could not be missed, and, although Helena might disapprove, Charlene thought that this might make up for other things she'd done.

The driver got warily back into the truck, looking at her as though she could at any moment change back into the monstrosity; which in truth she could. For the rest of the journey, the driver behaved himself, acting like a changed man, however, after a few more miles he seemed to come to a decision, and pulled over again.

"Sorry, you'll have to walk from here," the driver reached across, flinging open the cab door.

"Was it something I said?" Charlene asked, in a quiet voice.

"I think I need some time alone," the driver said, slamming the door behind her.

He drove off quickly, watching the girl disappear into the distance, not see her literally disappear, nor her arrival on the top of the trailer, with a mild pop of sound.

"It will get us a few miles more. I guess that he'll pull into the next service station and try to forget all about me," she muttered to thin air.

"Would it have been so bad to indulge him, Charlene?" John asked.

The stony silence that followed was all the reply required.

It turned out that got another thirty miles closer before the driver pulled over and called it a day. They'd made it about a hundred miles closer in a day; that meant that they had six days to make it the rest of the way.

"Do you think we should try for another lorry?" Charlene queried, looking at the others.

"I don't think so. Even if you change form, and our, rather amorous, driver friend does not blab about the strange encounter, people might make a connection; however accidentally," ruminated Helena. "Let's try walking off the road for a little, and see how much time we can make, perhaps even change the route, so that people cannot make the connection."

Helena looked at the road signs, "that, says Moulins is a few kilometres down the road, so let's keep within sight of the road until we hit the town, then we need to head South East, to get to CERN," she said indicating to the left slightly.

Charlene changed into a male form, similar to the farmer's picture, but younger.

"Err, Charlene, you might want to make your form a little less effeminate," Jack joked.

The rest laughed, except John; who seemed as preoccupied as ever.

Charlene looked at John, her face changing slightly.

"Now you just look worried," Jack commented, her face turning towards him suddenly and becoming less worried, and angrier.

"That's better," he grinned, making sure he was out of easy attack range.

Haines activated the link to the remote cameras; his team had managed to make some serious inroads into the alien security. By making slight adjustments, here and there, they had created several blind spots that, on casual examination, were covered by cameras. The cameras looked in on various sections of the machine and its accompanying equipment. The team had even found how the machine was being powered and arranged for a series of small adjustments and shorts along that line. Also, they had managed to make several minor short circuits on critical systems, until increased activity, and approaching repair teams, had forced them to get out of the area before they were detected.

"Assessment?" Haines asked the other two.

"It will take them a few days to find everything, more if they fix them in the wrong order. I think we are on schedule now," Gareth smiled, in a semi-relaxed manner. He'd been overconfident only once; the top of his leg still ached from the explosion which had taught him better.

"We won't be able to do that again. They've installed a buffer transformer, between the shield and the actually shield power source," Ricks informed them. "Let's hope we've bought enough time."

"Yes let's," added Haines.

"So what do we do while we wait for Selena, and her crew?" Gareth asked.

"We have a few days, so, let's gather what intel. we can, safely, and watch for the others."

"And if they don't turn up as expected?" Ricks said pessimistically.

"Then we improvise and finish this one way or another," Haines said, with a calm and dreadful finality.

It had been three days, since they had arrived in Geneva, and caused the enemy so many problems, and we're starting to get worried when a familiar face showed up for a coffee at a cafe they had been watching, known as a haunt of Selena.

"Marceux has arrived," Ricks observed.

Gareth looked at Haines who nodded, "he's one of hers?" sounding surprised.

"No, he's one of Krinelli's. It seems our girl, has bigger connections than we knew," Ricks, was referring to one of the most significant sources of independent security in the region.

Haines seemed either unimpressed, unaware of the implications or unsurprised; it was hard for Ricks to judge.

"Perhaps he owes her a favour?" Gareth supplied.

"Perhaps," Haines said in an unsurprised tone, looking slightly cagey at that point.

Ricks was suddenly suspicious, "you knew?"

Haines closed his eyes then nodded, sometimes he hated how smart Ricks was.

Gareth made the next jump of logic. "He's one of ours, isn't he?" The tone was of sad irony. "What about the others of that group?"

"He was a deep undercover agent, feeding us intel.," he lifted his hand, "he was semi-retired at that point anyway. He was not involved in the Cadiz killings," referring to a large loss of agents when they were betrayed, by someone in the European arena, "I took care of that one."

"So they have started to arrive. Let's send them what we have found, then we can start to organise." Gareth Started.

"No," they both looked at Haines questioningly. "We wait a day; let them get settled, and make sure they are not attracting attention, or already compromised. Then we call our, not so mysterious boss, and get his take on the situation. Then we call GhostKnight and see if they're in position and arrange for our troops to do what they say is needed."

"And what if they are wrong, like Cadiz?" Ricks queried these amateurs taking the lead.

"Then we do what we say is needed; and all hope to God that we are right," he said with a little smile.

"And if we are not?" Ricks said pessimistically again.

"Then, you can explain to him, in person, why we let his world be destroyed!"

"Are we in range of CERN yet?" Jack asked wearily. After their initial success in getting a lift, and the rather disastrous behaviour of the driver; the number of trucks dried up; rides it seemed were few and far between. It was the weekend, of course, but for a modern country, the roads seemed remarkably empty of large trucks, and when they did pass-by they were either not going in their direction, refrigerated, combination sealed, or just plain too small. So, they had decided to stay off the roads, and go cycling, or flying; for those that could. What they had not counted on was just how isolated Charlene's life had been. When she looked at the bicycle for the first time and said "I've never ridden one of these before. How do you do it?" they had all starred at her in consternation.

"How can you not have ridden a bicycle before?" Jack asked.

"We walked on the island, and before that, I was too young," she shrugged.

"Do you know how to swim?" John asked sarcastically. Did she not have any real-world skills?

"Sort of; if you count a few lessons in the pool, and a bit in the sea," she replied, casually dismissing the question.

She started out trying to 'port, but she soon became so hungry that they had to steal a sizeable amount of food for her, and that ended that plan. It ended up with her arms around Jack's neck, holding on for dear life, on a bicycle that he'd 'found'; John just shaking his head slowly on a bike next to them.

They'd spent the next few days alternately, riding and hiding from French people for nearly two hundred miles. It was slow, but sure and hassle-free progress, and of course, some people had seriously saw rumps after unaccustomed days of riding.

When the hills before Geneva loomed before them, they took a risk and used their powers to get them up and over them. Simon finally got his flight systems calibrated, giving them the all clear, "the power should be enough to get me and Isabella clear when it's time," he'd confirmed over the comms, John exulting at the news, nearly slipping Helena's grasp.

Before they had started the weather was fair and fine, unfortunately, when they hit two thousand feet, Mother Nature decided that she'd had enough of being kind, and a brisk wind picked up, with dark clouds gathering from the West. When that happened, Simon worried about his power systems that it had taken so long to repair and suggested that they land and seek shelter. As the wind picked up, they others were forced to agree, as the Flyers started having severe trouble with gusts of wind and sharp flying rocks.

"Let's set down on the lea ward side, out of the wind," Jack suggested, then he summoned up his shield, creating a makeshift shelter for them all.

For once, John looked happier, glancing at him and said, "I don't know if I've ever said this to you before Jack, but you're a handy person to have around."

"Why thank you sir!" came the wind drowned response, the wind intensity creeping up, and the visibility dropping as a late spring mountain snow began to fall, turning into a chill blizzard.

"Oh great!" Simon commented, "is everything against us?"

"No, not everything. There have been no avalanches yet," muttered Helena under her breath. Then came a sound through the darkness. At first, they thought it was just a loud gust of wind, when a loud pulsing noise started coming towards them, Helena fearing that the mountain had heard her. They could only distinguish it vaguely, but as it closed, the source of the sound became unmistakeable; when seen just a few tens of feet away, a Ghe'Dar saucer, using the bad weather as cover, skimmed the mountains they were in, at almost zero feet, heading South, from Geneva, at speed.

"That blows it," said John, cursing.

"What?" Simon asked, trying to shout over the wind.

"Well, if that ship is not the one attached to the machine; there must be another base somewhere."

"After we stop the invasion, I imagine we will be a bit busy, cleaning up pockets of the enemy," Helena pointed out.

"Your probably right about that," Charlene interjected.

"Count on it," Helena said, hunkering down against the wind, even with the shield in place.

The storm lasted several hours, with the snow building up on the shield so that when, finally, the wind died down there was a sizeable crust covering the shield. The team decided it was safe to move, even with the snow still falling a little.

As the shield collapsed, the snow covered them all, giving them all a wakeup call especially as some had managed to doze a little in the intervening time.

They moved a little more cautiously given the sighting of the ship, but they saw no more, and there was little sign of others moving in the weather. They hit the end of the snow line at dawn on the next day, the twenty-seventh.

"We should start to keep an ear out for the others on the comms. within the next day or two," Helena ordered Simon and John.

"I'll set my systems to alert us to signals on that frequency," acknowledged Simon.

John was looking out towards Geneva. "I cannot see the machine," he observed, "it should be visible from here."

"My guess, is that the defensive field we encountered from the inside, provides some form of camouflage, like my suit, only substantially more sophisticated," speculated Simon.

John looked at him, in a quite hostile manner, until Jack added.

"Well I can see where it is," he pointed exactly where John was looking, "even from here I can see the power radiating from it like a volcano, although there are a few systems that seem to be fluctuating. Seems that they are having power problems," he pointed to several areas just beyond the field.

"Well let's get down there. Then we can start to make our way to somewhere safe." Helena started to drift down the hillside, Simon picking up both John and Charlene, carrying them both down, although close, they did not speak to one another on the way down, and while it was not the fastest way to travel they finally made it to the small town of Peron.

"What now?" said a decidedly annoyed Simon as they settled just out of town, his power systems needing to be replenished soon, and his muscles stiff from carrying the two non-flyers in the same position for hours.

"It's unlike that the Ghe'Dar will be interested in anyone around this small town, so we should be safe until we get a signal."

"Well, I don't know about you but, I need power. I'll go find a sub-station and convert the local power to my frequency. It will take a couple of hours recharging, and the drain will be visible to the French grid technicians."

"Ok, You, me and John can go sort you out," Helena decided.

"Jack and I will get some food," trust Charlene to think about food first, but it was her power source, so not so surprising.

"Good morning, Mr. Starling," the customs official not phased by the major celebrity arriving, as the business lunch he was attending that evening had been well publicised, enough that a few paparazzi has descended for pictures of visiting VIPs.

"And how long will you be staying for?" The official having to go through the routine even for the rich; especially with the press watching like hawks, for any scrap of news.

"For a few days. There is a particularly interesting show on in a few days that I have always wanted to see," he pointed to a poster marked, 'Gospel for 100 Voix'.

"That is just next door to the airport," the official pointed out.

"With my schedule, anything further is impractical." Craig knew ironically he'd not really have time for the show with his actual schedule.

"Mais Oui. Go on through, Monsieur," and he waved Craig through.

It felt strange not having Helena with him, but he knew she was with the new team in Poole. He'd contacted a few resources to deliver some equipment to the Geneva warehouses, having some hardware on his jet too; namely his armour.

While his briefcase was scanned, his jamming system blocked the actual image of the comms system in there which allowed him, amongst other things, to monitor the contact frequencies of several assets in the area.

He was met by a hotel chauffeur, everything going smoothly. Three days to go he thought. Who'd have believed it, he thought, looking around at the airport. Not a sign of panic, other than the usual last-minute rushes to get flights and no indication that the world was under threat of invasion. Nothing. All was normal, well normal for humans that is. Yet, somewhere close by, was an enemy force, just waiting to destroy humanity, somehow. He hated not being in the know and was tempted to put out a call to his resources, but realised that if he were near the enemy, they would be monitoring all the available channels, and he did not want to risk tipping them off. He'd have to trust his people to get in touch with him directly. One reason for publicising his visit was to allow him to communicate with them without giving away who he was actually telling. In a manner of speaking even the paparazzi were being drafted into this war, although they did not know it.

As he arrived at his hotel, he was met by the porter and a bellhop. Nothing but the best for him, after all, why not have the best when you could afford it. At the desk he enquired about messages, the receptionist automatically checking.

"There are many messages for you, sir," the woman said, in her best professional voice. He noticed that the Duty manager was hovering, trying to get his attention.

"Yes?" Craig turned slightly.

"I'm Michael, the duty manager, sir. There was a package delivered for you earlier by courier. I took the liberty of placing it in the hotel safe."

"Good thinking," he complimented the manager, having expected something, although not a package. "I'll take it up with me."

"Excellent, sir. If you'll just follow me."

The man led him around the back of the counter into a small room with a sturdy door, that Craig noted, had a security camera trained on it.

The safe was actually behind a thick, solid steel grill.

"Impressive," he murmured.

"We take the safety our customers valuables seriously here, Sir!" the sharp-eared manager said with pride.

"Well thank you, I must say though that perhaps a guard as well would be better." Craig was a little critical, but the manager smiled.

"The reception staff are all security trained."

"Excellent," he said meaning it sincerely. One more resource available, if the worst came to the worst.

The package was a small brown cardboard box, Craig handling it carefully as he received it from the safe. "I'll see my room now," he instructed, more than asked, the manager leading him background, signalling the bellhop to guide the customer to his floor while passing him the key to the room.

"Executive Suite Three, Floor 5," he reminded the young man.

"Of course. If you'll come with me sir," the bellhop guided him to the lifts.

Craig unpacked his luggage carefully, as it was crammed with his own equipment, few clothes at all; he tended to get new ones in theatre as it were.

Delicate listening instruments, special glasses; the usual spy paraphernalia, plus his own kit; armour points, power packs and a set of hand weapons, that were based upon his own patented technologies. He also has a high-temperature plasma cutter; for cutting through obstacles, an electro-pulser; for stunning opponents that he wanted for questioning and finally a twin fusion pulse gun, designed to go through all known armours. It did not have many charges, but it had a kick like no other, and he'd sent an order of those, plus its bigger brothers to a warehouse for use at CERN. They were rejected at the last minute by the military, after massive budget cuts but he'd kept the first order himself for emergencies, and registered it destroyed. This counted as one serious emergency, so he'd put them in play.

He also unpacked a decoder for the M.I.X. communications, which included a special pack Isabella had beefed up, since the last hack attack. He hoped she was alright. Much as Helena had reported she was a capable operative, she was unlike Helena, without any real combat abilities, other than the basic self-defence training they'd insisted she take. He was surprised when Helena had rather insisted that she went, which had not been like her at all, but he was sure she had her reasons.

He decided now was a good time to check out the package which had been delivered to the hotel, doing a UV scan of it using a penlight. Sure enough, there was that strange fingerprint and the same watermark, confirming it came from the same people as the letter.

Opening it, carefully, he found a few things of interest: a fried transistor, which he recognised as coming from his old suit, meaning the power systems were fried, by some sort of electromagnetic pulse, or battle damage, next came a copy of the strange writing the team had found at Troyes and finally came a letter. Perhaps an explanation?

"Hello Craig, time to explain what we know and what is going on. I hope you're feeling open-minded today, the simple fact you have received this message means that you're taking this seriously. I'm glad, as you really need to. It gets stranger," this should be interesting, and the letter went on to explain the threat, what had happened during the initial battles and the resulting travel back in time by the team, which left Craig was shaking his head in disbelief as he neared the bottom.

"We have had time to study the information we acquired and think we now have the means both to close the portal and destroy the invaders, but we need a distraction only you can arrange. Await the signal to attack with any air forces and ground forces you can muster."

"We are en-route to take positions once the target is revealed, we will be in dark all-in-one suits. One of our number will contact the force with targeting information; call sign, Chi'mera."

Craig looked at the name and realised, the Klerks were involved. He knew them all and had sent Charlene on the mission only days ago. It could be Charlene who had named herself Chi'mera, having somehow tapped into the mitochondrial gene's potential. If they survived this, he'd need to explore her powers to see how the gene had affected her.

He set the letter down and started to think, understanding the non-standard communications now he knew the regular channels were seemingly compromised, perhaps even the people that used them too, and he could not call for other organisations help, for the same reason. Also, they could not call for his help too soon; otherwise they might have a paradox and, as he understood it, that could be even worse.

He shook his head again. They had done remarkably well to get this far, given they must be absolutely terrified of doing anything to affect the past they knew, the consequences being, potentially, catastrophic. But it looked like they'd pulled it off, the plans were in place, the troops were in place, mostly and now the General was in place.

He set up the comms, a relay to his phone, and set off to have a look around the town. If he knew the agents, which he did, they would be scoping the town and CERN out, looking for clues as to what was going on, and what they could do to gain an advantage. He should know; because they were trained to do that. The professionals were on the case now, and he knew they simply must not fail.

"There is no sign of your contact, Selena," muttered Marceaux, into a blue tooth earpiece.

"He's there, probably watching you and thinking whether he should kill you or not," replied Selena from a truck several blocks away.

"He is the professional, yes, I don't think he will hold our last meeting against me."

"He was not the one you knocked out, to get the information. It was Ricks," she reminded him.

"I get them mixed up," he admitted, "they are so alike in their mannerisms."

"Haines is the one that forgives easily. Ricks is not; you might want to remember that since you'll probably be working with them soon."

"I can handle, Ricks," he said confidently.

"If you mess this up, it won't be Ricks you'll have to deal with, it will be me and 'Pappa.' Understood?" the line went silent for a few seconds.

"Understood," the voice was cold, but the message was understood plainly. 'Pappa' was known for his particular brands of punishment; few would want that to happen to them.

Another man walked up to Marceaux. Quite small, barely five foot, in a long coat and a wide-brimmed hat, "hello there my friend. I wonder if you could give me directions."

Marceaux looked up and saw the man hat down, "I only know the way to Oblivion."

The hat lift to reveal an old friend, "same here. I want to know the way to the end of the world," he said, laughing.

There were few Marceaux called friend, but Francois Whiley was one of them.

"They called you in too. I thought that you were in India, with, what was her name, Illiana."

Francois tilted his head, "yeah, I heard that rumour too. Alas, she thought of marriage, and I suddenly remembered how much fun single-life was, even with you around."

They both laughed at that. There was a click behind them, making them both jump. A woman came up to them, with an old Instamatic camera, "picture?"

"Leave off, Eve, I still recognise you behind that old thing," Marceaux complained.

The woman wearing a heavy fur coat, stylish hair and the latest shoes, slowly lowered the camera, revealing that she was no stunner, but, for someone in their late fifties, she exuded an air of grace and majesty.

"That is no way to talk about Francois," the woman laughed, Francois's face indicated he did not appreciate that joke, but he indicated another seat.

"So where is Selena?" she asked.

"In the shadows, as always. She asked me to meet you two so that we can coordinate," Marceaux's message to the others, indicating he was in charge.

"So, what was so important, that all of us are meeting in broad daylight, in a place that barely anything has ever happened?" Eve asked.

"She did not see fit to tell me. However, she has brought in, just about, every favour she has ever had, to get us all here. So, whatever it is, it's BIG. Bigger than Archon," he referred to the operation he knew the others had been involved with before; some bank heist.

The others shuffled nervously. "We don't know," Eve kicked Francois, hard.

"Save the denial. I'm not interested." Marceaux said.

"So what are we waiting for?" Eve asked.

"The boss to call us," Marceaux replied casually.

"Can we not just go see her?" Francois asked.

"She's not the boss, as I understand it," the others looked at him, expectantly.

"I don't know, but, at a guess, I'd say we are now working for the big boys. So, no mistakes and don't even think of backing out," he said with meaning to Francois, who was suddenly looking around nervously.

"Relax. If they'd have wanted you for anything, they'd have taken you straight off," Marceaux said, enjoying the man's discomfort.

"Easy for you to say, my competitors would rather see me dead than alive."

"Oh, you mean Cherdal and Herwell. I hear that our targets already retired them for you," Francois relaxing, then sitting bolt upright.

"Both? In under a month," Marceaux replying with a very slow nod.

Francois looked very serious, "that must have taken someone very good."

"Very good!" Marceaux said, looking at Eve and winking.

"Ok, I'm in. But I get first shot at taking them down. I've never met anyone that good before, present company included," he shrugged apologetically.

Eve grinned, "that's probably why you're here then."

Francois was suddenly lost in thought, "I really should have brought my full kit."

Marceaux rolled his eyes. "That would have set off every alarm in the airport from miles away," he joked, and all three laughed.

"They all seem happy," said Ricks looking down the 'scope.

"It's just nerves. They don't know what they are up against yet. Still, they are the best and might give us an edge, and we'll need every edge we can get," Haines commented, looking at the phone and checking his watch. It was time to make the call.

CHAPTER 19

MAELSTROM

Haines set his comms to the required frequency and carefully initiated the call, which was answered almost immediately, a signal indicating the call connection had been made. They were close to getting some answers now.

"Hello there," came a familiar voice.

"Can I speak to my friend?" He had to confirm this, beyond any doubt.

"I'm GhostKnight, and you're not my friend, at least not yet," came the rather snippy reply. Good enough, if someone had managed to get the equipment from their contact that might have caught them out.

"And you are?" nice, GhostKnight caught on quick, "Alpha One."

"Sorry don't know any Alpha One. Perhaps you have the wrong number?" He was challenging him? Boy, he did catch on quick, as they had not given their code names to him. How could he prove himself, ah yes, he'd mentioned the reason for their meeting.

"I'm sure ELE can vouch for me."

"Ok, are you sure this is secure?" came the question they all wanted to know.

"No. But it's as secure as we can make it," Haines tried to reassure him, as best he could.

"Which, knowing the enemy, is not really," replied GhostKnight.

"So just who, or rather what, are we dealing with. If we don't know soon, we'll be too late to do anything, and since we've already scouted the area, we already know the biological weapon story is fake. Is this really what it looks like?" getting really frustrated with the lack of knowledge. I mean talk about secretive; just how bad could it be.

A few seconds later, another voice came on the line. "WitchFire to Alpha One, confirm Code designation." WitchFire was here? He'd heard of her, of course, most of the top M.I. had heard; whispers of the super-powered types here and there. Both Gravitron and WitchFire were in the field. He was getting a cold feeling in the pit of his stomach.

"Foxtrot Romeo Zero One, Paris, Alpha One," he responded in a low tone.

"Ok. Time for answers," and she took a few minutes to brief him, on what had happened and was going to happen, where he should place his men and where to collect the appropriate equipment.

Haines had had some bizarre briefings in his time, from mysterious murders to truly bizarre cults, this one beat them all by several miles. It was simply stunning. He rang off, noting that the line had still been secure, to the systems knowledge, at the end of it.

Ricks was looking at him strangely when he realised he was looking at the phone, even though he'd rung off.

"I," Haines slowly lowered his arm, Ricks staring at him.

"I've never known you to fall speechless before."

Haines gulped, then, with a tremendous mental effort, got himself under control.

He walked over to Ricks and put his hand on his shoulder. "This is the big one, my friend. Before I tell you even part of what I just heard, I would just like to say it has been an honour working with you," the other man gulped a little. They had worked together for years, but rarely had the man shown such, sentiment. It scared him more than any words he'd ever said before.

"You make it sound like it's the end of the world already," when the other just nodded, he shuddered.

"It may well be my friend, it may well be." He suddenly stood up tall, his face suddenly became incredibly determined, "but, it is our job to make sure it is not," he shook himself. "Right. Let's meet up with our resources, brief them as to what to expect, then let's plan us a battle, because, Ricks, my old friend, we are going to War!"

They had all meet before, in one way or another; but meeting all together in an old tavern anti-room was strange. Ricks had insisted that they leave their electronics at home. Strangely, Selena had asked that they not drink the wine, but have water instead; some found that suspicious, because of their nature; so no one had touched either since arriving.

Everyone became jumpy when Haines entered, with Ricks and Gareth close behind.

Some, who had not known who their new employer was, started to get up to leave and were quickly sat back down by those more in the know. After the scuffles finished, Haines spoke.

"Yes, surprising as it may seem, we are to work together on this one. I am Alpha One, for those few that don't know me, and since the rest of you know me, I will just put this down straight; no one backs out, refuses or betrays us. It's as simple as that; because we are dealing with a threat that, if we fail, won't leave us with a world left to live on, or hide in."

There was a buzz of disbelief, the audience being the ultimate sceptics.

"I have been ordered, by superiors to provide cover for a strike force against a target at CERN, and we will be provided with special equipment to do this," a few sly looks around the table, indicated people thought they might make a profit on this deal after all. "For those that might cut and run, I can guarantee you that, should anything go missing; I will make it my life's mission to hunt you down and end your days in the worst way imaginable," the passion in his voice was shocking for most, terrifying for the rest.

"Our target is not CERN itself, but an installation just North of it, on the French side of the border," he was passed a map by Ricks.

"Paper maps?" commented one person.

"The enemy is monitoring all communications and has decryption software that can hack almost any network, including the military one. Ours, have had some upgrades, last a bit longer, before they get penetrated," there were a few signs of alarm, but understanding, about the confiscation of their equipment.

"Who are we actually dealing with?" as Marceaux.

"Their name would mean nothing to you, and they may be monitoring for it so let's just call them terrorists," Haines giving a glance towards Selena, who nodded.

"The site is heavily fortified and guarded," he pointed to the site just above the CERN main site, to a square about a hundred meters across, next to the road.

"Don't bother trying to see it initially, it's camouflaged," not adding it was actually invisible.

"Then how can we target it?" came another voice.

"We are not there to target it directly. A specialist strike team is doing that, and you are under orders not to attempt to damage the installation; unless you want rapid orbital insertion."

"Ah," and the voice subsided.

"The strike team will deactivate a section of the perimeter defences, and we will enter holding against the enemy, and drawing their forces to us."

"With them isolated, can we attack? If we kill all their troops," the same voice that mentioned targeting asked.

Haines stood taller, bristling, "Ok. Let's get one thing straight. These will not be easy targets; they have state of the art body armour, weapons, targeting and air superiority, plus they may well get re-enforcements," murmurs going around the room. "This will not be a fight like you have ever had before, this will be a battle against a superior military force, worse than anything you've known and willing to die rather than fail." He laid it on thick, but he was pretty sure, from what WitchFire had said, that everything he put out there was true; the professionals around him saw that truth and wondered.

François looked at Haines. "So; we are to get equipment. I'd like to see it before we use it and get some practice. I'd still prefer my own weapons, I'm used to them," others murmuring similar sentiments.

Selena moved next to Haines. "Silence!" She threw that authority around well, Haines thought.

He raised a hand placating, "I know you'd all prefer your own kit, but trust me when I say, the equipment we are getting is, how should I put this politely; in a higher league."

Gareth, who'd entered with a rucksack, flipped it off over his head, opening the top, pulling out what looked like a sub-machine gun, although it no real barrel as such, just a hand sized circular doughnut.

"Since we don't have names for these as such, let's just call them grav-guns," Gareth aimed at one of the men, who laughed at the click when nothing happened, save a whining that filled the air. Half a second later the cynic was catapulted back six feet, pinned by a tremendous force to the wall. After about thirty seconds he collapsed, on the chair still under him, panting.

"What the **** was that?" Francois asked.

"I'm not a scientist, but I have been told that these should be able to knock back the enemy in a similar fashion," Haines shrugged.

"There are larger two-man versions. We'll pick them up in the day. The morning of May the first, about two am."

"Why then?" Asked two people at one.

"We have another strike team on site, and that's when they will be in position."

Selena stepped forward at this point, "we have our instructions gentlemen. Now a few points of order. Let me explain about the water,"

Craig sat enjoying a coffee when the call came relayed from his phone answering service, "Hello Mr. Starling, there's a call from your personal secretary," the other Helena monitoring.

"Afternoon, sir; just checking you have everything you need there," her voice was slightly strained but otherwise unstressed; asking if he was all set for the battle.

"Can you think of anything else?" last chance to call in any other resources.

"You can relax sir, we have this covered." So, everything was in place, now it was just a matter of making sure that no one gave anything away, and everyone knew their place. He'd called in a big favour from the French military attaché, he could have done it the other way, but he preferred exercise more diplomacy this time, the attaché having arranged for a helicopter display team to perform an air show in the region. Craig had told him that he had got some clients that wanted to see their capabilities, not informing him that he was going to acquire them. He'd have a hell of a bill afterwards, but that happened during significant operations, and this was as big as they got: he hoped.

The evening of April the thirtieth was a tense time for all involved, the M.I. strike team starting to make its way, in various appropriated vehicles, towards CERN, early morning still revealed a few other cars on the road. As they travelled carefully to the facility, they ran into a slight problem about half a kilometre short of the objective.

"There's a checkpoint ahead, not usually a problem, but this close to the event the enemy is bound to scrutinise things extremely closely, and I can see armed guards there, side-lining some vehicles for security checks," Ricks said with some binoculars to his face.

"Alpha One to Bravo Group. Divert north from the target, and deploy," judging that it was getting to the stage where stealth was less important than just getting into position. Alerting the enemy now may force more of a fight to get there, but the enemy would just as easily be diverted that way, as any other.

"Badger Leader, to all ground units, watch for friendly air units, advancing from the rear," came a brief message on the line.

Francois and the rest had thought that Haines was in charge, this message turned the ante up a notch. "Alpha one to all units, we're getting air support," ignoring all the startled muttering, in the background.

"We have thirty minutes to reach our positions," pointed out Ricks.

"Let's hustle people. Wait for clear targets before advancing beyond point Sierra, or this will all be for nothing," he reminded them. "Let's go."

GhostKnight, in his black outfit, was listening in on the M.I. channels, as the forces started moving into position, though knowing that they were there, did not make it any easier to see them, the night vision goggles only aiding in obscuring the area in a blurry light aura.

"You see them?" asked Titanium, camouflaged beside him.

"A few glimpses is all, Special Forces of some kind."

"You might say that," Helena added from cover, trying not to actively use comms so close to the enemy.

"It's nearly time," came Simon's voice, looking at his HUD. "If I read this right, our other selves are already in there. Let's move up."

"Not yet, remember we did not see ourselves, and Chi'mera will have a Ghe'Dar ship's view of the battlefield. We need to wait until the forces are fully engaged, then move like lightning," Helena looked at Chi'mera who did not have her goggles down yet. The woman actually looking like a man at the moment, only her eyes giving her away, those golden flecks positively glowing at the moment; literally.

The Ghe'Dar base commander received the message from England, Blavnic reporting that their security was compromised and that a squad of enemy commandoes, some powered, had managed to free some prisoners. The commander appeared apparently unconcerned. The report continued that they had escaped through a portal to, an unknown destination and that all bases should be on alert for intruders.

The commander looked at the last part and shrugged if you can imagine an armoured squid shrugging. What could a few humans do here, at the centre of military operations of the invasion, guard by the Elite? The entity paused, then reluctantly, set the defences on yellow alert; the Airsleds would be warmed up, and patrols placed around the shield perimeter. No need to go to Red alert, but caution would prevent any possibility of blame, should something, untoward happening. It had no idea that is was already too late.

Gravitron was at a thousand feet, watching the scene from above, in a camouflage bubble making him immune from detection by any kind of scanner, gravity-bending all EM radiation around it. Even through the alien's camouflage field, his own onboard scanners were detecting, gravimetric fluctuations, consistent with a power build-up inside.

"Echo One to Badger Leader. Ready for takeoff."

"Echo One, Badger Leader. Takeoff, vector two seven zero, weapons free on Christmas lights. Confirm"

"Confirmed control. Weapons free on targets. ETA 2 minutes."

Things were about to go crazy; he'd best get to a safe distance, he thought pulling back to just within striking distance.

On this quiet May morning, all was peaceful, the sky was clear enough that the stars shone brightly down on Geneva, couples walking in the starlight and the commercial aircraft silent, already on the late runs elsewhere.

It was an idyllic mountain scene that shattered as reality was split asunder in the middle of the valley floor, as a segment of the Ghe'Dar shield disappeared, the weird machine inside being revealed and a loud whining noise filled the night air. The various waiting groups responded with amazement at the scene inside; flying machines, explosions, blasts of energy and a hole in the fabric of reality forming, the air thrumming and crashing, with the sounds of war, erupting at the edge of the city.

Haines and his groups were about ten metres from the shield when it dropped right in front of them. "Go," Haines yelled, waving the others forward, the group rushed forward hands heavy with canvas bags and large carry crates, some carrying two sets of kit; their own, that they had been told they could try, and the ones they'd been told was probably the only type that would actually work on their targets. Most were stubbornly clinging to the belief that they could fight these enemies as usual; he just wanted to see their faces when they fail, their egos deflated, for once.

The three groups, Bravos One, Two and Three were up at the perimeter in a few seconds. The first team, including Francois, unpacking their weapons, taking aim and firing, the projectiles failing to do anything except bounce off their targets.

Haines saw the look on their faces and found it was no where near as satisfying as he'd imagined it would be. By the time he'd gotten over his disappointment, the professionals had smoothly switched weapons and gotten the enemy in their sights again.

The new grav-pulse weapons buzzed out in unison, proving to be highly effective, damaging the Ghe'Dar's shields and armour with equal ease. Once the teams had engaged the enemy, phase two began; Bravo three, the non-weapons experts, using lasers designators to illuminate Airsled targets, to guide in air-to-air missiles.

Helicopter's rotors approached, come in behind them, firing four Laser Guided Missiles (LGMs), going overhead, three hitting home, with just one sliced out of the air, by a sled's energy pulse; the battle was joined, intensifying rapidly.

While that battle spread from the breach, Haines hung back, analysing the enemy attacks, which seemed remarkably weak up front for the number of troops that they had seen in their scouting mission.

Then he caught sight of the ongoing battle with the enemy near the machine. Two, no three, attackers were blasting the guards and the Elite troops, near a grounded saucer next to the machine.

At first, Haines thought that one of the attackers, armoured and flying, was Gravitron, although the weaponry seemed different from what he'd remembered, also he'd seen Gravitron in action, the armour was distinctive, while this seemed plainer, almost primitive in comparison. When it went down in a heap, he thought the attack had failed, but a blur in a camouflaged outfit, ran into the fray, unarmed, also falling under the enemy's barrage before he could attack them. Haines was about to order his troops forward, when a large hand descended on his, from another armoured being, only partially visible.

"Easy there! Keep them busy here, we'll deal with this," came a metallic voice.

Haines did a double take, another armoured unit, except this one was had reflective panels one it. "Your pal over there is getting his butt kicked. Ain't you going to help?"

"All in good time. I and the others have our orders. This must be done to that schedule, although there may be a few casualties on the way." The hand disappeared, as did the rest of him. "Hold here. I'll call out 'Grab the Ball' if we fail. Then it will be up to you."

"Good luck, then," he said to thin air, returning to watching the battle, even more intently now.

Another combatant entered the fray; one with smooth golden armour on, using some sort of harpoon to fight their way through the enemy line, ignoring the remaining troops and running forward, vanishing into the ship.

Meanwhile, his eyes were drawn to two women moving at the fringes of the battle, one carrying a staff of some kind, which she used to ward off enemy troops with what looked like, a force field.

The other armoured figure recovered from the enemy attacks, flying up and blasting a slew of the guards, followed by a character that Haines recognised, even though he only knew his codename, "ah! There you are GhostKnight." The fire he unleashed, dropping more of the enemy. It looked like they might win through to the enemy ship. But why were they heading there and not to the machine; he could only guess.

Haines could see that the enemy was no longer doing so well, for although their air force was holding the few helicopters at the breach, their ground forces were getting pummelled at the rear, and they did not have many more remaining. He refocused in on the women. What were they doing? He could see one had a laptop and was furiously tapping away. Was she controlling a drone or ROV of some kind?

The armoured figure flew into the ship, leaving a few guards plus their commander to deal with a soldier battling against them.

Now the AA batteries opened up, not on the helicopters, but on the Airsleds.

Haines looked at the women, the smaller one pointing at the turrets. So that's what she'd been doing.

Then the Machine blasted the sky with four lashes of energy, and a portal ripped space open, allowing the invasion to begin. Haines face dropped; they had been so close. Even as he thought it, a colossal ship started to appear and glided slowly through the portal aperture. What could they do against that?

Gravitron too felt the change, with part of the shield down he could scan the area in detail. A huge gravitational shift having rippled from the machine, opening the portal, and his even his suit, usually immune to such effects was feeling the change.

He was fighting the urge to get in there, but he knew that he'd not been present then, so he had to let them try their way first, or he'd ruin literally everything, watching as his M.I.X. team started to move in from the left to join the fray.

Haines saw WitchFire fly the unarmed man into the saucer, the time for action getting close. He also noted that a few of the laser designators had gone, "Ricks, watch that left flank, I think they are trying to limit our air cover effectiveness."

"Got it. Francois; support the right," barked Ricks forgetting the codenames for once.

The marksman were hitting the Airsleds from cover, aiding the helicopters by trying to taking out the rear gunners, only having succeeded once, as the sleds had shielding, so he'd switched to targeting the ground troops moving against the well-hidden designators, who they were finding incredibly hard to find, even in the light brush.

He hit one trooper who fell, only to get up again, looking for the attacker, "Merd. Armoured and protected," he muttered, he really wanted that kit. "Well, if all I can do is knock you down, let's see if I can knock something bigger down on you, and he aimed for the undersides of the Airsleds flying above those troops; perhaps the shielding was thinner there. Everyone had a weak spot, he just had to find theirs'. His grav-gun remained packed, but the armour-piercing rounds now came into play.

At the other end of the portal, the Ghe'Dar fleet command, having seen the portal open ahead of schedule, had ordered two Motherships through the portal, to secure the target area. They could only go in one at a time, but the other area was shielded, so there should be no rush. Once that area was locked down, they could expand the bridgehead and create a full-blown spaceport. With the enemies' military resistance, in effect, neutralised by the mind control of their leaders, the Ghe'Dar could feast on the life of the new world; as they had done on hundreds of other planets.

The other Fleets arrival was weeks away yet, and the Homeship, the moon-sized vessel they called home, was months off, however, mainly because it needed the special portal generator to be in position at this end of the vortex, protected by the other fleets.

Thousands of scout ships moving in squadron formations neared the portal, ready to provide air support, once the big guns were in place. A Hundred Motherships, or more, waited behind the command-ship, four times their size, to begin their subdual of the human cities, as well as transports of every kind; viral pods, dropships, troop ships, trappers and food cages, all waiting for the command.

"Attention fleet. Fleet Admiral Gohox commands you, be ready. Prepare to advance. For Blood. For Glory. For Victory." He imagined them all drooling, impatient for battle and lust for flesh. Soon, very soon they would feast once again.

"GhostKnight to Bravo One," Jack called Haines.

"Roger, GhostKnight" Haines was not surprised to hear him, he'd just seen him with the girl outside.

"Advise strike team two, entering the theatre, left flank, rear."

He turned his head, and saw, four moving just up to the shield.

"Got you GhostKnight, thanks for the warning."

Then one of them stumbled and dropped as they passed the shield, looking out of it.

"GhostKnight, you're one down!"

Helena and John, and been behind the rest, moving slowly so as not to warrant Ghe'Dar attention, when she crumpled, as they passed the shield.

John had seen his chance, using his stun gun to catch her leg, making it look like she'd clipped the shield, or a stray bolt had hit her. He caught her, hiding the stun gun in his hand.

"Damn! Helena's been hit by something!" He yelled aloud, flipping the gun into his pocket. She looked totally out of it, not surprisingly having just received a jolt of fifty thousand volts of electricity.

"We cannot leave her here," said Jack. "I'll take her to the centre of the lines, once she recovers she can help out from there."

"I'll take her," said John, the voices in his head quieter now that he'd done what they asked. Strangely, however, the pain in his wrist and stomach was seemingly more pronounced. "I'll be there and back in no time," he dashed off, moving at high speed, and, upon arrival draping her over an equipment box next to Ricks, who did not even have time to draw a weapon on the intruder.

"Look after her, she's just received a shock," I'll bet, he thought.

"We'll take care of her," Ricks replied not recognising the man, but considering the speed at which he'd arrived indicated he was probably M.I.X., maybe even the one he'd seen before, being gone before Haines could pay any attention to the exchange.

Haines glanced at Helena, saw the staff and did a double take, "she was just on the ship!" he exclaimed.

"Must have been guards in there, she's out cold," Ricks crossed to her, lifting her head and placing a coverall under it, "I'll get her comfy. I doubt she'll be coming around anytime soon," noticing a slight burn on her suit, near her thigh.

John got back, as fast as he'd gone. Now it was all up to Simon, except, when he'd left two people were waiting for him, now there were three.

"Who's that?" he asked, pointing to a man in a dark camouflage outfit.

Jack and Charlene turning to see the third man, creeping behind them.

"Easy there, Alpha Two, M.I.6, I'm here to help," he introduced himself, lowering his weapon carefully.

Charlene looked at him and casually scanned him for Ghe'Dar tech, "he's clean," she informed the others.

"You cannot be here," Jack said. "There are only supposed to be four,"

They all looked at each other. There were four; with Helena gone, and Titanium getting ready for the rescue, Gareth made four. John suddenly went extremely cold. The plan to get Helena out of the way could well have caused a paradox; which had possibly been the whole idea, but because of this stranger, they were still on track.

"Why does there need to be four?" Gareth asked perplexed.

"Never mind, er, Alpha Two," Jack replied, "just keep down, things are about to go seriously weird. I want you to stay right here when it does, understand?"

"Ok," Gareth nodded.

When the saucer suddenly veered away from the machine, Titanium was standing rock still, not five feet from Isabelle, who was head down, trying extremely hard to avoid the Ghe'Dar troops, that were searching for her. He was finding it difficult not to reassure her, and Jack, as he flew in, desperately trying to get her to the scout ship.

He saw the wires ripped from the saucer's external conduit link, and the machine, almost immediately, starting to discharge to its outer shell and the ground, as power built up within the fateful discharge.

"Oh Shit," Gareth said as he saw the machine starting to fire off bolts of strange purple energy to anything metallic that stood out.

"Get ready, Chi'mera," John regarded her with tension in the air between them. She casually looked at him and rippled, her nano-suit hiding most of her golden armour, John saw Gareth's eyes bulge a little.

"I know what I need to do Pile Driver, you just get ready to provide the cover."

"I'll do that," Gareth volunteered, reaching over his shoulder and revealing a heavy duty grav-pulse gun, John and Jack looking at him and nodding.

"Ok. Make sure that none of those Airsleds sneaks back here, and no more come through that hole," John said, pointing to the sky, the mothership nearly all the way through.

Jack was there, able to see her, but, so could the advancing Ghe'Dar. He cursed that he could fly no faster. Finally, he got close enough to reach out to her.

"Isabella, it's Jack, hold out your hand, I'll try to get us to the ship. It looks like they might need us in there."

"Ok, Jack, get us out of here. I've had enough field work," she said lifting her hand for him to grasp, which he did as hard as he could, willing both of them invisible. Unfortunately, this time his needs went unmet, causing him to grit his teeth when he realised that she could still be seen, both of them now vulnerable to the Ghe'Dar.

The Ghe'Dar had had a hard time trying to locate the ghostly warrior who'd been plaguing them; indeed he'd eluded their best tracker, but now it is evident that he was trying to help the human female to escape. They aimed their rifles at the empty space above the human female, preparing to fire.

Gareth started to take a bead on the soldiers, but John put a hand on the rifle and shook his head, "they are already dead. They just don't know it yet," John watched as the scene unfolded just as before, dooming all near the machine.

At that moment, an unusually large bolt of power leapt from the open pyramid and struck the ground within five meters of Isabella and, like a massive pebble in a lake, reality rippled, then shattered around them, as the exotic energy from the machine unleashed its' full potential. As if in unison, similar bolts wound out from the other corners of the building, striking the sky, causing the veil of the world to peel back around the pyramid, which acted as a centre point, in an otherwise chaotic kaleidoscope of otherworldly colours and images.

One quarter of the tear was wreathed in fire, sheets of it ripping across a blood red sky; strange flying creatures circling around the rent seemingly unable to cross; no earthly animal could replicate the horror of these fanged and burning forms, with six wings four arms, two bulky legs and fanged mouths that emitted cries of despair and suffering.

Another segment of the shattered sky pulsed with absolute blackness; not the dark of the night sky or the blackness of space, but the absence of light; any light. And from that darkness radiated a malevolent pull on the viewer's soul, a conscious hunger and absolute evil.

Opposite the machine, the ground giving way, revealed a world covered in plants; or rather semi-organic plants, moving and swaying in a disturbing different motion, the animals in that strange jungle also moving disjointedly, almost mechanically; as though they were cybernetic in nature. A feeling radiated beyond them, one of unity, but with a strange sense of emptiness too, as though something was missing.

Then the ground underneath Isabella opened up or rather faded away. Far beneath her writhed a world covered in strange, mouthed worms, or threads, cities drowning in wave after wave of black, slick, vermicular, life forms; devouring everything in their path. Buildings crumbled under their weight, seas boiled with their feeding frenzy. Birds that feed on the horrors, dropping from the skies, as the hunters found they were the prey, of this apparently unstoppable menace.

Isabella dangled helplessly from Jack's hand, starting to slip. "No! Don't let go. Don't let me fall," she screamed at him. Other screams filled the air as the Ghe'Dar ground troops, without any support, fell that great distance and were absorbed into the worms; disappearing under their mass, as they landed.

Jack tried to hold on. But he knew he was not strong enough; he looked her in the eyes, "I'm sorry. I cannot hold you."

She misunderstood and yelled, "no don't let me go!" gripping even tighter. He felt his grip going, as her desperation stopped the blood flow to his hand. As his wrist went numb, his grip failed, and Isabella fell screaming, the last thing he saw, was Isabella falling towards that grizzly mass. He closed his eyes and, after a few seconds, silently prayed for her; that she would not suffer too much. He did not really know Isabella, as John did, but no one, not even the Ghe'Dar, deserved the fate that awaited below. When he opened his eyes again, the rents had closed and reality was back to normal.

Fortunately, even as the world began to peel back, Titanium was dropping too, in his attempt to rescue Isabella, falling below her by several meters and lining her up as he fell.

There was just one problem, he was indeed falling rather than flying. As reality had shattered around him and he'd dropped, so had all his power levels; apparently, there was an invisible dimensional boundary between the two realms which he had crossed, causing most of his systems to crash, sending them both into free fall. Not only was Isabella doomed, but now, so was he, as he doubted that he'd be able to compensate for the dimension differences before he smashed into the ground, or encountered the same fate that awaited Isabella, above him.

"Something's wrong," it was Jack, near Chi'mera, looking towards the machine.

"What do you mean?" John's head whipped to Jack.

"Titanium's power levels just dropped to virtually zero," he said, "he's going down!"

He did not know how he knew that because his sight showed nothing; he just did.

Chi'mera dropped the rucksack, with the override machine in, that she'd been just about to put on her back. Jack could see there was hesitation in her every move. She wanted to help, but her instincts and the warning she'd received paralysed her, blocking her natural compassion.

"I sorry," was all that she could voice, frozen in place.

Jack looked around, frantically scanning for anything to save the imperilled pair, spotting only an Airsled; too slow, they'd both be dead before it reached them. He looked at John.

John thought desperately. If Simon crashed, before he could save Isabella, they would both die as well as the world being lost, not that he genuinely cared about that if Isabella was gone.

As the remorseful Jack above Isabella, shut his eyes, John spoke the command.

"Chi'mera, Salvare-ei!" He spoke the word given to him by the dream creature.

Her eyes went very wide, and her pupils dilated to their extreme limit. Years of post-hypnotic suggestion, training and discipline kicked in. With a spasmodic release, she launched herself vertically into her battle kata and vanished.

Simon was at eight thousand feet, Isabella barely visible, many hundreds above him, when Chi'mera appeared, mid-air, right in front of him, her face fixed forward. A tentacle flashed out from her wrist, grasping him tightly, as he felt the sensation of teleportation for the very first time as agony swept over him.

They appeared a short distance from the falling Isabella, and another tentacle flashed out, grabbing the girl. Her astonishment amplified her relief; the others were here to save her, she realised starting to weep tears of pure gratitude.

However, Chi'mera's teeth were gritted in extremis, having recovered an awareness of her circumstances, radiating terror and desperation, "I can't do it, Simon, my powers exhausted just getting here," the pain palpable, regret sincere, "we're all going down."

Isabella, who'd just registered the rescue being attempted, started to express her gratitude, when she saw Chi'mera's face mouthing 'sorry' and realising that she was being told that they were all now doomed. It was just as she screamed again that a bolt of energy arced down from the shattered sky to strike the nearest metal object; Titanium.

Power surged through his systems, overwhelming, but not damaging them, thanks to the strange green circuits which, previously deactivated, now burst into life; shielding the rest of the system from damage, boosting power levels sufficiently to halt the groups descent and transferring power and a strange set of coordinates to Chi'mera's systems. Upon receipt, her teleportation system immediately kicked into life powering up for another jump. The Dimensional power surged past Chi'mera, sheathed in her armour, and carried on to impact Isabella, blazing around, and cocooning her in, its' purple embrace, causing her to scream in despairing-agony.

As Chi'mera and Titanium disappeared, teleporting to safety, Isabella resumed her fateful fall, power ripping through her, shredding her form. Above her the sky closed up, sealing her off from her friends and the battle above.

Seconds later she was engulfed in a dark, writhing, razor-sharp teeth and oblivion.

Chi'mera and Titanium appeared in a blaze of purple energy, just as the saucer disappeared into the portal, having damaged the mothership. For a second or two, they stood as if stunned by the magnitude of their failure, then Chi'mera simply collapsed twitching to the floor from exhaustion, Titanium just slumping to his knees.

John, Jack, and Gareth were just feet away, looking at them, John specifically looking expectantly at Titanium, who stood there, with empty arms. When he realised Isabella was not with them, he fell to his knees too and bent over, head in hands.

Jack, however, bolted to Chi'mera's side, feeling for a pulse, Simon looking at her too, still a little stunned, "she used all her power to try and save us."

John's head came up at that, "then where is she?" he growled.

Simon looked down, "we tried but were hit by a bolt from the machine, it channelled through us, into Isabella," uncomfortably trying to justify what happened, as Jack was checking her over.

"Her heart's stopped," Jack said, starting CPR.

Simon looked down, "let me try," pushing Jack to one side, and put his armoured hand over her chest, firing a bolt of electricity at her heart, it sizzling around the armoured cage she still wore.

"Damn. Her own powers may end up killing her. I cannot get through that armour."

Then Jack remembered how his bolts had penetrated the Ghe'Dar's armour.

"Perhaps," he lifted his hand and started to relax his mind, as Helena had taught him, a vibrant green light, flowing over and through Chi'mera.

As he did this, he felt dizzy, in an almost elated fashion, as though he'd suddenly had a great weight lifted from him, a great sense of well-being filling him,

Chi'mera giving a huge cough. After a couple of seconds, her eyes opened, just to see John bearing down on her.

"Where is she? Simon said you had her," he grabbed her shoulders and started to shake her.

"PileDriver! Stop!" Titanium hoisted the enraged man by his arms, easily removing him from the girl, restraining him to let Chi'mera get up.

"I had her. I tried to get a lock on to her, but my system is not powerful enough move three people at once; even if it had been with the boost from the portal, that same dimensional energy blocked the targeting scanners. I could not have ported her, even if I'd have had the power.

"You were always against trying to get her," he snarled, trying to wrestle free of Titanium's rigid grip. "You could have done more, you could have,"

"You heard her," Jack joined in, "she tried, and almost died trying to get Simon back."

John glared at them all but finally admitted defeat. He'd lost her. After all the madness and plotting, all the pain and suffering, he'd lost her. What cruel irony that he'd nearly lost another person, and the entire world, to end up with the same result.

A vast thunderclap above them broke him out of his reverie. From the portal, a huge pressure wave expanded, hitting the ground like a huge hand. Titanium withstood it, but the others were flattened, knocked to the ground like paper dolls. The Ghe'Dar soldiers, with force fields and armour, resisted it, but the Airsleds engines were overpowered, all suddenly impacting on the ground.

The damaged Mothership, was thrown sideways, impacting the edge of the portal again, this time fatally, as it also impacted the forcefield, which wreathed it in destructive energy, causing it to explode, raining fragments throughout the shielded area, some landing on the machine, damaging it slightly; the portal, however, remaining active. Fortunately for the human air force, the shield blocked the effects of the wave from striking them, although their ground forces were also flattened by the impulse. On balance, the odds were still fairly even, until a group of Ghe'Dar scout ships came through the portal.

"We must act now," ordered Gareth, seeing the new forces still coming through the portal,

Titanium looking up and nodding.

"It is Time! That's us going back," said Chi'mera, standing tall, and shifting into her normal form, visible even through the armour. She grabbed the rucksack.

Gareth twigged, "you're the shapeshifter?" He'd thought the shifter was the enemy.

"I am Chi'mera," and there was something more than Charlene in her voice.

"I will end this incursion," and she vanished.

"Si.., I mean Titanium, keep in touch, we'll go help the others."

The armoured figure nodded and faded into the background.

"Gareth, get us back to your lines," Jack was saying, John seemly withdrawn and unresponsive to the need. When Gareth touched his shoulder, his eyes locked with the Agents, and he shook off the hand.

"You two go. I have a score to settle," John growled, head coming slowly up orientating on the Ghe'Dar forces, making a decision.

"That won't help her, you know," Jack said realising what he was about to do.

"But it will help me!" he said and, like a shot, he was off at full pelt, to exact vengeance.

"Should I get him back?" asked Simon.

Jack looked at the ferocity with which the man went at the Ghe'Dar troops.

"I don't think he'd thank you for it, and we cannot spare you anyway," Jack smiled mirthlessly, "besides, it will let him work out his repressed anger. In all honesty, I'd rather fight the whole Ghe'Dar fleet than face him at the moment," a point that Simon could well understand.

After a few short teleports around the machine, Chi'mera found herself in the entrance of the portal machine. She opened the door and ran inside, looking around and trying to get her bearings, her HUD showing a small trail off to the right. Bolts of energy and fallen parts of the now destroyed mothership hampered movement, but the trail arced through well-shielded portions of the machine. The whole area danced with electrical discharges and energy bolts; it seemed that the machine was getting more and more unstable.

An alarm barred out over the noise in Ghe'Darian. Chi'mera adjusted her hearing so she could understand it, not something she did naturally.

"System Alert. Power at One Hundred and Ten per cent and climbing. Computer systems unable to maintain portal cohesion. Require emergency action. Auto repair systems offline."

Fair enough, it wanted emergency action. She darted through the, strangely narrow, superstructure of the machine, to an area, that Simon identified as, a potential spot for the control systems. She looked around, doing some mental translations, of the displays.

"Waveform, Output, Dimensional Integration?" Hmmm. Nope, not there.

She turned, "matter feed, Magnetic flux strength," Blazes. She closed her eyes. There were so many dials, and they stretched all over the place.

Internally she scanned the area tracing line after line until one cluster looked like it controlled the actual power. Then, getting back to the urgency of the moment, she leapt into action; porting the distance to the panel and scanning it visually.

"Control interface, Security Overrides. Oh." On the panel, was a scanner, for a tentacle. Chi'mera grinned, nice security measure for the system, and on a planet full of humans, only the Ghe'Dar would have been able to control the machine, if it were not for her. She was indeed the only one that could save the planet; the other her had been right.

She unpacked the device that Simon had fashioned and clamped it to panel where an interface slot matched the one Simon had created, matching the control nodule they had got from the comms. tower in London. Getting two pieces of debris, Chi'mera threaded them through the holes Simon had pointed out and bent them into the edges of the panel. As she pushed the device down, to the matching port, the device latched on snugly.

Her hand became a tentacle, fitting the interface perfectly, the screen coming up in Ghe'Dar, "scanning, scanning. Identity confirmed. Commander Kelnarth, 8964," the Ghe'Dar security officer from the channel portal.

A helmet descended from the lowest part of the ceiling. The Ghe'Dar liked their neural interfaces, probably because it allowed them hands-free control, figuratively speaking. Chi'mera changed fully into a Ghe'Dar to allow the helmet to fit properly, and once again that strange neural interface changed Charlene's perception to see the bigger picture.

This time, she understood more, and initiated a high-speed link from the database, directing the technical specs for the Ghe'Dar machine to both Simon's device and her own internal memory. Unlike the ships, the machine did not have external sensors, par say, however, she was shown the state of the device, and the portal it generated. It was enormous; there were thousands of ships on their way down its length, with a small number already trying to find space in the shielded area.

In the machine, messages were queued up from the invading fleet to release the shield, from irate commanders desperate to break out from the bridgehead, and demands that the machine portal be opened to allow troops and mechs. down.

Chi'mera directed the interface, "initiate Emergency Action Four, direct input from terminal interface," and Simon's device went to work, shutting down communications locking doors, other interfaces including the helmet. The automated repair system, just to her right, fuzed and sparked, exploding into plastic fragments.

"Time to go," Chi'mera muttered to herself, realising there was no waiting for Simon. She looked up, and ported to the rim of the machine, precariously balancing on the edge about five inches wide, and looking down, 'porting to where Simon was. Previously, she'd have been exhausted by using her power so much, now they were more natural, practice, it seemed, really did make perfect, unless the dimensional bolt had somehow energised her systems in some fashion. One more thing to check out after this was all over.

"Impatient?" came Simon's voice from right next to her.

"You neglected to say that the machine was going to blow up," she snapped back to where the voice came from.

"Sorry," not really sounding sorry at all, "natural side effect of power being sent through circuits at a hundred times the normal amplitude. I did not think you'd have missed what would happen," he was blaming her, for an oversight? Still; this was Simon she was dealing with here. More sparks of power came from the machine, but they were tight, controlled and all up."

"Shouldn't we run?" Chi'mera asked.

"No point. If this goes wrong, the planet will go with us."

Chi'mera gulped. He might have warned them. Oh, actually she thought he might have. Too late now anyway.

"Three." Simon was counting down. The machine's noise was cycling up.

"Two." The machines arms snapped closed, ten times faster than they'd opened.

"One." The machine went quiet.

"Zero," and Chi'mera felt him push her down underneath him, the world pausing.

Starling had landed giving mobile ground support to the beleaguered earth forces. In him, the Ghe'Dar found a superior enemy. Their weapons, designed to penetrate normal armour, hit his shield and found it impenetrable even to their Elite weapons.

When the machine exploded, his sensors went haywire. Blinded by the magnitude of what he was sensing, he merely looked.

The machine gave a slight mini-whine, then erupted in a pyrotechnic display of gravitational surges and dimensional forces, ripping through the sky above it. The small scout ships were catapulted back through the portal, smashing everything in their way, including each other. Motherships, with the power to level cities, tankers, full of exotic fuels, troopships, with thousands of Ghe'Dar each aboard where all slammed and destroyed, by the cataclysmic forces hurtling back through the portal, towards the bulk of the waiting fleet. As the massed energy and explosions hit the other side, the mighty Ghe'Dar, scourge of a thousand worlds, were delivered their first defeat in millennia. The fifth fleet, all its ships and support craft were vaporised or crushed, as the portal exploded, then reversed and imploded, causing a massive gravity well, or black hole, to open up, right next to the fleet. Not even the Ghe'Dar could escape Nature's most destructive force.

Back on Earth, on the ground, the whole battle stopped, the shield having failed totally, the portal disc rippling and folding in on itself. Not a sound could be heard for a few seconds, as the other saucers remaining, just hovered there, while their crews recovered and tried to understand the enormity of what had just happened. The humans were deafened and stunned by the noise, but it was they who renewed their assault first.

A new wave of human forces was now revealed by the failure of the shield; more helicopters, armoured vehicles, and Gravitron striding forward leading them in.

Quarter was not even thought of, as these beings were invaders, that would have feasted on humanity; they not only did not deserve quarter, they did not even have the concept. Nor, did they have the idea of surrender, retreat or mercy.

The scout ships were not weak, and they had Airsled support, but without re-enforcements, their situation was not good.

"Echo two to Gravitron. Clear site, repeat, clear site. Incoming," came a voice over the secure comms. It was a military channel, but the voice was in heavily French-accented English. On his radar, several blips were coming in, just sub-sonic.

"Gravitron to attack units, fire in the hole. Evacuate, evacuate, evacuate."

Chi'mera and Titanium looked at one another. "There is no way we can find the others and get them out in time."

"Leave it to me. I'll need you to zap me," he looked at her, confused and reluctant.

"No time. Do it!" Golden armour rippling as her armour appeared over her suit.

As he raised his arm to fire, she slammed her hand on to her badge. As the bolt hit her armour, she shouted "Chi'mera: Rising!"

Teleport circuits, in all the team's suits, initiated simultaneously; each badge glowing with the Chimera symbol, startling all of them. They all vanish and appeared several hundred meters away with groans of pain, and splitting headaches. It was her safety net; she'd build separately powered secondary teleport nodes into each of their suits, to save them. The extra power stopped it from killing her, but she still collapsed to her knees, even with Simon's extra power. The suits badges all melted with the dimensional power coursing through them; useless.

As the team all looked at her bewildered by the move, the Ghe'Dar ships all erupted as missiles, fired from incoming jets ploughed into them. Some, already damaged, exploded, knocking the ones closer to the ground causing them to explode, but not as expected; it simply blew up as a normal building. Chi'mera had looked concerned as the ships hit; she looked to Titanium for the answer.

"I diverted all of the exotic matter into the portal-stream to collapse it," Simon explained the machine had not exploding more extremely. "It seemed the logical thing to do, given your concerns."

"Let me guess, something else that neglected to tell us," she said sarcastically, almost vitriolically, "because we should have known."

John was covered in blue ichor, but on his knees crying; whether from exhaustion, or from the grief they could not tell.

Eventually, all the Ghe'Dar ships were downed, their troops killed; it was over. A dark armoured figure descended from the sky.

"Well done team, but it's time for us to depart," came the metallic voice of Gravitron. "We'll let the locals deal with the fallout."

"What about the machine, and all the technology?" Simon asked eagerly.

"I'm sorry Titanium, but the other teams will deal with that," as he said it, more explosions could be heard; demolition charges, ripping through scout ships and the machine.

"You're destroying it all?" Simon started to move trying to grab it before it was ruined, but the other armoured figure stepped forward to restrain him.

"Some things are best left for us to discover ourselves," Gravitron held on for a few seconds, then released Titanium.

"What about Alpha Two and the others?" Chi'mera asked.

"They know their jobs, and what to do. We've had situations before, that required the utmost discretion. A little white lie about an anti-gravity experiment going wrong, energy discharges and a few people visited to remind them of what actually happened, is usually all that is needed," the team were shocked, but Gravitron just looked around surprised.

"What? You'd tell them that the planet was nearly invaded, everyone under their control and that we saved the world? No. It does not work like that."

He pointed to Titanium, and he picked up a numb PileDriver, "we tried to save her," he did not lift his head when picked up.

"Some people cannot be saved," John did not know if Gravitron was talking about Isabella, or himself; as he felt about as lost as he could be at the moment.

411

The two armoured figures linked hands, and the whole team flew off with the supersonic boom being covered by more explosions on the ground.

Haines looked up at the sound, Selena sliding up beside him.

"We lost Francois and several others you know," She reported, eliciting a curt nod.

"For a sniper, he fought well. They all did," he handed her an envelope.

"What's this?" She asked starting to open it.

"They; are pardons for your people," She looked in his eyes, seeing a strange dullness in them. For the first time since she'd known him, he looked shell-shocked.

"Posthumously, for those that died. Only for crimes on British soil, but, well, payment for their services." Selena felt a small tear forming in her eye, lifting her head and dared it to get any bigger.

"This was not part of the deal. Why?" Selena leaned closer.

"Too many battles without recognition, in the dark places of the world. The boss," he emphasised the word, but his own voice betrayed that he agreed, "thought this was suitable, given that they just help save the world."

Selena's eyes softened. Haines looked at her; his own eyes were distant, but they focused on her and saw the tear. "Don't cry for them," he lifted her chin, "let's celebrate that they had a great victory instead; after all François proved he was better than them; something he'd always wanted, wasn't it." She was a little hesitant, but then she nodded, and they went somewhere to celebrate the fallen.

As the left, they walked past. Dr. Sayes partially concealed from everyone by a small armoured vehicle. He watched the departure of the armoured figures, including the smaller golden form. "That is the one. It is compatible. It can do what must be done," and he vanished in a silent ripple of azure energy.

Marceaux clutched his prize; a Ghe'Dar pistol and a powerful grenade of some kind, grabbed while the others were demolishing the Ghe'Dar remnants. He was smuggling it out of the area, heading to an arranged meeting with some clients, buyers of advanced tech., that would pay him a small fortune for this.

As he turned a corner, he ploughed right into someone else.

"Ah, there you are," Gareth greeted him pleasantly. He'd pelted hell for leather away from the machine, as soon as he'd recovered from the impact of the first pressure wave. "Taking a few souvenirs, are we?" the agent looked meaningfully at him, then his bag. Marceaux thought about trying to deal with the agent until Ricks waved jovially from behind him.

He sighed, handing over the items. "No use saying that they are worth a fortune, is there?" their returned look said it all.

Gareth leaned forward, "here is your payment," and he passed him an official looking document. Marceaux opened it up sceptically and read it, getting more and more interested.

"This is, real?" he looked up from the document, his hands trembling.

"It is. The English ambassador talked to the French ambassador, a day or two ago. We did not explain the reason we were asking to quash the indictment, but we explained that it was for extraordinary cooperation with the security services." Marceaux's eyes glistened. "You can go home; for the first time in twenty years."

Marceaux cleared his throat, "thanks. I think that might actually be a better payment."

He stood up and walked off, fading into a growing crowd of people that were arriving to view the devastation.

Gareth looked around, grabbing a Gendarme, indicating that he should keep the people away. He looked at the sky at the now-vanished M.I.X. team.

"They could have waited until it was all explained," he muttered to himself. Except it was not their style or their job; it was his. He sighed, starting the damage limitation. After this, he needed a holiday. The Bahamas would be pleasant this time of year, and now that they were safe, he could probably spend a few weeks there undisturbed.

CHAPTER 20

ALIGNMENT

The team landed at Geneva airport, after a few seconds flight, a trick Craig had learned very early on in his Gravitron career; shoot off fast so that observers lose sight of you, then land, before they can get to their scanners, making it appear as though you'd just vanished. Besides, he had an aircraft ready to fly them all back to England.

Simon, reluctantly, removed his armour and allowed a technician to store it in the hold, of the huge, seven-three-seven jet. The rest, casually strolling on to the plane, using the mobile ladder; although John was hardly looking up at all.

"Will he be alright?" Helena asked Chi'mera; somehow no longer thinking of her as Charlene; that person was gone, drowned by circumstance and the others that were a part of her. The voice that answered was deeper than the original, proof that the name fitted.

"Only he will know if he will be alright. We can help as best we can, but I fear that only time can truly heal his inner wounds."

Craig walked up into the aeroplane, indicating they should head aft, to the central section. As they passed the first-class section, through a curtain, they saw a radically different configuration from a standard commercial plane. A lounge, with sofas, tables, and a mini-bar, plus a monitor surrounded desk.

"Please be seated. The pilot says we'll be cleared in a few minutes, but the military has started to arrive and they tend to want the air to themselves."

"Sounds like you've done this before," commented Simon, a little surprised.

Craig actual laughed. "This? Hell, no; thank god," he started pouring some drinks from a brandy decanter, "but things like this, yes. It's my job. And now, it would seem yours too," the others all looked at him.

"Congratulations, on your first successful operation. I'll say it because no one else will know. To anyone else, this was just another day at an experimental facility. I'm sorry that I cannot offer much other than a new career in both intelligence and saving the world, as well as my own deepest thanks."

Simon reached across the table and got himself a glass, he was not usually the kind, but he'd decided that this was a special occasion, in fact, he fervently hoped it was unique.

"Unfortunately, the job is not even remotely finished," Craig apologised lifting a heavy, red, folder from behind the desk. "These other incidents need investigating," the team groaned, but he calmed them, "don't worry there are not all for you. It was just an illustration of the workload. Most of these can be done by technicians, statisticians, and other M.I. departments," the team relaxing a little. "Your jobs will be to investigate things that are more, unusual than they can handle. Helena," and all eyes went to her, "has sent a file on the abilities that you have exhibited, which at first glance, will prove exceedingly useful in any number of situations," there were a few accusatory looks, which she ignored.

"However, I have a feeling that for the most part, you will be the last resort, rather than the first, as keeping your ahem, talents, a secret is paramount," and he swept them with a glance, "too many answers would be required if others knew of your existence."

Craig indicated them all, "we will hide you by giving you new identities and a cover that will withstand the most rigorous check by people such as ourselves from other countries. Should you develop additional talents, inform Helena directly, so that we can either help develop it or at least know that they are available for use. The simple fact is, you no longer have the luxury of privacy, in this regard; if you have an ability, I need to know of it."

"What if we don't want to?" growled John, getting a severe stare from Helena.

Craig stood was unphased, leaning forward on the table, "imagine what would have happened, if Simon had not alerted me of the need to find you?" There were some sickened looks, around the team, as the images hit home, "exactly, the Ghe'Dar would have waltzed over the Earth and would now be tucking into several years-worth of human meals; and on that point, we must now dig out their infiltrators, dupes, collaborators, and slaves."

"But there is another, more important, reason that I must impress is something that I take very seriously indeed," he looked at Charlene, "if you start hiding things, we will be forced to consider it a sign that you are untrustworthy." He glanced at Simon, then Jack, who put on an air of innocence, and finally to John, who was almost looking right through him. "If we cannot trust people in this line of work, they are retired." He looked meaningfully at them all, "I hope it does not come down to that, but you need to know that what retirement actually means,"

John looked up and in a slightly insulted tone said, "this is a job for life right,"

Craig looked at him and just nodded, triggering a small wave of thoughtful faces around the team. He sat again, deciding that he'd said all he needed to on that. "We'll need to go through the cases and see where best to apply your talents."

"There are some obvious things that you will have to do, in addition to working on cases. John you will have to return the A.G.E. company car, and other equipment. I'll replace those with my own tech that needs to be issued to you. Jack, you will have to meet your agent and work up a routine that you can use in your new identity. Fortunately, as Harry Hidden, you have an ID that works just as well in your new life as it did previously, indeed probably better. Simon, I'm afraid you will have to lose your professorship, but since you will be working with us to assess the Ghe'Dar threat and tech, you will probably be busy here initially rather than on other cases. You'll be here, giving you time to build a properly designed custom suit, rather than a second hand, modified suit," Craig grinning at Simon's hurt look, him being rather proud of his jury-rigging.

"He's not disparaging your work Simon," Chi'mera put a reassuring hand on his shoulder. "I think he's saying," and she received confirmation from Craig, "that, if you could save the world using that suit, he is expecting miracles, once you really get your teeth into designing your own." Craig nodded at Simon, who puffed himself up with the compliment.

"Well, the first thing we do is," the seatbelt sign went on.

"Ah, we are cleared for taxiing," Craig started.

"Saved by the bell," Jack muttered to Chi'mera.

"Yes," she breathed a sigh of relief. The problem of Sylvia was really something she should deal with, but with the information aired, it suddenly receded from immediacy. Now was not quite the time, but soon. Soon.

John put his belt on automatically but had barely heard a word from the others.

All he heard and saw, was Isabella falling a second time, a third, a fourth; and a voice repeating over and over again, "you are Mine. You are Mine. You are MINE!"

When they were alone after the initial debrief Chi'mera cornered Craig.

"Your condition has worsened," she informed him bluntly. He tried to look shocked.

"Chi'mera," he warned her.

"Using your power is causing your cancers," she said observed gravely. "The grav. forces must be mutating your cells, and unlike Simon and me, they cannot automatically regenerate the damage, that's why Helena had to keep curing you."

Craig's head dropped trying to avoid her eye, but it confirmed a sudden suspicion.

"You knew all along, didn't you?" Craig looked up in defiance, but Chi'mera's stare was too fierce.

"I, suspected; one of the other reasons you were brought in," he admitted.

"My work cannot help you; I'm afraid," she pronounced, causing Craig to frown.

"When I linked into the machine, I downloaded a vast amount of Ghe'Dar knowledge, much to do with portals to help with the machine's deactivation, should Simon's machine fail. Ghe'Dar technology, is based, almost exclusively, around dimensional and transport theories, to allow them to continue their conquest of other planets and realms."

"My Nanites would be affected by your powers, causing, potentially, even more, damage because of the fields generated by your body."

Craig's look was one almost of relief in the tone, but hope was not gone entirely.

"I'm sorry Craig; this is one battle I cannot win. At least not to my knowledge," indeed her face was filled with deep regret that he could not be helped.

"It was a long shot at best Charlene," he started to lift a hand to put on her shoulder, but her face came up more fierce than sorry.

"We'll see. I'll be dammed before I give up just because of one little problem," and she went back to her seat, muttering and cocking her head slightly, thinking the problem through again and again.

Helena sat with Craig for the rest of the flight, while the others, finally including Charlene, just flaked out, resting from their recent monumental exertions.

Jack was relaxed, but his recent efforts, with his new power, had shown him that he could be some much more than just a combatant. He could heal and the book, which had become his constant companion, had taught him he could be whatever he wanted to be.

Then there was Helena. Ah yes. Now there was another book he would like to read; carefully. Carefully and slowly. His mother always said; "If a job's worthwhile, take the time to do it properly," he intended to do just that.

Chi'mera was thinking too. She had so much to think about, now that she'd both the time and a clearer mind to do so. She was trying to review all that'd happened over the last month and found that some memories were still blocked from her, in a way she could not understand. There were many things in her head; different personalities, created by the Demon's shattering of her mind. There were different mental images, of the people she knew; that were in effect the different parts of her own mind. And there were different technologies available to her; not all which she could access, even with the cataloguing of her systems.

But aside from them, there was something else, a more profound feeling, that she'd passed only the first test, a deep-seated knowledge that she, and indeed the rest of the team, were just starting on a path, either side of which lay the dark abyss of oblivion. They were the Guardians of this world and the realm it lay in. And their task had only just begun, and somewhere down the path lay the Demon; and beyond that something so terrible that it had no real name, a terrible darkness that, even now, was moving to destroy everything.

Troyes France. A small laboratory in the university.

Dr. Sayers, or rather the being who'd set himself up as such, sat and perused the news reports of the CERN incident, as it was being relayed on the news media.

The reports stated that a magnetic containment failure had caused a building to be catapulted into the air and create a sound and light show, for several minutes in the area.

'Expert' witnesses, used this interview to explain how safety procedures were successfully initiated, and that the EMP had been minimised. Images were particularly fuzzy the reporters were unable to get close for love nor money. Various political figures argued to and fro about safety and how the site should be moved, or even closed. It was all rather dull and familiar, humans being such limited creatures.

However, he regarded the screen showing four that were less limited. They did not know how far they had yet to go, but it looked like one of them might be the one he was seeking, for so many millennia; one that could restore the balance of his own realm and help him defeat his greatest foe. Still, she was a just one new factor in the equation, but one to be watched, carefully.

He'd planted a few small units in the university; that her companion had installed in his own equipment. They would monitor their progress and, in time, he would make contact and explain what was needed. In a few years perhaps. But he was patient. It was not as if time was a factor for him or his realm; he would watch and wait. If she failed, then he would know that she was not the one, and trans-shift to the next reality in line. Still, there was something about her. His golden eyes regarded her image with great interest, something stirring in his human form: his heart rate increasing slightly and his skin flushing. He'd not experienced these reactions before and did not really understand their function, still another thing to be catalogued and studied as he waited.

London M.I.X. headquarters. Craig's Private Office.

"Your reports have been incomplete of late, miss," Craig Starling rarely got angry, he rarely needed to, his staff and his agents knew what was expected of them, and that failure to comply had consequences; usually fatal, and almost always dangerous.

Helena fidgeted, rarely having seen this side of her boss before, and she did not like being on the receiving end of it.

"I sent all details relevant to the mission sir. I," she stopped, as he put a figure on her lips.

"You knew about Sylvia's appearance and did not tell me?" He did not shout, his intensity being far worse.

"I," the finger was pushed further into her lips.

"What possessed you to remain silent, knowing what Sylvia wanted from Charlene."

"I did not," She was trying to justify it to herself too, but she had other priorities.

"And what if she'd have caught her," he finally bellowed.

A figure appeared behind Helena, slightly in the shadows, and pushed her out of the way.

"What, Who?" Craig stepped back but in the relaxed style of someone ready to defend himself. Few knew that his powers were generated from within, rather than from his suit, it was his most significant advantage over most. Secrets could keep you alive.

"I am the reason she did not tell you; Craig Starling, Head of M.I.X, Gravitron." The figure stepping forward in impressive robes, sporting mystic symbols, large and ornate.

"I am the leader of the Magic Circle, a group dedicated to protecting this realm, from its various mystic threats; just as you deal with the more mundane ones." He stopped a few feet from the gradually relaxing Craig and waited for him to catch-up.

"Helena is one of your Circle," Craig twigged almost immediately.

"And had been for many years, since her mother passed on the mantle to her; as was Sylvia for a few years."

"You know about Sylvia?" Craig immediately starting to pump this new source for information.

"More than you can imagine, and more than I can tell. Sylvia, although even she does not realise it, was as badly affected by the encounter with the Demon as Charlene was. I know. I was there."

Both Helena and Craig started at that.

"Let me explain; as much as I dare," the old man sat in thin air, a stool appearing under him, and placed his hands palm up on his knees.

"The realms have been in harmony, since the dawn of time; Good versus evil, Chaos versus Order, that is the nature of things, staying in balance. However, in a distant realm; something happened; something truly Catastrophic, so catastrophic, that all of reality was disrupted."

Craig looked at Helena; who sat raptly attentive, this apparently being new to her too.

"Here, the shock waves were physically manifest; the dark ages, wars, pestilence and the like. In other realms; it was worse. The Ghe'Dar were forged in one such realm and have spread like a plague across the universe," Craig stood raptly, although he activated a recording unit to capture all this for later analysis.

"But I digress. The chaos in the other realms, allowed two old foes to attack the realm of the Guardian of life; Chimera."

"I thought Chimera, was a monster from Greek myth," Craig interrupted.

"History is always written by the victor, and, in this case, the demons won," the old man's head drooped slightly.

"I thought there was only one Demon, master," Helena interjected, confused, her master shaking his head, and smiling grimly at that point.

"The Demon that controls Sylvia and her coven thinks' itself a Demon Lord, but it is a puppet compared to the real entity that faced Chimera in battle," he placed his hands together.

"I will not mention their names, as they are powerful and would almost certainly hear me across the barriers that guard this realm. Never the less I will say that Chimera was isolated from her realm, in some fashion, and the greater demon slew her. Or so it thought."

"However, Demons, by their nature, cannot understand the tenacity of life. Chimera hung on, and sent a call for aid, then hid I know not where. It called to the Circle here, in dreams and portents."

"All very interesting, I'm sure but," Craig was silenced when the old man raised his hand.

"It reached out and touched Sylvia," he shook his head still bewildered by the choice.

"She was a promising young student of mine; gifted even, and full of the joys of youth; possibly why the message found her. I cannot explain, to someone like yourself, how the message was received, but somewhere in her soul she was profoundly altered." He stood, "she started saying that she needed to master older magics, ones long sealed away by myself, and my predecessors; that she needed more power, to fulfil ancient prophecies."

"What prophecies?" Helena asked.

"We do not know. Most of Sylvia's history is a mystery to us, but our ways are not founded on history, but skill. From her accent, she came from Eastern Europe, with little enough in the way of earthly things. We took her in, finding she was already skilled in many things; healing the mind, teaching and most importantly learning. She was skilled in finding things and teasing information from clues, using them to find what she needed."

"She played you!" Craig stated, knowing Sylvia's ploy as the one she'd used on M.I.X., offering up someone that could find what her audience needed, then using their resources to find what she wanted. The old man scowled, then nodded. "She got what she needed from the Eldarin; a set of prophecies, and their associated artefacts, some dating back before man walked the earth. I will not burden you with their content, and you'll not ask."

"Probably, as you say, we were played," he raised his hand, "however, she was played, by both the Chimera and her enemies too," he raised his other hand. "When the puppet Demon briefly contacted this world, two things happened; Charlene's mind was shattered yes, but Sylvia's spirit was shattered too. The darker side, obsessed with power and control, continued on the path that the real Sylvia had started; but somehow forgot the real reason she'd started on that path, remembering only the need to acquire power. The other shielded Charlene from the darker one's power and continued on the path that the prophesies dictated. Neither whole, but both following the prophesied path."

"There are two of them?" Craig was bewildered.

"The other is shielded from us; probably for fear of letting her other self, sense her, but we can see her work occasionally, a word here, a whisper in the wind there. She is moving far more subtly than before, but she is doing something."

"What master?" Helena asked puzzled.

"We don't know for sure, but we suspect she is guiding people to their proper places in fulfilment of the prophecies,"

Craig stood up, "that is all really fascinating, but it still leaves me with an aid that I cannot really trust any more. Why did she not just tell me all this?"

"One; she did not know it all, and you might have given away the information, quite unintentionally. Sylvia, as you may know, is quite capable of entering minds and would have stolen vital information, then slain you. I can prevent her from entering your mind, but even if I blocked her, it would give away that you had become involved and you would quickly become a target for various other, ahem, powers."

"So why tell me now?" Craig raised his hands and pointed around the room.

"Because now Chimera is here. It can protect the information in ways I cannot."

"And the rest of us?" Craig pointed out.

"All associated with it are protected; even I cannot see your actions now," he pushed Helena forward a little towards Craig. "She is loyal to you Craig Starling, she can be trusted to see this through to the end," there was a strange timber to the words. Craig looked at the man, as he started to fade, "I will leave this in your hands, daughter."

"He's your father?" Craig looked at her, drawing back a little to see her face fully.

"It's just a form of address, Craig. He calls all the woman in the Circle, daughter, after all, we are younger than him by many years."

The world had just got that bit clearer and so much stranger.

While Craig debriefed Helena, the others wearily moved back into their quarters at the base, which now seemed so clinical, when compared to the more organic French cottage, Jack almost immediately starting to plan on how to redecorate. He'd initially planned the furniture but decided this time to wait for the actual home person, Helena, to add her thoughts on the process.

Simon parked his armour in the engineering bay, but almost immediately began writing down schematics, equations, and ideas on one of the schedule boards around the bay. At the same time, John went straight to the Gym and started a rather furious work out until he was exhausted, the others pretending not to notice that he was actually making his hands and feet bleed.

Charlene, back into her original form, just sat apparently reading a book, although, to anyone that knew her at all, this was totally transparent. What she was actually doing was visiting her control room, the HUD displayed, getting more extensive and more complicated, increasingly more controls available and deciphered from the original Ghe'Dar into English, but even that didn't hold her attention now.

She stood before Chimera; the three head monstrosity somehow projecting a calming persona, a deep feeling of well-being and precious life, the deep scars on it, welling up with dark blood, and it limped slightly as it approached her.

"Greetings Guardian, Charlene, Chi'mera" its' mouths did not move, but spoke instead to her very soul, "I had sensed your coming into being, from across the boundaries of space, and knew it was time. Now, I have seen you in battle, seen that you tried to save lives, even though you knew that it might have the direst consequences for others, even for yourself. Still, you tried. For that reason, you have been chosen. You will take my place as Guardian, take on the mantle that I once held, the Guardian of Life."

There was no way to express the weight that Charlene suddenly felt on her shoulders; it was as nothing, yet felt like the weight of the world.

"The enemy that defeated me so long ago will try to destroy you, using powers you can only yet dream of. It is an agency of both evil and chaos, and it will wield both to try to claim the power over life," the creature started drooping. "The fading powers I have, I bequeath to you, Guardian. In time you will find a means to use them, perhaps in ways I never have." A stream of golden lights flowed from it to her, filling her with a feeling of peace and contentment, as well as an urgency she'd never felt before.

"The other powers that you will need, you must learn yourself," it drooped more.

"Wait. What must I do?" Charlene pleaded for desperately sought information.

The creature started to fade, becoming a golden outline, then a cloud, then a faint mist, as it departed this realm a final thought impinged on her soul, "seek out your mother, she has the answers."

Charlene knew that it had fulfilled its task, but still wished it had instructed her better. Now it was up to her, and she was ill prepared to take up the responsibility handed to her.

As she sat there, stunned by both the appearance, then the surprise departure of the Chimera, she noticed that her HUD had a new area, entirely different displays that just looked, well, weird. What she assumed were Mystic symbols instead of language, and displays that confounded her senses, wavering on the edge of her sight, skipping out of view when looked at directly. Another mystery to be solved, no doubt, however, it was blocked from her touch even in here by a thin, but impenetrable, veil. The spirit transfer had affected her in other ways too, with all her power levels raising higher than had previously been possible.

In her mind's eye, a familiar figure appeared to her right; her mother, Sylvia.

"Ah I was wondering about that," the figure commented quietly.

Charlene mentally turned to her, "what are you really? Just another part of me, or actually part of my mother?"

The figure smiled, "we are all part of our parents, in that we are taught by them and learn lessons from them. In this case, however, you are correct to question my actuality, as I am not like the other figments you see here. I truly am part Sylvia Nymonia, your mother; or rather a part of her spirit that I gave to you when you were born. This part of me allows me to protect you from my other self, as it falls more under the influence of the demon. I'm an insurance policy that I cannot destroy my own daughter, at least until the demon comes into this world when it can bring its' full power to bear. Then, his will will consume me totally, despite my strength."

"What makes you say he will enter this world?"

"The Guardian created the barriers long ago to protect life from those from the Demon Realm. With its passing, the barriers, already failing, will fall much faster. They cannot be fully breached yet; but in the not too distant future, the demon will have the power to do so; partially, thanks to me," the figure bowing its' head slightly, but not elaborating.

"For now, you must hunt the darker part of me, capture her and bring her before the Magic Circle. Then, and only then, can you learn what can be done to stop the Demon from invading, and laying waste, to this realm." The figure started to fade, then briefly reappeared.

"I love you, dear daughter. I'm am sorry that you were the one chosen and that I needed to train you so hard, for this task, but I have always loved you; and I am so totally proud of you," and she was gone.

When Helena returned from her briefing, she saw Charlene, tears in eyes, reading Romeo and Juliet. She walked past pretending not to see them.

Craig Starling gathered his team, with Helena by his side, having decided that they would keep their recent visitor a secret for now.

They were all sat in the upstairs office, in front of the big screen, which had a small presentation laptop, that Isabella had once used, the room in near dark, the roof shutters closed and locked.

"I thought it was time to tell you what M.I.X. has planned for you," he said starting a video feed on the laptop. The video was footage from the various news agencies around the globe, reporting on the CERN accident.

"The official footage, with a little adjustment, corroborates the stories that were handed to the press, while all phones in the area were hit by the machines power discharge, either wiping them or totally corrupting the data, so we have little to do in that regard."

He clicked his remote, and a map appeared marked with various red dots. "Before she left the Ghe'Dar base at Poole, Isabella manage to transmit this map of Ghe'Dar activities," there were dozens, perhaps hundreds; most small but others, nine of them, that were significantly larger. London, Paris, Moscow, Beijing, Tokyo, Sydney, Delhi, Cairo and Washington DC."

"As you can see; the Ghe'Dar still have bases right across the world, and with the destruction of the fleet, these become our main priority. Although we cannot deal with all of them ourselves, we will spend the next few days getting in contact with trusted' people in those areas, and make sure that those bases are captured or shutdown."

"The computer tells me that the mind control signal is still being broadcast, so they are still active, although it's weakened considerably, probably due to the loss of the machine. I think it safe to say that, as soon as the bases are captured, that will stop. They are not stupid, they will see that their invasion has failed and will go to ground until they can think of what to do next. I doubt they will be much of a problem for a time, being isolated on an alien planet. At least, that is what I would do," he started to turn.

"They will not!" Charlene interrupted vigorously stopping Craig and causing all of them to look at her.

"How do you know?" Craig countered.

"I have been inside their computer systems, reviewed their history and seen how they think," she stood gesturing at the dots on the screen.

"So how do they think?" Helena asked.

"They are a military force used to winning campaigns that last for decades, sometimes centuries. They will quickly reorganise, with the highest-ranking officer assuming command, and will move immediately to a new plan, then they will quickly counter strike."

"But they cannot win without their fleet and more ground troops," Craig objected.

"With all due respect sir, they don't see us as their equals, or even as intelligent really; we are food. They will not see their fleet's destruction as a sign of our strength, or even as a major setback. They will see it as their fleet's failure and will proceed to show that they can invade this world, despite the incompetence of the others."

"But," Helena started

"They will become even more aggressive, use less-overt tactics and be more vicious than before; they have contingency plans in place for virtually every eventuality, and they will move to one of them, continuing their invasion," Charlene said with a certainty in her voice that sent chills through everyone.

"So, what will they do?" Craig looked at Charlene, trusting her knowledge.

"I have no idea; it could be any one of the plans they have used in the past, or something totally new," and therein lay the problem. They were dealing with beings that were capable of doing just about anything to succeed.

The Ghe'Dar were not through with them yet, not by a long way.

Blavnic looked at the control panels and remained unmoved. The invasion it had signalled, implemented; then spectacularly failed within minutes. The main staging area obliterated, the portal to the fleet had been destroyed and may troops lost. It was a severe failure, but the Ghe'Dar were used to long campaigns, sometimes many cycles long and initial mistakes had occurred before. It was, however, the first time in its career it'd seen one, and it did not enjoy the sensation it evoked.

As the Supreme Commander had been at the machine site, it called up the mission command profile and checked who was next in line of command. As it turned out, it was Blavnic, not really surprising as chief intelligence officer, but protocol dictated that it be checked.

It activated a secure, and untraceable, comms unit from the command helmet. "This is Agent Blavnic, Henceforth I am taking command of the invasion task force, so noted for Historical records on this date," it transmitted several files to all the bases.

"Initiate protocol one-five-beta-one-four. Current base commanders are hereby promoted to force commander and are ordered to join me at the following location for the initial re-tasking briefing; Supreme Commander Blavnic out."

They would lose time and materials abandoning their production bases, and the humans would know that they were abroad, but the bases would self-destruct, and they would get no technology or information from the ruins. They might even believe that they had won; it mattered little. Protocol 15B14 had always been a particular favourite, and a chance to use it was something that it had never hoped for; fate now giving it such an opportunity. With the development of the new Nanites, it could be implemented even more efficiently, provided the latest information the human spy proved workable.

That was not the problem. During the recent battles some being, probably one of the ones who'd fought it, had accessed the secure database and obtained knowledge of the Ghe'Dar. Before, the humans were of little concern, being so low on the evolutionary scale; now, it appeared they were higher than initially assessed, and indeed the one who had that knowledge was now a top priority. They needed to find and eliminate that individual, tough enough even in a small population like this, but they had accessed the network using a stolen ID. Next time they attempted to use that ID they could locate them using a tracking program and eliminate them once and for all; there was the possibility that the new converts might be of assistance in that task, a final test of their enhanced abilities.

Fortunately, the intruder had only penetrated the military network, not the separate Intelligence network, so they just knew of the military resources on the planet, not the more secret infiltration units scattered around the world. The base in the UK was compromised, but the others were still safe, and the humans could have no information on them.

It put on its usual human disguise and left the base, walking into the sea through the concealed plunge pool. Seconds later, the station started to collapse, as focused seismic implosion devices all over the ceiling and walls activated; melting circuitry and collapsing rooms; the bodies of the failed experiments, guards and converts being buried under several thousand tons of liquefied rock, tidal sea water rushing in through the now depressurised pool. Blavnic was sure that, when the humans arrived on the island, they would find only a useless mass of rock and metal. Blavnic was content to move to the new plan. Subversion had initially failed, but now the new protocol added indigenous terror groups to the mix, which should prove more effective against this particular species, as it'd initially proposed.

Blavnic was also already working on how to get another scientist interested in developing z443 technology; they needed those portals. Perhaps the Koreans, or an emerging terrorist group, would find the technology appealing?

Blavnic's personal stealth ship awaited on the seabed ready to take it to Bermuda, where the intelligence network would already be initiating the first stages of the new operational protocol. The humans might provide a little sport before they succumb to the might of the Ghe'Dar; but they would succumb.

Waiting in a small boat above, D.I. Dilock felt had rather than heard the small quakes from the island and called in the local emergency services. They found a deserted set of damaged buildings and an old mineshaft which had collapsed, creating a large, deep, crater, where once the compound stood. The guard appeared dead, though the dog had managed to leap to safety through the security gate. There was no sign of the people who'd investigated the compound.

Dilock looked at the ruined area and had a niggling feeling that he had not seen the last of them. "This isn't over," he muttered.

Craig Starling looked at the map and continued with the rest of the briefing.

"I intend to keep you together, as a team; dealing with the bigger problems." He pointed to the big spots. "The smaller bases can be dealt with by the military and intelligence forces; once they are cleared of those who were mind controlled. You will be held in reserve for the problematical ones."

"What about our previous jobs, and our lives?" Jack asked.

"Well, there is good news and bad news about that," Craig said standing up again.

"M.I.X. will be employing you from now on, so you will have a salary, benefits and the usual corporate perks. This will become your base and lodgings for the foreseeable future." There was suddenly a commotion, and questions bombarded him, forcing him to slam his hand down onto the table.

"However," he said loudly enough to drown out the moaning and complaints, "you will all have immediate assignments, to keep you busy, while the world recovers from, and forgets, this incident."

"I am working on a more permanent 'cover' for you, but it's not ready yet, and it will take some time and effort to arrange." He picked up four folders, passing one to each of them. They all looked rather sullen, but each looked at their new assignment.

Jack saw that he was to develop his act. He was given a small list of clubs to work in and the name of an entertainment agent, probably an M.I.X. plant, Jack thought; but hey it was a start. The location was Birmingham, where he was to investigate some disappearances, not scientists this time; but teenagers and young women.

Simon looked at his and saw it was a suit design project. Fair enough, but it would take him weeks to get the ideas that he already had, even into the design stage. He noted that there was an early design for one of Craig's suits as a general guide.

John saw that he was to attend a set of M.I. courses. He'd already made the grade on similar training, so it was not really any different, also meaning he would be kept away from the others, while he grieved for his Isabella.

Charlene looked at hers' and frowned. She was not going back to A.G.E., as it was known to have been infiltrated, but to a higher-level company in the BioTechnica chain, A.C.E. to see if the company was also implicated in the Ghe'Dar invasion. She'd already been placed on the transfer list to their main labs in Oxford; boy, this guy worked fast.

"Now; I suggest you all get some rest and food, as de-briefing will begin tomorrow.

Sylvia Klerk, the former High priestess of the Coven, sat in her inner sanctum and pondered the latest series of events in her ongoing battle to regain her power. She had sensed it; the Guardian was gone. It had re-entered the world, after staying on the fringes of existence for centuries, then merely faded, passing over to the other side.

But, at its' passing a new presence had taken its place in the world, young, vibrant and powerful; potentially, more powerful even than the previous Guardian. She did not need to guess who this was. Somehow, the Guardian had located her daughter and had passed its powers to her. How it had managed to find her, where she could not, was beyond her knowledge, but she would need to find a way to locate her daughter, bring her to this sanctuary and perform the Ceremony of Inversion, thus passing her daughters power to her.

"The Time of Transition," mentioned in many of the prophesies she'd stolen during her flight from Rumania, had begun. As the time had approached more and more of the words had made sense to her until she finally saw the primary players clearly. The Huntress, obviously her daughter. The Golem, one she guessed was some sort of robot or android. The Enforcer, one she had few clues on, but that would turn to her side according to one of the scraps she held and finally the Phantom, one of the more dangerous of the group from her perspective, as another scrap said he would thwart the forces of darkness many times, even if they succeeded in vanquishing the Guardian.

There were others; the Dark Samaritans, the Fallen Angel, the Thrice Named One, the Fox and the Other, the one she trained at the moment that also featured, but those four were the main targets for her and the Coven.

The problem with the prophecies was that they were not complete, they had several different strands, and some were actually contradictory in a none consistent manner. There were three main streams; one followed the Guardian through to its succession, another the Demon to its triumph and the other was piecemeal scattered around, but not truly contiguous with either of the others. Also, the principal streams had details relevant to the reader hidden by layers of spells and second meanings and translational puzzles designed to keep the reader, her in this case, uncertain of the true meaning.

Now was the time she'd waited for, the time to seize the power of the Guardian and free herself from her master's control. And then? And then, she would have all the power she would ever need; to control the Coven, or all Covens and perhaps, even to rule the world itself.

Geroth, D.I. Blackmoore had felt the shift, in reality, a trembling of the good as their champion and protector died and strangely even he, as an agent of the one who'd achieved that dark victory, felt the darkness closing around him.

His inner sanctum grew gloomy and cold, and he knew that his master was coming again. He clutched the ring of control he'd seized from his high priestess those six years ago, and tried to draw strength from it, a strain as always, as the ring resisted. He needed to re-corrupt it, a process he'd discovered in the old temple under Oxford while researching the prophesies that Sylvia had obtained in her investigations for M.I. X.

He had to admit he was genuinely impressed by her skills in playing both the Magic Circle initially, then M.I. X. She considered herself a master manipulator, but she'd been betrayed by her own lieutenant, while she'd given birth to the Other; that strange thing she had conceived using the essence of her master, that she now trained in the most ancient of temples the Coven controlled. Only the master truly knew its potential, but Geroth suspected that the Demon's control of Sylvia was not as complete as the master thought, despite his constant vigilance again her inevitable treachery.

The presence of his master grew stronger than ever before, not surprisingly, with the guardian dead. With a conjunction due, his master would soon have the opportunity to enter the real world, and perhaps bestow the promised power to him and the Coven. Not to need to hide in the shadows, to stride out with his master and walk amongst the cowering and sniveling masses as their ruler and king; that would be worth all the effort and work he'd put into the Coven. More importantly, his master might then give back the stolen youth he'd endured with the recent failures and setbacks.

"Geroth?" The inky blackness started to form a face, not fully formed, but horrific enough in the details to make his skin go cold, and eyes dry up, the face turning to reveal the missing parts of its visage, as the presence continued to build. He dropped to his knees involuntarily, something which had never happened before, a reflex induced by his master's closeness to actual existence.

"Master!" the words were ripped from his throat.

"The Guardian is dead but has appointed a successor. You have failed!" The tone was one of impending death.

"No master, the barriers are still failing," desperation gave his mind the information that would save his life, "and we have traced the chosen south to a location near one of our Covens. We are close to her capture. I promise," pain ripped through his arms as they raised in supplication, he began choking, gasping for precious air.

"Aaarrghh, master, I promise. We will have her within the month. On my life," miasma filled air, whispered from his mouth, only to be gulped back in again, causing him to cough and wheeze even more.

"You Promise? You dare use flimsy promises, that you have failed to deliver before?"

"No Geroth! Not on your life. On your SOUL! Which I will rip from your still breathing corpse and torment for millennia with promises of release, should you fail," a black, blood-soaked, claw appeared beneath the face and grasped the writhing High priest, hoisting him into the air and began crushing his head against the ceiling.

"You WILL deliver her, or you will be the next sacrifice to me," and he was dropped onto his own sacrificial altar, a dagger floating from the head of the altar, to press against his throat, "do you understand?"

"Master, yes, master," the dagger dropped to the floor, the presence vanishing; leaving the terrified man to quiver in place and stare at the blade on the floor for a long time while heaving in clean air to his tortured lungs.

There was a knock on the door, and the door opened revealing Sylvia.

"What do you want, Hag?" fear, and suffocation, made him even less welcoming than usual to his rival, and his strength would not withstand her at the moment.

"Ah, is this a bad time?" he knew, she knew, it was, and he pushed the control ring forward to remind her that he still had it. Usually, this cowed her, giving her pause for thought. This time however the look she gave was strangely sympathetic look. No, wait, that look was one of pity! How dare she?

"You are in pain, Geroth, let me take that from you," and she lifted her hand, drawing his pain away; suddenly being engulfed in pain herself, which she channeled it to where she needed it, the Other screamed in agony, as power engulfed it in its' cage below.

Geroth relaxed, feeling his pain vanish, chilled by what Sylvia was doing to the Other. It may be demonspawn, but it was also her child, and she was channeling his pain into it. After a few seconds, the screaming stopped as his agony was negated. He expected Sylvia to either continue and try to drain his power, or to attack him for control of the Coven, but the spell ended, and Sylvia bowed and started to leave, not waiting for gratitude, which she did not expect anyway.

"Wait!" the high priest stood again, still a bit wobbly, holding the alter for stability.

"Why?" he found words difficult, not daring to look at the mirror, feeling drained entirely and because of the rebuke from his master's last visit.

"Why, what?" Sylvia smiled a chill smile, "why take your pain, why not attack when you're so weak, why channel the pain to the Other?"

"Yes," he struggled to speak, but also to look her in the eye. In some ways, he was more scared of her than his master. She nodded, as though going through the reasoning in her mind.

"We share a master, and he commands me to achieve the full growth of the Other in an unnatural timescale. To force that, it is required to endure many things others cannot, pain being one of them." She was speaking as though to a pupil, rather than the head of the Coven, but her candor was immediately suspicious to him but fascinating; unless she was lying. "Therefore, I need to channel that pain to achieve the master's goal. I will not fail." The smile became deeper and almost pure evil, and Geroth knew why. She was using his pain to guarantee her own success, and thus suggest elevation to High priestess again.

"As to why I did not attack, just look at your body and answer the question yourself."

He thought about it for just a moment then the answer became obvious. While he had the power, and he controlled the Coven, he also paid the price. He was almost tempted to force her to communicate with the master in his stead, but he knew deep down why he could not. Firstly, the master would not talk with underlings. Secondly, she would not be punished as harshly as he would be, being a true adept at magic and finally, she would probably use the communications to her advantage, thus loosening his hold on the Coven. Somehow, in his taking control of the Coven those years ago, he now realised he'd played into her hands and he could not escape the role without losing his life.

As if reading his mind, Sylvia softened her smile to one of Pity again, making him grind his teeth in anguished frustration. He wondered if the Demon too was all part of her plan.

"Sleep well, oh great High Priest," and she turned and left, without dismissal.

Geroth pondered; he was caught by his own ambition, between a Demon and a Powerful Adept, in a way that required desperate measures. Perhaps the scroll, describing how to use Mystic Ichor, could give him a clue on how to extricate himself while maintaining his power in the Coven. Perhaps. Perhaps.

Firstly, he needed to get to the Chosen, overcome her and her allies; then get her back to his sacrificial altar. All of that within a month; a terribly short timescale, but it needed to be done. It was time to unleash the stored power of the Coven and its mystic constructs on the world; damn the consequences, and any resistance. That meant a trip to Bournemouth for him to where his agent last informed him of the Chosen's location.

The time had come to begin the hunt, and unleash the Dark Hounds.

EPILOGUE · QUESTIONS

Jack and Helena were in an office, in the base's tower, just off the main area, where the others were debriefing, with Craig. She had a pot of her favourite tea, and Jack was having, a large, red-bull.

"As I said it was just a feeling," Jack was rolling a card over his fingers until it dropped off the end vanishing. Helena wondered what he was doing, but the look on his face was a little confused, as he looked around. Then a strange look came across his face, and he flicked out his hand, accompanied by a slight blur of movement across the room, a card appearing embedded deep in the wall opposite, almost like it was made of steel.

"That was weird," he said, standing up and crossing the room, tugging the normal feeling card out easily enough. He shook his head slightly and came back across the room with it.

"I gather that was unintentional?" Helena asked, looking at the wall, then starring at him, his head nodding. Getting back to their conversation, she indicated that he should get comfortable again. "I know this is probably going to sound all mystic; hey, perhaps it is, but we should investigate where all these feelings come from," obviously thinking hard. "You've had a few of them, even before you started to gain your powers; that cannot be down to pure chance, given what we have just been through. It stretches coincidence just too much, for my liking."

He frowned but nodded, playing with the card again, more carefully this time.

"Incidentally, perhaps we should talk to your mother too."

He looked strangely at her. "Why?" What did his mother, devout churchgoer though she was, have to do with this.

Helena raised her cup of tea to her lips then stopped, "over hundreds of years, white magic has been hidden from the general population, mainly because the uninformed people were too superstitious to understand its true origin." She put her cup down. "During those years there were custodians, guardians if you will, that kept the forms and the knowledge intact." She stood up, "at least that is what the circle knows, but, what if, there were other, underground Covens, ones that protected magic secrets; or there were secrets that were lost, which had been accidentally rediscovered." She looked at him.

"You're saying my mother is a witch?" He laughed, a little incredulously, at the thought. His mother could barely do the simple crosswords let alone read the symbols he'd been exposed to.

"No, of course not, at least that would stretch it a little," she thought more. "No. I guess what I'm saying is this; in olden times power was held by the women of the old tribes, here and in Europe. There were sisterhoods, covens and the like all over the known world. Perhaps, without realising it, your mother may have somehow, retained this power and passed this power to you."

Jack stood up, scoffing at the idea. "Really? That is your theory. That is seriously ridiculous?" He'd read about magic and seen it happen, things that a month ago would have been beyond his imagining, why was this now suddenly so farfetched. Because he supposed, he was a sceptic and just did not want to believe, or perhaps because it was his mother.

Helena smiled and knew he was stubborn; time to throw a dagger of her own. She made it a big one. As he passed a calendar next to the coffee machine in the corner, a real knife flicked past his nose, and embedding itself in a date; his birthday.

He looked startled at her, "if you're so against the idea; think about this. Your mother is a devout church going right," Jack still shocked that she'd thrown the dagger, looked at it sideways but nodded, paying full attention. "And as a devout churchgoer, she says prayers right!" He just nodded again, unable to say anything pertinent. "So, ask yourself this; what has she been praying for," he suddenly regarded her with a strange look.

"And if she has been praying so hard, for so long; who has been listening?" Their eyes met, and understanding came to his eyes, which suddenly went very wide.

Birmingham. Mid-evening, mass end, at Edgbaston Old Church. It was just starting to empty, and the altar servers had cleared up, but there were a few still praying.

Grace Somerfelt knelt and said her daily prayer.

"Dear Lord, I do not pray for myself. I pray for all those that need help, for those that suffer, for the poor of the world, the weak and helpless," Every day for twenty years, since the loss of her dearest husband, she'd come here to pray for those others who'd lost their loved ones.

"Give those that need help, aid, the suffering, comfort, the weak, strength and the helpless," the prayer was ingrained into her memory, mainly because she had said it as she'd raised her children, they were mostly lazy couch potatoes now, but that did not stop her from thinking about them every time she said the prayer.

"In the name of our Lord. Amen." She started to rise when a voice started her a little from behind.

"Why do you not pray for yourself, even occasionally, Grace?" asked the Vicar.

"I know we say that prayers should be for those in need, but in all the years you have been here, you have never once asked for something for yourself." He was a white-haired old man, everyone called him the Herder; mainly because he had about fifteen cats in his house.

"Now, that would not be right. Others have had more needs and always will," she sounded shocked at the question, especially given what the bible said.

"But the lord does say, 'Ask, and you shall receive.'" the softly spoken vicar, adding a firm tone unusual for him.

"He does, but he also says 'Don't put the Lord thy God to the test,'" not quite right, but the thought was there.

"You'll never admit it will you," he said quietly to her, touching her arm in sympathy.

"I don't need help. My boys are fine. Who knows?" she looked up at the ceiling of the small church, "perhaps if he's listening, he might help them find jobs and get out of the life I've had to lead," she sniffed a little at that.

"You said Jack had got some kind of job, a few weeks ago?" He asked hopefully.

"Yes, but then it's all gone quiet again. He always one to be a bit fanciful, and his head in the clouds. Always building contraptions in that garage of his, never out working," she sighed, "I pray for him too; but sometimes I do despair." She got up off her knees and walked slowly out using her stick to help her, unaware she was being watched.

In the shadows, the figure watched the encounter.

"Ah my dear lady, you will be so surprised when next you meet your son and his new friends," and he faded away, to check on the others, aware that time was catching them all up. Soon the real battle would begin.

About the Author

Born in a small Northern England town in the sixties, to some remarkably hard-working parents, my early life was as idyllic as you could imagine; friends, play and the rest. It was during that play I used my imagination to make characters and stories. At this time, my brother brought back a role-playing game back from university, and I was hooked. We used to role play for many hours, much to the frustration of my parents, who wanted a practical, hardworking son.

However, after moving schools, things changed, I'll skip the details, but to put mildly, life went downhill. That nearly prevented any career, but I recovered eventually, starting my first job.

I managed to get reasonable results in my exams and started a career in Chemistry, then in Computing, which I remain to this day. Still, the stories stayed with me, just biding their time until I took my most significant move yet; down South.

Here I met a friend that role-played with a group. He offered to introduce me, and I've never looked back since. That role-playing group finally led me to start to create a character for one of our role-playing games, which in turn became this book.

As this book took shape, I began to expand to the stories that I used to create. Now they are all queued up ready to get written; a real story maker at last.

DEDICATION

For Jade and Emma, my little Chimera and Lesley, my Isabella.

Lightning Source UK Ltd.
Milton Keynes UK
UKHW010725200722
406119UK00001B/260